MURDER
in
CHIANTI

MURDER

in

CHIANTI

CAMILLA
TRINCHIERI

Published by
Soho Press, Inc.
227 W 17th Street
New York, NY 10011

Library of Congress Cataloging-in-Publication Data

Trinchieri, Camilla, author.
Murder in Chianti / Camilla Trinchieri.

ISBN 978-1-64129-285-6
eISBN 978-1-64129-180-4

1. Mystery fiction. I. Title
PS3553.R435 M87 2020 DDC 813.54—dc23 2019059167

Interior design by Janine Agro, Soho Press, Inc.

Printed in the United States of America

10 9 8 7 6 5 4 3

MURDER
in
CHIANTI

GRAVIGNA,
A SMALL TOWN IN THE
CHIANTI HILLS

ONE

Monday, 5:13 A.M. The sun wouldn't show up for at least another hour, but Nico got out of bed, shrugged on a T-shirt, pulled on a pair of shorts and socks, and laced up his sneakers. Bed had stopped being a welcome place, both back in the Bronx brownstone he and Rita had lived in for twenty-five years and here in this century-old, two-room farmhouse he'd rented since May.

He set up the moka and, waiting for the gurgling to start, made the bed. Since he'd begun making his own bed at age three or four, he never walked away with it unmade. A neat bed started off the day with order, gave him the sense during childhood that all was well despite his father's drunken temper, his mother's fear. He knew it was all an illusion, but somehow it had helped then. And now, when he was trying to find order again.

A quick gulp of espresso shook him fully awake, followed by a forbidden cigarette that he smoked at the open window. Back in the Bronx apartment, he had happily lived by Rita's house rules. Now he had the unwanted freedoms that came with being a widower. Bad language when he felt like it, dressing like a street bum, a cigarette after morning coffee. An extra glass of wine or two with dinner. A good nighttime cigarette. Small stuff that would never be worth it.

The air was still chilly in the early morning, which Nico welcomed as he set off for his three-mile run along the winding road up to Gravigna. It was steep going and dangerous in the predawn light. And even at this hour, cars whizzed past in both directions, their drivers on their way to work. But Nico's morning run was like making the bed, a ritual that made him feel in control of his life, all the more necessary after the loss of his job, followed by Rita's death.

When the town appeared, perched on its own small hill, Nico stopped to catch his breath and take in the view of Gravigna, with its medieval castle walls, its two towers, the proud steeple of the Sant'Agnese Church. In the meager predawn light Nico could, with the help of memory, make out the hundreds of neat rows of vines that covered the Conca d'Oro, the golden bowl below the town that had once only grown grain. He had marveled at the sight the first time he'd seen it with Rita on their honeymoon. "Our fairyland," Rita had said then, and he had laughed, both of them dizzy with love.

Every three or four years, whenever they could afford the trip, they'd come back. It had been her childhood hometown. Rita's parents, who had immigrated to New Jersey when she was six, had come back to die and be buried here. Rita asked to be buried next to them. He had obeyed, bringing her to her birthplace and immediately heading back. But he no longer had anyone in New York. An only child with parents long gone, ex–work colleagues who shunned him. And he missed Rita and her fairyland. He came back to be close to her and what family she'd had left—her cousin Tilde and Tilde's daughter, Stella.

A pink-gray light had begun to scale the surrounding hills. It was time to go back and prepare the tomatoes. No going off in his old Fiat 500 to the town's only café, Bar All'Angolo. The friendly bar owners; the schoolchildren, mothers and workmen crowding the counter; and the tourists sprawling over the tables made him feel less lonely, and the delicious whole wheat cornetti that came fresh from the oven made the place all the more tempting.

This morning, however, Nico was happy to break his routine. He had a job to do. Instead of his usual slow walk back, he started to jog home. Twin motorcycles rent the silence of the morning with their broken mufflers. A few cars passed, one honking loudly to announce its presence behind him. Another, a Panda, whizzed past, only a few inches away. Just another crazy Italian driver. Nico reached the stairs of his new home with a wildly beating heart and no breath left in his lungs. Maybe he was too old now for round-trip jogs. As he stretched his calves, he looked up at the sky. A cloudless blue vault, the start of another glorious Tuscan September day.

THE DOG RELIEVED HIMSELF against a tree and meandered into the woods, sniffing for food that hunters or lovers might have dropped. The snap of twigs was followed by a chain of snaps. The dog froze, its ears at attention.

"Where are we going?" a voice asked.

The dog silently crouched down under a bush.

"I know these woods," another voice answered. "I'm taking you to the meeting place."

"Why here, and why at this ridiculous hour?"

"You wanted privacy, didn't you? You'll only get that in the woods, when everyone is asleep. If it were hunting season, we couldn't even come here."

"We've already been walking for half an hour."

"Consider it a step toward repentance."

"It hasn't been easy to live with what I did."

"You've certainly waited long enough to make amends, but don't worry. The money will be enough to wipe away even your sins."

"Are you sure this will happen? I have to fly back tonight."

"Shh. Relax. You'll get what you came for."

A TEN-MINUTE SHOWER RESTORED Nico. Cargo pants, a clean shirt, bare feet and he was ready. The previous night's pickings from the vegetable garden he'd started as soon as he'd signed the lease for this place awaited him in the room that served as both a kitchen and living area. Two baskets of ripe, luscious plum tomatoes sat on the thick pinewood table. He picked one up, felt its weight in his hands. A lot of work and love had grown these beauties. Nico turned on the oven and started slicing the tomatoes in half. After salting them, he drizzled extra virgin olive oil gifted from his landlord's grove, added a spattering of minced garlic, and spread them, cut-side down, over four trays.

A gunshot rang out just as Nico was sliding the first tray into the oven. The sharp crack made his arm jerk. Tomatoes spilled to the floor.

"Shit!" Hunting season wasn't opening for another week, but some hotheads were too eager for boar meat to follow the law. Aldo Ferri, his landlord, had warned him about the boars showing up en masse now that the vineyards were loaded with ripe grapes. The farmhouse Nico was renting was close to a dense growth of trees, the beasts' favorite habitat. They were mean, ugly animals who could grow to weigh over two hundred pounds. Aldo had suggested Nico pick up a hunting rifle to be on the safe side. No, thanks—he was through with guns of any kind. Last night was the first time he'd heard gunshots. They'd come in short, distant bursts. This one had been much closer.

Only one shot. If this guy was after boar, he must be a damned good marksman. A wounded boar would spare no one.

Nico stared down at the tomatoes on the floor. Some had landed on his feet. Hell, what was the rule? Thirty seconds? A minute? Well, Rita would have to forgive him. He'd swept the kitchen two days ago, and he needed every single tomato for the dish Tilde was letting him cook at the restaurant tonight.

With the tomatoes back in the oven to roast, it was time to enjoy the rest of this new morning. Nico ground some more coffee beans, put the moka over a low flame, cut two slices of bread, and filled them with thin slices of mortadella and a sheep's milk caciotta. Probably a lot more calories than two whole wheat cornetti, but not caring about that was one of his new freedoms.

He put his coffee and the sandwich on a tray, shrugged on a Mets sweatshirt, and stepped out to the best part of the house: an east-facing balcony overlooking part of the Ferriello vineyards and the low hills beyond.

There was just a slim ribbon of light floating over the horizon, enough light to see that the wooden beams holding up the roof were empty. No sleeping swallows. They didn't usually fly off so early. That gunshot must have scared them away. Or maybe early September was simply time to move on. He would miss them, if that was the case. The evenings that Nico wasn't helping Tilde at the restaurant, he'd gotten used to sitting out on the balcony with a glass of wine to wait for the three swallows to swoop in and tuck themselves in between the beam and roof for the night. He didn't mind cleaning up their mess in the morning. They'd become fond of each other.

Nico was halfway through his breakfast sandwich when he heard a dog yelping. A high-pitched, ear-busting sound that could only come from a small breed. Maybe it was the mutt that seemed to have made a home next to the gate to his vegetable garden. A small, scruffy dog that always greeted him with one wag of his bushy tail and then lay down and went to sleep. Nico had checked the garden the first time to see if the dog had done any damage. Finding none, he let it be.

Nico leaned over the balcony and whistled. The yelps stopped for half a minute, then started off again, louder this time. Nico whistled again. No pause this time. As the yelps continued, Nico wondered if the dog was hurt. More than possible. The vineyard fences were electric. Or it could've gotten caught in some trap. The yelps seemed to be coming from the left, past the olive grove. What if a boar had attacked the dog?

WITH HIKING BOOTS ON and the biggest knife from his new kitchen in hand, Nico traced the sound of the yelps. They led him past the olive grove, up a small slope of burned-out grass and into a wood thick with scrubby trees and bushes. The yelps got louder and faster. He was getting close. Then silence. Even the birds were mute. Nico broke into a run.

The dog almost tripped him. There it was, between his boots, with a single wag of its tail. "What the—" The dog looked up at him with a perky expression that clearly signaled, *I'm cute, so pay attention to me.* Toto, the cocker spaniel he'd had as a kid, used to give him that exact same look whenever he wanted a treat.

"I got nothing on me."

The dog raised a paw. It was red.

Nico bent down to get a better look. Blood. On all four paws. The thick undergrowth had masked the prints. He checked the animal for cuts. Nothing. It was filthy, but fine. The mutt must have found the spot where the boar or other wild animal had been hit with that one shot.

"Come on, you need a cleanup." Nico tucked the dog under his arm and turned to walk back. The creature squirmed and fought his grip, letting out a growl. "Fine, suit yourself, kid." Nico put it down and kept walking. The dog stood in place and barked. Nico didn't stop. The dog kept on barking. Nico finally turned around. Toto would do this when he was trying to tell him something. Once, it had been a nasty rat underneath the porch. No rats here, but maybe he should go along with it.

He turned around. "Okay. What?"

The dog shot off deeper into the woods. Nico trudged behind him. "This better be good, mutt."

At the edge of a small clearing, the dog sniffed the air a few times, then lay down, his job complete. When Nico reached the spot, he let out a long breath. What the mutt had been trying to tell him was a doozy.

About twelve feet in front of them, at the far edge of the clearing, a man lay on his back, arms and legs spread out at an unnatural angle. What had been his face was now a pulpy mess of flesh, brain and bits of bone steeped in blood.

Nico's stomach clenched. It wasn't the sight that got to him—during his nineteen years as a homicide detective, he'd seen worse and quickly numbed to it. No, it was the surprise of finding a body here. He'd walked away from that job, his old life, and come to Italy to find peace. He wanted to be near Rita, near her family, and far from violent death. Murder seemed to have no place in the beautiful Chianti hills.

"Come on, let's get out of here." His phone was back at the house. Nico bent down and swooped the mutt back up. No protests this time. He took another long look at the dead man without getting any closer. This was a crime scene, and old habits persisted. To blow off a man's face, you needed a shotgun, not a rifle. Close range, maybe four feet. So it was probable the victim knew his killer. Blood would have splattered all over him. Find the bloody clothes, and you had the perpetrator. Nico's eyes scanned the ground around the body. No shell that he could see. Either the murderer had picked up his brass, or it was somewhere in the underbrush. Not his job to go looking. His eyes shifted back to the body. A six-footer at least, judging by the length of his torso and legs. Big belly poking out of his jeans and a gray T-shirt mostly covered in blood. Some dark-red letters on it, or was that more blood? Nico leaned as far forward as he could without taking a step. Not blood. Two letters. *AP.* Blood covered the rest of the word or logo. At the man's feet were gold running shoes spotted with blood. Michael Johnson sprinters. If this man had ever been a runner, it was a very long time ago. White socks peeked up from the Nikes. On his wrist, more gold—a very expensive-looking watch. Maybe a knockoff. Hard to tell, even up close. Chances were the killer hadn't been interested in that. Unless something or someone had scared him away.

Nico looked down at the mutt huddled in the curve of his elbow. "You?" He surprised himself by smiling. "Sure thing." He turned his back to the dead man and, with the dog tucked under his arm, started walking back to the house. About twenty feet back into the woods, Nico felt the ground soften. Nico looked down. He'd stumbled on a patch of wet ground. Elsewhere the ground looked perfectly dry. It hadn't rained in days. Nico took another step and spotted an upturned leaf. It held water. Pink water. The killer must have washed himself. There was no water source that he could see. Nico continued his walk home. Solving homicides wasn't his job anymore.

NICO GAVE THE DOG what was left of his mortadella and caciotta sandwich and put it out on the balcony. He'd stick it in a bath later. He had a call to make: 112, the Italian emergency number, was the logical choice, but he'd prefer to talk to someone he knew first. Tilde was busy preparing lunch at the restaurant. She was a rock, but the news might upset her.

Maybe Aldo, his landlord, a cheery, likable man who seemed to have a lot of good sense. It hadn't taken much effort to convince him the run-down farmhouse that hadn't been lived in for thirty years would make Nico a cheap new home.

"Gesú Maria! On my land?"

"I don't know. I found him about two kilometers into the woods past the olive grove."

"Not mine, thank the heavens. The German who owned it died a few years back, and the heirs put it up for sale. I wanted to expand and had the ground tested two years ago. You can't grow grapes on that land. Too loamy. Loamy soil makes for inferior wine. There's a rumor that some—"

"Who's in charge around here?" Nico interrupted. Aldo was a talker. "Polizia or carabinieri?" He had no idea who was called when. All he knew was that the carabinieri were part of the Italian army, and that there was no love lost between the two police forces.

"Carabinieri. I'll call Salvatore, the maresciallo. The station is in Greve. If he's there, it'll take about twenty minutes for him to make the trip."

"Thanks. I'll wait here."

"I'll bring him over. Thanks for letting me know. Wait till I tell Cinzia. She's going to flip out! We're booked solid today. Seventeen Germans—"

"Someone has to get over there fast. Every second counts in a homicide investigation."

"You sound like a TV detective."

"I just want my part in this to be done."

"I'll call Salvatore right away."

"Thanks." Nico put down the phone. He had to keep in mind that Tilde was the only one who knew he'd ever been a cop. And only a patrol cop, which was what he'd been when she had first met him. Rita had sworn her cousin to secrecy, afraid the townspeople would shun him. The Rodney King beating had happened only a few months earlier.

SITTING ON A STONE trough by the front door, Nico smoked the one of the two-a-day cigarettes he hadn't been able to enjoy earlier. The mutt lay at his feet, snout between his still-bloody paws. Cleanup could wait. The dog was a part of the crime scene. So were Nico's hiking boots. He'd changed into sneakers, his boots next to the mutt. It was just past eight. The sun was warming things up, not a trace of cloud in the sky, and the tomatoes were nicely charred and out of the oven. He took another drag and felt the tension release. The morning's discovery would soon be over. A walk and a talk with this maresciallo, and he would return to his new Tuscan life.

A dark-blue sedan with distinctive red stripes on its hood appeared at the top of the dirt road that led to Nico's rustic house. Nico quickly stubbed out his cigarette, forgetting that no Italian was about to tell him he was killing himself. The dog sat up and started a series of high-pitched barks.

"Shut up."

The dog looked at Nico with what he would swear was a puzzled expression.

"You heard me."

One last bark in protest, and the dog lay back down.

"Good boy."

Christ! A man's face had been blown off not more than a few hours ago, and here he was, acting like his eight-year-old self when his mother had brought home Toto. Nico raised his hand to acknowledge Aldo in the backseat. In front were two men, the driver's blond head tall above the steering wheel and the front passenger's head lying low.

Aldo came out first. He was a big man in his late forties with a round, jovial face and a wine-barrel paunch. He was wearing tan slacks and a bright leaf-green T-shirt with the purple logo for his wine on it. He waved back at the car. "Who would have thought we'd have a murder on our hands today, eh, Salvatore?"

A dark-haired man in a tan shirt and jeans stepped out of the passenger seat. A black nylon jacket was tied around his waist. "The murder is in my hands, Aldo. Yours have to make good wine."

THE MARESCIALLO WALKED TOWARD the house, recognizing the man out front from his last visit to Bar All'Angolo. He had assumed then that he was just another American tourist, a man who'd held no interest to him. Now he saw the man as loose-limbed, big-shouldered, at least two heads taller than himself, on the short end of sixty with retreating gray-brown hair. He did not have the open, optimistic face he observed on so many Americans. Kind, naive faces bad at spotting danger. People who kept their wallets or cameras within easy reach of a thief and then came to the carabinieri with hope in their eyes. Hope the maresciallo was rarely able to reward. This man's face was closed off, though there was intelligence in his eyes, which were the color of steeped tea leaves. Had he only discovered a body this morning, or did he have something more to do with it?

THE OFFICER WAS SOMEWHERE in his forties, at the most five-six, with a full head of hair black enough to seem dyed. A stocky, muscled frame and a chiseled face, handsome, with large liquid eyes, thick lips, an aquiline nose. A face Nico had seen before but couldn't place. The man was smiling.

"Salvatore Perillo, Maresciallo dei Carabinieri. I should wear uniform, but no time." Up close, Nico saw that Perillo's hair had too much shine to be dyed. Perillo offered a hand. "Piacere."

Pleasure it's not was on the tip of Nico's tongue, but he stopped himself. He conformed to Italian politeness and shook the hand. "Nico Doyle." Perillo's grip was strong enough to crunch bone. Nico squeezed back.

Perillo nodded as if to acknowledge a tie, then took back his hand. "I have questions, but forgive, my English not so good."

Before Nico could explain, Aldo stepped between the men and said in Italian, "Nico's Italian is good. Italian grandmother, Italian American mother and Tuscan wife. Accent American." He grinned, seemingly happy to impart information the maresciallo didn't have. Nico recognized the same proud tone Aldo used to explain the mysteries of wine-making to the busloads of tourists who came to his vineyards.

The fact that Nico was pretty fluent in Perillo's language didn't seem to affect the man one way or another. "And the father?" Perillo asked in Italian.

"Irish," Nico answered in Italian.

"An explosive combination, I've been told." The maresciallo's Southern accent was strong.

"You've been told right."

"I usually hear the truth when I'm in civilian clothes. With the uniform, not so much." Perillo looked down at the dog sniffing at his heels. "Is that blood on his paws?"

"Yes, the dead man's. The dog led me to the body."

"Yours?"

Nico found himself answering yes.

Perillo bent down and scratched the dog's head. He got the one wag for his trouble. "What's his name?"

Toto was the first idea that popped into Nico's head. No good. And they were wasting time. "I call him OneWag." He used English words for the name. To say the same thing in Italian would have required too many letters. "I'll show you the way now."

Perillo eyed him for a moment. Nothing showed on his face, but Nico suspected the maresciallo was surprised he'd taken the initiative. "Yes, please lead the way. My brigadiere will stay here with the car. Is it far?"

"About three kilometers into the woods."

"Ah, the woods!" Perillo's glance went down to his own feet. He was wearing brown suede boots that looked brand-new. "At least it hasn't rained." He gestured toward the woods. "Please. I will ask questions as we walk."

"Maybe it's faster," Nico said, not used to being on the receiving end of an interrogation, "if I explain and then you ask questions."

Perillo seemed amused by this. "The Americans are prisoners of speed. Tuscany, the whole Italian north, is closer to the American way of thinking, but I come from Campania." They started walking, Aldo trailing behind them, OneWag running ahead. Nico was surprised Perillo was letting Aldo tag along. The fewer people on a crime scene, the better, but again, he reminded himself, it wasn't his investigation.

"We have a different approach," Perillo was saying, "although in this case, you are correct. Time brings heat, flies, maggots. I'm sure it was a very unpleasant sight in the first place, one perhaps you are not eager to repeat and therefore wish to be over with. Best to deal with it quickly. As for understanding the story behind this death, I fear speed will not be possible. Our investigations are not like on *Law & Order* or *CSI*. And so tell me, Signor Doyle," Perillo said, addressing Nico using the formal lei, "what facts are you so anxious to remove from your thoughts?"

"A few minutes after seven this morning, I heard a single gunshot. It sounded fairly close by. I assumed it was some hunter who couldn't wait for the season to start. But it could be the shot that killed this man."

"We will see. No need for you to speculate."

"Of course."

"Please continue, Signor Doyle."

"Please, call me Nico."

"For now, let us keep up the formalities."

They stepped into the woods. There was no path. Nico was grateful that OneWag led the way. Under different circumstances, the walk would have been a pleasant one. The morning silence was now broken by bird chatter, the dark underbrush splotched with the sun breaking through trees. A light breeze ruffled the leaves. While Perillo kept his eyes on the ground, careful of where he placed his new suede boots, Nico explained that he'd been led to the body by the dog's desperate-sounding yelps. "I thought he was hurt."

"Where were you when you heard the dog?"

"On the balcony, having breakfast."

"If the body is three kilometers into the woods, you have very sharp ears."

"OneWag has a very sharp voice. It was early and quiet. It's possible I was on alert because of that gunshot. Just one—that surprised me. When I heard the yelps, I followed them and saw the mess. On my way back, I found a patch of wet ground and some pinkish water. My guess would be that the killer washed some blood off there. I don't remember where it was, exactly."

"We'll find it. Did you step in it?"

"Yes. You'll want my boots."

"Indeed," Perillo said, looking at Nico with renewed interest. OneWag's barking stopped Perillo from going any further.

"It's just there," Nico said. "In the clearing behind those laurel bushes. The dead man's at the far edge."

"Stay here, both of you, and hold the dog," Perillo ordered. He squared his shoulders and walked ahead with a determined step.

THE MARESCIALLO WAS FIRST overtaken by the thick metallic smell of blood and the frenzied buzz of the flies. And then he saw the body at the edge of the clearing. He shrank back a step, closed his eyes and crossed himself. It was indeed an ugly sight. What had he said earlier? *Time brings heat, flies, maggots. I'm sure it was a very unpleasant sight in the first place.* He regretted his pompous tone. It was an unpleasant trait that always surfaced with strangers. What Signor Doyle had discovered was a gruesome act of hate. The dead man's face and half his brain blown away, spread across the grass like pig fodder.

Who was this poor soul? What had he done to deserve such violence? Certainly not a local, not with those shoes. Perillo took off his new boots, his socks. He had forgotten shoe covers. Bare feet were easily washed. He took out rubber gloves from his back pocket and slipped them on.

Slowly, he walked in a wide arc below the man's legs, trying to remain on clean grass. He circled the legs and stopped near the man's hips. Perillo reached into the pocket. It was empty. He leaned over the body and tried the other one. It had nothing that would tell him the identity of this poor man, but deep inside he found a hard object. He pulled it out, careful not to move the body, and studied it in the palm of his hand. With some luck, it would lead him to some answers. Luck and hard work.

Perillo slid the object into an evidence bag and took out his cell phone. He punched in the number of headquarters in Florence.

NICO BENT DOWN AND tucked OneWag under his arm, receiving a lick on the chin for his effort. Aldo waited a few minutes before tiptoeing forward.

"Oh, my God." Aldo's knees buckled as he peered beyond the bushes.

"I did warn you," Nico said.

Aldo backtracked slowly, wiping his face with a handkerchief. "You think he got shot in the face so he wouldn't be recognized?"

Nico had wondered about that himself. "He may have had ID in his pockets."

"You didn't look?" Aldo's hands kept kneading his handkerchief.

"I know not to mess up a crime scene."

Aldo looked at his watch. "I've got to get back. Seventeen Germans coming for a wine tasting and lunch, and forty Americans busing in from Florence for dinner. It's going to be a hard day."

"The hard day's mine, Aldo." Perillo walked through the laurel bushes with his suede boots and socks tucked under his arm. "This murder makes it a good day for you. You have a much better story to tell your guests than how wine is made." His tone was jovial, his face anything but. "Regale them with a few details, they'll be thirsty for more, and you'll sell some extra bottles. Go home and enjoy a few glasses of your Riserva. It will erase the ugly sight you insisted on coming here to see." He turned to Nico, who was staring at his bare feet. "Blood and suede is a disastrous combination, Signor Doyle."

Aldo asked, "Did you find ID on him?"

"No. He was wearing white athletic socks and gold running shoes, which makes me think he's an American, although I might avoid telling that to your guests. He was also wearing a gold Breitling watch, worth around five thousand euro."

"That eliminates robbery as a motive," Aldo said.

"Possibly, if he was the kind of man who went around without a cell phone, wallet, credit card or driver's license," Perillo said, "although one can be robbed of many things besides expensive accessories. Their life, for one." He turned to Nico. "Thank you, Signor Doyle, for being my Cicero on this terrible occasion. I am sure your expectations of Tuscany did not include a gruesome death. I do request that you give your boots to my brigadiere, who is by the car. I also need you to come to the station in Greve this afternoon for a deposition. At that time, I will take your fingerprints and a DNA sample."

"My fingerprints are on my residence permit, and I didn't go anywhere near the body."

"I don't doubt your word, but nevertheless. The DNA requirement is fairly new and meant to eliminate confusion. A good idea, for once. We Italians often make more confusion than is strictly necessary. As for your fingerprints, it will save time. It takes a while for the carabinieri to gain access to residence permits. Leave the dog with me, please. He may have picked up something of interest in his paws and fur. The technical team and medical examiner are on their way. Don't forget, Signor Doyle. At four o'clock. The signage in town is clear. You won't have a problem finding the office."

Nico glanced at the dog, who looked back with a sharp tilt to his head as if he knew something was up. "I don't have a leash for him." He was having a hard time letting him go. "I could stay here until they come."

"We cannot have you stay here while we do our work. Lay aside your fears. We will treat him with hands of velvet." Perillo undid the nylon jacket tied to his waist and lay it flat on the ground. "Put him here."

Nico did as he was asked. Perillo quickly zipped up the jacket around the dog, tied the sleeves and lifted the bundle up. OneWag peeked out of the opening and barked at Nico.

"Go home, Aldo. You too, Signor Doyle."

Nico gave OneWag a quick scratch behind his ear and turned to go. The dog barked louder.

"Try to forget what you have seen here. It is not representative of our beautiful country."

Nico could not help thinking of all the Camorra killings he had read about in Perillo's neck of the woods, but the maresciallo was right about his expectations of Tuscany. They did not include murder or a stray dog.

TWO

It was eleven-thirty when Nico arrived at the restaurant with his pan of roasted tomatoes. At noon, Sotto Il Fico—Under the Fig Tree—would open for lunch.

"Buongiorno," Nico said.

"Not for everyone, I hear." Elvira, Tilde's mother-in-law, was at her usual armchair in the back of the narrow front room, which held the bar and a few tables. The draw of the restaurant was its large hilltop terrace, which held a huge sheltering fig tree and a serene view of a patchwork of perfectly aligned grapevines below. Elvira was wearing one of her seven housedresses—she had one for each day of the week. Today's was white with red and pink checks. She was a widow with crow-black dyed hair, a corrugated face that made her look older than her sixty-two years, a small, sharp nose and piercing water-blue eyes that didn't miss a single trick. Rita had nicknamed her "the seagull" for the way she seemed to hover around people, looking for tidbits to snatch up.

"Salve." Behind the short bar by the door, her son, Enzo, Tilde's husband, reached for a grappa bottle. He had his mother's angular face and black hair streaked with gray, and always wore jeans and a Florentine soccer team's T-shirt. He poured grappa into a small glass and held it out. "Poor Nico. This will restart your motor."

So the news had already gotten out. "No, thanks, I'm fine," Nico said.

"I wouldn't be fine." Enzo drank the grappa in one swig. "No one's ever been murdered in Gravigna." He gave the grappa bottle a longing look but put it back on the shelf. "All over the world, people are killing each other for no good reason. This country is drowning in shit, and now there's a murdered man in our woods."

"I'm sure it wasn't anyone you knew." From what Nico had learned of the town, only Sergio Macchi, the butcher with two restaurants, was rich enough to afford that watch, and Sergio didn't have the dead man's belly.

"Of course not." Elvira turned her gaze on Nico. "I hear the dead American had no ID."

Nico walked up to her. "Who says he's American?"

"I do," Elvira declared. "He was wearing gold sneakers and thick white socks. You can always tell someone's nationality by his socks and shoes. Germans and Scandinavians wear brown or gray socks with sandals, of all things. Asian women wear little socks with drawings on them and feminine heels. The English, argyles and sensible leather shoes."

Nico lifted up his pan. "I'd better get this into the kitchen."

"I was hoping you'd changed your mind about that dish of yours. The tourists want Tuscan food, not something invented in the Bronx."

"Rita invented it, and she was Tuscan."

Elvira waved him away. "Go on, get yourself in the kitchen. Tilde thought you'd chickened out."

"I did not!" called a voice from the kitchen.

"Ever since she heard about the murder, she's been acting like she's walked into a wasps' nest."

"Mamma, she's upset. We all are." Enzo reached back to the shelf and poured himself another grappa.

Elvira shook her head and went back to folding napkins. Nico sometimes marveled at the relationship between the two women. It wasn't exactly a positive one, surprising considering how closely they worked together. Elvira owned the restaurant, and her contribution to the place was folding napkins from a rickety gilded armchair rescued from the dump—one that she would forever claim a Roman contessa had bequeathed her. When she wasn't folding, she solved the crossword puzzles in the weekly *Settimana Enigmistica*, eyes ready to snap up at every arrival. Enzo, her forty-year-old son, manned the bar and cash register. When he was feeling energetic, which from what Nico had seen wasn't often, he'd slice the bread as well. Tilde and Stella ended up doing the hard work, cooking and serving with part-time help from Alba, a young Albanian woman. Nico was only too happy to lend a hand.

Tilde was in the kitchen, a long, narrow room with scarred wooden counters and walls covered from hip level to ceiling with worn copper and steel pots and pans. She was rapidly slicing mushrooms for her apple, mushroom, and walnut salad, a lunchtime bestseller. She pecked Nico's cheek while spritzing the just-cut slices with lemon juice. "I heard. Sorry you had to go through that."

"You mean Elvira or the dead man?"

That got a half smile out of her. "Both. Are you okay?"

"Yes." Nico put the pan of tomatoes in a far corner. He didn't need them until this afternoon. "Are you?"

"The wasp bit me, but then it died."

Nico grinned. "I believe it. We all know you're armored in granite, but it's still only armor. Having a murderer nearby is scary. There's nothing wrong in admitting that."

HEARING ABOUT THE MURDER was horrible, but it was mention of the dead man's shoes that had stuck a knife in her chest. It had been twenty-two years. Tilde had managed to almost entirely erase the thought of Robi, but now his drunken boast haunted her. *I'll return covered in gold.*

"Was the dead man really wearing gold sneakers?" she asked.

"Yes, and a big fat gold watch." Nico walked past the small window overlooking the dining terrace and saw Stella under the fig tree, setting tables. He waved at Rita's goddaughter. "Ciao, cara." He was hoping for her usual heartwarming smile but only got a nod. Understandably, the murder had gotten to her too.

"Let me do this." Nico slid the pan of zucchini lasagna ready for the oven to one side and stood next to Tilde.

She handed him the knife. "Very thin. And don't forget the lemon."

"Yes, I know, I know." It wasn't the first time he'd done the slicing. "I'm aware that news travels fast in a small town, but how did Elvira know about the socks and shoes?"

Tilde waved a dismissive hand in the air. "She found out from Gianni. He works for Aldo. I thought you knew that."

Gianni was Stella's boyfriend, a handsome young man with the arrogance of youth. Stella liked him as much as Tilde disliked him. Tilde stirred a pot of cooling navy beans that she would serve with tuna and the sweet red onions from Certaldo, Boccaccio's hometown. Beans of any kind were a staple of Tuscan cooking.

Tilde offered him a spoonful of the beans. "You need reinforcement after what you've been through. Help yourself to anything."

He was being offered food as tranquilizer. Looking would have to be enough for now.

Next to the pot was another Tuscan staple, also a Sotto Il Fico bestseller—pappa al pomodoro, a thick soup of stale bread, tomatoes, garlic, basil and vegetable broth, topped by a generous squiggle of extra virgin olive oil. Tilde's pappa surpassed all the others he and Rita had tasted over the years. If Tilde had a secret ingredient, she didn't share. Every time he walked into the kitchen, no matter the time, the pappa was already made.

Tilde saw him eyeing the pot. "Maybe someday I'll tell you," she said.

"I won't hold my breath."

"That's wise. Does Salvatore know you were a police officer?"

"No, and you're not going to tell him. You're on a first-name basis with him too?"

"Everyone knows him. He goes to Bar All'Angolo whenever he gets a chance. That's where the cyclists hang out. He's an avid cyclist. He and his pals sometimes drop by for a late lunch after a Sunday race."

Cycling was an Italian passion, Nico had quickly discovered on his first visit. On the weekends, there wasn't a road in Tuscany that wasn't overrun by racing bikes either whizzing downhill or straining uphill.

Tilde said, "You must have seen him before."

"He did look familiar."

"Salvatore Perillo is a good man. Solid." She turned to look at Nico. She had a small face with wide, caramel-colored eyes that softened her severe expression. The red cotton scarf wound around her head covered the same beautiful long, chestnut-brown hair that had been Rita's pride before it turned gray. Tilde was forty-one, and her hair had not lost its rich color. She had been a stunning, smiling beauty in the photos Nico had seen of her as a teenager. With the passing years, her soft beauty had changed into something harsher, unsmiling. And yet she claimed to be happy. Rita had blamed the change on too much work.

Tilde wiped her hands on the long white apron that sheathed her perfectly ironed beige cotton dress. Nico had never seen her in slacks or in a wrinkled item of clothing.

"You could help him solve the crime," she said.

"Why?" The last of the mushrooms were done. He picked up a green apple.

He wanted to add *I have no experience in solving crimes*, but Tilde didn't deserve a lie. The omission was bad enough. Tilde had never been told he'd moved from being a uniform to homicide detective.

When he'd protested years ago, Rita said, "You don't know Italians. All they'll want to talk about are your cases. It would ruin our vacation. You deal with such gruesome, ugly stuff, and I'll never understand how you stomach it."

He'd been angry at the time, unaware until then how much she disliked his new job. He didn't have much stomach either for the gruesome part of homicide, he explained, but he wanted to right what was wrong, give the victims' families justice.

Rita accused him of wanting to play God. He reminded her a detective's salary was better than a patrolman's. They'd hoped to start a family. Twenty years had passed since then.

Tilde opened a big jar of Sicilian yellowfin tuna. "We need this murder solved quickly. The whole town is scared, excited, curious. Enzo's phone hasn't stopped ringing. I had to turn mine off. Just what we need right now, for the tourists to get scared and leave. Besides, I'm worried you'll get bored and go back to America."

"It's hard to be bored in such a beautiful place," Nico said. He was sad at times, which was to be expected. His footing here wasn't solid yet, but he was working on it. When he wasn't helping out at the restaurant one of his three shifts a week, he walked the streets, listening, striking up conversations at the bar, at the newsstand, at the trattoria in the piazza. He had nothing to take him back to New York. His police career was over. "You're the only family I've got, and I'm staying right here. I like helping you with the restaurant."

"But I feel bad I can't pay you."

"What I need is friendship, not money. Besides, you feed me when I'm here."

"We close in October and won't reopen until April. What will you do then? Of course, you're welcome to eat with us anytime you want, but still, the winter months here can feel very long."

"I'll perfect my cooking skills and hire myself out to the competition."

"Such a man. Your dish tonight better be good."

"It will be. I wish I could reassure Stella she has nothing to be

scared of." He'd been watching her weave through the tables with
sagging shoulders, head down.

"It's not the murder. She had a fight with Gianni."

"Serious?"

"Very, and I hope she has enough sense to break it off."

"That's harsh. She loves him."

"She'll get over it."

Tilde's angry tone made Nico pause and study her. He knew
she loved her daughter very much, and he wondered what could
make her dismiss Stella's feelings so quickly. He watched her put
the zucchini lasagna in the oven and waited.

She slammed the door shut. "Stop staring at me. I'm not a
witch. Stella has a university degree in art history, but Gianni
wants her to stay here and be a waitress. Yesterday she disobeyed
him and went to Florence to apply for the competition exam to
be a museum guard."

"I would think her degree was enough." From what he'd seen
of Italian museum guards, all they did was sit in a chair and make
sure visitors didn't get too close to the art. At least they had the
advantage of sitting, a privilege American guards didn't seem to
have.

"All state jobs can only be won by passing a competition with
flying colors," Tilde said. "Even if Stella gets top marks, there's
no guarantee she'll get it. Here, people get ahead because of nep-
otism or bribes. Stella wanted to teach art at the university level,
but her professor wasn't esteemed enough to mentor her, so now
we have to pin our hopes on the guard job. A state job is good.
I think they have about twenty openings and more than three
thousand people are applying. I don't hold much hope, but at
least she should be encouraged to try. Gianni told her he'd leave
her if she got the job."

"He's just scared of losing her."

She pointed a serving fork at Nico, eyes narrowed. "Don't you
side with him."

It was the first time he had seen her this upset. "I'm just saying. Want me to talk to him?"

"No. I want her to get to her senses and leave him." Laughter and German words drifted in from the front room.

"Enough talk," Tilde said. "Our first lunch guests are here."

"I'll help Stella serve."

"You're a gift from God," Tilde said with a peck on his cheek and a push out the door.

THERE HAD BEEN QUITE a crowd at lunch today, thankfully unaware of the murder in the area. Nico and Stella were too busy rushing about to talk to each other until it was time for him to go to the carabinieri station. The maresciallo was waiting for him by now, but Stella was more important. They had just finished clearing all the tables. He took her hand and led her to a seat under the shade of the fig tree. Before sitting down, he kissed her cheek. "How are you?"

Stella was almost a young replica of Tilde. The same oval shape of the face, full mouth, straight nose, a fair, clear complexion, thick chestnut-brown hair she had just had cut to intentionally uneven lengths, one side covering her ear and the other barely touching the top of her ear. Nico had watched Tilde blanch when Stella came back from the hairdresser. "Good cut" had been her only comment. What was different was the color of her eyes, a transparent jade green that no one else in the family claimed.

Stella furrowed her brow. "Did Mamma ask you to talk to me?"

"No. My feet hurt, and I want to see that beautiful smile of yours."

She responded with a quick, throaty laugh. "Sorry, I've dropped it somewhere and now I can't find it." She leaned over the chair and clasped her arms around his neck. "Poor Nico, it must have been terrible for you. Weren't you scared?"

"No reason to be. He was dead. I would say repulsed is more accurate. What's truly horrible is the cruelty we are capable of."

She dropped her arms. Fingers started twisting at the hem of her top. "It's scary. You found him in the woods behind Aldo's place, right? Mamma has always forbidden me from going there by myself. I don't know why. Nothing bad's happened there before today. Gianni thinks it's just a power play on her part. Says it's a great place to pick mushrooms."

"And I suspect a good place for lovers too."

Stella shook her head. No smile, no blush. "There are other places. I do wish Mamma and Gianni got along. I feel pulled in two."

"She's thinking of your future."

"I know. So am I, and Gianni's being a perfect pill about it. Zio Nico, are you sure you're okay?"

"I am, and please don't be scared. The carabinieri will find the killer quickly." Nico stood up. "Ciao, my bella. Thanks for worrying about me." He kissed her cheeks. "See you tonight. You'll have to tell me if you like my dish."

She stood up too, pulled the now wrinkled hem of her top down over her jeans. "I'm sure it will be delicious, and there will be none left for us." The shadow of her beautiful smile appeared on her face.

"Ah, the light is coming back."

"Your doing. I love you."

"Me too."

A quick hug and he walked away. He was going to be very late for his appointment.

NICO GOT ON THE panoramic 222 road that snaked from Siena through the Chianti hills, ending just south of Florence. The 500 started belching as soon as he floored it, and what should have taken only fifteen minutes took twice that. He knew from the start that the price Enzo had asked for the car was over-the-top, but they both understood that Enzo was asking for help in buying a new espresso machine for the restaurant, and Nico had gladly paid. Now he felt like cursing.

Once on the main road in Greve, the car stopped belching, but traffic slowed to bumper-to-bumper pace. He read the banner flying over the street. The reason for the traffic jam became clear. The Chianti Classico Expo, the biggest wine-tasting event in the region, was starting in three days. As he neared the intersection that led to the big medieval piazza that was the heart of the town, he heard shouting punctuated by hammer blows. He had read about the event in the local paper, but this morning's discovery had wiped it from his mind. Even if he'd remembered, he hadn't been about to leave Stella with more than thirty diners to take care of all by herself. For once, even Enzo had been busy pouring glasses of wine and making espresso drinks at the bar. There was nothing Nico could do about it now. The maresciallo would understand. Or not. He didn't care. This was a courtesy. Anyway, Italians were always late.

The red light was taking forever to change, and he couldn't see any signs telling him where to go. Nico leaned out the window and asked a woman overloaded with shopping bags where he could find the carabinieri station.

The middle-aged woman, dressed in a rumpled yellow linen suit, beamed at him. "Ah, thank the heavens. I will show you." She quickly walked in front of his car, opened the passenger door, pushed the bags to the floor, and dropped herself onto the seat. There was barely enough room for her.

Nico stared. She smiled. "Trust me."

He hated those two words because they rarely delivered, but her face was kind, which reassured him. Not that he thought he was being carjacked. Manipulated, maybe.

The light changed to green.

"Turn right here," the woman said, pointing a red-nailed finger. "Cross the bridge. Turn left at the next street. See the sign?" She said it slowly, in a soft, low voice, as if addressing a foreign child. His accent had given him away.

Nico did as she said. Halfway up the hill, she asked him to

stop. "I live in that villino." She extended a hand to him. "Maria Dorsetti." Nico shook it and mumbled his name. Something about this woman flustered him.

She did not ask him to repeat it. "Thank you for saving me the climb. At the top of the hill, turn right, then left. You'll see a café to your left, a park to your right. The carabinieri station is just across the street from the park. I hope your business with them is not unpleasant." She tilted her head, waiting for him to respond.

He said, "Thank you."

Clearly disappointed by his terseness, she gathered her shopping bags and struggled to get out of the small car. She waved at Nico as he took off.

As he climbed the hill, he noticed in his rearview mirror that she stayed on the sidewalk and watched him drive off. Nico remembered the time he and Rita had gotten lost trying to find Dal Papavero, a famous restaurant in a village above Gaiole in Chianti. Rita had asked for directions from the only person they could find on the road—a teenager kicking around a soccer ball. The boy offered to take them there. Rita accepted before Nico could stop her. "He's going to take us where he wants to go," he had muttered in English. Rita had laughed, her way of shutting him up. The boy got in the backseat, gave Rita directions, and seven winding uphill kilometers later, Dal Papavero came into view. The boy didn't live in the tiny town, wouldn't accept a meal or money. He said he did it because they were lost and he was bored. Rita watched him kick his ball back down the hill.

With dessert, a delicious torta della nonna, "grandmother's cake," Nico had gotten a lecture on trust.

"BUONA SERA, SIGNOR DOYLE." Perillo stood behind a large desk placed at the end of a deep room. The distance from door to desk gave him the time to study the people who came to complain, snitch, lie, or tell the truth. It gave him a head start.

Perillo watched the tall man stride confidently into the room.

Not smiling, but at ease with his surroundings. Most people, even honest ones, were nervous walking into the carabinieri station for the first time. Not this man. Perillo had discovered several interesting facts about Signor Doyle, thanks to the Internet.

"I'm sorry I'm late. I wasn't expecting so much traffic."

"An apology is not necessary. Your dog is waiting for you under the desk. He behaved very well."

"Hi, pal." Nico bent down.

The dog ignored him. His coat had turned into sparkling white fluff. His paws were clean too. Some fur had been trimmed off.

"Somebody gave you a bath." He reached down and stroked the dog's long ears. "You look good."

Still no response. Was he hurt? "What did you do to him?"

"The technicians examined him with great regard. His fur was carefully combed out to catch whatever might have been trapped there. His paws meticulously scrubbed. I do not believe he will solve our murder, but it is best to be thorough. We also took an imprint of your boots. As you seemed anxious about the dog, I brought him back to your house when they were through. You weren't present, so he came here. I was afraid he might run away. I left your boots by your doorstep."

"I was at Sotto Il Fico."

"Good restaurant, but I find their zucchini lasagna too thin. Only three layers of pasta, no tomatoes, no ricotta, just zucchini, herbs and béchamel. A poor man's meal, which is what Tuscan food is all about, after all. In the South, where we are far poorer than the Tuscans, our lasagna are small mountains of pasta filled with a richness for which we can only thank Apollo, the sun god."

"You washed him."

It sounded like an accusation, something Perillo was used to from indignant tourists and, too often, his wife. "My wife took it upon herself. We live upstairs. I didn't think you would mind. He needed it badly." He said it with a slight reproach in his voice. Tit for tat. "She also shined your boots."

"Please thank her for me. Let's get on with the deposition, then." Nico's tone was brusque. The maresciallo supposed it was easier to be annoyed with him than with the mutt.

He pointed to a chair on Nico's side of the desk. "Please, sit."

Nico sat down, taking care to make sure his feet didn't hit the dog. He heard voices coming from another room. He wondered how many carabinieri worked here. Perillo pulled up a wooden armchair to the other side of the desk and sat down. "Would you like to dictate to Daniele?"

At the sound of his name, the young man who had been at the wheel of the blue Alfa Romeo appeared from another room in his well-pressed summer uniform—lightweight black slacks and a blue short-sleeved shirt. "Good day, Maresciallo." He took his place in front of the computer at the far end of the room.

"He'll transcribe your words directly into the computer. He's very skilled." It was thanks to Daniele's ability to navigate the mysterious web that Perillo had discovered Conor Domenico Doyle's interesting past. The name Conor was on his birth certificate. But by the time he'd joined the police force, Conor had disappeared from his name. Why erase a name? Daniele had unearthed more. The Venetian police weren't the only ones with a computer expert on staff.

"I would prefer to do my own inputting," Nico said, his pride kicking in. He was also fast at the computer, having typed countless reports. He welcomed the challenge of writing in Italian.

"You're familiar with the Italian keyboard?" Daniele asked, a Venetian lilt to his words.

He hadn't thought of that. "Can I write it out in longhand?"

"Certainly." Perillo held out a hand. Daniele quickly filled it with several sheets of paper and extracted a pen from his front shirt pocket. Perillo handed over the sheets to Nico. "Please add your phone number and address at the bottom."

"Of course."

Daniele stood behind his superior in an at-ease position.

Perillo pretended to read a report on the disappearance of ten cases of wine from a Castellina in Chianti vintner. The matter had quickly been solved, thanks to a tip from the vintner's wife. All ten cases were in his mistress's home.

"Done," Nico said, and handed over a single sheet. Perillo held it back out for Daniele to type up.

While the young man's fingers flew across the keyboard, Nico nudged OneWag with his foot. The dog looked up at him for a moment, then stretched his small body as far as it would go, as if to say he didn't have a care in the world.

In two minutes, Nico's typed deposition was back in Perillo's hands.

"Please reread it." Perillo slid the paper across the desk after having read it a second time. "In typing it up, Daniele made a few grammatical corrections."

"I'm sure there were more than a few."

"No," Daniele said. "Only a few. Your Italian is good."

Nico knew that was bullshit. "Thank you." He had always been lousy at written Italian. It had nothing to do with how people spoke.

Daniele, who looked no older than eighteen, blushed. With his pale skin, rosy cheeks, blue eyes and straight, wheat-colored hair, he could have been mistaken for a midwestern farm boy. Or a Tuscan nobleman. The portraits in the Uffizi were full of men and women with his fair coloring.

Nico compared his own handwritten deposition with Daniele's typed one. Nothing had been altered except his many mistakes, which he hoped to remember. His life was now a continuing learning process, mastering written Italian being only the first step, and not an easy one at that. He signed the typed version and slid it back across the scratched, ink-stained wooden desk. At his precinct, the desks had all been metal, and the walls filled with details of cases they hadn't solved yet, photographs of the victims and whiteboards covered in the latest rundowns of each case in black Magic Marker, the salient points underlined in red.

In the room he was sitting in now, the pale yellow walls held a large map of the area, a photograph of Greve's famous Piazza Matteotti from the days when wine was sold from horse-drawn carriages. Next to it, an aerial view of tens of stands offering wine tastings, fronted by crowds.

Perillo caught him looking and shook his head. "Chianti Expo keeps us busy. It's good for the vintners, a headache for us and the idiots who drink too much." He turned to Daniele. "Where's the kit?"

Daniele jumped up and rushed out of the room.

"Is he new?" Nico asked, remembering his own anxiety when he'd first joined the homicide squad. After the first week, Joey, his first partner, had presented him with a cigarette box filled with joints. All they did was add five pounds to Nico's girth.

"Six months on the job and his first murder. We don't get too many of those. Fast learner." They both watched Daniele come back into the room, this time at an intentionally measured pace.

"Now for your DNA," Perillo said. "Go on, Daniele. You know how to do it."

Daniele straightened his shoulders, opened the sealed plastic envelope, took out a large Q-tip. "Open your mouth, please."

Nico did as he was asked and had his mouth swabbed. Fingerprinting was next.

When Nico had wiped his fingers clean with the tissues Daniele offered him, Perillo stood up. "Good. That's done." He wanted to talk to this man, draw him out, but fair was fair. Conor Domenico Doyle had had a very bad start to his day.

"The rest of the afternoon is all yours now."

Nico didn't move. Curiosity wound itself around his head like a snake. "Have you been able to identify the dead man?" Here was Eve, biting into the apple.

Perillo held back a smile of satisfaction. Once a police

detective, always a police detective. A cliché. But clichés were just truths made insignificant by too much repetition. "Not yet. Without a face to show around, it isn't easy. I've contacted all the hotels in the area."

Daniele's chair squeaked. Perillo waved a hand at him. "With Daniele's help, of course. He's invaluable."

Daniele's cheeks reddened again.

"The hotels are going to get back to us if any of their guests don't show up tonight. As for the three families who live near the crime scene, no one heard a thing. Or so they claim." In truth, he had only spoken to the wives, the men having gone to work for the day. He would need to return there this evening.

"The medical examiner and forensic team came down from Florence and did their work. They combed the area, but the murder weapon, a shotgun, was not found. Nor the casing. Maybe the medical examiner will find the pellet embedded in what was left of the man's face, so we at least know the gauge of the gun."

"Will that take long?" How fast would Perillo get results from Florence?

"I can assure you it isn't as fast as what you see on *CSI*. By the way, your assumption that the single gunshot you heard killed the victim seems to be correct. At least, the times match. The body's on its way to Careggi as we speak."

"The hospital in Florence?" Stella had been born there. The eighteenth of August. Every year, Rita sent her a gift.

"That's right. That's where our legal-medical institute is. Oh, we took his fingerprints, of course, and we're having them checked on the national database in Rome and by Interpol. It may be days before we get results. We're not as fast as you Americans."

"Don't believe what you see on American TV programs. We take our time too."

"Glad to hear that." With a smile on his face, Perillo extended a hand. "Thank you for coming by, Signor Doyle. I look forward to sharing a coffee. Maybe some morning at Bar All'Angolo?"

This man wanted something from him. Nico could feel it. Maybe it was just the standard Italian curiosity about American life and politics, and Nico was just being paranoid. He shook Perillo's hand. "I'm there most mornings around nine." Nico leaned down to pick up OneWag from under the desk, but the spot was empty.

"He's by the entrance, ready to go," Perillo said. As Nico walked to the door, Perillo added, "I've been wondering how the dead man got to that clearing."

Nico turned around. "You didn't find a car?"

"No car, no scooter, no bicycle."

"Three possibilities. He walked, the killer drove him there or the killer took his car."

"Perhaps, but we found no tracks. Only some freshly broken twigs. It barely rained on Sunday, so the ground is still hard. What I ask myself is, why did the murder occur at that time? It was still dark when you heard the shot. And why that particular spot?"

"I suppose that's for you to find out."

"True enough. But please stay in the area for the next few weeks."

Nico didn't like the sound of that. "Am I a suspect?"

"No, a witness."

Nico scooped the dog up, nodded to both men and left.

WHEN THE DOOR HAD closed, Daniele asked, "Do you want to involve him in the case?" He hoped so. Americans knew how to solve problems. If Steve Jobs were still alive, he'd have figured this out in the blink of an eye.

"The higher-ups in Florence have unfortunately assigned Substitute Prosecutor Riccardo Della Langhe to this case, and I can definitely say that exchanging ideas with an ex–New York City homicide detective will be far more beneficial than listening to Della Langhe's idiotic pronouncements." He wasn't about to let on to Daniele how unsure he felt about solving this brutal killing. It was complicated. Unknown victim, possibly American, valuables left behind. He had dealt with only one previous murder in his career, easily solved. It didn't help that Della Langhe, prejudiced against anyone from the South, considered him dumb.

Perillo opened his drawer and stared at the messy contents as if they could offer a solution. Eventually slammed the drawer shut.

Behind him, Daniele stood up straighter, steeling himself for an outburst.

"We're going to prove that arrogant jerk wrong," Perillo said out loud. "We're going to solve this ugly crime quickly, Daniele. We have to."

Daniele relaxed his posture. "Yes, Maresciallo. Maybe we can talk to Signor Doyle, who certainly must have solved many murders in his nineteen-year career?"

"Perhaps, Daniele." Exactly what he was thinking. "But right now, it's time for you to go back to calling the Florentine jewelry stores you so expertly unearthed on your computer."

The list was endless, much to Daniele's dismay. He enjoyed navigating the depths of the Internet to extract the gems Perillo needed. He found talking to people awkward, especially over the phone, without knowing what to expect beforehand. The one advantage, which his mother repeatedly pointed out, was that at least no one could see him blush when shyness made him trip on his words.

"Excuse me, Maresciallo. The dead man was American, so surely the bracelet is American?"

"The technicians did say his *clothes* were American, gold shoes included, but that does not necessarily make *him* an American. New York alone receives millions of foreign tourists a year, and they buy and buy and buy American clothes made in some cheap-labor country by children." Perillo picked up the suede leather jacket—Italian lambskin, cut and sewn in Florence—he had carefully draped over a chair and flung it over one shoulder. "No, dear Daniele, be careful of jumping to easy conclusions. The phone awaits you. I'll go and talk to the four jewelers here in town. One of us might get lucky. Ciao."

Daniele watched his boss saunter to the door on his soft new suede boots and matching jacket. He knew where the maresciallo was going first. The café next door, for his tenth or twelfth espresso of the day. How the man didn't have the jitters from all that caffeine was a mystery to him. Daniele looked at his phone, then the screensaver on his computer, a picture of an ascending line of cypress trees silhouetted against a clear blue sky. A picture that had ended up on countless postcards. He loved his job, most of the time. He liked his boss. The world behind the cypress trees would have to wait. Daniele picked up his cell phone and keyed in the numbers in his notebook.

THREE

Nico and Tilde sat outside at the restaurant, looking out at the dark valley sprinkled with the lights from distant towns. The sky had its own faraway lights and a moon reduced to a smile. The view Sotto Il Fico offered its diners was its biggest drawing card. The food was good, but the view was spectacular. It was now past midnight, and the place was empty. The only nearby sound came from a light breeze teasing the leaves of the fig tree. The tables had been cleared, the dishes and kitchen cleaned. Enzo had taken his mother home. Stella had gone off with Gianni. It was time to relax with a glass of 2013 Sammarco, a "Super Tuscan" red wine Enzo had introduced him to.

"Looks like Gianni's changed his mind," Nico said. "Stella has her smile back."

"A short-lived smile. I know my daughter. He brought her flowers. It's a ploy. He has to make her love him again before renewing his demands. She knows that."

Nico heard anger in her voice. Where was it coming from? He couldn't believe Enzo had ever treated her that way. He was a good man. Un pezzo di pane, Rita had once called him. A piece of bread.

"I'm glad to see my fusilli alla Rita sold out." He wasn't showing off so much as changing the subject.

"Compliments, Nico. They were delicious. You added just the right amount of garlic, arugula and oil. Did you see Elvira sneaking forkfuls from Enzo's plate when she thought we weren't looking?"

Nico laughed. "I guess she liked it, not that she'll ever admit it."

"Not even on her deathbed."

"I'm sorry we ran out. I would have roasted more tomatoes, if I'd had more. I picked my plants clean."

"You'll find many more at Sunday's market in Panzano. We can go together if you want."

"That recipe is yours now," Nico said. "I want to offer different dishes."

"Any recipe of Rita's is welcome here."

"How about mine?"

Tilde laughed. "I'll have to taste them first."

"Done." They clinked glasses and drank. "This wine is heaven," Nico said.

"Yes, it smooths out the wrinkles of the day, and you've had a major one."

"And your wrinkles?"

Tilde heard the concern behind the question and didn't like that her emotions had been readable. "They're on my face, but I can only blame them on age, not the day. How did it go with Salvatore? Did he figure out who the dead man is?" Nico could tell she was trying to pivot away from herself.

"Not yet. I believe he's assuming the man wasn't a local, thanks to those shoes, I guess."

Robi's drunken boast came back: *I'll return covered in gold.* Tilde shook her head to toss the words away. "A mosquito," she explained when Nico looked curiously at her.

"Perillo's put the word out to hotels in the area and I guess asked a few real estate agents. A man with that kind of watch might have rented an apartment. I wouldn't think he was the Airbnb type, but you never know. It's going to take a while. This whole area is rented out this time of year."

"Find the unslept bed."

"It's a start. I imagine there are plenty of guests or renters who find other beds to sleep in while on vacation."

"I wouldn't limit it to vacation time." Her voice had gone sharp again.

Nico leaned forward, trying to glimpse Tilde's expression in the dim light of the mosquito-repelling candle. Had Enzo cheated on her? Rita had once claimed that cheating was part of an Italian man's DNA.

Tilde caught him peering at her. "It's not what you think. Enzo has been very good to me."

"You deserve it."

She shook her head. "I wish I did." She hadn't returned Enzo's love when they'd gotten married, feeling that she didn't deserve him after what had happened. He had loved her enough for both of them. He still did. She would forever be grateful to him.

Nico didn't know how to respond to the sadness in her voice except by returning to the murder, which seemed to interest her. "It looks like the shot I heard was what killed the man."

"Is that significant?" When didn't seem as important as who.

"It establishes time of death. That can be important. Funny thing. Perillo's wife gave OneWag a bath, turned him into a big pom-pom."

"OneWag?"

"His tail produces one wag at a time. That's it."

"So you've given him a name. Does that mean you're keeping him?"

"I'm not ready to keep anything besides myself, but I'll feed him and make sure he has water."

"Help yourself to our scraps."

He lifted a plastic bag from the floor. "I have." Nico finished the wine and leaned back in his chair. In the distance, a blinking light moved across the darkness at a steady pace. He watched it move, trying to make out what it was.

"What are you looking at?" Tilde asked.

"That moving light. What is it?"

"When Stella was little, she called it a fairy light. She wanted to watch it until dawn. I see you're hooked too." Her beautiful, beloved daughter. She was hiding something from her mother. Something that she suspected had nothing to do with Gianni. Worry about her daughter and the detail of the gold shoes were making her frantic. "A light blinking in the dark, moving toward some unknown destination. That's what it must feel like when you're trying to solve a murder."

Nico remembered only too well. "What is the light, then?"

She laughed. "It belongs to a garbage truck making its rounds. I suppose Salvatore will also be picking through a lot of garbage on his way to a solution. I don't envy him."

"Neither do I." He just hoped the maresciallo's light was bright enough.

ONEWAG WAS CURLED UP in his usual spot by the vegetable garden gate. Nico spotted him easily, thanks to his flashlight. "Hey, brought you something." He waved the bag in the air, plastic rustling. "Not that you deserve it after that snub at the station."

The dog sat up and gave Nico his "I'm listening" tilt of the head. No wag and no running to the food. It made Nico smile. This mutt was as proud as any Tuscan. The people, at least, had a right to their pride. The Italians owed their beautiful language to the Tuscans, according to Rita. On their honeymoon, she had made sure to point out the greatness of Tuscan art, their architecture, and always Dante's *Divina Commedia*. Endless quotes from the *Inferno*, *Purgatorio*, and *Paradiso*. He understood nothing of the poet's arcane Italian, as he had not understood Chaucer in high school, but loved her, and that was enough reason to listen.

"For you, surviving is enough reason to be proud," Nico told the dog. "Okay, you keep your dignity. Here." He dropped the bag on the ground and opened it. "Buon appetito." He walked the thirty steps to the house, unlocked the door, turned on the neon light of the ground floor—one large room where the farmer had once kept his pig, now cleaned up and filled with Aldo's discarded wine barrels—and climbed upstairs.

Nico flicked the switch and watched as the glass bowls of three brass lamps slowly lit up his new home. Brick flooring in both rooms, as well as ceiling beams cut from discarded wooden railroad tracks. In a corner of the main room, a large cast-iron wood stove. In the cold months, the balcony would hold enough wood to get him through the winter. The wall abutting the bedroom and bathroom held a blackened stone fireplace the farmer's wife must have used for cooking. There was no stove when Nico stumbled on the house on one of his long walks. Aldo had planned to demolish the place and build two apartments, but he didn't have the money for it, and so they agreed on a five-year lease. Nico had chosen the place not in spite of but because it belonged to another time—and needed a good cleaning, a new bathroom, a brand-new stove. He would fix it up, maybe in the process fixing himself.

The work on the house was almost finished now. He wanted winter to arrive so he could see what more he needed to do. Nico quietly opened the balcony door and checked on his three swallows. They were home, asleep.

All was well, except for a man whose face had been blown off. Lying awake in bed, Nico found himself reliving his discovery. Would the poor man find justice? In his career as a detective, too many crimes had gone unsolved.

In his sleep, Nico dreamt the dog climbed into the bed and slept at his feet, keeping them warm.

PERILLO PARKED THE CARABINIERI'S Alfa Romeo in Gravigna's main piazza. He wanted his presence noted. It was his wife who had suggested he wear his uniform to make his visit to the town more official. A murder had been committed nearby, and the townsfolk needed reassurance. The weather helped, with clear skies and a light breeze that would later take the bite out of a hot sun. Perillo checked his watch. Eight forty-five. He'd timed his arrival well. By now, the grade-school children would be in class halfway up the hill, and the older kids in their high school in Greve. Not being a parent, he was awkward at dealing with children. The parents would reassure them far better than he could.

"Buongiorno," Perillo said, tilting his hat to the foursome of old men sitting on the benches surrounding the fountain. They were typically a happy lot, grateful to be alive, to be able to discuss the Viola, the Florentine soccer team, their ailments and what they'd eaten the night before.

As soon as he approached them, they crowded around him, assailed him with questions.

"Who was the victim?" "Was he a local, an Italian tourist, a foreigner?" "There's a rumor he was a rich American. Is it true?" "Should we lock our doors at night?" "Was the dead man robbed?" "Was it a hunting accident?" "Are you going to find out who killed him?"

"Of course, I am," Perillo said, waving down their questions with his arms. "I assure you, this is not a random killing. Nothing was stolen. You are not in danger. But it's important that if you see something, hear something, know something, please come forward."

Perillo watched the foursome go back to their benches, shaking their heads and muttering, unconvinced.

Carletta, the lavender-haired waitress of the trattoria facing the piazza, was readying the outside tables for lunch. "Keep me safe," she called out as Perillo walked by. If she was afraid, her smile masked it well.

A truck parked on the other side of the street was making its weekly delivery to Luciana's tiny flower shop. Luciana seemed too busy with the delivery of her beloved flowers and plants to worry about murder at the moment.

A few doors down from Luciana, Bar All'Angolo was crowded with locals in a huddle at the far end of the long space, hands gesticulating in the air as they argued, questioned, pontificated about the murder. Perillo walked in. The tourists, seemingly ignorant of the news, sat near the open French doors and enjoyed cappuccinos and hot cornetti. Sandro, the tall, handsome co-owner of the café, stood behind the cash register, ringing up orders, dispensing change, selling bus tickets to Florence and the neighboring towns. Jimmy, the other co-owner and Sandro's husband, manned the espresso machine and the oven.

Perillo went straight to the group of locals at the back of the bar. He knew these men and women had come to the café to share their curiosity and their fears. It was his job to make them feel safe again.

Perillo repeated what he'd said to the foursome outside.

A few of his cycling pals contributed their own words. "Salvatore will find the killer in no time. Let's stay calm. We're in good hands."

Some nodded. Others looked skeptical.

Perillo raised his hands again. "I'm sorry, I have no information to give you right now. I can promise you this. I will discover who the murdered man is and find his killer." *God willing*, he thought as his stomach fluttered with doubt. Why was he so dumb as to ever promise anything? "What is most important is that if you come to know anything, no matter how trivial it might seem, please let me know. Call me or come by the station if you want privacy. Is that understood?"

Everyone nodded.

"Good. Now go on with your day."

The group seemed more relaxed as they edged away from him. Perillo thanked his cycling friends for their trust in him. They were all going off to train for the big amateur race at the end of the month. He would have loved to have donned his racing gear and gone off with them, but until this murder was solved, his five-speed Bianchi Vittoria would be staying at the station.

"You've got a big one in your hands this time," Jimmy said.

"Here, console yourself with this." Jimmy handed him a sugar-covered ciambella. "Espresso corrected with grappa, coming up. Breakfast is on us."

"Thanks." Perillo took a big bite and let the cream filling ooze down his throat. He needed the consolation after the promise he had just made. Last night's visit to Aldo's three male neighbors had yielded a zero. The search for the jeweler who might have sold the bracelet he'd found in the victim's pocket hadn't yielded any results yet. Two hotels had each reported one missing male guest and three female guests. Perillo didn't worry about the missing women, at least not yet. He hoped, with all his heart, that their absence was due only to the joys of the Chianti vino and the attraction of the Italian male. The two missing men had gotten his hopes up.

Perillo had sent Daniele on his motorbike to the first hotel in Radda in Chianti. He'd picked the Panzano hotel because it was on the way to Gravigna. While he was en route, both hotels called within ten minutes of each other to say their missing guests had stumbled back in and were fast asleep in their rooms. He immediately called Daniele but got no answer. He blamed it on the young man's motorbike making too much noise and texted him instead: GO BACK TO GREVE. THE FLORENTINE JEWELERS LIST IS WAITING FOR YOU.

Perillo looked around the room. Could his killer be among the many locals who kept running in for that quick boost of espresso, then back to their jobs? They were good, hardworking people, from what he knew of them. The hunters among them aimed their rifles at boars, shotguns at hares and birds. To blast a man's face off took so much rage. Where could that come from? Greed? Then why leave an expensive watch on the man's wrist? Jealousy? Revenge? No, those gold shoes excluded a local.

Perillo's thoughts were interrupted by Beppe, a slouchy eighteen-year-old, rushing in and shouting, "Two espressos in paper cups!" like his life depended on it. "Double the cups, so I don't burn my fingers."

Sandro took Beppe's five-euro note and gave him change. "Our espressos taste better with a 'please' after the order."

Beppe pocketed the coins and picked up the cups. "What century do you live in?" He spotted Perillo. "Salve, Salvo." He grinned at his own bad pun.

"Salve to you." Perillo hated the nickname Salvo but let the kid feel clever. He was sure it didn't happen too often.

"Have you solved that murder yet?" Beppe asked.

"In fact, I'm here to arrest you."

Beppe's eyes opened wide. The tiny coffee cups in his hands trembled.

Behind the cash register, Sandro laughed. "Come on, Salvatore's kidding."

Beppe blinked. The cups steadied. "That's not funny."

"Neither are you," said Jimmy over the sound of steam foaming up milk for a cappuccino.

"I don't try to be," the young man said in his defense. He turned back to Perillo. "So who's the dead guy? I bet him and the killer are somebody we know." Beppe looked around the room, his face flushed with excitement. The bar had thinned out. Only a few tourists remained. "That would be something, eh?" he said, looking back at Perillo. "Every newspaper in the country would write about us."

"*La Nazione* already has." Nelli, who ran the art center, was reading about the murder in one of the copies of the Florentine paper the café provided for its customers. "What I don't understand is, why would a grown man wear gold sneakers?" A woman in her forties, with pale blue eyes, a welcoming face, and a long braid of graying blond hair, she favored muted colors in her wardrobe and her landscapes.

"To hide the grave sin he visited on another," Gogol announced as he shuffled into the bar, wearing a heavy overcoat and bringing with him the usual overpowering smell of cheap cologne. Luckily, most tourists considered him an added attraction, some asking to take his photo. He was a gentleman somewhere in his seventies who liked to wander through the town, offering to quote any verse from *The Divine Comedy* for a euro. It was the overcoat he could not part with, even in the worst summer heat, that had given him his nickname. Almost no one remembered his real name.

"What sins are you hiding underneath that coat?" Nelli asked. She had offered to buy him a new one countless times and been refused. The one Gogol wore looked as old and wrinkled as he was. At least they were both clean, thanks to the staff at the old-age home on the outskirts of town.

"No sin, gentle lady. It keeps my dreams safe."

"What dreams can you have?" Beppe asked in a tone Perillo instantly disliked.

"Dreams of a blameless life."

"Beppe," the maresciallo called out, "why don't you bring your mother her espressos before they're too cold to drink?"

Beppe caught the hint with a disgruntled look on his face. As he stepped out of the open door, Gogol quoted his favorite poet. "'I understood that to this punishment are damned the carnal sinners who let pleasure vanquish reason.' I offer this verse for no charge except 'a resting space bestowed.'"

Gogol walked to a table by the open French doors. Some people thought him stupid or mentally disabled, and no, he wasn't as quick as the lizards he'd tried to catch as a boy, but he did know Sandro and Jimmy wanted him to sit near the open air. He sat and took a bite of one of the many crostini he had taken from Sergio Macchi, the butcher, who handed them out to anyone who walked into his shop, along with a glass of red wine. This one was with lard, like the ones Gogol's mother used to make for him. He opened a napkin, placed a salame crostino in the exact center and pushed it in front of the opposite chair.

Jimmy leaned and whispered to Perillo, "That's for his new friend. Five minutes maximum till Nico walks in."

"How do you know?" Perillo asked.

"They've bonded. Nico treats him to breakfast every morning. He says Gogol reminds him of his wife."

"That bad?"

"No, Rita was all of one piece. It's because she liked to quote Dante a lot."

"I'm glad he's coming. It's time I get better acquainted with Gogol's new friend." Perillo left the café to light a cigarette and wait.

OneWag saw him first. The dog scurried across the piazza on his short legs, fluffy tail high in the air. Nico turned a corner, running after him and yelling.

Perillo laughed as the dog stopped at his feet and sniffed his shoes. Sleek black leather ones this time. The dog licked a drop of cream from the left shoe, then sat down. Perillo bent down and scratched behind the dog's ears.

Nico reached the sidewalk out of breath. "That's the first and last time this dog is tricking me."

"Buongiorno, Nico." Perillo put out his cigarette against the wall. Americans detested smoking. "I think you have a rascal on your hands."

"Sorry. Buongiorno, Maresciallo. I was afraid he'd get run over."

"Salvatore. The formalities are over. From now on, let's proceed on a first-name basis."

From now on? Proceed? Nico had the distinct feeling Perillo now knew he'd been a homicide detective—easy enough to find out on the Internet. The good, at least. Maybe not the bad. "Okay, Salvatore it is." Maresciallo Perillo was a mouthful.

Perillo saw Nico's recognition. He needed to tread carefully. He wished them to be friends first of all, even though he'd met this ex–homicide detective only the day before. He sensed they shared a love of justice. He didn't know why Nico had been forcibly retired from the police force, but he was convinced that whatever Nico had done had been done for a good reason. Perillo always prided himself on being a strong judge of character. This man was also clearly tutto di un pezzo, all of one piece. To ease the tension, he looked down at the dog, busy gnawing at a paw. "No leash?"

"I wasn't planning to take him anywhere," Nico said. "He slipped into the car without my noticing and jumped out before I had the chance to stop him."

"He probably doesn't need one. Strays know how to take care of themselves." The dog stopped gnawing and looked up at him. "Clever mutt knows he's being talked about." Perillo bent down, gave the dog another scratch behind his ear and said, "Sharing a cup of coffee comes with the elimination of formalities."

Befriend the dog, befriend the owner, was that what Perillo was up to? What Nico wanted was for Maresciallo Perillo to leave him alone.

Gogol waved from the open French door. "Ciao, amico."

Nico waved back with a big smile. He'd just been given an excuse. "Thanks for the offer. Maybe some other time? I don't want to disappoint Gogol."

"Of course. Some other time." Perillo held out his hand. Nico shook it and strode inside the café, followed by OneWag, his nails clicking against the tile floor. In the States, dogs got kicked out of communal spaces, but this café was a free country. "Buon-giorno, Sandro, Jimmy. The usual for both of us."

"Salve" came from both. He gave Sandro exact change. Jimmy called out, "One Americano, one doppio espresso corretto and four whole wheat cornetti coming up!"

The few remaining locals in the café turned to look at Nico. Stared more than looked. He steeled himself against the questions that he was sure were coming. Tragedy, for most people, was always followed by a nasty, all-consuming curiosity. Murder in a small, quiet village would prompt the ultimate version of this.

A couple of men nodded at him by way of saying hello. After a long minute, they turned back to whatever they were having, murmuring amongst themselves.

Nico relaxed as he realized he'd been wrong. They were certainly curious, but they didn't ask. Maybe out of respect, but probably because he was not one of them.

AS NICO WALKED OVER to Gogol's table, Perillo made his way to the parking lot behind Macelleria Macchi. He would try again tomorrow. Maybe by then, he would have some concrete details about the murder to offer the American detective. As Perillo took out his keys, his phone vibrated in his back pocket. Perillo slipped it out and swiped a finger across the screen. "Yes, Daniele, what is it?"

"I kicked the ball in the net." The loud excitement in his voice reverberated in Perillo's ear.

"Calm down, I can hear you. You found the jeweler who sold the bracelet?"

"Yes, but not in Florence. Here in Radda. Gioielleria Crisani. It's just past the Fattoria Vignale hotel. I know you told me to go back to the office, but I thought since I was here . . ." Daniele stopped and waited for the reprimand.

Perillo was thrilled but wasn't going to let it show. "This time you got results. Next time, check with me first. I'm coming to talk to them, but first I have to go back and get the bracelet."

"I have it with me."

"Ah." Perillo held back from saying "Good." Daniele was young and needed reining in. Not unlike Nico's stray. "I'll be there in fifteen minutes."

NICO SAT DOWN ACROSS from the old man wrapped in his overcoat. The pungent smell of his cologne was almost gone, thanks to the fresh air coming in from the open doors.

Gogol nudged his chin toward the salame crostino in front of Nico.

"Thank you." He wrapped the crostino in the napkin. "I'll eat it later." He could smell the cornetti coming out of the oven. "I'm sorry I didn't show up yesterday."

"We took care of him," Jimmy called out.

"Thanks. I'll pay."

"No need," Sandro said. "You're a good customer."

"You did not appear because," Gogol said, "'the river of blood draws near, wherein are boiling those who harm others by violence.'"

Nico picked up the words "blood" and "violence." "Yes, there was a murder."

Jimmy carried over a tray with their breakfast, to which he'd added a jar of his homemade raspberry jam. Nico watched Gogol grin with happiness as he slathered jam onto his hot cornetto. It was a sight that started Nico's mornings on good footing. Too bad he'd needed to roast the tomatoes yesterday instead of coming to the bar. He would have made Gogol happy, and someone else would've found the body. He picked up his own cornetto.

Gogol pressed a finger on the back of his friend's hand. Nico understood that he was about to say something he considered important. Two days ago, Gogol had pressed his finger on Nico's forearm before revealing that his mother didn't know who his father was, but God had forgiven her, and she was in Dante's *Paradiso* with the poet.

Nico prepared himself for another quote he would not understand, but this man deserved to be listened to. "Yes, tell me."

"The dead man is a not a good man," Gogol said. "Better dead."

Nico put his food back on the plate and looked into Gogol's water-blue eyes. People said the old man was simple, but anyone who quoted Dante at will had to have some intelligence. "You know who he is?"

"Stay away. He will hurt you." Gogol rubbed his hands over his face as if needing to wipe it clean.

"The dead man will hurt me?"

"Salvatore. Stay away."

"Why?"

"Bad man."

"Why is the maresciallo a bad man?"

"No!" Gogol slapped his hand on the table, spilling his coffee. It dripped onto the floor. "I go now. Tomorrow, if I live." It was his usual way of signing off.

"You will live, and you will tell me more tomorrow."

"'Through me is the way to the lost people,'" Gogol quoted, as he tightened his coat around his body and slowly made his way out of the café.

"Don't take him seriously. He's the lost one, unfortunately." Sandro brought over a mop and started wiping the floor. "You're manna from heaven for him. Not just because you feed him. Not many people really listen to him. They might give him a euro but they don't hear a word. I'm surprised you understand Dante's Italian. I had a tough time with it in school."

"I only catch words, not whole sentences. I tried to read *The Divine Comedy* in English to make my wife happy, but gave up pretty quickly."

"And yet you listen. Good for you."

"The man deserves that much." What Nico really listened for was the words between the quotes, the man behind the Dante screen. He hadn't found him yet. And what did Gogol have against the maresciallo?

"Has Gogol ever had trouble with the law?" Nico asked Sandro.

"No. We'd know if he had."

Jimmy, who was washing down the counter with a sponge, joined in. "In this town, even your farts aren't secret. Not that anyone really cares. Live and let live. You picked a good place to live."

"I know." Live and let live was exactly what he needed. Nico stood up, and OneWag followed his lead.

Sandro moved the pail out of Nico's way. "Don't worry about what Gogol said. He and Salvatore get along fine, but since he really likes you, please do us all the favor of smashing that cologne bottle of his."

"I can try to talk him out of using it."

Jimmy laughed. "You've got as much a chance at that as winning the lottery."

FOUR

The historical center of Radda, the medieval heart of Chianti, was a pedestrian-only zone. Perillo drove down one tree-lined viale that skirted the village, then back up the other side. As he expected, no free parking spots. September, with weather that restored the soul after the gagging heat of August, was his favorite month, but also the month the tourists poured in, thanks to the mild sun and all the wine and food festivals. They brought in much-needed money, but Perillo resented their taking over as though the place was theirs. His wife's complaints didn't help. Endless lines at the food shops, crowded cafés, bread selling out early, the best tomatoes gone, restaurants reserved weeks ahead when it had always been possible to reserve the very same day. Not that he ever took his wife out to a restaurant.

Lost in the iniquities brought on by tourists, Perillo drove right by his uniformed brigadiere standing in front of Gioielleria Crisani.

Daniele waved. "Maresciallo!"

Perillo saw Daniele in his rearview mirror and braked. The Fiat behind him swerved to avoid hitting the carabinieri car. Perillo shrugged an apology as the driver passed him, holding back what Perillo knew was a deserved vaffanculo. He turned off the motor, got out and joined Daniele, who was looking at his double-parked car with dismay. Perillo didn't care. Double parking was a privilege that came with the job. It was unfortunate that everyone else thought they had the same privilege.

"We won't be long." Perillo rang the bell by the door and

was buzzed in. The store was a small, narrow room with every available space covered by glass cases displaying glittering and expensive jewelry. He was reminded of the Ponte Vecchio stores he'd seen with his wife in Florence. This one had no view of the Arno in the back, but the young woman behind the display case was just as enticing a sight. Black, wavy hair falling to the shoulders framed a marble-white oval face, full bare lips, large, dark eyes nesting below a thick fringe of black eyelashes and perfectly shaped eyebrows. Perillo took his eyes away to look at the ceiling. The sight of good-looking women lightened his heart, but the sight of the two video cameras, one above the door, the other above the young woman, made it jump.

"Buongiorno, Signorina." He took out his identification.

She held up a graceful hand, devoid of any jewelry. "No need, Maresciallo Perillo. Daniele told me you were coming."

Perillo looked at his underling. "Daniele?"

"I gave her my full name." Daniele was smiling like someone who'd just found the end of a rainbow.

God, Perillo thought. This woman calls him by his first name and he's already in love! Lovelorn men were useless. Perillo turned back to the woman. "And your name is?"

She smiled. "Rosalba Crisani."

"You are the owner?"

"My mother is."

Perillo held his hand out behind him. Daniele understood and dropped the bracelet in his palm. Perillo spread the bracelet and its dated charm on the velvet cloth on the counter. "Now, Signorina Rosalba, I see that you have two video cameras in the store, which is a very good thing for you and I hope for me. Were they running the day someone bought this bracelet?"

"Only the tape from the camera above the door." She pointed to the video camera on the ceiling behind her. "This one was being fixed that day. I'm sorry." She looked chagrined.

"It's not your fault," Perillo said. There was a sweetness to her that made him want to reassure her, despite cursing his own bad luck. "It would have been far worse if you had been robbed that day. I hope it's working now."

"It is."

"We will want to see the tape from the working camera."

"I'm sorry. We tape over them at the end of each week."

Perillo held back a groan. Annoyed, he asked, "Then why did you tell us about the other camera not working? You would have taped over that one too, correct?"

"Daniele told me I had to tell you everything." She offered her pretty smile as if it was of help.

"I did, Maresciallo."

Perillo turned to look at his brigadiere. "I don't doubt it." At the same time, Daniele surely asked for her phone number, email, Twitter handle and whatever else young people used to communicate these days. Dio, to be young.

Daniele, who knew to stay in the background when Perillo was questioning witnesses, stepped up to the counter to explain. His face was watermelon-tinged. "I had a fruit juice at the bar by the hotel, and she was having a coffee next to me. I introduced myself and asked her where I could find a jewelry store."

Perillo softened, remembering how many times, at Daniele's age, he'd used "Do you know where I can find . . ." as a pickup line. He turned to Rosalba. "Please tell me everything you remember about the man who bought this bracelet."

"There isn't much to tell. He came in last Wednesday, just as I opened the shop at eleven."

"You open at eleven?"

"Yes. Tuesday to Saturday."

Perillo pointed to his watch. "It is now ten of ten. Why did you open so early?"

Rosalba looked at Daniele, then back at the maresciallo, her expression not in the least bit puzzled. "Daniele asked me to."

She was either obedient by nature, or Daniele had made quite an impression on her. "The man came last Wednesday," Perillo repeated.

"Yes. Daniele said it was important to be exact, so I looked up the sale on the sales log. I'm trying to get Mamma to list our sales and receipts on the computer, but she doesn't trust it, so it took me a while to find it."

Perillo nodded. It never paid to hurry a witness along.

"Sales have been very good lately."

"I can see that." There were quite a few empty spaces in the display cases. "Can you describe him?"

"Big man. Fat belly," Rosalba said. "Dressed in jeans and an old polo shirt with a golf club embroidered on the pocket. Just the golf club, no lettering. I noticed because my mother used to play golf with my stepfather whenever she got the chance. I'd take over here, and off she went. She doesn't do that anymore. He died two years ago." She addressed this personal fact to Daniele, who voiced that he was sorry.

There was no emotion in her tone, Perillo noticed. "Can you describe the buyer's face?" he asked.

"I didn't look at him really. Old. Maybe fifty?"

Perillo wanted to laugh. Fifty was middle age. He was about to hit that milestone himself in three years, and young women like Rosalba had stopped looking at him long ago. "Can you go into more detail?"

"He wore a blue baseball cap pulled low in front, so I couldn't really see his eyes. He had a big nose. Dark, leathery skin. Lots of wrinkles."

"Anything written on the cap?"

"LA Dodgers."

Perillo let out a sigh of satisfaction. Gold sneakers, baseball cap. An American, then, just as he'd thought.

Daniele leaned toward Perillo and quietly said, "The watch."

Perillo nodded. "Forgive me, Signorina, one last question.

Did you happen to notice what kind of watch your client was wearing?"

"A Swatch, I think. Nothing fancy. He wasn't dressed like a rich man, if that's what you're asking."

Rosalba's answer didn't surprise Perillo. A foreigner wearing an expensive gold watch would attract muggers. The victim had been prudent enough not to wear it everywhere, yet he'd had it on the morning of his death.

"I'd like to send a sketch artist from Florence to draw his face according to what you remember," Perillo said. "She'll show you different lips, eyebrows, eyes, chins. It might jog your memory."

Rosalba didn't answer right away. Her expression showed she didn't relish the thought of getting more involved. Perillo couldn't blame her. Rosalba, with her perfect diction, hair styled down to the strand, her pretty silk dress, came from a world that shied away from the sordid. "Has the man done something wrong?"

"He died."

"Oh." Rosalba traced her finger over the bracelet. She kept her head down when she spoke. "I'll try if it will help."

"Thank you. A few more questions."

She lifted her head. No smile. "Please, ask."

"Did he pay with a credit card?"

"No. All cash, which surprised me. The bracelet and charm cost fourteen hundred euros."

Daniele whistled and caught Perillo clenching his jaw. He was going to get a good talking-to after they left.

"It's heavy, eighteen-carat gold," Rosalba said. "The chain isn't hollowed out. He gave me three five-hundred-euro notes. I don't like holding large amounts of cash. It's dangerous. As soon as he left, I closed the store and ran to the bank. Luckily, it's just around the corner. I was sure he was American, you know, the baseball cap and"—a car honked loudly out on the street—"he didn't say buongiorno after I buzzed him in, which made me immediately think he was a foreigner, but I was wrong." She had to raise her voice because of the continued honking. "He spoke pure Tuscan. You know, how some people substitute their consonants with an 'H.'" By "some people," she meant ones outside her social class.

Perillo covered his disappointment with a smile. "'Hasa' instead of 'casa.'" He'd been so ready to bet the man was American. Hoped for it. They had passports. Their names and passport numbers were recorded in the hotels they slept in or by the real estate agents who rented them fancy villas. They paid with traceable credit cards. A Tuscan could disappear in the crowd more easily. On the other hand, a murdered American would stir up the American press and maybe their police. The botched Amanda Knox case had left a nasty stain on Italian law enforcement.

Rosalba flashed a smile at Daniele for a second, then turned to Perillo. "Your brigadiere is Venetian. What about you?"

"I'm from Hampagnia."

She laughed. A light, musical sound that made Perillo's heart jump.

The car on the street kept honking. Perillo took a quick look outside and threw his car keys to Daniele. "Take that man out of his misery."

Daniele was happy where he was, but he had no choice. Keys in hand, he gave Rosalba's lovely face another look and left to move the car.

"Did he talk about the date he wanted you to inscribe?" The Maresciallo turned over the round charm to show the date—1/1/97. "Say anything about what it stood for?"

Rosalba knitted her well-groomed eyebrows together. "He did say something. What was it? He got very nervous and excited when he talked about the date. He asked to see all the different fonts we had available. It took him a long time to decide on cursive. He was giving it to someone he loved very much, that was clear to me. I hope she gets the bracelet."

"She will when we find out who she is." As long as she wasn't the killer. Perillo pocketed the bracelet and gave Rosalba a card with both the station's and his own phone number and email. "In case something comes to mind." He suspected she already had Daniele's personal information. Perillo held out his hand. "Thank you. We'll call you when the sketch artist is ready."

"All right." She shook his hand and held on to it. "I hope you find her."

"So do I."

On the street, the car was gone. Daniele, the moralist, had refused to park in the now-empty space because it was in a no-parking zone, which meant he was now circling Radda looking for a spot. Perillo debated between waiting and getting an espresso at the nearest café. He opted for the espresso and rang Rosalba's bell. At the buzz, he opened the door and offered to bring her one.

"No, thanks, Maresciallo, but I'm glad you came back. I was about to call your cell. What the man said about the date popped back into my head. He said it stood for the day he did something both despicable and wonderful."

"Thank you. That's helpful." He had no idea what it meant, but it was something to chew on. He started walking in search of a café when up ahead he saw the squad car reversing into a legal parking spot. The luck of the young!

Perillo crossed the street and joined Daniele just as he was getting out of the car. "You and I need to talk."

"Sorry, I shouldn't have whistled back in the store."

Perillo got in the driver's seat. "You showed initiative today, and I like that, but you can't fraternize with anyone involved in this case. Besides, she'd chop you into hamburger meat and feed you to her dog. Now, get on your motorcycle and follow me back to Greve."

Daniele flushed with anger.

AFTER BUYING *LA NAZIONE* and yesterday's *New York Times International Edition* from Beppe at the news shop, Nico and the dog strolled up to the castle at the very top of the hill. All that remained was crumbling walls and a restored tower. He liked to take in the clear views of the valley the grounds offered. He could see Aldo's winery spread out mid-valley. He thought he could spot his new home, the dark speck near the Ferriello olive grove. Behind that speck was the wide expanse of woods where he'd found the body. Death was following him around, even now. He whistled to OneWag, who came running. It was time for flowers.

On the way back down, Nico stopped to say hello to Tilde and ask if she needed any help. She was alone in the kitchen, rolling small balls of spinach and ricotta in her palms, which the Tuscans called gnudi, which she would later serve in brown butter and sage. The word meant "naked." He found them delicious, but when he tried to make them, they always fell apart.

"That's another secret you're going to have to share," Nico said.

"No secret. Experience."

"Okay, I'll try again. How are you?"

"Fine. Busy."

"Where is everybody?"

"Enzo drove Alba to the Coop. Elvira is getting her color touched up, and my daughter is late."

"Gianni?"

"No, she stayed at a girlfriend's. Or so she said. Not that she has to lie to me. She's very nervous and down. Gianni, the museum exam, who knows? Daughters are impossible. You're lucky you never—" Tilde clasped her hand against her mouth, her eyes wide with regret. "I'm sorry. Please forgive me."

He wiped ricotta and spinach from Tilde's chin with his handkerchief. "There's nothing to forgive." After Rita miscarried for the third time, they'd locked away their dream of having children. "Come meet my dog." He'd ordered OneWag to stay outside, and to his surprise, the dog obeyed.

"Bring him in."

"Into the restaurant?"

"Why not? My clients' shoes walk the same streets his paws do."

"Well, look at him," Tilde exclaimed when Nico carried in a panting OneWag. "His portrait is in the Uffizi, next to a naked lady. You have to go see it." She turned on the cold water at the sink and reached for a bowl. "Put him down. He's thirsty." She placed the full bowl on the floor. OneWag licked her hand and eagerly lapped up the water. The climb to the castle had been too steep for his short legs.

Tilde picked up the quickly emptied bowl. "Any news on who the man is?"

"Not that I've heard. You'll have to ask Salvatore."

"What's taking so long? The whole town is on edge."

"You certainly are."

"No. I worry about the poor soul who's waiting for him to come home."

"Yes, there is that." How many times had he brought bad news to wives, husbands, mothers, fathers, children? Sometimes their reaction had been a clue that led to the killer.

Tilde waved him away. "Today's not your day to help out, so go. I'll see you tomorrow at lunchtime. If you want an olive loaf, Enrico, by some miracle, still has a few left." Enrico had a shop halfway down the hill that supplied the restaurant's bread. The olive loaves usually sold out by nine-thirty. It was now past ten. "But you'd better hurry."

"Thanks. See you tomorrow." Nico kissed her on both cheeks, part of the Italian hello and goodbye.

Halfway down the hill, Nico spotted Gianni trudging up in jeans and the leaf-green and purple Ferriello T-shirt Aldo's employees all wore. He was a not particularly tall young man, with a trim body and a handsome face crowned by a mess of curly dark hair. Gianni waved at him and stopped.

When Nico reached him, Gianni gave him a hug and the double-cheek kiss. A first for Gianni, who usually just said hi and went on his way. "Ciao, Nico. All is well, I hope?" He was all smiles.

"Everything is fine."

OneWag ambled over from the gutter, where he'd been on the lookout for intriguing smells and stopped to sniff Gianni's sneakers carefully.

"Glad to hear that after what happened. I've been meaning to tell you you've been great. You know that?"

"I have?"

"Helping Stella at the restaurant. I can't thank you enough."

"Stella is family."

"She's lucky to have you. You're reasonable, not like her mother. I don't know why Tilde dislikes me so much."

Nico didn't like getting into other people's affairs, but he was on Stella's side. A controlling boyfriend was not good news. "Stella loves you, Gianni. Be grateful for that. Don't try to control her. Even if she listens and doesn't take the exam, she will end up regretting it and taking it out on you. It's only an exam. She might not win the job, and even if she does get the job, it doesn't mean she'll stop loving you. Have faith in her."

Gianni laughed and gave him another hug. "Right you are, Nico. I've been an asshole. I got her so upset I risked losing her even before she takes that dumb exam. I told Stella she can do whatever she wants. I love her and I'm going to marry her." He showed off a wide grin.

"Good. And maybe you can come by in the evening and help Stella at the restaurant sometime."

Gianni dropped his grin. Nico regretted his remark. It was unnecessary and not his place to have said it, but there was a cockiness to Gianni's remarks that had gotten under his skin. The young man had looked so obviously pleased with his generosity toward Stella.

"Ciao, Gianni. What I do for the family gives me joy. No thanks needed."

ONCE BACK AT THE main piazza, OneWag ran across the street, aiming straight for Luciana's shop, just two doors down from Bar All'Angolo. Nico yelled his name just as a car rushed past the dog.

New flowerpots the truck had brought that morning lined the outside of the shop. OneWag sniffed the first one, a white cyclamen.

Nico hurried across the street. "Don't you dare!"

The dog ignored him and sniffed the next plant.

Nico watched, ready to snatch OneWag at the first hint of a raised leg. He would buy the plant, of course, but he'd have a hard time facing Luciana, who was Tilde's good friend. Hers was the only flower shop in the village, and every petal and leaf was her tesoro, her darling. She was capable of banishing him. He'd have to drive to Panzano to find flowers for Rita. It wasn't far, but he owed Luciana his loyalty. She had arranged the wreath of yellow roses he had requested for Rita's burial and refused to accept payment.

Luciana appeared in the doorway. A forty-year-old woman with a wide face, hazel eyes, a chiseled nose and a mass of thick henna-tinted curls that could pass for chrysanthemums. A black tentlike dress covered her large body. "Buongiorno, Nico, bello."

He looked up and smiled at her addition of "bello" to his name. Beautiful or handsome he had never been—not even as a baby, as his mother liked to remind him. "Buongiorno, Luciana."

She looked down at the paper bag on his arm that read DA ENRICO. "How many did you get?" Enrico was her devoted husband, a man half her size in height and width.

"Two." The small loaves were made with soft, chewy seven-grain bread dotted with salty black olives. "I reserved for tomorrow."

"I should start doing that. You'd think he'd set aside at least one for his wife. Not a chance. His customers come first." She moved aside to let Nico pass. "Come and see! The truck brought some lovelies in this morning."

Nico looked down at OneWag, who was examining his third flowerpot, one crowded with blue asters. Rita would like those. "I'm worried he'll lift his leg on the flowers."

Luciana shook her curls. "Not this one; I already know him. He's a smarty. I give him a treat, he sniffs and leaves his signature somewhere else. Come on, little one. You too. I've got sunflowers that will turn your head. And biscuits for the little one. You can have one too, if you want."

OneWag scampered inside, followed by Nico. "No thanks, Luciana." He looked at the new plants. More cyclamens, mostly red. Small flowers that looked like asters and were called settem-brini because of the time they flowered. Early chrysanthemums, the Italians' flower of choice for the Day of the Dead. Rita would never, ever have those on her tomb. For her, only flowers that stood for life. While Nico browsed, OneWag got his biscuit, which he took outside to eat.

"That dog has manners," Luciana said. "Someone must have owned him once. Maybe Titian. Have you been to the Uffizi?"

"Years ago, with Rita. I'm clueless about art."

"Look it up on the Internet. Titian's *Venus of Urbino*. The little one's on the bed, fast asleep. You've got yourself a Renaissance dog."

"Tilde told me about the painting. What I need to do is take him to a vet."

"You don't have to. He's had his shots."

"You took him?"

She nodded. "I would've brought him home too, but Geisha, my Siamese, would have scratched out my eyes. I'm so glad you've taken him in." She lunged at Nico and pressed him against her big, soft body. "You are a good man."

Nico held his breath, every nerve in his body wanting to

squirm free. He hadn't welcomed Rita's hugs either. He hadn't been hugged in his childhood, despite his Italian mother and grandmother. They only hugged their own unhappiness. And his father only liked to use his fists on his wife and his son. At fourteen, Nico had hit him back, and the man had walked out for good.

Luciana must have sensed his discomfort. "Don't worry. I still love my Enrico." She let him go. "I will tell you this. I am relieved you were the one who found that poor man. You are a big-city fellow, more used to violence than us Gravignesi."

"I suppose that's true."

"Can you imagine one of us finding him? A child, even? Terrible. Thank you for being the one."

Nico didn't know how to answer that. "I'll take the blue aster plant outside."

"Ah, Nico, you break my heart. Always you pick my darling of the week. I was going to take it home, believe me, but for you and Rita, I give it up gladly."

She said that every week. Nico thanked her, paid and kissed the cheeks she offered. On the way out, he left one of Enrico's olive loaves next to Luciana's handbag.

NICO WAS HALFWAY OUT of the parking space in front of the salumeria when the blue Alfa screeched to a halt next to him. "Ehi, Nico," Perillo called out from the open window. "Have you eaten at Da Angela yet?"

Nico's response was a sigh.

"No? I know you're loyal to Sotto Il Fico, but you have to try this place. It's in Lucarelli, twenty minutes from here. My treat. How about tonight?"

Damn! Why couldn't this guy leave him alone? In the backseat, OneWag reached up to the open window and barked a welcome. "What is it you want, Maresciallo?"

"Salvatore, please." Perillo left the motor running, got out of his car and leaned down to meet Nico's face at the open window. "I know about your old job and your forced retirement." His voice was low now. "Don't worry. That information stays with me."

Shit, Nico thought.

"I don't—"

"Daniele found the information online. Don't worry, he's as silent as a tomb."

"So you know. Now what? Are you planning to blackmail me?"

"Dio mio!" Perillo jumped up from the window, hitting his head against the top frame. He rubbed the top of his head. "How could you think that? Daniele suggested I ask for your help. It was a good idea."

"No!"

"Why not? You've spent as many years seeking justice as I have. And doubtless with many more cases like this."

"There's a reason I was fired."

"That's regrettable for you, but changes nothing for me."

"It wasn't regrettable. It was deserved."

"That doesn't change the fact that you have expertise I don't have. I've dealt with only a single murder in my career. Holy heaven, New Yorkers must have murders every day."

"That's not true by any means."

"I know. I'm just trying to make a point. Much more than in the villages of Tuscany, you would agree?"

"I don't have the data, but I suppose so."

"Let's have dinner together. If you don't wish to get involved, we can discuss other things."

"How can we talk about the murder with other people around?"

This question was good news for Perillo. "First we eat, drink a good bottle of Chianti Classico, then I drive you home and we strategize like two generals fighting a war. Do you accept?"

"If I don't?"

"I will do the best I can to find who killed this man. He

was not American, we discovered this morning from the young woman who sold the man a charm bracelet with a mysterious date on it. He was Tuscan."

Nico recognized the setup game. His partner had been an ace at it when interrogating suspects. Dangling a new detail in front of them and waiting for them to swallow the bait. No harm in playing along. "What bracelet?"

"I will tell you this evening." Perillo reached into the back window and scratched OneWag's head. "Forza, convince your friend. You can come too. We'll eat in the garden." He put his scratching hand back in his pocket and turned to face Nico, laughing. "Asking for a dog's help is the sign of a drowning man." There was the truth. No more saving face. Honesty was best with the American.

Nico leaned over the steering wheel and crossed his arms. He'd heard of Angela's from Tilde, who'd said it was excellent. A good meal, a report on the food for Tilde, maybe discovering a new dish or two to add to Sotto Il Fico's limited menu. And also listening to what Perillo had to say.

He sat back up. "I don't have any lifesavers to throw at you, but I've been told I'm a good listener. I pay for my own meal." No way was he going to owe this man.

"As you wish. I'll meet you here in the piazza at eight." Perillo prayed the restaurant wasn't booked solid, as it was most nights.

As Nico watched Perillo drive away, Gogol's words came back to him. *The maresciallo talk to you. Stay away. A very bad man.*

TILDE HAD JUST FINISHED stuffing al dente rigatoni with a veal and broccoli ragout when Stella slipped into the kitchen. As Tilde poured a light tomato sauce over the pasta, she looked at her daughter's unsmiling face. Damn that Gianni. Tilde put the saucepan down and wiped her hands on her apron. It was time to have another conversation with her beautiful, unhappy daughter before Elvira and Enzo came back.

Stella raised a hand in protest. She could tell what was coming. "Don't, Mamma. I'm sorry I'm late." She didn't sound sorry. "What do you want me to do? Set the outside tables?"

"Isn't that what you do every morning?"

Stella sighed loudly and went into the main room to get the cutlery. Tilde followed her. "Did you get a chance to study for the exam last night?"

Stella opened the heavy drawer of the oak chest that hugged the wall behind Elvira's chair and ran her fingers through the forks, making as much noise as possible.

"There's no need to act like a child. You know I worry."

"Yes, Mamma, I know you do. And I did study. Not a lot, though. I couldn't stop thinking about the man who had his face blown off." Stella looked back at her mother, completely pale. "I'm scared."

"Oh, Stella, sweetheart." Tilde enfolded her daughter in her arms. "That man's death was terrible, but it has nothing to do with us."

"Are you sure?"

Tilde cupped Stella's chin and peered into her daughter's green eyes. "Of course I'm sure." If only she could believe that. Those damned gold sneakers. It was ridiculous to think they had anything to do with Robi. "Please don't worry."

Stella pushed herself away from her mother and dropped down in Elvira's chair. She started leafing through her grandmother's *Settimana Enigmistica.* "I just have the creepy feeling that the man who died was the same man who was following me for a couple of days."

"What man?" The thought of a strange man following her daughter took the breath from her.

"I don't know. An older guy. I kept running into him in weird places. The first time I saw him, he gaped at me with this stupid grin on his face. He didn't say anything or try to touch me; I would have hit him if he had."

Tilde felt her knees weaken. She held on to the doorjamb. "Was it someone who came to the restaurant?"

"I don't think so. I couldn't really tell. He was wearing a baseball cap pulled down low over sunglasses. The first time I noticed him was in Panzano. He was at Dario Cecchini's butcher shop, drinking a glass of wine." Stella did not add that when the man saw her, he nearly dropped the glass. The next day, when she went to pick up Gianni in her Vespa at the vineyard, she thought she saw the man driving behind her. Gianni told her she was crazy and started to make fun of her. Having her fear dismissed so quickly angered her. She was beginning to think her mother was right about Gianni, but what other man was going to love her as much as he did?

"Why do you think he's the man who got killed?"

"I don't know. He was so creepy."

Tilde rubbed her stomach to calm herself. Her beloved daughter, prey to men's hunger. She knew where that could lead only too well. She had lived with that fear from the day Stella was conceived. "Darling, you are beautiful, and men will always look at you, no matter how old they are. Maybe you made him remember when he was young and in love, or maybe he just wanted to fall in love one more time."

Stella looked at her mother in amazement. "Since when were you a romantic? Feet on the ground, Mamma, please. I don't want you getting sappy on me. He was probably looking at my breasts."

Tilde laughed in relief. This was the daughter she knew. Sassy and down-to-earth. "You do have to get used to men staring at you. There's no need to be scared." She too had to stop being scared. She had let her imagination run away with her. "Just be careful."

"Yes, Mamma. I've heard it all before." It was her eyes the man had liked. She'd bumped into him again at the big Coop in Greve. He'd bared his teeth at her, like he was ready to bite into her. "You cannot imagine how happy you make me," he whispered. Gianni was with her and threatened the man with his fist. She dragged Gianni out of the supermarket as fast as she could, the shopping she needed to do completely forgotten.

"You know that old turd," Gianni accused when they were out on the street. He seemed not to believe her when she said she didn't. His ridiculous jealousy was one of the reasons her feelings for him were cooling.

She kissed Tilde's cheek to reassure her. "I'm not stupid. I can take care of myself."

"But you were scared of this man. Did you think he might hurt you?"

"No. It's just the way he kept staring at me like we knew each other. Then the murder happened, and for some reason I linked the two." Stella stood up and grabbed a handful of forks. "Come on, Mamma. Time to work."

"Right you are." Tilde pushed the old memory back into the hidden recess of her mind where she had kept it for twenty-two years and went back to the kitchen to toast the bread crumbs she would sprinkle over the rigatoni before putting them in the oven.

THE SMALL CEMETERY WAS on a hill behind the town, enclosed by a high stone wall and the stately cypress trees that acted as a cemetery's logo throughout Italy. It was a modest place. The one mausoleum, a sixteenth-century marble temple edged with Doric columns, had belonged to a humbler branch of the Medici family whose villa now housed Gogol's old-age home on the outskirts of town. The rest of the grounds were covered with stone and marble gravestones neatly divided by narrow dirt aisles, many with enameled photos of the dead. Only a few embellishments. A two-foot-high marble angel wept over a child's nineteenth-century grave. A stone basket filled with meticulously carved grapes sat atop the grave of a man who had died the year before. A faithful stone dog lay atop another grave. Flowers real and fake graced every grave, even the ones from past centuries. The Gravignesi cared for their dead.

Nico and OneWag passed through the open wrought-iron gate and walked to the water fountain in the corner. Nico picked up one of the empty plastic water bottles left there by other visitors for anyone to use and filled it. Water gurgled from the old spout. OneWag, thirsty again, sat up on his hind legs, a trick he'd picked up watching fancy dogs beg for a treat. Nico lifted him up and let him catch as much water as he could. With the full bottle in one hand and the dog under his arm, he walked to where Rita rested next to her parents. He watered the cyclamens he knew Tilde had brought for all three, then placed his own aster plant over Rita. He straightened up and stood, looking at the neatly carved letters of his wife's name, the numbers that marked the years of her life, at the bottom, the words BELLA, DOLCE DONNA E MOGLIE, "beautiful sweet woman and wife," words he had thought of in English, but had wanted in Italian so that all who came here would know how wonderful she was.

She had died fourteen months ago, and her face, her voice were beginning to fade. He missed them both.

OneWag sniffed the air loudly and dropped into a crouch with a low growl. Nico heard footsteps and tucked OneWag under his arm. "Shh. No acting out on holy ground."

"'Bella, dolce donna.' A beautiful inscription."

Nico turned around to see who had spoken.

The woman noticed the startled look on his face. "Please forgive me." She offered her smile. "I didn't mean to interrupt your thoughts. I simply want to thank you for giving me a much-needed ride on Monday. Remember?" She held out her hand. "Maria Dorsetti."

He shook the offered hand. "Nico Doyle." He didn't mumble this time. "Yes, I do remember. You gave me directions to the carabinieri station in Greve." She had a pleasant face and large, rich brown eyes that kept a steady gaze on him. Today, she was wearing a perfectly ironed pale blue short-sleeved linen suit that showed off her good figure. Nico shifted OneWag to his other arm. Making conversation with this attractive woman in front of Rita's grave embarrassed him.

"The meeting went well, I hope."

Was she just making conversation, Nico wondered, or was she the meddling kind? "The maresciallo is a very nice man," he offered as an answer as he nervously stroked OneWag.

"Of course he is. We depend on him and his men to keep us safe. I'm sorry we are meeting again in such a sad place." Actually, though, she considered it a happy event. There was a gentleness, a childlike lost quality to this man that had attracted her right away. American men had a reputation for being kind, she'd read somewhere. She'd been foolish enough to hope she would spot him over the weekend among the hundreds of people at the Chianti Expo, perhaps share an espresso with him later to counter all that wine tasting. Or even a meal. Her other widowed friends had told her often enough that she was foolish to hope their lives would change, but as Ungaretti concluded in a sad poem she studied in school, she had never been so coupled to life.

"I buried my husband here four years ago." Maria waved to the wall of tombs at the upper end of the cemetery. Four rows of loculi that looked like filing cabinets. "My inscription isn't as loving as yours. Just his name and the years he lived."

OneWag squirmed against Nico's grip.

"I see your dog has gotten impatient. I'm sorry to have disturbed you." She stepped closer. He inhaled her scent and recognized it as sandalwood mixed with something else. Tilde had given him a box of sandalwood soap at Christmas. He found the smell comforting.

"Goodbye, Signor Doyle. Maybe we will meet at one of the wine stands this weekend. I'm going on Friday when it opens at eleven. I like to watch the people flowing eagerly into the piazza." The crowd's chatter and laughter getting louder with one wine tasting following another lifted her spirits. "Podere San Cresci offers very good wine."

"Thank you for the tip," Nico said. He understood that she was giving him the opportunity for a date. Maybe after four years, she had put grief aside.

Maria hesitated for a moment. When Nico added nothing, she lowered her head and walked away.

OneWag yelped. Nico had been holding him too tight. "Stop it!" He loosened his grip and bent down on one knee. With his free hand, he fidgeted with the aster plant. Months after it had become clear that he and Rita would never have children, he'd brought home a hairy ragamuffin of a mutt from the ASPCA, a dog he'd instantly taken to. Rita had burst into tears and asked him to take it back. She couldn't accept a substitute for the child they could not have. And she wouldn't adopt a child, for reasons he was never able to understand.

He held up OneWag close to the gravestone. "Look what found me, Rita. He needs a home."

FIVE

Daniele's motorbike zoomed into the parking lot at the station just as Perillo got out of the Alfa Romeo. He acknowledged his superior with a curt nod. Perillo supposed his words about Rosalba turning him into hamburger meat still stung.

"Ehi, Dani, I'm going for a coffee." He knew he'd been a little rough. "Come on, my treat." When he'd been stationed in Naples, he'd never had to pay. Cafés and restaurants were only too glad to see him scare the pickpockets away. Tuscans weren't as generous. They also didn't have as many pickpockets.

Daniele shook his head. A coffee or a fruit juice wasn't going to do it. "I'd better see if any messages have come in. We've been gone a while."

Perillo pointed a finger at him. "Good thinking. I'll be fast."

When Perillo walked into the bar next to the station, he was greeted by the grumpy bartender with a torn rotator cuff thanks to thirty years of making espressos. "What's the count so far?"

"Eight, maybe."

"How about a glass of milk?"

Perillo snorted. "You want to kill me?"

"Caffeine will kill, not milk. Caffeine and cigarettes."

"If everyone stopped drinking coffee, you'd be out of a job. I need the jolt. I've got a big one on my hands."

The bartender put the espresso cup on the counter and took the euro Perillo gave him. "This isn't like the last one, eh?"

"Nothing like it." He'd solved the other murder in two days.

An Albanian had stabbed another Albanian to death over a woman. Back in the late nineties, the Albanians had poured into Italy, fleeing the war in their homeland. Most had come with good intentions. A few less so. An Italian thief Perillo had sent to jail several times had come into the office to announce he was changing careers because the Albanians had taken over his territory. There was nothing politically incorrect about admitting it was a fact. People stole when they couldn't find work. There was work here in the vineyards, in construction. They were hard workers. The Africans were still coming too, but too many drowned en route. Now the government wasn't allowing them in. How could anyone turn desperate people away?

Perillo drank his espresso in one gulp, raised his hand in salute to the bartender and walked out, jabbing a cigarette in his mouth. He was about to light it when his phone rang.

"Are you coming back?" Daniele asked.

"After I smoke a cigarette." The carabinieri stations were now smoke-free by order of some high-ranking health nut. "Why?"

"There's news."

"I'll be there." He shoved the cigarette back in the pack and hurried back to his office.

DANIELE SAT BY THE phone at his desk, next to his computer, his face beaming with excitement.

Good news, then, Perillo sensed, and felt his stomach do a tarantella step. "Yes?"

"The Avis car rental company from Florence just called and said one of their cars was supposed to have been returned yesterday. The employee remembered that the man who rented it said he was going to Radda in Chianti."

"Did you get the name?"

"Yes, and the make and license plate number." Daniele took his time looking over his own note. "A metal-gray Fiat Panda, license plate SI 182144."

Daniele was certainly getting back at him. "Name, please."

"Robert Garrett."

Mother of God and all the saints! An American. Not their dead man. Perillo threw down his car keys on the desk and sat down. He turned to face Daniele, whose desk was in the back of the room, where his keyboard tapping was less noisy, allowing for Perillo to think, which he felt compelled to do at times. "What do they want from us? To look for their car when we've got a murder on our hands and the substitute prosecutor calling any minute to ask why we haven't solved the case yet? Tell Avis they're going to have to send their own people looking."

"Substitute Prosecutor Della Langhe called while we were in Radda. Do you want to hear the message?"

"Not on an empty stomach. Give me the short version."

"He expects you to call him first thing tomorrow morning. Tonight he has a gala at Palazzo Vecchio and can't be disturbed."

Perillo looked up at the ceiling and silently asked if a kind God would send him some good luck for once. "How long has it been since we found the man? Twenty-eight hours?"

Daniele looked at his watch.

"Stop that, I don't need to know. It's been no time at all, and already Count Roberto Della Langhe or whatever his title is wants results. All we've got is how much the bracelet cost and that a Tuscan with a weathered face bought it."

"A Tuscan who wasn't wearing an expensive watch. Maybe he bought the bracelet for somebody else?"

"What are you saying?"

"Fourteen hundred euros is a lot of money. Maybe the dead man hired this man to buy the bracelet for him because he didn't want anyone to know about it. It could also explain what he was doing in the woods so early in the morning."

"And what was that?"

"Maybe he was meeting someone and didn't want to be seen."

That made sense. "Wait a minute. Are you saying this Robert

Garrett who was going to Radda in Chianti and didn't return his car might be our dead man?"

"The technicians confirmed that the victim's clothes were American brands. According to Avis, Garrett's passport said he'd come from California."

AP, the only legible letters on the blood-soaked T-shirt. "Napa Valley is in California," Perillo exclaimed with a quick burst of excitement.

"Exactly! The 'AP' on his T-shirt. And gold shoes. Maybe he was from Hollywood. I've read that movie people love glitter."

Whether the man was from Hollywood or not, his briga-diere, who'd been on the job only six months, was possibly onto something. Why hadn't he considered that the Tuscan might be a go-between? "I'll send Dino and Vince to look for the car. Call the other carabinieri stations from Florence to Siena and ask them to help."

"I think we should try the roads surrounding Gravigna first."

"You think so?" Perillo asked sarcastically.

Daniele felt his cheeks go hot. "Yes, Maresciallo. He died there."

"Indeed he did," Perillo said. He knew he was being a resentful idiot. "Good thinking, Brigadiere Donato. When you're finished, come upstairs and we can have lunch together."

Daniele shot out of his chair so quickly his chair almost over-turned. An invitation to share a meal with his superior upstairs was a first. An honor. Every day, the smells of Signora Perillo's cooking wafted downstairs to tease his nostrils and make him salivate. "Thank you, Maresciallo."

Perillo walked to the door, opened it and waited for Daniele to follow him. "My wife's made veal involtini stuffed with mush-rooms and spinach."

Daniele still stood by his chair, his face pale.

"What's the problem? You're not hungry?"

"I am, but I'm a vegetarian, Maresciallo."

Perillo lifted his arms in a sign of resignation. Of course,

Daniele the moralist! "So my wife will heat up what's left of last night's eggplant parmigiana. No dead animal in that. Now get going. The day won't last forever."

AT EIGHT THAT EVENING, Nico sat on a bench in the main piazza of Gravigna while OneWag circled the area in search of new scents and what tourist tidbits the pigeons and sparrows hadn't gotten to yet. The sun had fallen below the hills, but the day's light seemed reluctant to cede its place to darkness. The old men had gone home. At one end of the piazza, the trattoria was filled with locals and tourists. Lavender-haired Carletta with nails to match was serving the few intrepid tourists who preferred the outside tables despite the cool air. The florist and newspaper shop had closed. Behind the closed glass doors of Bar All'Angolo, Jimmy was mopping the floor while Sandro buffed the long steel counter. The glass balls of old cast-iron streetlamps burst into life just as Perillo stopped in front of the café.

After his visit to Rita, Nico had gone to Panzano to do some shopping at the small Coop, the nearest supermarket, then gone home and eaten lunch. OneWag got half a can of dog food he barely touched, preferring Nico's salame. After lunch, Nico had settled on the balcony with the Italian translation of Jo Nesbø's latest thriller. The dog preferred the sofa.

Maresciallo Perillo's request for help kept interrupting Nico's reading. It left a mark he recognized. The one left by a man in need. A need far lighter than the one the murder suspect in his last case had left on his conscience. Responding to that woman's need had cost him his job. But he had no regrets. He would do it again. And tonight, he would listen to the Maresciallo, even if Gogol thought the man was bad. Maybe because of it. Finding out made life interesting. Besides, Nico was willing to bet Perillo didn't hold a candle to some of the men he'd met in his line of work. And if he could help solve the case, why not? He had nothing to lose except boredom.

"WE'RE IN LUCK. I nabbed the last table in the garden," Perillo announced as soon as OneWag settled in the backseat of the Panda and Nico buckled his seat belt. He shifted into first gear. He swung the car onto Route 222, which would take them toward the village of Lucarelli and Da Angela's restaurant.

Nico inhaled deeply and was relieved the car did not smell of cigarette smoke.

Perillo heard the intake of breath. "Ah, no, my wife would divorce me if I smoked in our car."

Nico smiled. "Mine was the same. No smoking in the house, either."

"We have a balcony."

"We didn't. It was just easier to give it up. Now I've gone back to having one or two a day."

"I admire your restraint. I love it too much."

They both knew they were exchanging easy talk, a warm-up.

They climbed up a winding road. Perillo drove fast, cutting the curves. It wasn't dark enough to see oncoming headlights yet, and Nico chose to keep his eyes on the wall of trees whisking by, then the suddenly revealed scenery below.

"We've made some progress. First, the jeweler." Perillo went into detail about his visit.

"Do you believe her?"

"That she sold the bracelet to this man? Yes." He turned to look at Nico just as the Panda approached another sharp curve. Nico held his breath. "Why would she make that up?"

"Your brigadiere is very handsome."

"Well, I suppose he is," Perillo conceded, "but with her looks, she wouldn't have to make up lies, I assure you."

It was clear to Nico that Daniele wasn't the only man smitten by this Rosalba, which didn't make for clear thinking. "Maybe I'm too cynical."

"I didn't think cynicism was an American trait. It's an Italian specialty."

"It comes with police work. If she's detail-oriented, a sketch artist will help."

"I thought of that, although we may not need one." Perillo told him about the missing car rented to an American. He was about to go into Daniele's theory of a go-between when, just before the umpteenth curve, a car barreled past them with only a few inches to spare.

Nico's heart missed a few beats, or so it felt. He'd always been a careful driver. "Stodgy," according to Rita. "Slowpoke Doyle" in the squad room. "Let's continue this conversation when we're not in motion."

Perillo laughed. "As you wish. Just remind me never to give you a ride in our Alfa. That one can do two hundred fifty-seven kilometers per hour. I think that's about a hundred sixty of your miles."

"I'll be sure to remind you."

ROSALBA LOOKED UP FROM setting the table when she heard the front door. "Ciao, Mamma, I'm in the dining room."

"What's for dinner?" Irene called out as she walked down the hall. The apartment was large and crammed with the heavy, dark furniture Rosalba's great-grandfather had chosen when he'd bought the building that housed his jewelry shop. The other three apartments had been sold to keep the business going during the lean years. The furniture stayed. Rosalba's mother had tried to sell it, but no one wanted antiques anymore. Italy was going modern.

"Pina made stuffed zucchini. They're warming in the oven. How did it go?" Rosalba prayed the trip to Florence had been successful. She needed her mother in a good mood.

"Florence was a nightmare. I had to elbow my way through Piazza Signorina just to sit down and have a lemonade at Rivoire."

"Will he design for us?"

"It depends on how much I'm willing to pay him." Irene clicked across the marble pavement in her heels, impeccably dressed in a red silk Valentino dress she'd bought at the Barberino Designer Outlet three years ago. "He showed me some lovely designs he can make in gold, silver and even steel. I don't see the purpose of having steel jewelry. You might as well put a series of paper clips around your neck and call that jewelry." She pecked at her daughter's cheeks. "But *de gustibus non disputandum est.*" She stepped back and surveyed the T-shirt and pants Rosalba had changed into after closing up the store. "Not attractive."

Rosalba puffed out a sigh. She wasn't in the mood for this. "I was tired. It hasn't been a good day."

Irene's hand reached down to realign a knife and spoon. Now they lay in perfect parallel. "You didn't sell anything."

"I did. Six hundred and twenty-three euros in cash with a fifteen percent discount. Eight twenty in credit cards, full price." Proving her mother wrong gave her the boost she needed. "The carabinieri came by this morning."

Irene raised an eyebrow, waiting for more.

"They showed me the bracelet and asked if it came from our store. They said he was dead and they wanted to know what he looked like. He must be the man they found dead in Gravigna."

"Of course. His face was shot off."

"I expected you to be upset." Her mother's face had gone white when she'd told her that the man who bought the expensive bracelet had asked if Irene Crisani was now the owner of the shop, claiming he was an old friend of hers. Rosalba has answered with a simple "Yes."

"People get killed all the time for one stupid reason or another." Irene refolded a napkin. "Did they ask about the video cameras?" She had pressed the delete button on both tapes with a stomach-wrenching combination of joy and anguish.

"Yes."

"And what did you tell them?"

"That one was being fixed and we'd erased the tape in the working camera at the end of last week. They're bringing in an artist from Florence to make a sketch of what I remember of his face. What should I remember?"

"Whatever you want. He's dead."

AS SOON AS NICO and the maresciallo entered the restaurant, they were greeted by a woman in a flowered dress and espadrilles. "Ciao, Salvatore. It's been forever."

"I know, Angela, I regret. Too much work." He kissed her cheeks and introduced Nico.

"Piacere." Angela shook hands with Nico. She was in her forties, with a fleshy, round face and smiling gray eyes. A frown appeared on her face when she noticed OneWag looking up at her. He had no collar, no leash.

"He's an angel of obedience," Perillo said.

"We have a cat."

Nico had forgotten that every Italian restaurant had at least one cat. "I'm sorry." He picked up the dog. "I'll leave him in the car."

Perillo stopped him. "Rocco eats with us. Don't worry, Angela. He's under my tutelage."

"But my cat isn't. If he gets his eyes scratched out—"

"I'll arrest her."

Angela's smile came back. "Good idea. She can have her kittens in jail."

"Again?"

Angela shrugged. "What can I do? Romilda is a nymphomaniac, and my mother refuses to have her fixed." She picked up two menus and led them to the garden. "Take that last table in the far corner. I'll take Romilda upstairs."

Perillo took the menus. "Thank you, Angela, you are indeed an angel."

Nico and Perillo sat down facing each other. A baffled Nico held on to OneWag. "Why did you insist on the dog? And his name isn't Rocco."

"He is an Italian dog. He should have an Italian name. The one you chose is also impossible for us to pronounce properly. Call him what you wish, of course, but for me he is Rocco. I insisted he stay with us because he needs reassurance you will not abandon him." Perillo had taken care of many street dogs as a kid. He had identified with their need to be loved. "It is clear to me that he is a wise dog. If he disobeys, you may put him back on the street. He knows this. Put him down and command him to stay. See if I'm wrong."

Curious, Nico put the dog down on the dirt floor. "Stay here."

OneWag looked up at the man, undecided on what to do. The words were new to him, and so many different smells and bits of food on the ground called to him. But the low voice called too. This man who fed him and did not kick him wanted him to do what?

Nico leaned down and patted the ground. "Stay."

OneWag curled up underneath the chair. Gestures, he understood. And now the word "stay."

Nico sat up, surprised. "You're a dog expert."

"No, just on strays."

"You've owned many?"

The American was looking at him with an honest, unsuspecting face. He was waiting for an answer. Perillo looked down at the menu. Good, Angela was serving la peposa tonight. Domenico Doyle, a man whose help he sought. Should he tell him? "No," he said out loud in answer to Nico's question and his own. "I never owned one, but there was an abundance of strays back in Pozzuoli." He did not add that this meant both dogs and humans, sleeping on the streets, eating food from garbage cans, stealing anything they could get their filthy hands on. Years of it. He could still pick a wallet from a pocket without being caught.

He'd tried it just a few weeks ago, to see if he still had that ability, and put the wallet right back without Daniele noticing.

The angry edge in Perillo's voice made Nico curious. "Why did you choose to become part of the carabinieri?"

"Where I come from, I had three choices. I could be a man of the cloth, a man of the Camorra or a man of the law. I don't believe in God. I don't believe in killing people. I didn't believe in the law back then, either, but it was by far the better choice. Besides"—Perillo's face broke out in a grin—"I liked the uniform."

Nico recognized the pat answer. "Do you believe in the law now?"

"Do you?" Perillo asked, wondering how Nico had lost his job.

"I took an oath to uphold the law, but sometimes the law as we have worded it is imperfect." He had indeed broken the law and been fired for it. The law had deemed his actions wrong, but in his mind, what he had done was right. "Sometimes, the law does not take into account the despair suffering can bring. Sending a guilty person to jail isn't always the right answer, and too many times, the innocent end up there."

"Good. I see we think alike. The real reason I became a carabiniere? The jokes. There are thousands of them. A ship goes down at sea and the entire crew drowns. Surprisingly, two carabinieri survive. 'How come you didn't drown like the rest?' the rescue crew asks. One answers, 'We're not allowed to drink on the job.'"

Nico laughed.

"One more for you. Why do the carabinieri smile during storms?" Perillo waited. Nico shrugged. "Because they think the lightning is a series of camera flashes. Now, let's order before I tell any more dumb jokes."

Nico sighed. "When I was growing up in the States, we had Polish jokes. Sometimes, you need a little laughter."

Perillo raised his arm and called Angela. "Nico, you trust me to order for you?"

"Please do."

Angela strolled over, her eyes on OneWag asleep under the chair. "You were right. He's the picture of obedience. Bravo, Rocco. Now then, gentlemen, what do your stomachs desire tonight?"

"A bottle of your house red—"

Nico lifted a forefinger. "Excuse me, but I'd like to start with a glass of white wine first."

Perillo looked at Angela apologetically. Asking for white wine in Chianti was almost an insult.

Nico noticed the look. "I'll switch to red for the main course."

"Good." Perillo continued his order. "A platter of your crostini—you pick the tastiest ones—and la peposa for both of us. We'll see if we have room for dessert later."

"What's la peposa?" Nico asked.

"Ah," Angela said, "you're in for a delight." She pulled out a chair and sat down.

Perillo sat back, satisfied. He had ordered the dish for a specific reason. One of many admirable traits he had discovered in Americans was their curiosity about his country, and Angela never missed a chance to tell the story of la peposa.

"It's a historic meat dish," she began. "Chianina beef cooked in red wine with lots of pepper kernels, garlic, rosemary and sage, served on toasted bread to soak up the sauce. It was invented in my hometown, L'Impruneta, where we have been making the best terra cotta tiles in the world since the Middle Ages. The work was hard, and the men had to stay by the burning furnace all day, so they came up with the idea of cooking their lunch next to the tiles. Not only will it fortify you, but you will be eating an exquisite dish that fed the men who built Brunelleschi's cupola for the Duomo of Florence. Without la peposa, who knows if the cupola would still be with us after almost seven centuries?"

"Thank you, Angela," Nico said. A fun story with perhaps some truth to it. "I look forward to eating history."

"And we both need fortification," Perillo said. "You've heard about the murder?"

Angela's hands clasped her cheeks and she stared at Nico with wide eyes. "Oh, holy Jesus, are you the one who found him?" Her voice was loud, and some diners turned to look at Nico.

"It was the dog who found him first," said Nico quietly, not enjoying the attention.

"But I have to find out who killed him," Perillo said.

"Of course you do," Angela snapped. "It's your job."

Perillo laughed. He could always count on Angela for a put-down. And he always deserved it.

Angela stood up and put the chair back in place. "No house wine for you tonight. I'll open up a bottle of Brunello di Montalcino. It's on us. I'll bring it right away, plus some scraps for Rocco."

"Thank you," Nico called after her, "but his name isn't Rocco."

"Resign yourself, friend." Perillo leaned forward and said in a low voice, "Now, let me tell you about Daniele's theory and what the substitute prosecutor thinks."

"After dinner," Nico said. A few diners were still openly staring and muttering to each other. "Let's discuss the case on my balcony with a bottle of duty-free Johnnie Walker Black that's been waiting to be opened since May."

Perillo grinned. "Excellent whiskey, excellent idea. A judicious amount of liquor will illuminate the brain and further cement collaboration."

For the next two hours, they shared opinions on the latest news from both countries while polishing off all the crostini, wiping the peposa plates clean, and draining their bottle of 2010 Brunello di Montalcino.

SIX

Daniele was in the barrack's kitchen filling a plate with freshly drained bigoli and thinking of Rosalba. He dressed the thick noodles with olive oil, capers, a couple of smashed anchovies, pitted green olives and a coating of toasted bread crumbs. It was a dish his mother had made for as long as he could remember, a dish that had become his go-to whenever he was down. The maresciallo's remark still stung. Rosalba might be rich, better schooled than he was, but he'd felt something special pass between them. He knew her smile had been for him, not the maresciallo. How old was his superior? Forty-five? Maybe beyond that. He was getting old. Daniele plunged his fork into the heaping mound of thick pasta strands and twisted. The maresciallo was jealous, that was it. Even before taking his first bite of the pasta, Daniele felt better.

After his meal, Daniele went downstairs to the computer in the maresciallo's office that only he used and now considered his. He knew he had to stay away from Rosalba until they had closed the case, but there was no harm in looking her up. He went to Google and typed in her full name. To his surprise, there was no trace of her on the Internet. Not on Facebook, Instagram, Pinterest or Twitter. Only Gioielleria Crisani showed up on a dull website with shots of the store's display cases filled with jewelry and no one behind them. Had he designed the website, Rosalba would have been front and center, her smile bidding online searchers to walk into the store. The "About" page told him the store was run by Irene Castaldi, née Crisani, third-generation owner of Gioielleria Crisani, started in 1952 by her grandfather Tuccio Crisani.

No wonder he couldn't find her. Her last name was Castaldi, not Crisani. He went back to look for her on social media. Still nothing.

Why was a beautiful girl like Rosalba trying to stay hidden? Maybe her parents were old-fashioned, afraid their beautiful girl might be found by sex-hungry men. Well, it wasn't sex he was looking for—not right away, at least. A connection would be nice. He'd been assigned to Greve six months ago, and he still hadn't found a girl he wanted to be with for more than five minutes. He would turn twenty in January. It was time he got a girlfriend.

Daniele's fingers flew over the keyboard to find Rosalba's parents in the Radda in Chianti registrar's office.

Irene Crisani, born in 1975 and married Giorgio Castaldi in 1999 in the Basilica of Santa Croce.

Rosalba Crisani, born in Milano in 1997.

Damn! Rosalba was two years older. She'd never consider him.

THE NIGHT AIR HAD turned chilly, but Perillo wanted to smoke, and so the two men, stomachs full of excellent food, settled out on the balcony on two uncomfortable metal chairs. The three swallows were asleep, tucked in their usual spot between the beam and ceiling. OneWag was curled up at Nico's feet, thanks to Perillo's insistence that the dog deserved a roof over his head.

Nico poured the whiskey into two glasses, handed one to Perillo and placed the bottle on the small table between them. "You had two theories for me."

"First the more probable one. It's about the Tuscan who bought the bracelet. Daniele thinks he might have been a go-between."

"Possible, although why would the victim feel he needed a go-between? How much did the bracelet cost?"

"Fourteen hundred. He paid with three five-hundred-euro notes."

"That's a lot of money. If the Tuscan was a go-between, he must have been a friend of the victim."

"Maybe even the one who killed him."

"Possible. As for why hire a go-between, our dead man might not have wanted to be seen. It would explain why he was out in the woods so early." Perillo took a sip of his whiskey and smacked his lips with approval. "What's the first thing you did when you were assigned a case?"

"I always made my own list of the facts I had at that moment. Facts, no opinions or conjecture. They were written on the whiteboard, of course, but I liked to have the list with me at all times. When new facts came in, I'd add them to my list and tuck it in my pocket."

Perillo lit a cigarette. "You're a methodical man."

Nico lifted the small pot of geraniums on the table and handed Perillo the under-dish to use as an ashtray. He laughed as he said, "I guess I thought that the facts in my pocket would eventually make their way to my head and illuminate me."

"The only facts I have are: A dead man's face was blown off at close range. The pellets we found tell us the weapon was a twelve-gauge shotgun, manufacturer unknown since the killer took the casing with him. It's the type of gun that's probably owned by every hunter in Tuscany, which means most of the male population. Next up, a tanned Tuscan bought a bracelet with a mysterious date on it. And finally, a missing gray Panda that may or may not have been rented by our dead man. Every dumpster in the vicinity is being checked for bloody clothes, and so far, nothing. No autopsy report yet. No news about the fingerprints. This wealth of information I can certainly keep in my head."

"The killer must have been covered in blood. The best way to get rid of bloody clothes would be to burn them. Have you looked into unexplained bonfires in the area?"

Perillo raised his arms in a gesture of despair. "Every day a farmer or a vintner is burning something, even if the wind is high and they risk burning acres of surrounding land. I have to call the prosecutor assigned to this case tomorrow morning. I dealt with him once before, when his seventeen-year-old daughter claimed her Morris Mini had been stolen while at a party in Greve. We found the car after two days, parked in the garage of the boy she had spent the night with. Della Langhe wanted the boy arrested for theft, but I spoke to his daughter, a nice girl, not one of those spoiled, the-world-owes-me-deference types like her father, and suggested that she would feel better about herself if she told Pappa the truth. She did, and Della Langhe has never forgiven me for knowing she slept with a boy she'd just met. He will not take kindly to my not having much to report. Besides, he thinks all Southerners are slow."

Perillo liked to talk. Nico was grateful for it, after so many evenings on the balcony with only sleeping swallows for company. "I had a few difficult district attorneys in my day. Beware of ones running for political office. If it's a front-page kind of case, they won't let the truth get in their way."

"Ah, then America is not so different."

Nico thought his country was very different—99 percent of its citizens paid their taxes, for one thing, but he went back to the subject that had brought them together. "Your case raises many questions."

"Too many." Perillo flicked ash over the balcony railing. Nico's vegetable garden was below. He didn't like the idea of finding ash on his zucchini and pushed the terra-cotta dish closer to the maresciallo. "Please use this, if you don't mind." He leaned back in his chair and took a sip of his whiskey. "In your office, you wondered why the victim was in the woods so early in the morning. Now you think it might be because he didn't want to be seen, but what was he doing there? Was he meeting someone? Perhaps the person he was going to give the bracelet to? Or was the bracelet incidental? Who could it have been for?"

"A woman, of course."

"Nowadays not necessarily, but probably a woman. Someone who lives here, presumably. The date, a New Year's Day twenty-two years ago, what does it stand for? The New Year? A wedding? A birthday? Why give this as a gift so many years later?"

Perillo dutifully flicked his ash in the dish as a smile of relief crossed his face. His American friend was hooked on the investigation. "If he was meeting someone, the logical explanation for the place and time is that he didn't want to be seen. But what if the person who was meeting him also wanted secrecy?"

"Or maybe he wasn't meeting anyone. Maybe he was hiding because he knew he was in danger."

"Too many questions for one maresciallo and a young brigadiere." Perillo leaned back in his chair and hugged his elbows. "You will help, yes?"

Nico had to admit he was intrigued, but he still had no interest in becoming involved with an official case. "As I said, I'll listen."

"Your ears are good, Nico, but I need your New York mind." Perillo lifted his glass. "Let us toast to America and Italy, Salvatore and Nico, with your excellent whiskey."

Nico raised his glass.

"Cin-cin, amico," Perillo said.

"To your health."

"And Rocco's."

"OneWag's."

They clinked glasses.

IT WAS A FEW minutes past midnight when Perillo got home; Daniele was waiting for him outside the carabinieri station.

"Why still awake, Dani?"

"The substitute prosecutor wants you to call him immediately."

"At Palazzo Vecchio?"

"He's in his office. I guess the gala was a bore. He didn't sound happy."

"Mother of God and all the saints!"

"Sorry, Maresciallo."

"'Sorry, Salvatore,' and you don't need to apologize. You should have just left a note."

"I was afraid you wouldn't see it."

"You're right. There's been too much food, wine and whiskey tonight, but an important connection has been forged."

"I'm glad. Shall I put the moka on?"

"No, thanks. Go to sleep, Dani. I'll go face my penance in the office."

"I was hoping to listen in."

"I like your enthusiasm, although you might regret it."

Before calling Della Langhe, Perillo made himself a drink with bicarbonate of soda and water. It would stave off the hangover that was sure to come. There was nothing he could drink, unfortunately, to stave off Della Langhe.

The prosecutor answered on the first ring. "Perillo, your report is unacceptable."

"It has only been two days, Maresciallo."

"I am perfectly aware of how long it's been since that poor devil was atrociously murdered. The idea of having a man's face blasted to pieces no bigger than confetti"—*There he goes with his florid imagination*, Perillo thought as he stirred his awful drink with his finger—"is repugnant to me. A man's face is the mirror to his soul." Della Langhe was both handsome and vain, and Perillo had often caught the procuratore looking into whatever reflective surface he passed. Perillo was guilty of stealing glances of himself here and there, as his wife occasionally pointed out. In his case, it had nothing to do with being handsome, which he was not. His vanity came from having survived.

"We will find the man who did this, Maresciallo. But there are quite a few questions in this case that will take time to answer. Would you like to hear them?"

"I'm a busy man. I am only interested in answers." Busy, but he had time, as always, for his closing speech about the evil of today's youth, how the rejection of sound Christian values was leading the world to utter chaos. He was probably thinking of his daughter.

"Maresciallo, I am in perfect agreement with you." The last time Perillo had gone to church was for his own wedding twelve years ago. "Let us hope this new Pope will bring our young ones back to the church. As soon as I have some news, I'll let you know. I am not, may I point out, the only slow one. I haven't been sent the autopsy report yet."

"Ah, yes. The autopsy report. I have it here."

"I should have been sent a copy."

"I'm sure you were. Ah, no, I have the second copy here. Yet another clerical error. Let me see."

Perillo slurped the last of his drink, not caring if the man heard him. Merda, how long had that autopsy been sitting on Della Langhe's desk?

"Ah, Perillo," Della Langhe exclaimed smugly. "This could change everything."

Perillo did not rise to the bait.

"Maresciallo, your silence makes me wonder if you are interested."

With this man in his ear, his headache was only getting worse. "It is my duty to be interested. I did not wish to interrupt."

"I did not think you capable of such thoughtfulness. This man's death, as horrid as it was, may have been a mercy killing. Dr. Rotunno has written here that the man had at the most six months left to live. His body was riddled with metastasized cancer. The possibility of a mercy killing lifts my heart. Finding the perpetrator may turn out not to be so urgent."

Perillo was tempted to remind the substitute prosecutor that mercy killings were still considered murder by Italian law. He controlled himself. "Difficult to establish whether it was a mercy killing."

"I speak of it as a possibility, Maresciallo, not fact. I will have my secretary fax you your copy of the autopsy. Urgent or not, keep me informed, Perillo. We're in full-blown tourist season. The Chianti Expo starts tomorrow. We want our wine drinkers to be happy, not fearful."

Keep me informed. Six months to live. Mercy killing. Perillo's head couldn't make sense of it, not without another espresso. A double, corrected with grappa.

AT NINE FORTY-FIVE THAT morning, the local coffee and cornetti crush had abated at Bar All'Angolo. Now it was the tourists' turn. Nico had come earlier and had been lucky enough to snag a table by the open French doors. He was happy to sit. His legs ached after running an extra two miles to fend off last night's food and drink. His Dante-quoting friend was very late. Nico yearned for a whole wheat cornetto, but he didn't want to offend Gogol by not waiting for him. He whiled away the time reading *La Nazione*, skipping the crime section. He wasn't avoiding the paper's account of the murder, although he was sure it wouldn't tell him anything he didn't already know from Perillo. He was avoiding the cruel, sometimes petty crimes that filled this section every day. An elderly lady robbed by two men pretending to be carabinieri. A metal donation bin that collected clothes for the poor, broken into and ransacked. Teenagers beating up a sleeping immigrant who had survived the boat crossing from Africa. Because of Rita, he had always held Italy to a higher standard than the States. She believed Italy was a fairyland, and therefore so did he. Even now. It was why he wanted to help Perillo, despite his reservations. Solve the murder and wipe this corner of the world clean again.

Nico stretched his legs in front of him and looked out onto the piazza. It was another clear day with a breeze that would later keep heat at bay. The week's only rain had been on Sunday, just enough to wash dust from the vines and his vegetable garden.

The retired men were sitting on their usual benches chatting, one of them smoking a Toscano cigar. No Carletta with her lavender hair setting up the outside trattoria tables outside today. The restaurant was closed on Wednesday. On the far end of the piazza, the weekly fish truck was doing brisk business. Were its goods frozen? The Mediterranean was at least forty-five miles away. Many restaurants, even those close to the sea, served frozen fish, but there was always an asterisk that warned the customer. Nico constantly marveled at how a peninsula surrounded by the sea had the most incredible selection of frozen fish in its supermarkets. He preferred his fish fresh.

Nico looked at his watch as Sandro walked over with a small tray. Where was Gogol? Before he worked any further with Perillo, he wanted to know why Gogol thought the maresciallo was a bad man.

"It's time to eat," Sandro said as he slid the tray on the metal table. "This is Jimmy's last whole wheat cornetto, just out of the oven, your Americano and yesterday's cornetto for the dog. You've been stood up, amico."

Nico dropped the stale cornetto into OneWag's open mouth. "Maybe he's sick."

"In all the years I've known him," Jimmy said, "he hasn't missed a day of spewing Dante to the tourists. My bet is he's pissed with you."

Nico waited until he'd swallowed a bite of his cornetto before asking, "About what?"

"Something to do with Salvatore, probably," Jimmy said. "You might have misunderstood him."

"Jimmy has sharp ears," Sandro said.

"I can see that."

Jimmy leaned over the counter. "Like I said, you fart and the whole town knows about it, me included. You'll have to forgive me."

"What did I misunderstand?"

"Salvatore's a good man, and Gogol knows it. He must've been talking about someone else."

"According to town gossip," Sandro added, tugging at the earring on his left ear, "Gogol hasn't had a friend since his mother died. We put up with him. We give him money every once in a while. The kids make fun of him. We make sure no one hurts him, but that's all. It doesn't necessarily make us feel good about ourselves, but it's good to know someone cares."

"I do." Nico finished his cornetto and Americano and got up. He wasn't quite sure what it was that had made him latch on to Gogol. Yes, Rita and Dante had to do with it, but there was more. He saw Gogol as a lost man, maybe one who reminded him of himself. "I'll stop by the butcher's to see if he's there."

"If he's not," Jimmy said, "come back. I'll give you a thermos full of coffee and a ciambella. You'll find him somewhere."

"Who was it who didn't care?"

Jimmy shrugged. Sandro busied himself counting change for a customer.

LUCIANA PEEKED OUT OF her shop as Nico and OneWag walked by. "Ciao, Nico. Thank you for the olive loaf. You're a dear. Enrico couldn't figure out how I got it. It's our little secret! Are you going to visit Rita? I've got some pretty daisies today."

"Thanks. I'll be going later."

"Well, stop by. I'll be happy to give them to you."

He lifted his hand in a salute and turned the corner. Sergio, the butcher, was a few shops up the road to the cemetery. Nico walked in. On one side, a long refrigerated counter held beautiful cuts of meat that Sergio, following Dario Cecchini's lead, imported from Spain. There wasn't enough pasture in Italy to meet the demand, Sergio had told him on one of his shopping trips for Tilde. There was no sign of Gogol, but against the wall on one side of the shop, a long marble table held plates of crostini topped with lard or salame. Nico picked one of each and wrapped them in a napkin. He turned down the plastic cup of red wine an aproned young man offered him.

Sergio was behind the counter, weighing a mound of bright-red beef diced in quarter-inch pieces to be used for beef tartar. He was big, handsome, all muscle, with a large steak tattooed on one of his biceps. On the wall behind him was a sign celebrating the rebirth of the great bistecca alla fiorentina, the thick, delicious Florentine T-bone steak that had been banned during the mad cow disease scare. Luckily for Sergio and his far more famous rival Dario Cecchini in Panzano, the ban had lasted only a year.

Nico lifted the napkin holding the crostini. "Thanks. I'll come back and pick up a chicken later."

"Anytime," Sergio answered without turning his head.

WEDNESDAY MORNING, DANIELE LEFT his room in the barracks at six ten. He had slept badly, thanks to Rosalba. Something was bothering him, but he couldn't pin down what. It wasn't just that she was older than he was. Maybe it was the man without a face who kept intruding on his dreams, frightening him. He went downstairs and peeked into the back office to exchange a few words with the brigadiere on night duty. Vince was slumped over his desk, fast asleep. Daniele woke him up.

"Go to bed. I'll take over."

"Thanks," Vince mumbled. "Nothing came in."

"Too bad. We could use some news."

Daniele went to the maresciallo's office, turned on the computer and started searching for a pirated download of *Wonder Woman*. He'd seen pictures of the Israeli actress playing Wonder Woman. She looked a lot like Rosalba.

The call from the carabinieri station in San Gimignano came through at six twenty. They had spotted the missing Avis car being driven on the outskirts of the town by a kid and his girlfriend. The carabiniere on night duty asked whether Maresciallo

Perillo wanted to pick up the car and the kids or the San Gimi-gnano station should take over.

"I'll let you know," Daniele said, and hung up. Should he wake the maresciallo? He'd gone to bed late last night and was sure to have a hangover. Besides, he never came down before eight. Could it wait? *Wonder Woman* was ready for download.

No. Duty came first, even if the maresciallo's mood would be black for the rest of the day.

Daniele picked up the phone and called upstairs.

NICO FOLLOWED ONEWAG, WHO had picked up the scent of Gogol's cologne and was scurrying down the road that led out of town. They found him sunning himself on the stone bench in the Medici garden behind the old-age home. His overcoat was open. Underneath, he was wearing pajamas. His feet were bare.

"I brought you breakfast." Nico sat beside Gogol and placed the thermos and the crostini between them.

Gogol snatched the lard one without looking at Nico. OneWag sat at the old man's feet, looking up with hope. "'I craved for peace with God on the last shore of life.'"

"You're nowhere near the last shore yet," Nico said. He under-stood this quote. Gogol didn't want him there. "I am sorry I made you angry yesterday."

Gogol chewed on his crostino.

Nico unscrewed the thermos top and poured Gogol some coffee. The old man ignored the offer. "I don't blame you for not coming to the café." Nico held on to the cup. "This sun feels good." The garden, a large, elegant space with winding paths and arched stone niches at one end, was now in a sorry state. A carpet of weeds covered the gravel paths. The boxwood hedges had dried out. The few moldy rosebushes that had survived des-perately needed pruning.

"I misunderstood you," Nico said. "The maresciallo isn't a bad man, is he? You were trying to tell me something else."

Gogol leaned down and gave the dog what little was left of the crostino. "'If to thy mind I show a truth . . .'" He grabbed the thermos cup from Nico and drank. "Jimmy is a coffee artist. His brew brings happiness."

Nico leaned forward and turned his head. He wanted Gogol to look him in the eye. "What truth were you trying to tell me?"

The old man shook his head and bit into the salame.

"Gogol, do you know who the dead man is?"

"Dead is good."

"You do know. Who is he?"

"You are my friend. Stay away."

"If we are friends, tell me why I should stay away."

Gogol wrapped his arms around himself as though a cold wind were sweeping right through him. "Because your heart no peace will claim." He started rocking back and forth. "There will be much weeping and no singing. Your wife is a good woman. She knows."

"My wife is dead."

Gogol stopped rocking and wrapped his arms around Nico. "I go now." He rose from the bench and waved. "Tomorrow, if I live."

Nico and OneWag both stood up. "We'll walk you back to the villa."

"I am in no danger of straying into a dark forest. *You* are the one who must be careful. Part of your wife lives on."

Gogol had already strayed from a normal life, Nico thought as he watched the man shuffle up the incline that led to the old Medici villa, now a place for the infirm. What did his friend mean by part of Rita living on? Was it her memory? And what had she known?

SEVEN

On the way to San Gimignano, Perillo called Nico and filled him in on the latest. "Garrett's car's been found. We're on our way to pick it up and interrogate the two kids who stole it. And listen to this. When I got home last night, Della Langhe was waiting for me to call him. It made me sober up pretty quickly. The autopsy showed Garrett was in the late stages of cancer. He had only a few months left. Della Langhe thinks it's a mercy killing."

The phone call had come in as Nico was getting into his car with OneWag. He took a long breath to think over the possibility, then said, "The prosecutor thinks the victim hired a man to kill him by shooting his face off? And after being paid to kill him, he takes his wallet and credit cards but walks away leaving a five-thousand-dollar watch and fourteen-hundred-euro charm bracelet?" He shook his head. "No."

He heard a loud noise. Perillo hitting something. "No was my thought exactly. Murder it is. Ciao, Nico." He clicked off. "Caro Daniele, today is going to be a very good day."

Daniele smiled with relief.

A TALL, GOOD-LOOKING CARABINIERE in uniform greeted them outside the San Gimignano station. Perillo and Daniele were in jeans. "We've got the two kids inside. We fingerprinted them, but that's it. I thought you might want to be the one to question them."

"Thanks," Perillo said after he introduced himself and Daniele to Maresciallo Second Grade Davide Serroni. "The kids can stare at the walls for a while. Car keys?"

Serroni handed them over. "The car's in the back."

"That's good," Perillo said when he spotted the Avis Panda.

Daniele hitched his thumbs into his jean belt loops and looked to the fourteen towers that gave San Gimignano its fame. Once, the town had boasted seventy-two towers. One day soon he'd visit. "It's good that the car was found."

"That too, but what's also good is that it's still covered in dust and bird droppings, which means the kid who stole it didn't bother to clean it up. I'm hoping he didn't bother with the inside, either. If the car belongs to the victim, we should find some useful information." Perillo slipped on rubber gloves and opened the trunk. An expensive-looking tan leather suitcase took up most of the space. On top of the suitcase, a set of spread-out keys, looking like they'd been tossed carelessly there. Perillo picked them up. A brass ring held five different keys and an inch-long enameled wine bottle key chain. Three of them were stamped STAR, MADE IN THE USA and seemed to be house or office keys, while the other two were small. He picked the longer of the small keys and tried the lock on the suitcase. It fit. Perillo looked into the side pockets first and found neatly folded white sport socks. He lifted the clothes. Two pairs of tan slacks, one dress shirt, several polo shirts, T-shirts. No pajamas. No shirt with an embroidered golf club on the pocket. Underwear. A swimsuit. Blue New Balance sneakers.

While Perillo rummaged through the suitcase, Daniele was looking through the window on the passenger side, wondering if he'd ever love a girl so much he'd steal a car just to take her to see another town. He didn't have gloves with him, and not wanting to erase any possible evidence, he just stared at the inside, entranced.

A terry cloth towel lay bunched up in the well below the passenger seat next to a half-empty plastic liter bottle of water and three empty bottles of Peroni beer. A torn package of condoms was wedged between the front seats, making Daniele think they had been too much in a hurry to open it properly. The ashtray was full; all the butts had traces of lipstick on them. His eyes traveled to the driver's seat, which had a whitish smear on it. Daniele felt his cheeks get hot and looked away, spotting a blue fold of paper jutting out over the edge of the side compartment of the driver's door.

"Mother of God!" Perillo slammed the lid of the suitcase shut. "Where the hell is his passport?"

Daniele pointed at the driver's door, even though Perillo couldn't see him. "Over there, maybe?"

Perillo appeared from behind the trunk of the car like a Pamplona bull ready to trample anyone who got in his way.

Daniele took a step back, still pointing. "In the driver's-side compartment. Something blue is sticking out. Aren't American passports blue?"

"Right you are." Perillo unlocked the door on the driver's side and stuck his gloved hand in the side pocket. "Got it!" He held up the passport like a goalie showing off the soccer ball he'd just intercepted. "Bravo, Dani."

Daniele felt as tall as one of those towers in the distance.

Perillo opened the passport. The color photo showed a man with a wide face, chiseled nose, full lips and the usual expressionless gaze people adopt for passport photos. Handsome. Not many wrinkles. He looked much younger than fifty. The picture had probably been taken years ago.

"Surname," Perillo read out loud for Dani's sake. "Garrett. Given name: Robert. Nationality: United States of America. Date of Birth: The twenty-ninth of November 1974." That made him only forty-four years old. Perillo looked under Place of Birth and whistled.

"Is it our man?" Daniele hurried past the car hood to see for himself what made the maresciallo whistle.

"Unless you believe in such coincidences." Perillo held up the open passport for Daniele.

"Don't touch it. Just look under Place of Birth."

"Good God, and his mother," he said instead. "He's a local!"

"And not just from the region, but our very own Gravigna, Italy." Perillo flipped the page over. The bearer's address was listed as Delizioso Wine Company, Route 29, Napa, California, 94581. The foreign address and emergency contact had both been left blank. Perillo extracted a plastic bag from his back pocket, slipped the passport inside and locked the bag in the leather suitcase. With trunk and car doors locked, he said, "Let's go inside and interview those two idiots."

"It's thanks to them that we have the car," Daniele reminded him. He hoped they wouldn't be in too much trouble.

"They will get no thanks from me. Or you."

"Of course not, Maresciallo." But he *was* grateful. Now he had an excuse to see Rosalba again, to tell her she wouldn't need to see a sketch artist.

In the entrance hall of the station, the two teens sat on a wooden bench holding hands. The boy, with a chunk of hair falling over his eyes and both sides of his head shaved off, stood as soon as he saw Perillo. "I didn't know the car belonged to the murdered guy. I swear I didn't."

The girl stayed seated, tossing her long chestnut hair to one side. She smiled at Daniele. He did not smile back. "It was just sitting there," she said. "For two nights."

The carabiniere at the front desk pointed to the first door along the corridor. "Maresciallo, you can take them in there."

The boy grabbed the girl's hand and followed Perillo into a small, windowless room with a wooden table and four metal chairs. They sat down next to each other at the far side of the table. The girl was short and "in flesh," as Italians liked to say about someone chubby, wearing cutoff jeans and a spaghetti-strap top that showed off her abundant breasts. Her face might be pretty if she weren't sulking. The boy was tall, strongly built. He had on jeans and a sleeveless T-shirt that showed his deep tan ended midbicep. A boy who worked outdoors.

Perillo and Daniele sat down opposite them. Daniele took out his notebook and pen.

"Your names?" Perillo asked.

"We gave them to the fat guy at the desk," the girl said. "And where's your tape recorder?"

Perillo nodded his head toward Daniele. "He's my tape recorder, and an excellent one too. Please tell him your name, address and birthdate."

The boy leaned forward with an apologetic look on his young face. "We don't want to get into trouble. I'm Bruno Dini, and she's Katia Paccini. We both live on Via della Conca D'Oro in Panzano. She's at Thirty-One, I'm down the block at Fourteen. I was born February sixth, 2002."

"Too young to have a driver's license," Perillo said.

"I've been driving my uncle's harvester since I was twelve."

Perillo turned to the girl. "Your age, Signorina Paccini?"

"A woman should never reveal her age."

Bruno kicked her under the table. She kicked him back.

Perillo said, "You're not a woman yet."

Katia stuck out her lower lip in a pout.

"She was born July seventh, 2003." Bruno joined his hands together as if in prayer. "We're really sorry we did this, Maresciallo. We just wanted to have some fun. Katia's never been to San Gimignano. We were going to spend the day here, then drive the car back where we found it."

"And where was that?" Perillo asked.

"The San Eufrosino sanctuary. We both live with our families and go there at night sometimes to get some privacy. You must remember how it is for young people, Maresciallo."

Perillo wanted to kick the kid for that remark. Instead, he nodded.

"Only if the weather is good," Bruno said, looking at Katia. "We don't have a car, which I guess is obvious."

Daniele lowered his head to hide his smile. If you had a girl and lived with your family, the car became the bedroom. In Venice, the only place cars were allowed was in Piazzale Roma. His friends used to make out in gondolas. He'd tried it once, but the rocking made him seasick.

"Some important information for you, tape recorder." Katia eyed Daniele while she tugged at her top to reveal more of her breasts. "The car wasn't there Sunday night. Monday, it was parked behind the sanctuary. I was cold and we tried the door. No luck and no keys on the ground till last night. How they got there, I have no idea. I looked everywhere the night before. Even got down on my hands and knees. It was freezing, and I wasn't wearing much." She dropped her elbows on the table. "Got all that?"

Daniele kept his head down and wrote, praying he wasn't blushing. Of course he was.

Katia laughed.

Perillo stood up. He had the information he needed and had had enough of Katia Paccini. "Let's go, Daniele."

Daniele closed his notebook, slipped his pen in his pocket and followed Perillo without looking at the teenagers.

"What about us?" Bruno asked.

Perillo left the room without answering.

Katie wiggled her fingers like a two-year-old. "Bye, tape recorder. Don't let the battery run out."

As Daniele closed the door, he overheard Bruno whisper angrily, "Why do you always have to be such a bitch?"

"It's fun," was Katia's answer.

THE CARABINIERE STOPPED PERILLO as he headed for the exit. "What do you want us to do with those two?"

"Let them sit there for a bit and enjoy the San Gimignano air."

Once they were outside, Daniele asked, "You don't think they're involved with the murder?"

"They're dumb kids, but not quite dumb enough to kill a man and go joyriding in his car two days later."

"Kids do a lot of stupid things, though," Daniele said in a tone that indicated he'd passed that stage long ago.

Perillo lit up a much-yearned-for cigarette. "Of course. I did some pretty crazy stuff myself, but these two didn't blow our victim's face off with a shotgun."

"How can you be sure?"

"When I was a kid, I lived in a bad area and had to watch out for myself. After I was beaten up too many times to count, I developed an itch in my fingers whenever I met up with a bad one. Those two aren't bad. Just dumb."

Weird, Daniele thought, not sure whether to believe the maresciallo's fingers could serve psychic purposes.

Perillo was watching him. "Okay, I'll give you a more concrete reason. The killer clearly went through the victim's pockets. There's not a chance that besotted kid or his nightmare girlfriend would have left that watch and the bracelet."

Daniele rubbed his neck, as if that would hide the creeping redness. "What do we do now?"

"We need a tow truck to pick up the car and take it to Florence. Maybe we'll get lucky and the forensic technicians will get us some useful information about the killer before Father Christmas comes calling. We're taking the luggage with us. It should tell us more about our victim. And we'll take those kids home." Perillo took a long drag. "That girl really took to you."

Daniele found a pebble to kick. He knew she was just toying with him to make Bruno jealous.

"Rosalba and now Katia. You've got a way with women. Enjoy it."

There was nothing to enjoy. He hadn't been with a girl since he'd moved into the barracks in Greve.

Perillo stubbed out his cigarette on the sole of his shoe. "Dani, tell me the truth. How old do I look?"

Daniele stood at attention. This was a serious question. Age was the maresciallo's Achilles' heel. "Thirty-seven, Maresciallo. Thirty-eight at most."

Perillo laughed and slapped him on the back. "You're a good liar, Dani. That is an asset in our business." He tossed the cigarette on the ground and headed to the victim's car. "I want you to find out if those two kids ever got into serious trouble. Itch or no itch, it's always best to turn over every stone."

NICO WATERED THE ASTER plant and placed the fruit-juice bottle with Luciana's daisies in it under Rita's photo. He was relieved to be alone. The white of the flowers added a brighter sheen to the grayness of the picture. He resolved to bring more white flowers next time. He stood awkwardly, hands folded over his stomach, with OneWag curled at his feet. Gogol's parting words had left a stone of guilt in his heart, one he needed to dislodge.

You still live, Rita mia. In me, in Tilde, in Stella. You are unforgettable. Gogol, who shares your love for Dante, remembers you too. He thinks you know a gravely upsetting truth. I only know two truths. That you're gone, which still brings tears, and that I love you.

Nico leaned down, kissed Rita's photo and slowly walked down the path to the gate. The stone in his heart was still there, but it felt lighter now. He trusted somehow that Rita heard him. It was true that he had trouble summoning her face now when he woke in the morning. Her voice had retreated to a distance he could barely reach, but he would fight to keep her with him. Letting her go was like letting go of the beauty in his life.

OneWag trotted ahead of the man who cared for him, head and tail held high, eager to find somewhere smellier.

Back down in the piazza, the dog stopped by Luciana's flower shop to make a show of sniffing the flowers she kept outside. Luciana had cookies.

"No begging," Nico ordered as he walked past and waved. "Thanks for the daisies, Luciana." He was thankful she was waiting on a customer, which meant he wouldn't get one of her suffocating, breast-filled hugs.

OneWag assessed the situation with one glance. He ran across the piazza and aimed his small body toward the steep road that led to Sotto Il Fico. Nico followed the dog up the street and allowed himself a smile when OneWag stopped in front of Enrico's food shop. Yesterday, Nico had reserved two olive loaves for today. Had the dog stopped for the salty-sweet smell of the prosciutti hanging from the ceiling of the shop? Probably. Or was it the instinctual understanding some dogs had of their owner's next move?

There was a customer in the small shop. Behind the counter, Enrico was carving into a giant Parmigiano Reggiano wheel. After he'd extracted a chunk and wrapped it in butcher paper, Enrico dropped a round of mortadella on the slicing machine and worked his arm back and forth until five hundred grams of paper-thin slices sat neatly piled on oiled paper. Outside, OneWag gave a bark of protest. The smells had prompted a growl in Nico's own stomach. He'd already gained six pounds since coming here. Best to distract himself with something else. Had any new evidence appeared in the murder case? Was Perillo—fine, Salvatore—any closer to knowing the dead man's identity?

The Parmigiano and mortadella customer brushed past Nico, bringing him right back to the matter at hand. Food.

"Buongiorno, Enrico. Your arm must be aching after all that slicing."

"Salve, Nico." He was a short, slight man with a pale face and a half-crown of thinning hair hugging his head. "I started slicing as soon as I was tall enough to reach the handle. After forty years, I'm used to it. I've got your two olive loaves. And here's a slice of mortadella for you, and one for your dog."

"You'll have him at your doorstep every morning now." Nico stepped outside to give the dog his slice and got the usual one-wag response. Nico went back inside to taste his own slice. The meat was so soft and luscious he barely had to use his teeth. "Thank you. Delicious! I'll take a hundred grams of it. And some ricotta. Just enough for two people. I was thinking of trying my hand at making a ricotta tart."

Enrico sliced some more mortadella. "Ask Luciana for her recipe. She makes a good one."

"Thanks, I will if my attempt fails."

"Don't stint on the nutmeg." Enrico weighed the food, wrapped it in two separate parcels and rang up the amount on an old cash register. Nico paid him.

As Enrico handed over the change, he asked, "Any news about the dead man?"

The question surprised Nico, and it showed.

Enrico looked embarrassed. "You found the body and you've been seen with Salvatore, so some of us thought you were working together. You used to be a policeman, no?"

So that wasn't a secret anymore either. "I patrolled the streets, but I had nothing to do with murder." Why was he still lying? Rita was gone. At least Tilde deserved to know what his job had really been. The forced retirement he would keep to himself. Himself, Salvatore and Daniele.

Nico took the slim packages and the change. "For news, you'll have to ask the maresciallo. See you tomorrow." Nico pulled aside the beaded curtain that kept the flies out. "Come on, OneWag. Time to go to work."

Stella's boyfriend blocked his path halfway up the hill to the restaurant. "Can I talk to you, Nico?" Today, Gianni's face was darkened by a deep frown.

"Is something wrong?" Nico asked.

"No." Gianni's fingers nervously combed through his curls. "Well, yes. I need your advice. Let me." Gianni reached for Nico's bag. It made Nico feel like an old man, but he released his hold on the bag. Gianni was only being polite.

"Maybe we can sit on the church steps?" Gianni asked. "Out of sight of the restaurant?"

Nico nodded with what he hoped was an encouraging smile. If Gianni was having romantic problems again, he could listen for a few minutes. Tilde was expecting him to help with lunch. He followed Gianni the fifty uphill meters to Sant'Agnese, a largely restructured church dating back to the fourteenth century. If consolation was what Gianni was looking for, this would be the right spot.

Gianni didn't wait to sit. "Stella is pulling away from me, and it's tearing me apart. What makes it worse is, I have no idea why."

Nico welcomed the sit-down. He picked the third step and stretched out his legs. Gianni loomed over him, his hands stuffed in his jeans pockets. OneWag went exploring their surroundings.

"Sit," Nico said gently. "Did you tell her taking the museum exam was okay with you?"

"Yeah, if that's what she wants." Gianni dropped down next to him. "She talks about the museum job as her future, but I mean, is sitting in a chair for eight hours looking at old paintings and answering stupid questions a future? 'Hey, miss, where's the john?'" He imitated an American accent. "'I can't find the Botticelli, whadja do with it?'"

"There's no need for that," Nico said curtly.

Gianni looked at him in surprise. "Oh, sure. I forget you're American."

An apology would have been nice, Nico thought. "Maybe she doesn't believe you."

"Why wouldn't she? Tilde is getting to her. Stella has changed. I'm treating her like a princess. I tell her I'm going to marry her even if she ends up working in Florence. I'll get a job there too. What more does the girl want?"

"I'm afraid I can't answer that for you. I do think, though, that it would help if you treated Stella as a woman, rather than a princess. My wife taught me that what women want is respect first. It keeps the door open to love."

"Respect?" Coming from Gianni, it sounded like a foreign word. "What more do I have to do?"

"Ask Stella." Nico stood up. "Now, forgive me, Tilde is waiting for me."

"Of course. Put in a good word for me, will you? Tell her Stella's future is maybe with the job, but it's also with me. You can tell Stella that too."

Nico bent down to hide the disappointment in his face. He picked up his bag. Gianni persisted in being cocky and possessive, a bad combination. Nico straightened himself up and whistled. OneWag came running with a small red rubber ball in his mouth.

"No." Nico did not pronounce the word with any force, but OneWag took it as a command and let go of the ball. The three of them watched it stumble down the slope. Later, OneWag would retrieve it in the piazza below, and Nico would let him keep it. His no had been for Gianni.

SOTTO IL FICO DID brisk business at lunchtime, selling out of the zucchini lasagna, the stuffed rigatoni au gratin and the pappa al pomodoro. Nico gulped down the last portion of navy bean and kale soup served at room temperature. At three o'clock, the terrace had emptied except for two older Englishmen who were finishing the last drops of their 2013 Castello di Rampolla, a renowned vineyard they could spot in the distance. In the front room, Elvira napped on her armchair with the completed front-page crossword of the *Settimana Enigmistica* on her lap. Her pen had fallen to the floor. Enzo stood at his perch behind the bar, catching up on soccer news in the *Gazzetta dello Sport*. Stella was supposedly at home studying for the museum guard exam. Tilde and Alba, the Albanian helper, were wiping the kitchen.

Nico finished loading the dishwasher. They had been too busy cooking, plating and serving to say more than two words to each other until now.

Tilde asked as she hung up the scrubbed skillets on the brick wall, "Did Salvatore find out the dead man's identity?"

"Not yet. Look, there's something I need to tell you," Nico said.

"Ah, yes. Enzo saw you talking to Gianni up at the church. What did he have to say for himself?"

"Nothing interesting." Nico did not want to add to Tilde's bad opinion of Gianni. It was up to Stella to decide whether to keep him in her life or not.

"All right." It was clear she didn't believe him. "How was your dinner at Da Angela? I want to hear about every crumb you ate and every word you and Salvatore said to each other. You talked about the murder, yes?" The man's death and his gold sneakers still haunted her. Shooting his face off, erasing his identity struck her as an act of rage. It brought back the memory of her own rage from years ago. That was what scared her. That rage was still inside her. "Start with what the two of you ate. Anything we should be serving here?"

"Can we take a walk?"

Tilde took in Nico's serious expression. A walk meant he wanted privacy. Whatever he needed to tell her had nothing to do with food. "I've been on my feet since six o'clock this morning. I'm ready for a sit-down." She took off her apron, hung it on a nail by the kitchen door and walked out of the restaurant. Nico retrieved his package of food from the refrigerator and followed. OneWag trailed them both to the steps of the church, where he had sat with Gianni. From this vantage point, they had a good view of the medieval town. The new houses had been built on the other side, below the hill.

Tilde sat on one of the steps and offered her face to the sun, eyes closed. Nico lowered himself down next to her, and she sensed how tense he was. "Let me guess what you ate," she said to make the moment easier for him. Nico's dinner with Salvatore made her think she knew what he wanted to say. "A plate of the usual antipasto, salame, prosciutto, grilled eggplant, yellow and red peppers, zucchini. Pecorino cheese with a sweet onion marmalade from Certosa." She turned to face Nico, locking arms with him. "Then what? Pasta or risotto?"

Nico nudged her shoulder. He knew what she was up to, and it was working. "We had a historic meat course. La peposa. It was very good, although I would have liked a little less pepper. You should put it on the menu."

"We do on occasion. And Salvatore, what did he tell you about the murder? You're conspiring together to solve it, aren't you?"

Nico took a deep breath. "Rita will have to forgive me. But before I get into that, there's something you should know, something Rita asked me not to tell anyone here. I was a homicide detective in New York City for nineteen years before I left the force. Salvatore knows. That's why he wants me to help him. I'm sorry I didn't tell you earlier. I wanted to honor Rita's wishes."

"Bravo. I'm impressed." Tilde feigned surprise. Her aunt had told her the truth in that terrible last letter. A letter that had also told her Rita had stage-four cancer; a letter that had asked her to welcome and care for Nico once she was gone. Rita had correctly guessed Nico would move to Gravigna after her death.

Tilde took his hand in hers and squeezed. "Thank you for telling me. It must have been a very difficult job, and I'm proud of you."

"I'm not sure Rita felt the same."

"Of course she did. You were the earth and the sky to her. I imagine she was afraid for you. Not telling anyone meant you were safe. We women have funny ways of dealing with our fear. I worry that Stella won't get the museum guard job she wants, so I spend half the night on the Internet, memorizing the art in that museum. It's my good-luck charm for her."

Nico kissed Tilde's forehead. "I thought you would be angry."

Tilde let go of Nico's hand and stood up. "I think I used up my anger long ago. At least most of it." She looked back at the church, hoping Nico wouldn't see that she was lying. "I'm going back to work on dinner. You've done enough for today. I don't want to see you tonight."

"What about feeding me?"

"I don't trust you. You'll eat a single bite, then start serving on tables. Come up with a great recipe to feed yourself. Our menu could use another of your ideas. And don't let Salvatore take over your life. He's gotten bored with being married, and any excuse to stay out at night is good. Although I'll admit murder is an excellent one."

Nico was reminded of Gogol's words that morning. "You know Gogol, don't you?"

"Of course. He's one of our village landmarks. The castle, the church and Gogol. I've heard you've become fast friends."

"He got all worked up when he saw me talking to Salvatore. He said something odd. That there would be much weeping and no singing. That my wife is a good woman who knows the truth. What do you think he meant by that?"

Tilde felt a chill in her heart. "He's probably misquoting Dante. Or letting his imagination fly in the wind."

Nico lifted himself slowly. The church's steps were low, and he was still feeling the morning's run in his knees. "Maybe, but he was trying to warn me off something. I'd like to know what." OneWag, who had curled himself in the shade of a potted hibiscus, stood up, stretched and sauntered over to Nico.

Tilde hastily kissed Nico on both cheeks. She was eager to reach the safety of her kitchen, a place she considered her own, where she felt empowered. "Find a good recipe," she said simply, and walked away.

"I do have an idea. Easy, inexpensive. I just have to play around with it first." By the time his final sentence had ended, only OneWag was listening.

EIGHT

Daniele and Perillo had delivered Katia and Bruno to their homes, warning them to stay in town. The tow truck was on its way to San Gimignano to pick up the Avis Panda. On its way back to Florence, it would stop by the Greve station to collect Robert Garrett's suitcase, which had been carefully emptied by Daniele, its contents neatly laid out on two tables in Perillo's office.

"Make a list," Perillo said.

"Aren't we sending everything to Florence?"

"Yes, but the dead man is an American. I wish to be prudent. The Florence lab will make its own list. We will have ours, witnessed by—who's on duty today?"

"Dino and Vince."

"Witnessed by Dino and Vince. Go ahead, don't leave anything out. Toothpicks included." He caught Daniele hungrily eyeing his computer in the back of the room. "A handwritten list first, Dani." He opened his desk drawer, took out pen and paper and handed them over. "These are good items. They've been used for centuries. With these, no hacking, no computer malfunctions."

"Paper gets lost."

"Files get erased. You'll type it into your machine later."

A reluctant Daniele went back to the two tables and started writing. He listed the three most important items first. As soon as Daniele had written them down, Perillo slipped on a new pair of rubber gloves and transferred the listed items to his desk, where he could sit down and think about them. He had already read the information on the American passport back in the carabinieri parking lot in San Gimignano. Now he examined the hotel receipt that had been stuffed in a trouser pocket. Hotel Bella Vista, seven nights at 160 euros a night. No credit card numbers.

"He told Avis he was going to Radda in Chianti," Perillo muttered to himself. "Instead, he stayed in Panzano. Why not Gravigna, his hometown?"

Daniele always listened to Perillo's mutterings, hoping to learn something and also to have answers for him. "Judging from the other receipts we found, he was a Dario Cecchini fan. He ate at his top restaurant five of the seven nights he was here. Paid with cash every time."

"Maybe Garrett didn't believe in credit cards," Perillo muttered to himself. He'd paid for the bracelet in cash too. There was no cash in his pockets when he was found. The killer must have taken it. Maybe the dog's barks scared him off before he could grab the watch and the bracelet.

"Even kept the menu." Daniele waved the large sheet in the air. "'Leave all hope, ye who enter here. You're in the hands of a butcher.' I say, leave all your money ye who enter here. Fifty euros a meal. That's crazy."

"If we find the killer, I'll take you there."

"I'm a vegetarian, Maresciallo."

"That's right." Why did he keep forgetting things like this? Was he already going senile? "You liked the leftover eggplant parmigiana." He did remember the look of joy on Dani's face as he stuffed himself. "I'm sure they'd have something for you too. And don't 'Maresciallo' me."

"Signora Perillo is a very good cook."

"Yes, she is. Excellent, in fact." And a lovely woman. If only the fire between them hadn't flickered down to the strength of a single candle. "We have more important things to worry about here than my wife's cooking skills. Get back to your list."

"I never stopped, Maresciallo. Sorry, Ma—Salvatore. I can write and speak at the same time."

Something Perillo had never mastered. "Good for you." He picked up the third item on his desk. Another passport, Italian this time. He opened it. The photograph was of a much younger Garrett, the name different: Roberto Gerardi. This passport had been issued twenty-three years ago. The tax had been paid only that once, which allowed Roberto Gerardi to use his Italian passport for one year. Perillo slapped the passport down on the desk. "Why did Roberto Gerardi become Robert Garrett?"

"He became an American citizen."

"But why change his name?" Perillo said, more to himself than to Daniele. "Your given name is who you are. It represents you." He was proud of the name he'd been given by the Perillos, the couple who had opened up their home to him. On the streets of Pozzuoli, he'd been known as Sbriga because he was always hustling. He knew no other name until he was given the name Salvatore, "the one who saves." It should have been Salvato, "saved," but that was not a name anyone used. Salvatore replaced Sbriga. "You don't just throw your name away like it's garbage." And yet, ashamed of what he had been, he had done exactly that with Sbriga.

"Maybe that's what he wanted to do. I'll see if he had a criminal record here."

"Don't bother. You can't become an American citizen with a record. Or get a resident alien card."

"What a terrible name, alien. As if immigrants come from Mars."

"We're all aliens to each other, I think." Perillo watched Daniele write for a moment and remembered what Nico had said about making a list. Not a bad idea. He felt like he'd just been dropped into a high-walled maze where the exit would always be hidden. A list might help clear his head, arm him for the inevitable phone call to Della Langhe. He took out another sheet of paper and a pencil from his drawer. He'd always preferred pencil to pen. Mistakes were easily erased with a pencil, unlike in real life. He'd been lucky. He'd been given a choice and had the good sense to seize it.

Perillo bent over his desk and began in his best grammar-school handwriting. Signorina Bianchi, his teacher, had praised him for his neat, rounded letters. He chuckled as he remembered it was the only praise he'd received on starting school. Once he was done writing, Perillo folded the sheet of paper twice and started to tuck it in his pocket. A thought came to him and he unfolded it and added:

6. Remember to buy flowers for your wife. Just because.

List refolded and safely in his pocket, Perillo reached for the phone.

NICO'S CELL RANG JUST as he was slurping water from the faucet to cool his mouth. He'd been too eager to taste the ricotta tart he'd just plucked out of the oven. "Nico here."

"We've identified the victim." Perillo's voice sounded triumphant. "The dead man was Roberto Gerardi, a Gravignese, and also Robert Garrett, an American owner of a vineyard in Napa Valley called Delizioso."

"Good." He was happy for Perillo, but half his mind was concentrated on what he had just cooked. Nico's forefinger pressed gently on the surface of the tart. Still too hot. OneWag sat at his feet, hungrily gazing at Nico.

"His being American complicates things," Perillo said. "Your people will want to take charge, send a detective or two."

"They're not my people anymore." Nico walked away from the oven. "And they won't take charge. It's your jurisdiction. They might put some pressure on the embassy in Rome, but if they took charge, would it matter to you?"

Perillo thought over the question for a moment. If the Americans took over, they'd be the ones to have to deal with Della

Langhe's arrogance. That would be a relief. He and his men would go back to worrying about the pickpockets at the Expo del Vino opening tomorrow. Last year, more than twenty thousand people had shown up during the four-day festival. Only two wallets had been lost, one retrieved still full of money. A boring job.

"Yes, I would care," Perillo said. He wanted to rise to the challenge of this difficult case, prove to the procuratore that he had a brain, that he wasn't Southern Italian scum. "This is my case. Our case."

At the other end of the line, Nico felt an unexpected thrum in his chest. He had both loved and hated his job in New York. Loved it when justice was found for the victim and their grieving family. Hated it for the ugliness he faced with each murder. In his last case, the ugliness had been the victim's. He sighed loudly. Maybe with luck and some smart work, they could clean up the mess. "When you're done with everything you have to do today and your wife doesn't mind, come for dinner and we'll go over the new details. Bring Daniele. He's got some good gears in his head."

"Thank you. It's a welcome invitation. My wife is bringing dinner to a friend who's fallen ill. I have two bottles of wine to make our minds and a moonless sky shine with light." Never mind that the moon was almost full. Nico's willingness to collaborate thrilled Perillo. Maybe their minestrone of backgrounds—American, Venetian and Neapolitan—had a chance of cracking the case. He started to add *I made a list*, but stopped himself. Nico's suggestion had helped to clear his thoughts, but as a maresciallo of the carabinieri, he needed to maintain some dignity. "Daniele is a vegetarian," he said instead.

Too bad, Nico thought. He'd found a loose brick downstairs, which had given him the idea to make one of his favorites—pollo alla diavola, the devil's chicken. An easy recipe. All it took was a hot grill, a chicken split in two, well seasoned and brushed with olive oil, and a heavy brick to weigh it down and give it a crisp skin. "What about gluten?"

Perillo turned to Daniele. "Nico's invited us to dinner. I warned him you only eat sheep and cow fodder. Any gluten problems to add to that?"

"No, none at all. Tested negative when I was a baby." Daniele felt his chest warm, bringing a smile. He was being treated as an equal.

Perillo spoke into the phone. "We're fine with gluten."

"So I can serve pasta?"

"You can. We should be done here by eight, eight-thirty."

"Call me when you're on your way." Nico hung up. Perillo followed suit.

Daniele had just finished listing all the items in Gerardi's suitcase. He turned to look at his boss with a puzzled look.

"What, Dani?"

"I was wondering what happened to Gerardi's cell phone."

"Ah, that's right. It's missing." Perillo tried to keep the annoyance from his voice. He had overlooked that. He was getting duller.

"I bet it was a new iPhone and the murderer pocketed it. With what they cost here, I don't blame him." Daniele's face instantly reddened. "I mean, I don't condone—"

Perillo dismissed his brigadiere's embarrassment with the flick of a hand. "You're speculating again. Gerardi could have lost the phone. My wife is always losing hers, buying a new one and then finding the old one weeks later." He'd finally bought her a traded-in iPhone and activated the Find My iPhone feature. "The murderer could have taken the phone to cover their tracks."

"They communicated?"

"Maybe." Perillo sighed. *Maybe, could have, might have, what if.* Everything in the case was speculation. He'd put Daniele down out of pique, but now they needed to find the phone.

Noticing the maresciallo's dark face, Daniele regretted having brought up the missing phone. It was all about timing with his boss. He should have remembered that Perillo was tired. "I'll bring something typically Venetian tonight."

"Bravo. Nice idea." Perillo handed over the two passports.

"Get Vince or Dino to make photocopies of the American picture—it's more recent—and get it faxed over to *La Nazione* and *Chianti Sette*. Put everything back in the suitcase and make sure someone sticks around to hand over the suitcase when the tow truck arrives. Then you can play with your computer. Don't forget to get the typed copy witnessed. Then scrounge around and see what you can come up with for Bruno and Katia. If Della Langhe calls, stall. Not a word about the victim being American."

"I'll do my best, Maresciallo."

"I know I can count on you, and as a reward, tomorrow morning you can take a copy of the victim's older photo up to Radda to see if he's the man who bought that bracelet from the beautiful Rosalba." They had not found a receipt for the bracelet among Garrett's belongings. Too often a cash payment meant no receipt. That was the finance police's problem, not his.

As expected, Daniele blushed. "I'll go first thing in the morning, Maresciallo."

"The store doesn't open until eleven, but you might find her again at the café." Perillo slipped on his leather jacket. "On my birth certificate, the name Maresciallo does not appear."

"Yes, Maresciallo."

"Yes, Salvatore," Perillo corrected. Daniele was turning purple now. It was time to leave. "I'm off to Hotel Bella Vista. Who knows what hidden nuggets of information I might find there."

WITH ONEWAG FOLLOWING, HEAD and tail held high, Nico took the plate with the cooling tart out on the balcony and sat behind the small round metal table that must have once belonged to a café. The center held a fading painted ad for Lavazza Coffee. He plunged a fork into the now-cooled tart and tasted.

What a disappointment! The tart was much too bland. And here he had thought it would make a nice appetizer for the restaurant. For a toddler, maybe. Nico lowered the plate to the floor. "All yours, OneWag."

The dog approached the plate and sniffed. After one lick, he padded back inside to sleep on the sofa. Nico went inside and threw the tart in the garbage. "Come on, off to shop for food," he told the dog. "We have guests tonight."

OneWag jumped off the sofa and scrambled to the door with a small pink tongue protruding from his dog smile.

Nico smiled back.

THE WELL-NAMED HOTEL BELLA Vista sat on the crest of a hill facing away from Panzano. The wide stone building was embraced by a semicircle of tall chestnut trees. The front side faced a garden filled with late summer flowers, which ended with a descending slope marked by slanting lines of young grapevines. In the distance, a perfect view of Vigna Maggio.

"It has been a working farm since the early fifteenth century," said the woman, who had been pointed out to Perillo as being the manager of the hotel. A hotel guest listened by her side. "The original Vigna Maggio was built by relatives of the Mona Lisa Gherardini, rendered famous by Leonardo Da Vinci. It's perhaps the most renowned hotel in the Chianti region."

Perillo listened patiently, not wanting to interrupt with his sordid business. The manager, somewhere in her twenties, had a caressingly soft lilt in her voice, a lovely face with rounded cheeks, a pale complexion and long, blond wavy hair that fell loosely down her back and glinted pink in the sun, features he always associated with Tuscan women. She wore a long, loose skirt of deep-blue cotton with a white scoop-neck blouse trimmed with lace. Perillo thought she could have walked out of an eighteenth-century portrait hanging in the Uffizi.

The manager sensed a movement behind her and turned to face the man. "Oh!" She seemed startled. As this was official business, Perillo was in uniform. "I'm sorry. I didn't see you."

"I just need a minute of your time, when you've finished."

"I need to be off," said the guest, an older woman whose face had surely been tightened by a surgeon's hand. "Thank you so much," the guest said. "I'm sure our stay here will be a delight."

The manager smiled. "My pleasure." She turned to Perillo and held out her hand. "Laura Benati. I'm the manager here. How can I help you?"

He shook her hand, introduced himself, and showed her the hotel bill. "Your guest Robert Garrett is the man we found murdered in the woods."

Laura's only reaction was to study the hotel bill more closely, as if it could tell her that Perillo was mistaken. "You found him on Monday morning, didn't you?"

"Yes."

"He paid the bill Sunday night in cash. He said he had to leave very early Monday. He seemed very excited, and had a lot to drink at the bar that night, which he hadn't done the other nights he stayed here. I thought he was just nervous about flying back home to the States."

"Did he only speak English to you?"

"Yes, although he did have an accent, and quite a strong one. Spanish, I thought."

"He was Italian." No harm in revealing that much, even if Della Langhe hadn't been informed yet.

"Odd, I didn't spot it. Are you sure the dead man is Garrett?"

"I am. I won't go into how we know, but there is no doubt that the murdered man was Robert Garrett. Has his room been cleaned out?"

"Yes, and rented to the signora you just saw. He did leave a dirty polo shirt in one of the drawers. I was going to mail it to him."

"Did you by any chance find a cell phone? His is missing."

"No, I'm sorry."

Perillo had no doubt Garrett/Gerardi had a cell phone—everyone and their grandmother did, but it was best to ask anyway. "Did you ever see him use a cell phone?"

"The guests aren't allowed to use their cell phones in the hotel's public spaces. Some naturally pay no attention, but if they're quiet, I let them be. If he did, I didn't notice. My job keeps me rather busy."

"Did he have visitors or anyone asking for him? Phone calls?"

"Not while I was at the front desk. I'll have to ask the two girls who take over from me. Why don't you come inside while I fetch the shirt and call them?"

Perillo followed Laura to the hotel. The wide front hall had a beamed ceiling, old tapestries on the walls and dark furniture scattered here and there. On the floor, a gleaming expanse of old terra-cotta floor tiles for which Tuscany was famous.

Laura suddenly twirled to face him. "One odd thing did happen. You must know the man everyone calls Gogol?"

"Who doesn't. What did he do?"

"Tuesday, the day after the man you say is Garrett was killed, Gogol walked into the front garden laughing loudly and clapping his hands. He had never come here before. He was making a lot of noise, and I had a hard time getting him to leave." She put on a smile she didn't mean. "I'll get the shirt for you and make those calls. While you wait, can I offer you a coffee?"

"Thank you. A coffee is always welcome." Perillo followed Laura to the bar at the back of the hotel, a small room with wooden bookcases filled with books in various languages covering three sides of the room. Perillo had to weave his way between two small leather sofas and armchairs to reach the bar. Behind it, a man who looked to be on the wrong side of eighty was drying a glass.

Laura flung her arm toward the bartender. "Meet Cesare, the man who holds this place together. Cesare, this is Maresciallo Perillo of the Greve Carabinieri. Cesare has been working here since the dinosaur age. We can't live without him."

Cesare grinned, all his teeth still in place. "I'm really the ghost of the original owner, who died in 1891. I was a bad one in my day and am paying my dues by humbly bartending until the end of time."

"Cesare likes to tease, and the foreign guests eat it up. The maresciallo would like a coffee. Excuse me, I'll be right back with the shirt."

Cesare shrugged and put the dry glass away. "I guess I have to be serious with you. Anything stronger than coffee?"

"No, thank you. An espresso will be fine."

"So I finally get to meet the man who keeps order in these parts. What has kept you away from this nice hotel and our bar?"

"You haven't needed me."

"But now you're looking into the death of that man found in the woods."

"Yes, I am."

"The look on Laura's face told me. Her face was a burst of sunshine before you showed up. Now she's a storm cloud. And she's gone to get a shirt—perhaps the shirt one of our guests left in his room?"

"You would have made a good carabiniere."

Cesare turned to the large shiny espresso machine, filled the holder with fresh coffee and fit it into the machine. "All it takes is knowing how to add. I learned that in the third grade." After less than a minute, Cesare placed the espresso on the wooden counter in front of Perillo.

"Addition with calculus thrown in, I think." Perillo took a sip. Cesare went back to picking up glasses from the mini dishwasher behind the counter and drying them. "How long have you worked here?"

"I've been behind this bar since I was eighteen."

Two sips and the cup was empty.

"Did you ever serve a guest who called himself Mr. Garrett?"

"He was a strange one. Liked an Aperol Spritz every night. I can make you one now, if you want. On the house. It's refreshing."

"I don't go for orange drinks. Did he look familiar?"

"Never seen him before. Aperol Spritz is the latest craze from Venice. Prosecco, Aperol, soda water. Three, two, one is the formula. Signor Garrett would have just one and take it to his room."

"Was that what made him strange?"

"What was strange was that he kept to himself for five days and on the sixth, Sunday night, open sesame, the cave opened and he couldn't stop talking. Like he knew he wasn't going to get another chance. He boasted a lot about his success in America. Repeated himself. It sounded to me like he was the one who needed convincing that he'd done all right with his life. His American had an accent. Italian, I thought."

"You thought right."

"I wanted to ask him, but I've learned that asking isn't always welcome. Listening is the most important part of my job."

"And what did you hear?"

"That for all his bragging about being rich, he was very nervous about something. Insecure. He said he had an important meeting in the morning that was going to make things better. I wanted to ask, what things? He had all the money he could want, according to him, a great big house overlooking the Pacific. He showed me a picture. Again, asking isn't part of my job."

"He was dying of cancer," Perillo said, divulging a fact that was going to be in the papers tomorrow.

"That might explain it, I guess. He did mention that the purpose of his trip here was to heal. Maybe he was meeting up with a doctor, maybe one who was going to sell him some crazy cure. When people are desperate, they'll believe anything."

Was it his cancer that had brought Garrett home? Perillo wondered. The man had booked a flight back to California, which meant he hadn't planned to die here. Maybe the fact that he was dying had prompted him to come back. To do what, heal somehow? The cancer had been too far along to hope for a recovery. Perhaps to take care of something?

Cesare noticed the maresciallo was lost in thought. "Maresciallo, yours is a tough job. You need a break from murder. A glass of 2013 Panzanello Riserva on the house?"

"Did Garrett mention anything about a gold bracelet he'd just bought?"

The bartender was about to answer when Laura walked into the room. "I'm sorry I took so long," she said. "The housekeeper had locked the shirt up in the linen closets. I had to track her down for the key."

"I know nothing about a gold bracelet," Cesare said after a look at Laura.

"Neither do I," Laura said, holding out the shirt, seemingly eager to get rid of what had belonged to a murdered man. "The girls said no one called or asked for Signor Garrett." Tucked in the pocket of the shirt was a piece of paper. "I wrote down their numbers in case you want to ask them yourself."

"Thank you. Not that I don't believe you."

She nodded. "Do have a glass of wine." What she meant was, *Take this and leave.*

Perillo responded to Laura's words at face value. "Thank you, I'll pass on the glass, but how much is the bottle? I'll take two." It would save him a trip to the wine store. He couldn't show up at Nico's empty-handed.

"Consider them a welcoming present from us," Laura said.

"Too kind, thank you, but I must decline." Daniele would be proud of him. His wife less so. She wasn't happy about his pay.

"We're not trying to bribe you," Laura said with an annoyed look on her face.

"I know, but it's policy," a policy to which Perillo suspected too few colleagues paid attention.

Laura placed the shirt in his hands with determination. "I understand."

Perillo noticed the golf club embroidered in red on the pocket of the blue shirt. This was the shirt Rosalba had mentioned, the one Garrett had worn to buy the bracelet. He was glad it was now accounted for, but it would tell him nothing more. "Thank you for the coffee and the shirt. If you ever need help, let me know."

"I hope you'll come back without us needing your help," Laura said, playing the welcoming manager with clear insincerity. He didn't blame her—a carabiniere on-site in uniform wasn't the best for business.

"Come back for another espresso anytime," Cesare said, tossing a wet dish towel over his shoulder. "I hope I was of some help."

"You were. Your last name, please? For the report."

"Cesare Giovanni Costanzi."

"Thank you. Thank you both."

Laura accompanied Perillo to the entrance of the hotel.

"If you think of anything that might help with the investigation, please call me." He wished he had a business card to give her as he'd seen the TV detectives do, but he'd never had the need for one. "I can give you the number if you have something for me to write it on."

"I don't think anything else will come up, but if it does"—if it did, she wasn't sure she would tell him; she hated the thought of the hotel's name being connected to the gruesome murder—"I can easily look up the number. Here's my card."

Perillo took the card and they shook hands. Laura stood at the entrance and watched as Perillo stopped and took in the view, then walked down the gravel path to the carabinieri car he'd parked just outside the gate for all the guests to see. Tomorrow, even if they didn't read Italian newspapers, her guests would discover that a fellow guest had been murdered. How many visitors would she lose? She had nothing against Perillo. He was a nice man just doing his job, but she hoped to never see him again. He brought trouble with him. No, she was wrong. He *followed* trouble and she didn't like trouble. No one did.

"What did the maresciallo ask you?" Laura asked when she walked back into the bar.

Cesare sipped the Panzanello Riserva wine he had offered Perillo. "It's what he told me that's interesting. Gerardi was dying of cancer. That explains why it took me a while to realize who he was. It's been decades, and he was all swollen, I guess with steroids."

"Why didn't you tell the maresciallo you recognized him?"

"Sixty years a bartender, I know when to keep my mouth shut."

NINE

Nico had just finished the pasta sauce when Perillo called to say they were leaving Greve.

"Good. I've left the downstairs door open." The two carabinieri were his first dinner guests. Tilde never had a free evening. The one night of the week the restaurant was closed, she inevitably wanted to stay home. He'd put on clean khakis and a dark-green polyester short-sleeved shirt. Both needed "a touch of the iron," as Rita used to say, but sweeping a hot gadget back and forth without burning anything was a skill Nico had yet to master. At least cooking was easier. Nico dipped a coffee spoon into the sauce and tasted, a hungry OneWag watching closely.

"Sorry, you'll have to wait. Guests come first." Nico added a pinch of salt and pepper, used the wooden spoon to mix it all up. It was a nice sauce, nothing to be ashamed of. Thinly sliced leeks, broccoletti and mushrooms browned in butter, then wetted with a little white wine. Once the wine had almost evaporated he'd added vegetable broth, salt and pepper and let it simmer until slightly thickened. The last touch was whisking in a few tablespoons of mascarpone. Tonight he was going to serve it with penne, although any pasta would do the sauce honor. If Daniele and Perillo liked the dish, Nico would suggest it to Tilde. While cooking, he'd even come up with a name: Pasta Nico's Way. He was getting arrogant in his old age. Well, at least he was trying to make a mark in the kitchen, if not at solving crimes.

He filled the large pot with water, put it on the gas flame and placed the sea salt next to the pot as a reminder. Rita had taught him he had to wait until the water boiled to add the salt, other-wise the water would take forever to boil. In his zeal to eat, often he'd toss in the pasta and forget the salt.

Nico filled a small bowl with Castelvetrano olives from Sicily and chunks of Parmigiano Reggiano. He poured himself a glass of Aldo's white wine and took the bowl and his glass out onto the terrace. Clouds had slipped in and darkened the sky. The air was cooling. Dinner would have to be inside. He had no tablecloth or place mats, just cheap plates and cutlery he'd bought at the big Coop in Greve. As he went back inside and set the table he could hear Rita clucking her tongue. All the stuff in their Bronx home, he'd given to the Salvation Army. He didn't need to take any more weight with him.

DESPITE THE COOLING EVENING, the three men sat on Nico's balcony, listening to the crickets. Perillo had shown up wearing jeans, a blindingly white starched linen shirt, his leather jacket and his new suede ankle boots. Daniele had tried on two pairs of slacks and the three dress shirts his mother had given him before he left. After long minutes of uncertainty, he'd decided on black pants and his favorite dress shirt, a striped blue one. Seeing him in the parking lot, Perillo had whistled his approval. The "Dani bloom," as Perillo had dubbed it, followed.

Nico and Perillo smoked, wineglasses in hand. Nico stuck to his white, Daniele and the maresciallo with the first bottle of Villa Antinori Toscana. As the breeze shifted and smoke came his way, Daniele pushed his chair a little farther and tried to ignore the smell. The sky was dark early tonight, the moon having disap-peared behind a thick screen of clouds. The swallows were safely asleep in the balcony rafters. The bottle of red was half-empty. The only thing left in the small bowl of olives and Parmigiano Reggiano was a thin sheen of oil.

The pasta timer rang, calling for the cigarettes to be put out, the glasses gathered and the three men and one dog moved inside.

Perillo poured a glass of red and handed it to Nico. "Time to switch color. You're in the land of the Super Chianti, Nico, not at some fancy New York cocktail party."

"How do you know anything about New York cocktail parties?" Nico asked as he drained the penne.

"Television, where else?"

"I planned to switch for the pasta course." He had always preferred red, but its high tannin levels upset Rita's stomach, and so white wine was all they drank on Saturday nights when he wasn't on a case. Now in the evenings, his first glass was always white, a tribute of sorts. Nico poured the penne back into the pot, added the hot sauce, mixed well, and let the pasta cook in the sauce for a couple of minutes. After placing a mug filled with freshly grated Parmigiano Reggiano on the table, he served his guests directly from the pot.

"Buon appetito."

"Bravo," Perillo said, after taking a couple of bites. "This is tasty." He managed to keep the surprise out of his voice. He lifted his glass in a toast. "To Italian American cooking."

Daniele lifted his glass. "Very good, Signor Nico."

"Cut the Signore. My name's Nico."

Perillo winked at Daniele, who dropped his head to hide his cheeks. All three dug their forks into the penne. The smell wafting down from the table had OneWag's stomach turning somersaults, but in the past few days he had learned optimism. Something was likely to come his way, and so he curled himself at Nico's feet. With optimism came patience.

The three men ate in silence for a few minutes, too hungry to interrupt their enjoyment of good food with talk of murder.

"His picture will be in the paper tomorrow," Perillo said finally, his plate empty. "I put in an appeal for people who knew him to come forward. So far, I've gotten nothing from the Gravignesi, but maybe people in the nearby towns know something."

"Won't people be too scared to talk?" Daniele asked. His plate was empty too and he looked longingly at the pot that still had some pasta in it. "They might be worried about becoming implicated in the murder."

"Maybe, but some are going to want to show off what they know," Perillo said. "They'll start talking amongst each other, and someone will be happy to bring the information to us. I'm friendly with the locals, thanks to my Sunday cycling jaunts. People don't see me as a menace. I've shut my eyes to a few things, which always pays off. Information will eventually come to us—if not directly, indirectly."

Nico tore off a piece of olive loaf and gathered up what was left of the sauce on his plate. "Maybe we'll find out what enemies Gerardi left behind when he took off for the US."

Daniele watched Nico's swiping with envy. His plate still had sauce waiting to be scooped up, but his mother had insisted it was impolite. "Did you know that's called 'making the little shoe'?"

"Thank you, no, I didn't." Nico had known that, but why disappoint? He pushed the olive loaf toward Daniele. "Help yourself, and there's plenty more pasta in the pot. There's only salad and fruit after that." He waited until Daniele and Perillo had refilled their plates to ask, "Did you get ahold of the prosecutor?"

"He was off to a reunion of the Five Star Party, probably kissing ass. I spoke to Barbara, his secretary, a woman I admire and respect. She knows how to listen, often makes good suggestions. I asked her to advise the American embassy in Rome that we had a murdered Italian American on our hands."

Nico clinked his wineglass against Perillo's. "I hope you kept me out of it."

Perillo wiped his lips with a paper towel. "I thought it best." Nico was now a friend. He didn't want to embarrass him by having the embassy look into his career. "Barbara will hold off telling Della Langhe until the morning, since he told her he could be disturbed only if it was a national emergency, and in her opinion the Garrett/Gerardi murder is only an international blemish."

"And so it is." A grateful Nico poured more wine into their glasses. "Let's drink to the three of us finding the murderer."

Daniele raised his glass, happy to be part of the three, but worried about the consequences of not calling Della Langhe. "Won't we get into trouble?"

Perillo drained his glass. "Oh, tomorrow he'll call screaming. I might have to temporarily lose my phone."

Nico picked up the empty pasta plates and, followed by OneWag, put them in the sink. What little was left in the pot he scraped into the dog's bowl, which earned him a grateful tail swish. "I hope the American embassy won't start breathing down your neck."

"I think the Americans have bigger problems than one murdered dual citizen to deal with these days." Perillo opened the second bottle of wine. "By the way, we didn't find a computer or a cell phone among Gerardi's possessions."

"He must have had at least a phone. You need to find that."

"I am certainly aware of that."

"Sorry, you're right. Old habits." His partner had always complained he liked to state the obvious. Nico dressed the salad of fennel, olives, arugula and slivers of aged Asiago cheese with lemon juice and Aldo's olive oil.

Perillo did his dismissive hand wave. "I'm not going to waste my time—our time," he corrected, "guessing whether the phone was lost or stolen. We have to find it. The murderer must have communicated with him."

"Even if we find the phone, it'll have a password," Daniele pointed out.

Perillo shot him down with a look. "Pessimism gets us nowhere."

Daniele said nothing. Perillo obviously had no idea how long finding the password would take.

"I went to the hotel and got the missing shirt back," Perillo said. "The manager is too young to have known Gerardi, but Cesare Costanzi, the hotel bartender, is a local in his eighties. He certainly could have. I asked him if he'd ever seen Gerardi before his stay at the hotel. He said no, but he could be lying. When I confirmed Garrett was Italian, Rinaldi didn't even ask his name, which I find odd."

"Listening and not asking is part of a bartender's trade," Nico said.

"Rinaldi did also make that point."

"And he might not have wanted to get involved," Nico washed his hands and tossed the salad with his fingers. It was the best way to ensure all the ingredients were mixed well.

"Could be," Perillo admitted.

Nico washed his hands again and dried them. "I looked up Gerardi and his wine company on the Internet."

"I was planning to go online after dinner tonight," Daniele said through teeth he realized were clenched. The Internet was his domain. "I had too many things to take care of." He stole an accusatory glance at his boss.

Perillo ignored him and poured more wine in each glass. "What did you find out?"

"The company's website shows pictures of its buildings, its vineyards, the list of its wines, the usual stuff, but no history of the place, which is unusual. The other winery websites I took a quick glance at all had founding histories." Nico brought clean plates and the salad bowl over to the table. "Luckily, he was written up several times in the California newspapers. Serve yourself, please." He sat down. "Gerardi's story is one everyone likes, especially in the States. According to the articles I found, he arrived in Napa with very little money. After a few months working part-time with other immigrants at various vineyards, he was hired full-time by a small Italian American vintner, John Delizioso."

"Delicious." Perillo savored the English word. Repeated it. "An improbable name," he added in Italian.

"A good name for a wine company. The two men became very close, and the vintner sponsored Gerardi's American citizenship. He was a good worker, and when Delizioso wanted to retire, he sold Gerardi the vineyard at a very good price. Gerardi expanded it, added different varieties of grapes and became rich. How rich, the Internet didn't tell me. I did come across a speech he gave to the Napa Chamber of Commerce about a year ago. He was going to expand his company by buying land near Gravigna. He'd found an ideal plot and claimed he made a bid on it. We need to look into that."

"I'll look in the land register," Daniele immediately offered, "and see if any empty plots are for sale."

Perillo served himself a few slices of fennel. Salad, even with cheese added, was for rabbits. "Go ahead and look, but I haven't heard of any land available for wine-making. The only land up for sale is the fifteen-some hectares that include the wood where Gerardi was killed. Aldo had the soil tested, and it's not good wine-growing land."

Daniele drew the salad bowl close. "You could build a huge hotel on it."

Perillo shook his head. "Can't. It's marked for farming."

Daniele refused to give up. He'd been invited to dinner to put forward his opinions, and he would keep doing so. "I still think he could have been killed in that wood because he was trying to buy the land and someone else wanted it."

Perillo heard the anger in Daniele's voice and softened his tone. "No, Dani. The experts who tested the soil decreed that it's only good for hunting and picking mushrooms. No one is going to buy it to grow grapes."

"Experts can be bought," Daniele countered. He didn't enjoy the maresciallo's condescension and hated the fact that any so-called experts would lie for money.

"In his speech," Nico said, changing the subject, "Gerardi made a big deal about how he missed Italy and his hometown, missed what he had given up by leaving. He was nostalgic, and yet he never came back until now. What kept him away?"

"There's not much vacation time when you're running a vineyard," Perillo said. "Just ask Aldo. You're right, though. We need to find out what made him leave Gravigna, and what brought him back."

"Maybe the same thing that made him leave brought him back," Nico said.

"Could be." Perillo refilled Nico's glass. "The bartender at the Bella Vista said Gerardi talked a great deal about needing to heal here."

"That makes sense. He was riddled with cancer and wanted to live." Daniele covered his glass with his hand. He wished the maresciallo hadn't opened the second bottle. Too much red wine would affect Nico's taste buds and maybe change the taste of the Venetian surprise he had in store. Plus, he needed to keep his own head clear and not make any dumb remarks.

"You're right," Nico said, "but he must have known his cancer was too far gone for it to heal."

"Hope doesn't give up that easily, does it?" Daniele asked.

"No, it doesn't." Rita had held on to hope. Nico had steeled himself for the inevitable and only pretended he still had hope. "There are other ways of healing. Making peace with yourself is one. Asking forgiveness of someone you have hurt is another. Maybe that's why Gerardi came back. He must have relatives here."

"If he does"—Daniele could feel his heart beat a little faster—"the registrar's office will tell us." The office was in Radda in Chianti. He would go there first, phone in whatever he found out, then stop by Rosalba's shop. His thumbs started flying over his phone. Seconds later, he looked up with disappointment etched on his face. "They're closed tomorrow. I could try getting into their files."

"Don't," Perillo said. "That's illegal, and I don't want to be responsible for leading you down the crooked path. Not everything gets resolved by using a computer. I'll make a few phone calls in the morning and find an employee to open up for you. I'm also counting on the article in *La Nazione* to bring people to the office."

"Unless, as Daniele mentioned, they don't want to get involved with the police," Nico said. "I was always surprised at how many friends and relatives of the victim didn't come forward voluntarily. They had done things that had nothing to do with the murder—most times not very bad things—but if any of that guilt was involved, they stayed away or lied."

"We also need to know if he had any family in the States. I couldn't find any mention of a wife or children in the articles I read," Nico said. "And if he wrote a will, we should find out what's in it. If he did, it's probably with a lawyer in Napa. The Napa police need to be told. His house and office have to be searched for links to anyone here. That goes for his computer too. Gerardi might have corresponded with his killer here. Someone needs to go to his house and office, get into his computer. That's something for Della Langhe to ask the American embassy. That and how much money he had."

Perillo filled his wineglass again and took a long drink. "Unfortunately, that will take time. You think this murder was motivated by money?"

"Money, hate, unrequited love, revenge. All motivators. It's good to rule them out one by one."

Daniele cleaned out the salad bowl with the last of the bread. "There's something that's bothering me."

Perillo snorted. "You're lucky it's only one thing. I'm bothered about everything in this case." He drained his wine. "Go ahead, Dani. What is it?"

"Why did Gerardi tell the Avis people he was going to Radda in Chianti, but then not stay there? It's like he knew he was going to buy the bracelet in that town."

Nico took the empty salad bowl and the plates to the sink. "Could be he remembered the jeweler from the old days. I wonder how long that store has been around."

Daniele stood up. It was time to serve his Venetian surprise. "It was founded by Rosalba's great-grandfather in 1952."

"So, you've been looking up Rosalba on that lump of plastic you love so much," Perillo teased.

Daniele would have blushed if his face weren't already red from the wine. "I wanted to know how old she was."

"And?"

"Two years older, unfortunately."

Nico gave Daniele's sagging shoulders a pat. "It's not a death sentence. Today, young people don't care as much about age. Charm, looks and sexiness are what counts."

"And from the way Rosalba reacted to you," Perillo added, "I'd say she thinks you've got all three. Now that we have two dead on the table, what's the Venetian dish you've brought?"

"What do you mean, two dead?" Nico asked.

"That's what we call empty wine bottles. We also say there's a hole in the bottle. Come on, Dani, tell us what's next."

Daniele took his bag to the small counter next to the sink. "Not a dish. A digestivo. Un sgroppino."

"That's a new one to me," Nico said with an edge in his voice. Every Italian after-dinner drink he'd ever been offered—Fernet-Branca, grappa, limoncello, sambuca—had all tasted like cough medicine. But he didn't want to upset Daniele by not drinking. "What's it made of?"

"You'll see." Daniele unwrapped the three flutes he'd borrowed from the maresciallo's wife. He'd promised he would replace them if they broke, but she'd waved him away, too happy arranging the yellow roses the maresciallo had bought her.

Perillo hoped whatever it was had plenty of grappa in it. The day had been intense. He needed the jolt grappa always gave him. Grappa or the whiskey Nico had shared with him earlier.

Both men and the dog—the men anxiously, the dog calmly—watched as Daniele dropped six tablespoons of lemon sorbet into a bowl. He popped open a bottle of prosecco and poured two-thirds of a cup of the sparkling wine into the bowl. "Some people add an equal amount of vodka, but my mother was always afraid I'd get drunk, so we make it this way." With a whisk he used to foam up the milk for his morning cappuccino in the barracks, he blended the prosecco and sorbet together and filled the flutes. For that extra touch his mother insisted on, he wedged a slice of lemon onto the rim of each glass. "Ecco fatto!" He handed out the drinks and sat down.

Nico raised his glass. "Thank you."

"To our health." Perillo took a sip. Refreshing, but vodka would have made it a lot better.

"A real treat," Nico said after drinking. OneWag lay down on the floor, dropping his snout heavily on Nico's foot. Dogs had a language all their own. "Anything left in that bowl?"

Daniele had seen the dog's move. "Enough for a lick or two." He got up and placed the bowl on the floor. OneWag pattered over to the bowl.

The opening notes of "O Sole Mio" broke the quiet. Perillo muttered, "Shit." Daniele stiffened in his seat. Perillo took his time digging out the phone from his pants pocket. He squinted to check the number. Double fuck. He needed glasses.

"Della Langhe?" Daniele whispered.

Perillo shook his head. "Ehi, what's up? Is somebody making off with your beautiful wife?"

Excited words rumbled out of Perillo's cell. That the caller was a man was all Nico could make out.

"Who told you?" Perillo asked. He didn't think Laura or Cesare would be eager to spread the word about their murdered guest.

"Ah, Bruno." Perillo pressed a cigarette between his lips. He'd have to be satisfied with the pretense of smoking while he listened to the anxious sputterings. "The very same Bruno who stole our poor murdered man's car to take his girlfriend for a dawn joyride to the town of many towers and Vernaccia wine. The only good thing I can say about him is that he has good taste in locations."

While Perillo sucked on his cigarette and listened, Nico took the flutes to the sink. There was no point to eavesdropping on someone else's phone conversation if you didn't know who was on the other end of the line. OneWag gave one last sweeping lick of his bowl and scampered to the sofa to sleep. Daniele, more concerned about the glasses he might have to replace, joined Nico at the sink and took over washing them. The American's big hands didn't look like they were used to handling delicate things.

"Yes, I agree with you, Aldo," Perillo said, the jocular tone gone. "Your nephew is a jerk. And yes, I'm sure it's all his mother's fault, and no, I'm not going to tell you who our victim is."

"The news will be out in the morning," Nico said. "Tell him to come over now. We offer whiskey and the man's identity."

Perillo relayed the invitation to Aldo and clicked off. "He'll probably fly over. You think he might be involved?"

"Too soon to know, but I bet he can tell us something about Roberto Gerardi. It's a small town. He's bound to have known him."

TEN

While waiting for Aldo, Nico put out a bowl of fruit salad. He added a mug filled with sugar next to it on the table. As heavy footsteps made the stairs creak, OneWag jumped off the sofa, parked himself in front of the door and barked his head off.

Nico barked back. "OneWag!"

The dog turned to look up at Nico, understood he meant business and with a huff went down on all fours, ready to jump at the intruder if the situation called for it.

Aldo burst into the room with his face flushed from the effort of the stairs. He was wearing his usual entertain-the-tourists uniform: jeans and the bright leaf-green and purple Ferriello T-shirt. He waved a bottle like a man who'd found a lost treasure. Aldo had told Nico he was in love with every single bottle of wine he produced, a love he was always eager to sell.

"I thought vin santo, the wine of hospitality and friendship, was just the thing to keep us safe from murder. It's new this year. Wait until you taste it. Made with half merlot grapes, half cabernet."

"Stop selling it and uncork it."

Aldo dropped his full weight onto the chair Nico had vacated and handed the bottle and corkscrew to Daniele. "Sorry, they ate all my cantuccini." He shifted position to face Perillo. "So tell me. Who is it?"

"First, let's have a taste of this holy wine. We could all use some of that, right, Dani?"

Daniele turned his back to Perillo as he uncorked the bottle.

Aldo clasped his knees and tried to lean forward, but his belly got in the way. "Come on, tell me."

Perillo enjoyed keeping Aldo in suspense, his revenge for the measly discounts the vintner had given him last year when he'd treated his wife to a Super Chianti for her birthday. "Tell us how you make it. Does a priest bless it?"

"Stop it, Salvatore." Aldo, who loved to expound on his own wines and his olives, was in no mood for games now. "Christ, tell me who it is."

Was it simple curiosity, Nico asked himself, or was he afraid?

Daniele sat down in his chair and poured the wine into the three flutes he had just washed. He would abstain. Mixing red wine, prosecco and sweet wine would hammer nails into his head.

"No, I'm sure Nico and Daniele want to know about the production of this special wine," Salvatore replied. "I hear it's expensive and takes a long time to make. We'll enjoy it more if we know the process. You tell me, then I'll tell you. It's only fair."

Nico stayed by the sink, flute in hand, and wondered if keeping Aldo on tenterhooks had another purpose besides annoying him.

Perillo lifted his flute. The wine's amber color turned gold in the light. "Just pretend we're foreigners."

Aldo resigned himself with a loud exhale. "One: you need perfect grapes. No rot. Two: they're dried until they shrivel like raisins." He spoke quickly. "Three: they get pressed. Four: into oak barrels they go. Five: I wait from three to seven years, depending on how intense I'd like the wine. It is very costly and time-consuming." Aldo pressed against the back of his chair, which creaked in protest. "Your turn."

Perillo complied. "Roberto Gerardi."

The flush on Aldo's face disappeared, and his expression went dead for a moment. He stared at Perillo. "Are you sure?"

Perillo nodded while Daniele quietly spooned fruit salad into his dish.

After what seemed like a full minute, Aldo let out a laugh from the bottom of his stomach.

From the sofa, a disrupted OneWag sleepily lifted his head.

The blood rushed back to Aldo's face. "That's a good one. So Roberto Gerardi got his comeuppance. Never thought I'd see that! He left years ago. No one around here has heard news of him since. Why the hell did he come back?"

"That's what we need to find out." Perillo forked a pineapple piece and put it in his mouth. "You knew him. What can you tell us?"

Daniele followed Perillo's cue and started eating, careful not to make a sound. He didn't want to miss anything. OneWag settled back to continue his slumber.

Aldo wiped his large hand over his face. When it came down, all trace of laughter was gone. "I guess you'd find out anyway, so I might as well tell you. I don't want you to think I'm the one who killed him, though, because I'm not."

Nico leaned against the narrow kitchen counter. He liked watching, getting a first impression from a distance. It was something he'd picked up from Rita when she took him to see his first abstract art show at MoMA, back when he was still a patrol cop. The paintings were just a jumble of colored splotches and lines to him. She told him to step back to see the whole and allow the painting to speak to him. He did step back, and just sometimes, he saw something that he maybe understood. Oddly, Rita's advice about viewing art stuck with him once he made detective. When he needed to interrogate a suspect, he would let his partner do it first as he stepped back to watch. Watch the body, the twitches, the shifting, the breathing. Hear the words last.

Perillo took a sip of vin santo. "Why would we think you killed him?" He raised the flute. "This is good, by the way." Far too sweet for his taste, but Aldo only ever wanted praise.

"Gerardi worked for me for a couple of years."

"When was that?" Perillo asked casually, wanting Aldo to think they were just having a conversation between friends.

"I hired him to work at the winery twenty-four years ago. The first year Ferriello Wines made a profit. A small one, but still, not a year I'm likely to forget." Aldo's stomach started shaking with breathy laughter. "You know what's funny? I'm not making this up. Last time I saw Roberto, I told him I never wanted to see his face again. And now he's gotten his face blown off. Cinzia will get the shivers when I tell her."

"What did Gerardi do for you?" Perillo was willing to wait to see what was so funny.

"It was Cinzia's idea to hire him. He was working at a hotel in Panzano. Roberto was good-looking, well spoken. He knew a little English and French, enough to show tourists how we make wine, walk them around the vineyard. He could charm them into buying more than they'd planned on. He was a real asset." Aldo paused, his eyes on some distant point beyond the room.

Perillo waited, plucking another piece of fruit from the bowl, playing the disinterested listener.

Daniele had cleaned his plate and sat still, his stomach muscles clenched in anticipation.

Nico leaned against the kitchen counter and sipped the sweet wine. The murdered man had been important to Aldo. So something had soured.

"But he stopped being an asset?"

Nico regretted the question as soon as he asked it. This was Perillo's case. He was just a bystander.

Aldo lifted his head slowly. Anger burned in his eyes now. "Roberto was someone I trusted completely. I was still learning the wine and olive oil business. I needed help, and he gave it to me."

Perillo could repeat Nico's question, but he preferred approaching this from another angle. As the Tuscans said, with patience, you won everything. "Do you know anything about his life outside of work? Any relatives?"

"A lot of time has passed. His parents were dead. I think he had a married sister somewhere, but they weren't close. I don't know her name."

"Did you two socialize outside of work? Ever meet any of his friends?"

"If he had friends, I didn't know them. The two of us went out for pizza occasionally when Cinzia was off somewhere. Sometimes we drank too much."

"What did you talk about?"

"Just gripes about too much work, too much rain, not enough sun, lazy workers, women troubles. His, not mine. Look, I wish you'd stop interrogating me. I told you, I didn't kill him." Aldo was quickly clenching and unclenching his hands now.

Perillo straightened his back, aware of the impatience flickering across his face. "I'm not interrogating you, at least not while we are in Nico's home and sharing the wine you've brought. I'm asking questions because we're dealing with a very ugly murder, and I'm hoping you know something about Gerardi that could help us. *You* are the one who's said we might think you killed him."

Nico opened the kitchen cabinet to get the bottle of whiskey. There was one glass left, and it looked like Aldo needed it.

Aldo stretched his fingers. "One night, Roberto got very drunk and confessed he was very much in love with someone. Wanted to marry her. There was some kind of trouble with her though, something about her family being against it. He did have a reputation for womanizing, which might be the reason he was having trouble with the family. He wouldn't tell me who she was."

Nico filled a glass, walked slowly to the table and placed it in front of Aldo.

Perillo looked at the half-filled glass of whiskey with great envy. "Anything else you can think of that might help us get a sense of the kind of man he was?"

Aldo downed the whiskey in one go. "Well, the bastard stole from me."

From me were the key words there, Nico noted. Aldo could have said *from the winery* or simply called him a thief, but it was the personal affront that mattered, not the action itself.

"I even loaned him some money, idiot that I am."

"What did he steal?" Perillo asked, wondering if there had ever been rough patches in Aldo's relationship with Cinzia. She'd been the one to bring Gerardi in. Men couldn't stop looking at Cinzia. Even he'd had his own inappropriate thoughts there.

Aldo leaned back in his chair and fixed his eyes on the now-empty whiskey bottle. "It was Arben who figured it out. He was the most ambitious of my Albanian employees, and at first I thought he was just smearing dirt on Roberto because he was after his job. Well, he got it. It took a few years, and now he can run the place without me. Arben's a very good man." Aldo looked up. "I'm the godfather of his first child," he said proudly. "Our families get together a lot. You know, I hired quite a lot of Albanians and Kosovians after they fled their countries and came here. Sure, they were hungry, but I discovered they were good workers, and cheap."

Perillo let Aldo ramble. He always talked too much.

"I'm ashamed to say, though, I haven't always trusted them. They get into fights with each other, don't they, Salvatore?"

"So do Tuscans."

"Yes, yes, of course, but I was just trying to explain why I didn't listen to Arben. Roberto was Tuscan, and I trusted him. Arben was a foreigner, and therefore I didn't believe him. Arben understood that and was too proud to insist. That's how stupid I was. When I found out Arben had told me the truth, I punched Roberto in the face. He punched me right back. Arben and the others had to separate us. That's when I fired him and told him I never wanted to see his face again."

"What did he steal?" Perillo asked again.

Aldo looked surprised. "My wine, of course. What else could he steal? That's all I've got."

What about a wife? asked Nico silently.

"He stole straight from the barrels. Siphoned off the wine just before we bottled it. A bottle or two at a time, not so much that we'd notice."

Nico asked, sitting with the others at the table, "How did Arben find out?"

"One night, we had a big group of Americans here. Arben was upstairs helping with the dinner because Cinzia wasn't feeling well. She's in charge of feeding the guests. We always serve a dinner or lunch with the tour, and once it was over, it was part of Roberto's job to escort the group across the courtyard to the dining room in the other building and eat with them. The guests came, but Roberto showed up late. I was too busy talking about the wines they were drinking to notice anything. After everyone had left, Roberto included, Arben went down to the basement and checked the barrels. He noticed wine on the floor under several of the spigots. He'd made sure the floor was spotless before the guests came. Arben went back upstairs to the bottling and labeling room and noticed a few empty bottles were missing. He'd noticed missing empties before and told me about it, but a missing empty or two went with the territory, I told him. That night, after everyone left, he told me he thought Roberto was siphoning off wine. I accused him of being jealous. It's a miracle Arben didn't walk off the job that very night. I know I hurt his pride, and maybe he decided to stay to prove me wrong. After that night, whenever we had an evening tour, Arben would offer to help Cinzia. She couldn't have been happier. What we didn't know is that he'd set up a camera in the barrel rooms that he turned on just before the guests went down there. Early the next morning, he'd go back to turn it off. He gathered three months' worth of stealing before he showed me the videos. I had, thank God, the good grace not to ask him why he waited so long."

"Thank you, Aldo. For the moment, I don't believe you shot Gerardi's face off, but tomorrow, who knows?"

Aldo flung his arms in the air. "Good God. You're joking, right?"

Perillo clinked his empty flute against Aldo's empty whiskey glass. "Don't I always?"

Aldo let out a grunt that might have been a laugh. "You do, and I put up with it." He stood up. "Thank you for the hospitality. By now, Cinzia must be jumping out of her skin to know who it is."

"I'll have to talk to Cinzia too," Perillo said. "She might know more about his love life."

Aldo scowled. "What are you implying?"

"Sometimes men confide in women."

"He didn't get anywhere near her."

"I'm not saying he did, but she's the one who pointed him out to you. She might know something you don't."

Aldo seemed mollified. "All right, I'll tell her."

Perillo stood up and the four of them shook hands.

After the door closed and Aldo's footsteps disappeared, Perillo asked Nico, "What do you think?"

"After twenty-two years, he might still carry a grudge against Gerardi, but not one major enough to kill him."

"Unless he didn't tell us the whole story," Daniele added. This job was making him cynical.

Perillo picked up his leather jacket. "We'll find out. But for now, I think it's time to bid our host good night. Pack up the flutes, Dani, and we'll go. Good night, Rocco."

OneWag lifted his head, wagged once and went back to sleep. Nico was surprised the dog reacted to the name. "You'll turn him into a schizophrenic."

"Italian dog, Italian name. Anything else is against nature." At the door, Perillo remembered and turned around. "Your friend Gogol made a first-time appearance at the local hotel yesterday, laughing loudly and clapping. Laura, the manager, had a difficult time convincing him to leave. Maybe you can find out why?"

"I can try."

Once the maresciallo and his bridgadiere were gone, Nico washed the pots, dishes and tableware, dumped the empty wine bottles in the recycling basket and sponged the table and the sink clean. He dried his hands and walked over to the sofa. "Bedtime, OneWag."

The dog uncurled himself and waited.

"No dice." Nico walked to his bedroom. "You've got four legs. Use them."

OneWag turned over and began scratching his ear, which didn't itch. Next, he busied himself with gnawing his front paws, which were perfectly clean. After what the dog considered a suitable amount of time, he jumped off the sofa and, tail held high, slowly made his way to the bedroom.

THE NEXT MORNING, THURSDAY, the sky was a thick gray cap leaking heavy rain. With OneWag still nestled between the sheets, Nico took his espresso out on the balcony. A flutter of wings brushed his face as the swallows left their sleeping quarters to swoop through the curtain of rain, not caring if they got soaked. The vegetable garden would be grateful—Nico had forgotten to water it last night—but he knew Aldo and the other local vintners wouldn't be happy to see the rain dilute the sweetness and strength of their grapes. Enough water had fallen during the summer to satisfy the humidity required by the vines. With the grape harvesting only five or six weeks away, heat was needed to produce a good year.

Aldo. Had he told Perillo everything he knew about Gerardi? Perillo seemed confident that they would find out more, but unpleasant actions and events often managed to stay buried.

Nico brushed his teeth, washed his face and, after peering at himself in the cracked mirror, decided to forgo shaving. After last night's drinking, what he really needed was a long, brain-clearing run. He'd gone out in far worse weather, but this morning he had work to do. Perillo was going to be dealing with Della Langhe and whoever showed up in his office to tell him what they knew about Gerardi. Daniele had to reach into the annals of his computer to dig out what he could about Gerardi and the land Aldo had wanted to buy. Nico had assigned himself the job of eavesdropping and questioning Gogol. Roberto Gerardi's photo was in the paper this morning, and the sooner he got to Bar All'Angolo, the better.

OneWag lifted his head from the bedsheets and watched as Nico dressed quickly in jeans and a long-sleeved polo shirt. "Come on, you lazy mutt. We're off." The dog jumped from the bed and scampered over to the adjoining room. He sat at attention in front of his empty food bowl.

"It's whole wheat cornetti this morning." Nico slipped on his parka and opened the door. A blur of orange and white streaked by him.

THE FERRIELLO WINE SHOP/DINING room was a large, handsome beamed room that gave out to a sprawling covered terrace facing a well-tended lawn and, beyond that, an olive grove. Perillo's shoes squished—he had managed to step into a puddle as he'd gotten out of his car—across the smooth, polished floor, leaving a trail of wet footprints. He had come alone in civilian clothes, although this was an official call that technically required a uniform and another carabiniere to act as a witness. Throughout the years, he had learned to bend the rules. He also wanted Aldo's wife to feel his was a friendly visit.

On the terrace, a couple was seated at a table well away from the dripping awning edges. Above them was the drumming sound of rain. Perillo watched as Cinzia poured them two generous glasses of a Ferriello red. What had brought these two foreigners here for a wine tasting at nine o'clock in the morning, and in this weather, was beyond his comprehension.

Cinzia walked toward him with a teasing smile on her face.

"Ciao, Salvatore." She was a petite, slender brunette originally from Rome, with sparkling eyes and a pretty face. She stepped inside the room and Perillo followed.

"Here for a wine tasting?" She waved the open bottle. "They're having a Chianti '15 vintage."

"Too early for me."

"An espresso, then?"

"Gladly." He sat on a barstool in front of the counter at the far end of the room. Cinzia went behind the counter and into a small kitchen partially hidden by a wall of shelves filled with photo albums of the wine dinners they'd hosted for scores of tourists throughout the years. Perillo peered. The older ones showed a thin, eager-looking Aldo, a long-haired Cinzia by his side.

"Aldo hired Gerardi twenty-four years ago, at your suggestion. Is that right?" Perillo asked, remembering what Aldo had said the previous night.

"Wrong." Cinzia lowered the flame on the stove and placed a small moka over it. "I hired Robi."

Perillo noted the more intimate name, Aldo having called him Roberto.

She came back to stand behind the counter, the sparkle in her eye gone. "I can't stomach Robi's death. And the way he was killed. Shooting his face off like that, wiping out his identity. That's pure hate."

"Maybe. It could also have been to serve the killer, gain him time while we blundered about trying to find out who the victim was."

"I'm sure you didn't blunder."

"We don't usually, but this time . . ." Perillo shook his head. "How did you meet him?"

"I was having lunch with a friend from Rome at Hotel Bella Vista in Panzano, where she was staying. Robi was our waiter. The only one in the place, and most of the tables were taken. He handled the crush beautifully. And the women were lapping him up. That was important. My friend was so smitten, she ate every meal at the hotel during her week's stay."

"You must have been smitten too, if you hired him."

The moka stopped gurgling. Cinzia slipped back into the kitchen. "Sugar?"

"No, thanks. I've had my limit today."

She poured two cups and set them on the counter. "I enjoy looking at a handsome man. No sin in that. I convinced Aldo to hire him because men like to be the wine buyers, but women have veto power. We were also both exhausted. I'd come up with the idea of hosting lunches and dinners for tourists. We started offering simple Tuscan specialties—a platter of salami, crostini, then panzanella or ribollita. But the main attraction still had to be our wines." She drank down her coffee and wiped her mouth with a napkin. Perillo did the same. "The idea really took off. There were only four of us at the vineyard. We needed extra help just for the events. Buses were bringing people in droves from Siena and Florence."

"Did you know anything about his love life?"

"Robi liked to brag a lot about his conquests, but I didn't believe him. I think he was just a lost soul who needed to feel important. He loved the attention the tourists gave him, which worked well for us."

"Did he talk about anyone in particular that you can remember? Parents, friends, a girlfriend?"

"When I hired him, he told me both his parents were dead, and that he had a sister he wasn't close to. A few weeks before we found out he'd been siphoning off our wine, he said he was getting engaged and showed me a pair of earrings he had bought in Florence—two coiled silver snakes with tiny green eyes. I guess they were pretty, but snakes give me the shivers. I asked who she was. He wouldn't tell me because her parents didn't know yet. I wondered if he was making the whole thing up. For all I know, those earrings could have been his sister's."

"You weren't curious?" His wife wouldn't have let the matter go until she'd found out who the girl was. He often thought she'd have made a very good carabiniere. He'd once been tempted to enlist her help but stopped himself in time.

"I didn't ask questions. My only interest was that he show up on time and do his job well, which he did until he got it into his head to start stealing from us. If I come up with anything that might help, I'll call you. Now I have to get back to those two Belgians and try to unload a case of Ferriello Chianti '15 vintage."

Perillo got off his barstool. His shoes had stopped squishing. The damp was all in his socks now. "Thanks, Cinzia. I appreciate it. And thanks for the coffee."

THE CAFÉ WAS NOISY and crowded, with no seats available. The doors were shut to keep out the slanting rain. The smell of coffee, hot butter and damp clothing filled the room. Nico opened his rain jacket and, after lowering a dry OneWag to the floor, raised a hand in salute to Sandro and Jimmy. They were too busy behind the counter to look up. Breakfast was going to have to wait.

OneWag went off on a hunt of his own, sniffing between legs to find choice tidbits of flaky cornetti, fallen sugar from the ciambelle. Paper napkins with drops of spilled jams or custard he licked carefully. Paper was not part of his diet.

Nico leaned against the wall and scanned the bar for signs of Gogol, just in case the news had brought him out before his usual time. It hadn't. The place notably was filled with locals this morning. It was either too early for the tourists or they had shown up and left, finding Bar All'Angolo already packed with locals. Nico knew only a few of them by name. Luciana the florist was standing next to the counter with her Enrico, master of the olive loaves. Sergio the butcher, who looked at least forty, was telling the couple he was too young to have known Gerardi.

Enrico gently reminded him that twenty-two years ago, Sergio was twenty years old.

Sergio was quick to rebound with a smile. "I thought he had left town thirty-two years ago!"

Beppe, the son of the newspaper vendor, was in a corner nearby, telling a small pack of students that he had known right from the start the dead man was a Gravignese.

"Why were you so sure?" asked a pretty girl with tiger-striped leggings that matched her backpack. "Are you psychic?"

The attention made Beppe stand taller. "I guess I am."

"Is the killer here now?"

Beppe shifted his weight back and forth as he glanced around, unsure of what to say. "I can't tell. It's too crowded." He smiled at the girl, hoping she accepted the excuse. "Maybe he is."

"Maybe he's up your ass!" The girl and her companions laughed loudly.

Beppe's eyes went wide with surprise and hurt. The girl started to say something else, surely something equally mean, but a distant honking of the bus sent the students running en masse out of the café. Beppe retreated into a corner and started playing with his phone.

Not a fighter, Nico thought. An assessment, not a criticism. He'd only learned to fight back bullies thanks to his fist-happy father, the only good lesson he'd ever gotten from the man.

Some locals he didn't recognize huddled together over the tables, pointing to the two copies of *La Nazione* that the café provided. Others clasped tiny espresso cups, their free hands either placing food in their mouths or dancing in the air to emphasize a point. The voices were subdued rather than excited. No one seemed terribly sad or shocked by the brutal murder of one of their own.

"I knew his father," said one of the old men who, in good weather, always sat on the piazza benches. Somewhere in his eighties, he had a long, thin face with an equally long prominent nose and a surprisingly full head of fluffy white hair. Now, he sat at the center table holding the newspaper close to his chest. Nico changed position against the wall to hear the group better.

Ettore, a fellow pensioner sitting next to him, reached for the paper. "Gustavo, let me see, let me see."

Gustavo held on. "He ran the gas station outside of Radda. A good man. Can't say as much for the son."

"You shouldn't speak ill of the dead," objected Nelli as she walked in, arms filled with posters for the children's art show next week. "Hi, Nico."

Nico nodded in greeting. He didn't want to call attention to himself, aware he was still considered an outsider.

"You're wrong, Nelli," Gustavo said. "Once they're dead, that's the only time you can speak the truth. They can't get back at you."

"Where's the rest of the gang?" Nelli asked. Gustavo and Ettore were always with two fellow pensioners.

"It's raining," Ettore offered.

"They're afraid of shrinking," Gustavo said. "Ehi!" Ettore had grabbed the paper away.

"I paid for that, so don't mess it up." Gustavo looked up at Nico. "I like a neat paper."

"So do I," Nico answered. So much for remaining unnoticed.

Ettore stared at the two photos: Gerardi twenty-two years ago and Gerardi now. "Poor Robi. He didn't age so well."

"Can't you read?" Gustavo pressed his finger at the article below the photos. "Cancer all over. Six months to live. Why kill him, I say."

"Maybe he didn't tell his killer he was sick. I barely recognize him in the second photo."

Nelli dropped her pile of posters on the table, accidentally tearing a page of the paper. Gustavo let out a yelp.

"Don't worry. I'll buy you another one." She called out to Beppe, who was still in the corner entrance by his phone. "Do me a favor and get another copy of *La Nazione*. Tell your mother it's for Gustavo. She'll understand. And don't get it wet. I'll pay later."

Beppe rushed out, happy to have a task.

Gustavo looked placated. "My wife used to iron the paper when it got wrinkled."

"Your wife should have been locked up in a madhouse."

"*His* house was the madhouse," Ettore said. "Robi was a looker. Thought he was a rooster in a henhouse. I say a jealous husband killed him."

"Twenty-two years later, with him looking like that?" Nelli turned to Nico, who was still leaning against the wall like the proverbial fly. "That couple behind the column are getting up. Grab their chairs. I need to sit, and I bet so do you."

Nico had been too busy eavesdropping to notice. As he walked over to the chairs at the other side of the room, he wondered if Nelli wanted him out of earshot for a moment, then quickly dismissed the thought. He hurried, though.

As they sat, Ettore peered at Nelli above his glasses. He was also somewhere in his eighties, with a shiny bald scalp, jowled cheeks and kind eyes. "Now, I recall that when you were a pretty girl of eighteen or so, handsome Robi conquered a corner of your heart, and maybe something more."

"You recall incorrectly. All of my heart was taken when I was sixteen by the man who became my husband—now ex-husband, thank the heavens. I will admit to not minding looking at Robi when the occasion presented itself, which wasn't often. He was always off somewhere with his fiancée."

Gustavo grunted. "What fiancée?"

"I never met her."

Gustavo looked around the room. "Did this fiancée have a name? Did anyone ever see her?"

"I didn't," Nelli said.

No one else answered.

"If no one saw her, she didn't exist." A mischievous grin added more wrinkles to Gustavo's cheeks. "It's an old ploy to make women want you more. Used it myself in my younger days."

Ettore laughed, showing off all his gold crowns. "No woman wanted you."

Curious about the mysterious fiancée, Nico interrupted from his seat behind the pillar. "I heard Gerardi was madly in love."

At that moment, Beppe darted in and dropped a plastic bag on Gustavo's lap. Just as quickly, he darted back out.

Nelli stood up and gathered her posters. "Maybe he was, maybe he wasn't. Robi was a slippery man."

"Who, then?" Ettore asked, perking up at the possibility of learning a gossipy tidbit he could take back to his wife. "Who was Robi in love with?"

Gustavo took out the pristine newspaper from the bag and spread it out on the emptied table. "Himself." He turned to the sports section. "Who else?"

Nelli hugged her posters against her chest. "You're turning into a nasty old man, Gustavo."

Gustavo shooed her away with his hand. "Always was."

"How about a cappuccino, just the two of us?" Nico suggested to Nelli.

"Excellent idea," Nelli said. "As far away from this meanie as we can get." She kissed Gustavo on top of his head, then pecked Ettore on the cheek. "How you put up with him is beyond me."

Ettore shrugged as though it was beyond him too.

Nelli walked to the table where Nico was sitting, dropped her posters on a nearby table and sat down. The rain had let up, and the place was now almost empty. The people who had gathered early at the café were now taking their talk of the murdered among their own to homes, offices, shops, workstations and all the vineyards of the golden valley.

Nico went to the counter and ordered two cappuccinos from

Sandro. "Did you know this Robi?" he asked casually as Sandro handed out his change.

Sandro shook his head. "I'm thirty-two."

"But recently? Did he ever come in here?"

"Not that I noticed. Jimmy, did you see him in here?"

"Who knows? I don't look at faces when I hand out coffee."

"Stop talking to Nico," Nelli called out to Jimmy, "and I'll take a ciambella with my cappuccino, please. Nico, you might as well order your cornetti. Gogol won't show up today."

"Coming up," Jimmy called. "But since when is Gogol afraid of a little rain?"

"He isn't. He's gone mushroom hunting."

Nico brought the cappuccinos and the ciambella to the table. Two whole wheat cornetti were in the oven.

"Do mushrooms pop out that fast when it rains?" Nico asked as he sat down.

"Depends." Nelli leaned over the table. "I made that up." Her voice was low. "I think Gogol will probably be hiding in his room for a few days."

Nico lowered his voice too. "Why?"

"I imagine he's scared, now that he knows who the dead man is. He attacked Robi once. By the tower behind the church. It must have been a Sunday, because I was walking to church. Robi was a few feet in front of me, and yes, I was taking a good look at his nice ass and having impure thoughts I wasn't about to confess in church. Just as Robi reached the tower, Gogol pounced on him, swinging a thick tree branch. I screamed. Of course. Robi easily stopped him. He wrenched the branch out of Gogol's hand and threw him on the ground with a single punch to his chest. I asked Robi if he was going to call the carabinieri, begged him not to. He walked away without answering. He must not have said anything, because nothing came of it."

"Were there other witnesses?"

"Not that I noticed. I was on my knees, trying to help Gogol stand up. The poor man was crying, hiding his face in his hands, shaking his head. He was very upset." She would discover the reason days later.

It was hard for Nico to think of Gogol as violent. He did live in a world all his own, but Nico had always instinctively sensed that violence did not enter into it. And yet, it had. The smell of warm cornetti hit his nose. He waited until Jimmy had placed them in front of him and walked off to ask, "Did Gogol offer any explanation?" He remembered what the manager of the hotel had told Perillo. Gogol, for the first time, appearing in front of the hotel where Gerardi had stayed, laughing loudly.

"I asked him why he was angry with Robi," Nelli said. "He wouldn't answer. After I got him on his feet, I asked him again. All he said was 'a river of blood.' I suppose that's what he was hoping for, a river of Robi's blood." There was no reason for anyone else to know, she thought.

"'A river of blood.' Gogol quoted that to me yesterday. A line from *The Divine Comedy*, I think. Did you ask Gerardi about the attack?"

"I never saw him again. A few weeks later, I found out he'd left town shortly after the incident."

"I'll talk to Gogol. Try to reassure him. I know he's not the killer." Nico's heart told him that, though his head had room for doubt.

"Of course not. He's petrified of guns. Gustavo told me the kids used to shoot at him with BB guns when he was young. Gustavo was probably one of them."

"You don't think Gerardi was in love with anyone?"

Nelli leaned back and bit into her ciambella. She took a sip of her cappuccino, then looked at Nico with an indecipherable expression. "If he was, it wasn't me, although back then, I wished it with all my heart."

ELEVEN

Perillo held the phone away from his ear as Della Langhe went on one of his tirades. After a few minutes of being told he was incompetent, that he was unnecessarily complicating Della Langhe's life, that if the case wasn't solved quickly his career would be in jeopardy, Perillo tried to interject with, "It's not my fault Gerardi became an American citizen."

The substitute prosecutor seemed to grasp this, because his tone changed. "My secretary has already contacted the American embassy. As soon as they inform us of the name of his lawyer and whether he had any family there, she will inform you."

"We also need to know if he corresponded with anyone in Italy."

"Whatever information the Americans give us, I trust you will then act quickly."

"I assure you, Maresciallo, that I don't waste time. As we say back home, the rooster crows in the morning."

Della Langhe sniffed over the phone. "I wouldn't know about roosters, and Southerners do not have a reputation for haste. Keep me informed." The line went dead.

Perillo slammed down the phone and made for the door of his office. "I need a cigarette." Daniele followed.

Outside, the rain was coming down in thick sheets. Perillo stood under the eaves and took drag after drag. Why was he saddled with a pompous ass like Della Langhe for this case? Why not a reasonable substitute prosecutor? Maybe there weren't any reasonable ones. He'd heard Della Langhe had gotten his job because he was in deep with the conservative party, who was now in control. But in Italy, no party stayed in control for long. Elections were coming up in March. There was hope. This time, he'd vote against Della Langhe's party. In the past, he had left the ballot blank in protest. Politicians were all liars.

Daniele stayed on the other side of the entrance. Rain splattered on his shoes. "Do you think it will let up soon?" He was hoping the maresciallo would calm down and find a registrar's office employee so he could ride his motorbike up to Radda, get the name and address of Gerardi's sister and finally tell Rosalba she wouldn't have to deal with the Florentine sketch artist. By now, she must know they'd discovered the identity of the man who'd purchased the bracelet. He didn't have to go, but he wanted to see her, and he was more comfortable armed with an excuse. He had dreamt about her early that morning. The two of them were holding hands, their faces close. He'd leaned in to kiss her just as his alarm went off.

Perillo finished his cigarette in silence and tossed the butt into a wide puddle at the bottom of the stairs.

Daniele winced. He would pick that up later and throw it in the garbage.

Perillo ignored the wince and asked, "Did you look into the records for those kids?"

"I did. Bruno Dini and Katia Galli. No arrests. Same for the bartender at Hotel Bella Vista. I also checked to see whether there was any land for sale in the area. I came up with nothing."

Perillo nodded and lit another cigarette. Daniele hovered.

"What is it?"

Daniele hugged the wall, trying to protect his shoes. He had spit-shined them late last night in anticipation of his trip to Radda. "The registrar's office is closed."

Della Langhe's words were burning a hole in his stomach. "Yes, you told me. I'll get on the phone and see if I can find someone to open up for you."

Daniele nodded. Waiting was good. The rain might stop.

"I just need a few minutes, Dani."

"Yes, Maresciallo." Daniele retreated backward through the open door.

"Yes, Salvatore!" Perillo yelled after him and took out his phone.

NICO WAS PUTTING A wet OneWag into the 500 when his phone rang.

"No need to come at lunch," Tilde said. "With this rain, very few people are going to show up." Sotto Il Fico had only five indoor tables.

He dropped into the driver's seat. "I'll come by anyway. You've seen the paper?"

"Heard it thanks to Elvira, who read the article out loud over breakfast like I was illiterate."

"Did you look at the photograph?"

"No need."

"Then you knew Gerardi?" He heard Tilde's intake of breath.

"In Gravigna, everyone thinks they know everyone. That doesn't mean they do." Her voice had turned steely.

"And you?"

"I saw him around."

"I'd like to find out whatever you, Enzo and Elvira know about him."

"I thought you weren't getting involved."

Nico didn't remind Tilde that she had been the first to suggest it. "Perillo asked for my help. I reluctantly agreed." During last night's dinner, as Perillo, Daniele and Nico talked about the murder, his reluctance had melted away. He was working on something important again. Something that needed resolution. Being part of a team, puzzling things out together was what he most missed about his years as a homicide detective. "Anything you can tell me will help."

"You should be looking at his life in America."

"He was killed here." The phone beeped again.

"That doesn't mean a local killed him," she insisted. "The wine festival in Greve brings Americans in by the dozens. The opening is tonight. Go look for your killer there."

That was Tilde's local pride talking. "I'm sure Perillo and the substitute prosecutor in Florence will look into the American angle. So will the American police. Can I come talk to you about him?"

"I don't have that much to tell. I'll feed you lunch if you want. We'll talk afterward."

"When Elvira has gone off to take her nap." He'd said it to make Tilde laugh but was met with silence.

Nico's phone rang as soon as he clicked off.

"I'm afraid we'll have to wait a few days to know about Gerardi's American life. And no one is around to open up the registrar's office," Perillo announced. "According to a grandmother I got ahold of, the whole group went off in this rain to the castle of Meleto to celebrate a birthday. They'll be back in the late afternoon. I'll get someone to open up the office then. Della Langhe can't blame this delay on me. The employees are all Tuscan."

"What did he say?"

"He yelled for a bit, then insulted me by saying Southerners are not known for their haste. Is that something you believe?"

"I've heard that said about all Italians." Nico wasn't about to say that the reputation was worse from Rome on southward.

"Yes, yes, I know. You Americans want to fly through your lives, then end up with a heart attack. 'Who goes slowly goes far and stays healthy,' is the saying here. Not so today for Daniele. He was like a racehorse at the starting gate, pawing at the ground and waiting for that whistle."

Nico laughed. "That's called love."

Perillo remembered how love had made him crazy for a while. Four women he had loved; only one endured. The craziness of it had now been replaced by comfortable habit, warmth and a hint of boredom. "With that beauty, good luck to Dani."

"Did anyone answer your appeal for information?"

"A lot of people came in, worried about their safety. I assured them that they had nothing to worry about. It wasn't a random murder, and we're not dealing with a serial killer."

"What about a murderer who's lost his mind?"

"I wasn't about to point out that possibility. I don't believe it, anyway."

"Don't rule it out. In my experience, you have to keep every possibility on the table."

Perillo nodded. "A few men came in to offer information, which amounted to nothing. They didn't know him well, didn't like him, saying Gerardi thought himself the only rooster in the henhouse. They didn't know anything about a girlfriend or even his sister's name. Arben, the Albanian who works for Aldo, confirmed Aldo's story about Gerardi stealing from him. He just flew back yesterday from two weeks in Tirana. He offered to come in and show me the boarding passes. I told him not to bother. I did get one phone call that sounded interesting. A woman, says she knew Gerardi very well. She wouldn't give her name, but she's coming in after she's done shopping. Anything on your end?"

"I was about to call you. Nelli, the art center director here, told me that Gogol attacked Gerardi with a tree branch here in the piazza right before Gerardi left town. She asked him why. Gogol's only response was, 'A river of blood.' That could be one of his usual Dante quotes, but it could be that he wanted actual blood. I'm on my way to the home to see if he'll talk to me. I'm also going to ask Tilde and her family if they know anything about Gerardi that might be useful." Twenty-two years ago, Tilde was in her early twenties. If Gerardi was as handsome as Nelli said, Tilde would have at least noticed him, and Elvira would have known what gossip there was about him.

"See if you can find out who he was in love with. If he walked out on her, whoever it is could still be carrying a grudge."

"Nelli didn't know. Neither did Ettore and Gustavo. Do you know them?"

"Sure I do. Half of the Bench Boys. I gave them that name because I can't keep their names straight. Thanks, Nico. I appreciate your help. Ciao for now."

"Ciao." At the sound of the phone's click, OneWag jumped in Nico's lap and pawed at the window.

"You're not going anywhere."

OneWag dropped his head between his paws and whimpered his protest.

"Don't try that on me. Be reasonable. You'd get soaked."

OneWag looked up at Nico's determined face. After a few seconds, the dog dropped his head back down and closed his eyes. At least he had the comfort of knowing this man would never abandon his car.

Nico got out of the passenger seat, shut the car door and unfurled his umbrella. There was no place to park near the "house of rest," as Italians called an old-age home. As Nico walked the five hundred meters to the home, he hoped his own old age would be filled with much more than rest.

THE WOMAN AT THE front desk raised an eye in Nico's direction and went back to crocheting her yellow wool and reading the newspaper. He noticed it was open to the page with Gerardi's two passport photos. "Gogol's gone. Who knows when he'll be back." She kept her head down, showing a scalp covered by thin, short, curly white hair. He could see through to the pink skin beneath. Nico didn't know her name, though Gogol had once referred to her as Cerberus, the three-headed dog guarding hell.

"How did you know I was going to ask for him?"

"You're Gogol's friend."

Nico held out his hand and introduced himself.

She reluctantly set down her crocheting, shook his hand quickly and went back to her work. "Lucia," she muttered, keeping her last name to herself.

"Do you know where he went?"

"Mushroom picking. What else can you do in this weather?" She raised her eyes for a moment with a look that questioned his mental capacity.

He knew that many of the guests at the home had mental disabilities. "One could stay dry at home."

"Gogol was too happy for that. Took one look at Robi's photos and laughed his head off."

"He was happy Gerardi was dead?"

"Seems so to me. It didn't surprise me." She looked at the strip of yellow wool and started counting loops. "Whatever happened between those two must have been nasty. Gogol has always been a good man. No trouble at all, if you don't mind his Dante gibberish."

"Are you referring to the time Gogol went after Robi with a big tree branch?"

"Robi was able to stop him and no one got hurt, God be praised." She crossed herself and brought the gold crucifix that rested on her chest to her lips.

"You have no idea why?"

She was back to swinging the crochet hook in and out with a twist of her wrist. "No one does. Robi said they'd never even spoken to each other. Gogol must have just been seized by some anger from his childhood. He's never been a hundred percent, and the kids used to bully him mercilessly."

"Could Gogol have killed Robi?" Nico asked just to see her reaction.

"May God forgive me for saying this," she said, kissing the crucifix again, "but humans are basically cruel. Cain killed his brother. From then on, we have been killing each other. God isn't even trying to stop it. The world turned away from God from the moment Eve stuck her teeth in that apple. We do not merit the life He gave us."

"Did Robi merit death?"

"I would say he was not a God-fearing man, but I'm sorry Robi had to die in that terrible way. To think that he would have died naturally six months later in his own bed. Only God knows why this happened to him. As for Gogol, God's light shines on him. He cherishes all life. Gogol promised to make me a potato and mushroom omelet if he found enough porcini. He'll be back by dinnertime."

"Gogol cooks?"

"When something makes him happy, he stirs it up in the kitchen. There's nothing wrong in his head when he's cooking."

"You wouldn't know where Gogol went mushroom picking, would you?"

"The woods behind the Ferriello Vineyard is his favorite spot, but he could be anywhere. I'll tell him you stopped by."

The woods behind the Ferriello Vineyard had been where Gerardi was killed. He needed to find Gogol. "Thank you, Signora Lucia."

"Signorina, and proud of it. As a young girl, I suffered men's ways and promised myself to keep them at a distance. My life couldn't have been more pleasant." Her head stayed bent over her work. "I won't forget."

Nico walked away, wondering if "I won't forget" meant telling Gogol he had been by or her suffering of men's ways.

DANIELE PARKED THE BIKE, took off his helmet, removed his plastic poncho and spied himself in the door of the ceramic shop next to Gioielleria Crisani. Wanting Rosalba to forget he was a carabiniere, he had dressed in newly laundered jeans and a striped red and purple birthday present from his mother. As he looked at his reflection, his hopes of making a good impression on Rosalba sank to nothing. His boots, the bottom of his jeans and the lower half of his face were dark with mud. He unlocked his motorcycle seat and took out a towel. He wiped down his face, put the towel and the helmet under the seat, locked the bike and filled his lungs with air, then pressed the buzzer.

The door opened. Daniele looked up to see an older replica of Rosalba standing behind the counter. The same round face, large dark eyes, full lips, long black hair coiled back in a loose bun reflected in the mirror behind her.

Irene Crisani eyed the boy with his cheap shirt and his muddy boots dirtying the floor. At the most, he could afford a small silver trinket for his girlfriend or his mother. "Can I help you?"

Not an exact copy of Rosalba, Daniele decided. Her warmth was missing.

"Good morning." He tried to imitate the maresciallo's officious tone. "I need to speak with Rosalba Crisani."

Irene looked at Daniele with renewed interest. What need did this boy have to see her daughter? Was he another one of Rosalba's strays? She often wondered where Rosalba had gotten her overfriendly genes. Certainly not from the Crisani side of the family. Maybe from her charmer of a father.

"She's not coming in today." A lie. Rosalba was taking over after the lunch break. "I'm her mother." She didn't bother to give her name. "You can tell me."

He took out his carabinieri identity card. "Brigadiere Daniele Donato. Maresciallo Perillo and I are looking into the murder of Roberto Gerardi." The shine in her eyes disappeared, Daniele noticed. Or perhaps it had never been there. It was just that the rest of her had so instantly recalled Rosalba. He explained his previous visit to the store.

"Yes, you asked about a bracelet my daughter sold to a man. She told you all she knew. What is it that you want from my daughter now?"

Irene's condescending tone didn't sting Daniele. He disliked her for it but was grateful. Disliking someone always made him feel as though he had the upper hand. It stopped him from blushing. "I wanted to show her the picture of Gerardi, to see if he was the man who bought the bracelet."

"She saw the photo in the paper and told me she was almost certain he was the same man."

"Almost certain?"

"The man wore a baseball cap pulled low. I will ask her to call the maresciallo if you don't believe me."

"I believe you, and please thank her for her cooperation."

Irene nodded. She had no intention of mentioning this brigadiere.

"Rosalba is too young, but perhaps you knew Roberto Gerardi?"

Irene fiddled with the gold bands on her wrist. "I doubt my age is reason enough to assume I knew him."

The bracelets kept clinking. For a moment, Daniele felt bad about her discomfort. "I'm sorry, Signora Crisani. I'm not very good at explaining myself. Your age has nothing to do with it. It's the fact that Gerardi knew this shop. If not you, maybe your husband or your father knew him?" Daniele was aware he was going out on a limb. Gerardi could have just as easily found the shop by chance, but he had told Avis he was coming to Radda. Why say that and end up in Panzano? Maybe because he knew he would buy his bracelet here, the only jewelry shop that had existed here twenty-two years ago. Daniele had double-checked that last night.

Irene placed both her hands flat on the glass counter. Below the glass, the display of glittering jewelry seemed to smile back at her. Looking at the necklaces, bracelets and rings always calmed her down. They were her riches, her strength. The shop had thrived under her ownership. She didn't miss her father, a cruel man who had stunted her life. Her husband, whom she'd met only after her father's death, had loved her, and in return she'd given him what little love she had left. "I'm afraid I can't answer for them. My father and husband are both dead, and whether they knew that man or not is buried with them."

"Thank you, Signora. Please do tell Rosalba I stopped by." Daniele suspected she wouldn't, but for some reason his questions had made Rosalba's mother sad. For that he was sorry, even if he disliked her. Sorry, but curious.

Outside, the rain had stopped.

SITTING AT HIS DESK, Perillo glanced at his watch as his stomach growled. One o'clock on the dot. Lunchtime. His cell phone rang. Punctual as ever, Signora Perillo informed him she'd just thrown the pasta into boiling water and he should come up. Today, she was offering spaghetti loaded with roasted yellow peppers and Parmigiano Reggiano, a dish he cherished. Since he'd given her those flowers, she'd been as sweet as those yellow peppers she was about to serve. The main course was breaded chicken breast and fennel and olive salad. As always, an espresso would be his only dessert.

As Perillo hung up, his mouth already watering, the office phone rang. He let out a long sigh and for a second or two thought of letting the call go unanswered. No, spaghetti took nine minutes to cook al dente. Whatever it was, he'd make it brief.

"Yes?"

"There's a woman to see you," said Vince from the front desk. "She's got information on the dead man. She said she called earlier. Should I tell her to come back?" Vince knew how Perillo felt about his lunch break.

"No, send her in." Perillo understood that people who had information, or thought they did, wanted to be treated with importance. Making him wait until she had finished shopping was a clear indication that the woman felt very important. If he didn't see her now, she might not offer any information. "Please call upstairs and tell my wife to keep the plate warm for me. That I'll come up as soon as I can."

The woman walked in through the door Vince had opened for her, burdened by two large shopping bags from the Coop. "Here I am at last."

A pleasant-looking woman in her late forties, Perillo guessed, dressed in a beige ruffled blouse and matching skirt that showed off a good figure. She looked familiar, but he couldn't place her.

She lifted her heavy shopping bags as though she was ready to do some bodybuilding. "I should have brought these home first, but I knew you were anxious to know more about Robi."

Then you could have done your shopping afterward, Perillo thought as he stood up and said, "Very kind of you." He extended his hand. "Maresciallo Salvatore Perillo. And you are?" Still holding on to the bags, she shook the tips of his fingers. "Roberto Gerardi's sister."

His hunger pangs disappeared. "Very good. Please, have a seat." He waited for her to settle her bags onto the floor and sit before sitting down himself.

Her light-brown eyes didn't blink. "There's nothing good about it."

"I'm sorry. That was insensitive of me."

She waved his words away. "Oh, you can be as insensitive as you like. Robi was not a very nice man to me—or my husband, for that matter. We already know each other, by the way, although it's clear you don't remember me. Too old to leave an impression, I guess." It wasn't a lament. She sounded very matter-of-fact about it. "When I was young, it was different." She smiled, reminiscing. The smile made her more attractive.

"I'm sorry. I'm so focused on your brother's murder, everything else has ended up locked away in some cubicle in my head. Please tell me about him."

"I take care of the Boldini villa, just down the road from here. They spend most of the year in Milan. We had a theft there two years ago. You came over with another carabiniere. You never did find the thief. Whoever it was stole my cell phone and laptop. Do you remember now?"

"Yes, of course. You're Maria Dorsetti." He also remembered being suspicious when he'd discovered that the Boldinis' expensive objects and silverware had been untouched, only Maria's things having been taken. Nothing else in the villa had been disturbed. No locks broken, no windows smashed. No other thefts in the neighborhood. She'd kept calling him for news, wanting him to come and check the villa again. After a few weeks, he'd filed the case away, judging her a lonely woman needing attention. "I'm sorry we didn't find the thief."

She shrugged. "I'm the one who should be sorry. I was wasting my time." Maria Dorsetti sat back in her chair and crossed her arms below her chest. It would muss up her blouse, but the weight of her arms gave her comfort. "I didn't know Robi was here. I have no idea why he came back, unless he wanted to settle an old score, but he could have at least come over. He knew where I lived.

"I didn't hear from him at all, not even when my husband died four years ago. When I let him know, he sent a five-thousand-dollar check and not a word of condolence. I guess he thought money spoke for itself. Five thousand dollars certainly wasn't going to replace my husband, but it did help." Her words flowed like water from an open faucet. A lonely woman who had found her audience. "After that check, nothing. I did write from time to time, giving him tidbits of gossip. What was going on in Gravigna. Who got married, who had children, who did what." The truth was, he'd been the one who kept writing, asking all sorts of questions about one woman in particular. "Gravigna's our hometown. I was too proud to ask outright for money. I hear he was wearing a very expensive watch when he died. Does that mean he was rich?" She gave her cheek a gentle slap. "How greedy of me. I apologize, but I am, after all, his only living relative."

Ah, so that was it, Perillo thought. This was all for show.

"Oh, but maybe not. He could have a family in America. Do you know if he did? It would be nice. Maybe I could fly over and meet them." She stopped again and this time patted her chest. "I'm sorry, I'm nervous. I wish I could have loved him." She pulled down on her blouse to smooth out the wrinkles that had formed. "When I was a young girl, I envied his good looks. He had such beautiful green eyes. Mine are the color of mud." She gave a flirtatious, girlish laugh, perhaps hoping Perillo would contradict her.

"The American embassy in Rome is looking into his life in America," Perillo said. "As soon as I have information, I'll let you know. You mentioned he might have come back to settle old scores. Did he have enemies here?"

"I imagine a lot of husbands were mighty relieved when he took off."

"Any specific husband?"

She straightened her back as if offended by the question. "I don't know anything about the women who threw themselves at him." He claimed not to have bedded any of them, but he had always liked to boast about his affairs around town. It had been a way to keep his great love secret, she'd decided. "Who I love is no one's business," he'd replied when she'd pressed him for the name. Calling his sister "no one" was insulting, she'd told him. He didn't budge.

"Do you know of anyone who might have wanted your brother dead?"

"I just told you, I don't. I'm so angry at him for not giving a damn about me." She started to cry and reached for a tissue in her purse. "I'm sorry. He died in such a horrible way, could've lived a full life."

"He was very sick. Cancer. It was in the newspaper article. The medical examiner thinks he only had about six months to live."

"Oh. I didn't read to the end. It was too upsetting." Maria wiped her eyes and looked at Perillo, her eyes softening. The news seemed to give her some relief. "Maybe that's why he didn't

get in touch. Didn't want me to see him so sick. Poor Robi."
She moved to the edge of her chair to be closer to Perillo. "That
explains his coming back here, then, doesn't it? He was making
amends and saying goodbye. If he hadn't been killed, he would
have come to me. I know he would have."

"Making amends to whom?"

Why had she used that word? Foolish. "I don't know." To the
nameless woman. Something had gone wrong between them. It
had been what drove him to leave. "I'm not a good man," Robi
told her a few days before he left. "I don't deserve any love. Not
even yours." There was good reason not to reveal her name to
the maresciallo, a name she had discovered only by the questions
Robi asked in his letters.

Perillo's cell phone started to belt "O Sole Mio." He glanced
at it. His wife, probably furious. He cut off the ringer. "You are
his only relative?"

"Yes. It was just the two of us."

"Do you have children?"

"I am not blessed." The expression on her face was noncom-
mittal.

"Your brother worked for Aldo Ferri for a while."

"He loved that job. Robi told me he liked Aldo so much, he
left his wife alone. That's my Robi, his bird always ready to fly
into a new nest. At least toward Aldo, he showed some respect."

"Wasn't he in love with someone then?"

"Well, isn't that what you tell a girl when you want to get her
between the sheets?"

"Do you have any idea who the girl was?"

"He never told me about his personal affairs. We weren't close,
you know. My husband disliked my brother, and I didn't much
like him myself. He was arrogant. Why would he stick with one
woman when he could have any girl he wanted?" She looked
straight at Perillo. He wouldn't guess she was lying. Liars turned
their eyes away, she learned from the police shows.

"You can't think of anyone who had a vendetta against him?"

"Not from here. He left twenty-two years ago. Who holds on to hate that long? Besides, all he did was fool around. We're not in Sicily. We don't have honor killings in Tuscany. Maybe someone from America."

"Maybe. I do have to ask you this."

Maria eagerly leaned toward the desk.

"Can you tell me where you were Monday morning between five and seven in the morning?"

Of course, Maria thought. Just like on TV. She smiled at Perillo to show she understood he was only doing his job. "I was in bed, of course. I sleep at the Boldinis' villa when they're away. No witnesses, though, alas." A smirk this time.

"Do you own a shotgun?"

"My father did. He went hunting every Sunday. That he would kill on the Lord's day infuriated my mother. She always refused to cook his kill."

"Do you still have it?"

"No. He loved that shotgun so much, we buried it with him. A year later, Mamma was dead too. Then my husband. Now my brother."

She looked crestfallen, but Perillo wasn't sure if that was genuine. "When you're not at the villa, where do you live?"

"The new development in Gravigna, via Moro Twelve. I've rented it to an English couple for the month." She reached over the desk and took the maresciallo's pen and a Post-it and wrote down her address and cell phone number.

Perillo took the Post-it and stood up. "Thank you. If you think of anything else that might help, please call. I'll get one of my men to drive you home."

She laughed. "How kind of you." She leaned over the desk and gave him an awkward hug. "You'll let me know what the embassy says? And if there is a will. I know I sound crass, but if I inherit even a little money, it will be like winning the lottery."

"I understand. I'll let you know as soon as I know. I have to ask you to make an official statement and sign it." He picked up her shopping bags and walked her to the door. "Vince in the front room will take it down." He would have preferred to have Daniele take the statement—Vince always insisted on writing in long hand to show off his meticulous handwriting. There was a chance Vince would still be writing when he came back down from lunch.

"I do have to ask you not to take any trips until your brother's death has been cleared up."

Her expression brightened. "Am I a suspect?"

"I may have more questions." Certainly she was a possible suspect. The only one he had so far. "Vince!"

Vince showed his round, curly-haired head in the doorway, his mouth working on a focaccia sandwich. "Please take Signora Dorsetti's statement, then get Dino to take her home."

Maria blew Perillo a kiss he did not acknowledge.

UPSTAIRS, IN HIS ONE-BEDROOM apartment, part of the barracks, the kitchen clock showed it was 1:52 P.M. He called to his wife. She didn't answer. Neither did the cat. The bedroom door was closed. The table was now set for one. He found his meal in the warm oven. As he slipped his hand into an oven mitt, he made a mental note to get her a box of chocolates.

TWELVE

Nico parked the 500 on the bald patch of earth that had once been for farming equipment behind his new home. He held the door open and OneWag, who'd been fast asleep, took his time to stretch and examine what might need cleaning or scratching.

"Come on, mutt. You've got a job."

OneWag's ears perked up. He understood that something was required of him, which was much better than being locked away upstairs. The dog jumped out of the car and looked up at Nico. Expectation made him wag his tail—once.

"We have to find Gogol." Nico started walking toward the path edging the olive grove, the path he had taken Monday morning looking for a hurt dog.

OneWag followed, nose in the air, taking in the smells. Olives ripening, their green tartness softening, the dark richness of wet earth. Pine sap. From far away wood burning. Nearby, his master's sweat and his own damp fur. Nothing that didn't belong in their surroundings.

They reached the woods. Birds stopped singing and the light became a lacy pattern of sun and shadow. Gogol was somewhere in here, Nico was convinced, but not because it was his favorite spot. Twenty-two years ago, Gogol had attacked Gerardi with a tree branch. The other day, he had shown up at Gerardi's hotel for the first time, laughing his heart out. He was happy the man was dead. And now, Gogol could be laughing where Gerardi had been killed. Maybe where he'd killed him?

OneWag scrambled to keep up with Nico's fast-scissoring legs, his own panting tongue bobbing to the rhythm of his shorter steps.

As Nico got closer to the site, he was purposefully loud as he walked, crushing twigs. He didn't want his presence to be a complete surprise.

A thick oak loomed in front of Nico and the dog, its thick branches twisted with old age. Stepping to one side, Nico walked past it. OneWag instead stopped and stood still, swiveling his snout from left to right like a periscope. The dog turned his small body to the right. He whimpered a warning to Nico and took off.

Nico heard only the sudden rush of crackling twigs. OneWag had picked up Gogol's scent! He ran after him.

A hundred yards farther, underneath another old oak, Nico found OneWag with his head deep in a wicker basket. "What are you doing?"

OneWag retrieved his head from the powerful-smelling mushrooms, lay down and stretched his hind legs behind him, looking very pleased with himself. He had found food. Far more important than a smelly old man.

Gogol had to be nearby. "Gogol, it's Nico. Where are you?"

"'Turn your eyes to the valley,'" Gogol quoted.

There was no valley to turn to, but Nico followed the voice.

Ten feet deeper into the woods, Nico found Gogol rocking on his knees in front of the clearing where Gerardi had been killed. A forgotten strand of police tape hung limply from a branch. Raindrops dripped from the tree leaves onto his face.

Nico knelt next to him. "Come with me. This is no place for you."

Gogol pushed him away. "His is the place of justified violence." He laughed, a raucous sound like rock rubbed against rock that seemed to come from the bottom of his soul. "Roberto Gerardi boils in hell." He stopped rocking and turned to Nico. "I burn too. I saw it and did nothing."

"You saw the murder?"

"The murder of a heart. Her body twisting, turning, his body a weight to carry for a lifetime. I heard the moans, mournful sounds escaping through fingers set on silence."

Nico assumed Gogol was quoting Dante again until he heard him say, "I drown in shame, friend. You understand?" Tears mixed with raindrops.

"You witnessed a rape?"

"Carnal violence. And did nothing." His body shook with sobs now.

Nico held him. "You were scared."

"He died for the grave sin he visited on another. I breathe, I eat, I shit, but I too have died. When I quote the great poet, I quote from hell."

OneWag nudged his head against Gogol's thigh. The old man picked up the dog and held him under his coat.

"Who was raped?" Nico asked.

"You will not know from my mouth. At least I can keep silent."

More questions would come only after Gogol calmed down. Part of Nico hoped Gogol had only imagined this terrible thing. "Let me take you home."

Gogol lifted one of OneWag's long, furry ears and dried his eyes with it. In response, OneWag licked his face. "My mushrooms." He scrambled to his feet with Nico's help, holding the dog tight. "I must gather my mushrooms. Thank you, friend. I go now. Hell's gatekeeper is waiting for me to make dinner."

"I'll take you home."

Gogol gave one last look at the clearing where Nico had found Gerardi. "He left in shame. He came back to die for it." He handed the dog to Nico and they set off for his old-age home.

PERILLO WAS AT THE café next to the station, having his midafternoon espresso, when Nico called and related what Gogol had said.

"That's all I could get out of him." Gogol hadn't spoken a

word during the ride back. On seeing Lucia at the front desk, he'd proudly shown off his basket of precious mushrooms and hurried off to the kitchen.

Perillo paid for his espresso and walked out, not to be overheard. His stomach tightened into a fist. "Do you believe him? I mean, his circuits are a little jammed up, aren't they?"

"Gogol's not crazy. I want to believe him. He was overwhelmed with pain and shame. He must have witnessed a rape, and that could be the killer's motive."

Perillo tried to release his muscles by letting out a long, silent breath. "Maybe he just saw heavy-handed sex. People get off on being rough sometimes."

Nico walked out onto his balcony, needing to rest his eyes on the soaked colors of nature. "We have to at least consider that a rape may have occurred and look into it."

"How?" Perillo stood rooted in place, his stomach still tight. "Even if the victim went to a doctor, her files will be private."

"Asking around. Jimmy at the café says you can't fart without the whole town knowing about it."

"And yet no one knows who Gerardi's love was. Besides, there's no shame involved in farting. Embarrassment at most, which is not the case with rape. And how the hell would you ask someone if they've been raped?" Perillo searched his jeans pocket for his cigarettes. "Mother of God and all the saints!" He'd left them on his desk. "When did this supposedly happen?" He started walking to the station. "Did he at least tell you that?"

"Gogol said, 'He left in shame.' I take that to mean it happened not much before Gerardi took off. It might even be the incident that prompted him to leave. It could also explain why Gogol attacked the man with that tree branch."

"That's one supposition after another grounded on very threadbare fact." Perillo spoke sharply and instantly regretted it. He needed to calm down, and a dose of nicotine was exactly what he needed. "Let me get to the office."

Nico waited on the phone, surprised by Perillo's resistance to the news. The possibility that a woman had once been raped by Gerardi was tragic and a very strong motive for murder, even after all this time. He'd expected the maresciallo to want to look into it immediately.

Perillo walked into the station, nodded as he hurried past Vince, who quickly stood and shoved his mortadella sandwich into a drawer—there was no eating allowed on front-desk duty. In his office, he put the phone back to his ear. "I have a possible suspect."

"That's good news."

"Remember when I told you that a woman had called with news?" He wiped his face with his handkerchief. "Well, she took her time showing up, but it turns out she's Gerardi's sister—younger, by the looks of her. She didn't seem in the least bit upset that he was dead. She was up-front about them not getting along, angry that he hadn't been helping her financially." The maresciallo grabbed his cigarettes and walked back out. The mortadella sandwich was back in Vince's mouth. Perillo ignored him and parked himself under the eave of the entrance to smoke. "She's hungry for his money, that's clear. Immediately asked about his will. A strong-willed woman is the impression I got. And not a very nice one. I know that doesn't make her a killer, but she has an obvious motive. She has no one to corroborate that she was sleeping in the villa she works at early on Monday morning. I'll call her back for more questioning once we hear from the police in California. We can't move forward until they answer our questions. Did Gerardi have a family there? Did he have a will? Who benefits from it? Was he in contact with anyone here? We have to wait, that's all."

"I hope you're not going to ignore what Gogol said."

"I won't. We'll talk about it some more face-to-face, and I hope to come up with some delicate way of asking around that won't get me kicked out of town. Not tonight, though. We've got the Chianti Expo opening in a few hours, and I have to show up with my men armed and in uniform to reassure the crowd that we'll protect them." He looked up at the now-clear sky. Good. No hint of more rain. "Come hear the band play. They're pretty good."

"I do miss the old days when people didn't show up wielding AK-47s," Nico said, "but I'm sure you and your men will do a wonderful job."

"Thank you. I'll be in touch as soon as Della Langhe has news for us." Perillo headed back to the café for a shot of grappa. The cigarette hadn't helped. Gogol's revelation had brought back the violence of his childhood—he could feel it in the pit of his stomach. He didn't even taste the grappa.

NICO SHOWED UP AT Sotto Il Fico near the end of the lunch hour. He was hungry and hoping to catch Enzo and Elvira so he could ask them about Gerardi. Enzo was at his usual post behind the bar, making two espressos. Elvira commanded the small room from her rickety gilded armchair in one of her seven housedresses, this one dark gray with pale flowers, matching the gray light of the day. Her hair, freshly dyed, sat like a matte black cap on her head. She didn't look up from her weekly crossword magazine. Of the five tables in the room, only one was taken, by a German couple, judging by Elvira's shoe classification. Sandals with socks, soaked through.

"Sit, Nico, sit," said Enzo as he brought the espressos over to the couple.

Nico leaned his umbrella in a corner by the door and wiped his shoes on the doormat. "Let me say hello to Tilde. She was expecting me later."

"I hear you," Tilde called out from the kitchen. "You couldn't wait, could you?" She sounded angry.

"Sorry. Hunger got the best of me."

"Is the dog with you?"

"Left him at home. I was afraid it was going to rain again."

Tilde popped her head out of the door that led to the kitchen. She had wrapped her hair in a blue bandana, and her face was sprinkled with flour. "Too bad. I had some good tidbits for him."

"I'll take them home. You're making pasta?"

"Olive oil cake," Tilde snapped, and withdrew her head.

"She's nervous today," Enzo said apologetically. "Stella's taking her museum exam Monday afternoon in Florence."

"Wonderful," Nico said. "Does she need a ride? I'll happily drive her there."

"I wish you could. Gianni's taking her on his motorbike. He's suddenly discovered being nice to her pays off." Enzo leaned over the bar and lowered his voice. "He says he has you to thank. Don't tell Tilde."

Nico laughed. "I won't."

"Stop muttering, you two, and you, Nico, shouldn't settle for dog food," Elvira said. "Tell her to give you the chicken rags." Her voice was loud enough for Tilde to hear. "It's an old recipe of mine."

"It was your mother's, not yours," came from the kitchen.

"My mother was *mine*, therefore the recipe is mine. My cranky daughter-in-law has finally deigned to offer it to our patrons."

Nico sat down. He knew the chicken would appear without his asking for it. One did not deny Elvira without good reason. Enzo poured him a glass of the house red, an unlabeled Sangiovese that came straight from a barrel. "Now we know who it is. Poor Robi. I knew him. He used to eat here a lot. Mamma had a soft spot for him. Gave him extra portions. Tilde wasn't in the kitchen then."

Elvira looked up at her son. "But she was here every day. I was convinced she came here looking for Robi."

Enzo lifted his arms in exasperation. "Mamma! Stop it. We were engaged already."

"Well, women often change their minds. In my heart, you

are the handsomest son a mother could have, but Robi, well, 'la donna è mobile,' as Signor Verdi puts it." She closed her eyes as if to summon the past. "An Adonis with charm, Robi could inflame any heart, even mine, which as you know is diamond-hard." She lifted her chin with unabashed pride.

Nico laughed. "Elvira, yours is all an act."

"It isn't in the least." This time all of Tilde appeared at the door, her face now clean of flour. Underneath a long, white chef's apron, she wore a burgundy dress with ruffled sleeves. "Tell the truth, Elvira. You were hoping I'd fall in love with that horrible man so I wouldn't marry your son."

Elvira went back to her crossword magazine.

"Chicken rags coming in a minute." Tilde disappeared again.

Nico waited while the Germans settled the bill with Enzo. Once they'd left, he asked Enzo to sit with him. Enzo obliged.

"Was Gerardi horrible?" Nico asked.

"No, the opposite in my view. He boasted about his conquests, which is what turned Tilde off, but it was just talk. He was in love with someone."

"Did he tell you that?"

"No, not in words. I'd known him since we were kids. He was older, and I used to look up to him. He was nice to the younger kids. He gave us soccer lessons, refereed our games. He brought us cookies his sister made. He was always kind of serious, but once in a while, all he would do was smile. I thought he was getting high. I got up the courage to ask him if he was doing marijuana or something. He laughed. 'No, a much stronger drug. The strongest drug there is.' I assumed he was talking about love."

"Or heroin," Tilde chimed in from the kitchen.

Elvira looked up from her crossword. "Robi was clean. A good man."

Nico asked Enzo, "When was this? How long before he left?"

"At least two years. I hadn't fallen in love yet, and I wanted to ask him questions, but he never spoke about it again after that once. Said I'd find out soon enough. And I did, when I met Tilde."

"Love was no drug for you," Elvira remarked. "You burn a low flame."

"Which lasts much longer than a bonfire." Tilde placed the chicken rags plate in front of Nico and kissed her husband's head. "I love that low flame and always will. It kept me sane. Still does."

Nico thought of Rita. She had kept him sane too, but her love had been strong. He took a bite of the chicken. "It's very good."

Elvira puffed up her chest. "Of course it is."

"Why the name 'chicken rags'?"

"The chicken breast is sliced very thin and sautéed with radic-chio, cut into strips. A little olive oil, salt and pepper, a dose of balsamic vinegar, push it around the hot skillet and serve. It ends up looking like rags. There's a beef dish with arugula that's done the same way, but without the vinegar. Simple, easy to eat and good for you."

"Thank you. It's delicious. I'll try making this at home, and if I ever write a cookbook, I'll call it 'Elvira's chicken rags.'"

"No, 'Elvira's mother's chicken rags.' Give credit where it's due."

"What was your mother's name?"

"Giuseppina Gioia Maria Consolazione. But stick to 'Elvira's mother.'"

Nico drank the wine and finished the rags. While Enzo made him a coffee, Nico turned to Elvira. "What was Robi like, besides being clean and good."

"Why?"

"Curiosity."

Elvira crossed her arms over her chest. "Don't lie to me, Nico. The whole town knows you're helping that idiot Perillo. He needs all the help he can get, and if you want my opinion, find the woman Robi loved and you might have your killer."

"Why do you think that?"

"Enzo is right. Robi was very much in love. He told me so himself, but when I asked who she was, I got the silence of a tomb. Why not tell me?"

"Maybe she was married."

"Or engaged."

Tilde strode out of the kitchen. "Are you implying"—she stopped at Elvira's feet, towering over her—"what I think you're implying?" Her voice was knife-sharp.

Elvira stiffened and looked up at her daughter-in-law. "Well, we don't know who this great love was, do we? And Robi did come here a lot."

"He came here for good inexpensive food and to chat with his childhood friend, your *son*." Tilde dropped down on her haunches. "Elvira, why do you hate me so much?" Her voice was soft now.

Elvira riffled through the pages of her magazine.

Tilde put her hands on Elvira's lap. "I have a heart as hard as yours. The only person you're hurting by hating me is your son."

Elvira looked up with wet eyes. "I miss my husband. He won't be coming back. I miss my son even more."

Enzo walked over to his mother and squeezed her shoulder. "Mamma, we spend most of every day together."

"You go home with her."

Tilde stood up and retreated to the kitchen. Nico followed her. "I'm sorry you had to witness that," she said, slipping the olive cake into the oven.

"I wanted to give the three of you some privacy, but I didn't want to leave without saying goodbye." He'd hated every moment of the exchange. It brought back the memory of the conflicts between his own parents, which had always ended the same way.

Tilde wiped the counter clean of flour. "Italian mothers and sons can never be separated. She still insists on doing his laundry and ironing his shirts, which is fine with me. Less housework."

With the counter cleaned, she untied her apron. "I've set the oven alarm for the cake. Let's go outside. It's cooler and out of earshot."

"Enzo won't mind?"

"He doesn't need me. We have this confrontation three or four times a year. She makes some especially nasty remark, I ask her why she hates me, she goes into her 'My son no longer loves me' nonsense. Enzo reassures her of his undying devotion, and for a month or so, she's nice to me. Then it starts again. My husband has the patience of Sisyphus."

Nico laughed. "Rita liked to claim that for herself whenever I left a mess."

"I know full well my lovely aunt was a neat freak. Remember the time she came in here at dawn and scrubbed down the already perfectly clean kitchen? I'll admit, the pots gleamed for months."

They walked outside. The storm clouds had floated away. The leaves of the fig tree still drooped, dripping their morning's load of rain onto the metal tables and chairs, making soothing *plink* sounds.

"Wasn't Sisyphus punished for testing his wife's love?" Nico asked.

"I don't know, but Enzo's mother certainly tests mine." She opened the small window that allowed whoever was in the kitchen to see the tables. Now she would be able to hear the oven alarm. "Enzo told you about Stella?"

"Yes. She's taking the exam on Monday."

"God, I pray she gets in. It's not a great job, but it's a start. If you still lived in America, I would have asked you to sponsor her. She's such a bright girl, and I don't want her stuck with a self-serving jerk like Gianni. He has no ambition, perfectly happy to label wine bottles for the rest of his life."

"If Stella loves him, though, that's what matters, isn't it?"

"That's the thing. I'm not sure she does. And he's noticed it. That's why he's being so nice to her." She leaned her head against

Nico's shoulder. "I know, enough. Stella will have to sort out her life by herself, but that doesn't mean I don't have jellyfish in my stomach." She straightened her back and met Nico's gaze. "You're here for a reason that has little to do with hunger. I'm ready for the interrogation now."

"I won't ask any questions if you don't want me to."

She tapped her shoulder against his arm. "Ehi, what kind of detective are you?"

"A lousy one." He'd always been diligent at his job, but never a star. He didn't have the necessary ambition or hardness. "You're family. I don't want to pry."

"If you don't, Salvatore will. I'd prefer it be you. Ask away. I have nothing to hide."

"Elvira implied—"

Tilde finished the sentence for him: "That I was Robi's secret lover. I wasn't."

"Do you know who was?"

Tilde stretched out her arm and held her palm up to catch a raindrop from the tree. "I don't."

Nico suspected Tilde was lying. Her posture had gone completely rigid, the outstretched arm trembling. If she did know, Tilde must have her reasons for not telling him. He wouldn't push her for the name. Not today, at least. "Gerardi had a gold bracelet in his pocket when he died, a bracelet he'd bought a few days earlier in Radda. It had a charm with the date January first, 1997, engraved on it."

Tilde withdrew her arm and looked at the one drop that had fallen in her palm. She could see a fraction of her life line through it. She blew on the drop, and it broke apart. That date explained why—no, it had to be a simple coincidence. January 1, 1997, was a date she would never forget. "That's the day I told Enzo I would leave him if he didn't marry me. I gave him a month."

"Weren't you engaged already?"

"A we'll-get-married-someday kind of engagement. Mamma

Elvira was holding on tight. I finally got fed up. We got married three weeks later. Elvira has never forgiven me for strong-arming her precious son."

"No regrets?"

"I've got a good husband and a wonderful stubborn daughter, what else could I wish for? I ignore Elvira. So, what else do you want to ask me?"

"I heard some disturbing news from Gogol that might be able to help us with the case. He says he witnessed Gerardi raping a woman."

Tilde's face blanched. "A rape? Did he say who she was?"

"No. He was completely silent after that. He was upset he didn't do anything to help her."

"No." Tilde's hand swiped the air in front of her. "No, I don't believe it. Gogol gets confused. His mind doesn't work properly. I refuse to believe a woman was raped. It's too ugly, too cruel. Let's not talk about it anymore, please." Tilde walked back inside, Nico right behind her. "Let me deal just with chicken rags, olive oil cakes and tonight's dinner menu. I don't want your help tonight. Go to Greve and taste all the wines at the Chianti Expo. No more talk of hideous crimes, please."

The delicious smell of cake wafted through the kitchen doorway. "I'm sorry I upset you."

"You're only doing your job. Before Salvatore comes around asking, tell him I don't know of anyone getting raped in this town. Ever. Now take the scraps for the dog and let me do my work."

Enzo was still reassuring his mother of his undying filial love when Nico left the restaurant. The wet grayness of the day clung to the old stones of the church and the buildings that led down to the main piazza, matching Nico's mood. The encounter with Tilde and her family had left him sad. He had no desire to go to the Chianti Expo, to hear the Friends of Chianti's band play or listen to eight mayors of the Chianti Classico municipalities go on and on about how flawless their wines were. He certainly didn't want to see Perillo or Daniele. His questions had clearly upset Tilde, his wife's closest family and a woman he respected and loved. He regretted getting involved with Gerardi's murder. He would go to the Expo tomorrow when the booths opened, he decided. Tonight, he would taste his own perfectly good wine at home with dinner.

Walking down the hill to his car, he passed Enrico's shop. Its grate was down, but the shop door was open. Food shops in Italy closed from one to five in the afternoon, sometimes five-thirty.

Nico stopped and looked at his watch. It was three o'clock. "Hey, Enrico, no siesta for you?"

"Doing a little cleanup."

Enrico's shop was always spotless. Nico suspected the shopkeeper was taking a break from Luciana's hugs—and her cat.

"Need anything?" Enrico stepped out of the darkness of the shop and lifted the grate halfway. "You look like you need something."

An astute man, Signor Enrico. But his need had little to do with food.

"It's all right. You can't sell me anything now, and I'm too lazy to come back later." He had every intention of parking himself in his chair on the balcony and sitting there until the swallows came home.

"You are right. I can't sell to you now. I'll sell to you tomorrow when the shop is open and you pay me. I give to you today."

That was the Italian way, the law only serving as suggestion. Nico was tempted. He slipped under the grate and entered the shop. "Thank you, Enrico. I'll take fifty grams of finocchiona and a chunk of Parmigiano Reggiano." It would be his dinner. He wasn't in the mood to cook.

Enrico sliced the salami, cut a chunk of cheese from the Parmigiano wheel, added a thick slice of cooked ham on the house for OneWag and handed Nico the package. "Two olive loaves tomorrow?"

"Two olive loaves tomorrow and today's bill," Nico said. "A domani."

"A domani," Enrico repeated to Nico's back.

THE AFTERNOON HOURS WENT by, Nico sitting on his balcony with OneWag. First, they watched the swallows flutter in short loops over the neat rows of vines and the grove of olive trees under a now bright, sunny sky. Swallows represented loyalty, freedom, hope, he had read somewhere, and finally the three of them came to sleep on his balcony. Their presence gave him a sense of home. Rita would have been "tickled pink," an expression she'd fallen in love with when she'd first immigrated to the States as a teenager.

As the afternoon glided on, Nico's sadness wore off, replaced by questions. Why would Tilde have reason to lie about the identity of Gerardi's great love? Her body language, the complete stillness of her expression told him she knew. Why was she protecting this mystery woman? Didn't she realize that woman could be the killer? Or did Tilde know the woman was innocent, meaning to protect her from a painful interrogation and town gossip? With OneWag asleep, Nico let the questions swirl in his head unanswered, and after a while, he nodded off too.

What seemed only minutes later, he awoke to the sound of the dog scratching at the front door. "Coming." Nico stood up stiffly and was surprised to see a dipping red sun leak its pink-orange light down the length of the horizon. He let OneWag out and followed. The vegetable garden needed to be checked after a hard rain. An earthworm wiggled past his foot. He hoped there were many more to aerate the soil. As always, a few snails were gathered by his salad patch. He picked them up and put them in the pail he kept for weeds. Later, he would drop the snails on the grass behind the house—a great distance away for a snail, but he suspected he would find the very same ones in the garden a few days later. He picked a small bunch of string beans and a head of lettuce for tonight's salad and whistled to OneWag for them to go back inside.

Nico dropped Tilde's scraps into the dog's bowl and added Enrico's ham gift. OneWag skittered over on nails that needed cutting, too hungry to bother with his usual one wag of thanks. Nico poured himself a glass of red wine. He was beginning to sag again. The change from day to night always brought him down. It was when he missed Rita the most. Best to concentrate on dinner. He put a small pot of water on the stove to cook the string beans. As he waited for it to start boiling, he cut up and mixed it with OneWag's dry food. The dog gave one impatient bark and began wiggling with anticipation.

Washing the lettuce was next. The leaves were a beautiful light green. The color made him think of Stella's eyes. The same translucent color. Gerardi's passport photo flashed through his mind. Green eyes. And Elvira had implied . . . Was it possible Stella was Gerardi's daughter? Stella had been born prematurely.

Nico turned off the stove, his appetite gone. He went out on the balcony with his glass and lit a cigarette. His swallows had flown off again, but he would wait for them to come home. The pieces fit together. Stella could very well be Gerardi's child, but he wished with all his heart it wasn't so.

THIRTEEN

At ten o'clock Friday morning, a small crowd was already lining up at the Chianti Expo cashier's booth. Most of the guests bought their tickets and immediately wandered off to have breakfast at one of the café porticoes. The Expo didn't open until eleven. Foreign wine buyers and tourists had already shown up for what was considered the most important Chianti Classico showcase in Tuscany. A week later, Panzano would have her own smaller showcase, Vino al Vino, but this one was the oldest and the biggest. Sixty-six producers of Chianti Classico, a wine marked by the Gallo Nero black rooster insignia, were here.

Daniele strutted up and down the four aisles between the booths in his summer uniform: short-sleeved blue shirt, dark-blue trousers with bright-red bands running down the sides. A white bandolier crossed his chest. Last-minute preparations were still being made at many of the booths. Wine bottles wiped clean and displayed according to vintage year and importance, wooden crates stacked neatly, signs with the vineyard logos pinned across the backs of the booths.

After his second go-round, Daniele made his way to the Ferriello Wine booth at the north end of Piazza Matteotti. He was hoping to catch Arben, Aldo's Albanian assistant, during a break, which didn't look like it would be anytime soon. Arben and Gianni were still unloading crates from a large handcart parked in front of the bronze statue of Giovanni da Verrazzano, the Greve native who explored North America. Aldo's wife, Cinzia, was lining up bottles on a shelf below a map designating the

Chianti Classico region, while Aldo uncorked some bottles. All four wore Ferriello T-shirts.

"Ehi, Carabiniere, keep us safe, eh?" Cinzia said, with a wink and a smile.

He looked down at his feet. "Yes, Signora."

"Welcome," Aldo said. "Cinzia, meet Daniele. He's Salvatore's right hand and makes a great sgroppino. Come by when there aren't too many people and taste some wine."

Being called Salvatore's right-hand man made Daniele find the courage to look up. "I can't afford your wines, I'm afraid," he said, taking off his hat. Oblique rays of sun were already heating up the piazza. His head needed cooling in more ways than one—Aldo's wife's breasts looked like they might tear through the T-shirt.

"For free, Daniele," Aldo said. "You keep us safe, we thank you. Tell Salvatore too. He hasn't been around."

"I will. Thank you." The last he'd seen of the maresciallo, he was back in the office calling Substitute Prosecutor Della Langhe to see if any information had come in from California. He was glad he wouldn't have to listen to the curses that came afterward, information or no information. The man brought out the worst in the maresciallo. "Good luck with sales today."

"Thanks." Cinzia flashed her smile.

Feeling his cheeks burn, Daniele put his hat back on and approached the handcart behind the booth. Gianni was lifting the last crate. Daniele had seen him here and in Gravigna, usually with his arm around the same pretty woman. He envied his having a girlfriend.

"You can't leave that here," he said to Gianni, hoping Gianni would take the handcart and leave him alone with Arben.

Gianni, his arms around the heavy crate, stopped to look down at him, a full head taller than Daniele. "Like I don't know that? That uniform has gone to your head."

Arben elbowed Gianni. "He's just doing his job." He extended a hand toward Daniele. "Arben Kazim." He was a short man with a torso rippled with muscle, full dark hair and eyebrows, a strong nose and chin.

Daniele happily shook his hand and introduced himself. "Daniele Donato."

"I'll take the cart back to the van." Arben started pushing it across the wide piazza. He was headed for the parking lot across the main street, Daniele guessed. His patrol territory was technically within the piazza, but he needed to ask Arben a question. He scanned the area. Vince and the other men were walking the aisles, eyes peeled for trouble. Five minutes was all he needed.

Daniele hurried to catch up with Arben. "I need to ask you a question about Roberto Gerardi."

"I don't have anything good to say about the man." Arben's Italian was fluent; his accent was detectable only on the vowels. He had lived in Italy twenty-four years, one of the eight hundred thousand Albanians who had reached the eastern coast by sea.

"Being around him so much, two years, I thought—" Daniele stopped to catch his breath. Arben was walking so fast.

"Yes, two years."

"Maybe you knew something about the woman he was in love with."

"I know where he fucked her."

Daniele clasped his bandolier to control his excitement at the lead. "Where?"

Arben didn't answer until they reached the covered parking lot, opened the back of the van, hauled the cart inside, locked the door and lit a Toscano cigar.

Daniele stepped away. The smell was vile. "A Toscano isn't really Tuscan," Daniele said, repeating what the maresciallo had once told him. "The tobacco is from Kentucky."

"Where's that?"

"America."

Arben smiled. He had incredibly white teeth for a smoker, Daniele thought.

"Marlboro Man country."

"Where did Gerardi take the woman?"

"Oh, he took her all right. And from the floor creaking and both their moaning and groaning, she knew how to give back. It was upstairs in the abandoned farmhouse Aldo owns, the one where the American lives now. We used to store our old barrels on the ground floor, where the farmer who'd been there before had kept his animals. One day Aldo told me to grab one of the barrels. That's when I heard them."

"Did you ever go upstairs when they weren't there?" He would have wanted to. Maybe.

"Only once. It was clean up there, just a big bed with fancy sheets and a cashmere blanket. A table, two broken chairs. I guess they weren't interested in sitting."

"No personal belongings besides the bedding?"

"Towels in the bathroom, nothing more. I didn't search the place, I just wanted a look. I'll tell you, that blanket was just asking to be swiped. That would have shaken up that thieving turd, but then I figured he couldn't afford a blanket like that. I'd be stealing from her, whoever she was. Maybe she could afford ten cashmere blankets, but I don't steal from women. I give." He winked at Daniele and took a long drag of his Toscano.

"You never saw her?"

"No. Sorry."

"After Gerardi left town, did you go back to the house?"

"I confess I did. Maybe whoever she was was going to entertain other men in there. I was going to leave my phone number, but the place had been totally cleared out. I did find an earring stuck between the floorboards. A curled silver snake with green stones for eyes."

Daniele's heart skipped. Gerardi had shown Cinzia Ferri the snake earrings he was going to give to his lover. "Did you keep it?"

"Dreaming of a snake can have many different, powerful meanings in Islam, mostly bad. I keep it under my pillow to keep me from dreaming snakes."

Daniele's heart was drumming so fast now it hurt. "Fantastic! The maresciallo will need to take it."

"Only if he gives it back at night."

"Yes, yes, he'll understand about the dreams."

"No, he'll think all Muslims are stupidly superstitious. We're not! Just me."

"He won't think that. Italians have countless superstitions."

Arben threw his Toscano on the concrete floor and stepped on it. "I have to get back. We open in thirty minutes."

Daniele straightened his bandolier and readjusted his hat in an attempt to calm down. The maresciallo would be proud of his detecting skills. Daniele thanked Arben as he followed him out of the parking lot.

"What made you think I might know something?"

They wove their way between cars stuck in gridlock on the main street. "You were competitors, from what Signor Aldo told us. That means you watched Gerardi, hoping to catch him in a mistake. You caught him stealing, so I asked myself what else you might have observed."

Arben slapped him on his back. "Good thinking."

Daniele wiped his cheeks with his hands as if getting rid of sweat. It was a new ploy he'd discovered to hide his exaggerated blushing. "Did you tell Signor Aldo what you heard in the farmhouse?"

"I don't interfere with anyone's fucking. It's a right given to man and woman by Allah."

They shook hands when they reached the piazza. There was now a long line at the two ticket booths. Ten euros for a wineglass embossed with the Chianti Expo logo, a red cloth holder and six tasting pours of wine.

IT WAS ALMOST LUNCHTIME when Nico parked the 500 a good distance from Greve. With the Expo in full swing, he was lucky to find a spot just off the main road. He welcomed the walk, despite the hot sun and OneWag pulling back against his unfamiliar and unwelcome leash. He replayed the morning in his head, what had been said and not.

Anxious to get to the café in case Gogol had shown up early in order to avoid him, Nico had skipped his morning run. When he walked in with OneWag, Nico said hello to Jimmy and Sandro. They waved back. He looked around. A few students with bulging backpacks were already there, stuffing themselves with ciambelle and cornetti. No Gogol, but Nelli was sitting by the open French door, reading the paper, a cappuccino raised to her lips. His first lucky break. Nelli was Gogol's friend.

Nelli looked up as OneWag ran to her. She'd conquered his heart by stooping down and rubbing his ears whenever they met. The dog leapt onto her lap and licked her chin. Nelli smiled as Nico approached. He admired how easily smiles came to her. And there was nothing fake about them.

"I'm glad you came in early," Nelli said. "I can give you this in person." She handed over something wrapped in the paper. "OneWag will never forgive me"—she kissed the top of the dog's head—"but I think it's best for him."

Nico sat down next to her and opened the package. A red harness collar with a tag engraved with Nico's name and phone number and a matching leash. "I hope you don't mind, they're old. My dog was about the same size as yours."

"How nice of you. Thank you, but don't you want to get another dog?"

"No. Too painful." As soon as the words were out, she apologized, putting a hand on Nico's arm. "She was just a dog. I know her death doesn't compare to—"

"Please, don't apologize." Nico clasped her hand. "Pain is pain, for the loss of any loved one."

"Thank you." She looked up at Nico with her welcoming face and warm smile.

Nico felt a rush of emotion that, seconds later, made him uncomfortable. He took back his hand. "How did you get my phone number?"

"I had to convince Tilde I only needed it for the dog tag." Despite being aware of Nico's discomfort, Nelli kept her smile as her rejected hand kneaded OneWag's ear. She resented Tilde's assumption that she was out to snare Nico. He was a nice man with good looks and kindness to spare, but she wasn't looking for a relationship. Friendship would be nice, though. "She's very protective of you." She'd almost said "possessive."

"Tilde has been very good to me. She, Enzo and Stella are the only family I have left."

Nelli changed the subject, asking, "Is Salvatore any closer to finding out who killed Robi? I know you two are friends."

"Even if I knew I couldn't tell you, but I'm glad you brought it up. How well do you know Gogol?"

"Pretty well. Why?"

"Is he crazy?" He'd denied the possibility to Perillo, but maybe he was wrong. "Does he ever make things up?"

"I'm not a doctor, but we've been friends since I was a little girl. He would come by the house and give me *Divine Comedy* lessons I wasn't the least bit interested in. Georgio, that's his real name, lost his mother when he was maybe nine or ten. Father unknown. The old townspeople say he was pretty normal until she died. I think he just couldn't accept a reality that included his mother's death, and so he made up his own. His mother became Beatrice, Dante's great love, who also died young. By spouting Dante, he keeps his mother alive. The coat he refuses to take off? That's his mamma hugging him." Nelli put OneWag on the floor and sat back in her chair. "Now you're going to think *I'm* the crazy one."

"Not at all."

Sandro came by the table to deliver Nico's breakfast.

Nico thanked him and waited until he was back behind the counter. OneWag was busy wandering the café, licking up crumbs. Nico leaned over the small table and in a low voice told Nelli what Gogol had said at the murder site.

Nelli pressed her hand against her mouth and closed her eyes. "Could he have made that up?"

"No."

"How can you be sure?"

She opened her eyes filled with tears. "Because he asked me back then if I was the woman Robi had raped. He was pretty sure it had been someone else, but he wanted to be certain it wasn't me. This was after Robi had left."

"Why didn't you give this information to Perillo once you found out the murdered man was Gerardi?"

Nelli pulled her hands over her face. "I was going to. But then I thought he'd try to find out who'd been raped and accuse her of killing Robi." Nelli dropped her hands on the table. They were spotted with gray and yellow paint. "I couldn't do it. Whoever she is, she's suffered enough. I don't know if you can understand."

"I do understand what abuse can do to any human being." His mother had certainly suffered enough of it. And his understanding of another woman's suffering had ended his career. He and his partner had been first to the murder scene. A man, shot multiple times, lay on his back by the entrance. A woman was on her knees still holding the phone, trembling. A very slight woman, much younger than she looked, he would discover. An intruder had shot her husband, she said in a thin whisper. He walked over to her, helped her up and sat her on a nearby armchair. She explained that she was in the bathroom when she'd heard the shots. She'd rushed out, but the man was gone. He owed money, she said. She didn't know how much. He loved to gamble.

And loved to hit her, Nico suspected. July. No air-conditioning.

Despite the heat in the room, her legs were covered in dark stockings, arms hidden by long sleeves. He remembered how carefully his mother would hide her bruises. When his partner walked into another room, he lifted one of the woman's sleeves and saw the burn marks.

She pushed the sleeve down quickly. "I bruise easily."

"I understand that oil splatters when you cook." He realized he was feeding her a more believable answer. He was going to help her. Gently, he asked where the gun was.

She shook her head. "No gun." Her eyes darted to a full garbage bag by the door.

"Your husband was going to take out the garbage," Nico said.

She clutched his hand. "Yes, yes. You see, I forgot to do it."

And he was going to make her pay for forgetting. "Let me take it out for you."

"Thank you," she said in her meek voice.

His partner was back in the room and nodded, understanding he was going to look for the gun. When he found it, he slipped it inside his jacket without giving it a thought. "No gun," he told his partner, hauling the garbage bag back in. He still remembers the stink on his hands from the rotting garbage. "Maybe the others will find it in there."

That night, he wiped the gun clean and threw it in the Gowanus Canal. The woman got off on reasonable doubt. A few weeks later, Rita died. Nico went bar crawling with his partner shortly afterward. In a drunken stupor, he'd confessed about the gun.

"When did Robi leave?" Nico asked Nelli.

"Sometime in January."

"Did Gogol tell you who he thought the woman was?"

"No. I didn't want to know. I was actually jealous of that woman for a disgusting minute or two. Afterward, I was so ashamed of myself, I sent half my savings to a center for abused women in Florence."

"And yet you really have no idea who Gerardi was in love

with? Please forgive me, but I find that odd. Women in love usually know who their competition is."

"You think he raped his girlfriend?"

"If he did rape her, that would give her a motive, but even if she wasn't raped, she might have useful information. I can't believe no one knows who she is."

"I followed him once. I could tell he was going to see her by the way he was dressed. Pressed pants, new shirt, polished shoes. I got on my Vespa and followed him up to Radda. He went into a jewelry store there. Crisani's. Before Robi went in, he combed his hair with his fingers, tucked in his shirt. I just knew she was in there, but I didn't have the courage to follow him inside. I hid behind a car across the street and waited to see if they'd come out together. Instead, an older man followed him out, screaming at him. I jumped onto my scooter and swung away, not wanting Robi to see me. I went back a few days later and walked into the store, and there was this stunning girl behind the counter. About eighteen. The man who had shouted at Robi came out from a door in the back as soon as I stepped in. I pretended I was looking for a charm for my mother's bracelet. He dealt with me, she only watched. My mother doesn't own a bracelet. I muttered something stupid and left, convinced I'd found Robi's great doomed love. At least, that's what I hoped. I was twenty at the time, and all I read was romance novels. What else was I supposed to think?"

"Why doomed?"

"Crisani is a well-known jeweler, and Robi came from nothing. Not the ideal husband for a rich girl. I told myself that was the reason for the secrecy."

"The girl might have been an employee, but you could be right. Why didn't you tell Perillo?"

Nelli sighed. Men really didn't understand, not even nice ones like Nico. "For the same reason I didn't tell him what Gogol had asked me way back."

Nico nodded. "Of course. This girl could have been the rape victim."

"That's right. Besides, that the Crisani girl was Robi's beloved is just another one of my theories, not fact."

Nico remembered Aldo's comment while explaining his relationship to the victim. Gerardi had told him he wanted to marry a woman, but the family was opposed. "You've been a great help, Nelli. Thank you for telling me."

"I trust you."

A smile came to his lips, unbidden. "Now let's enjoy our breakfast."

"I've already had mine."

"If you keep me company, I'll treat you to another cappuccino."

"Add a custard-filled cornetto and I'm in." Her wonderful smile came back.

BY THE TIME NICO reached Greve's Piazza Matteotti, he was carrying an exhausted OneWag. He stopped and let a sudden breeze cool his face. It was just past eleven o'clock; the Expo had opened. Nico hated crowds, but he had to speak to Perillo.

Nico walked to the first restaurant under the portico and asked the waiter setting up for lunch for a glass of water. He poured the water into a clean ashtray and put it on the floor. OneWag lapped it up happily. The waiter, a young, skinny black man in jeans and a colorful tie-dyed shirt, brought another full glass. "This one for you. Plain, no gas," he said with a strong accent. A man who knew the value of water and compassion. One of thousands who were still crossing the sea from Africa, blessed not to have drowned and lucky enough to have found a job.

Nico drank the water and held out the glass and a five euro note. The waiter took only the glass. "Water is free. Come eat, then leave money."

Nico nodded, thanked him and returned the now-empty

ashtray to its original place. He looked above the door and made a mental note of the restaurant's name. He would come back and eat here, maybe invite Nelli.

"Signor Doyle!"

Nico didn't need to turn around to know who it was. "Signora Dorsetti." This time she was wearing something fancy, a shiny apricot-colored dress with ruffles at the hem and sleeves.

"How wonderful that you're here. And your sweet dog."

"It's nice to meet you again." Nico picked up OneWag. "I hope you'll excuse me, but I need to see Maresciallo Perillo."

"Something to do with the murder?" She gave him no time to answer. "Robi was my brother, you see. As I told the maresciallo, I know nothing about his new life or his old loves. Nothing at all. I think the maresciallo doesn't believe me. I can't blame him. Brothers and sisters should be close, confide in each other." She smoothed her dress. "Robi was a complicated man. Very proud, quick to anger when he didn't get his way. But I can't think of why anyone would want to kill him. Maybe for money, but that can't be, because whoever it was didn't take his watch. I hope he left me something. If it's a great deal of money, though, then I'll be a suspect, won't I?" She laughed as though the mere thought was ridiculous. "Please, come have an espresso with me. Three minutes and you're free. Surely you have three minutes to give a grieving sister?"

Nico let out a long internal sigh. "Of course, Signora."

"Please, call me Maria. When we were children, Robi used to call me Marimia. How would you say that in English?"

"My Maria."

"Not as pretty. Robi adored me then. I'm ten years younger than him. I was his pet." She sat down at the nearest table, already set for lunch. "Do sit. I think he stopped loving me when I got married. He was such a jealous man."

Nico obliged and placed OneWag on his lap as insurance. He felt assaulted by this woman's unwanted speech.

The African waiter appeared, then smiled at both of them. "Good day, Signora. The usual?"

"Too early for my beer, Yunas. Two espressos."

That he might want something else was clearly a possibility that hadn't occurred to her. "No coffee for me, please," Nico said. "But another glass of water would be welcome."

Yunas smiled. "Plain. No gas."

"Thank you."

"Yunas is from Ethiopia. Italy is full of Africans now. We'll soon have only cappuccino-colored children. Some people get very upset at the thought. I don't." She smiled proudly.

Nico wondered if she expected a compliment for her tolerance.

"Now, tell me about you, Nico."

"There isn't much to say." Before he was forced to supply information he had no desire to give, Yunas appeared with their order. Nico seized the glass and gulped down the water.

Maria realized he was going to rush off. "My brother's death must have greatly upset Tilde Morelli." Nico froze. "You're related, I hear."

"Yes, she and my wife are cousins." What was this woman getting at? Nico put his glass down and reached into his pocket to pay the waiter. "I think his death upset many people," he said curtly.

Maria tilted her head. She'd been very circumspect with the maresciallo, but this man was being rude. She wanted him to regret that. "They were very close, you know."

Her words felt like a punch to the stomach. Nico stood up, dropped a ten-euro note on the table. "I'm sorry. I really do have to go."

Maria felt something bubble inside her. Rejection in any form made her seethe. Americans had a reputation for being nice, even gullible. Who did Nico Doyle think he was? She'd only been trying to help, thinking he must be lonely.

"I'm sorry, Maria."

She acknowledged his apology with her sweetest smile. She was good at hiding her feelings, always had been. She had her pride to think of. This was a stupid man who deserved to have his face slapped.

Nico tucked OneWag under his arm again. "You caught me at a bad time."

She flicked her wrist in the air. "I'm afraid the good times are gone for everyone."

"I hope not for you," he said, and walked away.

"I'll have my beer now," she called out to Yunas when Nico was out of earshot. She thought of poor dead Robi, her only sibling, coming back without planning to see her, not even calling. He'd left her to lick his own wounds on another continent. Made himself rich too.

Maria crunched on the chocolate square that came with her coffee. *I hope not for you.* Well, that was unexpected. Maybe even sweet. As the chocolate melted in her mouth, so did her anger. There was yet still a chance at good times.

DANIELE SAW NICO MAKING his way to the northern end of the piazza and met him halfway.

"Where's your wineglass?" Daniele asked Nico after they greeted each other.

"It's a little early for that. I'm here to talk to the maresciallo."

There was urgency in the American's voice. Something new had come up. Well, he had something new too. "I left him in his office, calling Della Langhe. I don't know if he's still there." He started to pet OneWag. It helped slow his racing heart. "I have something I need to tell him too, something that could be important, something Arben told me."

Nico could see that Daniele was dying to tell him whatever it was. Daniele kept absentmindedly petting the dog, who surprised him with a lick on the wrist.

Deep in thought, Daniele didn't notice. Would the maresciallo mind if he told Nico what Arben had said? After all, he'd enlisted Nico to help them. He mulled the possibility over for a minute, then let out a sigh. No. After dealing with Della Langhe, his boss would be furious. He gave Nico his full attention. "I'd come with you to the station, but I'm on duty."

Nico saw Daniele's disappointment and said, "We'll wait for him then."

SOME TWENTY MINUTES LATER, Nico stood in the shade behind the statue of Verrazzano and finally saw Perillo stride into the piazza in full uniform, hat slightly askew on his head and boots shined to a gleam. He looked taller, handsome, important. Relieved to see him, Nico waved. He was eager to share Nelli's information. Maria Dorsetti's comment about Tilde he intended to keep to himself for now.

Daniele, who had just patrolled the piazza, spotted the maresciallo and stood up straighter. To his surprise, his boss was in full uniform, which had been required only at last night's opening. Well, the maresciallo could be a bit vain. The men at the station sometimes made fun of him for it behind his back. Daniele thought it was disloyal and never joined in. His boss did look good in full uniform, except for the dark expression on his face. "Good news?" Daniele asked, knowing the answer.

"News. But not good. Gerardi wasn't married. The police finally got a subpoena to search his home and office. They took his laptop but haven't looked through it yet. The computer at the winery only had production and client lists. So for now, no copy of the will and no personal correspondence."

"He didn't have a safe in the house?" Nico asked.

"No. He did have a safe deposit box, and according to the Delizioso manager, before Gerardi left for Italy, he added his lawyer's name for it at the bank and left him the key. The lawyer's secretary claims she knows nothing about a key, and the lawyer's on vacation, not responding to calls or email."

"The police can get a subpoena to open it."

"They're trying, but Gerardi's bank demanded a death certificate first, which then had to be translated into English and notarized. The American embassy in Rome took care of that yesterday, but so far no news."

Daniele asked, "What about the manager? Are the police looking into him?"

"He's been with Gerardi since he took over the Delizioso. According to all the employees there, he was devoted to his boss. Plus, he knew Gerardi was dying. They all knew. Why have someone kill him?" Perillo spread his arms in protest. "We've got nothing."

Nico gave Perillo a pat on the shoulder, relieved that nothing involving Tilde had come out. "Murder cases require patience."

Perillo shook his head. "What they don't need is Della Langhe. He broke my eardrum with this information, then threatened to send down some 'experienced men' from Florence, as if it were my fault we're still in the dark. I told him to go ahead and send. Of course, he's not actually sending a goddamn soul, because in about an hour, he'll calm down and realize what an idiot he is." Perillo turned to Daniele. "Are you religious?"

"I go to church on Sundays." He'd done so since birth. His mother made sure no Sunday Mass was missed. He used to fall asleep as a child. Now he found it restful.

Perillo reached into his trouser pocket and slipped a ten-euro note into Daniele's hand. "If that lawyer isn't found by Sunday morning, go light some candles for us. If he is, give it back. It will be the seed for a Dario Cecchini meal."

"I don't eat meat."

"Ah, right."

Daniele stuffed the money into his pocket. He would add five euros of his own, even though he didn't actually believe the candles would help.

Cinzia spotted Perillo and wiggled fingers at him. Their booth was only a few feet away. Perillo waved back. Aldo shot him a glance and went back to pouring wine into several raised glasses.

"Salvatore, Nico," Cinzia called out. "When this is over, you're all coming to our house for our best wine and my cacio e pepe spaghetti."

"You mean the Expo?"

"No, the murder investigation. Hope it's soon."

"It will be," Perillo answered with false confidence.

"We have things to tell you too," Daniele said loudly, his eagerness taking over.

Perillo looked at Nico.

"Yes, I have something new."

"Very good. The more information, the better. But this isn't exactly a good spot to discuss anything except wine. Let's go to the pharmacy instead of the station. It's just around the corner. The pharmacist is a friend of mine, and he'll give us his back room while we talk."

IN A SMALL, HOT room filled with unopened cartons of medicines, shampoos and creams but no chairs, Daniele told Perillo and Nico about the love nest, the snake earring Arben had found and kept. He didn't mention why.

"Bravo, Dani. Get the earring from Arben tomorrow morning. Unless it has the jeweler's markings on it, I'm not sure it will be of much help. But whether it is or not, excellent thinking on your part."

Daniele felt his cheeks get hot. Was he supposed to be proud? Disappointed? Both, maybe. But he was still convinced the forgotten snake earring would help to solve the puzzle of the mystery lady.

Perillo leaned back against a wall of well-stocked shelves. "Now you, Nico."

Nico told him what he had learned from Nelli.

"So you think Gogol really witnessed a rape?"

"Nelli believes him." Nico noticed Perillo go pale.

"For now, let's concentrate on the earring," Perillo said, pulling himself together. "Maybe it's one of Crisani's. Thanks to you two, we have a new lead. We're already short-staffed at the Expo, so pursuing it will have to wait until tomorrow morning. I'm sorry, Nico. I would love to have you come with us to Crisani's, but I'm afraid it's not possible."

"Of course." Nico was just as happy not to go. He had Tilde to worry about. Tonight, after dinner, he had more questions for her, unsure he wanted to know the answers.

FOURTEEN

At eleven at night, the downhill slope that led to the main piazza was empty and dark. Tilde lowered herself onto one of the church steps just above Sotto Il Fico and placed the bowl of string beans on her lap. On each side of her, a line of terra-cotta pots filled with pink geraniums disappeared up the dark stairs. She reached into her apron pocket and took out a cigarette, lit it, took two puffs and placed the lit cigarette carefully on the step. Her fingers started snapping one end of the string beans. The lamp outside the restaurant barely gave her enough light, but after years of experience, Tilde could have snapped those string beans in pitch black.

Nico sat down next to her. "I didn't know you smoked."

"I don't." She avoided looking at Nico. Instead, she looked straight ahead, the snapping mechanical.

"Rita used to snap both ends," Nico said as a warm-up.

"Italian string beans are thin, they don't need it."

"How are you cooking them?"

"In tomato sauce, but I know you're not here for cooking tips. Go ahead, ask your questions." Her tone was angry.

Nico reached for her hand. She pulled away, picked up her cigarette and took a deep drag. "I gave up smoking when I was pregnant."

Nico leaned in, his voice low. "Tilde, I don't want to pry in your affairs, but I'm worried you're not telling me the truth about Gerardi, and if Perillo decides to question you . . ."

"I don't remember what I told you."

"If you don't, that means you were making it up."

"No, it means I am very tired, Nico, so let's get this over with. I'm not Robi's mystery woman. I knew Robi the way I know most of the people who live here. We were friendly in a 'hi, how are you' sort of way, whenever we happened to run into each other."

"His sister says you and Gerardi were very close."

"She can say whatever she wants."

Nico put his hand on her arm. This time, she let it stay.

"He didn't harm you, did he?"

Tilde looked at her half-smoked cigarette. "Why, am I trying to kill myself?" She stubbed it out on the stair, put the butt in her pocket and turned to face Nico. In a perfectly level voice, she repeated his question, adding, "Why would you ask me that?"

Nico softened his expression. Even in the semidarkness, he could see that her face was wiped clean of emotion. He wished he could hold her, as Rita would have done. "Because of what Gogol witnessed."

"If you insist on talking about it, I'll ask you a question. Did he see who she was?"

"Does that mean you believe him?"

"Why shouldn't I? If Gogol saw a rape, he saw a rape. I just don't want to talk about it. I already told you that."

"If Gogol did see who the woman was, he won't say. That's why I brought it up again. I'm sorry, but after what Maria said . . ." He let the rest of the sentence drop.

She started snapping peas again. "How awful for Gogol."

"Worse for the woman."

"Yes, much, much worse." She snapped faster.

"It wasn't you?"

"If it were, I wouldn't kill him for it. I'd have erased it from my mind by now. I'm sure whoever it was has dealt with it." Tilde stood up with the bowl in the crook of her arm. "Women are much more resilient than you think."

Nico got on his feet. "Rita showed me that every day."

Tilde stood on her toes and kissed both his cheeks. "Thanks for worrying about me, Nico. I'm fine. I really am."

Nico very much wanted to believe her.

AT NINE SHARP THE next morning, the Crisanis' seventy-year-old housekeeper, Pina, answered the door. Seeing Maresciallo Salvatore Perillo and Brigadiere Daniele Donato standing on the landing in their well-pressed uniforms, she let out a small cry.

Perillo smiled to reassure her. "Nothing to be afraid of. We're only here to have a word with Signora Crisani."

Pina straightened her back to cover her embarrassment. "There is no Signora Crisani here. Maybe you mean Signora Castaldi?"

Perillo cast a look of reproach in Daniele's direction. He should have been told of the married name. "Yes. Signora Castaldi."

"Good. If you wanted Signorina Crisani, you'd be out of luck. She's at the seashore."

Daniele's shoulders slumped. Expecting to see Rosalba, he'd dreamed of her all night.

"Who is it?" asked a woman's voice from the apartment.

"Two carabinieri, Signora. They want to speak to you."

"Then let them in."

Pina stepped back and, with a grim expression, opened the door wide.

Irene Crisani Castaldi appeared in the large, dark foyer, wearing a long, red caftan made of a light material that billowed as she walked on bare feet. Her nails, toes and lips all matched the rich red of the caftan. Long, black hair hung over her shoulders. A stunning woman, thought Perillo. She barely looked older than her daughter.

"Come in." Irene had a deep, harsh voice that seemed to contradict her beauty. "Pina, make us some coffee and bring your lemon pound cake." She turned to Perillo and said in a flat tone,

"She's a wonderful baker." From her lips, it didn't sound like a compliment.

Perillo introduced himself and Daniele. With a nod of acknowledgment, Irene led them into a large room overstuffed with heavy furniture and dark oil paintings. "Forgive my attire. I wasn't expecting anyone at this hour." In truth, she never expected anyone at any hour, except for her daughter and faithful Pina, who had brought her and then Rosalba up. They were the only people she loved. The rest of her heart was reserved for her grandfather's jewelry store. Would these two men understand that devotion? She doubted it.

"Please sit down." She floated down into a brocaded armchair and arranged the caftan around her legs. Perillo watched her as he undid the bottom button of his jacket in order to sit on the sofa. The sofa was a deep one, and Perillo was now on edge. Either his wife had moved the button or he had to go on a diet, a prospect he'd planned to avoid. What he found more interesting was the fact that Irene Castaldi wasn't in the least nervous or intimidated. They were either wasting time, or she was a very good actress. But Pina, the maid, had cried out on seeing two carabinieri at the door. For Perillo, that was a first.

Irene sat back in her armchair. "How can I help you, Maresciallo?"

Daniele took out his notebook and sat at the far end of the sofa. Perillo leaned forward, elbows on knees. "I'm hoping you can help us with information about the murder victim, Roberto Gerardi. I believe you knew him before he left for the United States."

She frowned as if trying to place the name. "If I did, I don't remember. Twenty-two years is a long time."

Daniele looked up in surprise.

Irene noticed and smiled at him. "I know he left twenty-two years ago because I read it in the paper."

Perillo kept his eyes on Irene. Daniele really did need to learn to keep a straight face.

"Robi, as everyone in Gravigna calls him"—had her eyes just widened at the nickname, or was it wishful thinking on his part?—"had told a friend he was very much in love with a woman and wanted to marry her."

Irene reached for a cigarette and was about to light it when Pina came in with a silver tray holding a silver coffee service, delicate cups, a stack of small plates and a large one with sliced lemon pound cake. Pina kept her eyes on the shaking tray. Perillo wondered if his presence had anything to do with that shaking.

"Thank you, Pina." Irene put her cigarette and lighter down and indicated the wide wooden bench in front of the sofa. "Just set it there. We'll serve ourselves."

Rosalba is rich, Daniele thought sadly as he eyed the moist, pale-yellow slices of pound cake. They smelled of lemon and vanilla. He would never be able to afford her.

Perillo accepted the coffee, added three sugar cubes and stirred for a long time. "No cake for me, thank you." Accepting coffee from an interviewee was perfectly fine. A cup of coffee was like a glass of water. Accepting food placed them at a disadvantage, made them indebted to her. "Gerardi used to meet this woman in a small abandoned farmhouse belonging to Aldo Ferri. Gerardi worked for him then."

Irene picked at the pound cake slice. "A place filled with mice."

Perillo leaned forward, almost hitting the coffee cup with his knee. "Was it?"

Irene put the plate back on the bench and lit her cigarette. "Aren't all abandoned houses filled with mice?"

Perillo scanned her face. Her cool control had changed. To what? Defiance? Anger? Not at him. At something, someone more distant.

"Your father was a difficult man," Perillo ventured.

"Yes, he was." Pina had begged her to walk away, make her own life, but her father made it clear that he would disinherit her if she did. She had promised her grandfather, who had no love for his son, that she would one day take care of the business, that it would always belong to a Crisani.

"That must have been hard for you."

"No more than for most children who lose their mothers early."

"Gerardi mentioned that there were problems with the relationship. It seems her family didn't approve."

"I suppose that's sad for him, but why are you telling me this?"

"Gerardi was seen entering your jewelry store a few weeks before he left."

"Not mine back then. My father's. It became mine on his death fifteen years ago." His death had brought her a joy she was no longer ashamed of. "Many people went into Crisani's."

"But I imagine not many were kicked out of the store by your screaming father."

"Any little thing set my father off." She took a deep drag of her cigarette. On the exhale, she did her best to wipe her thoughts clean.

Perillo noticed the change. She was once again controlled, calm. He had no evidence she was the mystery woman except for the discovery of the earring—a coiled silver snake with tiny green eyes. Maybe it was the same pair Gerardi had shown Cinzia, an engagement present for the woman he loved.

"Please tell me the truth, Signora Castaldi."

"What truth? There are always many versions, don't you think? My truth is that I didn't kill Gerardi."

"Were you Roberto Gerardi's lover?"

"No." Irene stood up abruptly. "If you have nothing else to ask me, I really must get dressed and get to work. I open at eleven."

Perillo and Daniele stood. "Thank you for your time." Perillo planned to come back when Irene Castaldi was in the shop and talk to the housekeeper. Pina had been genuinely frightened at seeing them. Either she had been up to no good or she was frightened for her employer.

Irene walked the two carabinieri to the door. "I'm sorry to have disappointed you, Maresciallo."

"Don't be. Being disappointed is part of our job. As is being persistent."

As Irene lowered her head to turn the lock, several strands of her long hair fell over one side of her face.

"Thank you for your time," Perillo said as she opened the door. As he stepped across the threshold, Irene's fingers tucked the fallen strands behind her ear.

Daniele stared, inhaled deeply and said, "What a beautiful earring, Signora."

Irene quickly covered her ear with her hair. "Thank you," she said with a stiff voice.

Perillo stepped back into the foyer. "Let me see?"

"An unusual design," Daniele said, eager to keep this part of the interrogation on his plate.

She didn't uncover her ear. "A present from a friend, nothing special. I have far more beautiful earrings in the store."

Daniele reached into his pocket and took out the earring Arben had given him that morning. "Did your friend give you this one too?"

As Irene's eyes dropped to the silver snake earring, its sheen tarnished by twenty-two years of neglect, a tidal wave of pent-up emotion washed over her. Irene stared so intently that Daniele closed his fist over the earring, afraid she might try to snatch it.

Irene took her eyes away. She had turned ashen.

Daniele asked, "Do you need to sit down?"

She nodded. He took her arm, walked her back into the living room and sat her back in the armchair. Perillo followed.

"A glass of water?"

"Yes," she said in a threadbare voice. "Tell Pina it's for you. Keep her in the kitchen, please."

Perillo sat down on the sofa, impressed by Daniele's initiative. His young brigadiere had pinned Signora Castaldi into a corner.

A minute later, Daniele came back from the kitchen with an apologetic face. Behind him came Pina carrying another silver tray, this time with the glass of water on a doily. She took one look at Irene and turned to glower at Perillo. "What have you done to her?"

Irene waved Pina away. "It's nothing, Pina. Please leave us alone."

Pina put the tray with the glass of water on the bench, then straightened up to her full five feet two inches. Her anger seemed to turn into stone. In a glacial voice, she said, "As you wish, Signora," and retreated on slippered feet.

While Irene drank the water, Daniele eyed his boss. Perillo nodded. Daniele sat at the other end of the sofa as before and took out his notebook. He understood that his time with Signora Castaldi was over.

Irene put her glass down and sat back in the armchair. Some of her color had returned. "Where did you find it?" Her voice was still weak.

"In your love nest. The abandoned farm."

"When?"

"Shortly after Gerardi left town."

"Who?"

"That is of no concern to you."

She looked at Daniele and held out her hand. "Please?"

"I'm sorry, Signora," Perillo said. "You will get it back when we have found his killer. Now, I think it's time you told us the truth."

Irene reached for the ear that hadn't been exposed and removed an earring identical to her other earring and to the one Daniele had in his pocket. She held it out for them to see. "I kept the box, you see. When I couldn't find it, I went to a jeweler in Florence and had a copy made."

"The eyes are different," Daniele said.

"They're onyx. I didn't want them to be identical, and black seemed appropriate. I turned down his marriage proposal, you see. I loved him very much, but my father made it very clear that he would have nothing to do with me ever again. He was a widower, and I was his only child. Once he died, there would have been no more Crisani Jewelry. I couldn't accept that." She sat up. The wave had receded. The strength that had allowed her to carry on without regret all these years was back. "It was a painful decision, but the best one under those circumstances."

Perillo leaned forward. "What circumstances?"

"He'd stolen from Aldo Ferri. He was fired."

Before Daniele could control himself, the words slipped out. "Maybe he needed the money to pay for these earrings."

Perillo shot out a curt "Daniele!"

"That was the problem. I was rich, and he was poor and probably always would be." She had loved him in spite of that, or because of it. She no longer remembered. What she did remember was the pain of that decision. Irene looked down at the coiled black-eyed snake in her hand. She had always liked money too much. It was that simple.

"Gerardi became a successful owner of a California winery." How successful, Perillo hoped to discover over the weekend.

"I likely helped with that," Irene said. "Anger is an excellent motivator. I knew it was Robi when I read about the gold sneakers. When I told him it was over between us, he was furious, spat out insults. His last words to me were, 'I'll show you, you bitch. When I come back, I'll be wearing gold shoes, that's how rich I'll be.'"

"But he didn't come here to show you how rich he had become?"

"No. After I broke up with him, I never heard from him again. I guessed that the dead man was Robi from the description of the shoes, but once the newspaper confirmed his identity, I was surprised he hadn't gotten in touch to show me how wrong I'd been to leave him."

"He bought a bracelet in your store and he didn't ask about you? That's hard to believe."

"He did. He asked my daughter if I owned the store."

"You recognized him from the tape. That's why one camera supposedly didn't work and the tape of the other had been wiped clean."

"Yes, I'm afraid so."

He could have her arrested for tampering with evidence, but to what purpose?

"It must have given him perverse pleasure to buy such an expensive bracelet from my store, and in cash."

"As you know, the charm on the bracelet was engraved with the date January first, 1997. Does that mean anything to you?"

"No. We broke up a week before Christmas, and I spent the holidays out of town. My father thought it prudent to send me on a ski trip to Switzerland, in case I changed my mind about Robi."

"Where were you between five and seven o'clock Monday morning?"

"Why would I kill Robi? If anything, Robi might have wanted to kill me."

"I have to ask the question, and I need you to answer it."

"I was asleep in my bed until seven-thirty, when Pina brought me a coffee. She arrives at six and won't be able to corroborate my being in bed before that."

"Was your daughter here?"

"No. She came home from Siena, where she was visiting friends, later in the day." She looked at Perillo with a defiant expression. "I didn't kill Robi, but I'm afraid I have no alibi. Even if Rosalba had been here, she would've been fast asleep."

"You don't love him anymore?"

"You can't love a dead man, only your memory of him. Did he ever marry?"

"No."

"I see." She had made up a whole life for him in her mind. A wife and three boys and a wooden house with a nice backyard, like the American homes she had seen in the movies. He owned a pizza restaurant—all he'd ever wanted to eat was pizza. Sometimes she'd imagined him owning an auto repair shop. He was good with his hands.

Irene stood up. It was time to let the past go. "I think I've answered enough questions. I really need to get dressed."

Daniele and Perillo got up awkwardly, the sofa being very deep. They both shook down their trouser legs. Perillo followed Irene to the front door. He had one last question for her. One he had held off on for a purpose.

Daniele went back into the kitchen to thank Pina for the coffee and her lemon pound cake. She was rolling a sheet of pasta on a marble-topped table. "Signora wouldn't listen to me. Her father would have come around and forgiven her." She lifted her head to look at Daniele. "You're too thin. There's more pound cake in that bundle over there. Take it and enjoy, but don't go around saying I bribed you."

Daniele grabbed the bundle and planted a kiss on her cheek.

In the foyer, as Irene was about to open the door, Perillo said, "Just one more question, Signora. Forgive my crudeness, but I need to ask. Did Gerardi force himself on you or anyone you knew of after you turned him down?"

Irene clasped her throat. "God no! Did someone accuse him of that?"

"It seems so."

"When?"

Perillo studied Irene's blanched face, her widened eyes, the shock in them. She wasn't the one. "It happened between your breakup and his departure."

"I don't believe it."

"If you have to leave town for any reason, please let me know first."

Daniele slipped behind Perillo, holding the pound cake bundle so Irene wouldn't see it. He wasn't sure she'd approve of Pina's generosity.

Perillo extended his hand. Irene took it gingerly, still shocked by the news. "Thank you for you time, Signora Castaldi. Goodbye."

Irene stood at the door as they walked down the stairs. "I don't believe it," she repeated in a voice too low for them to hear.

FIFTEEN

Lucia, Gogol's gatekeeper of hell, looked up from her crocheting as Nico approached the front desk of the hospice. Her expression was grim.

"He's waiting for you in the garden, God knows why. I don't know what you did to him, but that poor man has barely eaten since you brought him back. He burned the mushroom omelet for the first time ever. He's still asking me to forgive him." She pointed the crochet hook at him. "You upset Gogol again, and you'll answer to me."

"Right you are," Nico said, and pulled a growling OneWag out the back door.

GOGOL WAS RAKING THE leaves on the winding gravel path of the garden. His coat lay neatly folded on the bench where they had sat together before. The morning was sunny but still had a night's edge of coolness. Nelli had told Nico that Gogol never took off his coat. Something had changed.

"Good morning," Nico called out as he undid OneWag's leash. The dog scurried over to the old man and waited for a head pat. Gogol obliged. "Good. We're friends now, yes?"

OneWag licked his hand. Gogol laughed.

Nico realized he had never heard Gogol laugh before. It was a beautiful sound. He walked over to where the old man had amassed a small pile of fallen leaves. It was too early for the big shedding of trees. "I have breakfast for us. The usual salami and lard crostini." Nico waved the bag. Gogol's head stayed bent down, laugh gone. He swept his rake back and forth, raising dust.

"Your gatekeeper said you were waiting for me."

The rake kept grating against the gravel. OneWag barked, but Gogol didn't stop.

"Do you want me to leave?"

"'The tangle of pathways contain my blindness.' I woke up with Ungaretti this morning. Dante will forgive me, I think."

"Is that why you're raking the path? To see again?"

"Not the woman. As the poet said of himself, I am a man of sorrow. All I need is an illusion to give me courage."

"What illusion will help you to tell me what you know?"

Gogol dropped the rake, walked to the bench and put his coat back on. Nico and OneWag followed. Once seated, Gogol held out his hand for the bag of crostini.

"I woke up hungry this morning."

"Good. Take all of them. Lucia told me you haven't eaten much lately, for which she blames me."

"She's angry because I burned the omelet and didn't go back for more mushrooms."

Nico opened the bag, placed a paper napkin on the bench and lined up the four crostini on it. "Lucia is angry with me because she cares about you."

Gogol's fingers went from salame to lard and back again, undecided which to take first.

"You usually go for the lard right away."

Gogol grabbed the salame crostino and bit into it. "My mother was the one who loved me," he said with his mouth full. "She took most of me with her." He swallowed, then took another bite. "A little bit of me must be coming back now. I haven't remembered Ungaretti since my school days."

"A few days ago," Nico said, "you told me to stay away from the maresciallo. I think I understand why now. You saw who the woman was. I remember your words. That my heart would claim no peace if I didn't stay away. You wanted me not to get involved with the murder investigation, because you were afraid it would lead to the rape. You said my wife—"

Gogol squeezed Nico's arm, his eyes on his face. "The illusion I need to give me courage?" He looked down and held out what was left of his crostino for OneWag. "The impossible illusion that what I saw will not hurt a beautiful woman and her child."

"Tilde and Stella. Stella a child of the rape."

"Stella is good and beautiful. She is a child of love, not carnal violence."

Nico knew there were thousands of beautiful, good children born after their mothers had been raped, but he let Gogol keep this illusion. He was angry with himself for having told Perillo about the rape. Tilde would become a suspect. Maybe even Stella. He knew in his blood that Tilde could not have killed Gerardi, as sure as his heart was beating. But what could he do to protect them?

Gogol had looked up at his pained face and understood. "Let us both have the courage of silence."

PERILLO'S CELL RANG JUST as Daniele drove out of the parking space a few doors away from the shuttered jewelry store.

Perillo listened for what Daniele thought was a long time. He couldn't understand the words, but the voice on the other end of the line was female. The maresciallo's wife, maybe. Today was Saturday, market day in Greve. It wasn't the first time she'd given him a list of vegetables to bring home for the night's dinner. Daniele loved going to the market and feasting his eyes on shiny red, orange and yellow peppers in a basket, opened heads of escarole that could be mistaken for enormous flowers, the red sweet onions from Certosa, and deep orange apricots, dark purple plums.

"The station or the market first?" Daniele asked after Perillo hung up.

Perillo slapped his thigh and grinned. "You can give me my ten euros back. That was Della Langhe's secretary, the wonderful Barbara. Gerardi's computer is now an open book. Any content that might shed light on the case will be sent to the American embassy today. We should receive it by tomorrow. And the good news doesn't end there. Gerardi's lawyer has finally returned. He was off scuba diving in the coral reefs in Australia, and here I thought there weren't any left. What's important is, he's getting on a plane to Los Angeles in a couple of hours. He's already instructed his secretary to scan Gerardi's will and relevant papers. We'll get them by email soon."

"What about the papers in the safe deposit box?" Daniele asked.

"That'll be next, unless the police get to the bank first. By the time the lawyer gets home, the banks will be closed. Whatever's in the safe deposit box will have to wait until Monday. The best part is, Della Langhe will be in Capri for the weekend, which means I get to keep dealing with Barbara."

Perillo picked up his phone again and pressed Nico's number. "Our first lady has been found, thanks to Daniele here."

"The owner of the jewelry store?"

"She was wearing the matching earring. She says she's the one who left him, and I believe her. She chose money over love. She was asleep at the time of the murder, has no alibi, and she was truly horrified when I asked her about the rape. She's not the one."

"She might be a very good actress."

"I consider that a very small possibility. There's more." Perillo relayed the information he'd gotten from Della Langhe's secretary. "I'm feeling good. Finally we have information to work with."

Information that might hurt the people Nico loved. He asked, "Do you know who the beneficiary is?"

"The lawyer didn't remember, as the will was prepared four years ago, but he thinks Gerardi might have wanted to update it. They had an appointment set for this Monday."

"I see."

"You don't sound as excited as I am."

Nico tried to put more energy behind his voice. "You're getting closer to a solution, and that's good news."

"*We* are getting closer. This is a team effort, don't forget that."

"I haven't." That was the trouble. How could he be loyal and honest at the same time?

"I'm feeling good, Nico. So should you. Come by the station after the Expo closes for the day. We need to drink to continued health and safe travels for Gerardi's lawyer."

"I can't," Nico lied. "I'm helping Tilde at the restaurant." He wasn't needed at Sotto Il Fico thanks to Gianni, who'd taken his advice and was helping Stella wait on tables. Nico planned to show up for dinner anyway, but he wasn't going to say anything to Tilde. She had denied the rape. He could only respect her need for privacy. As Gogol had said, part of his wife lived on in Tilde and Stella. His ardent hope was that Gerardi's papers made no mention of them.

"Too bad," Perillo said. "I'll call you as soon as something comes in. Ciao, Nico." Perillo pressed to end the call and turned to Daniele. "Come on, Dani, let's go grocery shopping and make you and the wife happy. She gave me a long list of vegetables. You're having dinner with us tonight."

Daniele blushed, with happiness this time.

BEFORE GOING HOME, NICO stopped by Luciana's shop and picked a small pot of pink baby roses. Luciana was too busy with three different customers to give him her usual hug, one he would strangely have welcomed today. He paid and made his way up to the cemetery with OneWag at his side. He followed his usual ritual of filling a watering can and watering Rita's old flower pot, which was still in bloom, and added the roses. He then watered her parents' boxwoods. OneWag dropped down by Rita's tomb, head between his paws. With a faithful dog's

instinct for his master's mood, he understood these visits were
sad ones.

Nico sat down on the grass beside him and silently spoke to
his wife. *Gogol told me you were a good woman. I think he meant
because you didn't tell me what happened to Tilde. I would have
liked to know the truth because I'm sure you suffered. Maybe I could
have helped. I'm not angry or disappointed. Your loyalty was to the
women of your family. You were always a good woman, the best. I
promise to do my best to protect them.*

Nico leaned in and kissed Rita's photo. OneWag licked his
hand.

"WE'VE GOT A FULL house tonight," Elvira declared from her
chair as Nico walked into the restaurant. "We could have used
your help a little earlier."

"Sorry, I'm not on duty tonight. It's Gianni's turn."

Elvira huffed. "He's useless. Too taken by his good looks, in
my opinion. He goes on and on with the clients, trying to show
off the very little English and German he knows, and ends up
getting their orders wrong. Poor Enzo and Stella are constantly
scrambling to set things straight. I won't tell you the mood Tilde
is in. I would help, but my sciatica is in full furor."

Nico kept a straight face. Elvira had been soldered to that
armchair since Nico had first seen her years before. She gestured
toward the terrace. "Go out there and help, for God's sake, and
get rid of that sad face."

Nico faked a smile. "At your service, ma'am."

Elvira let out a raucous laugh, strongly resembling donkey
braying. "You've got that right. I'm the general here. Now get
going."

Nico passed the kitchen. "Ciao, Tilde. I'm in."

Without looking up, Tilde squeezed a double ring of chocolate sauce over two plates of panna cotta and handed them over.
"Table six, left corner."

"I know where table six is. I'm not new."

She looked up, saw who it was. "Sorry. It's a little hectic tonight."

"What's Stella doing here? Shouldn't she be studying?"

"You tell her that."

Nico delivered the panna cotta to table six, where a young couple was too busy gazing at each other to notice the incredible view or the food. Honeymooners, he decided. Gianni passed by him and flashed a smile. "See, I listened."

"Bravo."

Behind Gianni, Stella made an exasperated face.

Nico made the rounds, taking orders. Panzanella, eggplant parmigiana, rigatoni with mushrooms and sausage. As he worked, weaving in between Enzo, Gianni and Stella, his mood lifted. When Nico got a chance to pass by Stella, he whispered, "I meant well."

She squeezed his hand.

"Shouldn't you be studying for Monday's exam?" he asked.

"My head needs breathing space. It's turned into Google for art. All you have to do is click, I've got the answer. The photographic memory helps."

"Good for you."

THE EVENING COOLED AND daylight dimmed. Only two tables were still occupied.

"So you were telling the truth," Perillo announced as he strode out from behind the huge fig tree in jeans, a short-sleeved shirt and his precious suede ankle boots. "You're working tonight."

Nico looked up from clearing a table at one end of the restaurant. He waited until Perillo was close to say, "Why would I have lied?"

"May I steal you away from your duties?"

"Please do," Stella said as she gave table two their check. "He deserves jail time for enlisting Gianni to help me."

Perillo was stopped short by her deep-green eyes. He'd seen and admired them many times, but they now reminded him of something they hadn't before.

"Stella doesn't appreciate excellence," Gianni said from somewhere behind the tree. "She'll learn."

Stella stomped over to where a seemingly exhausted Gianni was leaning against the kitchen wall, sneaking a cigarette.

"What I appreciate is humility and honesty." She snatched the cigarette out of Gianni's mouth and crushed it underfoot. "Restaurant staff is not allowed to smoke."

Nico couldn't see Gianni's expression, but didn't want to stay for the fight that was sure to come. Luckily, Stella knew how to take care of herself, and Tilde was in the kitchen, ready to step in even when she shouldn't.

"Let's go," Nico said, and walked the dirty dishes to the kitchen. Perillo followed, carrying two water glasses from another table.

Tilde was cleaning the counter with watered-down bleach. "Thanks for stepping in and helping at the last minute." Enzo looked up from stacking the dishwasher. "Ehi, Salvatore, we've missed you. Help yourself to a drink at the bar."

"Thanks, next time." Perillo gave Nico's arm a light punch. "Last minute, eh?"

Nico shrugged. So the lie was out. "Good night. See you at the Panzano market tomorrow? Nine o'clock."

Tilde nodded, her ear tuned to the ominous silence coming from the terrace. Nico helped himself to the leftover bag of meat Tilde always reserved for OneWag. He and Perillo passed a sleeping Elvira on the way out.

Perillo stood under the restaurant lamp and lit a cigarette. The rest of the street was dark, windows shuttered for the night. Perillo offered his pack to Nico.

"No, thanks."

"Where's Rocco?"

Nico shifted weight from one foot to the other. He had the

feeling this wasn't a friendly visit. "I left OneWag home. Why did you come here? You have news?"

"No. I was hoping you had something to tell me."

Nico stopped himself from speaking. It was impossible to remain loyal to Tilde and be truthful with Perillo.

Noticing how tense Nico was, Perillo put a hand on his shoulder. "Halfway down the hill, there's a side street that leads to a terrace with benches. A good place to talk, unless couples have gotten there first."

The terrace was empty. They sat on the bench closest to the railing. In front of them was a sea of black, dotted with a few distant lights. Crickets made their usual racket.

"You once asked me why I became a carabiniere," Perillo said in a low, soft voice. "I gave you an incomplete answer."

"I don't need to know." One intimate revelation would demand another.

"I want you to know. You noticed a reaction of mine when you told me about Gogol witnessing a rape. I heard the surprise in your voice, just as I heard the lie when you said you were working at the restaurant tonight. I'm certain you have the same ability. It's a skill that comes with our work, from years of watching reactions, listening to lies."

"Yes, I've counted on that ability, but I've made a lot of mistakes."

"Don't we all? I felt like one big mistake as a kid. I had a mother who didn't give a damn and no idea who my father was. So I lived on the streets, grabbing food from garbage cans, stealing whatever I could get away with. When I was eleven, I got caught with my hand in a woman's handbag by a carabiniere, Maresciallo Francesco Perillo. Instead of dragging me to the station, he took me home to his wife. He cleaned me up, fed me and told me what I made of my life was up to me, that I had choices. 'Stay with us for a month, follow our way of life and see if you like it. If not, you're free to leave.'"

"That's a pretty easy choice."

"Yes, if you have at least a shadow of common sense. I ran away after two nights. I missed my street friends, especially this wonderful girl, Ginetta. She was older, thirteen or fourteen, and always looked after me. If she had food or money, she shared it with me. And I did the same with her. I went looking for her and didn't find her. My street pals avoided me. I thought it was because I'd stayed with the maresciallo for two nights."

"They saw that as a betrayal?"

"That's what I thought, but I kept asking where Ginetta was, and finally Mimmo—he was the oldest of the group—told me the truth. Ginetta had gone looking for me in another part of town. The carabinieri found her hanging from a tree wearing only her bra. She'd been gang raped. Afterward, she tore her dress into strips to commit suicide." Perillo leaned back on the bench and pressed a hand against his eyes.

Nico had no words.

Perillo slowly took another cigarette from his pack and lit it. "I was ready to kill. I wanted to find whoever they were, smash their heads in, slash them to pieces. I wandered all over Pozzuoli, asking questions armed with a knife. I got beaten up for it more than once, but finally I remembered the man who took me in. A week later, I was at his door. If anyone was going to find Ginetta's rapists, it was his people. He took me back in and promised the carabinieri would look for them."

"Were they ever found?"

Perillo shook his head and took a long drag of his cigarette. "Ginetta, Francesco and his wife, Bice, made me a carabiniere. I still miss all three of them."

"Francesco and his wife died?"

"Yes, nine years later. One after the other in a matter of weeks. Cancer."

Nico eyed Perillo's cigarette pack. Perillo handed it over.

Nico took a cigarette and lit it. "Thanks." They leaned back on the bench and listened to the crickets for a few moments.

"As you know, I was kicked off the police force," Nico said.

"The reason for that is yours to keep."

"One confession merits another. Rita was dying when I did what I did. My captain found out from my partner and offered me a deal. Instead of publicly denouncing me, which could have gotten me a two-year jail stint and given his leadership a bad name, he officially kicked me off the force for some trumped-up infraction."

"And the deal?"

"Keep my mouth shut."

"Fair enough. Any regrets?"

"I miss some of the men I worked with. I miss not helping to find justice, but what I did was right, so no, no regrets."

"I'm glad," Perillo said. "And now, to our problem at hand. I've been trying to understand the reason for the date on the charm bracelet. Could it have to do with the rape Gogol witnessed? I thought it was perhaps a birthday instead, but Daniele's checked the birth records of Gravigna and nearby towns. Gravigna, zero births. In nearby towns, seven boys. I doubt the bracelet's for them. Have you spoken to Gogol again?"

"I have."

"Did he tell you when he witnessed the assault?"

"I didn't ask. I should have, but I didn't want to upset him again. I'm sorry."

"Please talk to him if you can—the information he has is very likely what we need to solve this case. I should be the one to ask, but I'm not his friend. I'd get Dante for an answer, and I don't believe *The Divine Comedy* talks of dates." Perillo noticed Nico had withdrawn, become a reluctant investigative partner, and after seeing Stella tonight, Perillo thought he knew why. "Gogol knows who the woman is, then."

"If he does, he didn't tell me."

"No, he wouldn't."

Nico said nothing.

"I understand," Perillo said. Family came first. "You're under no obligation to tell me anything." And maybe he was wrong. Stella's green eyes weren't necessarily proof. Perillo put out his cigarette and stood up. "Good night, Nico. Tomorrow or Monday, we'll know more. I'll call you as soon as that information comes in."

Nico looked up. It was too dark for Perillo to see if there was surprise on his face. "We're still in this together, yes?" Perillo asked.

Nico slowly nodded, a gesture Perillo guessed at rather than saw.

LATE SUNDAY NIGHT IN Greve in Chianti, the madhouse of the Chianti Classico Expo was over for another year. How many tickets and wine had been sold would be tallied Monday and bragged about Friday in the regional paper. The sixty-one exhibitors were gone, their stands dismantled. The carabinieri had gone home as well. A tired sanitation crew was busy putting Piazza Matteotti back to its pristine condition. Under one of the arches, Maria Dorsetti sat at a café table. The café was closed, but she had convinced Yunas to leave one table out for her. In the spur of the moment, she had splurged on a bottle of Fontalloro. At home, she would have been alone. Here she watched the crew working and the people sauntering home. The wine was an extravagance, but money was coming her way. Robi had no one but her. She knew he hadn't married. He'd told her as much in one of his emails after she'd asked. She deserved this money. She deserved this superb wine. It was her time to get.

AT THE FARMHOUSE, NICO roasted the red, yellow and orange peppers he'd bought that morning at the Panzano market. He was discovering that cooking absorbed him and pushed any other thoughts, pleasant or not, away. He wanted to offer Tilde a new recipe. It was time-consuming but worth it, he hoped.

Once the skins had blackened, Nico removed the peppers from the oven and sealed them in a sturdy paper bag to let them steam. It made it easier to remove the skin. Once cleaned of skin and seeds, each half was laid out on a cutting board and joined by some crumbled sausage meat and onion Nico had sautéed earlier. He carefully attempted to roll the pepper half around the meat, but the filling kept falling out or the pepper tearing. Another fiasco. Nico washed his hands, poured himself half a glass of wine and went out to sit on the terrace. OneWag followed.

Nico lifted the dog onto his lap. He needed to think how he could protect Tilde and Stella once Perillo figured it out. It was clear he was already suspicious. All he could do was stand by them and beg the maresciallo to be discreet.

AT ELEVEN O'CLOCK THAT Sunday night, Daniele and Perillo were still in the maresciallo's office. To pass the time, Perillo was teaching Daniele how to play Scopa, a card game Neapolitans loved. Emptied dishes sat piled on the maresciallo's desk. His wife had sent down dinner, a dish called "stingy spaghetti" because it had no meat, just garlic, oil, pecorino, potatoes and string beans. Perillo was too anxious for news to care what he ate, but Daniele happily cleaned his plate. He was now beginning to figure out how to use the strange-looking cards when Perillo's phone rang. The maresciallo rushed to answer, scattering his cards on the floor.

Barbara from Della Langhe's office in Florence was on the phone. Gerardi's lawyer hadn't sent anything yet, and she was going home. "I'm sorry, Salvatore, but you have to remember that California is nine hours behind Italian time. The chances of anything coming through tonight are very slim. Unfortunately, tomorrow Della Langhe will be back, and I'll have to show whatever information comes in to him first. I can't sneak anything to you."

A tired and frustrated Perillo let out a string of obscenities.

"Salvatore, please understand, it's too big a risk," Barbara protested. "That man is waiting for the chance to get rid of me and replace me with some young busty blonde." Barbara was fifty-two and liked to boast an airplane could land on her chest.

"Forgive me, Barbara. Of course I understand. Thank you for giving up your Sunday."

"Glad to. Gave me a chance to read a good book in holy peace. Let's keep our fingers crossed the information comes in overnight. The boss never gets to the office before ten. I'll get in at eight, and if anything has come through during the night, I'll send it over directly."

"Good idea, thanks."

"Good night, Salvatore. Golden dreams. Give a kiss to Dani."

"You too. Good night." Perillo put the receiver down and stood up.

Daniele handed him the cards he'd picked up from the floor. "Tomorrow's the day, then." He was unable to hide the relief in his voice. They could quit waiting. He was having a hard time keeping his eyes open, and he had never liked playing cards. He always lost.

"Tomorrow, the next day, who the hell knows." Perillo threw the collected cards on his desk. "Our beds are calling. Check your machine by eight tomorrow morning, in case Barbara has sent something. By the way, she sends you a kiss."

Daniele's eyebrows swept up. "Why? She doesn't know me."

"She thinks you have a sexy voice."

Daniele's cheeks responded for him.

"Good night, Dani."

In a dream that night, it was Rosalba who thought Daniele's voice was sexy. Even in sleep, he blushed.

SIXTEEN

At eight fifteen Monday morning, chewing on a ciambella filled with strawberry jam, Daniele turned on his computer. He was able to take two more bites before the desktop came on. Jam dribbled on his chin as he clicked on Barbara's email. "Good morning," followed by two emojis—a thumbs-up and a kiss. She had included an email from the lawyer with an attachment labeled "The Last Will and Testament of Robert Garrett."

Daniele's stomach did a flip as he knuckled the jam off his chin, put what was left of the ciambella aside and sat down. The lawyer's email had come in on Monday, 5:15 A.M. Italian time. In his email, the lawyer explained that the banks were closed Sundays, and so he was unable to access the safe deposit box. He planned to go to the bank on Monday afternoon after taking care of some urgent matters regarding other clients. He left his phone number in case there were any questions.

After taking a deep breath, Daniele clicked download and called the maresciallo.

AT BAR ALL'ANGOLO, NICO was having his usual breakfast with one eye on the door, hoping to see Gogol shuffle in with his overcoat and overpowering cologne. Instead, Nelli walked in, bringing with her the smell of oil paints and Marseille soap. Not an unpleasant combination, thought Nico as he pulled out a chair for her. He was glad to see her, and Gogol would be too, were he to come by.

"Sorry, I've been working," Nelli said as OneWag jumped

onto her lap. An orange streak adorned her cheek. Multicolored dabs covered her T-shirt. She wore no makeup. "I have a small show at the art center next week. I hope you'll come?"

"I'll be glad to, though I don't know much about painting."

"In my case, that's good. I did a small portrait of this little guy—it didn't come out too badly. I see he's wearing his collar today."

"He took to it right away but not the leash. Whenever I attach it, he lies down and refuses to budge."

"He wants to maintain the freedom of being a stray." Nelli's wide eyes, a light, transparent brown flecked with black, rested on Nico's face for a moment. "You look a little glum. I hope it's not because of Gogol. You have to give him time. He knows you're a friend."

How to answer. He couldn't tell her what made him sad. He took a bite of his cornetto, chewed slowly and swallowed. An idea came to him. "I failed at cooking a dish. More than one, in fact. My last attempt was roasted peppers rollatini stuffed with sausage and onions."

"Sounds delicious."

"It sounded delicious to me too. I wanted to surprise Tilde and offer it to the restaurant. It's labor-intensive but relaxing. I was so sure it would work out, which shows how arrogant I am."

"Mix everything together and add some Parmigiano Reggiano, and you've got a wonderful sauce for any pasta."

Nico smiled at Nelli. "Fantastic. Why didn't I think of that?"

"Because you were so focused on one thing, you didn't consider the other possibilities. It's a male weakness, I think."

"Not this male." Perillo suddenly appeared behind Nelli. He was dressed in a freshly pressed plaid shirt, pressed jeans and his usual suede boots. "A one-track mind wouldn't get me far in my job. Good morning to the two of you."

"Ciao, Salvatore," Nelli said. "You look sleepy." She looked at both the men and sensed she was now a third wheel. She put the dog down and started to stand. Perillo stopped her with a hand on her shoulder.

"No need to leave. I just need Nico to translate something into English for me. I'll bring him back."

Nelli got up anyway. "I have work to do." She resented Salvatore's assumption that she wanted Nico to come back, even if it was true.

As Nico went to pay for his breakfast, Perillo said, "I have a question for you, Nelli. Nico told me what Gogol asked you." He didn't want to utter the word "rape" in front of a woman. "It makes me think Gogol really did witness the violence."

Nelli gripped his arm. "You have to believe him. He doesn't invent things."

"Did he tell you when it happened?"

She let go of his arm. "Nothing specific that I remember. He asked me about it maybe three weeks or a month before Robi left."

"Thank you."

Nico came back. "Ciao, Nelli. Thanks for the cooking tip. I'll try to keep my mind open to all the possibilities."

"I'm counting on it," Perillo said as Nelli watched them walk out. She realized that she was counting on it too.

"YOU HAVE NEWS?" NICO asked, feeling his stomach clench.

Perillo nodded and kept walking until the two men and the dog reached the terrace where they had spoken last night. Luckily, it was still empty.

They sat on the same bench, which in daylight offered a view of the rooftops of the newer part of town. Beyond them, a distant patchwork of vineyards, each one going in a different direction. OneWag scouted the area for interesting tidbits, found none and wandered off.

"The lawyer scanned the will over," Perillo said. "We got it this morning. The sister inherits seven hundred and fifty thousand dollars, which sounds like a good motive to me. Gerardi's manager and three employees get the winery and vineyards and three million dollars to run it. They all knew Gerardi was dying, which removes any reason to have him killed."

Greed wasn't the only reason people killed, but Nico wasn't going to point that out. "Didn't Maria Dorsetti know he was dying?"

"Not according to her statement. She said she hadn't been in contact with her brother in four years, since her husband died."

"You only have her word for that."

"That's true. There are generous bequests to the gardener, the housekeeper, other employees. Our victim was a very generous man. Even Aldo gets something. I guess it's penance money for the wine Gerardi siphoned off and the loan."

"How much?"

"Ten thousand dollars. Not enough to kill for."

"Thank God. I like my landlord."

"There's more. Remember the piece of land next to Aldo's property? Where Gerardi got killed?"

"The one Aldo had tested for planting vines?"

"Yes, where the ground was decreed too loamy for wine making. Gerardi bought it eighteen months ago. Maybe Daniele was right to suggest the people who tested the ground were paid to declare the land wasn't wine-friendly."

"If so, that puts Aldo back on the suspect list."

"Daniele is getting another tester to check the ground."

Nico stood up and walked the perimeter of the terrace. "Need to stretch my legs. I ran too far this morning." What might come next was getting to him. There was nothing wrong with his knees. "So," he said, on his second round. "Who gets the land?"

"The will predates Gerardi acquiring the land. The lawyer added the information because he thought it might be connected to the murder."

One down, Nico thought. How many more to go? He sat

back on the bench, willing his stomach to relax. "Anyone else get anything?"

"Oh, yes. Five million dollars' worth. Five million dollars that corroborate Gogol's story."

Stomach clenching, Nico reached for one of Perillo's cigarettes. "How so?"

Perillo flipped opened his Zippo and offered a light. "The money goes to three different organizations that deal with rape and domestic violence. To me, that says Gerardi was making amends. Maybe his success changed him, or the cancer, but the will shows he regretted what he'd done." He was still holding up his Zippo. "Do you want to light that cigarette?"

"No." Nico removed the cigarette from his mouth and looked at it. The wet filter showed teeth marks. "Sorry. I took it without even asking."

"Friends don't have to ask, and there's more where that came from."

"Anything from Gerardi's computer yet?" There was a good chance he had written to his victim. Maybe even asking forgiveness.

"No, it should have come in yesterday. Somebody's sleeping on the job. I asked Barbara to give the embassy a nudge. Actually, I said a kick in the ass, but that's not very diplomatic." A clickety-click sound made Perillo turn around. OneWag's long nails tapped the tiles of the terrace floor. He stopped at Nico's feet and looked up.

"Good timing, Rocco," Perillo said. "We're done."

The dog jumped up onto his owner's lap. His breath smelled of mortadella. Nico started kneading his ear and felt his own body ease. The only Italian woman in the will, then, was Maria Dorsetti.

Perillo stood up. "I'll call you when more news comes in. Ciao."

Nico smiled for the first time that day. "Thanks for letting me know."

"We're still partners." Perillo gave OneWag a scratch on his back and walked away.

Nico stayed seated and let his mind turn to Stella. Her exam was in the afternoon. He called her. "When are you leaving?"

"At eleven-thirty. I don't have to be there until three."

He looked at his watch. It was just past nine. "Can I see you before you go?" There was something he wanted to give her.

"Sure. Gianni and I are having an early lunch. We'll be there in an hour or so. Come by and wish me luck."

Good. That gave him some time to go home and work on Nelli's suggestion.

WHEN NICO CAME BACK to Sotto Il Fico, Elvira was napping and Enzo was in the kitchen with Tilde, checking what to write on the day's menu. Nico uncovered the large bowl of sauce he was carrying. "Add this too?"

Tilde looked down at the jumble of peppers, onions, sausage meat and Parmigiano Reggiano. She slowly inhaled its perfume. "Good with rigatoni. Thanks. Write it in, Enzo. I've already got the water boiling for Stella. She gets the first portion."

"I added some dried hot pepper."

"Bravo. A little heat activates the brain. She'll need it today."

Nico looked out the kitchen window. The terrace was set up for lunch, but no diners yet. "Is she here?"

"At the corner table, her favorite. Where I can't see her from here. Gianni's with her."

He had hoped to catch her alone. "I want to give her my old rabbit's foot for luck, but not in front of Gianni." He'd only make fun of it. "Where's her purse?"

"That's nice. Thank you." She was also going to slip something inside Stella's bag. "Her bag's hanging behind the kitchen door."

The only thing hanging on the peg was a worn black backpack. Nico stuck his head back into the kitchen.

"A backpack?"

"Her bag's in there."

Nico unzipped it and dropped the small package into Stella's handbag.

"Do you think you can stay?" Tilde asked from the kitchen. "With Stella gone, I could use your help."

"Of course." He welcomed the idea. It would keep his mind off worrying. He went out on the terrace and kissed Stella's cheeks. "In the mouth of the wolf, my dear."

"Shit" was her answer. It was the obligatory one, but Nico still didn't understand what one had to do with the other.

While Nico was wishing Stella good luck, Tilde dug into her apron pocket and fished out the rosary she had bought after she gave birth. Stella had given her back her belief in God. He would watch over her baby. She went behind the kitchen door and pushed the rosary deep into the backpack, where her atheist daughter wouldn't find it and have a fit.

GERARDI'S EMAILS STARTED COMING in while Daniele sat in front of his computer, eating his share of the casserole Perillo's wife had prepared: fettuccine with zucchini and string beans, coated with a tomato and béchamel sauce. As his loaded fork made its way to his mouth, Daniele read the first one. His fork crashed on the plate. They had their murderer.

Perillo picked up his phone from the kitchen table. Across from him, Signora Perillo crossed her arms on her chest and gave her husband a don't-you-dare look.

"Are they in English?" Perillo asked with a full mouth.

"Italian. I'll read the first one. It's dated August twenty-ninth. It must be the last one he wrote."

"Go on."

Daniele cleared his throat. "'Ciao, Maria. I have not written often and you know why. Your incessant requests for money were not met for a reason, which you very well know. You and your husband turned your back on me twenty-two years ago when I needed it most. I left Italy for various reasons, you being one of them. However, that's in the past. Now it's time to make amends. I have cancer and do not expect to live very long. You will receive money when I die. How substantial that amount is will depend on how my trip back home goes. I'll text you once I'm there. I do not have your telephone number. Robi.'"

"Get ahold of Maria Dorsetti now."

"I'm scheduled to take over for Vince at the front office in fifteen minutes."

"He'll have to wait."

"I'll bring him a sandwich."

"Better make it two." Perillo clicked off and plunged his fork into the fettuccine. He had plenty of time to finish lunch, maybe even a coffee at the bar.

Seeing her husband eat with such gusto, Signora Perillo unfolded her arms and went back to eating.

ELVIRA SAT IN HER armchair folding napkins, looking extremely annoyed. "If you're going to cook for a restaurant, you have to make more," she said as Nico walked by to receive a well-earned espresso from Enzo. At three-thirty, the few diners still on the terrace were having their coffees. Nico was eager to gather OneWag from wherever he'd wandered and go home.

"The amount you brought was ridiculous," Elvira complained. "What was it? Eight portions? They were gone in the blink of an eye."

"It was my first attempt at this sauce." Nico wasn't about to mention that it was the result of a failure. He'd never hear the end of it. "I wasn't going to make a huge batch and then have Tilde reject it."

Elvira straightened her neck as far as it would go. "I do think I should be able to give my approval or disapproval of the food that is served in *my* restaurant."

Enzo handed Nico his coffee. "Mamma, you should thank Nico. He wasn't even supposed to work today."

"He's helping Tilde and getting some very strange ideas in his head."

Nico laughed and sat on the barstool to drink his three sips of espresso. "I'm not trying to take over the restaurant."

"Not while I'm alive." Elvira put the napkins on the side table and slowly stood. "It's time for my nap."

Enzo rushed out from behind the bar. "I'll bring the car around."

"No, I need a walk, and as punishment for not allowing me to taste what several guests told me was a delicious pasta dish, Nico will accompany me home."

Enzo looked at his mother with disbelief. "Mamma, you asked them if it was good?"

"Of course. Don't look so aghast. How else was I going to know what it tasted like?"

Nico walked to her and offered her his arm. They made their way slowly to the door. "They would never tell you if it was bad. You're the owner."

"I'm perfectly aware of that. I asked them what dish was their favorite." She turned to her son. "Don't pick me up tonight. I feel a cold coming on."

Enzo shook his head. His mother felt a cold coming on every Sunday. "Rest up and drink lots of liquids." Her favorite TV program would be on.

ELVIRA LIVED A SHORT walk away, in a ground-floor apartment behind the church. Nico followed her past a narrow kitchen into a living room overstuffed with dark furniture. The only bright spots came from the white crocheted doilies on the armchair and sofa and two narrow windows that overlooked a large courtyard lined with blue hydrangeas.

"That's part of the castle," she said when Nico walked to the

window to look out. "I like to say I live between God and roy-
alty, although the royals are long gone and God with them." She
settled herself in the worn velvet armchair. "Sit." She indicated a
spindly-legged settee opposite her. Nico doubted it would hold
his weight and chose the sofa. As soon as he sat down, his rear
end was welcomed by a sharp spring. He winced.

Elvira nodded with satisfaction. "Men always think they know
better. It's an old home. My husband grew up here. When his
parents died, my husband was only too happy to come back to
what he considered his real home."

"Did you mind?"

"I did, but said nothing. Men were obeyed in my youth. I've
made up for it since. I'd offer you coffee, a must when you enter
an Italian home, but you've already had yours at the restaurant.
I've brought you here to set you straight."

"About what?" He had no idea where this was going.

"You're wrong about Stella."

"What do you mean?"

"Stella was born early and, like all newborns, her eyes were blue.
The village tongues started flapping. A small town breeds gossip.
Enzo getting Tilde pregnant before marriage wasn't shocking, so
the tongues decided Enzo was forced to marry Tilde. My daughter-in-law has always been a strong, outspoken woman, which
many women don't like, and which is the very reason I like her."

Nico tried to keep a straight face, but she saw through it. "I
know. I'm not always nice to her. Showing affection was not
something I was taught. I do care for her. It's that sometimes I
want to roll back time, have my husband and my son still with
me. I shouldn't complain. I have a sweet, loving son with a backbone that Tilde holds up nicely. That was my job once." She
looked down at her lap, smoothed her blue housedress over her
knees.

Nico moved to another part of the sofa. He sank. No springs
at all.

Elvira looked up. "Where was I?"

"Tongues flapping."

She sucked in her lips, took a deep breath, exhaled. What she was about to say clearly pained her. "When Stella was six or seven months old, her blue eyes became the beautiful green you see now. The minute those eyes went public, the flapping tongues retreated behind closed doors. Walking on the street with the baby, we got silence. It meant their thoughts had turned uglier. To them, it was clear that Tilde was Robi's mystery woman and Stella was his child."

Nico wanted to point out that Elvira herself had implied that Tilde was that woman just the other day. Instead, he said, "The maresciallo has been asking about this woman. No one pointed to Tilde or to anyone else."

"Because green eyes are proof of nothing, and they know it. Besides, the women in this town don't betray each other." Elvira looked at Nico with reproach in her eyes. "You also think Stella is Robi's child."

"What makes you think that?"

"You've been asking Tilde questions, and she's upset. She's good at keeping a tight grip on her feelings, but I've known her a long time. She's kept her jaw clenched since you spoke to her on the church steps." She unclasped her pocketbook next to her, fished out a small iron key and waved it at a heavy dark bureau wedged between the two windows. "Please unlock the second drawer and bring me the photo album."

Nico did as he was asked. There was a knot of expectation in his stomach. He gave Elvira the album and went back to the sunken spot on the sofa.

Elvira carefully wiped the embossed leather cover with her handkerchief and placed the album on her lap. "I will show you why you and those tongues are wrong." She slowly leafed through the crumbling pages. Each page was covered in small black and white photos with wavy white edges. As she leafed through, many photos fell out of their corner holders. Elvira let out a loud satisfied breath. "Here she is." She held out the album. "Be careful, or we'll have photos all over the floor."

Nico carefully took the album and put it on his own lap.

"On the right-side page." The pitch of Elvira's voice rose. "Can you spot her? She has green eyes and is the very image of Stella."

Nico saw several close-ups of a beautiful smiling girl with big clear eyes. They may have been green or blue, though the photo was in black and white.

"She was christened Anna, but when the color of her eyes turned jade, they started calling her Giada. She was Enzo's paternal grandmother, Stella's great-grandmother. I met her, and her eyes were as green as Stella's. I am witness to that." There was great conviction in Elvira's voice. "You see, Nico? Stella's green eyes have nothing to do with Robi."

"Yes, I do." He only hoped it was true.

MARIA DORSETTI SETTLED HERSELF in the hard wooden chair, smoothed out the wrinkles of her beige linen skirt and looked up at Perillo with a smile on her face. She was nervous and trying hard not to show it. "I agree," she said in answer to the maresciallo's accusation. "The statement I signed the other day was incorrect. I knew Robi was coming, but what was the point of telling you? He died before he could get in touch with me."

"I have only your word for that, which isn't worth much now." Perillo ruffled the papers on his desk, looking for copies of the emails Maria Dorsetti had sent her brother. One was particularly interesting. He looked back up at Maria. Her smile was still there.

"In his last email, your brother makes it clear that the size of your inheritance depends on his trip here. Do you have any idea why?"

She shrugged. "A while back, he mentioned that he was buying some property here. Maybe he needed to pay for it, which meant less for me. How much do I inherit, by the way?"

Perillo ignored her question. "Gerardi had an appointment with his lawyer today. The lawyer believes he wanted to change his will, which is something he implies in his last email to you. His being killed before going home lets the old will stand. That benefits you directly."

Visible fear gripped her face. "You think I killed him."

"Did you?"

"No." Her chin started trembling.

"I have one more question." With the palm of his hand Perillo spread out the emails, found the one he wanted and slipped it across the desk. "The email you're looking at, dated in August of last year, seems to be in answer to some questions your brother asked you."

She held the copy in front of her face and squinted. She was too upset to reach in her handbag and take out her glasses. "Yes, I sent that."

"You tell him Tilde and Enzo are still married, that Stella has grown into a real Tuscan beauty. You add that her green eyes are the envy of all the girls in Gravigna."

"I was answering his questions."

"Why did you think he asked them?"

"It's obvious. He was still in love with Tilde. You obviously haven't figured it out yet, have you?" A flash of smugness crossed her face. "She was his mystery lady, and her daughter is the result." She smirked.

"When I asked you at our first meeting if you knew who his mystery lady was, you said you didn't."

"Of course I said that. Women honor each other's secrets."

As long as it's convenient, Perillo thought. "You've made two false statements, which is a violation of the penal code. You will be tried. Go home, call your lawyer and don't even contemplate leaving the area." He was glad to be rid of her for now, but he would need to search her home and the villa she took care of. She had raised a few questions that needed answering. He sat back, satisfied not only by his wife's delicious fettuccine casserole but by the conviction that he was so near to the end of the case.

SEVENTEEN

The sky was fading to a gray-blue, and the birds had started their evening racket. OneWag was stretched out on the grass next to the rudimentary fence Nico had put up around his vegetable garden. Perillo stood behind the chicken wire, held up by dried branches of varying lengths as he watched Nico weed his zucchini patch. He had just finished telling him about the emails and the Maria Dorsetti interrogation.

"She's the one, then."

"Everything points to her. Tomorrow I should have the warrant to search her home and the villa she works at. I can search for arms and drugs on my own, but I want to get into her laptop and phone, and that requires Della Langhe's approval." He took hold of one of the branches and shook it gently. The chicken wire danced with the movement. "You need to get yourself a real fence. Any rabbit can break right through here."

"I'll get to it this winter. I was in too much of a hurry to start planting. It's been a dream of mine. For now, let the rabbits in. Look at this." He held up a zucchini the size of a pineapple.

"Good for soup."

"You think?"

"With lots of leeks, shallots, carrots, celery. No tomato paste."

"Do all Italian men cook?"

"In my household, the wife reigns in the kitchen. Sometimes after work, I read the newspaper in the kitchen and watch her with one eye. When she goes back to Pozzuoli to visit her mother,

I put what I've observed to some use." Perillo shook his head. "Doesn't compare."

Nico stood up and brushed the dirt from his pants. "I know what you mean." He looked around the small garden, at what had once been, before the murder, a neat garden with neat rows of plants. Bamboo sticks held up the coiling branches of string beans. Some of the string beans were as thick as thumbs. In another row, bamboo sticks kept tomato plants erect. A few small tomatoes peeked out from their leaves. The lettuce was overgrown. Something was eating the eggplant leaves. At the four corners, he had planted climbing red roses. The roses were now gone, and the leaves of one plant had started shriveling. "I've been neglecting this place."

"But you've been helping me."

"Have I?" Nico walked out of the garden with two zucchini and tied a string to lock the gate. "I don't think I've been helpful to you. I should have told you from the start I was never a very good homicide detective. I'm not sure why you wanted me involved."

"I've had to deal with only one murder, easily and quickly solved. You, how many?"

"I didn't count."

"There's your answer. Are you on waiter duty tonight?"

"No, Alba and Enzo are taking over."

"My wife has abandoned me tonight. She's playing bingo at the church." Perillo lifted his arm to show Nico a wine bottle. "What do you think?"

Nico looked up. "Not a bad idea." Certainly better than drinking alone. "I'll throw in a zucchini frittata and another bottle of whiskey."

ALL THROUGH THE AFTERNOON, Tilde worked mechanically, her head and heart focused on what she had inadvertently found in Stella's bag. She kept her phone by her side, looking at it every five minutes, hoping, praying Stella would get in touch. She forced herself not to be the one who called. She wouldn't be able to hold back. *Come home, Stella, call, Stella, come home* became a refrain swirling in her head for hours.

At 8:10 P.M., as Tilde was dishing out the last of the ribollita, her phone rang. "Hi, Mamma, I just got out. I think I did all right."

Tilde held her breath. Not now. "Good," she managed to say.

"It wasn't half as hard as I expected. Really. Of course, I won't know for a few months, but I think I did really well."

Tilde was silent.

"Mamma, are you there?"

A quick intake of breath, and Tilde was back in the moment. "Yes, of course. I was so nervous for you. I'm glad it went well. When are you coming home?"

"Tomorrow morning. The last bus is at ten, and we want to celebrate my getting through this. Here comes Gianni. Bye, Mamma. Keep your fingers crossed for me!"

"Of course. See you in the morning." Tilde would need far more than crossed fingers to help her daughter.

NICO AND PERILLO WERE out on the balcony. The swallows had returned and settled in for the night. The frittata was eaten, the Panzanello Riserva bottle empty. They'd moved on to whiskey and were watching the sunset when "O Sole Mio" rang out from Perillo's phone.

"The lawyer got to Gerardi's safe deposit box," Daniele said. "He found a revised handwritten will, which he's scanned and sent over."

"Hold it." Perillo reached for a cigarette, lit it. "Go on." He was a little fuzzy right now. Smoking helped him concentrate. "How is it different?"

Daniele told him.

Perillo clicked off and met Nico's anxious eyes. "Gerardi wrote out a new will." Nico wasn't going to like it.

"What's it say?"

"That green eyes don't lie."

Nico closed his eyes and emptied his glass.

DANIELE WAS SITTING IN front of the computer in the maresciallo's office when Perillo came back from dinner with Nico.

"What are you doing still here? Frying your brains on that
computer?"

Daniele turned off the screen before anyone saw it and managed not to blush. "The printout is on your desk. It's incredible
that he had nothing to do with her for twenty-two years and then
he gets sick and leaves not only the land, but enough money to
build a palace on it, if she wants. If we can prove Signora Dorsetti
knew about this will, she's finished."

Perillo glanced over the handwritten sheet. The letters
wavered. Nico's frittata was good, but too light a dish to absorb
the drinking they'd done. "I'm off to sleep. Get to bed, Dani.
We're going to need sharp brains tomorrow."

Daniele reluctantly turned the screen back on, put the computer to sleep and promised himself he'd wake up very early to
pursue the idea that had popped into his head that morning.

Stella was in the kitchen in her bathrobe, dipping a slice of
pandolce in her caffelatte when her mother walked in.

Tilde's heart jumped. "Oh, good morning." She thought she'd
have more time before facing Stella.

"Ciao." There was no enthusiasm in Stella's voice.

"I didn't expect you this early. When did you get in?"

"I took the ten o'clock bus last night. You were still at the
restaurant, so I just went up to my room to sleep."

"What happened to your celebration with Gianni?"

"I realized that the exam had drained all the energy out of me.
I just wanted my bed." She wasn't about to tell her mother that
Gianni had been horrible to her.

Stella's eyes were glued to her coffee cup, Tilde noticed. Why wouldn't her daughter look at her? What was she hiding? *I took the ten o'clock bus*, she'd said. *I*, not *we*. Another fight with Gianni? Far better that possibility than . . .

Tilde interrupted her own ugly thought by pouring what was left of the coffee into a cup.

Stella stole a glance at her mother. Stone face, rigid shoulders. "I found the rosary. That was sweet, Mamma." She didn't believe there was a God looking after anyone, but on the bus home, she'd been surprised at how fingering the beads comforted her. "Can I keep it?"

Tilde kept the surprise off her face. "Of course. It's yours."

Stella told herself to keep talking. "Did Nico show you what he gave me? A rabbit's foot key chain." Stella got up and went to the counter to cut herself another slice of pandolce. "I know he meant well, but I found it a little creepy. Please don't tell him."

Tilde drank the tepid coffee in one gulp. "Sit down, Stella."

Stella raised her eyebrows at her mother's harsh tone. "That's what I was planning to do, Mamma. Sit and eat my second slice of cake and wait for you to ask me all about the exam." She walked back to the table, sat, placed the slice directly on the table and waited. A lecture was coming. About Gianni still being in her life, not that he would be anymore. But Mamma didn't know that. Or maybe it was about not telling her she'd be home last night, or not coming home right after the exam to share her excitement with the people who really loved her, or not putting the slice of cake on a plate. Or who knew what else it could be? She loved her mother so much, but recently, ever since that man had been killed out in the woods, she sometimes found it hard to breathe near her.

Once Stella was seated, Tilde reached into her pocket, took out a handkerchief and slowly unfolded it.

"Where did you get this?"

Stella gasped and tried to grab it back.

"Don't touch it!" Tilde yelled.

"It's not yours."

"What was it doing in your backpack?"

For several minutes, mother stared at daughter, and daughter stared at the object in mother's hand. Then Stella told her.

SHORTLY BEFORE ELEVEN, NICO was watering the vegetable garden before going to the restaurant. Gogol hadn't shown up for breakfast again. Neither had Nelli. He missed them both.

OneWag waited by the open gate until Nico's back was turned to sneak into the garden, which had become forbidden territory ever since he was caught scratching at the dirt under one of the roses. He planned to scratch some more dirt, even make a hole.

Nico's phone rang. He turned to reach his back pocket and out of the corner of his eye caught OneWag pushing himself forward on his stomach. "Out you go," he said, and turned the hose on him for a few seconds. A wet OneWag quickly rolled over and offered his dirt-covered belly as a peace offering. The phone kept ringing.

"Forget it!" Nico freed his phone from his pocket. "Out!"

OneWag rolled back over, got on his feet, shook himself violently and, with tail held high, trotted out as if that had been his intention all along.

Nico pressed the green button and put the phone to his ear. "Hi, Tilde. How did Stella do yesterday?" He'd called last night to ask, but Tilde hadn't answered.

"I need you to meet me at the carabinieri station in Greve in half an hour."

"What happened? Is Stella okay?"

"I'm not going to explain over the phone. Be there, please."

"Of course."

"Half an hour." The line went dead.

Nico called Perillo and told him about Tilde's request. "What's going on? Did she find out about the second will?"

"There's no way she could have. I'm in the dark too—she

called the station right after we got back from searching Maria Dorsetti's home and the Boldini villa. Tilde called and said she had something important to show me. Her tone could have melted Antarctica. Whatever it is, we'll find out soon enough. I came down hard on the sister, but she insists she's innocent. Claims she would've been happy even if Gerardi had left her only a thousand dollars. That all that matters to her is that her brother remembered her. We found no traces of a shotgun, and Daniele's checking her computer now. Maybe Tilde will surprise us and confess."

"That's not funny."

"I'm sorry, Nico. It's possible that she killed him. She had a motive and a gun—"

Nico said, "No," and clicked off. It was not a possibility.

NICO WAS ALREADY THERE when Tilde marched into the maresciallo's office, followed by an angry-looking Stella. Two empty chairs were waiting for them in front of Perillo's desk. Nico sat to one side. Daniele stood by his computer, ready to sit and start transcribing if needed. As soon as Stella sat, one of her legs started jittering rapidly. Tilde remained standing and opened her handbag. She took out tweezers and carefully clasped a hundred-dollar bill, which she dropped on Perillo's desk.

Both Nico and Perillo peered at it. The bill was strangely smooth, even though it was clearly old. In one corner was a series of brown smudges.

Tilde hovered over the desk. "That money has been washed and ironed, but you can still see the bloodstains."

"Thank you, Tilde." Perillo could observe that for himself. He wasn't sure about the smudges being bloodstains. "Now, please sit. Let's have this conversation without me craning my neck, shall we?" The two aspirins this morning hadn't helped much. He'd just taken another two.

Tilde sat down and reached over to clasp Stella's hand. Stella's other hand became a fist pressed against her lips. Nico could see she was fighting tears. His own body was stiff with dread. Gerardi's pockets had been emptied of money, and here was a hundred-dollar bill with what looked like dried blood on it. And Stella . . . he wanted to hug her, to tell her it would be all right. But he couldn't bear to look at her.

"Where did you get this?" Perillo addressed the question to Tilde, although Stella's clenched jaw told him she had the answer. There was no need to rush things—the truth liked to take its time.

Tilde explained that Stella had gone to Florence yesterday to take the museum exam. "I wanted her to have a rosary for protection. I didn't want her to find it because she thinks that's all mumbo jumbo. So I tried to hide it at the bottom of her bag, and my fingers found what I thought was a piece of paper."

In the far corner of the room, Daniele took notes. Nico could hear the clicks of his keyboard.

"Why did you take it out?" Perillo asked.

"I was going to use it to wrap the rosary. When I saw what it was, I kept it."

"It's the only bill you found?"

"I was so shocked when I saw it that I didn't look to see if there were more."

"Why did you wait until this morning to show this to me?"

"Like any mother, I wanted to talk to Stella first. I didn't expect her until this morning, and wasn't aware she'd already come back last night."

Perillo turned to Stella and, in a gentler voice, asked, "Can you explain this hundred-dollar bill?"

"It's not mine!" The words came out as a bark.

Perillo's tone remained level. "Why was it in your bag, then?"

"It wasn't." Stella's leg stopped bouncing, and she leaned forward in her chair. "It was in my backpack with my overnight stuff and Gianni's." Her face was now a startling white. "That money is his. Don't ask me how I know because I'll tell you, and it's not a nice story." Stella stopped to swallow.

Nico swiped the plastic water bottle from Perillo's desk and offered it to her. He could see tears welling up in her eyes.

Stella grabbed the bottle and gulped half of it down. She clutched it to her chest and sat up tall. The tears stayed floating in her eyes. "I walked out of a grueling three-hour exam feeling like I'd just won my future, and my boyfriend, instead of congratulating me, accused me of stealing his money. He wouldn't let up. He was sure I'd taken it. He grabbed my bag and threw everything out on the street." She turned toward her mother. "That's how I found the rosary and the rabbit's foot." She looked over her shoulder. "Thanks, Zio Nico." She turned back to Tilde. "I told you the exam was easy so you wouldn't worry, but I know I did very well. I know I'm going to get that job, and Gianni can drop off the edge of the earth for all I care. I'll never forgive him for treating me like a thief." Her tears finally fell. "How could he do that? When he claims to love me more than anything in the world. How could he? You'll be happy, Mamma. It's over between us. I told him I never want to see him again. I took the bus home early."

Tilde, demeanor completely changed, reached over to hug her daughter. Nico wanted to do the same. Stella backed away. "Mamma, I'm fine. I really am." She wiped her eyes and gave a throaty laugh. "I just had to get my anger off my chest, even in front of a maresciallo of the carabinieri."

"Thank you for being so honest." Perillo picked up the office phone and asked Vince to call the café next door for five espressos and more water. He smiled at Stella. "I think we need refueling before we go on. If you need a cigarette break"—he was badly in need of one—"please feel free."

Tilde shook her head. Stella said, "I don't smoke."

Perillo closed his eyes in resignation. One day, caffeine would be enough, but it wasn't yet.

"Do you have more questions?" Stella asked, turning back to him. "I'd like to get this over with."

"I understand. Did Gianni explain how he happened to have this American money?"

"He says he found it on the floor of the Coop in Panzano."

"Do you know why he didn't convert it into euros?"

"He said he was going to do it in Florence. The streets are full of exchange booths, and he could shop a better deal. He was going to use it to pay for some of the hotel."

Perillo shot a questioning look at Nico, who said, "The banks give you the best rate. I always used the ATM in Gravigna."

"But Gravigna is the town where a bloody murder occurred," Perillo added, forgetting for a moment Nico wasn't the only one listening. "A bank clerk might wonder about a hundred-dollar bill with suspicious brown smudges on it."

Stella frowned. "What are you saying? You think that money has the dead man's blood on it?"

"Or the blood of someone who cut his finger," Perillo said with a reassuring smile. "Or melted chocolate." Borrowing Tilde's tweezers, he slipped the hundred-dollar bill into a clean envelope and dropped it in his drawer. "Does Gianni know your mother found the money?"

"She forbade me to tell him."

"She did well. Please don't let him know."

"I never want to speak to him again, but why shouldn't he know?"

Perillo's smile reappeared. "I think it's best for your mother's sake that I let him know *we* have it."

Stella looked at Tilde, who nodded. "I guess you're right. They've never gotten along."

"Thank you for coming in, Stella."

In one graceful movement, Stella was on her feet. "I didn't want to."

"Still, thank you." Perillo stood and extended his hand. She shook it reluctantly. "You can go home now."

Tilde got up from her chair.

"No, Tilde, please stay. Something has come up, and I need your help with it."

Tilde looked at her watch. Ten past twelve. "I have a kitchen to run."

"This is important. Nico, can I ask you to take Stella home?" Talking to Tilde with Nico present would be awkward. His American friend was too emotionally involved.

Nico understood and shook his head. "Tilde asked me to be here."

Tilde understood that Salvatore's "something has come up" meant he was going to question her about Gerardi. Nico would try to defend her and make the situation even more painful. Tilde reached for Nico's hand and squeezed it. "Go, please. Stella needs company right now. Take her home."

"Don't worry, Mamma." Stella wrapped her arm around the man she'd thought of as her uncle since she'd been a little girl. "The two of us will take over in the kitchen until you're back. Ciao, Maresciallo. Ciao to you too." She waved at Daniele in the far corner.

Caught off guard, he waved, cheeks flaring. It wasn't dignified brigadiere behavior, but she had smiled at him despite what had to be a broken heart.

Daniele was wrong. Stella felt much better now that she'd gotten Gianni off her chest and her heart. She had the urge to skip out of the carabinieri station, do cartwheels in the park out front. She'd done the right thing. Where there was love, there was trust. Watching her parents had taught her that. Her love for Gianni had been dwindling for some time, and now it was over. Finished. Later on she might cry a little, or even a lot, because she'd be alone. Right now, she was her strongest self.

As Stella walked toward the door, she asked Nico, "Why is a poor rabbit's foot lucky?"

"I wish I knew."

TILDE WAITED UNTIL THE door had closed to sit down again. With arms folded, she gazed at the man she knew not as a maresciallo of the carabinieri, but as Salvatore, who loved her pappa al pomodoro and argued about Sunday soccer moves on Mondays with Enzo. He was fumbling with a sheet of paper, clearly uncomfortable. She was about to put him out of his misery when the bar boy walked in carrying a tray with a water bottle, an empty plastic cup filled with sugar packets and five plastic cups of coffee.

"The espressos, Maresciallo."

"You took your time," Perillo grumbled, eyes still on his desk. He didn't know the best way to start with Tilde. With the dead man's crime? With the hastily drafted new will? The will, yes. It would naturally segue to the rest.

"Sorry, Maresciallo. Where shall I put them?"

Perillo looked up. "Renzino!" He raised his eyebrows, held them high, exaggerating his shock. "What the hell have you done to yourself?" The boy's appearance was a welcome distraction. "You used to be a handsome kid." He had completely shaved both sides of his head. The top boasted a mop of fire-truck-red hair.

Renzino's deep laugh wobbled the tray, almost spilling the coffees.

Tilde quickly took the tray from him and placed it on one side of Perillo's desk.

Perillo's eyebrows relaxed. "What did your mother say?"

Another rumble of laughter from Renzino's nearly sumo-sized belly. "This was her doing."

"She must love you very much. Close the door behind you, and have Vince pay you from the petty cash fund. I'll bring the tray back later." Perillo looked at the five espressos at his elbow and offered Tilde a smile. "Two each. That's good."

"None for me." Tilde uncapped the water, emptied the cup with sugar packets, poured from the bottle and drank.

In the far corner, Daniele did not move to pick up his espresso. He knew what was coming was embarrassingly private and hoped Tilde would forget his presence.

Silence followed while Perillo drank the first coffee, then the second. "Did you have any contact with Gerardi after he left Italy?"

"No."

"He never wrote to ask how you were?"

"No."

"It seems he got that information from his sister. Gerardi discovered he had a short time to live and came home. But he didn't come here to die. He was flying back to California the day he was killed. I need to know what brought him back after twenty-two years if I am to solve his murder."

"He didn't come back for me."

Perillo knew he was talking in circles, but he couldn't bring himself to ask the question. "Did you have any reason to hate him?"

"Not one enough to kill him."

Perillo stood up. "Excuse me. I'll be right back." He took the evidence bag with the hundred-dollar bill and quickly walked to the door. In the corridor, he signaled Vince, who came forward with his heavy, rocking gait. "Get in the car and rush this to the lab in Florence. Have them check for blood and fingerprints. Tell them we need the results yesterday." That message delivered, Perillo stepped outside to light a cigarette. This time, he needed strength more than concentration. After two long drags, he put the cigarette out under his heel and went back in.

"Sorry," Perillo said, sitting back down behind his desk.

Tilde closed her eyes. "Why don't I just tell you what you want to know?"

After a moment, she reopened them and wet her lips. "In 1996,

I went to a New Year's Eve party that Nelli Corsi was throwing."
She spoke with no inflection in her voice, as if she was telling a
story she had no interest in. "I was supposed to go with Enzo. I
was engaged to him by then, but he came down with the flu."

Tilde took another sip of water. Why not just say it in three
words? She looked down at her cup. It was empty now.

"I wanted to ring in the New Year with him anyway," she
continued, "but his mother wouldn't let me, so I went to the
party by myself. There were about twenty of us. Sandro and
Jimmy from the café. Luciana, Enrico. Robi, who looked mis-
erable. Nelli was in love with him then and tried to cheer him
up. We drank, ate, danced to records. It was fun. The New Year
came, we all kissed each other and it was over. Outside, it had
started snowing lightly. I'd come on foot, and my family lived
on the outskirts of town. It was a twenty-minute walk. Friends
offered me a ride, but I said no. I've always liked walking, even
in bad weather, and I'd had too much to drink. The walk would
clear my head. I'd just passed Aldo's winery when Robi came up
beside me in his car."

Listening to her, Perillo thought of Ginetta. If she were still
alive, would she be telling her story years later in the same mechanical way? Would she still be screaming?

"He offered to take me home. I told him I was enjoying
myself, that I was nearly there already. 'Please,' he said. 'I need
someone to talk to.'" She could still hear his soft, pleading voice.
"He'd seemed so down at the party, I couldn't say no."

"He drove for a minute or two and stopped the car next to
the small chapel at the edge of the road. He said he knew Enzo's
parents owned Sotto Il Fico and asked me if I was marrying Enzo
for money. No, I said. Would I marry him if he was dirt poor, he
asked. No, I would wait until we both had good jobs. I wanted to
have children. He told me I was a liar, that all women wanted was
money. I argued with him. He called me a whore and slapped
me, then dragged me out of the car. I was screaming and fighting,

but Robi was very strong. Yes, Roberto Gerardi raped me. That's all you wanted to know, isn't it?"

Perillo looked down at his papers, feeling shame.

"He raped me, but I didn't kill him."

Perillo held out the sheet he'd been fumbling with earlier. "This was found in Gerardi's safe deposit box in California."

Tilde put the empty water cup on the desk and took the sheet. It was a printout of a handwritten letter. She read it twice before putting the paper down. "He wanted to leave three million dollars and ninety acres of land in the town of Gravigna to his daughter, Stella Morelli?" Her voice had turned into a rasp.

"Unfortunately for Stella, it's not legal as it is not signed or witnessed," Perillo said, "but he did want to make this his last will and testament. He had an appointment with his lawyer for the day after his death."

"The man was delusional!" Tilde slammed the draft of the will on the desk. "Even if he had signed it"—her face was white with anger—"Stella would never have taken that money."

"It would have changed her life. Yours and Enzo's."

"My Stella is not his daughter."

"She was born nine months after the rape, give or take a few days."

"She was born premature."

"Her eyes are the same color as Robi's." Thanks to Daniele's research he could add, "Only two percent of the world's population has green eyes."

"Stella's eyes are the same color as Enzo's grandmother's." Tilde filled the empty cup with water again and drank all of it down. Some color returned to her face. "Stop being the maresciallo for a moment. What are you getting at, Salvatore? Do you really think I could shoot a man's face off?"

"I'm getting at something you don't want to say out loud."

"What? I'll repeat it over and over until there's no breath left in me. I didn't kill the man who raped me. And I never told anyone I was raped. Not a single person." It was a lie, but she wanted to keep Enzo out of this. She had told him only after he'd found the paper results from the lab. He had cried with happiness. She hadn't realized that he too had had doubts about being Stella's father. On January 1, 1997, they'd been engaged for five months but had not yet made love.

"How are you so sure Stella isn't Gerardi's daughter?"

Tilde crushed the plastic cup in her fist.

Perillo turned to Daniele, crouched behind his computer, inputting Tilde's words. "Dani, please take the bar tray back. They're in short supply over there."

Daniele shot up, grabbed the tray and happily rushed out of the office. Tilde's story had upset his stomach.

"Thank you," Tilde said.

Perillo acknowledged her thanks with a nod.

"To answer your question, I had Stella's DNA tested. They confirmed she was Enzo's daughter, as I had hoped. If you want, I can show you the lab report."

"I'll take your word for it. Why didn't you want to tell me?"

"You don't understand the shame I've experienced. Of being raped first of all. And again, for doubting she was Enzo's daughter. A mother should know."

"You had every reason to doubt. Thank you for bringing in the hundred-dollar bill, and thank you for telling me the truth."

"You believe me, then."

"I do."

"Will you question Gianni?"

He spread his hands in a gesture of regret. "I'm afraid I can't discuss police matters with you."

Tilde rose from her seat and took back her tweezers from the desk. "Well, I'm glad to hear it's a police matter."

Perillo stood up and took Tilde's hand. A good, solid woman who had gone through something no one deserved.

"Take care of yourself, Tilde."

"I don't have to. I have a good husband and a wonderful daughter, and Zia Rita has left me the gift of Nico. Bring your wife to the restaurant every once in a while. She deserves a night off."

"Yes, she does."

Perillo walked Tilde to her car. As soon as she drove off, he smoked a quick cigarette. Daniele walked back from the lounge. "Get into uniform," Perillo ordered. "We're paying an official call. Meet you at the car in ten minutes."

Upstairs, Perillo hurriedly got into his own uniform and went to the kitchen, where Signora Perillo was sautéing onions. "I'm not going to make it back for lunch."

She kept stirring without even turning around.

On the counter next to the stove, Perillo noticed a box of Arborio rice. "What am I missing?"

"Risotto with porcini mushrooms."

"What bad luck! Can you make it for dinner instead?"

"You might not be here for dinner, either. I'll save you some."

He kissed the back of her head. "I'll miss you."

"You'll miss my risotto."

He gave her behind a loving pat. "That too."

EIGHTEEN

At the Ferriello Winery, Perillo found Aldo watching over the machine that placed perfectly positioned labels on his wine bottles. In the open adjoining room, Arben was stacking bottles in wooden crates with two Kosovian helpers. "We've got a big shipment going off to China in two days," Aldo said.

Daniele stood near the machine, transfixed by its seamless automation. His grandfather had labeled his wines with a brush and a bottle of glue, but then, he produced a maximum of thirty bottles in a good year.

"Why the uniforms? Are you here to arrest me?" Aldo had a grin on his face. The Chinese order they were fulfilling was a big one.

"No, we need to talk to Gianni."

"He came in this morning in a coal-black mood. What's he done?"

"Nothing for you to worry about."

"He works for me. Of course I worry about it. Anyway, you missed him. He ran off about ten minutes ago." Aldo kept his eyes locked on the labeler. It was an old machine, and sometimes it hiccupped, mangling the labels. "Bad timing on his part, but I remember what it's like to have troubles in love, so I let him go. I expect him back in half an hour. Cinzia's in the reception room. She'll give the two of you a glass of red while you wait."

"Thanks, but we have to attend to something else. Call me when he gets back, but please don't mention to him that we've come by. That goes for Arben too."

Aldo looked up with a frown. "This sounds serious."

"It isn't, but some people get nervous about a visit from the carabinieri."

Back in the car, Perillo called Nico. "Are you at the restaurant?"

"Outside." He had gone there hoping to find out from Tilde how her conversation with Perillo had gone.

"You can't talk?"

"That's right."

"Gianni's there."

"Very much so."

"Keep him there. We're coming."

"WHO WAS THAT?" GIANNI asked Nico, his handsome face scrunched up with suspicion.

Nico slipped the cell phone in his back pocket. "Luciana, the florist."

Tilde had arrived fifteen minutes earlier and told Nico, "Keep him out of my restaurant."

Gianni heard her and leaned against the wall under the lamp outside the front door, resigned to waiting. "It's the only exit," he muttered to himself.

Nico grabbed Gianni's arm and led him to the church steps, always a good place to talk, maybe even to get him to come to his senses. Perillo could take his time. There was no danger of Gianni leaving, not until Stella was present to hear him out. "Come on, let's sit."

Gianni let himself be pushed down onto the steps.

"Stella is rightfully upset, you agree with that, don't you?"

"Yes, yes, yes! I was awful, but she has to understand that she's my woman. She's mine and I'm hers. I'm going to marry her. She can't just leave me. It's not fair."

"Why were you so upset when you couldn't find the money?"

"It's what I was going to use to pay for the hotel. We were

going to celebrate. She just didn't understand how important it was for me."

"The celebration or the money?"

Gianni turned to stare at Nico like he was dumb. "Both. I needed one for the other."

"Your reaction was very strong."

"And how would you have reacted? I put the money in the backpack, and when I went to get it, the money was gone. The only other person who had access to the backpack was Stella. What was I supposed to think, that it flew away?"

"Maybe that it dropped out the way it dropped out from somebody's wallet or pocket in the supermarket. That's how you found it, isn't it?"

Gianni looked at Nico with narrowed eyes. "Stella talks too much. And so do you." He leaned back on the stairs, crossed his arms and didn't say another word.

Eight or ten minutes later, Perillo and Daniele appeared from the side street next to the church. "Gianni Baldi."

Gianni sat up and stared at the two carabinieri standing above him. "That's me."

Perillo introduced himself and Daniele. "I have some questions I need to ask you."

Gianni scrambled to his feet. "God, don't tell me Stella filed a complaint against me. I only yelled at her. I didn't touch a hair on her head, I swear it."

"Your treatment of Stella is not the reason we're here. Your home is just down the hill. Anyone home now?"

"No. My parents are at work."

"Good." Parents only got in the way. "We found the hundred-dollar bill."

Gianni's face did not light up. "Where?"

"A woman brought it in."

"Where was it?"

"That's not important. Let's talk at your home."

"Like hell it isn't. Stella is going to chop my head off."

"Hasn't she already?" An unnecessary comment, Perillo realized too late.

"You talked to her?"

"Let's just say I heard a rumor."

Gianni started stomping his feet on the cobblestone. "Shit, shit, shit!"

"Let's go to your place."

"You want to know about that money? I found it. Right on the floor of the Greve Coop, that's all there is to it."

"I need a few more details."

"Can't this wait? I need to talk to Stella."

"Afterward."

"I need to go back to work. We're preparing a big shipment to China. Three thousand bottles."

"Afterward."

Gianni glanced at the door of the restaurant, probably hoping Stella would appear. "Can't we talk here? Nico's a friend."

Perillo held out his arm to usher the way. "Let's go."

Gianni turned to Nico. "You come too. I want you as a witness."

Perillo snorted. "We're not going to beat you up. Answer a few questions and it's all over."

"I don't trust anyone in uniform. If it's only questions, you can ask them here."

"Come on, Gianni. Love can wait."

Gianni dug his heels into the cobblestones. "Not without Nico."

Perillo let out a long, noisy sigh for effect. He was happy to have Nico come along. The more eyes and ears, the better. "All right. Nico, you come too."

Gianni, sandwiched between the two carabinieri, walked halfway down the hill. Nico followed. Going along suited him fine, but he had to remember to keep his mouth shut and be the fly on the wall. In the meantime, two questions whirled in his head like lotto numbers waiting to be extracted from their cage. The hundred-dollar bill. Had Gianni really found it on the floor of the Coop? Had he found more? Gianni claimed he was going to use the hundred dollars to pay for the hotel, but Stella had said they planned to celebrate somewhere fancy. A room in a fancy hotel in Florence cost a hell of a lot more than a hundred dollars a night.

GIANNI LIVED ABOVE THE only laundromat in town. As they walked up the narrow flight of stairs, they could feel the pulsing of the washing machines underneath their feet. Gianni unlocked the door, and they entered into a large square room filled with light from a large sparkling window. One half of the room was a well-furnished kitchen. The second half, divided by a long table, was used as a living room. Underneath the window was a sofa covered by a blue-patterned cloth Nico had seen at the Greve market. One armchair. On the wall hung a calendar featuring Our Lady of Sorrows.

"So, ask," Gianni said, standing on the kitchen side of the table with his arms crossed.

Perillo took his time sitting down on the sofa. Daniele took out his notebook and pen and seemed not to know where to place himself. Nico sat on the armchair and leaned over to feel the texture of a jade plant. "Who's got the green thumb in the family?" Okay, so he wasn't keeping quiet, but he'd found that asking inane questions usually loosened up interviewees.

"Papà," Gianni answered, his eyes still on Perillo. "Go ahead, then. I'm not planning to offer you coffee."

Perillo patted the seat next to him. Daniele sat.

"Tell me how you found the money."

"I already told you."

"Tell me again."

"Are you hard of hearing?"

Nico intervened. "There's no need for hostility, Gianni. Just answer as best you remember."

As Gianni walked around the table and straddled a wooden chair, Perillo shot a glance of approval at Nico.

"Okay," Gianni said with a put-upon tone. "Let's get this over with. I found the bill on the floor at the Greve Coop."

"When did you find it?"

"I don't know. About ten days ago."

"Give me all the details."

"I was with Stella, who needed to do some shopping for her mother, and this guy kept staring at her, which freaked Stella out. I told him to get lost and he left. That's when I saw the money on the floor. I guess it belonged to him."

"You didn't find any other money?"

"I wish I had."

"Did you ever see this man again?"

"No."

"Do you own a shotgun?"

"Sure I do. Doesn't everyone?" Gianni raised his voice. "What the hell are you getting at? Do you think I killed that man because he was staring at my girlfriend? You're out of your head!"

"So you know the man from the Coop is the dead man. Why didn't you mention that before?"

"You didn't ask. What's it matter, anyway?"

Perillo fought hard to contain the urge to slap this young man. "There was blood on the hundred-dollar bill you found." He hadn't gotten confirmation it was Gerardi's yet, but he wanted to shake Gianni up a bit.

"So the guy cut himself. What's that got to do with me?"

"It depends on when the blood got there."

Gianni lifted his palms in the air. "I don't know what you're getting at. I told you how I got the money. I've got nothing else to say." He stood up and pushed the chair back under the table. "No, I do." He turned around, a finger pointing at Perillo. "You're fishing around because you've got nothing. And I bet Tilde has something to do with you being here. She can't stand me, and the feeling is mutual. Stella and I are going to get married whether she likes it or not."

Given Gianni's arrogance, that "she" could refer to Stella as well as Tilde, Nico thought. Stella had been wise to break up with him.

Nico stood. "I'm sorry, I need to use the bathroom." An old ploy. Whatever he found couldn't be used in court, at least not in the States, but it might give Perillo a leg up. He was also tired of just being a witness.

Gianni pointed a thumb to his left. "Second door to the left. Pull hard on the chain. It gets stuck sometimes."

"Thanks." Nico made his way carefully past the plant-laden coffee table and turned the corner to face a narrow corridor. He waited for Perillo to start talking again before opening the first door.

Perillo was going to ask to see Gianni's shotgun, but right now, they all needed to stay right where they were until Nico came back. "Where were you last Monday morning around six o'clock?"

"Here, asleep. Where else?"

Perillo smiled in answer to Gianni's sneering attitude. Was his antagonistic tone a cover-up for fear? "Was anyone with you?"

"My parents. My mother woke me up at seven-thirty with my caffelatte. She does that every workday. I've got to be at the winery at eight-thirty."

A mamma's boy then, Perillo thought. That explained some of his attitude.

Daniele, who had been quietly and quickly taking notes, felt a pang of envy. His mother had stopped offering him caffelatte in bed on his tenth birthday.

"Can anyone else corroborate that you were here at that time?" Mothers never told the truth about their children to the authorities. "Your father?" Not that fathers were much better.

"Papà leaves at five, except on Sundays. He's a mason working on that five-star hotel Vigna Maggio is building in Vitigliano. It was just me and Mamma." He leaned back against the table with a satisfied smirk on his handsome face. "Now, I've really got to get back to work."

Perillo stood up slowly and adjusted his uniform, taking up time and waiting for Nico. Daniele followed his lead. It wasn't like the maresciallo to waste time, but Nico hadn't come back yet.

"I'll need to speak to your mother," Perillo said. He would also have to speak to Stella, who had been with Gianni when he'd supposedly found the money.

"Sure. Mamma'll vouch for me." They all heard the toilet flush. Gianni walked to the front door, twirling the key chain. "You'll find her at the post office in Panzano."

"I'm not finished yet," Perillo warned, not moving.

Gianni spun around. "God Almighty, now what?"

"You need to come to the station and sign a statement."

Gianni pointed at Daniele. "He's been taking notes all this time. I'll sign them here."

"Notes won't do. We need a formal statement. You can come with us now."

Nico walked in from the corridor, pushing his shirt into his cargo pants. "Everything okay, Gianni?"

"Well, you weren't much of a witness, and now they want me to go to Greve and sign a statement."

"It's just procedure," Nico said. "Don't worry about it." He turned to Perillo. "Gianni's quite late for work. Can't he come this evening?"

Gianni looked relieved, and Perillo understood. Nico had something to tell him first. "No later than seven. Now, we need to take your shotgun."

"What for?"

"To eliminate it as the weapon that killed Gerardi."

"I didn't kill him! How many times do I have to say it? No

wonder you guys are known for being slow. How many carabinieri does it take to sink a submarine?"

"That one's old," Perillo answered. "Fetch your shotgun now. When you come to the station later, I'll tell you some better jokes."

"Do I have a choice?"

"For the jokes, yes. The shotgun, no."

"I'll get it for you, but I want it back by next Sunday. I'm going hunting with my buddies."

"We'll try our best."

BACK ON THE STREET, Daniele asked Nico in a whisper, "You didn't really have to go to the bathroom, did you?"

"No, but once you get there, why not?"

Daniele hugged Gianni's shotgun to his chest and smiled. He was catching on.

Nico was staring at the laundromat. "Did forensics look at those machines for blood?"

"Then you think—"

Perillo cut Daniele off. "They did. Plus the Caritas dumpsters where people leave clothes. Nothing. Now, let's get this shotgun back to the station. Vince will have to make another trip to Florence."

"I can do it," Daniele offered. He'd never been to the renovated Cathedral Museum. He'd finally see the real Baptistery doors.

"No, Dani. I need you with me."

Daniele knew the real reason the maresciallo didn't want him to go. He would take twice as long. Vince was a speed demon.

As the three of them walked down to the main piazza, Daniele asked, "How many carabinieri does it take to sink a submarine, though?"

"I'll tell you a better one," Perillo said. "A carabiniere runs to his maresciallo. 'Our squad car got stolen.' 'Did you see who it was?' 'No, but I got the license plate.'"

"That's not funny."

"The police think it is. Don't get discouraged, Dani. Being the butt of jokes gives us a perverse pride."

IN THE PIAZZA, THE benches were deserted. The old men were home eating a hearty three-course lunch, pasta and some meat with cooked vegetables. For dessert, whatever fruit was in season. For dinner later, it might be a light soup and cold cuts. A full stomach at night brought nightmares. In between, around five o'clock, they would come out again to chat, complain, maybe start up a game of cards. Luciana's flower shop was shuttered. The café had only a few clients. It wasn't coffee time yet. The outside tables at Da Gino were almost full. The best place to talk was in the squad car. As Perillo and Daniele were getting in, the lilac-haired waitress, Gino's daughter, Carletta, waved at the group.

"Why is her hair that color?" Daniele asked.

"She's young. You've made another conquest," Perillo said.

"No, she's waving at you."

"Well, maybe. I got her out of trouble once." He turned to Nico, who was sitting in the backseat. "I'm listening."

"I think you have your man. Unless Gianni can explain why he has a thick stash of euros in his house."

"Where was it?"

"I got lucky, because his room was a holy mess. It looked like it hadn't been cleaned in a lifetime, which works in our favor. I took out a clean handkerchief"—a Rita must-have—"and started poking around. I noticed the guitar was full of dust, except around the rosette and the strings over the sound hole. I took it down and shook it a few times. Some bills fell out. I pressed my eye against the hole and saw more. Lots and lots of hundred-euro bills, bills I suspect were originally dollars. I put back the bills that fell out, rehooked the guitar and went to the bathroom."

"You think Gianni killed Gerardi for his money?"

"The watch Gerardi wore did announce he was rich, but

Gianni would have had to know the man was carrying that much cash."

"But how would he get Gerardi to walk into the woods at that time of the morning?"

"Exactly. I think that cash was an extra bonus."

Daniele snapped his fingers. "Gerardi kept writing to his sister asking about Tilde, so much so that she thought Tilde was the mystery woman. When she told him Tilde had a daughter and the dates matched up, he assumed Stella was his. That's why he came back."

Nico felt the blood drain from his face. "She told you."

"Yes," Perillo said. "Tilde also told me she has proof that Stella is Enzo's biological daughter. She's no longer a suspect."

Nico's heart pumped fast with joy. "Thank God."

"The date on the bracelet charm, January first, 1997, is the date of the rape." Daniele was on a roll. "What Gerardi thought was the date of Stella's conception. He saw it as her real birthday."

"Sick, but the only date he knew himself," Perillo said. "I wonder if he saw giving that bracelet to Stella as a form of apology."

"If Gianni didn't kill for money, then why?" Daniele asked.

"That might not necessarily be the case. We'll ponder it later," Perillo said. "We've got to get this shotgun to Florence. If our luck holds out, it will have traces of Gerardi's blood. Gianni is obviously not good at thorough cleaning. Let's meet up at the station after lunch. Three o'clock okay with you, Nico?"

"Fine."

"Thanks for thinking so fast."

"The bathroom trick is very old. I'm surprised Gianni didn't catch on. By the way, his parents' bedroom is the last room in the hallway. Gianni could have easily slipped out without them knowing and been back in time for his caffelatte. Ciao for now, and buon appetito."

"Buon appetito to you too."

Nico wanted to walk up the steep road back to Sotto Il Fico and give Tilde, Stella, Enzo and Elvira a big hug, but it was the height of the lunch hour. The hugs would have to wait. Right now he was hungry. A mortadella and caciotta sandwich was waiting for him at home, plus OneWag. He missed the little guy.

"WHAT THE HELL HAVE you done?"

OneWag hid his face between his dirt-caked paws. In front of him, the rosebush was lying on its side, roots exposed. Next to it, a deep hole.

Nico didn't move from the open garden gate. He wanted to be furious, but his good mood prevented it. "Get out of there!"

OneWag stuck his face in lower. The little mongrel had been clever enough to figure out how to slip out the long wooden stick Nico used to close the gate. At least he'd ruined the one rosebush that wasn't doing well. But while digging for what?

"Out, I said."

The dog turned on his back, legs in the air.

Nico stepped into the vegetable garden. "That's not going to work." He noticed OneWag had something in his mouth. He walked in closer. "That better not be one of my vegetables."

No, it was something plastic. He tugged at it. OneWag let go. A sheet of thin plastic. Nico took another step and looked into the hole OneWag had dug. It was full of small pieces of soft, clear plastic. He reached into his pocket and took out his phone.

"Has Vince left for Florence yet?"

"He's leaving now," Perillo said. "Why?"

"Tell him to stop by my place first. My dog dug up something forensics needs to look at."

Taking advantage of the moment, OneWag snaked his way behind Nico, his long ears dragging dirt. It was back to the streets for him.

"What is it?" Perillo asked.

"I think it's the plastic poncho our murderer used to keep the clothes clean. It's been cut up into slivers."

"Bravo, Rocco. I'll send Vince over right away."

"His name is—" Nico started to say, but Perillo had already hung up. By now, OneWag was past the gate, ready to start running.

"Where do you think you're going?" Nico asked. "Come here."

OneWag started to snake his way back, his small body tensed for a kick or a whack with a stick.

"Walk on your paws. You're dirty enough as it is."

OneWag stopped. Nico saw he was trembling and picked him up. He brushed the dirt off his face, his ears, his silky fur. He held the dog tight against his chest to soothe the tremors. He remembered the poor dog had likely experienced some terrible things. "It's okay. You did a good thing this time." He turned OneWag's snout so they were eye to eye. "No more digging in our vegetable garden, okay? You got that?"

OneWag blinked. Nico let go of his snout and got a lick in return. Nico put him down. "Off you go." OneWag trotted out, tail held high, and dropped down on the grass outside the gate.

Vince showed up five minutes later, and he and Nico gathered all the plastic pieces and carefully dropped them in the evidence bag. On the way back to his car, he dropped a cowhide bone for OneWag. "Rocco should join the carabinieri," he called out as he gunned the motor and raced out of the driveway, spitting gravel in every direction.

THE THREE OF THEM sat in a shaded bench in the park facing the carabinieri station. Perillo was in his usual jeans and crisply ironed shirt. Daniele had kept his uniform on. OneWag sat at Nico's feet, chewing on Vince's gift. At three in the afternoon, no one was around. They could speak freely, and Perillo could smoke.

"All right, we think Gianni is the killer," Perillo said. "Now, let's go over the possible scenario. He sees Gerardi staring at Stella at the Coop and confronts him."

"What's more important is that Gerardi sees him with Stella," Daniele adds. "Am I right?"

"Yes. Gianni is a possible conduit to Stella. After Gianni confronts him, Gerardi asks him to meet somewhere else so he can explain his interest in Stella. I don't think he makes his plea outside the Coop with Stella nearby. They meet that day or the next, and Gerardi explains Stella's his daughter, and that she's going to inherit a lot of his money. He begs Gianni to convince Stella to see him. From how she reacted in the Coop, he knows she's scared of him. Maybe he offers Gianni some money. Gianni sets up a fake meeting early in the woods behind Nico's house. Unaware that Gerardi is a dying man, he kills him."

"The woods behind Nico's house," Daniele repeated. "I forgot to tell you, I got the report from the other land experts. No vines are going to grow on the land Gerardi bought."

"Good," Perillo said. "Aldo will be happy to hear he wasn't cheated."

"So Gianni kills Gerardi," Nico said, "and in his mind, Stella inherits, which to Gianni means he won't lose her to some Florentine. She stays in Gravigna, and they get married and live happily ever after on her money. I do think Gianni is arrogant and stupid enough to think that's how it would have worked out."

Perillo stubbed his cigarette out on the sole of his shoe. He was about to toss the butt when he caught Daniele looking at him. "We'll have to wait for forensics to nail him." He pushed the butt into his pocket. Daniele turned away to hide his smile.

"I have a hunch," Nico said. "If it's right, maybe we won't have to wait for forensics. May I make a suggestion?"

"Why do you think I asked you to get involved?" Perillo asked. "Make all the suggestions you want."

"I only have one."

NINETEEN

Gianni showed up at the carabinieri station at seven o'clock sharp, still in jeans and his Ferriello T-shirt. He ignored Perillo behind his desk and walked over to Nico sitting in a chair a few feet away. "Did you talk to Stella?"

Before Nico could answer, Perillo said, "You'll talk to Nico about your love problems later. Normally, I don't allow people not officially involved in an investigation to sit in, but at your request, I made a concession this morning, and I'm making it again tonight. You consider Nico a friend, and I want you to feel comfortable. Now please sit."

Gianni sat in the chair placed in front of Perillo's desk. He was still looking at Nico. "She isn't picking up or answering any of my texts."

"Let us proceed with the matter at hand, please," Perillo said in a cutting voice.

Gianni reluctantly turned to face him.

"Brigadiere Donato has typed out what you stated this morning in your home." On cue, Daniele got up from his post in front of the computer and brought the two typed pages. Perillo read quickly, then summed up the contents. "You stated that you found the hundred-dollar bill at the Coop here in Greve after a man, who turned out to be Roberto Gerardi, stared aggressively at Stella and you confronted him. You did not find any other money. You never saw Gerardi again. At the time of the murder, you were home asleep. Your mother brought you a caffelatte at seven-thirty, as she does every workday morning. You did not kill Roberto Gerardi."

"Yeah, that's what I said."

Perillo held out the pages for Gianni. "Please read it carefully before you sign it. Making a false statement is a serious offense."

Nico noticed the slight tremor of Gianni's hand as he turned the page.

Gianni looked up. "Can I have a pen?"

Nico leaned forward in his chair. "Gianni, before you sign, I think there's some things you need to know."

"Like what?"

"When you confronted Gerardi outside the Coop, did he tell you why he was staring at Stella?"

"He didn't have to. She's beautiful."

"She is, but that's not the reason."

"Who cares what the reason was? I didn't like him looking at her like he was going to swallow her whole."

"He stared because he thought he was looking at his daughter."

"What the fuck are you talking about? No way is Stella his daughter."

"You're right. She isn't, but he thought she was."

Gianni shook his head, laughing. "No, he didn't."

"Why don't you think so?"

Nico's question silenced his laugh. Gianni stared at Nico for a few beats before answering. "Because, well, it makes no sense." His voice was loud. "She's Tilde and Enzo's daughter. She'll inherit the restaurant one day, and I'll help her run it."

Perillo intervened. "Do you know Maria Dorsetti?"

Gianni shot a surprised look at Perillo, as if he'd forgotten he was there. "No." The word came out as a spit.

"She's one of your mother's Friday-night canasta friends." Gianni's mother had told Perillo when he'd gone to the post office to check on Gianni's alibi.

Gianni ran his hands through his hair, his face flushed. "I don't know their names."

"Stella is Tilde and Enzo's daughter," Nico said in the soft, calm voice he'd always found useful. "What's important for you is that Gerardi, who was a millionaire, thought differently. He was dying, and he wanted Stella to inherit most of his wealth, but he needed to talk to her first. He had important things to get off his chest. Unfortunately, he never got to meet her or make official the will that would've given Stella more money than she could ever dream of. He was murdered, so the money goes to his sister, Maria Dorsetti."

Gianni leapt up to his feet, knocking down his chair. "No!" he yelled. "You're lying. You're all lying! Stella had nothing to do with that man."

Nico picked up the chair from the floor and set it back in front of Perillo's desk. "Sit down, Gianni. Yelling is what got you in trouble with Stella. It will get you into even more trouble here. If you sit down, Maresciallo Perillo will show you we're telling the truth."

Perillo pushed the copy of the handwritten will Gerardi had kept in his safe-deposit box across his desk.

"Read it," Nico ordered.

Gianni continued to stand and read, his lips quietly forming the words, eyes darting over each sentence twice. He turned to Nico when he was finished. "I've lost her for good now."

"Stella will want the truth."

"It won't win her back." Gianni slumped down in the chair and, with a grim expression, faced Perillo. "Well, here it is, then."

BY THE TIME NICO got back to Sotto Il Fico, the restaurant was empty of patrons. He walked in with Enzo, who'd just driven his mother home. He called Stella and Tilde in from the kitchen. Alba, their helper, had already left.

"Please, sit down," he said. "I have some sad news."

"Someone died," Tilde said.

"No."

"Thank God." Tilde sat at the corner table and raised her arm to invite Stella to sit next to her. Parental instinct taking over, Enzo sat on Stella's other side. The yellow light from the lamp above them cast a shadow under their eyes.

Nico sat down and faced them with the painful knowledge that he was about to wound his goddaughter's heart.

"Well, what is it?" Stella asked.

"This evening, in Maresciallo Perillo's office, Gianni confessed to Roberto Gerardi's murder."

Tilde gasped. Enzo wound his arm around Stella's shoulders. Stella stared, wide-eyed.

"Why?" she finally asked.

"He says Gerardi's sister offered him a thousand euros, to start with. After she inherited, she was to give him an additional hundred thousand euros."

"He said so?" Enzo asked.

"Yes. And Maria Dorsetti is being questioned right now, I believe."

"She'll deny it, of course. Does Gianni have proof?"

Gianni had kept proof, which he'd played for Perillo—two conversations with Maria recorded on his iPhone.

"I'm sorry, I can't say. I shouldn't even be telling you this much, but Salvatore Perillo is a friend." So much a friend he was going to ask Della Langhe not to mention Stella's name when he talked to the press. Her name would have to come out at the trial, but the wheels of Italian justice turned very slowly, a blessing in this case. It would give Stella time to brace herself, develop some armor against long-kept secrets that weren't hers.

"I understand," Enzo said. "It's hard to believe Gianni's the killer."

Stella shook her head in disbelief. "He killed a man for money?"

"He said he was tired of living with his parents," Nico said.

"He wanted to get his own apartment. He needed a new motorcycle." These weren't Gianni's main reasons, but he didn't want Stella to blame herself.

"It's not my fault, is it?" Stella asked as the lamplight illuminated the tears on her cheeks.

Tilde stroked Stella's hair. "Of course it's not."

"He thinks he did it for me, doesn't he?" Stella said. "That if he had lots of money, I wouldn't go to work in Florence. That I'd stay right here and marry him." Stella wiped her cheeks with the back of her hand. "Poor Gianni. He's so self-involved he can't see reality. I fell in love with him at first because I confused that with strength. Shit! I can't believe this." She slumped forward on the table and buried her head between her arms. No one said anything while she sobbed, then slowly regained her breath. After two or three minutes, she looked up and asked Nico, "What's going to happen to him?"

"He's being driven to a jail in Florence, if he's not already there. Eventually he'll be put on trial."

She sat up. "I'm going to see him."

"Stella!" Tilde cried out. "He's a cold-blooded murderer."

"I'm sorry, Mamma, but I'm going to see Gianni tomorrow."

Enzo squeezed Stella's hand. "You'll need permission. Let me talk to Salvatore, and then I'll drive you."

"I want to go alone."

Tilde covered her mouth to keep from intervening again.

"Please, let me drive you. You'll be upset." Enzo knew that on the way back, Stella's eyes would be too full of tears to see the road. "Thank you, Nico, for telling us about Gianni. I'm sure it wasn't easy, but I'm glad we found out from you and not the carabinieri."

"I've always thought bad news is best delivered by someone in the family," Nico said. As a homicide detective, one of his roles had been the total stranger announcing the death of a family member. He'd hated every second of it.

Tilde stood up. "Thank you," she said, and gave him a quick hug. Stella and Enzo followed suit.

"Good night," Tilde said as she was leaving. "If you're up to it, I could use you for lunch and dinner tomorrow."

"I'll get here early."

"We'll cook together. Food is a great medicine." Tilde linked her arm through Stella's. "Come on, darling. Let's go home."

Nico followed the three of them out of the restaurant with a heavy heart. It would take some time before their family would find peace again, but he would do everything he could to help.

TWENTY

Nico picked the last Sunday in October to celebrate Aldo's grape harvest with a cookout in his garden. Everyone needed a pick-me-up after the shock of Gianni's arrest. Nico had helped Tilde cook countless Tuscan meals in the past month. Now it was time for his Italian family and friends to be introduced to some old-fashioned American food. Not hamburgers and hot dogs, which they could find anywhere. Spare ribs lathered in barbecue sauce, accompanied by cole slaw and potato salad. If nothing else, the food would be a distraction, a conversation piece.

Tilde had resisted closing Sotto Il Fico for one day, even though the tourist season was almost over and fewer diners were coming to eat. To Nico's surprise, Elvira sided with him. "It will be good for Stella," she declared. It was what Nico hoped. Stella had become so withdrawn after her visit to Gianni. Nico suspected she still thought she was somehow to blame for what he'd done. Nico tried to talk to her, but she kept repeating, "I'll be fine, Zio Nico. Don't worry about me, I just need time."

Just days before, Nico had bought a grill, two bags of charcoal and some wooden chips. That morning, Aldo and Arben had driven over two long tables and helped Nico set them up. Tilde and her family arrived early. She brought the restaurant's cutlery, plates and napkins, insisting that plastic and paper had no place in a celebration. Luckily, Nico had already brought down his armchair for Elvira. She let him peck her cheeks, sat down, spread her green flowered housedress over her lap and went to work on the *Settimana Enigmistica* crossword puzzle. Stella, looking too thin but still beautiful, hugged him. He hugged her back tightly. He noticed she'd attached the rabbit's foot he'd given her to her belt. The results of the museum exam hadn't been announced yet. While Tilde and Stella set the tables, Enzo watched Nico light the charcoal and asked what ingredients were in the sauce.

Fourteen people were coming. Only Jimmy and Sandro had declined, as there was no one to staff the café for them, but they'd provided two large thermoses of coffee and refused payment. As more guests arrived, their generosity overwhelmed him. Nico had specifically told everyone to come empty-handed. Not a single person had listened. Luciana brought two aster plants that she put at the center of the tables. Enrico, a basket filled with his olive loaves. Signora Perillo offered a raspberry jam crostata and a smile, as Perillo stood beside her, happy his shy, pretty wife was willing to expose herself to what she would consider a crowd of strangers.

Daniele introduced Rosalba to Nico with blushing cheeks. He had never expected Rosalba to accept his invitation. He was sure her mother would prevent her from going; she had good reason.

"I hope there's enough for everyone," Daniele said as he handed Nico a wide dish filled with tiramisu, made by him in Signora Perillo's kitchen.

Nico thanked him. "A taste is all we need."

Aldo had insisted on supplying the wine. Cinzia brought what she insisted was just an appetizer, "in no way competing with the bones Nico is going to serve us." Her "appetizer" turned out to be a huge bowl of cacio e pepe spaghetti, which was devoured before it had a chance to cool. Nico understood it was Cinzia's payback for declining to celebrate the solution to Gerardi's murder with her and Aldo back when the news had first come out.

Perillo thanked Cinzia repeatedly, overjoyed to coat his stomach with cheese, pepper and spaghetti to protect him from whatever concoction his American friend was going to serve. Signora Perillo, on the other hand, stayed away from Cinzia's Roman dish. To be on the safe side, she had eaten at home.

Nico was tending the grill when Luciana cried out with her usual oversized enthusiasm, "That one's one of your best, Nelli! The very best."

"Thank you," Nelli said, and kept on walking.

Nico turned around. She was coming toward him, dressed in a yellow skirt and a light-blue blouse. It was the first time he had seen her without paint-splattered jeans. She looked lovely. "I'm glad you could come," he said.

"You sound surprised. I told you I'd be here."

"You did." Now he felt stupid.

"You don't take things for granted, then?"

"I don't know if that's true." Stupid, and now embarrassed.

"I brought you this." She handed over a small framed painting of Gravigna as seen from a few miles away. It was the same view he saw each morning on his run. He always stopped to stare at the town while catching his breath before turning back home. He had bought her painting of OneWag at her show two weeks earlier and asked to buy the landscape.

Nelli kissed his cheeks. He brushed his lips quickly against her cheeks. "You said it wasn't for sale."

"I wanted to give it to you."

"Thank you. I don't know what to say."

"There's no need for anything more than a thank-you. Who's the beauty with Daniele?"

"Rosalba Crisani. She sold the charm bracelet to Gerardi."

"Robi got it all wrong, didn't he?"

"What do you mean?"

"She's got his nose and his smile."

"Oh," was all Nico could say.

"I'll leave the painting inside the house, okay?"

"No, prop it up on that olive branch so we can all enjoy it."

His yard had one runaway olive tree from Aldo's grove. He was moved by the gift and wanted to keep looking at it.

Nelli did as he asked and walked away with a wave of her hand. "Ciao, Nico. I'm going for a glass of wine. Want one?"

Nico lifted his untouched glass. "Got it, thanks." He looked over at Rosalba, laughing with Daniele. He couldn't see any resemblance, but then, Nelli had known Gerardi when he'd been Rosalba's age. "Send Perillo over, will you, please?"

She smiled. "Got it."

Perillo made his way over quickly. "I don't know anything about grilling, so I can't help."

"Nelli just told me something."

"Rosalba?"

"You knew?"

"Thanks to Daniele. Last night I walked into my office to get my cigarettes and found Daniele at his computer. The minute I walked in, he shut the screen off. It's not the first time he's done it—I thought he was looking at pornography. He can do that all he wants, but not on the station's computer. This morning I asked him, 'What were you looking at last night?'

"He said, 'Nothing.'

"I told him to show me, and he did, albeit reluctantly. What he was looking at was Rosalba's birth date. She was born six months after Gerardi left. I suspect her mother didn't know she was carrying Gerardi's child when she broke up with him. She would've been only two months pregnant."

"Gerardi should've at least entertained the idea when he found out Irene had a daughter."

"Maybe he had too much anger toward her for rejecting him. Or too much guilt about the rape. A daughter from the terrible thing he did, someone he could compensate, would have made his guilt easier to bear."

"Was Daniele upset you found out?"

"He pretended not to be, but I'm sure he wanted it to be

his secret. There's nothing like knowing someone's else's secret to make you feel close to them."

"Ehi, Nico," Nelli called out by one of the tables. "Gogol's here."

A welcome interruption, Nico thought as he walked over. Enough with anything that had to do with Gerardi. As the Italians said, "Basta!"

Gogol had brought himself and his overcoat, but he'd left behind the powerful cologne. The left-behind cologne was his gift, Nico thought as he welcomed him. Nelli hugged him. OneWag sniffed the hem of his coat and his shoes and waited for the old man to acknowledge him. Perillo introduced Signora Perillo, who smiled with a slight bow of her head.

Gogol grinned at her. "You should be proud of your hero Ulysses, Signora. He took a mad leap and flew with swift wings and the plumes of great desire."

"Is that Dante?" Perillo asked.

"*Purgatorio* Four. My adaptation to fit the circumstances. A good man, Perillo. He brought justice." Gogol turned to Cinzia, who offered him a plate of cooled-down cacio e pepe. He dug into his pockets and showed her he'd brought his own lunch: yesterday's crostini from Sergio's shop. Then he took the plate anyway and dropped it to the ground.

OneWag didn't wait a second to bury his face in the pasta. Cinzia laughed, which brought Stella over. When OneWag looked up at her with bits of melted cheese on his whiskers, Stella laughed too. Then Tilde laughed, Enzo, Nico. Laughter spread down both tables. Daniele, Rosalba, Luciana, Enrico. Only Elvira paid no attention. Five Down was giving her trouble.

Once OneWag was through eating, the plate looked like it had just come out from the dishwasher. Nico hoped his guests would go home this evening with minds clean of the ugliness of murder and stomachs filled to satisfaction. He went back to the grill to work on the spare ribs. As he basted them with the sauce, he listened to the lively chatter amongst friends and family. He felt his body relax. The tension and sadness of the recent years seemed to melt away. He looked up at Nelli's painting of Gravigna, perched on a tree branch, and knew he was home.

ACKNOWLEDGMENTS

Writing this story has been a joy, thanks to the many friends I made while researching in Tuscany. They welcomed me and answered a flood of questions with smiles on their faces. A huge grazie to Lara Beccatini, who first introduced me to the ways of a small Tuscan town and stayed close throughout. Grazie to the team at Il Vinaio in Panzano: Paolo Gaeta, Teresa Barba, Brian Garcilazo, Carolina Gemini and Manjola Kurti. They fed me their wonderful food and filled my glass with excellent wine while I took notes. I am grateful to Ioletta Como and Andrea Sommaruga for trying to teach me the complicated wine business, Lorenzo Guarducci for answering my questions about guns, Bibil Vangjeli and Gianluca De Santi for feeding me breakfast every morning and introducing me to the local Maresciallo dei Carabinieri. Maresciallo Giovanni Serra's help is a priceless gift, and I send him a thousand grazie.

I am lucky to have a wonderful New York team of readers who give me advice and spot my countless typing mistakes. A heartfelt thank you to Barry Greenspon, Barbara Lane, Rose Scotch, Elaine Gilbert and Willa Morris.

I am grateful to Amara Hoshijo for her intelligent editing, and I am proud, once again, to be a Soho Press author.

To my patient husband Stuart, my love and trust.

Continue reading for a preview of the next Tuscan mystery

THE BITTER
TASTE OF MURDER

ONE

Gravigna, a small town in the Chianti hills of Tuscany
A Tuesday in June, 7:50 A.M.

Ex-homicide detective Nico Doyle parked his red Fiat 500 under a cloudless sky that promised another hot day and followed his dog across the deserted main piazza. It was too early in the day for tourists. The tables and chairs outside Trattoria da Gino wouldn't be set up for another two hours. The benches where the four pensioners sat daily to exchange their news were empty. In the far corner, Bar All'Angolo, open since 6 A.M., would offer him breakfast.

OneWag rushed into the café through the open door, nose immediately canvassing the floor. Nico followed, scanning the tables. There were only a few customers. Last week at this hour, he had found the place full of students chattering with mouths full of cornetti, their colorful backpacks getting in everyone's way. School had since ended, and they were now having breakfast at home. The few locals who didn't have to travel far for work were standing at the bar counter with espresso cups in their hands, talking among themselves.

Sandro, one of the café's two owners, was manning the cash register as always. He looked up.

"Ciao, Nico."

Some locals turned to nod their hellos.

"Salve," Nico replied to all. He walked to the cash register. "How goes it?"

"So far the morning is good," Sandro replied with a smile. He was a good-looking, lanky man somewhere in his mid-forties with a small gold stud shining in one ear. "It's still cool enough, but get your fan out. We're going to fry today."

"I've been trying to convince him to air-condition the place," his husband Jimmy said. Jimmy's job was to work the huge, very hot stainless-steel espresso machine at the far end of the bar and the oven that baked the most delicious cornetti this side of Florence.

Sandro shook his head. "Costs too much. Besides, it's bad for you. Freezes your guts like that ice water Americans like."

Jimmy shrugged and turned to start Nico's Americano. There was no need to order, as Nico always had the same thing. While Nico paid Sandro, OneWag's nails clicked back and forth over the tiles, his snout a periscope sweeping left and right. The café floor was usually scattered with sugar-laced crumbs. After two rounds across the room, the dog sat and barked a protest.

"Sorry, Rocco," Sandro said. "I swept. I didn't want those floppy ears of yours to get dirty." The Italians called Nico's dog Rocco. They claimed OneWag was too hard to pronounce and that an Italian dog should have an Italian name. The dog wisely answered to both with his signature one wag, which usually brought good things. In this case, a day-old cornetto tossed by Sandro and caught on the fly.

"Bravo!" Sandro clapped.

"No more, please," Nico said. The morning the small stray had led him to a murdered man, he'd been a skinny, dirty runt. Nine months later, his long white and orange coat was clean and fluffy, and his stomach looked as if it held a full litter.

Nico walked over to his usual table by the open French doors and sat down, as he had nearly every day since he'd moved to his late wife Rita's hometown of Gravigna a year ago. In that time, he had slowly made new friends. Gogol was the first, a man who lived in a reality all his own. A good man with an incredible memory. Gogol's ability to quote every stanza of Dante's *Divine Comedy* was what had first attracted Nico to him. Having breakfast with him became another part of this morning routine.

The old man stood by the door, wrapped in his strong cologne and the overcoat he wore in winter and summer. It had first earned him the nickname of Gogol, after the Russian writer whose most famous story was titled "The Overcoat." His face was a maze of wrinkles, his long hair clean and brushed. The old-age home where he lived took good care of him. His coat had been recently mended. "Another day to live through, amico," he said to Nico.

"Let's live it well, Gogol." Nico stood up and held out a chair. "I'm glad to see you."

Gogol shuffled to the table and took the chair closest to the open door, minimizing the effect of his cologne. He held up the two crostini he'd gotten from the butcher around the corner. "Our friend made them for me especially. A man with a noble heart." Gogol placed the two squares of bread carefully at the center. "'It pleases me, whatever pleases you.'"

"*Paradiso.*"

Gogol coughed a laugh. "*Inferno*, amico."

Trying to guess which *Divina Commedia* entry the quotes came from was a new game Gogol had suggested, hoping Nico would study the poetry. Back in the Bronx, Nico had once had his ears filled with Dante by his wife, who also loved quoting the Tuscan poet. He found old Italian too difficult; it reminded him of struggling through Chaucer in high school. Modern Italian he could handle pretty well, thanks to Rita's lessons and Berlitz.

Nico took the salame crostino, knowing Gogol liked the lard best. He rarely guessed the quote. "It sounded too nice for *Inferno*."

Gogol bit into his lard crostino, swallowed quickly and said,

"I begin to abandon hope of you ever climbing the slope. Also from *Inferno*. My adaptation for this occasion."

"Why abandon hope on such a beautiful day?" asked a voice with a Neapolitan accent.

Nico turned around. Maresciallo Salvatore Perillo stood outside the open French doors, chatting with a group of cyclists about to take off for the steep hills of Chianti. Perillo had been one of them until last year, having even won a few races. He was a short, stocky man with shiny black hair beginning to gray at the temples, a chiseled handsome face with large, dark liquid eyes, thick lips and an aquiline nose. He was out of uniform as usual, wearing jeans, a perfectly pressed blue linen shirt and, despite the heat, his beloved leather jacket flung over his shoulder.

Nico smiled, glad to see the man who had become a good friend since involving Nico in a murder investigation last September. They hadn't seen each other or talked in the last week. The maresciallo's carabinieri station was in Greve, nineteen kilometers away.

Nico pushed back a chair. "Join us."

Perillo stepped into the café, looked at Gogol hunched over the table and hesitated. "Gogol, am I welcome?"

Gogol grinned, showing his brown teeth. "You were Nico's Virgil through last year's journey into hell, or perhaps he was yours. Whichever it is, friends of Nico are welcome today. Tomorrow perhaps not."

"I'll keep that in mind." Perillo sat down next to Nico. Gogol made him uncomfortable. His overpowering cologne didn't help. The man was crazy, mentally disabled or putting on an act to get attention. Perillo eased his discomfort by bending down to pet Rocco, who was sniffing his suede ankle boots.

Sandro brought over two Americani and two whole wheat cornetti straight out of the oven, a Bar All'Angolo specialty. "Espresso for you, Salvatore?"

Perillo raised two fingers, then a thumb for his double espresso to be corrected with grappa. The inclusion of grappa meant things weren't going well with the maresciallo.

"That bad?" Nico asked before biting into his cornetto. The salame crostino, he pushed Gogol's way. The old man always ended up eating both.

"I will happily tell you." Perillo looked in Jimmy's direction, eager for his espresso. "No murders, may God be praised."

Sandro hurried over with the double espresso. Perillo thanked him and emptied the cup with one swallow. "Yesterday, Signor Michele Mantelli drove into Greve, found that the parking spots in Piazza Matteoti were occupied, parked his Jaguar in the middle of piazza, locked it and went off to lunch. In the center of the town! Can you believe it? There's perfectly good parking nearby. Of course, one of my men called the car removal service. What followed was Mantelli stomping into the station preceded by a hailstorm of insults directed at me. It was clear I had no brains, I didn't know who he was, headquarters in Florence would hear about this, I would be demoted and so on. You would not believe the fury of the man."

"Who is he?" Nico asked.

"A ball breaker. Michele Mantelli is considered a famous critic of Italian wines, said to have the power to make or ruin a new vintage. He runs a very successful biannual magazine called *Vino Veritas*, written in Italian and English and distributed globally. Also a blog, which he posts to monthly for thousands of readers. The pied piper and his rats, I say. If they only knew he was the head rat."

"I'm sorry he's gotten to you. Where's he from?"

"Milan, but he has an old villa in Montefioralle."

"Words aren't necessary," Gogol said. "The face shows the color of the heart."

"Well said, Gogol. My wife considers him very handsome." Perillo sniffed. "I suspect he's also a smooth talker when not shouting insults."

"I haven't seen Ivana since last year's barbecue. How is she?" Nico asked.

"She's fine. She was in the piazza getting bread."

Gogol chuckled to himself. "'The eyes of Ivana were all intent on him.' A very bad adaptation of *Paradiso*, canto one. Amusing nonetheless."

Perillo didn't look amused. He sat back in his chair and closed his eyes.

"Refreshed?" Nico asked after a minute of silence had gone by.

"It's a drug," said Perillo.

"The grappa or the coffee?"

"Love is a drug," Gogol announced. Clasping his hands on the rim of the table, he slowly stood. "The only woman I love is my mother. 'Watching her, I changed inside.' No point in guessing. Tomorrow, if I live." Gogol's mother had died when he was just a boy.

Nico stood up. "Tomorrow. I'm counting on it."

Gogol stepped through the open French door, his powerful scent leaving with him.

"That was abrupt," Perillo said.

"I think Gogol knows he annoyed you with that quote about your wife."

"He didn't, though." Perillo had mostly been annoyed at his wife's comment about Mantelli. *"That man is very pleasant to look at, don't you think?"* she'd asked with a smile on her face. He'd answered her with a long kiss. Ah, yes, that reminded him of why he'd come to the café.

"How are Aldo and Cinzia?" Perillo asked.

Aldo Ferri, who owned the Ferriello vineyard, rented the small run-down stone farmhouse at the edge of his olive grove to Nico. "Fine. They invited me over for dinner last week. Spaghetti all'arrabbiata. Just as good as Cinzia's carbonara." Nico bunched his fingers to his lips and released them with a kiss. "I convinced her to give me the recipe."

"You can get a recipe for that from any cookbook."

"Maybe, but I'd use hers."

"Has there been any tension between Cinzia and Aldo?" Gogol's comment—*"Love is a drug"*—brought back the scene he had witnessed last night. Luckily, he hadn't been seen. Perillo felt a sudden pang of remorse. Should he tell Nico? But maybe there was an explanation for what had happened. It would only be spreading malicious gossip.

"Not that I've seen." Nico watched Perillo's expression carefully. "Why are you asking about them?"

A couple walked in and ordered from Sandro in French-tinted Italian. Perillo heard laughter and turned to look at them. They were hugging, mussing up each other's hair.

"No reason. Just that I haven't seen them around in some time." He stood up. "I'd better get back to the station. Say hello to Tilde and Enzo for me. Tell them not to work you too hard at the restaurant. Be well."

Nico stood too. "I'm not working Thursday night. Any chance of dinner?" It was clear his friend was holding something back. Maybe he was having problems with his wife? Getting out of the house for an evening might help. Besides, he missed Perillo's company.

"Maybe. If no one does anything stupid or cruel. I'll let you know." Perillo walked over to the counter and paid Sandro for his corrected double espresso.

Nico waved goodbye to Sandro and Jimmy and, with OneWag running ahead, went to his car. Tuesday was laundry day, part of the routine he had set up for himself when he first moved to Gravigna. Back in the Bronx, he had made fun of Rita's need to follow a routine that wavered only when she fell sick. At the beginning of his new Italian life, he'd found that maintaining a routine helped him find his footing. Now that he was fully settled, it was possible he kept it up out of laziness.

There was no need for OneWag to join Nico in the car. The dog had his routine down pat. Nico would find him waiting in the heart of the medieval part of town, at the aptly named laundromat Sta A Te, which meant, "It's up to you."

Two hours later, his freshly cleaned clothes neatly folded in the back seat of his car, Nico started his work for Tilde and Enzo. His first duty was to pick up the restaurant's daily supply of bread from the grocer, Enrico. With the bread, Enrico gave him one of his coveted olive loaves and a ham bone. "The loaf is for you, the bone is for the little one. It's too hot to use it for soup. Where is he?"

"Thanks. He's gone to visit Nelli at her studio. She spoils him." Nico reached for his wallet.

Enrico raised his hand in protest. He was a small man with a pale face and thinning hair. "Friends pay for two loaves—one, no. Bring Rocco the next time. He's a good dog."

"He loves you."

Enrico chuckled. "He loves my prosciutto. The best in the area, if I do say so myself."

"Agreed. See you later." Nico lifted the large paper sack and turned to go.

"Watch out on the street. Some maniac zoomed past here a few minutes ago in his fancy car. Almost ran down one of my customers."

"I'll be careful." Nico looked down the slope. Only a few people and a struggling cyclist were working their way up the steep hill.

Hugging the bag of bread, Nico climbed the rest of the way. At the top, diagonal to the Santa Agnese church, stood Sotto Il Fico. A white Jaguar was parked in front, fully blocking the entrance.

Nico squeezed through the narrow space the car had left and called out, "Buongiorno."

"Nothing good about it," the restaurant's owner grumbled.

Elvira fanned herself with a large black lace fan she claimed was a gift from a Spanish admirer. The truth, according to Tilde, was that she'd bought it at the monthly flea market in Panzano.

"I'm sorry to hear that." Nico dropped the bread bag on one of the five indoor tables. He was used to her bad moods by now. "Is your arthritis acting up?"

She answered with a snort. A sixty-three-year-old widow with pitch-black dyed hair, a wrinkled face, a small pointed nose and pale blue eyes as sharp as a hawk's, Elvira oversaw the goings-on of her restaurant from an old gilded armchair in the front room. Today she was wearing a blue and green housedress, which meant it was Tuesday. She had seven, one for each day of the week.

"Where's Enzo?" Her son was in charge of managing the bar and the cash register and cutting the bread. Tilde, Enzo's wife and Rita's cousin, cooked the meals.

"He's on the terrace with that fraud who calls himself the world's best wine critic!"

"Michele Mantelli is here?"

"Yes, he marched in not ten minutes ago. If he doesn't remove his car in the next ten, I'm calling the carabinieri."

"He's already had a run-in with them."

"Good. He can have another."

Nico leaned toward the open door that led to the terrace. Mantelli was sitting in the shade of the huge fig tree that gave the restaurant its name and fame. All he could see was a crumpled white linen suit that matched a full head of long white hair. The man's face was hidden by Enzo, who was hovering over him.

"That man insisted on seeing our full wine list," Elvira said. "Enzo was just making me another espresso."

"I can make that for you, if you want," Nico offered. Enzo had taught him how to use the espresso machine behind the bar.

"No, I'll wait. Americans don't have the touch. That fraud claims he can teach us which wines to sell. 'I offer my expertise for free. I will mention you in my blog.' Enzo was beaming like a child being offered a yo-yo, showering him with thanks. Even offered him a free lunch!"

Tilde popped her head out of the kitchen. "A yo-yo won't get you anywhere with a kid these days. You need an iPhone." Tilde liked to correct her mother-in-law whenever she could. Elvira, possessive of her son, was often unkind to her. "Mantelli is a revered wine critic and will give Enzo some good suggestions," Tilde went on.

"Pfui. Enzo knows perfectly well what wines to offer. We taste each new vintage together and decide according to the price our clients can afford."

This meant, Nico knew, that Elvira decided. He pulled out a chair and sat next to her. "There's nothing wrong with hearing him out, is there?" She was at times unpleasant, but he couldn't help admiring her toughness. "And being mentioned in his blog has to be good for business, don't you think?"

Another snort in response. Elvira picked up the magazine on her lap and slipped on the glasses that hung from a chain on her neck. "I read from *Vino Veritas:* 'The 2015 ColleVerde Riserva offers hints of fruit, spices, scorched earth, espresso beans and herbs.'" She threw the magazine on the floor. "Scorched earth indeed! Who wants to taste spices or rosemary in their wine? Nonsense is what it is."

Nico picked up the magazine.

"Nico," Tilde called out. "You're needed in the kitchen."

"Throw that in the trash," Elvira commanded as he made his way to the kitchen.

"Coming." Nico took the magazine with him and, once out of sight, slipped it in his pocket.

Tilde was bent over the scarred marble counter, quickly shaping golf-ball-sized ground pork, egg, Parmigiano and ricotta meatballs in her hands. A long white apron covered her flowered dress. Her usual red cotton scarf enveloped thick chestnut brown hair.

Nico kissed one cheek. In Italy, it was usually both cheeks, but her other one was out of reach. "What can I do?"

"Take over for Enzo. Mantelli has him in his grips, and I need Alba back here."

Nico turned. Alba was wiping mushrooms clean at the other end of the counter. A sliced mushroom salad with apples and walnuts was one of the restaurants signature dishes. "Ciao, I didn't see you there."

"I'll kiss you later." Alba laughed. A pretty, round-faced woman in her early forties, she had never told Tilde her real name. She was Albanian, and so she said Alba was a logical choice. She also liked that the word meant 'dawn' in Italian. Coming here was for her the start of a new life. She'd fled the violence in Kosovo against ethnic Albanians and found her way to Gravigna. Her story was now a happy one. A good Italian man fell in love with her, and she with him. They married, and now she worked full-time at the restaurant, taking Stella, Tilde and Enzo's daughter's, place. She told everyone she met how blessed she felt.

Alba peered out the small window that looked out onto the terrace. "He's very handsome."

"And arrogant." Tilde rolled the meatballs with light fingers on a plate filled with flour, then dropped them gently in a hot sauté pan coated with oil. Once they achieved a nice brown crust, they would end up cooking in tomato sauce for thirty minutes. Eaten on their own or surrounded by buttered farro, they were heavenly. "Please, Nico, go out there and set the tables. Listen to what Mantelli is saying. I don't trust that man."

"You know him?"

"Just met him. Let's just say he gives me an odd feeling."

"Makes your nose itch?"

"Something like that."

Nico went back to the front room and filled a tray with plates, silverware and the clean cloth napkins Elvira folded every morning. She was now absorbed in a crossword puzzle in the *Settimana Enigmistica*. "Don't let Enzo make that man any promises," she muttered as he passed by.

"Of course," Nico said.

Mantelli was now sitting with Enzo at a corner table. Behind him under an overcast sky was the beautiful view of rows of vines spreading toward the horizon. In front of him was a half-empty glass of red wine and an open bottle. Enzo's own glass was empty.

Nico started setting the first table when he noticed a woman at the far end of the terrace fanning herself with a menu. He was struck by her beauty. She was dressed in tight white slacks and a spaghetti strap white top that hugged her torso. Long blond hair in a thick ponytail hung over one tanned shoulder. Huge sunglasses crowned her head. She looked very young, twenty at most.

Mantelli noticed Nico staring and waved him over. "Never mind Loredana." His voice was surprisingly high and thin. "Come taste this excellent wine. Luca Verdini started his vineyard only ten years ago. Makes him a novice, but his 2015 and 2016 riservas are jewels, and his regular wines are excellent. Verdini is getting a lot of attention these days, thanks to me. I spotted him first two years ago and wrote him up in my blog and *Vino Veritas*. You know it?"

"I'm afraid not," Nico said.

"Ah, you're American. Well, the Robert Parker people rated him a 93. I give him a 95. You must help me convince Enzo to stock it."

Mantelli poured two fingers' worth of the riserva into Enzo's empty glass.

Enzo took a sip, swished the wine in his mouth and swallowed. "It is excellent," Enzo said, "but his wines are too expensive. We're not a three-Michelin-star restaurant. We serve simple food."

"Great wines will turn simple food into manna," Mantelli said. "Drinking great wines helps to better understand the land and its people. Besides, Verdini is eager to spread the word about his wines. I'm sure he'd be willing to give you a discount." The wine critic added a splash of wine to another glass on the table and held it out to Nico. "Please, try."

Nico took the glass and slowly rolled a sip around his tongue as he'd seen Enzo do. He felt like an idiot, but he didn't want to look like a country bumpkin in front of this man. He swallowed. The wine burned the back of his throat. Scorched earth indeed, not that he knew what that tasted like. "Excellent, thank you." He put the glass back down on the table. "I have to get back to work." Enzo shot him a glance. "I'll need your help, too," Nico said, guessing Enzo had had enough of being lectured to.

Mantelli stood up, shook down his trousers and readjusted his jacket. Underneath, he wore a blue and white striped T-shirt, the kind Venetian gondoliers favored. A tanned hand brushed back thick wavy white hair that fell below his ears. He was tall, with wide shoulders and slender hips. A swimmer's body. A face soaked by sun. A strong broad jaw, the straight nose Roman statues were known for, full lips, heavy black eyebrows that looked dyed, and black eyes to match. He was somewhere in his fifties, Nico thought. And yes, noticeably handsome.

"I have work to do too," Mantelli said. "I think I've given you enough guidance for now. Thank you for your offer of lunch. I'll take a rain check and leave the bottle so you can enjoy the rest of the wine. You'll get hooked and buy, I know you will. And I'll see what I can do about a discount. Verdini owes me." He shook hands with Enzo. "Come, Loredana," Mantelli ordered without so much as a glance at her. He offered his hand to Nico, who shook it reluctantly.

"Not a nice man," Nico said as Mantelli and Loredana disappeared into the front room.

"Nice or not," Enzo said, "I'll have to order at least two cases." He filled his glass with the expensive wine and took a long sip.

"Because of his blog?"

"He can give our restaurant a big boost."

"Doesn't that feel a little like going along with blackmail?"

Enzo shrugged. "It's business. He probably gets a cut from Verdini and some of the others he praises in his magazine. I'll tell you one—"

Elvira's voice interrupted Enzo. She was giving Mantelli a piece of her mind about the car.

"You are correct, Signora," Mantelli answered in his high-pitched voice. "I am incorrigible, but please consider me a friend. Arrivederci."

If Elvira replied, Nico and Enzo didn't hear it.

Nico walked over to another table and set down the sheets of butcher paper the restaurant used for mats. "You were telling me something."

Enzo finished his glass and slapped the cork back in the bottle. "Your landlord, Aldo, I guess he doesn't play the game. Mantelli had some nasty things to say about Ferriello wines. 'Totally overrated.' 'Should be selling at half the price, if at all.' He said I should take Aldo's wines off my list."

"What did you say?"

"I said I trusted his judgment."

Nico looked up in surprise. "Ferriello wines are very good."

"I agree. Don't worry; I have no intention of dropping a single one of Aldo's wines from my list."

"I'm glad to hear that."

"Give me the tray, Nico. I'll finish setting the tables. I'm sure Tilde can use your help."

Nico handed over the tray and the mats. "Thanks. I have a food idea she might like."

"As long as it doesn't cost too much."

"Bread covered with scamorza and pancetta, then broiled. Sound good?"

"Yes, but Tilde's the judge."

"It will keep people drinking."

Other Titles in the Soho Crime Series

STEPHANIE BARRON
(Jane Austen's England)
Jane and the Twelve Days
* of Christmas*
Jane and the Waterloo Map
Jane and the Year Without a Summer

F.H. BATACAN
(Philippines)
Smaller and Smaller Circles

JAMES R. BENN
(World War II Europe)
Billy Boyle
The First Wave
Blood Alone
Evil for Evil
Rag & Bone
A Mortal Terror
Death's Door
A Blind Goddess
The Rest Is Silence
The White Ghost
Blue Madonna
The Devouring
Solemn Graves
When Hell Struck Twelve
The Red Horse
Road of Bones

CARA BLACK
(Paris, France)
Murder in the Marais
Murder in Belleville
Murder in the Sentier
Murder in the Bastille
Murder in Clichy
Murder in Montmartre
Murder on the Ile Saint-Louis
Murder in the Rue de Paradis
Murder in the Latin Quarter
Murder in the Palais Royal
Murder in Passy
Murder at the Lanterne Rouge
Murder Below Montparnasse
Murder in Pigalle
Murder on the Champ de Mars
Murder on the Quai
Murder in Saint-Germain
Murder on the Left Bank
Murder in Bel-Air
Murder at the Porte de Versailles

Three Hours in Paris

HENRY CHANG
(Chinatown)
Chinatown Beat
Year of the Dog
Red Jade
Death Money
Lucky

BARBARA CLEVERLY
(England)
The Last Kashmiri Rose
Strange Images of Death
The Blood Royal
Not My Blood
A Spider in the Cup
Enter Pale Death
Diana's Altar

Fall of Angels
Invitation to Die

COLIN COTTERILL
(Laos)
The Coroner's Lunch
Thirty-Three Teeth
Disco for the Departed
Anarchy and Old Dogs
Curse of the Pogo Stick
The Merry Misogynist
Love Songs from a Shallow Grave
Slash and Burn
The Woman Who Wouldn't Die
Six and a Half Deadly Sins
I Shot the Buddha
The Rat Catchers' Olympics
Don't Eat Me
The Second Biggest Nothing
The Delightful Life of
* a Suicide Pilot*

GARRY DISHER
(Australia)
The Dragon Man
Kittyhawk Down
Snapshot
Chain of Evidence
Blood Moon
Whispering Death
Signal Loss

Wyatt
Port Vila Blues
Fallout

Under the Cold Bright Lights

TERESA DOVALPAGE
(Cuba)
Death Comes in through
* the Kitchen*
Queen of Bones
Death under the Perseids

Death of a Telenovela Star
* (A Novella)*

DAVID DOWNING
(World War II Germany)
Zoo Station
Silesian Station
Stettin Station
Potsdam Station
Lehrter Station
Masaryk Station
Wedding Station

(World War I)
Jack of Spies
One Man's Flag
Lenin's Roller Coaster
The Dark Clouds Shining

Diary of a Dead Man on Leave

AGNETE FRIIS
(Denmark)
What My Body Remembers
The Summer of Ellen

TIMOTHY HALLINAN
(Thailand)
The Fear Artist
For the Dead
The Hot Countries
Fools' River
Street Music

(Los Angeles)
Crashed
Little Elvises
The Fame Thief
Herbie's Game
King Maybe
Fields Where They Lay
Nighttown
Rock of Ages

METTE IVIE HARRISON
(Mormon Utah)
The Bishop's Wife
His Right Hand
For Time and All Eternities

FUMINORI NAKAMURA CONT.
Cult X
My Annihilation

STUART NEVILLE
(Northern Ireland)
The Ghosts of Belfast
Collusion
Stolen Souls
The Final Silence
Those We Left Behind
So Say the Fallen

The Traveller & Other Stories
House of Ashes

(Dublin)
Ratlines

KWEI QUARTEY
(Ghana)
Murder at Cape Three Points
Gold of Our Fathers
Death by His Grace

The Missing American
Sleep Well, My Lady

QIU XIAOLONG
(China)
Death of a Red Heroine
A Loyal Character Dancer
When Red Is Black

MARCIE R. RENDON
(Minnesota's Red River Valley)
Murder on the Red River
Girl Gone Missing

JAMES SALLIS
(New Orleans)
The Long-Legged Fly
Moth
Black Hornet
Eye of the Cricket
Bluebottle
Ghost of a Flea

Sarah Jane

JOHN STRALEY
(Sitka, Alaska)
The Woman Who Married a Bear
The Curious Eat Themselves
The Music of What Happens
Death and the Language
  of Happiness
The Angels Will Not Care
Cold Water Burning
Baby's First Felony
So Far and Good

(Cold Storage, Alaska)
The Big Both Ways
Cold Storage, Alaska
What Is Time to a Pig?

AKIMITSU TAKAGI
(Japan)
The Tattoo Murder Case
Honeymoon to Nowhere
The Informer

CAMILLA TRINCHIERI
(Tuscany)
Murder in Chianti
The Bitter Taste of Murder

HELENE TURSTEN
(Sweden)
Detective Inspector Huss
The Torso
The Glass Devil
Night Rounds
The Golden Calf
The Fire Dance
The Beige Man
The Treacherous Net
Who Watcheth
Protected by the Shadows

Hunting Game
Winter Grave
Snowdrift

An Elderly Lady Is Up
  to No Good
An Elderly Lady Must Not
  Be Crossed

ILARIA TUTI
(Italy)
Flowers over the Inferno
The Sleeping Nymph

JANWILLEM VAN DE WETERING
(Holland)
Outsider in Amsterdam
Tumbleweed
The Corpse on the Dike
Death of a Hawker
The Japanese Corpse
The Blond Baboon
The Maine Massacre
The Mind-Murders
The Streetbird
The Rattle-Rat
Hard Rain
Just a Corpse at Twilight
Hollow-Eyed Angel
The Perfidious Parrot
The Sergeant's Cat:
  Collected Stories

JACQUELINE WINSPEAR
(1920s England)
Maisie Dobbs
Birds of a Feather

Mary Kassian speaks with rare insight, clarity, directness, and grace as she challenges the prevailing winds of our culture. She paints portraits of two contrasting kinds of women and sets forth a vision that calls women out of their dysfunction, pain, and deception, to walk in the light of God's redeeming truth and grace.

This book is extremely important, timely, and needed—I cannot think of any category of women (or men, for that matter) who could not benefit greatly from reading it and grappling with these critical issues. A "must-read" for women who desire to honor God with their lives and to influence others to do the same.

—Nancy Leigh DeMoss, author, host of Revive Our Hearts radio

This is a wonderful book with amazing insight into the hearts of women (and men!) who feel pressured by today's "wild" culture—and also deep, spiritual insight into the Bible's wisdom regarding the beauty of true womanhood as God created it to be.

—Wayne Grudem, Ph.D.
Research Professor of Theology and Biblical Studies
Phoenix Seminary, Phoenix, Arizona

Mary Kassian has done it again. With aplomb, grace, and wisdom, she sets the right course through some of the most treacherous and dangerous issues of our day. With just the right balance of truth and understanding, Mary calls girls and young women to a bold, strong, and biblical model of true womanhood—an understanding that honors God and shows the world a counter-revolutionary model of genuine womanhood. When Mary Kassian writes a book, women can count on sound advice and biblical wisdom from a gracious friend.

—R. Albert Mohler Jr., President
The Southern Baptist Theological Seminary

So much of life is broken because our standards come from the world rather than from the precepts of God's Word. Our young people are living in the rubble of destruction and need rescuing from the earthquake of the consequences of not building their lives on truth.

Mary's book *Girls Gone Wise . . . in a World Gone Wild* is a needed book for our times. May it grab our attention and drive us to His Word where Mary will take us.

—Kay Arthur, CEO and cofounder Precept Ministries International
Author of *The Truth about Sex: What the World Won't Tell You and What God Wants You To Know,* and *Return to the Garden: Embracing God's Design for Sexuality*

Girls today are growing up in a culture where "bad" has become the new "good." The glamorization of bad behavior among young women has become the new norm and left in its wake a tremendous amount of fallout and misery. Mary has penned a handbook for reversing the tide of the girls-gone-wild trend and replacing it with a new rank of girls-gone-wise. I can't wait to recommend this book!

—Vicki Courtney, bestselling author of *Your Girl* and *5 Conversations You Must Have With Your Daughter*

Many women today are eager for mentors. While a book is never a substitute for a real, live mentor, this one does connect women everywhere to the wise counsel of Mary Kassian. And we should heed her winsome, culturally relevant, and biblically sound words in *Girls Gone Wise*. This book provides an accurate gauge of the current feminine perspective in Western culture and contrasts it with the eternal wisdom found in Scripture. Easy-to-read, humble, humorous, and thoroughly sound, *Girls Gone Wise* is a book both long-time believers and new converts will benefit from reading. Highly recommended!

—Carolyn McCulley, author, *Radical Womanhood: Feminine Faith in a Feminist World*

This book sounds a clear and much-needed message regarding the ethics of biblical womanhood. Mary Kassian's energy and passion make it a readable book. Her eye-opening contrast between the wise and the wild make it a convicting book. Her faithfulness to Scripture makes it a compelling book.

—Susan Hunt, author, consultant for women's ministries for the Presbyterian Church in America

Girl's Gone Wise is a crucial message for such a time as this. In a culture where true femininity is in danger of extinction, young women desperately to catch a vision for God's pattern. Mary Kassian's relevant, practical, and biblically based insights give today's young women a clear, inspiring blueprint for the only version of womanhood that truly fulfills—God's version.

—Eric and Leslie Ludy, bestselling authors of *When God Writes Your Love Story*

Mary Kassian will help you navigate the overexposure we experience every day to messages that call us to be anything but what God created us to be as women. Her message will make you wise to that, and hungry to be what God intended. I think this would be a great book for moms to read with their teen girls. Though Mary navigates critical worldview issues and strong theology, she does it with a conversational and contemporary note in her writing voice. You'll never realize how hard you're thinking. It'll be too much fun!

—Dannah Gresh, coauthor, *Lies Young Women Believe*, founder, Pure Freedom

MOODY PUBLISHERS
CHICAGO

Editor: Cheryl Dunlop
Interior Design: Ragont Design
Cover Design: Faceout Studio—formerly The DesignWorks Group, Inc.
Cover Image: RF Shutterstock and Fotolia
Cover Photo: JDS Portraits

Library of Congress Cataloging-in-Publication Data

Kassian, Mary A.
    Girls gone wise in a world gone wild / by Mary A. Kassian.
        p. cm.
    Includes bibliographical references.
    ISBN 978-0-8024-5154-5
    1. Christian women—Religious life. I. Title.
    BV4527.K37 2010
    248.8'43--dc22

                                        2009049616

We hope you enjoy this book from Moody Publishers. Our goal is to provide high-
quality, thought-provoking books and products that connect truth to your real needs
and challenges. For more information on other books and products written and produced
from a biblical perspective, go to www.moodypublishers.com or write to:

Moody Publishers
820 N. LaSalle Boulevard
Chicago, IL 60610

3 5 7 9 10 8 6 4

Printed in the United States of America

for my k-pod,
the favorite tunes of my life

Brent
Clark & Jacqueline
Matthew
Jonathan

CONTENTS

WILD THING

"Wild thing . . . you make my heart sing.
You make everything groovy."

—The Troggs, 1966[1]

"Look carefully then how you walk,
not as unwise [wild] but as wise."

—Ephesians 5:15

From women exposing themselves for a camera crew on a beach in Florida, to cardio striptease classes in Los Angeles, to the infamous Manhattan Cake Parties, girls have gone wild! Many things that were once reviled as shameful—*Playboy*, strippers, wet T-shirt contests, and a porn aesthetic—are now embraced by young women as symbols of personal empowerment and sexual liberation. Videographer Joe Francis has built a multimillion-dollar empire on the backs (or I should say breasts) of college-age women who are willing to go wild on camera for the sake of a dare and a T-shirt. His multimedia *Girls Gone Wild* venture has become a household name and a distinguishing phenomenon of popular culture.

But as shocking as their behavior is, the phenomenon of girls going wild isn't really new. A generation ago, a British rock band called the Troggs paid tribute to the groovy, peacenik, hippy-beaded, flower-powered, grass-smoking, love-making Girl-Gone-Wild of that era, with what *Rolling Stone* magazine ranked as one of the five hundred greatest songs of all time: "Wild Thing." The fortuitous invention of the birth control pill ensured that she could be a Wild Thing and hook up in the back of a Volkswagen van without worrying about the usual risks of pregnancy.

The Girl-Gone-Wild of the 1920s was the flapper. She smoked, drank, danced, and had a giddy, risqué attitude. She bobbed her hair short, wore makeup, and went to petting parties. In an earlier era, the Girl-Gone Wild was the "bad girl" who crossed boundaries of propriety and wore clothing that was unencumbered by bustles, layers, or corsets. Her loose clothing and hair signified a "loosened-up" sexual standard. And let's not forget the Girl-Gone-Wild of the first century, who spent days getting her hair woven into intricate beaded creations that would rival the outrageous 'dos seen on models on the runway in Paris.

So does that mean that every woman who adopts the latest fashion is a Girl-Gone-Wild? And if we could set up a time-travel machine and transport a Girl-Gone-Wild from the past into our era, would she cease to be a Wild Thing because she isn't baring her breasts on video? Is a woman's "wildness" simply determined by the extent to which she is a fashion diva? Or the extent to which she pushes the boundaries of what's considered culturally acceptable? Although external appearance and sexual behavior certainly play a part in determining if a particular woman has or hasn't gone wild, the Bible teaches that there's a whole lot more involved than that. What's more, it teaches that Girl-Gone-Wild behavior isn't restricted to young single women. A woman can be a Girl-Gone-Wild at any stage of life.

It's easy for those of us who are older to distance ourselves from the bawdy college-age women who are sexting, or exposing themselves for cameras, or mud wrestling in a bar like pigs in a pen, or necking with other girls to turn on the guys, or adopting a *Sex and the City* multipartner lifestyle. It's easy to shake our heads, look down our noses, and self-righteously condemn them as Wild Things. It's easy to convince ourselves that if we don't happen to be young or single, and if we're not risqué, and if we stay a couple steps behind the cutting edge of fashion and propriety, that the Girl-Gone-Wild label couldn't possibly apply to us. But the truth of the matter is that it's not just over-the-edge, single, college-age girls who qualify as Wild Things.

According to Scripture, there is a measure of Girl-Gone-Wildness in all of us. I'll never forget the seventy-year-old woman who came up to me after a workshop with tears streaming down her face: "I came to your workshop to get some ideas about how to help my granddaughter," she said, "but I see now that it's *me* who is a Girl-Gone-Wild."

CONTRASTING WILD AND WISE

In this book, I want to contrast the attitudes and behaviors of a Girl-Gone-Wild with those of a Girl-Gone-Wise. I want to do this for two reasons. First, I hope that you'll grow in spiritual discernment, so you can spot the difference between wild and wise when it comes to the right biblical attitudes, thought patterns, and behavior for women. Second, I pray that this awareness will help you say yes to God's ideas about womanhood and no to the tremendous pressure to conform to the world's pattern and to the sinful tendencies in your own heart. My goal, in the final analysis, is that you might become more biblically savvy and godly in the way you think and conduct yourself in your relationships with men. As the title clearly indicates, I want you to become a Girl-Gone-Wise in a world gone wild.

Characteristics of both the wild and the wise woman are mentioned numerous times throughout Scripture, but perhaps nowhere more clearly than in the book of Proverbs. In this collection of writings, a Sage Father, Solomon, repeatedly warns his son to stay away from wild women. He talks about that kind of woman in some sixty-five verses, more than any other figure, even Lady Wisdom. In Proverbs 31, King Lemuel's mother chips in with some advice on how to spot and marry a woman who is wise. Don't worry. This isn't going to be another rehash of the Proverbs 31 woman. We've all heard our share of those. My approach is quite different. I intend to instruct by means of contrast.

Let me explain. When my middle son, Matt, played football, he had a pair of white practice pants. (White. Go figure.) Since Matt has always been an active, "let me at 'em" kind of a guy, he used to come home with all sorts of mud and grass and bloodstains ground into them. (White practice pants! White!!) Anyhow, it was my job to use Oxi-clean and Spray 'n Wash and bleach and to soak and scrub the stains out so that the practice pants would be clean for the next practice. (White! I never did find out which rocket scientist made that call.)

With some work, a substantial amount of elbow grease, and a lot of muttering under my breath, I managed to keep Matt's practice pants white. Ta da! Are you impressed? I was. I even thought about volunteering my services for a Tide commercial. But there's white, and then there's *white*. Halfway through the season, when Matt irreparably ripped his practice pants and I laid a newly purchased pair alongside, I saw that, in comparison, his old pants were not white at all. Lying beside the new white ones, the old ones looked grey. Comparison magnified the difference.

This book revolves around the story of the typical Girl-Gone-Wild as recorded for us in the Bible. The bulk of her story is recorded in Proverbs 7. Jesus' favorite and most powerful teaching tactic was the parable. We see this same method used by the Sage Father when he instructed his son to stay away from wild women. What I'm going to do is unpack the Proverbs 7 tale about the typical wild woman and contrast her characteristics with those of the typical wise woman. Over the course of this book, we'll look at twenty points of contrast. Like looking at my son's old football pants lying beside his new ones, it's the contrast between wild and wise that will magnify the difference.

The cautionary tale recorded in Proverbs 7 paints a picture of a typical Girl-Gone-Wild. For the purpose of the narrative, the author depicts her as a young, married woman—an ordinary, average, "typical" Jane Doe you could meet at the church down the street. But she could be any woman: young, old, single, married, divorced, widowed, childless; a mother, a teenager, a grandma . . . whatever. The point of the story isn't her age or marital status. It's about the "wild" characteristics she displays. As you'll soon see, these characteristics could show up in a woman of any age, of any marital status, at any stage of life.

Before we get into the text, I want to capture your imagination so you can picture the story happening in your surroundings—perhaps in the life of someone you know or even in your own life. If the Proverbs 7 cautionary tale about the Girl-Gone-Wild were told from today's vantage point, it might go something like this . . .

A TALE OF A MODERN GIRL-GONE-WILD

She stretched the satin sheet over the corner of the mattress. The sexual tension had been building for weeks. The looks. The banter. The innuendo.

It had started off innocently enough. They had both been volunteers for the big Easter musical. She was the backstage manager, and he was a stagehand. She discovered that his office was downtown, not far from where she worked. At her suggestion, they got together a half-dozen times for lunch and coffee—to discuss aspects of the production—just as friends, of course. They met at a cozy bistro tucked in an alley off Fifth and Main, a warm and homey place with checkered red drapes, booths aglow with candle-plugged wine bottles, rich operatic music, and delicious Italian fare.

The production ended, but their lunchtime get-togethers didn't. The thrill of the chase was too much to resist. Besides, he was such a good listener. He made her laugh. He understood. He empathized with her loveless existence. And the chemistry between them was electric.

Her heart quickened a beat. She plumped the pillows, arranged some cinnamon-scented tea lights, and scattered rose petals across the bed. After docking her iPod and sliding her wedding picture into a drawer, she went into the washroom to finish getting ready. A glance at her watch told her that her husband would soon be touching down in Seattle. The conference would keep him away for a week. The timing was perfect.

She carefully composed a text message: "I'm going to be lonely unless I happen upon a friend after Saturday night service. I hear it's Tuscany night at the bistro."

Her cheeks flushed with anticipation. Would he come? She felt certain he would. She had been reeling him in like a fish on a hook. And now it was time to make her big move. She touched up her hair and makeup, misted on some perfume, and stood back for a final appraisal.

Simple but sexy: tight designer jeans, stilettos, tank top. Oops. Too much skin and cleavage for church—better save that for later. She selected a little sweater from her closet. She'd whip it off on her way to the bistro. It would be too hot in there for a sweater. She smiled ever so slightly. Way too hot!

Later, her eyes scanned the church foyer. There he was. She moved close enough to entice him. She knew her craft. The toss of the hair. The ever-so-slight parting of the lips. The subtle display of her wares. The lingering sideways glance. The secret invitation was noticed by no one but the intended target. It gave her a rush to observe the effect it had on him. She waited until he selected his seat, and then positioned herself where he couldn't help but watch her. All through the service she kept sending little nonverbal cues to crank up the sexual tension. She caressed the back of her neck. Bent over to pick up a dropped pen. Licked her finger to turn the page. Every tiny move was calculated. Reel. Reel. Reel. She eased past him in the aisle on the way out, making certain he felt the brush of her skin. Another seductive look. Another toss of the hair. Reel. Reel. The fish was almost in the boat.

She waited for him in the corner of the bistro parking lot. After what seemed like an eternity, he appeared, walking from the direction of his office. Forget about Tuscany. This was the moment she'd been waiting for. She wouldn't be denied this chance at love. Grabbing hold of his shirt, she brazenly pulled him close and kissed him hard.

She could tell that he was tempted. She overcame his last bit of resistance with a barrage of smooth talk and flattery: "Thank God He sent you into my life. You're the answer to my prayers. You're the only one who understands me. You're the only one I can talk to. You are amazing! I feel so happy and safe when I'm with you. I finally found someone I can trust. Please come home with me. My husband's gone again. He's on the other side of the country and won't be back till the end of the month. I can't bear the thought of spending another night in that big house alone. I need you so much. I'm counting on you. I want to spend the whole night in your arms."

Her seductive words take hold. She kisses him again, fiercely. His breathing is thick. His hands begin to tremble. She takes a step back and holds out her car keys, locking her eyes with his—willing his fall. He only hesitates for the slightest second before grabbing them, helping her in, and driving off in the direction of her neighborhood.

He wasn't the first, and he wouldn't be the last. Though she's married now, she's had a history of revolving-door relationships with men. Consequences? She won't think about those. She's too caught up in the moment . . . and in the quest to fill the hole in her heart.

WALK NOT AS WILD BUT AS WISE

Did that modern-day take on Proverbs 7 sound at all familiar? Over the years, as I've ministered to women, I've heard hundreds of variations on the details, but it usually boils down to the same basic plot:

> *Rising Action:* Girl sees guy. Girl thinks guy will meet her needs. Girl seduces guy. Girl gets guy.
> *The Climax:* Girl has the whole thing blow up in her face.
> *Falling Action:* Girl doesn't find what she was looking for. Girl is damaged by messy emotional, spiritual, and relational fallout.
> *Resolution:* Girl buries her pain and starts looking for another guy.

I suspect most of you have also seen or heard of lives that have been damaged by this storyline. Maybe the damaged life is yours. The details may differ, but for untold numbers of women, the Proverbs 7 story isn't theoretical. It's real. The longing is real. The pull is real. The entanglement is real. The thrill is real. The sin is real. The inevitable breakdown is real. And the resulting devastation and heartache are real. Solomon points out that while this particular chick flick promises to be sweet as honey, those who buy tickets find themselves gagging on the bad taste it leaves in their mouths. They get a mouth full of "wormwood"—a strong, bitter-tasting plant that symbolizes bitterness and sorrow (Proverbs 5:4). So why do women sign up to be actors in this deceptive drama? The Bible says it happens because they are wild and not wise.

I doubt that anyone would disagree that wisdom is a valuable thing for women to have in their relationships with men. I think most women try to be wise and not stupid. But a quick glance at the current state of male-female relationships indicates that our own wisdom is woefully inadequate. We need a higher wisdom to guide our way.

All treasures of wisdom and knowledge are hidden in Christ Jesus (Colossians 2:3). So if we ever hope to be wise when it comes to male-female relationships, we need to align our thoughts and actions with His. We need to do what He says. The instruction of the Lord isn't just some good advice, in the same category as all the other "good" advice we get from friends, family, radio talk shows, reality TV, magazines, and pop psychology. The Bible says the Lord's instruction is *perfect*. It nourishes the soul. And it's *trustworthy*. It is what makes a woman wise (Psalm 19:7 NIV). A Girl-Gone-Wise is a woman who has committed herself to a relationship with Jesus Christ and who relies on Scripture to understand how she ought to conduct herself in her relationships with men.

What then, is a Girl-Gone-Wild? Wild is the polar opposite of wise. A wise woman's heart inclines her "to the right," but a wild woman's heart "to the left" (Ecclesiastes 10:2). Wild and wise go in two separate directions. This book equates "wild" with what Scripture calls foolish, wayward, evil, ignorant, or unwise.

In Proverbs 1:22, the Sage talks about three different types of unwise people—the simple, the fools, and the scoffers. The three Hebrew words all focus on moral rather than intellectual deficiencies. The first depicts the wild woman as lackadaisical or obstinate, unwilling to learn or do what is right. The second portrays her as being resistant to God's input and standards of morality. The third indicates that she is reckless, insolent, and rebellious. A Girl-Gone-Wise relies on God's Word to guide her conduct. A Girl-Gone-Wild doesn't.

Emily came up to me after a conference, wanting to know how to resolve her ongoing affair with her husband's brother. Her seven-year-old son hadn't been fathered by her husband, but by the man he called "Uncle." Emily had grown to despise her husband and wanted to start a new life with her lover, but they were hesitant because of the inevitable consequences. The son loved his "Daddy." And her husband, his parents, and the rest of his extended family had no idea of the long-hidden betrayal. Emily was convinced that she had married the wrong brother, and that it was God's will that she and her son and his real dad be together as a family.

I gotta admit, it was all I could do to keep from banging my fist against my forehead and exclaiming, "How could you be so *stupid*?!!!"

It's the thought that often crosses my mind when I listen to the impossible situations women get themselves entangled in. It's never, "How could you be so wise?", but always, "How could you be so stupid?" That's the thing. Sin makes us stupid. And I'm not exempt from this malady. Nor are you. None of us is beyond falling into the prideful assumption that we have enough smarts to make our own decisions about the way we live.

"Wild" is what we are whenever we disregard God and rely instead on the world's advice, or on what seems right in our own eyes. This was the mistake of Eve, the first Girl-Gone-Wild, who went with her own gut instinct instead of trusting and obeying the Lord. She fell for Satan's deceitful sales pitch (Genesis 3:1–5). The Evil One convinced her that:

1. God's ways are too restrictive ("Did God actually say?").
2. She wouldn't suffer any negative consequences by detouring from God's plan ("You will surely not die!").
3. She shouldn't let herself be denied ("When you eat, your eyes will be opened, and you will be like God!").

Eve fell into the trap of thinking that she had the right to judge the merits of the forbidden fruit for herself, rather than simply take God at His word. From her perspective, the fruit looked attractive ("a delight to the eyes"), harmless ("good for food"), and incredibly promising ("desired to make one wise"). So she took a bite. How many times has the Evil One used the same ploy? How many times have women fallen into the trap of viewing sin as attractive, harmless, and even promising? How many times have you?

Eve couldn't have begun to envision the ugly, painful, deadly consequences of her choice—in her own life, in her relationship with God, in her relationship with her husband, in her children, and grandchildren, and in every human being who would ever live. She bit because Satan convinced her that the fruit would be sweet. But tragically, from that day on, tragedy and bitterness dominated her life.

We are all Eve's daughters. All of us are born with Girl-Gone-Wild tendencies. Most of us have experienced bitterness, pain, and even death in our relationships. That's the bad news. The good news is that we have something infinitely more precious than Eve had. Because of the redeeming sacrifice of Jesus Christ on the cross, those who put their faith in Him get the gift of God's indwelling Holy Spirit and, therefore, a supernatural capacity to discern and follow the way of wisdom. God's grace is bigger than all of our sin. The power of Christ can transform even the most messed-up and broken Wild Thing into a Girl-Gone-Wise.

THE GIRL-GONE-WILD OF PROVERBS 7

Before we get into the twenty points of contrast between a Girl-Gone-Wise and a Girl-Gone-Wild, I'd like you to read the text in as it appears in Scripture. As always, God's inspired Word is rich with meaning and instruction that no paraphrase can mimic. We'll be coming back to this passage repeatedly throughout the rest of the book, so read it slowly and attentively. You might even want to read it a couple of times:

Be attentive to my wisdom; incline your ear to my understanding. . . . [The wild woman's] feet go down to death; her steps follow the path to Sheol; she does not ponder the path of life; her ways wander, and she does not know it. . . .

At the window of my house I have looked out through my lattice, and I have seen among the simple, I have perceived among the youths, a young man lacking sense, passing along the street near her corner, taking the road to her house in the twilight, in the evening, at the time of night and darkness. And behold, the woman meets him, dressed as a prostitute, wily of heart. She is loud and wayward; her feet do not stay at home; now in the street, now in the market, and at every corner she lies in wait.

She seizes him and kisses him, and with bold face she says to him "I had to offer sacrifices, and today I have paid my vows; so now I have come out to meet you, to seek you eagerly, and I have found you.

"I have spread my couch with coverings, colored linens from Egyptian linen; I have perfumed my bed with myrrh, aloes, and cinnamon. Come, let us take our fill of love till morning; let us delight ourselves with love. For my husband is not at home; he has gone on a long journey; he took a bag of money with him; at full moon he will come home."

With much seductive speech she persuades him; with her smooth talk she compels him. All at once he follows her, as an ox goes to the slaughter, or as a stag is caught fast till an arrow pierces its liver; as a bird rushes into a snare; he does not know that it will cost him his life.

And now, O sons, listen to me, and be attentive to the words of my mouth. Let not your heart turn aside to her ways; do not stray into her paths, for many a victim has she laid low, and all her slain are a mighty throng. Her house is the way to Sheol, going down to the chambers of death. (Proverbs 5:1, 5–6; 7:6–27)

In the next twenty chapters, we're going to unpack these verses phrase by phrase. They contain a wealth of instruction for women today. I wish I could get you to squeeze through the pages of the book and nestle down on a sofa in my den so we could talk about womanhood. I'd pour you a big steaming cup of my favorite African chai tea, and we'd share heart to heart. I have such a burden for you and for all the other daughters, sisters, and mothers of this generation. It's like we've lost our bearings and have no idea who we are or how we should live. So many of us are living with the brokenness, dysfunction, pain, and confusion that come from having gone wild.

As you read each chapter, make sure to visit the website Girls GoneWise.com, to download chapter questions for personal reflection. They'll help you apply the Word to your life. You can also download a leader's guide that will help you study the book with a girlfriend or with a group of girlfriends. Studying and discussing the book in a small group environment is the best way to learn. You'll also find additional Girls-Gone-Wise articles, resources, and a blog on the website. There, you can post your comments and interact with other women who are trying to figure out what it means to walk as wise and not wild.

The observer looking out from behind the lattice at the Wild Thing of Proverbs 7 could just as easily have been looking out at all the Wild Things of this generation. Update the fashion and technology, and not much has changed. The points of contrast between wild and wise are still the same. Lady Wisdom still calls. She cries aloud in the street; in the markets she raises her voice; at the head of the noisy streets she cries out; at the entrance of the city gates she speaks, beckoning women to listen. The Wild Thing of Proverbs 7 and all her foolish girlfriends ignore her. But Girls-Gone-Wise pay close attention. If you are wise, you will listen to Scripture's words of wisdom to figure out who you are and how you should live. You'll understand that "wisdom is better than jewels, and all that you may desire cannot compare with her" (Proverbs 8:11).

20 POINTS
OF CONTRAST

Point of Contrast #1

HEART
What Holds First Place
in Her Affections

Girl-Gone-Wild: **Christ Is Peripheral**	Girl-Gone-Wise: **Christ Is Central**
"Her feet go down to death; her steps follow the path to Sheol; she does not ponder the path of life; her ways wander, and she does not know it." (Proverbs 5:5–6)	"Her heart has not turned back, nor have her steps departed from your way." (Psalm 44:18)

H*e swept her off her feet.* I'm sure you've heard the expression. People often use it when a girl gets emotionally overwhelmed by and infatuated with a guy. He gains her immediate and unquestioning support, approval, acceptance, and love. Like Wanda, the high school senior who was swept off her feet by the star of the football team. She loved him so much and was so certain they would have a future together, that she gave up her virginity and self-respect. Their relationship lasted a scant month. Or forty-four-year-old Tammy—who was swept off her feet by Omar, a new convert with a Muslim upbringing and twenty years her junior. He was an exotic foreigner, with a desire for a green card. She married him weeks after they met, convinced she had met the man of her dreams. Or Amanda, who was swept off her feet and into an affair with a married co-worker. Or Bridgette, who was swept off her feet and left her husband and teenage children for a guy she met on the Internet. Or Gretta, a lonely widow, who was swept off her feet into bankruptcy by a dashing elderly gentleman who was just a tad too fond of gambling.

The idiom "swept off her feet" indicates that there is a strong connection between a girl's heart and her feet. That connection is the first point of contrast between a Girl-Gone-Wild and a Girl-Gone-Wise. A wise woman gives the Lord Jesus Christ first place in her heart. Her feet follow the inclination of her heart, so she makes cautious, wise, godly decisions about her relationships with men. A wild woman, on the other hand, does not have Christ at the center of her affections. Other things—such as her desire to have a boyfriend or husband, to gain security or approval, or to have fun—take center stage. Her relationship to Christ is peripheral, shoved off to the side somewhere. The wild woman's feet also follow the inclination of her heart, but since Christ is not at the center of her affections, she makes missteps in her relationship with men. "Her ways wander, and she doesn't know it."

THE WAY SHE WALKS

The Sage Father tells his son that he'll be able to spot a Girl-Gone-Wild by the way she walks. He advises him to check out a woman's "feet," "steps," "path," and "ways." He's not being literal here. He's not telling his son to look to see whether the woman sports a crisp French pedicure or calluses rough as concrete, whether she wears designer heels or hiking boots, whether she prefers swaggering through a barn or strutting down urban pavement, whether she sways her hips or marches like a commando. It's obvious that the "walk" that he and his son are talking about is primarily figurative.

Biblical writers use the word *walk* metaphorically to describe the way human life is lived in relation to God. A girl's walk has to do with the overriding inclination of her heart. Her walk demonstrates where her loyalty lies. It reveals whether her heart is inclined toward the Lord or toward other things—whether she's moving toward Him or away from Him, whether she prefers the path of uprightness or the path of wickedness, God's way or the world's way—whether she favors being wise or wild. Her walk is her prevailing pattern of behavior. It's the key to determining which way she's headed. According to the Bible, you can tell the difference between a Wild Thing and a Wise Thing by the way she thinks, what she talks about, and all the small, daily decisions she makes. Her small, individual "steps" all add up to reveal the dominant direction of her heart.

If Christ is at the center—if He is the one who has forever swept her off her feet—she makes sure that her attitude and speech and conduct are pleasing to Him. She seeks to walk in His way. Her eyes are ever toward the Lord (Psalm 25:15). Her steps increasingly follow His path. She relies on Him to make each footstep secure (Psalm 40:2). If, on the other hand, Christ is not at the center, then she will walk in her own way, in a way that is "right in her own eyes" (Proverbs 12:15). She will follow her own desires, turn aside from the straight and narrow, go after things she has no right to, and mess around with sin (Job 31:7). Her way will be "a way that seems right to a man, but its end is the way to death" (Proverbs 14:12).

The wild woman makes poor decisions concerning her sexuality and relationships with men. If she doesn't have a guy, then she's probably obsessed with getting one. If she does have a guy, she's probably not content with him and is having trouble with the fairy-tale-ending part of the romance. If she's between guys, she may be licking her wounds and wrapping herself up in protective layers, telling herself that she'll be more careful next time. In any case, she schemes, dreams, manipulates, connives, controls, clamors, seduces, dominates, cowers, compromises, explodes, and/or implodes in this area of her life. All the while, her spirit dies a slow, withering death. When it comes to her love life, her "feet go down to death; her steps follow the path to Sheol; she does not ponder the path of life; her ways wander, and she does not know it."

It's important to remember that although her steps wander, the Wild Thing of Proverbs is a very religious woman who moves in religious circles. Nowadays, you might find her at a youth group, on the worship team, in a Bible study, on a mission trip, or teaching Sunday school. She could be the leader of the women's ministry in your church. Or the speaker at your next women's retreat. She could be me. She could be you.

On the surface, the Wild Thing does a lot of things right. She professes to worship God. She offers "fellowship offerings" at church and appears to fulfill her vows (Proverbs 7:14). But a closer examination reveals that her heart really isn't into it. Christ is not at the forefront of her affections. He has not captivated her heart. She loves herself and her own pleasure more. She only follows the Lord as long as it's convenient, and as long as it doesn't interfere with her quest to get what she wants (Zechariah 7:4–7; Isaiah 58:3–7). She lives a religious life, but does not love Jesus wholeheartedly. Though she calls Him "Lord, Lord," she does not know Him intimately, nor does she eagerly and obediently follow His ways (Matthew 7:21–22).

Several months ago, my young adult son, Matt, phoned and told me about a girl he had started seeing. My first question for him was, "Is Christ at the center of her heart?"

"Well," he tentatively replied, "she's super nice. She attended a Christian school. She goes to church. She went on a mission trip last year. Her family seems solid. We get along really well."

"That's not what I asked." I explained, "What I want to know is if she bubbles over with Jesus. Does He occupy her thoughts, purposes, dreams, and desires? Does she long to know Him better and obey Him more? Is she into His Word? Is He the sun around which all her planets revolve? Does she love Him with her whole heart?"

"Umm . . . I'm not really sure," he stammered. "We haven't really talked about it much." (By now, he's probably sweating, because it's dawned on him that his lack of an answer is an answer. If he's gone out with her several times, and they haven't talked about Jesus, chances are Jesus isn't at the center of her heart, at the center of his heart, or at the center of their relationship.)

"Son," I gently advised, "there is *nothing* more important than a girl's relationship to Jesus. Nothing. If her heart isn't sold out to Him, then she's not the woman for you. Plain and simple. A heart for God should be your number one criteria for a wife—number one—at the top of your list. Above all, make sure she loves Jesus and gives Him first place in her heart."

Thankfully, my sons have learned to politely tolerate and listen to what they refer to as my "mom-lecture moments." I pray that they take the wisdom of my words to heart. And I pray that you do too. It's one thing to be acquainted with Jesus. It's another thing to uphold Him as the Lord of your life—and to let your relationship with Him dictate how you conduct yourself in all other relationships. As my sports-chaplain husband often tells his pro athletes, "You can talk the talk. But it doesn't mean a thing unless you also walk the walk."

THE HEART-FOOT CONNECTION

When I was a kid at summer camp, we used to sit around the campfire late at night, belting out any song that came to mind. It was always an eclectic collection, ranging from old spirituals ("He's Got the Whole World in His Hands") to action songs ("Hokey Pokey"), from rounds of "Three Blind Mice" to repetitive counting songs like "Ninety-Nine Cans of Soup on the Wall" . . . (the counselors at the church camp made sure we substituted "cans of soup" for "bottles of beer"). We also sang an old traditional folk song, "Dem Dry Bones." It started with, "Ezekiel connected dem dry bones; I hear the word of the Lord," and then continued with a lesson in anatomy: "Your toe bone connected to your foot bone. Your foot bone connected to your ankle bone. Your ankle bone connected to your leg bone . . ." and so on, until you got to the final connection: "Your neck bone connected to your head bone—I hear the word of the Lord! Dem bones, dem bones gonna walk aroun'—I hear the word of the Lord!"

This song comes to mind because I believe that any girl who wants to *hear the Word of the Lord*, feel His Spirit breathe life into *dem dry bones*, and experience what it means to *walk aroun'* in His power needs to be very mindful of the connection between her heart and her feet. Anatomically, your foot bone is connected to your ankle bone. But spiritually and metaphorically, your foot and heart are directly connected to each other. Maybe the campfire song should add the line: "Your foot bone's connected to your heart bone!"

That's the way it's always been. Throughout the Old Testament, God repeatedly asked two things of His people: (1) follow Me with your feet, and (2) love Me with your heart (Deuteronomy 11:22; Joshua 22:5). Under the terms of the old covenant, the "feet" part came first. It was necessary for people to keep all the rules (the Law)

27

in order to have any kind of a relationship with the Lord. But it may surprise you to know that the love relationship, and not obedience to the rules, was the main goal the Lord had in mind. His old covenant was a "covenant of love" (Deuteronomy 7:9 NIV). The rules were there because they made a love relationship possible. A holy, sinless God cannot enter into a relationship with a sinful creature. It is an utter impossibility. That's why the old covenant had a set of rules that defined God's standard of righteousness and a sacrificial system to atone for the penalty of falling short of that standard.

The sacrificial system of the old covenant had severe limitations. The sacrifices needed to be continual and were never quite "enough" to restore humanity to the sinless state that was required in order to approach and interact with a sinless, holy God. Because of the ongoing problem with sin, people's contact with Him, knowledge of Him, and relationship to Him were limited. Their feet and hearts continually strayed. They were unable to do what was necessary to remain in a committed love relationship. They couldn't hold up their end of the deal.

The Old Covenant didn't satisfactorily solve the problem of the sinful human condition. But God had the ultimate remedy in mind. Through the prophet Ezekiel, the Lord foretold:

> I will give you a new heart, and a new spirit I will put within you. And I will remove the heart of stone from your flesh and give you a heart of flesh. And I will put my Spirit within you, and cause you to walk in my statutes and be careful to obey my rules. (Ezekiel 36:26–28)

There it is again. The foot-heart connection. But this time, there's a different order—and an absolutely breathtaking promise. The prophecy pointed to a time when things would be radically different. The heart would come first. And the right heart wouldn't be the result of human effort. It would be the gift of God and a work of His Holy Spirit in the life of the individual. The feet would come second. The new heart would ensure that all who have it would walk in the way of the Lord. They would obey, not because they *had* to—contrary to the old covenant, there would be no obligation to fulfill—but because they *wanted* to. The new heart would contain the power, motivation, and guidance to walk the right way. Instead of being inclined toward sin, it would be inclined toward holiness.

Jeremiah prophesied that the new heart would have a far greater capacity to do the right thing, because God would engrave His ways directly on it (Jeremiah 31:33). Instead of relying on the external letter of the Law, the Spirit would provide internal guidance as to the intent of the command. (The Spirit might reveal, for instance, that imagining an affair is just as sinful as having one.) The capacity for holy living would be exponentially greater than under the old covenant, for God's Spirit would provide the impulse, guidance, and power to understand and follow God's Word.

God fulfilled the promise when He sent His Son to institute the new covenant in His blood. The sacrifice of Jesus Christ—the spotless Lamb of God—satisfied the requirements of God's justice and atoned for all sin. Through Jesus, we can receive the gift of God's Holy Spirit and enter into a close and intimate family relationship with our Father. We can be declared holy and enter into His presence boldly.

In the old covenant, the rules provided "the way." In the new covenant, Jesus is the Way (John 14:4–6). A relationship with Him sets us right with God. It results in a new heart and inspires and enables us to walk correctly, according to the directions in His Word. The heart-foot connection is still there, as it was in the old covenant, but God is the One who does everything. He gives us the heart, desire, and power to obey. It's a radically different approach.

So what does all this have to do with male-female relationships? We can draw several important conclusions. First, the way a woman relates to men has a lot to do with the state of her heart for God. Her behavior is a good indicator of the state of her heart.

Second, although behavior is a good indicator, it is not a *conclusive* indicator. A woman can have the "right" behavior, yet still miss the mark by failing to have the right heart. Conversely, a woman's heart may be right, but she could still be doing some things wrong. The Holy Spirit's conviction and instruction in her life might still be a "work in progress." Therefore, although it is our responsibility to evaluate behavior, discern right from wrong, and make judgment calls in our relationships, we need a strong dose of humility when doing so. Unlike the Lord, we are unable to see what is in a person's heart.

Third, when it comes to sexuality and male-female relationships, the Bible gives an *illustrative* list of behaviors that are out of step with God's way, but it doesn't provide an *exhaustive* list. Just because a certain behavior isn't prohibited in the Bible doesn't mean that it's a behavior the Lord condones.

For example, the Bible doesn't explicitly prohibit a girl from having her boyfriend sleep over on the couch at her apartment. I've heard several college students rationalize that if the couple does not have sex, this behavior is totally acceptable, that it's not sin. I agree that it technically doesn't go against the "letter of the Law." But it may be an offense against the Lord nonetheless. It may cause the girl and guy to toy with temptation, compromise purity of thought, engage in sensuality and impurity, dishonor the institution of marriage, disobey their parents, fail to flee the appearance of evil, muddy the reputation of the gospel in the eyes of unbelievers, and/or place their desire for convenience and pleasure above their desire to glorify Jesus Christ. They may have avoided the sin of fornication, but in all likelihood, there are a bunch of other sins they did not avoid. Furthermore, compromise of one protective boundary usually leads to the compromise of more protective boundaries. Couples who start with the intent of abstaining will often find that the circumstances are too tempting and, bit by bit, will give in to sexual immorality.

When the Holy Spirit writes God's law on our hearts, He calls us to a higher standard of purity than the "letter of the Law" ever did. Jesus did not come to abolish the Law or the Prophets. He came to fulfill them by having them blossom in the fertile soil of redeemed, Spirit-filled hearts (Matthew 5:17). The presence of God's Spirit increases our capacity to obey the Word of God and therefore our capacity for holiness. Through His Spirit's work in our hearts, the Lord wants to rid us of sinful behavior. But He also wants to rid us of sinful attitudes, thoughts, inclinations, and compromises. A growing love for the Lord inspires and empowers us to turn away from anything that is not completely spotless. When our hearts are captivated by Christ's glory, we are "transformed into the same image from one degree of glory to another" (2 Corinthians 3:18). And that affects our relationships with the opposite sex. As we become more and more holy, we become less and less tolerant of any hint of evil in our thoughts, words, or actions toward men.

Fourth, under the terms of the new covenant, success in our relationships with God does not depend on our personal resources or capabilities. God's Spirit provides us with all the power, love, wisdom, and self-discipline we need (2 Timothy 1:7). He equips us with *everything* we need to love Him and *everything* we need to be godly in our relationships. "His divine power has granted to us *all things* that pertain to life and godliness" (2 Peter 1:3, italics added). Therefore, proper conduct in our relationships with the opposite sex requires that we rely on Him. His divine wisdom, power, love, and self-discipline—and not our own—are what will enable us to do the right thing.

Fifth, though the order and the means have changed, the Lord still asks His children to do the same two things: (1) Love Me with your heart and (2) Follow Me with your feet. Our obedience is not a *requirement* for a relationship with God, but it is the expected *by-product* of it. Jesus said, "If you love Me, you will keep My commandments" (John 14:15).

GREAT AFFECTION

In the mid-1700s, New England and other colonies along the Eastern seaboard experienced a religious revival that historians call the Great Awakening. The people who became followers of Jesus at that time had a unique expression to describe their salvation experience. Instead of saying, "I've been born again," or "I gave my life to Jesus," or "I've become a Christian," they'd say, "I have been seized by the power of a great affection!" They'd say it with a loud voice and lots of enthusiasm. To get the inflection right, you have to put on a thick Philadelphian accent and divide the sentence into three separate phrases and emphasize it something like this:

> *"I have been SEIZED . . . by the POW'R*
> *. . . of a GREAT affection!"*

Try it. (Yes, out loud.) It sounds kinda cool. Being Canadian (and having no accent), I like to try to mimic the accents I hear in various parts of the continent. But more than that, I really like the idea that this declaration conveys. (Did you say it aloud? My dog came running and is staring at me, because I've hollered it out four or five times now.)

God fervently and unrelentingly pursues a love relationship with us. When the hearts of the New Englanders were "seized" by His affection, they responded with a fervent affection of their own. God's affection stirred their affection. They became passionate about Jesus. Jonathan Edwards, a well-known preacher at the time, made this observation:

> On whatever occasions persons met together, Christ was to be heard of, and seen in the midst of them. Our young people, when they met, were wont to spend the time in talking of the excellency and dying love of Jesus Christ, the glory of the way of salvation, the wonderful, free, and sovereign grace of God, His glorious work in the conversion of a soul, the truth and certainty of the great things of God's word, the sweetness of the views of His perfections, etc.[1]

For those who had been "seized," the great affection became the central focus of their lives. Edwards said, "The *engagedness of their hearts* in this great concern could not be hid, it appeared in their very countenances." They thought about Jesus. They talked about Jesus. They wanted to hear more about Jesus. They told others about Jesus. They read their Bibles. They sang worship songs on the streets. They stopped living the world's way and started living God's way. Bars emptied. Brothels went out of business. Broken relationships were restored. The poor, hungry, and needy received care.

Bottom line? The heart bone is connected to the foot bone. The more a woman's heart is seized with affection for Jesus, the more her life will be transformed to walk in His way. This is abundantly evident in the behavior of the people who were seized by the power of a great affection during the Great Awakening.

The first and most important characteristic of a Girl-Gone-Wise is that Jesus Christ occupies first place in her heart. He is the object of her greatest affection. A Girl-Gone-Wild loves the Lord little. A Girl-Gone-Wise loves Him much. The steps of her feet demonstrate the devotion of her heart.

THE HEART IS THE WELL

The inclination of a woman's heart is, by far, the most important factor in determining whether she will conduct herself in a godly way in her relationships with men. It's the most important point of contrast between a Wild Thing and a Wise Thing. As I constantly tell my eligible sons, "The first and most important thing to look for in a wife is a girl whose heart is overflowing with love for Jesus." A woman who attends to her heart will attend to her ways.

The remaining points of contrast in this book focus on the ways girls ought to "walk." But all these can be traced back to this first and central matter of the heart. The heart is the "well" from which all other behaviors spring. That's why the Sage Father instructed his son, "Keep your heart with all vigilance, for from it flow the springs of life" (Proverbs 4:23).

I hope you see the connection. I hope you understand that you will never get your behavior toward men or your relationships right until you first get your heart right before God. Girls-Gone-Wise cry out, as David did, "O Lord, teach me how you want me to live! Then I will obey your commands. Make me wholeheartedly committed to you!" (Psalm 86:11 NET).

Don't forget to download the chapter questions at www.GirlsGoneWise.com. They'll help you examine the condition of your heart.

Point of Contrast #2

COUNSEL
Where She Gets
Her Instruction

Girl-Gone-Wild: World Instructed	Girl-Gone-Wise: Word Instructed
"Her feet go down to death; her steps follow the path to Sheol; she does not ponder the path of life; her ways wander, and she does not know it." (Proverbs 5:5–6)	"She walks not in the counsel of the wicked, nor stands in the way of sinners, nor sits in the seat of scoffers; but her delight is in the law of the Lord, and on his law she meditates day and night." (Psalm 1:1–2)

magine this. Let's say I wanted to do an experiment to determine the effects of popular culture on a girl's ideas about womanhood and male-female relationships. So I lock her in a lab and expose her to mass media every waking moment of every day. Her schedule looks something like this:

- Television: 8 hours
- Radio/iPod: 4 hours
- Video games/Internet: 2 hours

- Hollywood movie: 1.5 hours
- Women's magazines/romance novel: 1 hour
- Newspaper: 0.5 hour

After a full day of constant exposure, the girl goes to bed and sleeps for seven hours. As soon as she wakes up, the bombardment resumes. Every day—seventeen hours a day, seven days a week, for seven months—it continues. I make her watch, listen to, and read all the latest and most popular entertainment and news. That's all I allow her to do. She's exposed to nothing else.

What do you think would happen? How do you think it would affect her?

I asked my twenty-year-old son, Jonathan. He said, "She'd become what she was exposed to, because she wouldn't have any other influence."

I agree. She would become what she was exposed to.

Here's the shocker. This scenario isn't hypothetical. It's real. It's based on actual statistics and projections. According to research studies, the U.S. Census Bureau estimates that the average woman will expose herself to 3,596 hours of mass media this year.[1] That's seven full months of exposure! The only difference between the average woman and the girl in my scenario is that the average woman's exposure is spread out over twelve months instead of being crammed into seven. And she isn't locked into a room. She has other things going on in her life, like going to school, working at a job, or caring for a family. What's more, no one is forcing the mass media down her throat. She willingly indulges.

The ingestion of mass media starts at a very young age and continues year after year throughout a woman's life. If your daily intake of TV, Internet, radio, and women's magazines is about "average," by the time you are sixty-five, you will have spent forty solid years of all-day-every-day time sitting under the tutelage of worldly wisdom. Do you think you could possibly remain uninfluenced by its counsel?

The problem with popular media is that they constantly lie about the nature of truth, goodness, and beauty. They offer counterfeit versions of what womanhood, male-female relationships, romance, sexuality, marriage, and family are all about. They lie to a woman about who she is, what gives her significance, what she should do to be successful, and where she should spend her time and money. Mass media typically portray sin as natural and harmless. The things God calls the lust of the flesh, the lust of the eyes, and the pride of life are the very things they uphold as highly desired (1 John 2:16). They twist truth. They call evil good and good evil, put darkness for light and light for darkness, put bitter for sweet and sweet for bitter (Isaiah 5:20). They promote sin and mock godliness. I understand that not all media are bad. Some media are extremely good and do provide godly counsel. But few women exercise the necessary discernment and restraint to ensure that the media they expose themselves to are godly and not ungodly.

Where a woman gets "counsel" on how to live is the second point of contrast between a Girl-Gone-Wild and a Girl-Gone-Wise. A Wild Woman gets her instruction from the world. A Wise Woman gets it from the Word. A Girl-Gone-Wise does not walk in the counsel of the ungodly, stand in the path of sinners, or sit under the instruction of those who scoff at God. Instead, she delights in the Lord's instruction, and constantly meditates on His counsel. "Blessed is the man who walks not in the counsel of the wicked, nor stands in the way of sinners, nor sits in the seat of scoffers; but his delight is in the law of the Lord, and on his law he meditates day and night" (Psalm 1:1–2).

LIFE OR DEATH CONSEQUENCE

Proverbs tells us that the feet of a Girl-Gone-Wild follow the path to sheol. *Sheol* is a Hebrew word that means ravine, chasm, or underworld. In the Old Testament, sheol is the abode of the dead; a gloomy place of shadows and utter silence where existence is in suspense and life is no more. The psalmist describes it as the "land of forgetfulness" (Psalm 88:12 KJV). In the New Testament, *sheol* is translated as the Greek word *hades* and the English word *hell*. It's a place of separation from God, a place of torment where the wicked dead await judgment. In the end, God will judge sin and cast the wicked, death, and sheol (hades) into the lake of fire to suffer eternal punishment (Revelation 20:10–15).

Death. Sheol. Hades. Hell. Those are very strong words. The behavior of a Wild Thing isn't trivial or inconsequential. How she conducts herself in relation to men ends up having a horrific eternal consequence—one that she doesn't envision and certainly doesn't intend. So how does this church-going girl end up on the path to hell? Why do her feet wander? How does she end up unwittingly taking steps toward the land of forgetfulness? Our text tells us this happens because she does not *ponder* the path of life.

To ponder is to think over, to consider carefully, to weigh. The mistake of the Wild Thing is that she doesn't intentionally think about how to live a godly life. She forgets. She goes about her daily business and neglects to walk in the way of the Lord. It's not that she willfully scorns God's way. She just doesn't expend the necessary time or effort to figure out what it is or how to walk in it. Instead, the way of the world subtly sidetracks her. Like an intravenous drug dripping into the veins of an unconscious patient on a gurney, worldly thoughts get into her system and numb her sensibilities. Her constant exposure to the world poisons the way she thinks and behaves. Because she doesn't intentionally ponder and pursue the path of life, she unintentionally wanders onto the path of death.

The Hebrew word for "wander" literally means to stagger, topple, stumble, or haplessly fall. It conveys the idea of instability caused by aimlessness. The Bible teaches that if we walk aimlessly—if we aren't intentional about pondering and walking the way of life—we will wander onto the path of death. Life and death are the only two options. A woman who neglects God's way will begin to walk the world's way. It's bound to happen. She'll become what she is exposed to. And the consequence of this misstep isn't trivial. It is potentially deadly. No less than heaven and hell, eternal joy and eternal damnation rest in the balance.

I met Judy at a women's retreat. She told me the story of how she and her husband, John, had slowly wandered away from God. John and Judy both grew up in Christian homes. They met at Bible school. He got his degree in theology. She got hers in Christian education. Upon graduation, they both secured staff positions at a church in the Midwest. Their hearts were filled with love for God and a sense of hope and possibility for the future. But after a few years, they became disillusioned with the daily pressure and grind of church life and politics.

They decided they needed a break, so they resigned, found secular jobs, and moved to the East Coast. There, they just couldn't seem to find a church they liked. Eventually, they stopped going altogether. Their Bible reading and other spiritual disciplines also fell by the wayside. Although they still thought of themselves as Christians, they rarely talked about their faith, nor did they do anything to grow spiritually. No Christian friends lived nearby. Their circle of friends was unbelievers they knew from work and the community.

One Friday night, a new couple in the neighborhood invited John and Judy over to have some drinks and play cards. Judy wasn't entirely comfortable with the idea, but reasoned it could do no harm. The two couples hit it off and became close friends. Their Friday night card games became a regular highlight of the week. Judy couldn't remember exactly when, but at some point, hearts turned into poker, and poker turned into strip poker. And then, after they had grown accustomed to shedding all their clothes, the stakes got even higher. Sexual favors and sexual dares became the bets they placed on the table. By the time Judy sought me out to pray for her, their Friday night poker games had escalated into full-blown orgies with increasingly depraved sexual behavior. She had become a sexual addict, in severe bondage to pornography and sexual perversion. I prayed for her, but to this day, I do not know if she ever broke free.

If a friend in Bible college had asked Judy if she would ever participate in a sexual orgy, Judy would have scoffed at the question. It was preposterous! Of course she would never do that! She wouldn't compromise her morals. How could she? She was a Christian. She loved Jesus. Yet eight years later, Judy had all but forsaken Him and was walking in the land of forgetfulness. How did it happen? Very simply. *She stopped pondering the path of life.* A. W. Tozer warned, "The neglected heart will soon be a heart overrun with worldly thoughts; the neglected life will soon become a moral chaos."[2] With the decrease of godly influence and the increase of worldly influence, Judy slowly became what she was exposed to. Without her even realizing it, her way began to wander. She began to walk in the counsel of the ungodly, stand in the way of sinners, and sit in the assembly of scoffers. Each step was just a small compromise. But bit by bit, she became more and more entangled in sin.

THE COUNSEL OF THE UNGODLY

Bit by bit is the way it usually happens. A woman who faithfully follows Christ does not suddenly wake up one morning and decide to jump into bed with her neighbor. To get to that point, she will have made a series of small compromises along the way.

Compromise always begins by listening to the wrong counsel. That's exactly how the first woman, Eve, fell into sin. When the Serpent approached her, she listened to what he had to say. That was her first big mistake. After listening, she engaged in a conversation with him. Instead of rejecting his point of view, she mulled it over and let it percolate in her mind. She stared at the forbidden fruit and thought about all the benefits he said it had to offer. She entertained the idea that God was selfishly holding out and that He didn't really have her best interests at heart. Contemplating the Serpent's point of view was her second big mistake.

Eve's third big mistake was that she began to accept his ideas. She adjusted her beliefs to accommodate them. God's ways were definitely too restrictive. The consequences of disobedience were certainly overblown. She had a right to be happy and reach her full potential—she shouldn't let herself be denied. Her fourth big mistake was that she acted on her thoughts. She took the fruit and ate. The compromise in her mind led to a compromise in her behavior. And it all started by listening to the wrong counsel. Listening led to contemplating. Contemplating led to accepting. Accepting led to acting.[3]

What would have happened if Eve had declined to listen to ungodly counsel? What if she had refused to contemplate any point of view that differed from God's? What if she had repudiated instead of accepted the Serpent's faulty ideas? She would have nipped evil in the bud. She would not have compromised. She would not have sinned. She would not have wandered onto the path of death. Eve's biggest mistake of all was that she thought she was smart enough and strong enough to handle things without God's input and direction. She didn't think that something as simple as listening to the wrong counsel could get her into trouble or interfere with her relationship to the Lord.

Most of us recognize the danger of blatant evil, so we tend to set limits on the type and extent of sin to which we expose ourselves. When a TV show or movie presents us with occasional nudity, immorality, adultery, or profanity, we try to weigh the danger level. If it doesn't go beyond some arbitrary threshold of what we feel we are able to handle, we tolerate it, thinking it won't affect us. But evil is not benign. Author Josh Harris says we might as well ask how much of a poison pill we can swallow before it kills us.

> The greatest danger of the popular media is not a one-time exposure to a particular instance of sin (as serious as that can be). It's how long-term exposure to worldliness—little chunks of poison pill, day after day, week after week—can deaden our hearts to the ugliness of sin. . . . The eventual effect of all those bits of poison pill is to deaden the conscience by trivializing the very things that God's Word calls the enemies of our souls.
>
> Does anyone really believe that if I disapprove of the sin I'm watching, or roll my eyes and mutter about Hollywood's wickedness, or fast-forward through the really bad parts, my soul is not affected? Yeah, sure—and if you don't actually like chocolate cake, eating it won't add to your waistline.[4]

Pop culture is brim-full with the counsel of the ungodly. It's a poison-laced pill. As Harris says, it deadens our conscience by "trivializing the very things that God's Word calls the enemies of our souls." So should we throw away our DVRs and satellite dishes, ditch movies, disconnect from the Internet, cloister ourselves in a room, and refuse to go to the grocery store lest we expose ourselves to the images on the covers of the checkout counter magazines? No, of course not. But it is important that we do not shrug off the seriousness of exposing ourselves to evil, particularly when the exposure is constant. We must be cautious, wise, and vigilant, and ensure that listening to the counsel of the godly—and not the ungodly—remains our top priority and practice. "Whatever is true, whatever is honorable, whatever is just, whatever is pure, whatever is lovely, whatever is commendable, if there is any excellence, if there is anything worthy of praise, think about these things" (Philippians 4:8).

I have talked to thousands of women who have fallen into sin because they were unconcerned about their exposure to worldliness and complacent about pondering the way of the Lord. You are mistaken if you think that going to church for an hour a week will counteract the influence of thirty-three hours of TV. Do not think that you can constantly listen to ungodly counsel and remain uninfluenced by it—especially if you are not in the habit of pursuing godly input. Daily exposure to the world's way without a counteracting exposure to God's way will kill you just as surely as ingesting bits of poison without an antidote will.

TUNING IN TO GODLY COUNSEL

A Girl-Gone-Wise knows that God's ideas are radically different from the ideas of popular culture. Therefore, she tunes out what the world has to say and intentionally tunes in to what God has to say. She recognizes her need for ongoing godly input. She ponders the path of life. She disciplines herself and is not complacent.

A Wise Woman regularly feeds and nourishes her soul with the counsel of God's Word. Her *delight* is in the law of the Lord, and on His law she meditates *day and night*. She takes great delight in reading her Bible (Deuteronomy 17:19; Psalm 143:8). She studies it (Acts 17:11), memorizes it (Psalm 119:11), meditates on it (Psalm 119:97, 148), fixes her eyes on it (Psalm 119:14–16), and, above all, applies it (Psalm 119:1–3). She esteems the Word of God as a treasure and her safeguard against the way of evil:

> If you receive my words and treasure up my commandments with you
> . . . then you will understand . . . every good path; for wisdom will come
> into your heart, and knowledge will be pleasant to your soul; discretion will
> watch over you, understanding will guard you, delivering you from the way
> of evil. (Proverbs 2:1, 9–12)

The Counsel of the Godly

A Girl-Gone-Wise also counteracts ungodly influence by seeking out the counsel of the godly. Godly counsel comes from godly people. Ungodly people give ungodly counsel. "The thoughts of the righteous are just; the counsels of the wicked are deceitful" (Proverbs 12:5). That's why the wise woman makes sure she spends plenty of time in the company of those who are wholeheartedly following God.

Like the psalmist, she takes "sweet counsel" together with other believers (Psalm 55:14). She gathers with them regularly to worship, hear instruction, study the Bible, engage in fellowship, and encourage each other (Hebrews 10:25). She seeks out teachers who do not shrink from declaring the "whole counsel of God"—godly preachers, speakers, and authors who stand against the tide of popular culture and boldly teach sound doctrine (Acts 20:27). She listens to musicians whose lyrics faithfully extol Jesus Christ and His Word. She nurtures her closest friendships with those who are on fire for the Lord, and not with those whose hearts are lukewarm or cold toward Him (Psalm 141:4; 1 Corinthians 15:33). She seeks and listens to the instruction of older, godly female mentors (Titus 2:3–4).

The Bible teaches that older godly women, who love the Word and have figured out how to get life right, are a vital source of counsel for younger women. They have richer and more seasoned stores of advice than friends in the same stage of life. These older women can offer invaluable wisdom and training. They've been there, done that, gotten the T-shirt, the battle scars, and the know-how (and know-how-*not*). A Girl-Gone-Wise knows that when she walks in the counsel of God's Word and the counsel of the godly, her steps will be sure.

LEAVING THE LAND OF FORGETFULNESS

There's a scene in C. S. Lewis's Chronicles of Narnia, in the story of *The Silver Chair*, that reminds me of the effect that popular culture often has on us. The children and their friend the marshwiggle Puddleglum, go down to the Underworld to rescue a Narnian prince from the Witch-Queen's evil enchantment. They free him from the Silver Chair and are about to head back to the Overworld, when the Witch intervenes. She does not try to restrain them; instead, she throws a handful of green powder on the fire.

"It did not blaze much, but a very sweet and drowsy smell came from it. And all through the conversation which followed, that smell grew stronger, and filled the room, and made it harder to think." Next, the Witch began to strum on a mandolin-like instrument with her fingers—"a steady, monotonous thrumming that you didn't notice after a few minutes. But the less you noticed it, the more it got into your brain and your blood. This also made it hard to think."[5]

After the Witch has thrummed for a while, and the sweet smell is very strong, she begins to speak in a quiet, soothing voice, coaxing the Narnians to forget. As they breathe in the sweet, drowsy fragrance of the green powder and listen to the steady thrum, they do forget. Her subtle scheme lulls them into believing that there is no Narnia, no Overworld, no sky, no sun, no Aslan—that her Underworld is the only world that exists or matters—that they want to stay there with her. The enchantment is only broken when Puddleglum does a very brave thing. With his bare foot, he stamps on the fire, stops the overpowering smell from interfering with their ability to think, and loudly declares truth.

Do you see the lesson here? Satan tries to lull us with the sweet smell and steady thrum of worldliness. He wants us to forget God and become enchanted with evil. Stamping out his influence and listening to godly counsel is the only way to escape his subtle, yet powerful scheme. I want to challenge you to do a very brave thing. For the next thirty days, tune out the world so that you can tune in to the counsel of God. Reduce the amount of time you spend watching TV and movies, reading women's magazines, and surfing the net—cut it in half, or cut it out all together. Use that time, instead, to fill your mind with truth. Take the *Girls Gone Wise 30-Day Media Reduction Challenge*, and share your experience on www.GirlsGoneWise. com. Let me know what you did and how it went.

I think you'll be pleasantly surprised. The Bible says that tuning out the world and tuning in to God will increase your joy. It says "blessed" is she who walks not in the counsel of the ungodly, nor stands on the path of sinners, nor sits under the advice of those who scoff at God; but her delight is in the instruction of the Lord, and on His counsel, she meditates day and night (Psalm 1:1–2).

Point of Contrast #3

APPROACH
Who Directs
Her Love Story

Girl-Gone-Wild:	Girl-Gone-Wise:
Self-Manipulated	**God-Orchestrated**

"And behold, the woman meets him . . . *wily of heart*."	"She trusts in the Lord with all her heart, and does not lean on her own understanding. In all her ways she acknowledges Him and He makes her paths straight."
(Proverbs 7:10)	(Proverbs 3:5–6)

Wile E. Coyote is a cartoon character that stars in a Warner Brothers Looney Tunes cartoon series. His adventures all follow a typical pattern. The Coyote dreams up a new, elaborate plan to help him catch the Road Runner. Sometimes he obtains complex and ludicrous contraptions from the fictitious Acme mail-order corporation to help him: a rocket sled, jet-powered roller skates, or earthquake pills, for example. Invariably, his plot fails. And it always fails in an improbable and spectacular fashion. Instead of catching his prey, the Coyote ends up burnt to a crisp, squashed flat, or knocked senseless at the bottom of a canyon. Nevertheless, he egotistically calls himself "Super Genius" and compliments himself on his great ideas even as he watches them (or himself) go up in flames. Regardless of how often he blows himself up, falls from dizzying heights, and is flattened or mangled, Wile E. Coyote remains undaunted and tries again to catch his prey.

Creator Chuck Jones apparently based the character of Wile E. Coyote on Mark Twain's *Roughing It*, in which Twain describes the coyote as "a long, slim, sick, and sorry-looking skeleton" that is "a *living, breathing allegory of Want*."[1] When Wile E. Coyote made his debut in 1949, the audience assumed that he was just hungry, and had a good reason to chase the Road Runner. However, it soon became apparent that Wile E. Coyote wasn't just a silly coyote trying to get a meal. He had reasons for stalking the bird that were more nefarious. Desire and obsession had gripped him. He was "a living, breathing allegory of Want." Even if he were to catch the elusive Road Runner, Wile E. Coyote wouldn't be satisfied—or at least not for long. Just like an addict hooked on alcohol, drugs, or gambling, Wile E. Coyote was hopelessly addicted to the chase.

As you've probably figured out, the coyote's name is a play on phonics for the word *wily*. Wile E. Coyote is a wily coyote. *Wily* means crafty, cunning, sly, devious, or designing, characterized by subtle tricks and schemes. When Proverbs introduces the wayward woman, it identifies her as "wily of heart." A wily woman is calculating. She uses all sorts of tricks and schemes to insidiously entice, manipulate, and entrap. Desire and obsession have gripped her. She is a living, breathing example of Want.

A woman's *approach* to romance is the third point of contrast between a Wild Thing and a Wise Thing. A Girl-Gone-Wild is crafty. She plots and connives to manipulate her own love story. The Girl-Gone-Wise, on the other hand, trusts God to orchestrate the script.

A WILY WOMAN

The Sage Father tells his son that a Wild Thing is "wily of heart." The Hebrew word means guarded, blockaded, or secret. The phrase conveys the idea of a woman who has an underlying personal agenda, and secretly and skillfully manipulates men in order to get what she wants. The corresponding Greek term means "ready to do anything," usually in the bad sense of tricky and cunning behavior. The wily woman (1) has a personal agenda, (2) wants a man to satisfy it, and (3) does whatever is necessary to make that happen.

A famous biblical example of a wily woman is Delilah. Her story appears in Judges 16. Delilah was Samson's new girlfriend. After they started seeing each other, five Philistine rulers approached Delilah and offered her a considerable amount of money to seduce Samson into revealing the secret of his enormous strength. She had no qualms about using men, so she fast-forwarded their relationship and cranked up her feminine charm. "Please tell me where your great strength lies," she pleaded, "and how you might be bound, that one could subdue you." It's not hard to imagine her resting her head on Samson's chest, slowly tracing the outline of his bicep, and coyly teasing him until he gave her an answer.

Samson teased her back. "If they bind me with seven fresh bow-strings that have not been dried, then I shall become weak and be like any other man."

The next time Samson came, Delilah bound him with bowstrings. She had men hiding in an inner closet, ready to ambush him. But when she called out that the Philistines were on the doorstep, Samson jumped up and snapped his restraints like thread.

Seeing that her first attempt didn't produce the desired result, Delilah reverted to another tactic. She burst into tears. "Behold, you have mocked me and told me lies. Please tell me how you might be bound." She continued to sob and would not be comforted until Samson gave her the information she wanted. New ropes would do the trick. If she bound him with new ropes, he would be helpless as a kitten.

On his next visit, she had new ropes on hand. She seductively joked about taming her big kitten as she bound him hand and foot. Once again, when she called out to warn him of Philistines, Samson easily broke free. Seeing this, Delilah pouted and feigned offense at his continued lack of trust. When Samson tried to embrace her, she gave him the cold shoulder and pushed him away. Not until he told her that weaving his long hair into her loom would deprive him of strength did she cheer up, abandon her black mood, and allow him to embrace her.

Her loom went flying on a following visit, when Samson demon-strated for the third time that he had not been forthcoming with the information she wanted. Delilah was incensed. She lashed out in anger and began to accuse and badger him until he was "vexed to death" and finally gave in to her demand:

> And she said to him, "How can you say, 'I love you,' when your heart is not with me? You have mocked me these three times, and you have not told me where your great strength lies." And when she pressed him hard with her words day after day, and urged him, his soul was vexed to death. And he told her all his heart. (Judges 16:15–17)

You know the rest of the story. Delilah sent for the lords of the Philistines, made Samson fall asleep on her lap, and shaved off his hair—which represented his Nazirite vow and his special relationship to the Lord. "Then she began to torment him, and his strength left him." The Philistines seized Samson, gouged out his eyes, and threw him into prison. And Delilah got her bag of money.

PLANNING EVIL—DEVISING FOLLY

Delilah was exceptionally clever in the craft of manipulation. She obviously knew how to flirt, seduce, admire, compliment, pout, cry, reason, argue, lie, accuse, nag, and do whatever else was necessary to achieve her goal. Most women regard manipulating a man to get money as sordid and disgusting. So you may think that you and Delilah have very little in common. But is manipulating a man to get attention, love, or a ring on your finger that much different? Or is pouting, crying, or nagging to get him to comply with your demands? Or orchestrating circumstances to paint him into a corner? Or doling out physical affection as a reward? Or withholding it as punishment? If you have a noble end in mind, does that justify the means? Can scheming and conniving to manipulate someone for your own gain ever be justified? Is your craftiness any less wily or reprehensible than Delilah's?

The Bible teaches that crafty, cunning human wiles are "follies" (1 Corinthians 3:19). Folly is tragically foolish (thickheaded, dumb) conduct that goes against the ways of God. Folly is essentially a lack of wisdom. A "fool" in the Bible is a person who lives life as if God and God's way were of no consequence. It can mean a woman who, either by ignorance or by deliberate and calculated premeditation, relies on her own cunning to orchestrate what happens in her romantic relationship(s). Folly is more than just plain silliness. It actually demonstrates a disdain for God's truth and discipline. "Fools despise wisdom and instruction" (Proverbs 1:7).

In God's eyes, there is no difference between deliberately planning *evil* and devising a foolish, manipulative *scheme*. Delilah's plot to manipulate Samson to gain money and a contemporary woman's scheme to manipulate a man to get something from him, fall into the same category. Both are sin. Proverbs 24:8–9 says, "Whoever plans to do evil will be called a schemer. The devising of folly is sin, and the scoffer is an abomination to mankind."

Delilah was a schemer—a vixen. She planned to do evil. But according to this verse, "the devising of folly" is also sin. In God's eyes, wily behavior is sinful behavior. It is evil. So even if a woman has a noble goal in mind—love or marriage, for example—using under-handed cunning and craftiness to reach that goal is unwise. The end doesn't justify the means. The woman who uses her wiles to manipulate a man is just as guilty of sin as the vixen who plots evil. The verse concludes by pointing out that both are scoffers and an abomination to mankind.

Wow. That's pretty strong language! Wily, manipulative women are "scoffers" and an "abomination." What does that mean? To scoff is to scorn, to show contempt, to treat with disrespect or derision, to make fun of. According to Scripture, a wily woman scorns God. She demonstrates contempt for Him. When she decides to manipulate men and circumstances for her own gain, she treats God with derision and disrespect. When she relies on her own craftiness instead of relying on the Lord, it is just as though she mocks and makes fun of God's ways.

An "abomination" is something that greatly offends God's righteousness and evokes His extreme hatred and disgust. It is something that gives off a horrible, odious smell and is abhorrent and reprehensible to Him. The definition reminds me of the time I walked into an apartment defiled by numerous cats. The cat litter and feculence hadn't been cleaned for months and was everywhere. The sharp, caustic stench was more than I could bear. I ran from the room with my nose and eyes dripping, coughing, gagging, and gasping for clean air. An "abomination" is to God's senses what that room was to mine. It disgusts Him. Examples of abominations include defective sacrifices (Deuteronomy 17:1), magic and divination (Deuteronomy 18:12), idolatrous practices (2 Kings 16:3), homosexual conduct (Leviticus 18:22), and sexual immorality (Revelation 17:4–5).

Would you have expected scheming and devising folly to appear on the list of things that are an abomination to the Lord? Do you realize how offended He is by foolish, manipulative behavior? A "heart that devises wicked plans" is near the top of the list of things He absolutely hates (Proverbs 6:16–18).

SNARES, NETS, AND FETTERS

If you flip through the latest women's magazines, you're bound to find a generous amount of advice on what girls need to do in order to attract, snag, and keep a guy . . . how to bait the hook, cast the line, reel him in, or net the catch. Incidentally, did you know that the average woman reads twelve magazines a month? The demographic reading the highest average number of issues in a month is women aged eighteen to thirty-four. They read more than thirteen.[2] (That's more than 150 each year—which is a lot of worldly counsel!) The statistics aren't broken down into the types of magazines, but I think it's safe to assume that the majority of magazines read by women in that age group feature tons of advice on male-female relationships. They specifically instruct women how to be crafty so they can get what they want from men.

Popular magazines and media tell a girl to calculate every move in a romantic relationship. They teach her how to get noticed, how to signal interest, how to strike up a conversation, how to flirt, how to drop hints, how to stroke his ego, how to inflate his desire, how to please him sexually, how to maintain his interest, how to ward off the competition, how to get him to commit, and so on. They teach her to be a vixen, a fox—not only in the way she looks, but also in the way she thinks and behaves.

The problem is that this approach to male-female relationships trains a woman to develop the instincts of a hunter. Her foxy manipulations fill her heart with "snares" and "nets." The only way she knows how to get and keep the attention of a man is to entrap him in her "fetters." To the male writer of Ecclesiastes, this is a fate more bitter than death. "And I find something more bitter than death: the woman whose heart is snares and nets, and whose hands are fetters" (Ecclesiastes 7:26). He laments that although it may be rare to find a male who does not revert to manipulation, finding such a female is nearly impossible (v. 28). He had never met a woman without a hidden agenda.

I asked my son and three of his single, young-adult male friends to help me brainstorm and come up with a list of categories for the types of wily female manipulations they and I had either observed or encountered. We boiled it down to five general categories: sexual manipulation, verbal manipulation, emotional manipulation, spiritual manipulation, and circumstantial manipulation.

Sexual Manipulation

No surprise here. The number one scheme of women is to use their sexuality to control or manipulate a man's behavior. This includes, but is not limited to, immodest clothing, flirting, sexual banter and innuendo, the "come get me" look and other nonverbal turn-ons, all types of physical contact, and giving (or punitively withholding) physical affection and intimate sexual relations and acts. The world teaches us that sexuality is a woman's primary tool and/or weapon. She uses it to get the man she wants and then uses it to get what she wants from him.

Verbal Manipulation

A woman can use words to coax, reason, nag, explain, bombard, insinuate, lecture, harangue, cajole, accuse, wheedle, convince, and otherwise proselytize the guy so that he gives in to her way of thinking. The man leaves the conversation feeling like she has tap-danced on his head. He agrees to change his mind and do things her way, but he has no idea why, like Samson, who was "vexed to death" when Delilah urged him and "pressed him hard with her words day after day." The only way he was able to stop her incessant, confusing verbiage was to give in to her demands.

Emotional Manipulation

Any girl knows that one of the best ways to manipulate a guy is to turn on the waterworks. Many a woman has gotten her way by shedding tears. And then there are the tactics of pouting, sulking, acting hurt, lashing out, or emotionally withdrawing. Or how about securing his loyalty by manipulating him into feeling threatened and jealous? Or what about the "If you really loved me you would . . ." line?

A woman one of the young men in the room had dated tried to manipulate him by appealing to his protective nature. She made up stories about guys following her and insisted that she needed to come see him because she was so afraid. She also magnified symptoms of a physical ailment whenever she wanted more of his attention. Not only that, but when he tried to end their relationship, she threatened to do something to hurt herself. (Yup. This girl sounds like a real zinger!) The "I-need-you-so-much-you're-my-savior-my-life-would-fall-apart-without-you" scheme appeals to the protector-provider in almost every man.

I'm not saying that emotions are wrong. Nor am I saying that women shouldn't express them. The problem is not when a woman expresses her feelings, but when she does so with the subtle, underlying intent to control and manipulate the man.

Spiritual Manipulation

I didn't think of this one right off the bat. My son did. It's an "extra" form of manipulation that Christian girls will sometimes pull out of their purses. This is the "I-prayed-about-it-and-I-know-it's-God's-will-for-us-to-be-together (even-if-you-don't)" tactic. It, too, is a subtle form of manipulation.

Circumstantial Manipulation

It amazes me how much time and energy some women expend to plot and set up circumstances that give them an opportunity to get a man to do something he would not otherwise do. For instance, take the girl who just happens to be walking past the building when he leaves work. ("Fancy bumping into you!" she says, after waiting for him for an hour.) Or what about the girl who shows up at his apartment soaked to the skin from getting "caught" in the rain. ("Whoops—oh my goodness, it *would* have to happen on a day I wasn't wearing a bra!") Or the one who somehow locks herself out of her apartment at midnight and needs a place to stay? Or the one whose parents simply couldn't get two days off work to drive her out to college? Or the one who "falls" and sprains an ankle so he has to carry her to his car?

An example of circumstantial manipulation in the Bible is found in the story of Amnon and Tamar:

> Amnon had a friend, whose name was Jonadab, the son of Shimeah, David's brother. And Jonadab was a very crafty man. And he said to him, "O son of the king, why are you so haggard morning after morning? Will you not tell me?" Amnon said to him, "I love Tamar, my brother Absalom's sister." Jonadab said to him, "Lie down on your bed and pretend to be ill. And when your father comes to see you, say to him, 'Let my sister Tamar come and give me bread to eat, and prepare the food in my sight, that I may see it and eat it from her hand.'" (2 Samuel 13:3–5)

Amnon follows through with the manipulative scheme. He feigns illness, gets his dad to send Tamar to fix him a bowl of hot soup, gets Tamar into his bedroom alone, and declares his love for her. He tries to kiss her and win her over, but when she resists his advances, he forces her to have sex. The sex would have never happened had he not slyly manipulated circumstances to make the opportunity possible. In this instance, it was the manipulative behavior of a man, and not a woman, that set up the scenario for sin. But the story demonstrates the point nonetheless.

The most memorable instance of crafty behavior is, of course, the serpent's manipulation of the first woman, Eve. "Now the serpent was more crafty than any other beast of the field that the Lord God had made" (Genesis 3:1). His crafty, underhanded brilliance operated in stark contrast to the beautiful naked innocence of the first man and woman. The devil's craftiness deceived the woman and brought about the fall of humanity. At that time, women and men lost the beauty of innocence, and were infected with the evil tendency to be crafty and underhanded with one another. What's more, because of God's specific sentence on Eve, the tendency to manipulate men is a sin to which all women are particularly susceptible. Later we'll see how men are susceptible to their own particular type of sin.

The Lord "frustrates the devices of the crafty, so that their hands achieve no success. He catches the wise in their own craftiness, and the schemes of the wily are brought to a quick end. They meet with darkness in the daytime and grope at noonday as in the night" (Job 5:12–14). Have you ever noticed that a wily woman is rarely satisfied? Oh, she may get the guy, the ring on her finger, and her way, but she doesn't get what she needs to fill that gaping ache in her heart. Apart from abandoning her selfish, manipulative tendencies and trusting the Lord with her heart, she, like Wile E. Coyote, will experience a perpetual case of "Want."

A RADICALLY DIFFERENT APPROACH

Girls-Gone-Wise adopt a radically different approach to male-female relationships than the Wild Things of the world. A Girl-Gone-Wise renounces "disgraceful, underhanded ways" and refuses to "practice cunning" (2 Corinthians 4:2). She rejects the worldly belief that in order to get a guy, a woman must manipulatively toss out the bait and reel him in. She refuses to play that game. Instead, she seeks to be godly, above-board, unpretentious, and without guile in her relationships with men.

She trusts in the Lord with all her heart and does not lean on her own understanding. In *all* her ways she acknowledges Him, and He directs her paths. She does what my friend Leslie Ludy did. She gives up control, hands her pen to God, and lets Him write her love story. As Leslie says:

> The One who knows you better than you know yourself, and who loves you more than you can comprehend, wants to take you on a journey.
>
> This journey is for anyone who is searching for the beauty of true and lasting love, for romance in its purest form, and who is willing to do whatever it takes in order to find it. This journey is for anyone who has made mistakes, whether small or big, and said, "It's too late for me to discover *that* kind of love." It's a journey for anyone who is tired of the same old scene of physically intense relationships, devoid of meaning and purpose.
>
> This journey is for anyone who will dare to dream beyond the cheap and diluted romance our culture offers and hold out for an infinitely better way. This journey is even for the skeptic, who doubts that such a way exists.

No matter where you are or where you have been, this invitation is for you. The very One who is the Author of all true love and romance is standing before you, asking you gently, *Will you let Me write your love story?*[3]

The invitation is for the married as well as the single. It contains no guarantee of finding the perfect man, or of having your man transformed into one. But it does hold the promise of a spectacular story line—one that can satisfy the deep desires of a woman's heart to an infinitely greater extent than crafting her own love story ever could. Jesus wants to lavish you with love. He wants you to taste and see that *He* is good. And that good things happen when you stop being wily and trust Him with your love story.

(There are questions for personal reflection and a testimony of a woman who trusted God to write her love story, on GirlsGoneWise. com. Surf on over and check it out.)

Point of Contrast #4

ATTITUDE
Her Prevailing Disposition

Girl-Gone-Wild: **Clamorous & Defiant**	Girl-Gone-Wise: **Gentle, Calm, Amenable**
"She is loud and wayward . . ." (Proverbs 7:11)	Her heart reflects the imperishable beauty of a gentle and quiet spirit, which in God's sight is very precious. (I Peter 3:4)

I remember striding down the school hallway with a couple of girl-friends in the early seventies, belting out the words of Helen Reddy's chart-topping song, "I Am Woman." We sang about being strong and invincible. We were determined to show the world that we were in control. The words of the song summed up our resolve: We were women, and we would ROAR in numbers too big to ignore—no one would ever keep us down again! We were perched on the verge of womanhood. And we were confident that we would be the first generation to get the meaning of womanhood right.

Feminism taught the girls of my generation that men had terribly oppressed our mothers and grandmothers, and their mothers and grandmothers before them. Patriarchy had forced women to conform to an image of womanhood that men had conjured up to serve their own needs and egos. Men had seized all the positions of power. They had kept women in a subservient position by nefariously convincing them that there was no nobler female title or occupation than that of "wife" and "mother." (Gasp! What a travesty! How could they? Will someone please cue some heavy, ominous background music?)

Feminists informed us that marriage and motherhood catered to the selfish male agenda. Men got to do all the important stuff—like punch a time clock and earn money—while they forced women to stay home and do the trivial, demeaning work of homemaking and raising snotty-nosed kids. (At this point, the ominous music gets even more ominous!) The workplace provided men with prestige and power, and their wives provided them with sex and servitude. This arrangement totally favored the male. All he had to do was bring home the paycheck, fix the car, and cut the lawn.

When it came right down to it, men were nothing but lazy, power-hungry bums who married women for the men's own selfish ends. (And this is where the sound track screeches to its scariest, nail-biting crescendo . . .) I am being facetious, of course. But it's hard to believe how completely taken we were by those ideas. I know that you may be thinking that staying home and raising children while your husband financially supports the family sounds idyllic. Unbelievably, feminism claimed that this arrangement was inherently oppressive. And for the most part, the women of my generation swallowed the ruse.

According to feminism, not only did men seize power by occupying all the important roles in society, they also seized it by laying claim to all the important character traits. Patriarchy promoted the idea that the powerful attributes of strength, assertiveness, aggression, initiative, leadership, control, independence, self-reliance, and self-sufficiency were more characteristic of the male gender. All of the weak, insignificant traits belonged to women. Society upheld kindness, gentleness, purity, warm-heartedness, tenderness, and submissiveness as noble feminine virtues. The women of the past bought into the idea that these virtues were both womanly and noble. But this, too, was part of the male plot to keep women subservient to men.

Thanks to the brave efforts of the feminist movement, we women got wise to patriarchy's villainous scheme. We learned that what we needed to do, in order to remedy the age-old injustice, was to reclaim the *power* that men had stolen from us. Man (and not woman) had defined what womanhood was all about. It was time for women to fix that. It was time for Girl Power!

Feminism instructed us that the way to exert power was to reject all the traditional "male-defined" rules about marriage, motherhood, morality, and the meaning and nature of womanhood. So that's what we did. We embraced education, careers, prominence. We despised all relationships and responsibilities that might hold us back. We moved marriage, mothering, and homemaking from the top of our lists to the bottom—or crossed them off altogether. After all, we were so much more enlightened than our foremothers were. The world had revolved around men, but it was our turn now. We would make it bow to our demands.

We decided that the role of a housewife was passé. *Charlie's Angels* seemed so much more exciting. So we redefined boundaries. We changed the rules of male-female relationships. We boldly pushed back against traditional definitions of gender and sexuality. We claimed our freedoms and our rights. We bought into the feminist promise that woman would find happiness and fulfillment when she defined her own identity and decided for herself what life as a woman was all about.

Over the next few decades, culture's definition of womanhood did change. The ideal went from a home-based, nurturing wife and mom (think *Leave It to Beaver*) to a self-indulgent, promiscuous, narcissistic professional (think *Sex and the City*). The media stopped portraying women as sweet, nurturing wives and homemakers, and started portraying them as ripped, in-your-face, male-kicking, sassy heroines who were tough, dominating, hypersexual, and above all in control.

Nowadays we hold in high esteem the assertive, aggressive, tough, calculating, controlling, independent, self-reliant, self-sufficient, brazenly sexual women. Traits of kindness, gentleness, faithfulness, purity, warm-heartedness, tenderness, and submissiveness have all but fallen to the wayside. They are devalued and even scorned. The reason I took you on a trip down memory lane was to show you why. Due to the impact of the women's movement, today's women reject the very disposition that makes women uniquely "feminine"—the one that distinguishes them as God's perfect counterpart to men.

The traits that we value for women are not always the traits the Lord values. And the traits we scorn are often the very ones that are precious in His sight. The biblical stance on the appropriate demeanor for women is extremely countercultural. It goes directly against the grain of how pop culture has programmed us to think. According to the Bible, a Girl-Gone-Wise is not tough and aggressive. Nor is she clamorous and defiant. She forsakes this attitude for a soft, womanly disposition.

THAT GIRL'S GOT ATTITUDE!

"She is loud and wayward" is how the Sage Father pegs the Proverbs 7 woman. The phrase definitely describes her behavior, but more than that, it sums up her prevailing state of mind. She's a sassy, defiant, my-way-or-the-highway kind of a girl. Nowadays, the father might have described her by saying, "She's got attitude!"

The Hebrew word *loud* implies murmuring, growling, roaring, or being tumultuous or clamorous. The description applies to an untamable beast that refuses to bear the yoke. "Like a stubborn heifer" is how the prophet Hosea describes this mind-set among people who refused to obey God (4:16). I think it's ironic that Helen Reddy talks about women roaring in the lyrics of her song, because that's exactly what a Girl-Gone-Wild does. She roars. And it's not so much the volume of her voice, although it definitely can include that. It's her insolence. Synonyms for this clamorous type of attitude are *sassy, brassy, cheeky, cocky, flippant, mouthy, saucy, smart-alecky, barefaced, brash,* or *pushy.* It's an attitude that pop culture promotes and even admires. "Girl, you've got attitude!" is more compliment than insult.

The second adjective describing the Proverbs 7 woman is translated as *wayward.* The Hebrew word means "to be stubborn and rebellious." It reflects a defiant, self-willed, obstinate, "nobody-tells-me-what-to-do" frame of mind. According to the Bible, an attitude of stubbornness toward people often reflects an underlying attitude of stubbornness toward the Lord (Ezekiel 20:38). Ours is a "stubborn and rebellious generation," whose heart is not steadfast, whose spirit is not faithful to God (Psalm 78:8).

A Girl-Gone-Wild is stubborn. She gets irritated and sullen when someone tries to correct or rebuff her. She is not willing to give in or change. She turns a stubborn shoulder (Nehemiah 9:29), plugs her ears (Zechariah 7:11), turns aside and goes her own way (Jeremiah 5:23–26). A woman like this "sticks to her guns." She will not budge. Her way is right in her own eyes. She is not open to input (Proverbs 12:15). One theologian uses the word *unmanageable* to describe a woman with this type of attitude. Another suggests *ungovernable*. The bottom line is that this type of woman refuses to be led—especially by a man. No one has the right to tell her what to do.

Clamorousness (loudness) and defiance (waywardness) go hand in hand. Clamorousness loudly insists, "You better do it my way," and defiance reinforces the idea with, "I refuse to do it yours." They are like two sides of the same coin. Pop culture preaches that women *should* have a clamorous-defiant attitude. It extols it as a virtue. Oh, it often dresses it up nicely and calls it something that makes it sound a bit more respectable—like self-confidence, assertiveness, or personal empowerment—but it really boils down to the same thing: the brash, rebellious attitude of a Girl-Gone-Wild.

"Ms. Stupidity" is what the Bible calls a girl with this attitude. I'm not kidding. That's equivalent to what the Bible actually calls her! It says that Lady Folly is rowdy; "she is gullible and knows nothing" (Proverbs 9:13 HSCB). Folly is empty-headedness, craziness, absurdity, stupidity. Proverbs says that a brash, rebellious demeanor is foolish. It specifically warns women against adopting this mind-set. The Bible is very clear that embracing a defiant attitude isn't liberating and wonderful, as the world would have us believe. It's downright stupid. "Claiming to be wise, they became fools" (Romans 1:22). Janet's testimony shows the negative effect a rebellious attitude can have on a relationship:

> Not long ago, my husband of thirty plus years left me for another woman. Listening to you teach about biblical womanhood has opened my eyes to why this happened. I know that he is responsible for his infidelity and betrayal, and I won't justify his sin. But I know that my bad attitude over the years probably drove him to it.

If I were to pick a word to describe my manner toward my husband, it would be "resistant." I was forever resisting him. If he came up with an idea, I suggested a different or better one. If he wanted me to do something, I dug in my heels. If he tried to make a decision, I objected. If he asked me to reconsider, I would refuse. I continually corrected him and put him down. And I always had a sharp comeback ready on the tip of my tongue.

You have to understand that my husband was not a demanding man. He was very kind. But because I believed that compliance was a sign of weakness, and that women should *never* subject themselves to men, I constantly undermined him. I would not let him lead. Even in the smallest, most insignificant matters, I absolutely refused to follow.

Looking back, I can sadly see how my constant resistance chipped away at his manhood and at our relationship. I resisted and resisted until he gave up, and walked away and into the arms of a woman who welcomed his strength. I was very foolish. If I had the chance to do it all again, I would try to do things God's way. Sadly, it's too late for me, but it isn't too late for all the young women you teach. The world may not believe it, but a gentle, quiet, submissive spirit doesn't demean women. This attitude is precious to God. If it would have been precious to me, I probably would have celebrated my thirty-second anniversary last week. Instead, I was mocked by an empty house and a heavy heart full of regret.

The world thinks a sassy, defiant attitude is the epitome of empowered womanhood. It breaks my heart when I see Christian women fall for this lie. The Evil One has deceived us. A rebellious attitude does not strengthen a woman, nor does it strengthen her love relationship. Quite the opposite, in fact. As Janet and countless others have discovered, rebellion diminishes rather than enhances a woman's life.

STEEL MAGNOLIA

A brazen, defiant attitude stands in stark contrast to the soft receptiveness that the Lord intended for women. When I think of His original design, the Southern phrase "steel magnolia" comes to mind. I'm a Northern woman, so I don't know all the nuances of Southern talk. I wouldn't know when to drawl, "Well bless your heart!" if my life depended on it. I'm just not the pink, frilly, fluffy type. Nevertheless,

I do like the phrase "steel magnolia", because to me it speaks to the essence of womanhood. The image melds beauty with perseverance, softness with backbone, delicacy with durability, sweetness with stamina. It reminds me of what the first man exclaimed when he saw the first woman. When Adam laid his eyes on her, he broke into an exuberant, spontaneous poem:

> "This at last is bone of my bones and flesh of my flesh; she shall be called Woman (*Isha*), because she was taken out of Man (*Ish*)." (Genesis 2:23)

The first man called himself *"Ish"* and the woman *"Isha."* This appears to be an extremely clever and profound play on words. The sound of these two Hebrew words is nearly identical—*Isha* merely adds a feminine ending—but the two words have a complementary meaning. *Ish* comes from the root meaning "strength," while *Isha* comes from the root meaning "soft."

The implication becomes clearer when we observe the biblical meaning of a man's "strength." The Hebrew root is commonly associated with the wisdom, strength, and vitality of the successful warrior. It carries the idea of a champion valiantly serving his people by protectively fighting on their behalf. Strength can also refer to a man's manhood—his virility (Psalm 105:36; Proverbs 31:3; Genesis 49:3). Woman's corresponding trait is her fertility—her unique capability to nurture and bring forth life. He is "strong" directed by inner softness. She is "soft" directed by inner strength.

The bodies of male and female reflect the idea of this complementary distinction. A man's body is built to move toward the woman. A woman's body is built to receive the man. But the pattern goes beyond the mere physical difference between men and women to encompass the totality of their essence: The man was created to joyfully and actively initiate and give. The woman was created to joyfully and actively respond and receive. The woman is the beautiful "soft" one—the receiver, responder, and relater. The man is the "strong" one with greater capacity to initiate, protect, and provide. Each is a perfect counterpart to the other.

Although our culture portrays the ideal woman as aggressive and tough—both physically and sexually—this is a far cry from what

woman was created to be. According to Scripture, it's woman's softness, her ability to receive, respond, and relate, that is her greatest
strength.

THE RIGHT STUFF

You don't have to be a girly-girl to cultivate a soft, beautiful womanly disposition. A woman who rides a Harley or spends her days in
chaps wrangling steers, can be just as womanly as the daintiest southern belle. Womanliness has to do with a female's demeanor rather
than her occupation, hobbies, or talents. It's more of an *internal* than
an *external* characteristic. It involves *who she is* more than it involves
what she does.

The primary passage that outlines the disposition of godly women
is 1 Peter 3:4–6. Peter talks about "the imperishable beauty of a *gentle*
and *quiet* spirit." He also talks about *deference*—a willingness to respond
that expresses itself in a married woman's life as her submission to her
husband. Scripture maintains that these three basic qualities are foundational to godly womanhood. A Girl-Gone-Wise is not clamorous and
defiant. She is (1) gentle, (2) calm, and (3) amenable.

Gentle

Godly women are gentle. Gentleness (often translated as "meekness") is a mild, friendly, kind, considerate disposition. Here are some
synonyms that my thesaurus lists for *gentle*:

affable, agreeable, amiable, biddable, compassionate, considerate, culti-
vated, disciplined, genial, humane, kindly, lenient, manageable, meek, merciful, moderate, pacific, peaceful, pleasant, pliable, soft, softhearted,
sweet-tempered, sympathetic, tame, taught, temperate, tender, tractable,
trained, warmhearted.

Gentleness isn't weakness. It's the strength of character that enables
a person to respond in a kind, considerate way to others' weakness—
to put up with their impositions and imperfections. In 1 Thessalonians 2:7, gentleness is portrayed as the type of disposition a nursing
mother has as she cares for and caters to her fussy child. Gentleness
is the reverse of being insistent on one's own rights, being rude or

pushy, or demanding one's own way. It's the exact opposite of the loud, clamoring attitude of a Girl-Gone-Wild.

Gentleness is a disposition in which we see the Lord's dealings with us as good and therefore accept them without disputing or resisting. Gentleness means we wholly rely on God rather than our own strength to defend ourselves against inconvenience, hardship, or injustice. It stems from trust in God's goodness and control over the situation. Gentleness isn't self-abasement. It's the mark of the wise woman who remains calm even in the face of other people's shortcomings.

According to the Bible, there are numerous benefits to having this type of attitude. The gentle "delight themselves in abundant peace" (Psalm 37:11). They constantly obtain "fresh joy in the Lord" (Isaiah 29:19). Jesus said, "Blessed are the meek [gentle], for they shall inherit the earth" (Matthew 5:5).

Calm

Calmness is the second characteristic of a Girl-Gone-Wise. Most translations use the word *quiet* to describe this attitude of serenity and tranquility. Being calm means being settled, firm, immovable, steadfast, and peaceful in spirit. A calm disposition is like a still, peaceful pool of water, as opposed to a churning whirlpool that's agitated and stirred up. It's the opposite of the anxious, distressed, disorderly, and clamorous spirit of the Girl-Gone-Wild. "For the wicked are like the tossing sea; for it cannot be quiet, and its waters toss up mire and dirt" (Isaiah 57:20). When women lack a calm spirit, they toss up all kinds of "mire" and "dirt" in their relationships.

According to the Bible, a calm spirit goes hand in hand with trusting the Lord. "In quietness and in trust shall be your strength" (Isaiah 30:15). God's love quiets us and is the source of our calm (Zephaniah 3:17). What's more, calmness and trust are both a result of righteousness: "the result of righteousness [is] quietness and trust forever" (Isaiah 32:17). "Quietness" has more to do with the state of our hearts than the quantity and volume of our words (although the one definitely influences the other). Even women who are gregarious, extroverted, and sociable can achieve a calm, tranquil spirit.

Amenable

A third aspect of a beautiful womanly disposition is the inclination to bend, comply, or submit. Godly women are amenable. The word comes from the French *amener* (to lead). An amenable woman is "leadable" as opposed to "ungovernable." An amenable woman is inclined to say, "Amen!"—which means, "Yes!" She's responsive to input and likely to cooperate. I believe that the Lord created women (all women) with an amenable disposition. He created us with a soft, deferent spirit—a disposition or tendency that joyfully responds and yields to the will of others.

Amenability is really a more sophisticated way of saying "respect." Amenability is an attitude that respects others and esteems God's proper lines of authority. An amenable woman gladly foregoes personal desires and preferences to honor that authority. Other words for amenability are *deference, homage, submission, reverence,* and *consideration.* Antonyms (opposites) include *insolence, irreverence, disesteem, disfavor, discourtesy,* and *rudeness.* The amenable disposition of a Girl-Gone-Wise is the exact opposite of the wayward, rebellious attitude of the Girl-Gone-Wild.

Amenability is the disposition that made Eve beam with joy when Adam named her. It's the disposition that made Mary respond to the angel's startling news of her coming pregnancy with "Behold, I am the servant of the Lord; let it be to me according to your word" (Luke 1:38). And it's the beautiful disposition that the Lord desires each one of His daughters to cultivate.

FEAR FACTOR

The beautiful softness of womanhood was severely damaged when Eve sinned. The Lord informed Eve that sin's horrible consequence was that her "desire" would be for man, but that man would "rule" over her (Genesis 3:16). Theologians have spent a lot of time figuring out what this verse means, but what it boils down to is this: Sin twisted the positive desire of woman to respond amenably to man into a negative desire to resist and rebel against him. It twisted the positive drive of man to use his strength to lead, protect, and provide for woman, into a negative tendency to abuse or refuse that responsibility.

Read that statement again. It's important that you understand the far-reaching consequences of how your womanhood has been affected by sin. Sin damaged woman's inherent softness. Sin also damaged man's inherent strength. That's why maintaining the right disposition can be such struggle.

The world leads us to believe that we must fight for our rights. It teaches us that we need to look out for number one. It teaches women that an attitude of clamorousness and defiance is necessary to ensure we don't become doormats or punching bags. It suggests that those who exchange the Girl-Gone-Wild attitude for the Girl-Gone-Wise attitude will surely lose power and be diminished. I call this the "fear factor."

First Peter 3:6 says that we are Sarah's daughters if we seek a gentle, calm, amenable disposition and *don't give in to fear.* If truth be told, the reason women are clamorous and defiant is that they're scared not to act this way. They're scared of softness. They're scared of vulnerability. In essence, they're scared of womanhood (and of manhood). They're scared that if they become soft and vulnerable, that they will be taken advantage of, and will be reduced to weak, quivering, spineless blobs, devoid of will or personality. They're scared that adopting womanly traits will cause them to be "less" and not "more."

Is it true? If you adopt a gentle, calm, amenable spirit, will it diminish your personality? Will you get stomped on? Will it make you less than who you are? That was Cindy's fear:

> I cut my teeth on feminist philosophy. I was a strong, independent, capable woman who wasn't afraid to elbow her way to the top. If I had to steamroll over some men in the process, well, so be it. I was loud, brash, self-confident, self-promoting, and aggressive, the epitome of what feminism taught me womanhood was all about.
>
> It was with great dismay that I discovered, in a Bible study, that God had a very different perspective on womanhood than I did. When I read adjectives like "quiet," "gentle," "meek," and "submissive," I balked. Being those things went against every fiber of my being. I was literally terrified that pursuing these traits would diminish me into a quivering bowl of jelly. I would lose my personality and become less of a person . . . less of who I am.
>
> Conviction won out, and I begrudgingly told the Lord I was willing

to die to self and be what he wanted me to be, even if it meant losing "me." I would be obedient and to try to cultivate the type of womanhood taught in Scripture.

It wasn't easy. I had to work hard at it, and I can't say that the process is complete yet. Did I sacrifice and give up some things? Yes, definitely. But it dawned on me the other day that I have gained so much more, and that my fear was unfounded. I didn't lose myself. In fact, quite the opposite happened.

In trying to be the woman God wanted me to be I found out who I really am. It's as though Jesus removed the ugly, cracked paint so that the beautiful pattern of the wood could shine through. The joy and peace are incredible. I love being a woman according to His design. And paradoxically, my personhood did not diminish. I am more "Cindy" now than I ever was before.

When it comes to attitude, you have a choice to make. Will you accept the deceptive lie that God's way will diminish you? Or are you going to fight the fear factor? Will you hang on to sin's twisted distortion of what it means to be a woman? Or will you be transformed into whom the Lord created you to be? Will you choose the clamorousness and defiance of a Girl-Gone-Wild? Or the gentle, calm, amenable spirit of a Girl-Gone-Wise?

SWIMMING UPSTREAM

"Wait a minute," you may argue. "Godly attributes are not unique to gender. They're the same for both genders. Women ought to possess strength, initiative, resourcefulness, and enterprise just as men ought to possess gentleness, calmness, and amenability. The Bible doesn't say that the last three attributes belong exclusively to women. It's just as important for men to be gentle, calm, and amenable!" To this, I answer yes and no.

Yes, these attributes are characteristic of both genders. And yes, men should seek to be gentle, calm, and amenable. (Just as women should seek to possess strength, imitativeness, resourcefulness, and enterprise.) But no, these characteristics are not the same in men as they are in women. Gentleness, calmness, and amenability look different in a man than they do in a woman. The texture is markedly different. In a man, the traits have a uniquely masculine texture. In a woman, they have a uniquely feminine one. His gentleness is strong and initiatory. Hers is soft and responsive. His gentleness moves out and toward. Her gentleness accepts and welcomes in. Therefore the traits should not receive the same emphasis for both genders. Some traits are uniquely important to what it means to be a man, and some are uniquely important to what it means to be a woman. The Bible identifies the ones that deserve special sex-specific attention.

The idea that women should cultivate a soft-spirited attitude is very countercultural. Those who accept and try to live out this idea will find themselves swimming upstream against the current—even against ideas about womanhood that are prevalent in the church. Our cultural milieu makes biblical concepts seem very abrasive.

I'm aware of how foreign some of these ideas may seem to you—especially if you are hearing them for the first time. When I was a young woman and first encountered some ideas about biblical womanhood written by some fuddy-duddy lady, I pitched her book across the room in disgust. I find it amusing to think that I am now the fuddy-duddy one, and that some of you may pitch *my* book across the room in disgust. That's OK. I understand. You don't have to agree with everything I say. All I ask is that you consider these ideas and hold them up to the light of Scripture to see if they are true. I have no doubt that this will be a journey for you, as it was for me.

The Bible has a spectacular vision for what womanhood is all about! With the right heart, the right counsel, the right approach, and the right attitude, you will be well on your way to being a Girl-Gone-Wise.

Don't forget to visit the website GirlsGoneWise.com to download some questions to help you apply what you've learned.

Point of Contrast #5

HABITS
Her Priorities and Routines

Girl-Gone-Wild: Self-Indulgent	Girl-Gone-Wise: Self-Disciplined
"Her feet do not stay at home; now in the street, now in the market, and at every corner."	"She looks well to the ways of her household and does not eat the bread of idleness."
(Proverbs 7:11–12)	(Proverbs 31:27)

Texans are familiar with the saying, "Red touches yellow, kill a fellow; red touches black, venom lack." This old reminder helps people distinguish between the deadly, venomous coral snake and the harmless milk snake. Both snakes have alternating bands of red, black, and yellow, but the order and pattern of the colors is different. Red-to-black-striped milk snakes are quite docile. Some people even keep them as exotic pets. But the red-to-yellow-striped coral snake's bite can be fatal. Its fangs inject a potent neurotoxin that paralyzes nerves and breathing muscles. Mechanical or artificial respiration, along with large doses of antivenom, is often required to save a victim's life.

Just as folks in Texas can tell a milk snake from a coral snake by looking at the order and pattern of the stripes, it's possible to differentiate a Wise Thing from a Wild Thing by observing the order and pattern of her conduct. Her priorities and routines are a dead giveaway. If the Sage Father were to dream up a ditty for his son about a woman's habits, he might come up with something like this: "Homeward-faced, wisdom-graced; out-to-the-max, wisdom lacks." A Girl-Gone-Wise is settled and self-disciplined. She puts first things first by giving precedence to intrinsic, home-based priorities. A Girl-Gone-Wise is restless and self-indulgent. She is undisciplined and gives precedence to the pursuit of extrinsic social pleasures and amusements.

OUT AND ABOUT

The Proverbs 7 woman is a prime example. "Her feet do not stay at home; now in the street, now in the market, and at every corner she lies in wait." The words *street*, *market*, and *corner* refer to the broad, public, open spaces in towns and cities where people in Bible times gathered. Markets were located at the city gate and were often ornamented with statues and colonnades. This is where merchants displayed their goods (2 Kings 7:18). Generally, the marketplaces of the ancient Near East were much like the open-air bazaars one can still see in many cities throughout Greece, Turkey, and Israel. Trade goods included ivory, ebony, emeralds, coral, rubies, wheat, honey, oil, balm, wine, wool, wrought iron, cassia wood, lambs, rams, goats, horses, gold, silver, bronze, iron, tin, lead, carpets of colored material, embroidery work, fine linen, purple cloth, clothes of blue, and choice garments (Ezekiel 27:12–25).

The point that the Sage Father was trying to convey is that the Wild Thing spent her time frequenting public places. She was always out and about. She wanted to be where the action was. She wanted to be amused and entertained, and to feed her appetite for attention and admiration. She was self-indulgent rather than self-disciplined. Shopping, hearing the latest gossip, having a good time, being noticed, and potentially hooking up with a good-looking guy took precedence over other, more important things. "Now at the mall, now at the club, now at the movie theater, now at the party, now at the game" is how the Sage Father could have described her habits, given our contemporary circumstances.

The problem was not so much that this woman went out, but that she went out at the expense of what she should have been doing. "Her feet do not stay at home." That means that her house was probably messy, her laundry undone, her mail unopened, her bills unpaid, her exam unstudied for, her pantry unfilled, and her supper unmade. What's more, she probably couldn't even remember the last time she read or studied her Bible, picked up a good, instructive Christian book, or listened to a sermon she downloaded from the Internet. When she was at home, her overriding purpose was to get herself ready to go out again. This girl could find plenty of time to paint her toenails, but couldn't possibly find time to paint the badly peeling fence. She was far too busy for that!

The Proverbs 7 woman was married. But undoubtedly, her habit of out-and-about behavior was established long before she had a husband. She had never learned the discipline of giving first priority to the things that deserved first priority. She had never learned to attend to her private life first.

Home is far more than a place of residence with a requisite set of domestic duties. One's home is her inner private sanctum. It's the "place"—physically and spiritually—where the most important stuff in life happens. Home is crucial. If a woman's surroundings are neglected, out of order, cluttered, and chaotic, chances are her inner, private life shares the same fate. And her habitual pattern of neglect affects far more than just her. It affects her husband, her marriage, her children, and, ultimately, her own capacity to live a godly, fruitful, productive life and to make a difference in this world.

EYE ON THE HOMEFRONT

The habits of the Proverbs 31 woman stand in marked contrast (vv. 10–31). The writer describes them in a poem he learned from his mother. The structure of the poem is a Hebrew acrostic. The starting consonant of each verse follows the order of the alphabet. The first verse starts with the Hebrew A, the second with B, and so on. It's like an A to Z guide of how to spot a great woman. The beautifully structured poem points out six key characteristics of the habits of a Girl-Gone-Wise:

bits are self-disciplined and not self-indulgent.

> looks well to the ways of her household and does not
> he bread of idleness." (v. 27)

2. She habitually attends to matters of personal faith and character.

> "She dresses herself with strength and makes her arms strong." (v. 17)

> "Strength and dignity are her clothing, and she laughs at the time to come." (v. 25)

> "She opens her mouth with wisdom, and the teaching of kindness is on her tongue." (v. 26)

> "Charm is deceitful, and beauty is vain, but a woman who fears the Lord is to be praised." (v. 30)

3. She habitually attends to the needs of her household.

> "An excellent wife who can find? She is far more precious than jewels." (v. 10)

> "She does him good, and not harm, all the days of her life." (v. 12)

> "She is like the ships of the merchant; she brings her food from afar. She rises while it is yet night and provides food for her household and portions for her maidens." (vv. 14–15)

> "She seeks wool and flax, and works with willing hands." (v. 13)

> "She puts her hands to the distaff, and her hands hold the spindle." (v. 19)

> "She is not afraid of snow for her household, for all her household are clothed in scarlet." (v. 21)

> "She makes bed coverings for herself; her clothing is fine linen and purple." (v. 22)

4. She habitually attends to kingdom mission and ministry.

> "She opens her hand to the poor and reaches out her hands to the needy." (v. 20)

5. She habitually attends to beneficial (and not idle) pursuits.

> "She perceives that her merchandise is profitable." (v. 18)

"She makes linen garments and sells them; she delivers sashes to the merchant." (v. 24)

"She considers a field and buys it; with the fruit of her hands she plants a vineyard." (v. 16)

6. She and her household reap the reward of her disciplined lifestyle.

"Her lamp does not go out at night." (v. 18)

"The heart of her husband trusts in her, and he will have no lack of gain." (v. 11)

"Her husband is known in the gates when he sits among the elders of the land." (v. 23)

"Her children rise up and call her blessed; her husband also, and he praises her: 'Many women have done excellently, but you surpass them all.'" (vv. 28–29)

"Give her of the fruit of her hands, and let her works praise her in the gates." (v. 31)

The habits of the Girl-Gone-Wise are very different from the Wild Thing. Both are busy, but they are busy with different things. The Wild Thing is busy indulging herself. She is constantly out and about, looking for a good time. And she neglects things on the home front. The Girl-Gone-Wise attends to her home life. Her habits are self-disciplined, self-sacrificing, and directed by the needs of her household. "Her feet stay at home."

FEET AT HOME

Having feet that "stay at home" has more to do with a woman's focus than her actual physical location. The Proverbs 31 woman obviously went to the marketplace on a regular basis. She managed her own wholesale business, trading linen garments and sashes. She was also involved in kingdom business, ministering to the poor and needy. But even though she physically went out of the home to do these things, she still maintained a homeward focus and did spend a significant amount of time in her home. It's important to note that a woman's physical location is not the only nor the main part of what it means to have "feet at home." Just because a woman stays at home physically

essarily mean that she is attending to her household. She
:rastinating, self-indulging, and living an undisciplined life
as the woman who is always out and about.

ı ne Bible teaches that God created woman with a uniquely feminine "bent" for the home. "Working at home" is on its top ten list of
important things that older women need to teach the younger ones
(Titus 2:5). It encourages young women to "manage their households"
(1 Timothy 5:14). It praises her who "looks well to the ways of her
household"—keeping her antennas up to the physical, emotional, relational, and spiritual well-being of everyone in her family, and making
sure that everything and everyone is connected and doing well
(Proverbs 31:27). The Bible casts women whose hearts are inclined
away from the home in a negative light (Proverbs 7:11).

A woman's role in the home is a hot topic. Feminism has taught
us to bristle at the idea that a woman's responsibility to the home is
any different from a man's. The very suggestion conjures up the classic, oppressive notion of woman being perpetually "barefoot, pregnant, and chained to the kitchen sink." So I feel as though I'm treading
on a field full of landmines here. One wrong word or phrase, and my
mailbox will explode with angry e-mails. I risk being vilified, mocked,
and misrepresented by bloggers in cyberspace forever. Nevertheless, I
believe that it is crucial that women understand their special connection to the home. God "wired" women with a unique homeward
bent. We can argue until we are blue in the face that it should not be
so—that men ought to function in the home the same way as women.
But Scripture and a simple observance of male-female behavior indicate that there is indeed a difference. Because of women's nurturing,
responsive spirit, we are equipped to be attentive and attuned to the
affairs of our households in a way that men are not.

The "ways of the household" involve the cleanliness and orderliness of its physical environment. But more important than that, they
involve the cleanliness and orderliness of its relational and spiritual
environment. Have you ever noticed that, generally speaking, women
have a far greater sensitivity to disorder than men do? (Just think of
the typical bachelor pad.) It has always amazed me that my husband
and sons can step over something that is out of place (like a jacket or
book on the floor in the hallway, for example) a hundred times with-

out even noticing that it is there. It's not that they are intentionally negligent, or averse to picking it up. If asked, they are glad to do so and to contribute to keeping the house clean. But until I draw their attention to it, or until the disorder becomes a significant problem, they simply don't see it. They don't notice that the item is out of place. I do! And it's the same way with "seeing" things that are out of order with a family member's emotions, relationships, or spiritual life. The guys usually don't notice it as readily. Most of you who have been married for a time can attest to the fact that women generally notice a problem in the home long before the men do.

This bent of woman toward the home is an incredible responsibility and an incredible blessing. I can't count the number of times my watchfulness for "things out of place" has saved my family from emotional and spiritual injury. I notice the "disorder" and deal with it with prayer, counsel, and correction. Or I draw my husband's attention to it so we can set it straight and deal with it together. We address the thing that is "out of place" before it becomes a chaotic mess.

I am not the type of woman who loves housekeeping chores (who does?), but over the years I have learned that my vigilance for physically maintaining order in my home is a reflection of what I do for my family spiritually. The two are interconnected. And both are necessary. Attending to the physical condition of a household is of little value if one does not attend to its emotional and spiritual condition. Attending to a household's emotional and spiritual condition is not possible if one does not also attend to its physical condition. Given my personality and gifts, and distaste for all things "trivial," this has been a very tough lesson for me. But I have learned that in order to "look well to the affairs of my household" spiritually, I must physically and practically order my priorities and routines to put first things first. The inward must precede the outward. My feet need to be "home" before they are "out and about."

A single woman might say, "I have no household. I need to get out and about so I can find a husband and get a household!" It's true that a single woman may have more discretionary time for socializing, but it's not true that she does not have a household. Nor is it true that she can neglect it and suffer no ill consequence. Every woman has a household—even if she is the only one in it. A Girl-Gone-Wise cultivates habits, routines, and priorities to keep her home life in order. This happens long before she is ever married. Home is not all she does, but it is what she does first.

FIRST THINGS FIRST

Most of us have a sense for what's important. We know that we ought to develop habits that nurture our personal faith and character, attend to the needs of our households, and minister to others. We know we ought to expend our energy on beneficial and not idle pursuits. However, ordering our lives to put first things first takes discipline. The Wild Thing sadly lacks this character trait. "The woman Folly is . . . undisciplined" (Proverbs 9:13 NIV). Unlike her wise counterpart, the Wild Thing habitually eats "the bread of idleness" (Proverbs 31:27).

The apostle Paul admonished believers not to be idle (1 Thessalonians 5:14). He specifically identified unmarried women as being susceptible to this sin (1 Timothy 5:13). When we use the word *idle*, we usually think of inactivity. We assume that an idle woman has lots of time on her hands. But "inactive" is not exactly what idleness means. The Greek word refers to someone or something that is not in good order. It means "careless" and "out of line." The word was used to describe an undisciplined soldier who would not keep rank but insisted on marching his own way or someone who failed to remain at his post of duty. In the Bible, idleness doesn't mean "doing nothing"—it means "not doing what you should." An idle woman is often busy. Perhaps even excessively busy. Our Proverbs 7 woman was constantly on the go, doing all sorts of things. But she was idle nonetheless. Women are idle when they have the wrong priorities. They are idle when they fail to stay at their post of duty, and busy themselves with other things instead. An idle woman's life is undisciplined and out of order. She does not do what she ought to do.

An orderly, disciplined life is a hallmark of those who follow Jesus. According to the apostle Paul, the grace of God trains us "to renounce ungodliness and worldly passions, and to live self-controlled, upright, and godly lives in the present age . . . zealous for good works" (Titus 2:11–12, 14). Paul set an example by his own self-disciplined lifestyle. He explained, "Every athlete exercises self-control in all things. . . . So I do not run aimlessly; I do not box as one beating the air. But I discipline my body and keep it under control" (1 Corinthians 9:25–27). He expected that all believers would follow his example.

To Paul, self-discipline was a discipleship issue. He wanted the older women to teach younger women how to live "self-controlled" lives (Titus 2:4–5). He implied that self-control was the virtue that ensured that a woman ordered her priorities in the right way. Self-discipline was so important to Paul that he warned his friends to "keep away from any brother who is walking in idleness" (2 Thessalonians 3:6). He didn't want his friends hanging out with undisciplined people and being influenced to adopt a self-indulgent, undisciplined lifestyle.

Is your life orderly and disciplined? Are you putting first things first? A well-known American journalist once said, "Don't waste your breath proclaiming what's really important to you. How you spend your time says it all. . . . There's no sense talking about priorities. Priorities reveal themselves. We're all transparent against the face of the clock."[1] There's a lot of truth in those words. Priorities reveal themselves in habits. If asked, most of us could come up with quite a good-looking list of priorities. Unfortunately, for most people, this list would itemize the things we know should take precedence in our lives, but that really don't. It's not what we *say* but what we *do* that reveals our true priorities. That's why I titled this chapter, "Habits," and not "Priorities." Looking at what you routinely *do* reveals what your priorities really are. For instance, if you routinely sleep in instead of getting up to read your Bible, then sleep is a higher priority to you than Bible reading. There's no sense trying to pretend otherwise.

If you were to evaluate your priorities based on your habits, would "what you do" match up with "what you know you *should* do"? I don't know about you, but for me, taking a look at my habits shows me how very far I still have to go in the area of self-discipline. My life is not as ordered and balanced as it should be. It seems that I am always reevaluating habits and struggling to keep priorities in the right order. But if there's anything I've learned, it's that the battle for a godly, self-disciplined lifestyle is ongoing.

In order to determine whether I am putting first things first, I need to clarify what should come first in this particular season of my life. I need to evaluate my habits to see if what I am doing lines up with what I should be doing. A high priority of every woman is to attend to her spiritual growth through the Word and prayer, and to attend to her personal health and physical fitness. Other priorities will differ, depending on a woman's stage of life and circumstances. A single college student will have her studies as a priority. A new mom's priority is to attend to the needs of her baby. A widow might put ministry first. A wise woman constantly checks her habits to see if she is putting things in the right order and giving everything the right emphasis. She prayerfully evaluates her life, clarifies her God-given priorities, and adjusts her habits to match.

Clarifying what we should do is a whole lot easier than actually doing it. The natural, sinful inclination of our flesh is to be self-indulgent and not self-disciplined. I want to sleep more than I want to get up with the alarm. I want to relax more than I want to exercise. I want to eat chocolate and drink Coke more than I want string beans and milk. I want to be entertained more than I want to work. I want to receive more than I want to give. I want others to wait on me more than I want to wait on them. I want to have fun more than I want to sacrifice. I want things easy. I don't want to be inconvenienced or to exert too much effort. My sinful nature is the reason I need help. I do not have the necessary motivation or self-discipline to do what I ought to do. It's just too tough. And there's usually no one to blame but me. My own desires interfere and keep me from doing what I want to do: "For the desires of the flesh are against the Spirit, and the desires of the Spirit are against the flesh, for these are opposed to each other, to keep you from doing the things you want to do" (Galatians 5:17).

Given my own strength and willpower, my ability to live a self-disciplined life is extremely limited. That's why I need to depend on my "Helper." The Lord gives me His Spirit to help me in my weakness. The Holy Spirit is the Spirit of power, of love, and of self-discipline (2 Timothy 1:7 NIV). The truth of the matter is, I don't have enough *power* to overcome the sinful pull toward self-indulgence. I don't *love* God or others enough to sacrifice my own comfort and pleasure for the sake of theirs. I don't have the *self-discipline* to make myself do what I ought to do.

On my own, I do not have the capacity to put first things first. But thankfully (and this is the wonder of the Gospel), it doesn't matter. The Lord gives me all I need. He provides the power, love, and self-discipline that I so desperately lack. Therefore, doing the right thing doesn't depend on me drumming up enough willpower. Success is a matter of depending on the Holy Spirit and not on my own capacity.

The "rubber hits the road" at decision time. I know what I should do . . . and I know that God gives me the power and self-discipline to do what I should do . . . so all that remains is for me to surrender my will to His and actually do it. I need to live by the Spirit and not by my flesh. And that's the toughest part. Every day, I make dozens of "rubber hits the road" decisions about whether I'm going to gratify the desires of my flesh or walk by the Spirit of God. All these decisions add up to a self-indulgent or self-disciplined pattern of living.

The alarm rings. I know I should get up. I know that God's Spirit gives me the power to get up. I know that if I don't get up, I won't have time to read my Bible, pray, exercise, straighten the kitchen, throw in a load of laundry, and put on a pot of coffee for my husband. So it's decision time. Do I gratify the desires of my flesh, or do I surrender my will and walk in the power of the Spirit of God? I stumble downstairs and rub the sleep out of my eyes. On the way to the laundry room, I pass by my office. Should I check my e-mail? There might be an important or interesting message in my inbox. I want to read my e-mail more than I want to read my Bible and definitely more than I want to exercise! So it's decision time again. Do I gratify the desires of my flesh, or surrender my will and walk by the Spirit of God? When I get to the kitchen, I notice that someone left an open bag of potato chips on the counter. I know I shouldn't have any, especially that early in the morning, but they're my favorite brand. It's decision time. Do I gratify the desires of my flesh and dig in? All day I make tiny decisions that are either self-disciplined or self-indulgent.

Ten p.m. End of the day. My son just flicked on an entertaining movie in the family room. I should be taking the meat out of the freezer, running the dishwasher, hanging up some clothes, checking tomorrow's schedule, and getting ready for bed. I know that a lack of discipline at bedtime often sets me up for an unproductive day tomorrow. But all I want to do is plop down on our comfy sofa, curl up in a blanket, and watch the DVD. It's decision time again.

Each day we make dozens and dozens of small decisions. Each individual decision seems trivial and inconsequential. But together they add up to a habitual pattern that is either life-giving or life-quenching. Paul warns, "If you live according to the flesh you will die, but if by the Spirit you put to death the deeds of the body, you will live" (Romans 8:13). The problem of the Wild Thing is that she gave in to her own sinful inclination and lived according to her flesh. She habitually chose to go out and about, looking for a good time. In the end, the consequence of her behavior was deadly. Her relationship with the Lord stagnated and died.

You can tell if a girl is wise or wild by the order and pattern of her habits. "Homeward-faced, wisdom-graced; out-to-the-max, wisdom lacks." The Girl-Gone-Wise recognizes the importance of daily habits. She orders her ways and lives a self-disciplined, rather than self-indulgent life. She keeps an eye on the home front, and diligently works to make sure all is in order there.

Point of Contrast #6

FOCUS
What Commands
Her Attention

Girl-Gone-Wild: Getting	Girl-Gone-Wise: Giving
"She lies in wait." (Proverbs 7:12)	"She opens her hand to the poor and reaches out her hands to the needy." (Proverbs 31:20)

She looked so cute. But her appearance was at odds with her inclination. Our pretty cat, Truffles, had a killer instinct. It was obvious by the number of mice and birds she dragged into my kitchen and triumphantly dropped at my feet. You could also see it in her eyes. Especially when she got the evening crazies. Her eyes had an intense, focused look—highly alert for prey. The tiniest bit of movement from any small object, and she immediately crouched into a predatory stance—ears pricked forward, tip of her tail flicking, every muscle taut, ready to pounce. If she ever spotted a bird through the window, she'd fixate on it, chatter her teeth, and emit a guttural growl.

And she didn't restrict herself to small prey. Once, our adorable tabby trapped an electrical repairman in the basement storage room. She positioned herself in the doorway, then snarled, spit, and threatened to attack when he tried to escape. Being a skilled predator, Truffles obviously derived pleasure from stalking, pouncing, chasing, and playing with her victim. She was always on the lookout for another good hunt.

The Sage Father of Proverbs likened a Girl-Gone-Wild to a predator. He advised his son that this kind of woman "lies in wait." She has a hunting instinct. She's always alert and on the prowl. The Wild Thing focuses on what she can *get*. She particularly wants to get the guy. The Girl-Gone-Wise, on the other hand, focuses on what she can *give*. The Wise Thing extends her hands outward. "She opens her hand to the poor and reaches out her hands to the needy" (Proverbs 31:20). The Wild Thing closes her hands inward. Hers is a predatory *me-focus* and not the productive *kingdom-focus* of the Girl-Gone-Wise.

CAUGHT IN A TRAP

In the last chapter, we learned that the Girl-Gone-Wild is always out and about. The reason she is out and about is that she is on the prowl. Like my cat, she gets the evening crazies. "Her feet do not stay at home; now in the street, now in the market, and at every corner she lies in wait." Lying in wait is traditional hunting behavior. The Bible often uses a hunting metaphor for people who take advantage of unsuspecting victims. It compares their behavior to animals such as lions and bears, which lie in wait to ambush their prey (Lamentations 3:10). But the hunting metaphor it uses the most is that of the "fowler." The wicked "lurk like fowlers lying in wait. They set a trap; they catch men" (Jeremiah 5:26).

Fowlers were professional bird catchers. They supplied the marketplace with doves and other birds that people kept as caged pets. They also sold wild pigeons and doves for temple sacrifices, and small birds such as partridge and quail for food. The many biblical references to the fowler and his hunting devices are likely due to the fact that Palestine lies on one of the main flight routes of certain migratory birds (Exodus 16:13). A fowler catching and selling birds was a common sight and thus a concept with which the ancients were very familiar.

The Bible refers to the "snare of the fowler" as an alluring but dangerous trap. Fowlers generally caught birds in snares or traps. A passage in Job uses six Hebrew words for traps, more synonyms for these objects than in any other Old Testament passage (Job 18:8–10). Scripture's point is that the traps of foolish, ungodly people are many and varied and highly dangerous. They are "snares of death" (Proverbs 13:14). And this is particularly the case with a Girl-Gone-Wild, who dangles herself out as bait to catch a man. Here's how the Bible describes her predatory hunting behavior:

- She lurks and "lies in wait" (Proverbs 7:1 1–12; 23:28).
- Her "heart is snares and nets" (Ecclesiastes 7:26).
- Her "mouth is a deep pit" (Proverbs 22:14).
- She "hunts down a precious life" (Proverbs 6:26).
- She traps him like a stag in a trap or a bird in a snare (Proverbs 7:22–23).
- Her "hands are fetters" (Ecclesiastes 7:26).
- "He who pleases God escapes her, but the sinner is taken by her" (Ecclesiastes 7:26).
- Like a bird, the young man rushes into her snare. "It will cost him his life" (Proverbs 7:23).

The Lord warned the men of Israel that getting involved with this ungodly type of woman would be "a snare and a trap for you, a whip on your sides and thorns in your eyes" (Joshua 23:12–13). The Sage Father agreed. He warned his son that taking the bait would lead to spiritual death (Proverbs 7:27). He directed his son to steer clear of Wild Things. He didn't want him falling for the wiles of a predatory woman.

If the father had written his proverbs for a daughter, he would have warned her against *becoming* a Wild Thing, for he knew that the trap of a predatory woman doesn't just snag the man. It also entangles her. Scripture makes it clear that predators are trapped by their own devices. "For in vain is a net spread in the sight of any bird, but these [predators] lie in wait for their *own* blood; they set an ambush for their *own* lives" (Proverbs 1:17–18). The wicked are snared in the work of their own hands (Psalm 9:16).

I want to make sure that you carefully note this point: *predators will not avoid getting caught in their own traps!* This is incredibly important for women to understand. I cannot stress it enough. Being out and about, dangling your body as bait, and lying in wait to hook a man isn't just bad for the man who walks into your trap; it's also bad *for you*! It's a foolish strategy. Ultimately, it will backfire. You will hurt yourself. You won't find the long-term, loving relationship you yearn for. Your own schemes will throw you down. You will be ensnared and injured by your own devices (Job 18:5, 7–10).

I think of Meagan, the twenty-two-year-old who has given herself away to multiple guys and has had her heart broken numerous times, yet fails to see that her Girl-Gone-Wild behavior sets her up for failure, and therefore refuses to change. I think of Gloria, the fifty-six-year-old who is on marriage number four, sobbing on my shoulder, "If only I could find a man to love me!" Or Vicky, the dental hygienist who, disappointed by the husband she caught in a club, became infatuated with her married boss and then turned her charms on him. I think of the thousands of women I have met who think that "getting the guy" is what life is all about. I think of the thousands more who have been deeply disappointed and hurt by the guys they've caught, but who nevertheless continue to "lie in wait."

LYING IN WAIT

A Girl-Gone-Wild expends enormous amounts of time and energy lying in wait. She is like the fowler who bides his time to lure the birds onto his net and then bides it again to determine when he should pull the cord. Biding time is the major part of his job. He repeatedly watches and waits. Where are they? Are they coming? Do they see the bait? Do I need to put out more? Here they come . . . I hope they keep moving in this direction. Are they close enough? Have they taken the bait? Is the bird in the net? Should I spring the trap? Will I catch my prey?

Like the fowler, the Wild Thing perpetually waits. She constantly scopes things out and evaluates the situation. She preoccupies herself with "the hunt." Thinking about it takes up a great deal of mental energy. She dreams up possible scenarios and schemes for the hunt. She talks about it with her girlfriends. She makes sure she reads the latest *Cosmopolitan* to find the latest techniques for it and constantly evaluates how it is progressing. She watches sitcoms and Blu-rays about the hunt. She texts her girlfriends to find out how they are faring in the hunt. She cries when it is going poorly. She's happy when she has a new prospect on the horizon and the hunt is going well. She's elated when she finally catches her bird. But her satisfaction is short-lived. She may busy herself with getting the bird tethered down and taking him to market, but she will soon grow restless. She's a hunter, after all. It's not long before she will return to the lipstick jungle to once again lie in wait.

Lying-in-wait behavior isn't restricted to getting a guy and getting married. It extends to getting other things too. After she gets the guy, the Wild Thing may turn her attention to getting the house, getting the furniture, getting a car, getting new clothes, getting a job, getting some kids, getting a break, getting her husband to change, getting the money to retire . . . Many women spend their whole lives lying in wait. They perpetually wait and watch for their next big catch, and hope that it will bring them the fulfillment they so desperately desire.

Predators "lie in wait" because they rely on others to satisfy their desires. They are greedy at heart. Their primary focus is to satisfy their own appetites. They are ravenously intent on filling their own stomachs. They will disregard the needs of others and steal or destroy to get what they want. The devil is the greatest predator of all. He prowls around like a roaring lion, seeking someone to devour (1 Peter 5:8). His motivation is utterly selfish. He ensnares people so that they might be "captured by him to do his will" (2 Timothy 2:26). The Girl-Gone-Wild operates with a similar motivation. A man is "taken by" her just as a sinner is "captured by" the devil (Ecclesiastes 7:26). The language indicates that the Girl-Gone-Wild is the perpetrator. Yes, men can be just as guilty of predatory sins, but in this instance, the woman is the one doing the "grabbing" and "taking." She is the one who is intent on getting.

The Girl-Gone-Wild captures a guy with the expectation that he will do *her* will. She expects that he will give her what she wants—a good time, love, acceptance, security, marriage, kids, a home. Almost everything that she gives him is bait. It has "strings attached." It's motivated by her desire that he will meet her needs in return. A girl will *give* a guy a peek at her hardware . . . to *get* his admiration. She'll *give* him a boost to his ego . . . to *get* him to engage in conversation. She'll *give* him physical pleasure . . . to *get* another date. She'll *give* him sex . . . to *get* him to love her. She'll *give* him what he wants . . . if it will *get* her what she wants.

Her heart is "snares and nets," and her hands are "fetters" (Ecclesiastes 7:26). A fetter is a chain or shackle fastened to somebody's ankles or feet. It's a means of restraint. When the Girl-Gone-Wild extends her hand and gives something to a man, it's with the hope and expectation that she will bind him to her with obligation. Because of her need and greed, she is incapable of loving freely like Jesus—with a pure, no-strings-attached kind of love. In the end, her "me-focus" doesn't deliver. She ends up forsaking the right way, selling out to sin, and having a partner that she has to restrain like a dog on a leash in order to keep him from wandering. She entangles herself in a terrible mess.

FROM PREDATORY TO PRODUCTIVE

The predatory behavior of a Girl-Gone-Wild stands in marked contrast to the productive behavior of a Girl-Gone-Wise. A Girl-Gone-Wise doesn't waste time "lying in wait." She's too busy putting first things first. She has a *kingdom-focus* instead of a *me-focus*. She's far more concerned about what she can give than what she can get. Why is her life so different? Because she believes the old creed that says, "The chief end of man is to glorify God and enjoy Him forever." To "glorify" something is to extol it and "show it off" or "make it famous." The wise woman's life is all about enjoying God and making Him famous. That's what commands her attention.

People intuitively get the part about "enjoying" and "glorifying." Everyone has an innate drive to enjoy and glorify something. The Girl-Gone-Wild wants to enjoy and glorify herself. Her me-focus governs everything she does. She tries to make men, sexuality, marriage, family, money, career, her volunteer work—everything in life—cater to her personal enjoyment and affirm her personal sense of self-worth. For her, that's what life is about.

The difference between the Girl-Gone-Wise and the Girl-Gone-Wild is not that one "enjoys and glorifies" something and the other does not. The difference lies in *what* each enjoys and glorifies. The overriding purpose of the Girl-Gone-Wise is to enjoy and glorify Christ in all she does. She seeks to enjoy Christ and make Him famous in her relationships. She seeks to enjoy Christ and make Him famous in the way she interacts with men. She seeks to enjoy Christ and make Him famous in her marriage. She seeks to enjoy Christ and make Him famous in her sexuality, in her family, with her money, and with her career. In everything she does—from the way she dresses to the way she orders her day—she seeks to delight in Christ and put His beauty and excellence on display. Getting love, getting a guy, getting "stuff," or getting herself to the point where she feels "self-actualized" isn't her overriding goal. Enjoying and glorifying God is. She focuses on building His kingdom—not on building her own. And that makes a major difference in how she interacts with men.

A WOMAN ON A MISSION

The Girl-Gone-Wise doesn't lie in wait for a man, because she doesn't need a man to fulfill her life's purpose. Although marriage is a good and legitimate goal, her life is about so much more. She has a profound sense of mission. More than anything, she wants to know Christ and make Him known. She wants to display His greatness by doing the good works that He prepared in advance for her to do. "For we are his workmanship, created in Christ Jesus for good works, which God prepared beforehand, that we should walk in them" (Ephesians 2:10). The Girl-Gone-Wise understands that regardless of whether she is single or married, her overriding purpose is to display Christ and to be busy with the kingdom work that He has for her in that season of her life. As my twenty-two-year-old friend Vanessa told me, "I just had this overwhelming sense that the Lord had a purpose for me that was not all about me. . . . The reason I'm here is so much bigger than that!"

I invited Vanessa over for coffee to talk about her focus in life. I had met her eight years before when she and my son were both in eighth grade. She and the rest of the kids in their class had come over to our house for a birthday party. Vanessa and several others hung out in the kitchen while I readied some pizza buns for the oven. It didn't take long for me to notice that Vanessa had a different focus than the other girls. The others had that "truffles" look in their eyes. They were intent on watching the boys and trying to get the boys' attention. You could tell by the way they dressed and did their makeup, the way they positioned themselves around the room, what they talked about, and the way they giggled and tossed their heads.

Vanessa didn't play that game. She seemed rather uncomfortable with the whole scene. But when I asked her about how she was planning on spending the weekend, she came alive. Her beautiful dark eyes sparkled as she told me about the quilt she was making to send to the family of a firefighter killed in 9-11.

Vanessa's dad is a firefighter, and when she watched the events of 9-11 unfold, she wanted to do something to reach out and comfort the kids who had lost their dads. That night, the fourteen-year-old knelt by her bed and asked the Lord what she could do to help. He gave her the idea to sew and send handmade quilts to wrap the grieving children in Arms of Compassion. The quilt would be "like a big hug of comfort." The next day, Vanessa took out a big pair of shears, cut up her dad's old firefighting uniform, and started making quilts. Her goal was to make three hundred quilts to send to all the children affected by the tragedy.

She soon realized that she couldn't do it alone. So she called up all the churches and youth groups and schools in the area, asking for volunteers. She made templates and patterns. She canvassed businesses for supplies: old blue jeans, cloth, sewing machines, cutters, mats. Soon, box after box of supplies landed on her doorstep. If she needed cloth, she prayed for cloth. If she needed batting, she prayed for batting. Department stores donated vans full of display material. The Salvation Army gave large boxes of old blue jeans. Laundromats offered cleaning services. Thousands of volunteers donated their time. Businesses gave money. Vanessa witnessed miracle after miracle as she asked the Lord to supply her needs. One time, she needed thread. So she specifically prayed for thread. Soon afterward she got a call from the Levi Strauss Company. They were shutting down one of their factories. Could she possibly use some massive cylinders of thread?

Vanessa's Arms of Compassion soon reached beyond the children in New York to sick kids at the local children's hospital, to families who lost homes in fires, to needy children and orphans in Nicaragua, and to many other people who were suffering and in need. Quilting volunteers delivered the precious handmade "hugs" as symbols of the love and compassion of Christ. "The needs were overwhelming," Vanessa explained. "Everywhere I looked there was a need." While the other girls were flaunting tight-fitting, low-rise denim to lie in wait for guys, Vanessa was cutting up denim to make patchwork quilts to give to those who were suffering and in pain. During her high school years, her Arms of Compassion wrapped more than six hundred hurting kids and families in homemade quilts.

Vanessa was a young woman with a profound sense of mission. And it wasn't long before the world sat up and took notice. When she was fifteen, the Governor General awarded her with the Queen's Golden Jubilee Medal for outstanding citizenship; she was the youngest Canadian ever to receive this honor. Other accolades followed—a Premier's Citizenship award, a Centennial Medal, and a Stars of the Millennium award. When she was seventeen, Soroptimist International, a worldwide women's organization associated with the United Nations, recognized her with yet another award. At that ceremony, she stood in front of thousands of women from nations all around the world and spoke of the importance of purpose, compassion, and making a difference in the lives of the poor and needy.

Vanessa shrugs and looks somewhat embarrassed as she lists off the awards. She wasn't really looking for awards. She just wanted to reach out to kids who were hurting. She just wanted to be faithful to what the Lord wanted her to do. "I just want to make a difference every day—whether in a small capacity or large."

It shows. For the past few years, Vanessa has quietly ministered to the homeless in downtown Edmonton. Last year, at age twenty-one, this remarkable young woman dropped out of college to care full-time for her mother, who is recovering from a brain tumor, and her father, who was stricken with lung cancer from his many years firefighting. It has been very, very difficult. But Vanessa is undaunted. When I ask the reason for her resolve she says, "You have to realize that life is bigger than you. It's bigger than what we can see. We all have a purpose. God has a purpose for each and every person."

Would Vanessa like to meet and marry her Prince Charming? Of course she would! But she knows that the God who satisfied her need for thread can also satisfy her desire for a husband. Vanessa doesn't have to take matters into her own hands. She doesn't have to worry. She doesn't have to lie in wait. She can busy herself with doing the things that are proper for women who profess godliness to do—the good works of the kingdom of God (1 Timothy 2:10). She knows she needs to be about His business. Like my eighty-one-year-old mom often says to me, "I'm still here. There must be something God wants me to do today."

Vanessa learned the importance of a Godward focus as a teen. Some of you may not have. But it's never too late. Whether you are eight or eighty-eight, you can shift your attention from a predatory *me-focus* to a productive *kingdom-focus*. Don't squander your life. Don't waste your time lying in wait. Christ is too important. Time is too precious. The needs are too great. Too much is at stake. Be like the wise woman of Proverbs 31, who opens her hand to the poor and reaches out her hands to the needy (31:20). Focus on kingdom business. Enjoy God and glorify Him. A Girl-Gone-Wise does not lie in wait for men or worldly "stuff." Instead, she busies herself with her mission and trusts the Lord to take care of the rest.

Point of Contrast #7

APPEARANCE
How She Adorns Herself

Girl-Gone-Wild: Unbecoming, Indecent, Excessive	Girl-Gone-Wise: Becoming, Decent, Moderate
"And behold, the woman meets him, dressed as a prostitute." (Proverbs 7:10)	"[She] adorn[s] [herself] in respectable apparel, with modesty and self-control." (I Timothy 2:9)

I was at a hockey game. But it was hard to focus on hockey. The low-rise skirts and jeans of the six young women sitting in front of me revealed everything from colorful thongs, to fleshy love handles, to the most intimate crevices of a woman's body. Their tops were equally immodest. I kept thinking very disturbing thoughts about where all the ice in my drink would land if I happened to spill it. At the end of the first period, I relocated to a different seat so I could enjoy the rest of the hockey game without the distraction of the skin show. It was that bad. And if I was having a hard time not staring, I can't imagine how difficult it was for the young men seated across the aisle to avoid gawking at the display and keep their minds on ice (the sheet of ice the players were skating on, that is).

The girls at the hockey rink looked more like hookers than hockey fans. In my city, hookers peddle their wares on a certain street downtown. It used to be easy to pick them out. They were the ones with the extreme high heels, micro-mini skirts or shorts, protruding cleavage, heavy makeup, and attention-getting hair. But if a prostitute from the street had seated herself next to those six girls, chances are I wouldn't have been able to tell her apart. She would have blended right in. Nowadays, there is little difference between the appearance of a prostitute and the appearance of what the world upholds as a sexy, attractive woman.

The hooker look has gone mainstream. You can see it paraded by women in malls, restaurants, schools, the workplace, and even in churches. Popular culture encourages very young girls to dress in a provocative manner. Toddlers play with dolls dressed in fishnets, miniskirts, and heavy eye makeup. Clothing stores sell tiny tank tops printed with Playboy bunnies and such expressions as "Hottie," "Porn Star," "Wet," "Princess," "Party Girl," and "No Angel." In 2002, retailer Abercrombie and Fitch produced a line of thong underwear with expressions such as "Eye Candy" and "Wink Wink." The thongs fit girls as young as seven.[1] From the adolescent Lolita to the middle-aged "cougar," looking "hot" is promoted by the media as a desirable, life-long pursuit.

The Sage Father tells his young son that one of the telltale marks of a Wild Thing is that she dresses "as a prostitute." It's important to note that the Proverbs 7 woman is *not* a prostitute. But *like* a prostitute, she relies on her "wares" to entice men. Looking "hot" is her aim. Though her desired remuneration is not as tawdry as money, she peddles her looks for payment of another kind . . . attention, self-esteem, acceptance, or affection, for example.

What does it mean to dress "as a prostitute"? It definitely involves how a woman puts herself together—the type of shoes, clothing, and makeup she chooses to wear. But far more than that, it has to do with her underlying attitude. A prostitute is excessively concerned about personal appearance. She believes that the payment she'll receive from men is dependent on her external packaging. Packaging equals payment. "Getting" depends on "looks." A Girl-Gone-Wild has this same sort of attitude. A Girl-Gone-Wild might try to look sexy or despair that she cannot. She might expend a tremendous amount of energy to make herself look like a "Pretty Woman" or be self-conscious that her body doesn't measure up. Her body type may prevent her from wearing the tight, highly revealing type of clothing that a prostitute commonly wears, but she would wear that type of clothing if she could. She believes that her level of "sexiness" and "hotness" will dictate whether men will buy into a relationship with her.

The prostitute-like mentality of a Girl-Gone-Wild will motivate her to dress in a way that is unbecoming, indecent, and/or excessive. Her counterpart, the Girl-Gone-Wise, has a very different mind-set. She neither obsesses over, nor neglects her appearance. Mindful of Christ, the Girl-Gone-Wise adorns herself in a way that is becoming, decent, and moderate. Her external appearance reflects the beauty of her inner self. Later, we'll take a look at what all that means, but first, I'd like to explore the biblical reason for covering our bodies. Why do we wear clothing anyway?

THE PURPOSE FOR CLOTHING

In the church, most discussions about clothing revolve around the need for modesty. Teachers place much emphasis on the fact that men are visually stimulated. Women are told that if they dress in a way that is overly sexual, they can tempt their Christian brothers to sin, and may end up in sexual sin themselves. The issue of clothing is thus often reduced to the question of the best way to help men avoid temptation: How low is too low? How short is too short? How tight is too tight? How sheer is too sheer? How much skin is too much skin? How stylish is too stylish? How do I reduce the chance that men will lust after me? How do I divert their attention away from my private parts?

Some try to come up with a checklist of what is and is not appropriate for Christian women to wear. Others propose that the best solution is to dress in clothes that are outdated or ugly: wear long, faded, baggy jean jumpers, along with white socks and sneakers, and pull your hair up in a bun. Some Christians believe that those who dress in colorful, stylish, attractive clothing, wear high heels, and get their hair styled are rather unspiritual, if not downright carnal. Frumpy and out-of-style equals holy. All this can leave a woman with the impression that curbing wrongful sexual desire and activity is the ultimate goal of the way she dresses. Taken to its logical end, this mentality supports the *burka*—the tentlike garment worn by women in some Islamic traditions that cloaks the entire body. If the ultimate point of clothing is to prevent wrongful sexual temptation and activity, then it makes sense that covering a woman's entire body would be the best way to accomplish that goal.

It's true that women must take care not to willfully tempt or mislead their Christian brothers. But curbing wrongful sexual activity is not the main reason behind the Bible's teaching on dress. Don't get me wrong. It is an important consideration. But it's not the main one. And those who focus on it can miss the point. How we ought to dress has something to do with curbing wrongful sexual activity, but it has a whole lot more to do with the Fall, when God originally covered the nakedness of human beings. It has to do with why we wear clothing in the first place.

NAKEDNESS AND SHAME

"What's the Problem with Nudity?" was the title of a recent program on BBC. The show pointed out, "All humans are sensitive to sexual modesty," even in cultures where nudity or partial nudity is normative. To find out if modesty could be "unlearned," the BBC took eight ordinary people—none of them nudists—and had them spend a few days together naked. The producers wanted to test some scientific theories that explain why naked bodies make us so uncomfortable. The big question was whether people could unlearn their naked shame.

The volunteers did unlearn their shame. By the final nude wine and cheese reception, they appeared to be entirely comfortable with each other's nakedness. As a parting challenge, the director asked them to walk out naked onto the street to waiting taxis. Emboldened by their experience, they suppressed any remaining shame and did so. In the end, the moderator concluded, "We're not born with sexual modesty," and added, "So long as everyone agrees, we can create new rules and avoid the risk of offense."[2]

Why does nakedness normally cause shame? The BBC suggests it's because of cultural conditioning. But the Bible has an entirely different answer. It reveals that there was once a day when there was nudity and no shame. "And the man and his wife were both naked and were not ashamed" (Genesis 2:25). Then sin entered the world. Adam and Eve suddenly became aware that they were naked. They felt shame, and tried to cover up.

> Then the eyes of both were opened, and they knew that they were naked. And they sewed fig leaves together and made themselves loincloths. And they heard the sound of the Lord God walking in the garden in the cool of the day, and the man and his wife hid themselves from the presence of the Lord God among the trees of the garden. But the Lord God called to the man and said to him, "Where are you?" And he said, "I heard the sound of you in the garden, and I was afraid, because I was naked, and I hid myself." . . . And the Lord God made for Adam and for his wife garments of skins and clothed them. (Genesis 3:7–10, 21)

Nakedness was natural and fitting for Adam and Eve when they were pure and innocent. But when that purity and innocence was lost, they became painfully embarrassed by their naked condition. Why? What's the connection between sin and nakedness? Why were they ashamed of nudity? Why did they feel the need to cover their private parts? What were they trying to hide? Who were they trying to hide from? Why were their fig leaves inadequate? Why did the Lord shed the blood of an animal to make them garments? How did He propose to solve the problem of their shame? As you'll soon see, these questions all relate to the matter of why we wear clothing and the appropriate attitude we ought to have toward adorning our bodies.

It all started when Eve decided that she wanted to be like God and call her own shots. The Serpent convinced her that she would receive all kinds of benefits if she did. He promised that a whole world of knowledge and experience would open up to her. ("Your eyes will be opened.") He assured her that she would be equal with God—that is, she could be her own god. ("You will be like God.") Finally, he promised that she would be able to decide for herself what was right and wrong. ("Knowing good and evil.")

The Serpent's promises came true, but in a horribly twisted way. Eve's eyes *were* opened to a new world of knowledge and experience— it was awful. She felt the horrible, oppressive force of evil wrap its ugly black tentacles around her heart. She *did* act "like God"—it was a farce. In trying to usurp His position, she enslaved herself to the Prince of Darkness, who was cast from heaven for the same rebellious sin. She *did* make her own decision about good and evil—it was a disaster. Apart from God, she was totally inept at discerning right from wrong. Eve's sin was self-exaltation. She arrogantly refused to acknowledge that God alone was God. When she took the fruit, she defied who He was and made herself out to be something that she was not.

After she sinned, Eve's eyes opened to the fact that she was not the goddess she had presumptuously made herself out to be. Nor was she the woman that God had created her to be. Not anymore. A massive chasm had opened up between what she once was and what she had become. For the first time ever, she experienced imperfection. She was flawed. Feelings of inadequacy swept over her like the rushing muddy waters of a Mississippi flood. She was not who she should have been. Her created beauty was marred. And this resulted in excruciating shame.

Shame is a negative emotion that combines feelings of dishonor, disgrace, unworthiness, and embarrassment. Eve's attempt to clothe herself was a pitiful effort to conceal her disgrace. The ugliness in her heart made her feel physically ugly. For the first time ever, she felt unattractive. Imperfect. Flawed. Self-conscious. Her nakedness felt too revealing and too vulnerable. So she tried to conceal the gap between what she was and what she should have been by covering her most intimate, vulnerable parts with leaves.

The leafy apron Eve stitched together may have helped a bit when it came to covering the shame she felt in Adam's presence. After all, Adam had also sinned and had donned a leafy loincloth to cover his shame. But neither she nor Adam could cover their inadequacy before the Lord. When God drew near, they realized that the leafy aprons didn't suffice. They still felt naked. Eve couldn't cover her sin. Adam couldn't cover his. Nothing could hide the dishonor, disgrace, and embarrassment of their rebellion against their Creator. They could not conceal the fact that they no longer measured up to who He created them to be. So they ran and hid from His presence.

Pre-Fall nakedness symbolized the purity and innocence of humans before God. Post-Fall nakedness symbolizes the inability of humans to make themselves presentable before Him. God did what Adam and Eve were unable to do. He covered them and made them presentable. He shed the blood of an animal—probably a lamb—and clothed them with its skin. By means of a bloody sacrifice, *He* covered their sin and shame. Do you see the symbolism here? Do you feel the surge of hope? God's merciful solution to Adam and Eve's sin, and their inadequate attempt to cover shame, was to clothe them with something infinitely more adequate. The skin of the sacrificed animal pointed to the time when God would sacrifice His Lamb—the Lord Jesus Christ—to atone for sin, alleviate shame, and clothe us in His righteousness. "And the Lord God made for Adam and for his wife garments of skins and clothed them" (Genesis 3:21).

The Lord did not pretend that nothing had happened. He did not tell Adam and Eve to strip off the silly leaves and go back to being naked. He knew that Adam and Eve could never go back to their sinless state. It was impossible for them to return to their naked and shame-free existence. In clothing them, the Lord confirmed that they needed something other than their own skin. Covering up was the appropriate response to the disgrace of sin. The shame of their fallen condition demanded a covering, not to *conceal* it, but to *confess* and *redeem* it. This is a very important point. Clothing bears witness to the fact that we have lost the glory and beauty of our original sin-free selves. It confesses that we need a covering—*His* covering—to atone for our sin and alleviate our shame. It testifies to the fact that God solved the problem of shame permanently and decisively with the blood of His own Son. It also directs our attention forward to the time when we will be "further clothed" with spotless, imperishable garments (2 Corinthians 5:3 NKJV, Revelation 3:5).

Clothing is an outward, visible symbol of an inward, spiritual reality. When you "put on Christ," He covers your shame and makes you what you should be. He offers you his garments "so that you may clothe yourself and the shame of your nakedness may not be seen" (Revelation 3:18). His covering makes us decent (Galatians 3:27). Without it, we are indecent. The physical clothing we wear is supposed to bear witness to that fact. It testifies that the Lord covers our sin and makes us presentable. That's why we need to cover our bodies in public. That's why public nakedness is inappropriate.

In private, within the covenant relationship of marriage, being naked is a very good thing! A husband and wife are presentable and shameless to each other within the context of their covenant. But when they are in public, they clothe themselves to bear witness to their covenant relationship with God. When we see Jesus face-to-face, He will transform our lowly bodies to be like His glorious one. But it's significant to note that even then, we won't go back to being naked. Immortal, imperishable clothes will replace our mortal, perishable ones (2 Corinthians 5:3, Revelation 3:5). Until that that time, we must wear clothes in public as a visible witness to our fall and redemption (Philippians 3:17). We must adequately cover up. As John Piper says:

> Our clothes are a witness both to our past and present failure and to our future glory. They testify to the chasm between what we are and what we should be. And they testify to God's merciful intention to bridge that chasm through Jesus Christ and his death for our sins.[3]

Piper also points out:

> Those who try to reverse this divine decision in search of the primal innocence of the Garden of Eden are putting the cart before the horse. Until all sin is gone from our souls and from the world, being clothed is God's will for a witness to our fall. Taking your clothes off does not put you back into pre-Fall paradise; it puts you into post-Fall shame. That's God's will. It's why modesty is a crucial post-Fall virtue.[4]

Let's relate this back to the BBC's question of "What's the Problem with Nudity?" and its conclusion that people can and ought to unlearn their naked shame. One practical implication of the divine decision to clothe the sinful human race is that public nudity is not a return to pre-Fall innocence, but a rebellion against God's remedy for sin. God ordains clothes to testify about the glory we have lost and to testify about His solution for this shame. Taking off our clothes in public or wearing revealing clothes, adds insult to injury. It is added rebellion. Doing this is like shaking my fist at God and saying, "I'm proud of my sin!" "I'm proud of my fallen condition!" "I don't need to cover up!" "I don't need You or Your clothes!" "I'm proud of my shame!"

Is this possible? Can people be proud of their shame? Can it be unlearned? Most definitely. The volunteers in the BBC study discovered that in an environment that encouraged nakedness, they could readily throw off personal inhibitions and be proud and unashamed of doing so. It comes as no surprise. The Bible informs us that sinners "glory in their shame" (Philippians 3:19). They take pride in defying God. They strip off clothing, morality, and God's directives, and unabashedly display their shame for the world to see. Instead of confessing their need for the clothing of Christ, they brashly proclaim that they feel "comfortable in their own skin." They glory in their naked shame.

The question is not whether shame can be unlearned. It can. The question is whether it *ought* to be. The passage in Philippians explains that those who glory in their shame walk as enemies of the Cross of Christ. When Jesus Christ died for us, He "despised the shame" of the cross and bore it in our stead. His death and resurrection removes our disgrace and the accompanying shame. Only when we cover ourselves with His garments can we truly be free of shame and disgrace. The appropriate response to this moral reality is not to throw off our clothing and inhibitions and thumb our noses at shame, but to be all the more careful about the way we dress.

CLOTHED WITH CHRIST

What then shall we wear? Paul tells us in Romans 13:14 to wear Christ. "*Put on the Lord Jesus Christ, and make no provision for the flesh, to gratify its desires*" (italics added). A Christian woman clothes herself with Christ. That's what she wears. That's how she covers herself. That's how she makes herself beautiful. The clothing of Christ is the most important item in her wardrobe. Her external appearance should display, and not deny or distract from, the righteous clothing of Christ that she wears. The visible should point to the invisible. The temporal should point to the eternal. The symbol should point to the reality. In the final analysis, your clothing is not meant to be about you—it's meant to display deep and profound spiritual truths about the gospel. That's why it's highly important that you wrestle with the practical question of what and what not to wear.

It's not an easy question. Pitfalls exist all around. Sin encourages us to throw off clothing and inhibition, and proudly display our nakedness. It tempts us to exalt external appearance and make clothing our god. It tempts us to deny the importance of appearance and walk around like slobs. It tempts us to become sirens. It tempts us to despise beauty and deny our femininity. It tempts us to slavishly follow contemporary fashion or haughtily spurn it by adopting the fashion of another era. It tempts us to think that clothing is overly important. It tempts us to think it is unimportant. It tempts us to be self-righteous about the way we dress and downright uncharitable toward the way other people dress. It tempts us to sin by remaining quiet and tolerating the flagrant unrighteousness of our sisters. When it comes to clothing and personal appearance, the dangers are many and varied. But Scripture gives us some clear advice on how to navigate our way through this quagmire.

To begin, the Lord wants His girls to be stunningly beautiful. But He repeatedly stresses that a woman's beauty—and her beautification—is something that primarily happens on the inside. "Do not let your adoring be external . . . but let your adorning be the hidden person of the heart" (1 Peter 3:4). The heart is where we put on Christ and the clothing of Christ. A wise woman commits more time and energy dressing herself up on the inside than on the outside. She is like the Proverbs 31 woman, who makes strength and dignity "her clothing" (31:25). The Girl-Gone-Wise *puts on* the new self (Ephesians 4:24). She *puts on* compassion, kindness, humility, meekness, patience, forbearance, forgiveness, love (Colossians 3:12–13). She *puts on* "the whole armor of God" (Ephesians 6:11). She *puts on* a gentle and quiet spirit (1 Peter 3:4). She clothes herself with these garments of Christ, "so that the shame of [her] nakedness may not be seen" (Revelation 3:18).

Spiritual adornment is the reality. Physical adornment is the symbol of that reality. The external clothing we wear is of secondary importance. But it is important nonetheless. In 1 Timothy 2:9, the Lord provides three critical guidelines that help Christian women figure out what and what not to wear. "She adorns herself with *respectable* apparel, with *modesty* and *self-control*." The three guidelines are:

1. Is it becoming or unbecoming? (*respectable*)
2. Is it decent or indecent? (*modest*)
3. Is it moderate or excessive? (*self-controlled*)

The word *adorn* (Greek: *kosmeo*) can also be translated as "to decorate" or "to beautify." It means "to put in order, arrange, make ready." Elsewhere, Jesus' parable talks about wise bridesmaids "trimming" (adorning) their lamps—ensuring that they are in good order, properly set up, and ready for the Bridegroom (Matthew 25:7). Women are to adorn their bodies in the same way. The three guidelines help us ensure that our looks are in good order, properly arranged, and ready to display Christ.

WHAT AND WHAT NOT TO WEAR

It appears that some of the wealthy women in the church in Ephesus were adorning themselves inappropriately—and very likely, quite provocatively. The way they dressed presented a problem. Their clothing was opulent, their jewelry was excessive, and their hairstyles were extravagant. Braided hair was considered a work of art and was very popular among Greek and Roman women. They intertwined elaborate braids with chains of gold or strings of pearls, and piled them high above their heads. Their big hair, low-cut togas, and mounds of tinkling gold bracelets were likely distracting fellow worshipers and setting apart the haves from the have-nots. They were dressing "as a prostitute," to attract attention. The worshipers sitting behind them may have felt the same as I did sitting behind those six young women at the hockey game.

In his letter to Timothy, Paul encouraged these primped women to evaluate their wardrobe in light of the overall purpose of clothing. He counseled them to dress in a way that was in keeping with their Christian character and to concentrate on what was most important. While their inner heart attitude was Paul's primary concern, he did cite three Greek adjectives that would help them govern their choice of clothing: *kosmio*, *aidous*, and *sophrosunes*. The English Standard Version of the Bible translates these qualifiers as "respectable," "modest," and "self-controlled." Other translations use a variety of other words to translate the Greek. These three terms are related; their meanings are very rich and overlap in some ways. They give us some valuable insight about what and what not to wear.

Is It Becoming or Unbecoming?

Kosmio is the descriptive form of the Greek noun *kosmos* (to put in order, trim, adorn or decorate), which is related to our English word *cosmos*—the universe. The Greeks regarded the universe to be an ordered, integrated, harmonious whole. *Kosmos* is the opposite of *chaos*. So when Paul told the women that their adornment should be *kosmio*, he meant that like the universe, all the parts should be aptly and harmoniously arranged with the other parts. It should be "becoming"—that is, appropriate or fitting for someone and/or something. Given the context, I believe Paul was implying that our adornment ought to be *becoming* on a number of different levels.

First, and foremost, your clothing ought to be becoming, congruous with, fitting to, and consistent with your character as a child of God. It needs to "match" the clothing of Christ. But it also ought to be becoming to your body type, becoming to your femininity, becoming to your husband, becoming to the other clothes you are wearing, and becoming to the occasion and place you intend to wear it. There's a tremendous amount of guidance in that small word, *becoming.* There's a "cosmic" amount, because it challenges you to evaluate your clothes, shoes, purses, makeup, and hair from multiple angles, as part of the harmonious, integrated whole of your life—to line up the seen with the unseen and the temporal with the eternal. It challenges you to bring a cosmic perspective to bear on your everyday decisions.

I like the word Paul chose. It has enormous implications. *Kosmio* means that a Christian woman's "look" ought to be consistently put together, inside and out. This challenges those who put an undue emphasis on external appearance as well as those who neglect their personal appearance. It's a corrective to women who dress extravagantly like the ones in Ephesus. It's a corrective to those who dress seductively like hookers. But it's also a corrective to those who think that "holy" means frumpy, ugly, unfeminine, and out of style. *Becoming* indicates that running around in baggy jeans and T-shirts all the time is just as inappropriate as being obsessed with stylish clothing. It means that a woman's appearance ought to be put together nicely. It ought to be pleasant and attractive—on the inside and on the outside.

Say that you're trying to decide whether to buy a certain skirt. You try it on, look in the mirror, and ask yourself, "Is this becoming?" Most women will ask and answer that question on the superficial level of "Do I like it and does it fit?" But Paul appears to be challenging women to take the question a lot further. He wants you to consider:

- Does it fit with who I am as a child of God?
- Does it fit with Christlikeness?
- Does it fit and flatter my body?
- Does it fit and flatter my femininity?
- Does it fit my age and stage of life?
- Does it fit my wardrobe?
- Does it fit my budget?
- Does it fit my needs?
- Does it fit the occasion?
- Does it fit the place I intend to wear it?

You get the picture. It all needs to fit. All of it. If the skirt is "becoming" in all of these areas, then you might purchase it. If it's unbecoming, then you shouldn't.

Is It Decent or Indecent?

The second word, *aidous*, is based on the Greek term for shame and disgrace. The word is a blend of modesty and humility. *Modesty* is how it's most often translated. When I think about a word picture that personifies this concept, I think of approaching God with eyes that are downcast. It's timid respect in the presence of a superior, penitent respect toward one who has been wronged, or the diffidence of a beggar in the presence of one from whom he seeks help. It involves a sense of deficiency, inferiority, or unworthiness. It suggests shame, but also a corresponding sense of reverence and honor toward rightful authority. It's the opposite of insolence, imprudence, disrespect, or audacity. Downcast eyes are the opposite of defiant eyes.

So what does it mean to dress with your eyes downcast? Does it mean that you are self-conscious? No. It means that your clothing tells the truth about the gospel. Your clothing shows the world that Jesus covers your shame and makes you decent. Your clothes cover your nakedness as the clothing of Christ covers your sin.

Dressing "with eyes downcast" means that you are not defiant toward God. You choose clothes that are decent in His eyes . . . not clothes that are provocative, seductive, and that honor nakedness. When you dress decently, you recognize that God ordained clothes to cover, and not draw attention to, your naked skin. You cover up out of respect for Him, the gospel, your Christian brothers—and out of respect for who He made you to be. Decency means you agree with the Lord about the true purpose of clothing and set aside your self-interest to dress in a way that exalts Christ.

So in that dressing room, trying on that skirt, you need to sit, bend, and stretch in front of that mirror, and ask yourself, "Is this skirt decent? Does it do what it should do? Does it properly cover me up? Does it showcase my underlying nakedness—or exalt the gospel of Christ?"

Is It Moderate or Excessive?

The final thing you need to ask yourself about the skirt is whether it is moderate or excessive. Paul uses the Greek word *sophrosunes*. It means "of a sound mind, sane, in one's senses; curbing one's desires and impulses, self-controlled, temperate." The word indicates that our adornment should be reasonable and not crazy. We ought to rein in our impulses and avoid crazy extremes in fashion, hairstyles, and makeup. We also ought to avoid spending crazy amounts of money or stuffing our closets full of crazy quantities of clothing. We ought to govern our wardrobe choices with a sense of moderation, simplicity, and self-control. If the skirt is crazy extreme, crazy expensive, or if it's crazy for you to be buying another one, then you ought to pass it up. Christian women don't get extreme, outrageous, or exorbitant, like *Sex and the City*'s Carrie and her Manolo Blahniks.

Understanding the purpose of clothing and asking yourself the three questions, "Is it becoming?" "Is it decent?" and "Is it moderate?" will help you figure out how to dress. And don't forget to include your "Helper" in the process. The Holy Spirit is an invaluable source of assistance when it comes to figuring out whether or not your appearance glorifies God. He cares about your clothes. He has a big stake in making sure you adorn your body the right way. "Do you not know that your body is a temple of the Holy Spirit within you, whom you have from God? You are not your own, for you were bought with a price. So glorify God in your body" (1 Corinthians 6:19–20). If your heart is right, and you seek the Holy Spirit's guidance, He will be your personal wardrobe consultant and teach you what and what not to wear.

A Girl-Gone-Wise presents herself in a different manner than a Girl-Gone-Wild. Her appearance doesn't scream, "Look at me!" The way she styles her hair and does her makeup enhances her looks, but doesn't clamor for attention. Her clothing doesn't invite onlookers to see or imagine her nakedness. She adorns herself in a dignified, God-exalting way. Her appearance is pleasant and attractive. Proverbs 31 points out that the wise woman is "clothed in scarlet," that "her clothing is fine linen and purple," and that "strength and dignity are her clothing." The implication is that everything she wears—both inside and out—is beautiful. She doesn't dress *as a prostitute*, but in the way that is "proper for women who profess godliness" (1 Timothy 2:10).

Point of Contrast #8

BODY LANGUAGE
Her Nonverbal Behavior

Girl-Gone-Wild: **Suggestive**	Girl-Gone-Wise: **Demure**
She captures him with her eyelashes. (Proverbs 6:25)	She does not resort to deceitful charm. (Proverbs 31:30)
". . . graceful and of deadly charms." (Nahum 3:4)	

She had the *look*. You know the one I'm talking about. It wasn't her sparkly halter dress, her snappy sandals, her perfectly-sprayed-on tan, her incredibly white teeth, her false eyelashes, or her big hair. It was *the* look. The provocative, over-the-shoulder, chin-tipped, sultry-eyed, flirty, tantalizing one. Her mom was instructing her how to pose seductively, walk with a hand perched on her writhing hips, and act all sexy and playful for the judges.

My daughter-in-law and I gaped in disbelief. The girl was only five years old! But what really fascinated me was what happened next. My husband walked into the room. He came in humming a tune, carrying a massive mug of soda and a plate piled high with munchies in anticipation of the family movie we were about to watch. When his eye caught the image of the young beauty pageant contestant on TV, he stopped dead in his tracks. A look of fury I have rarely seen darkened his eyes. With teeth clenched, he grimly ordered us, "Turn that garbage off! How *dare* they do that to that little girl?!!"

As women, Jacqueline and I were morbidly amused and critical of the mom teaching her five-year-old daughter the body language that a girl does not normally learn until she is much older. But Brent, as a man, processed the body language of this little girl in an entirely different manner. Her nonverbal communication told him and every other watching male, "Come get me! I'm available." That's why he was overcome with righteous indignation and holy anger. The thought that anyone would teach a five-year-old girl to send such a message was absolutely reprehensible to him. His outrage and protective fatherly instinct was so strong that I'm sure he would have dropped the snacks and crashed his way through the TV screen and onto that stage if he could have, to halt the pageant and administer a severe tongue-lashing to all the adults in the theater.

The look. The tilt of the head. The flip of the hair. The sway of the hips. The deliberate caress of a curve. The cross of the legs. The leisurely forward lean. The titillating exposure of skin. The brush of the bottom lip. The catlike stretch. The lingering touch . . . By the time a woman reaches adulthood she has learned how to move and position her body in a provocative way. If she chooses, she can hit the "sexual charm" button and turn it on. When activated, her body sends out alluring nonverbal messages to entice her chosen prey. Women, you *know* what I'm talking about! I don't think men have any idea how calculating women are when they employ this strategy. As Jacqueline said, "Not every woman chooses to use that artillery. But we all have it, and we all know how to use it. We can turn it off, or we can turn it on."

A discussion about a woman's appearance isn't complete without a discussion of her body language. The Girl-Gone-Wild uses suggestive body language to attract the attention of men. Her counterpart, the Girl-Gone-Wise, is demure. She does not resort to deceptive charm.

CHARMED!

She's an assertive, self-assured woman, and she has perfected the subtle art of attracting men. She knows how to flirt with her eyes, seductively tilt her head, and position her body in a provocative way. She's a classy dresser who chooses her wardrobe carefully—curve-hugging clothes that reveal just the right amount of skin. Tempting, but not distasteful. High heels are a must. Especially with those tight designer jeans.

Her closet needs constant replenishment. Clothes, jackets, shoes, jewelry, accessories, handbags. And she doesn't neglect her beauty regime. Makeup, manicured nails, styled and highlighted hair, tanned skin, whitened teeth . . . creams, lotions, perfumes. Magazines keep her up to date with the latest advice on interacting with men. She's become an expert at provocative body language, playful banter, and innuendo. She goes to church and Bible study, but her commitment to God is superficial. Her deepest desire is to be sexy, powerful, and alluring.

Who is this woman? You might be surprised to learn that the description (with a few minor fashion updates) comes from the pages of Isaiah. And it may surprise you even more to learn that her behavior was so reprehensible to God that He punished her and her like-minded girlfriends.

> The Lord said: Because the daughters of Zion are haughty and walk with outstretched necks, glancing wantonly with their eyes, mincing along as they go, tinkling with their feet, therefore the Lord will strike with a scab the heads of the daughters of Zion, and the Lord will lay bare their secret parts.
>
> In that day the Lord will take away the finery of the anklets, the head-bands, and the crescents; the pendants, the bracelets, and the scarves; the headdresses, the armlets, the sashes, the perfume boxes, and the amulets; the signet rings and nose rings; the festal robes, the mantles, the cloaks, and the handbags; the mirrors, the linen garments, the turbans, and the veils. Instead of perfume there will be rottenness; and instead of a belt, a rope; and instead of well-set hair, baldness; and instead of a rich robe, a skirt of sackcloth; and branding instead of beauty . . . empty, she shall sit on the ground. (Isaiah 3:16–26)

The women in Isaiah's time were guilty of using their finery to charm men. Years later, another prophet, Nahum, noted that a Wild Thing is full of "deadly charms" (Nahum 3:4). In Assyrian and Babylonian culture, charms were magic formulas that women chanted or recited to get a certain desired result. They believed that love-charms, spells, and incantations to the goddess of love were very effective at helping them bewitch the man of their dreams. Often they wore an ornament—a gem, a stone, a bead, a plaque or an emblem—on a bracelet or chain to symbolize the charm. Sometimes the ornament or stone had an incantation inscribed directly on it. A woman could wear any number of charms. Charm jewelry was very popular and fashionable throughout the ancient Near East.

To charm a man is to affect him by magic or as if by magic. Spells, potions, and incantations are not necessarily involved. A charm is *any* method of enchanting and compelling him. It's obvious that the women in Jerusalem wore charm jewelry such as crescents, pendants, and amulets. But that wasn't the only way they tried to charm men. The passage indicates that these women also tried to charm them with their flashy clothing. They were shopaholics. Isaiah's extensive list indicates that they had stuffed their closets full of shoes, handbags, clothes, and jewelry. These women were also obsessed with primping—meticulously styled hair, perfume, and cosmetic boxes are a few clues. They also attempted to charm men in the way they carried themselves—with their body language. The passage provides details about how they walked. This indicates that they had perfected the feminine art of the *look*. They swayed their hips. They strategically moved and positioned their bodies. They allured and enticed men like charmers hypnotizing snakes.

The women in Jerusalem may have impressed the guys, but they certainly didn't impress the Lord. He was dismayed that they had neglected the most important aspect of womanhood—the beauty of a holy heart—and had attempted to seduce men with their deceptive charm. God called them to task, but His daughters didn't repent. So as predicted, He punished them by having the Assyrians and Babylonians invade and decimate Jerusalem. The women lost everything. "Empty, they sat on the ground."

It's evident that God wouldn't like His daughters wearing any type of jewelry that was thought to contain magical power or influence. But the jewelry wasn't the only charm the Lord viewed in a negative light. Something about the way the women in Jerusalem dressed and primped bothered Him. Based on what we learned in the last chapter, it was undoubtedly that their adornment was unbecoming, indecent, and excessive. However, the charm that topped His list, the one He mentioned first, was their body language—their outstretched necks, wanton looks, wiggling hips, and mincing feet. The Lord was highly offended by the provocative way these women moved their bodies and directed their eyes.

NOT A HINT

What was God's issue? Is it wrong for a woman to be attractive and beautiful to look at? Is He saying that a woman shouldn't be charming? What's the problem with flirting and showing off your womanly wares?

The Bible makes a clear distinction between women who are truly "charming" and those who deceptively try to charm. Women who are charming are gracious, full of favor and elegance. Their selfless goodness makes them attractive from the inside out. Women who seductively try to charm have an underlying selfish agenda. Their intentions are impure. That's why Proverbs 31:30 says, "Charm is deceitful." There's a huge difference between a Girl-Gone-Wise who looks and smiles at a guy to show that she likes him, and a Girl-Gone-Wild who looks and smiles at a guy to try to attract him.

A Wild Thing turns on her seductive charm in order to get a man to be turned on to her. The Sage Father warns his son about a woman like this: "Do not desire her beauty in your heart, and do not let her capture you with her eyelashes" (Proverbs 6:25). The father didn't want his son to be enticed by flirtatious, coy glances. He wanted him to be aware of the danger of women who used body language to seduce men. One ancient commentator suggested that the word translated *eyelashes* could also be "the nets of the eyes." A Girl-Gone-Wild uses her eyelashes to "capture" men as in a net.

You might defend your flirtatious behavior by claiming that you don't intend to seduce a man to have sex—you're just playing and are not really serious. But suggestive body language implies or hints at something improper. The Bible's perspective on the sin of seduction includes more than just the type of seduction that leads to illicit sex. Seduction is *any* behavior that purposefully leads another person in the wrong direction. It's *any* behavior that falsely hints that evil is desirable or exciting. It's *any* behavior that entices someone to think about something improper. Even if she's just playing, the woman who turns on her sexual charm clearly *wants* men to think that sex with her is an alluring idea. That's seduction. And that's sin.

The other day, I heard a female talent-show judge compliment a contestant on how enchanting her "naughtiness" was. As if just a little bit of naughtiness is cute and doesn't matter. Naughtiness might not be an offense on your radar, but it's a crime on God's. A woman who gives any man (other than her husband) a "come-and-get-me" look is in effect telling a lie. She is thumbing her nose at God by hinting that illicit sex is desirable and exciting. She is sinning by willfully enticing a man's thoughts away from the path of virtue. Body language that implies or hints at a wrongful sexual act is just as heinous to God as performing that sexual act. Jesus told men that looking at a woman lustfully was just as sinful as having sex with her. So I'm sure He would tell you that giving the look to the stranger across the room is just as sinful as jumping into bed with him.

Seductive body language may have been one of the sins Paul had in mind when he told the believers in Ephesus, "But among you there must not be even a hint of sexual immorality, or of any kind of impurity . . . because these are improper for God's holy people" (Ephesians 5:3 NIV). This certainly deflates the theory that a wee bit of naughty is OK. According to Paul, not even a hint of sexual immorality or impurity is appropriate among believers. *Not even a hint!* That means that even the tiniest allusion, suggestion, or whiff of sexual "naughtiness" is *not* OK. It means the "I'm just teasing" excuse is not acceptable. "Teasing" doesn't negate the fact that this type of behavior is sin.

Nowadays, Christian teachers routinely address the problem of sexual sin in regards to men looking at porn and lusting after women, but they rarely address the problem of women inviting men to lust. Let me say this loud and clear to all you women: Suggestive dress and suggestive body language is sin. There's no getting around it. The woman who sends the invitation to look is just as guilty as the man who accepts it.

WANT-ON EYES

The Bible describes "the look" as wanton. (Not to be confused with the small round dumpling floating in your Chinese soup. Not *wonton*—*wanton*.) Just divide the word into syllables and you'll get the gist of the meaning. Want-on is someone whose attitude is, "I want (to get it) on." A woman who is wanton will come on to men. Wanton is lacking appropriate restraint or inhibition, especially in sexual thought and behavior.

The corresponding New Testament sin is *sensuality* (lasciviousness; Greek: *aselgeia*). The sin of sensuality appears in numerous lists of vices. The following verses demonstrate that sensuality is an evil from which all believers ought to flee:

"Now the works of the flesh are evident: sexual immorality, impurity, sensuality . . ." (Galatians 5:19)

"Let us walk properly . . . not in orgies and drunkenness, not in sexual immorality and sensuality." (Romans 13:13)

"Evil thoughts, sexual immorality, theft, murder, adultery, coveting, wickedness, deceit, sensuality, envy, slander, pride, foolishness. All these evil things come from within." (Mark 7:21–23)

"For the time that is past suffices for doing what the Gentiles want to do, living in sensuality, passions, drunkenness, orgies, drinking parties, and lawless idolatry." (1 Peter 4:3)

"Many . . . have not repented of the impurity, sexual immorality, and sensuality that they have practiced." (2 Corinthians 12:21)

If you take the Bible seriously, you have to admit that sensuality is a sin. Sensuality can be (a) characterized by lust, (b) expressing lewdness or lust, and (c) tending to excite lust. Provocative body language falls into one or more of these three categories. If you typically act like a vamp, then your body language is characterized by lust. If you come on to a man because you yearn for him, then your body language is expressing lewdness or lust. If you intentionally broadcast provocative sexual signals, then you are tending to excite lust. Whenever you hint or playfully suggest that you want to get it on with anyone other than the man you are married to, you are probably guilty of the sin of sensuality.

The definition of sensuality provides three essential questions you can ask yourself about your body language:

1. Is my body language characterized by lust?
2. Does my body language express lewdness or lust?
3. Am I intentionally inciting lust with my eyes or the way I move my body?

A Girl-Gone-Wise does not engage in inappropriate, sexually charged nonverbal communication. Her body language is demure. That means that she keeps her body language in check: modest, reserved, and free of impure sexual undertones. She takes God's disdain for sensuality seriously. She doesn't shrug off the Bible's warnings as outdated and prudish. The Wise Woman refuses to resort to any behavior that might lead her brother in the wrong direction. She does not hint, by way of innuendo, that evil is desirable. She is very, very careful to avoid any look or behavior that sends this ungodly message.

DANCING TO THE BEAT OF A DIFFERENT DRUM

Several years ago, my son and I were in a mall and walked past a seductively dressed young woman. I noticed that she gave him "the look" as she brushed by. So I asked him, "What do you think when a woman dressed like that comes on to you?" (My poor sons—I ask them such piercing questions.)

He thought for a long moment and then replied, "Well . . . I would have to say that it excites the male in me, but it doesn't attract the man in me."

Read that again. It's a pretty profound answer for a seventeen-year-old. And one that women of all ages should sit up and take note of. It's not very difficult to use sexual charm to pique the sexual interest of a male. But provocative dress and body language won't attract the heart of a godly man. Your provocative body language might get you some attention, but it won't get you the kind of love relationship you yearn for. And even more serious than that, it will interfere in your relationship with the Lord.

Body language is part of any romantic "dance" between a couple. The glances, the smiles, and the playful interaction are important elements that signal interest and move the relationship along. Nonverbal communication is an important part of all face-to-face interaction. Some psychologists say that it conveys 55 percent of the overall message. The point of paying attention to our body language is not to get rid of body language, but to make sure that our nonverbal communication is holy.

I hope you'll take an honest look at what your body language says and whether you are guilty of the sin of sensuality. If you are unmarried, I challenge you to stop reverting to deceptive charm in an attempt to attract men. In the way you dress and act, do not hint at any kind of sexual impurity. Do not resort to seductive flirtation. If you are married, I challenge you too, to stop using seductive flirtations to attract attention from men. I also challenge you to *increase* your sexually inviting body language toward your husband. The Lord gave you the capacity for that "come get me" look for a reason. Your body language toward your husband *ought* to be alluring and sexually playful.

Today, females learn to be sexually flirtatious at a very young age. This chapter about body language is radical stuff. It's extremely countercultural. It flies in the face of how popular media has taught this generation of women to interact with men. Truth may be grating, but only because it cuts away at the restrictive entrapping of sin. The disciples were once aghast with a standard that Christ presented as the ideal. Initially, it seemed far too radical and unattainable to accept (Matthew 19:6–12; Mark 10:9–12). You may feel the same way about some of the ideas in this book. I challenge you to think about them nonetheless. Wrestle with them. Study the Scriptures to see if what I am saying is true.

By now, you're getting the idea that Scripture's portrait of a Girl-Gone-Wise is radically different than culture's norm. As my one son exclaimed after encountering a truly godly young woman, "All those other girls are cut out of the same cloth. She's different. Everything about a woman who loves God is different." He meant it in an admiring way. The Girl-Gone-Wise is exceedingly attractive. Her attractiveness relies on the imperishable beauty of her inner self and not on seductive charm. She knows that "charm is deceitful, and beauty is vain, but a woman who fears the Lord is to be praised" (Proverbs 31:30).

Point of Contrast #9

ROLES
Her Pattern of Interaction

Girl-Gone-Wild: Inclined to Dominate	Girl-Gone-Wise: Inclined to Follow
"She seizes him. . . . He follows her." (Proverbs 7:13, 22)	Like Sarah, she submits to her husband, and to God's beautiful design. (I Peter 3:4–6)

The phone was ringing. Katy was calling for the eighth time that evening. She had called five times the evening before and nine times the evening before that. I knew what this seventh grader wanted . . . to speak to my youngest son, Jonathan. Instead of beckoning him to the phone, I normally took a message, so he could call her back at his leisure. My standard reply to her inquiry if she could speak to him was, "I'll give him the message and have him call you back."

Which he did. When it suited him. But that wasn't good enough for Katy. She was getting irritated that I was interfering with her desire to cajole my son into jumping through her hoops. Jonathan wasn't at home that particular evening, so I told her, "I'm sorry, he's not available."

Katy sarcastically snapped back, "Well . . . when *will* he be *'available'*?"

That was it. Enough. Enough Katy. I wouldn't tolerate disrespect from a cheeky twelve-year-old. So I called the phone company and blocked her number. And my husband and I challenged Jonathan to step up and refuse her advances.

The incident happened just before the era of students routinely using cell phones. I remember thinking about how aggressive young girls had become. It used to be that the girls waited for the guys to call them. A female phoning a male was very forward and inappropriate. Social etiquette stipulated that the male was the pursuer. But the feminist movement changed all that. Women became the pursuers. More recently, my sons have dealt with girls who text them every two minutes every waking hour of every day (and several times during the night), girls who ask them out, girls who stalk them on Facebook, and girls they have to block because "the woman won't take 'no' for an answer." (And these were "Christian" girls!) Females have morphed into hawkish predators. For a mom trying to raise godly sons, it's scary out there!

The rules have changed. Social convention now stipulates that women can and ought to be initiators in male-female relationships. They can take the lead. This may sound good in theory, but it doesn't work very well in practice. I constantly see the carnage resulting from this approach. I think of Heidi, a Christian woman who bought into the "roles don't matter" paradigm. She saw a guy she liked. She asked him out. She insisted on paying for half their dates. She called him. She kissed him. She brought up the subject of marriage. She negotiated the terms. She insisted on a hyphenated name. She made him give up his job and move because of hers. She made more money, so she made him stay home with the kids. OK. Now fast-forward ten years into their relationship: Heidi hates her husband. Her complaint? He's unmotivated. A deadweight. She has to beg him to do anything. He doesn't initiate. He's wimpy, whiny, and disgusting. She's the only one contributing. And she's exhausted.

Wait a minute, Heidi. Let me get this straight: You asked him out. You pursued him. You took the lead. You dominated the relationship.

Like putty in your hand, you molded him into what you wanted him to be . . . and now you hate him for it? What's more, you expect him to go against years of emasculation and suddenly become a man? Why should he? You're the "man" in your house—or at least you pretended that you could be.

Details differ, but I can't tell you how many "Heidis" have ended up crying on my shoulder, dismayed that their husbands are wimps and not men—that they are passive and won't lead. Inevitably, it only takes a few pointed questions to discover why. It's usually because, right from the start, the woman "wore the pants." That was the pattern of their relationship. She was the pursuer. He was the pursued. It doesn't take a rocket scientist—or a social scientist—to figure out that once established, this relationship pattern is difficult to change.

A major notion of this generation is that gender roles are insignificant and irrelevant. It doesn't matter who pursues. It doesn't matter who wears the pants. In fact, it's good if women take the wheel. Men have had their turn, and for far too long! While it has made for an interesting—though tragic—social experiment, this theory neglects to take the created design of male and female into consideration. It assumes that we get to decide for ourselves what manhood, womanhood, and male-female relationships are all about. However, according to Scripture, we don't. Our text in Proverbs reveals that a Girl-Gone-Wild "seizes" a man and compels him to "follow her." A Girl-Gone-Wise knows that this pattern goes against God's created design.

BACK TO THE DRAWING BOARD

Let's go back to the drawing board—not to take pen in hand and try to redraw the image of womanhood, like the generation of the sixties did, but to take a look at the model God drew. Genesis lays out His blueprint. The first chapter gives a zoomed-out view of the big picture. It displays the profound dignity of the human race and shows how the creation of humanity fits into the overall story of creation. It reveals that men and women are more like God than anything else in the universe, and that they share this status equally. Genesis 2 zooms in to capture the spectacular details. It reveals that God created each sex to be unique. Each has a distinct significance and function. Each perfectly complements the other.

The truth that God wanted to display through male and female was of paramount importance. So it stands to reason that He was highly intentional when He created them. Every action was significant. That's why Genesis 2 is so careful to provide a detailed, frame-by-frame rendering of the creation of mankind. God could have made men and women at the exact same time and in the exact same way. But the fact is, He didn't. The blueprint displays twelve markers that show how male and female roles are complementary, but not identical. Let's have a look and see, starting with what makes the male uniquely male.

UNIQUELY MALE
The Male Was Firstborn

> "Then the Lord God formed the man of dust from the ground and breathed into his nostrils the breath of life, and the man became a living creature." (Genesis 2:7)

The first thing to note about the creation of the sexes is that God created the male first. You might think that this fact is trivial or inconsequential, but the Bible teaches otherwise. The firstborn son held a unique role and position in the Hebrew family. He ranked highest after his father and carried the weight of the father's authority. He was responsible for the oversight and well-being of the family. He also served as the representative of all the other family members. This wasn't just a cultural quirk that the Hebrew people dreamed up. God gave them these directions. Their family structure followed the pattern He gave.

We can tell that the position of firstborn son was important to God, because He called Israel His firstborn son (Exodus 4:22). Adam was God's firstborn human being, but Israel was the first nation He adopted as His own. When Pharaoh stubbornly refused to release the Israelites from bondage, the Lord sent the angel of death to kill all the firstborn sons of all the families in Egypt. Those oldest brothers were the family representatives. As such, they were destined to die to pay for Egypt's sin. But the Lord graciously made a provision to save them. If they smeared lambs' blood on the doorposts of their houses, the firstborn sons wouldn't die. The lambs bore the punishment in their stead. The

Hebrew people followed God's direction and sacrificed lambs. Their firstborn sons were saved. The Egyptians didn't. Their firstborn sons died.

After this momentous event, God instructed the parents of every Hebrew family to redeem all their offspring by sacrificing a lamb at the birth of their oldest son (Exodus 11:4–7; 13:11–15). The oldest brother represented all his brothers and sisters. His redemption signified the redemption of them all. Conversely, his disgrace signified the disgrace of all.

God made Adam first. He was the firstborn—the head of the human race. He carried the weight of responsibility for the oversight and well-being of the human family. So when the human race fell, God held Adam responsible, even though Eve sinned first. The New Testament bluntly states, "In Adam all die" (1 Corinthians 15:22). The Lord held Eve personally responsible for her sin. But He held Adam responsible for smearing the entire human race with his.

Are you beginning to see the significance of Adam's position? The Old Testament sketches the outline, but the New Testament colors it in. The position of firstborn is all about Jesus Christ, the firstborn—the only begotten Son of God. He is firstborn among many brothers, firstborn of all creation, firstborn from the dead (Romans 8:29; Colossians 1:15, 18; Hebrews 1:5–6). His divine authority is greater and higher than every human authority, and the model on which all human authority rests. Jesus Christ is "the Last Adam" (1 Corinthians 15:45). He was the lamb that died to take the place of the first Adam and the human family he heads. "For as in Adam all die, so also in Christ shall all be made alive" (1 Corinthians 15:22).

So what does all this have to do with male and female roles, and young Katy aggressively stalking my son? It has a great deal to do with them. The New Testament says that Adam's position has ongoing implications for male leadership in male-female relationships. The responsibility that God put on the shoulders of Adam extends—in one way or another—to the shoulders of all other males. Paul tells Timothy that the reason males bear responsibility for spiritual leadership in God's family is that "Adam was formed first" (1 Timothy 2:13). He also teaches that every man bears responsibility for the oversight of his own individual family unit (Ephesians 5). What's more, this charge appears to extend to a general responsibility of all men to take the initiative and look out for the welfare of the women around them. Exercising godly initiative and oversight is a big part of what manhood is all about.

That leaves us with one of three possibilities concerning the fact that God created the male first. Take your pick:

a. God was crazy—His decision was arbitrary. It meant nothing. The position of firstborn means nothing.

b. Paul was crazy—he hated women. He egotistically tried to seize power for men. He was wrong to draw any significance from the fact that God created Adam first. He was wrong to suggest that Adam's position had ongoing implications for manhood and womanhood.

c. People who reject the idea of God giving men a unique responsibility to take initiative are crazy—they presumptuously think they know more about manhood and womanhood than God or His apostle Paul.

God made the male first. That *doesn't* mean he made the male better. But it *does* mean that He created him to bear a unique responsibility that differs from the female. (I suppose there's a fourth option you could add to the list—"Mary is crazy, and this book is crazy." Please don't pitch it across the room quite yet—there are eleven markers to come . . .)

The Male Was Put in the Garden

"The Lord God took the man and put him in the garden . . ." (Genesis 2:15)

The second observation we can make about Genesis 2 is that God took the man and "put" him in the garden. God created the male out in the wild, from the dust of the open desert. Then He led His firstborn male away from his place of creation and put him in a garden, in Eden. Why is this significant? Because later in the chapter we see that when a man gets married, he leaves the place where he was created in order to initiate a new family unit ("A man shall leave his father and his mother and hold fast to his wife," Genesis 2:24). It is as though God "puts him" in a new position of responsibility. What's more, the image seems to foreshadow Christ forsaking the home of His Father in heaven in order to pursue His bride, the church.

God put the male in the garden in Eden. The Hebrew word for "garden" indicates an enclosure, a plot of ground protected by a wall or hedge. It's an area with specified boundaries. The garden was a specified place in the land of Eden. It wasn't the entire land of Eden. It was more like a designated homestead within that land. Eden means "pleasure" or "delight." The Lord took the male to the land of delight and set him up in his own place, to be the head of a new family unit. But before the Father presented him with a wife, He took some time to teach him the specific roles and responsibilities of a man.

The Male Was Commissioned to Work

"The Lord God took the man and put him in the garden of Eden to work it . . ." (Genesis 2:15)

The word translated as *work* (Hebrew: *abad*) is the common word for tilling soil or for other labor (Isaiah 19:9). It contains the idea of serving someone other than oneself (Genesis 29:15). What's more, it frequently describes the duties of the priests in worship (Exodus 3:12). The man's life in the garden was not to be one of idleness. God's plan, from the very start, was that the man worked to provide for his family's needs. He was supposed to work to provide for them— physically as well as spiritually. God created men to be the providers. That doesn't mean that women don't contribute. But it does indicate that the primary responsibility for provision for the family rests on the man's shoulders.

The Male Was Commissioned to Protect

". . . and keep it." (Genesis 2:15)

God also wanted the man to "keep" the garden. The Hebrew word for *keep* translates as a verb meaning "to be in charge of." It means to guard, to protect and look after, to provide oversight. It involves attending to and protecting the people (Genesis 4:9; 28:15) and property (Genesis 30:31) under one's charge. It also extends beyond the physical to include a spiritual component of protection (Numbers 3:7–8). The Lord created men to be physically stronger than women are. Men are the protectors, more suited for a fight. The physical protection mirrors the spiritual protection that God wants men to provide for their families. Again, this doesn't exclude women from contributing. It simply indicates that if a robber crawls in through the window, the man is the primary protector. He's the first one to jump up and take the bullet.

The Male Received Spiritual Instruction

> "And the Lord God commanded the man, saying, 'You may surely eat of every tree of the garden, but of the tree of the knowledge of good and evil you shall not eat, for in the day that you eat of it you shall surely die.'" (Genesis 2:16–17)

Before the woman arrived on the scene, God explained the rules of the garden to the man. It was up to him to pass on this spiritual instruction to his wife. That's not to say that the man interacted with God on her behalf. No. She had a personal relationship with the Lord. But it does indicate that as leader of his newly minted household, the man had a special responsibility to learn and understand the ways of the Lord. This was so that he could fulfill his commission to provide spiritual oversight and protection.

The Male Learned to Exercise Authority

> "Now out of the ground the Lord God had formed every beast of the field and every bird of the heavens and brought them to the man to see what he would call them. And whatever the man called every living creature, that was its name. The man gave names to all livestock and to the birds of the heavens and to every beast of the field." (Genesis 2:19–20)

I smile when I think of what it must have looked like when the Lord brought the animals to the man to name. It seems to me that besides serving the purpose of making the man yearn for a suitable mate, this was a type of training exercise. To name something is to exercise authority over it (Genesis 5:2; Daniel 1:7). The Lord wanted the male to learn how to exercise authority in a godly manner. His first-born had a unique responsibility to govern. And the Lord wanted him to govern well. That's why the Lord closely supervised and mentored him through the naming process. The Lord wanted the male to learn to exercise his delegated authority with gentleness, kindness, wisdom, and much care.

The first chapter of Genesis indicates that "dominion over the earth" extends to women as well as men. God gave *both* dominion. So God's excluding the female from the process of naming the animals doesn't indicate that she lacks God's authority to govern. But it does indicate that the Lord does not view her authority to govern as interchangeable with the authority of His firstborn male. A man's authority is unique to what it means to be a man. A woman's authority is unique to what it means to be a woman.

The man was firstborn, but had no kin. He was head of a new household, but his were the only feet that trod within the walls. God commissioned him to work, but there was no one for whom to provide. He knew his mission was to guard and protect, but there was no one to look after. He had thought of new ideas, but had no one to discuss them with. He was bursting at the seams with the desire to love and serve, but as the day wore on and he named animal after animal, it became painfully obvious that no creature had anywhere near the capacity to receive what he so deeply wanted to give.

The Lord knew it. He could read it on Adam's face. It was the only thing in creation that was not good. But for the time being it was necessary. It was part of the man's training. Part of his preparation. The Lord wanted him to catch a glimpse of the full import of God's final and most magnificent work. He wanted the man to feel the longing intensely—to love and want a soul mate with such passion that he was willing to pay the ultimate price to win his bride. God knew that He had to wound His firstborn to create woman. It would draw blood. Having a bride would cost the man dearly. When the man named the last animal and turned back to his Maker, the Lord knew it was time. Time to make "her"—the one who would captivate the man's heart as completely as the vision of the Lord's coming heavenly bride had captivated His.

"Sleep." The man sank down as if dead, on the soft carpet of moss. The Lord extended His hand and pierced the side of his firstborn to extract a bloody mass of bone and flesh. I wonder if a lump formed in His throat as He saw the future toward which the image pointed. I wonder if His hand trembled as He began to shape and form. I wonder what thoughts flew through His mind as He carefully sculpted each soft curve. This final masterpiece tipped the scales and set it all in motion. When He was finished, He stepped back to look. He glanced past the flesh He had just formed to peer into eternity future at *her* and softly sighed. It was good. Yes! It was *very* good!

UNIQUELY FEMALE

God created woman from the side of man, so she's made of the same stuff—equal to man. But He didn't create her at the same time, place, or from dust, so she's also different. Male and female are equal and different. God made them to complement each other. We've already looked at six markers of complementarity that can be observed in the creation of the male. Six more markers appear in the creation of the female.

The Female Was Created from the Male

> "So the Lord God caused a deep sleep to fall upon the man, and while he slept took one of his ribs and closed up its place with flesh. And the rib that the Lord God had taken from the man he made into a woman." (Genesis 2:21–22)

In our culture, "Remember where you came from!" is a common admonition not to look down on one's beginnings. It's a warning to avoid pride and an overinflated sense of self-importance. We intuitively know that it's inappropriate to regard that from which we were made as lesser than us. We know that we are obliged to honor and respect our origins.

The same sort of idea is present in the creation of the female. Because woman was drawn from man's side, it was appropriate for her to have an attitude of respect toward him. He was the firstborn. In the New Testament we see that the fact that she was created from him— and not the other way around—is the basis of a wife honoring the authority of her husband. "For man was not made from woman, but woman from man. . . . That is why a wife ought to have a symbol of authority on her head" (1 Corinthians 11:8–10).

The Female Was Made for the Male

> "Then the Lord God said, 'It is not good that the man should be alone; I will *make him* a helper fit *for him.*'" (Genesis 2:18, italics added)

The second chapter of Genesis tells us that the female was created "for him"—that is, on account of the male. First Corinthians 11:9 reinforces that man was not created "for the woman;" rather the woman was created "for man." He explains that this is the basis for a wife respecting the authority of her husband.

For most of us, the idea of woman being created "for" man sounds somewhat negative, since it appears to imply that he has license to use and abuse her at will. But the Hebrew preposition carries no such overtones. It simply denotes direction. She was created for—that is, toward or with reference to him, or on account of him. She was created *because* of him. His existence led to hers. It didn't happen the other way around. Our adverse reaction to the idea that we were created "for man" serves to underline how very far we've fallen from the original created order. When the first bride was presented to her husband, her heart was undoubtedly bursting with joy to have been created for him. She was thrilled that his existence led to hers.

There's another important point here. Being created for someone indicates that God created the female to be a highly relational creature. In contrast to the male, her identity isn't based on work nearly as much as on how well she connects in her relationships. Woman is the relater-responder who is inclined toward connecting with others.

The Female Enriched the Male

> ". . . a helper fit for him." (Genesis 2:18)

God created woman to be a helper. "Helper" is another word that begs explanation. It's not a term that indicates a lesser status or the type of help that assists in a trivial way. The Hebrew word (*ezer*) is a very powerful one. It's most often used with reference to the Lord being our helper (Psalm 33:20; 72:12). An *ezer* provides help that enriches and makes the recipient more fruitful than he would be without that help.

God created the woman to enrich the man by providing invaluable support that without her he would not have. What the man lacks, the woman accomplishes. She makes it possible for them to receive the blessing that he could not achieve alone. Woman plays an integral part in the survival and success of the human race. Without her, man could not be fruitful—physically or metaphorically.

So does that mean that women exist to serve the selfish ends of men? Absolutely not. The phrase "fit for him" in Hebrew literally means "like opposite him"—like an image in a mirror. The term is unique to Genesis. It expresses the notion of complementarity. She's not exactly like him. She's like-opposite him. Corresponding. Harmonized. Suitable. An exact fit. She's a "helper," but more importantly, she's a helper "alongside."

The *alongside* part is extremely important. The purpose of woman helping man isn't about exalting the man. It's not about him. Her help contributes to the both of them achieving a greater, nobler, eternal purpose that is far bigger and more significant than their own existence. She struggles alongside for the same purpose for which he struggles. And what is that? The glory of God. The Lord says that He formed and created sons and daughters to magnify His glory (Isaiah 43:6–7). A woman helps a man achieve the purpose of exalting and displaying the jaw-dropping magnificence of the gospel of Jesus Christ and the glory of God. That's what she helps him do.

The Female Deferred to the Male

"The Lord God . . . brought her to the man. Then the man said, '. . . she shall be called Woman, because she was taken out of Man.'" (Genesis 2:22–23)

I think that the first male and female intuitively knew how to behave. He knew what it meant to be a man. She knew what it meant to be a woman. So when the Lord presented the bride to the groom, the man spontaneously broke into a poem that expressed ecstatic love and delight, and at the same time demonstrated his intuitive grasp of the nature of their relationship. He named her—thus fulfilling his responsibility to initiate and lead. She joyfully responded with deference. For both of them, it was the natural and beautiful thing to do.

When God presented Eve to Adam, you don't see Eve taking charge and saying, "Wait a minute, Adam, I'm going to name myself—thank you very much! In fact, I'm going to be the one doing the naming around here. I've thought of a great name for you!" No. That's not what happened. Adam and Eve acted according to their God-given bents. He initiated. She responded. The pattern of their relationship reflected who God created them to be.

The Lord created woman with a bent to be amenable, relational, and receptive. He created man with a bent to initiate, provide, and protect. As we talked about in an earlier chapter, Genesis 3:16 indicates that sin severely damaged the God-given inclination of both. Sin twisted the positive desire of woman to respond amenably to man into a negative desire to resist and rebel against him. It twisted the positive drive of man to use his strength to lead, protect, and provide for woman into a negative tendency to abuse or refuse that responsibility.

When a girl goes wild, she's overcome by the sinful desire to go against the created order and selfishly dominate a man. Like the Proverbs 7 woman, she becomes the one who does the pursuing—she "seizes him" and demands that he follow her lead. A Girl-Gone-Wild is inclined to dominate. Her counterpart, the Girl-Gone-Wise, is inclined to joyfully defer to and give the man the opportunity to set the pace in the relationship.

The Female Was the Male's Perfect Counterpart

"She shall be called Woman [*Isha*], because she was taken out of Man [*Ish*]." (Genesis 2:23)

In Hebrew, the name with which the male identified himself was *Ish*, while his name for woman was *Isha*. As discussed previously, *Ish* comes from the root meaning "strength" while *Isha* comes from the root meaning "soft." The idea goes beyond the mere physical difference between men and women to encompass the totality of their essence. The man was created to joyfully and actively initiate and give strength. The woman was created to joyfully and actively respond and receive it. Each was created with a unique role and responsibility to be the perfect counterpart to the other.

The Female Was Created in the Garden

> "Therefore a man shall leave his father and his mother and hold fast to his wife, and they shall become one flesh." (Genesis 2:24)

A final but highly significant observation is that the female—the softer, more vulnerable one—was created in the garden, in a place of safety. She was created in a place that was already under the protective authority of her husband-to-be. The male leaves the protective sphere of his household of origin to become the protector of a new household (Genesis 2:24). The woman doesn't "leave." She's the constant beneficiary of protection from the authorities God has put in her life. The Lord wanted to ensure that woman, His final delicate masterpiece of creation, would always be loved, cherished, and kept safe.

The fact that woman was created within the boundaries of a household also implies that women are to have a unique responsibility in the home. This is consistent with the idea that a woman metaphorically keeps her feet (and heart) centered in the home, rather than outside of it. For the woman, nurturing her relationships and keeping her household in order takes priority over other types of work.

LET HIM DRIVE

The Lord evaluated his equal-yet-different creation of male and female as, "Very good! Spectacular! Outstanding!" Do you agree with Him? Do you feel the same way? Do you try to bring your life in line with God's beautiful, unique design for the woman He created you to be? Or do you defiantly take pen in hand and scribble over His blueprint?

When we think about roles, we often make the mistake of thinking that they are primarily about what we do. Roles influence what we do, but the role defines the behavior, and not the other way around. People miss the point when they engage in endless debates about specific behavior, like whose job it is to take out the trash. Everyone wants a list of dos and don'ts, but the Bible does not provide such a list. Roles speak to *who we are* more than they speak to *what we do*. Roles are about who God created male and female to be. The Lord knows that we'll figure out what we ought to do when we figure out who we ought to be.

Let's think about how all this relates to junior high Katy chasing my son. Setting aside the fact that she was young and the fact that her calls were excessive, do you think that Katy pursing boys was healthy and appropriate behavior for a young woman? If Katy (who is now twenty) continued this pattern of relating to boys, what kind of a relationship do you think she would end up in? Do you think her style of relating supports who God wants her to be as a woman? Do you think it will result in Katy having a husband who assumes his God-given responsibility to be a man? Or will Katy likely end up crying on someone's shoulder in the future, because she'll eventually be clued in to the fact that her husband is a wimp? And that her effort to wear the pants in her house has become exhausting and frustrating, because it doesn't fit with who God created her to be?

Is it wrong for a woman to phone a man? No. Is it wrong for her to initiate from time to time? No. But if her habitual pattern of behavior is that she is the pursuer and he is the pursued, this is unlikely to change if and when the couple get married. When we were talking about it last week, my daughter-in-law astutely said, "I tell my girlfriends that the right roles start right at the start of a dating relationship. I rarely called Clark. Only if he called me, did I call him back, or only if there was a really good reason for me to call him. I didn't text him very much. I waited for him to ask me out. I waited for him to declare his love before I declared mine. I waited for him to give me a kiss. I waited for him to bring up the idea of marriage. I waited for him to propose. I held back so he could lead. I wanted a man who would be a man in our marriage." Smart girl!

So here's my advice to you—unmarried or married—who want to

be Girls-Gone-Wise: Let him drive. Wait for him to pick up the keys (physically and metaphorically). Hold back. Don't rush in. Give him a chance to initiate. Welcome his leadership. I know that nowadays men are plagued with the sin of passivity. This is primarily due to their sin nature, but also in part because women have shoved them out of the driver's seat and brashly taken the wheel. I know that many women ache for their men to step up and be men. What I advise all the Heidis crying on my shoulder is this: "Reclaiming your womanhood is the best way to help a man reclaim his manhood." We live in a world broken by sin. So this isn't easy. But a Girl-Gone-Wise inclines her heart to embrace her role as a woman and follow God's design.

Point of Contrast #10

SEXUAL CONDUCT
Her Sexual Behavior

Girl-Gone-Wild: **Impure and Dishonorable**	Girl-Gone-Wise: **Pure and Honorable**
". . . and kisses him." (Proverbs 7:13)	She controls her body in holiness and honor, and does not wrong her brother. (I Thessalonians 4:4–6)

S ex. Sex. Sex. Sex is everywhere. Movies, sitcoms, soaps, reality
TV, news stories, commercials, talk shows, billboards, magazine ads, and MTV. Sex sells everything from travel to tele-
phones to toothpaste. This current generation has more sex education,
sex books, sex columns, sex therapists, sex supplements, sex talk, sex
techniques, and sex toys than any other in the history of mankind. Sex
is the topic of Internet chatter, locker-room gossip, and watercooler
banter. We live in a sex-saturated world.

Given the modern-day obsession with sex, I'm going to say something that may sound radical: *We don't make as much of sex as we*

should. Oh, most women are overwhelmingly eager to indulge. They partake in worldly sexual pleasures like revelers greedily snatching up beads at a Mardi Gras carnival. They hang them up as cheap trophies to collect dust on the edge of their vanity mirrors and eagerly wait for the next big parade. Others scorn the festivity. They think the beads are tawdry. They were once mesmerized and collected a few strands, but the sparkle has worn off. Now the trinkets hang tarnished and neglected in the back of their closets. Been there. Done that. Got the necklace.

The problem is not that we value sex too much—but that we don't value it enough. We fool about with lust, sensuality, seduction, glossy-magazine titillation, movie-screen romance, illicit sex, obligatory sex, or boring sex, when divine pleasure is offered us. We are like a senseless child who refuses to trade in her dollar-store baubles for a gold locket. We don't make nearly as much of sex as we should. We are far too easily pleased.

Sexual conduct is one of the major differences between a Girl-Gone-Wise and a Girl-Gone-Wild. The sexual behavior of the former is holy and honorable, whereas the sexual behavior of the latter is not. The Wild Thing thinks that the way she conducts herself sexually is her own business—whether or not she collects sexual baubles is a personal matter and not all that important. The Girl-Gone-Wise realizes that her sexual conduct, both inside and outside of marriage, *is* important. What she does sexually is much bigger than her own personal life. It has meaning that connects to the cosmic, unseen, eternal realm. The Girl-Gone-Wise understands that sex is a big deal to God— and that He wants her to know and experience what great sex is all about.

It's my aim, in this chapter, to help you understand, from a biblical perspective, what great sex is all about. I believe that this understanding is necessary for both single and married women. Knowing what sex is all about will motivate a single woman to delight in sexual continence. She will understand that restraint is as much and as valid of an expression of the meaning of sex as the sexual act itself. Her sexual chastity contributes to the cosmic story. It testifies to the astonishing meaning of it all—and glorifies God.

Understanding what sex is all about will motivate a married woman to delight in having sex with her husband—to have a strong, "till death do us part," pure, unwaning desire to make love to him and to honor the exclusivity of their union. She will understand that sex is a God-given, delightful act that is, among other things, a testimonial act of worship. It is a means whereby a married woman glorifies God.

Most Christian discussions about sex and sexuality put the emphasis in the wrong place. They spend a whole lot of time focusing on what constitutes improper sexual conduct. They draw lines and boundaries that delineate pure from impure behavior. It seems to me that coming up with a list of "don'ts" somewhat misses the point. It tackles the issue from the wrong side. We can't hope to know which behaviors we should avoid until we understand the reason that we ought to avoid them. What's more, this approach lopsidedly focuses on behaviors to avoid, rather than attitudes and behaviors to cultivate. It can result in a pharisaical sense that we're getting our sexuality right, when in fact, we're getting it very wrong. Many married Christian women are guilty of wrongful sexual conduct, even though they may not technically be transgressing a specific biblical boundary. For example, a woman who is frigid toward her husband dishonors God's pattern for sexuality as much as the one who commits adultery does. A married woman who uses sex to punish or reward her husband is as wrong in her thinking about sex as an unmarried woman who hooks up with a guy just for the thrill of a fleeting night of pleasure.

The Bible's principles for sexual conduct take the issue of sex a lot further than a written list of dos and don'ts. They emanate from the heart of God. He wants us to cherish and value our sexuality as much as He does. He wants us to understand the cosmic, amazing meaning of sex and to honor that meaning with all our hearts. He wants us to delight in sex. Honor it. Think His thoughts about it. He wants us to live in such a way that our sexuality puts His glory on display. He wants us to be so familiar with the awesome meaning of sex that we will be able to spiritually discern whether any thought or behavior contradicts or detracts from that meaning. The more we embrace *why* God created sex, the more readily apparent it will become *what* constitutes appropriate sexual conduct. Understanding the reason for this amazing gift will help us honor and enjoy it in the right way.

SEX IS A BIG DEAL

To figure out what sex is all about, we need to look again at the creation of man and woman and the first marriage. In the previous chapter, we talked about the twelve markers of complementarity evident in Genesis 2. We discovered that God created man and woman to be equal, yet different. The difference in our anatomy mirrors our difference in makeup. What it means to be a man is different from what it means to be a woman. The question we're going to explore right now is *why*. Why did God create male and female? Why did He create marriage? Why did He create sex?

The meaning of sex can't be addressed outside of the context of what it means to be a man or a woman—nor can it be addressed outside of the context of marriage. Manhood, womanhood, marriage, and sex are indivisibly connected. Their meaning intersects. As you'll soon see, the meaning is a mystery that God hinted at from the beginning of time, but did not reveal until the death and resurrection of Jesus Christ.

Did you know that the Father had the death and resurrection of Jesus Christ in mind before He created the world or anything in it? Before He created male and female, He had a plan to redeem them. Paul makes this clear in Ephesians 1:4–11. He points out that God planned to display His glorious grace by adopting us into His family. He planned to accomplish this through the death and resurrection of Jesus Christ, "the Beloved." This was God's plan "before the foundation of the world." When God set about creating man and woman, He already had in mind the marvelous plan of Jesus dying to redeem His church-bride. He already had in mind the marriage that will take place between Christ and the church at the end of time.

In the first chapter of Genesis, we see the Creator reflectively pause before His final and greatest creative act. There was no question in His mind about what He was going to do. He had settled on His plan long before the foundation of the world. It was already in motion. At His word, the galaxies and planets, sun and moon had all formed and aligned. The earth had ripened with life: The ground had sprouted vegetation; the sky, sea, and land teemed with every sort of living creature. Everything was in place. Everything was ready. It all led up to this moment—and this moment pointed to another moment far off in time but eternally present in the mind of God. The significance of what He was about to do was deeper and more profound than even the angels could fathom. He was about to make man—and to make him male and female.

> Then God said, "Let us make man in our image, after our likeness. And let them have dominion over the fish of the sea and over the birds of the heavens and over the livestock and over all the earth and over every creeping thing that creeps on the earth." So God created man in his own image, in the image of God he created him; male and female he created them. (Genesis 1:26–27)

Take note of the language. It's significant. God said, "Let *us* make man in *our* image, after *our* likeness," and then He created man in His own image—male and female He created them. The discussion about the creation of male and female took place between members of the Godhead. It may have been between all three: Father, Son, and Holy Spirit. But at the very least, it involved the Father and his Son, as Scripture draws parallels between that relationship and the relationship of a husband and wife. When God created man and woman, He had the dynamic of His own relationship in mind. God created the two sexes to reflect something about God. He patterned the male-female relationship ("them") after the "us/our" relationship that exists within the Godhead. He used His own relationship structure as the pattern.

Paul confirms, in 1 Corinthians 11:3, that the relationship between a husband and wife is patterned after the relationship between God the Father and His Son. "The head of a wife is her husband, and the head of Christ is God." God purposefully created marriage to reflect the headship structure that exists within the Godhead. But He also created marriage and sex to reflect some other truths about the Trinity.

Jesus confirmed what Genesis says about marriage: "From the beginning of creation, 'God made them male and female.' 'Therefore a man shall leave his father and mother and hold fast to his wife, and they shall become one flesh.' So they are no longer two but one flesh. What therefore God has joined together, let not man separate" (Mark 10:6–9). Marriage is about union, communion, commitment, and family—and these things all point to the character and nature of God.

Marriage is about *union*—It's about the "oneness" of two individuals. Two become one. The word *one* stresses unity while recognizing diversity within that oneness. The same word is used in the famous Shema of Deuteronomy 6:4: "Hear, O Israel . . . the Lord is One." Jesus used the same language: "I and the Father are one" (John 10:30). The oneness of male and female in marriage is an earthly picture that helps us understand the oneness of God.

Marriage is about *communion*—husband and wife become "one flesh" through the physical union of their bodies. The physical act consummates their emotional and spiritual intimacy. The Old Testament expression for sexual intercourse is that a man "knows" his wife. Sexual intercourse equals knowing. Covenant love is all about "knowing" someone. It's communion of the most intimate kind. It's the deepest love that is humanly possible. "One flesh" expresses the idea that within the marriage covenant, husband and wife get to know each other intimately, in every possible way.

When Jesus talked about the divine love between Himself and His Father, He used the language of communion: "The Father knows me and I know the Father" (John 10:14). "The Father has loved me" (John 15:9). "The Father is in me and I am in the Father" (John 10:38). "I am in my Father, and you in me, and I in you" (John 14:20). John described the intimacy between God the Father and Son this way: "The only begotten Son, who is in the bosom of the Father" (John 1:18 NKJV). The terms "know," "in," and "in the bosom" indicate that the Father and Son experience a divine intimacy. Their relationship is one of closest communion. Communion in marriage bears witness to the spiritual, divine intimacy between the members of the Trinity.

Marriage is about *commitment*—the man commits to forsake all others and "hold fast" to his wife. The word means to permanently adhere oneself to. The Hebrew word refers to permanently soldering one piece of metal to another. It's used in Job 41:15–17 to describe how tightly a crocodile's scales are joined together. This joining of husband to wife is a permanent covenant, orchestrated by God. He joins two individuals together indivisibly. The indivisibility of husband and wife is to bear witness to the fact that Father and Son are indivisibly one (1 Corinthians 8:4–6). and that Christ is indivisibly one with His church (Colossians 1:18).

Marriage is about *family*—a husband and wife establish a new family unit. Their union produces children. The family relationship is a symbol that teaches us a lot about God. It teaches us about the relationship a father has to his children. It helps us understand the relationship between God the Father and His only begotten Son, the enormousness of what it meant for the Father to sacrifice His Son, and what it means for Him to adopt us as His children (Romans 8:29; Galatians 4:5–6).

In Romans 1:20, Paul sheds more light on why God created men, women, marriage, and sex. He says, "For his invisible attributes, namely, his eternal power and divine nature, have been clearly perceived, ever since the creation of the world, in the things that have been made." What does this tell us? It tells us that when God created male and female, sex and marriage, He put two very important truths about Himself on display: (1) His divine nature (the glory of who He *is*) and (2) His eternal power (the glory of what He *does*).

God created male and female in His own image. We don't fully understand what the image of God is all about, but two things are clear. First, being created in His image gives us enormous dignity, privilege, and responsibility. He has crowned us with honor and glory and given us authority over the earth. It's a breathtaking charge to go about the business of daily life and all the while reflect the image of the Almighty. And that leads to the second thing: what a mess we've made of this awesome dignity! The image of God in man is badly marred, sometimes even beyond recognition. It begs for redemption. Transformation. A type of re-creation. And stunningly enough, God stamped this vision and hope onto human beings in the very beginning, before they had even sinned.

When God created male and female, He provided an object lesson—a parable, as it were—of his entire redemptive plan. Manhood, womanhood, marriage, and sex are mini-lessons that proclaim the gospel (Colossians 1:23). They tell the cosmic story about the Bridegroom who loved His bride so much that He died to redeem her, and about how wonderful their wedding and union will one day be.

Throughout the Old Testament, God used the image of marriage to teach His people about the nature of His relationship to them. He was the husband; Israel was His wife. "For your Maker is your husband" (Isaiah 54:5). God likened their spiritual infidelity to a wife whoring around with other men (Ezekiel 16). Old Testament marriage imagery foreshadowed the mystery that remained hidden until the time of Christ. "In that day, declares the Lord, you will call me 'My Husband' . . . and I will betroth you to me forever. I will betroth you to me in righteousness and in justice, in steadfast love and in mercy. I will betroth you to me in faithfulness. And you shall know the Lord" (Hosea 2:16, 19–20).

Paul connects all the dots in Ephesians. In chapter 3, he explains that the mysterious plan came to light through the work of Jesus Christ (vv. 9–10). In chapter 5, he links the mystery of redemption (Christ loving and dying for the church) to male-female sexuality and marriage. "Husbands, love your wives, as Christ loved the church. . . . 'Therefore a man shall . . . hold fast to his wife, and the two shall become one flesh.' This mystery . . . refers to Christ and the church" (Ephesians 5:25, 31–32).

When God described the work of His Son as the sacrifice of a husband for his bride, He was telling us the ultimate reason why he made us male and female, and why He created marriage and sex. Christ and His bride are the reason. Sexuality is a parable—a testimony to the character of God and to His spectacular plan of redemption through Jesus. This spiritual truth is so magnificent that God chose to put it on display permanently. Everywhere. Men were created to reflect the strength, love, and self-sacrifice of Christ. Women were created to reflect the character, grace, and beauty of the bride He redeemed. He created marriage and sex to display the joining of Christ and the church in an indivisible covenant. History started with the covenant wedding and sexual union of a man and woman because it will end with the covenant wedding and spiritual union of Christ and His bride.

Manhood, womanhood, marriage, and sex exist to tell the story of Jesus, the Bridegroom who loved and gave His life for His bride. What is manhood about? Displaying the glory of Jesus Christ. What is womanhood about? Displaying the glory of Jesus Christ. What is marriage about? Displaying the glory of Jesus Christ. What is sex about? Displaying the glory of Jesus Christ.

Sex is the act that defines marriage. It consummates (completes) the marriage covenant. It is the act of ultimate significance because it represents the essence of what covenant is all about. Sex confirms that covenant means union, communion, intimacy, commitment, exclusivity, satisfaction, delight, and fruitfulness. God created sex so that a husband and wife might display, confirm, and enjoy their union—so that their physical bodies bear witness to the spiritual, supernatural, and legal joining that has taken place. Physical intimacy reinforces the fact that God has joined two individuals together in covenant commitment.

Through sex, a husband and wife affirm in the private realm what has taken place in the public and heavenly realm. They tell and retell the story to each other. Sex is the testimony. Sex bears witness that God has made two one. That's why God restricts sex to marriage. If unmarried individuals are physically intimate, they tell a lie with their bodies. They testify that a joining has taken place, when in fact it hasn't.

God created manhood, womanhood, marriage, and sex because He wanted us to have symbols, images, and language powerful enough to convey the idea of who He is and what a relationship with Him is all about. Without them, we would have a tough time understanding concepts such as desire, love, commitment, fidelity, infidelity, loyalty, jealousy, unity, intimacy, marriage, oneness, covenant, and family. We would have a hard time understanding God and the gospel. God gave us these images so that we have human thoughts, feelings, experiences, and language adequate and powerful enough to understand and express deep spiritual truths. The visible symbols display and testify about what is unseen. That's why the symbols are so very important.

Scripture is emphatic that who we are as male and female has very little to do with us and very much to do with God. The Lord says, "Bring my sons from afar and my daughters from the end of the earth, everyone who is called by my name, *whom I created for my glory*, whom I formed and made" (Isaiah 43:6–7, italics added). The storyline of gender and sex is ultimately not about us. It's about displaying the glory of our Creator and His spectacular redemptive plan. So when my husband and I make passionate love, we bear witness to the glory of the gospel of Jesus Christ. Our sex bears testimony to it. If my heart wanders and I lust for a man who is not my husband, I bring disgrace on the gospel of Jesus Christ.

Any violation of the exclusivity of the marriage covenant throws mud at God's beautiful parable. Given the powerful symbolism of gender, marriage, sex, and family, is it any wonder that Satan tries to destroy the image? Is it any wonder that these symbols are at the forefront of the spiritual battle? Is it any wonder that they are at the heart of so much brokenness, dysfunction, and pain?

NO MESSING AROUND

I hope you can see how understanding the "why" directs the "what" of our sexual conduct. Understanding that marriage and sex go hand in hand, and that the image is all about the covenant commitment, love, unity, permanency, and exclusivity of Christ's relationship to the church, answers a whole lot of questions about what and what isn't appropriate sexual behavior.

In the spiritual realm, would it be appropriate for Christ's bride to "mess around" with anyone other than her Bridegroom? Even just a little bit? On the other hand, would it be appropriate for her to shun her Bridegroom, refuse His approaches, or give Him the cold shoulder? The answer is simple. No. And I believe the answer is almost as simple when it comes to sex in the physical realm. We honor God with our sexuality by restricting physical, sexual expressions of intimacy to the confines of marriage, and by delighting in the joy of marital sex. Keeping sex exclusive to the marriage covenant and having great sex with one's spouse, is the right way for Christians to display the purity, unity, and fidelity of the church's relationship to Christ. It's the way we tell the story.

Physical intimacy is the sign of covenant commitment. The covenant is what changes the traffic light from red to green. *Sex testifies to the fact that a union has taken place.* So what are the implications for physical intimacy between unmarried couples? The simple answer is that it's wrong for two people to act as if they are married when they are not married. Our sexual behavior in the physical realm is to mirror the purity and faithfulness of Christ's bride in the spiritual realm. Therefore, if the behavior is inappropriate between a *married* woman and a man who is not her husband, then it is just as inappropriate between an *unmarried* woman and a man who is not her husband.

Would it be appropriate for a bride to seek to give or receive sexual pleasure outside of the confines of her marriage bed? Would it be appropriate for her to sleep over at a male friend's apartment? Would it be appropriate for her to passionately kiss anyone other than her husband? I think the answer is obvious.

Does this mean that couples should refrain from kissing or holding hands until they are married? The Bible doesn't say. And I don't think it's wise for us to enforce a set of rules and boundaries. That misses the point. But honoring the meaning of marriage definitely means bridling our passions and confining sex to marriage. Outside of the covenant relationship, the traffic control light is red. This is the standard for those who are married as well as those who are single. Unmarried individuals respect the meaning of sex by restraining their sexual appetites and saving most—if not all—expressions of physical intimacy for the covenant context for which God designed it.

Arguing that "just a bit" of messing around outside of the covenant of marriage is OK is as logically indefensible as justifying that it's OK for Christ's bride to mess around on Him "just a bit." Christ gave His life for the new covenant—it was bought by His blood. Faithfulness to the covenant is supremely important to Him. It is impossible and utterly unthinkable that He would ever be unfaithful to His bride. That's why Christ's standards for the covenant of marriage are so shockingly high. To those who don't grasp the significance of sex and marriage, they sound totally unreasonable. Christ's view on the exclusivity and permanency of the marriage relationship shocked His disciples. Jesus saw the marriage covenant as so binding, and its symbolic significance so profound, that in His mind, divorce and remarriage were out of the question. His perspective left His disciples gasping. His claim that lust is as sinful as adultery undoubtedly left the crowd gasping. Christ's ideal for covenant commitment and absolute sexual purity is radical.

Married or unmarried, a woman's sexual behavior is to present an image of the purity, faithfulness, and exclusivity of the church-bride to her one and only beloved Bridegroom. God takes marriage and sex very, very seriously. The Bible teaches that God intends sex to consummate the marriage covenant, and *not* to precede marriage. The Lord wants us to cherish and set apart sex to bear testimony to this exclusive, till-death-do-us-part relationship. This honors what sex is all about.

Hang in there. Keep reading. I think things will become even clearer when we unpack a passage that Paul wrote to new believers who lived in a sex-saturated culture not unlike our own.

UNCOMMON, SET-APART SEX

The moral climate within the Roman Empire was not healthy. Sexual promiscuity was common. People got divorced on a whim. The Roman philosopher Seneca observed, "Women were married to be divorced and divorced to be married."[1] Romans traditionally identified the years by the names of their consuls—but fashionable Roman women identified the years by the names of their husbands. One historian quotes an instance of a woman who had eight husbands in five years. Promiscuity and adultery also saturated Greek culture. One writer admitted, "We keep prostitutes for pleasure; we keep mistresses for the day-to-day needs of the body; we keep wives for the begetting of children and for the faithful guardianship of our homes."[2] There was no shame whatsoever in extramarital relationships.

It was to new believers in this sex-crazed Roman and Greek culture that Paul wrote the following passage:

Finally, then, brothers, we ask and urge you in the Lord Jesus, that as you received from us how you ought to walk and to please God, just as you are doing, that you do so more and more. For you know what instructions we gave you through the Lord Jesus.

For this is the will of God, your sanctification: that you abstain from sexual immorality; that each one of you know how to control his own body in holiness and honor, not in the passion of lust like the Gentiles who do not know God; that no one transgress and wrong his brother in this matter, because the Lord is an avenger in all these things, as we told you beforehand and solemnly warned you.

For God has not called us for impurity, but in holiness. Therefore whoever disregards this, disregards not man but God, who gives his Holy Spirit to you. (1 Thessalonians 4:1–8)

The young believers in the church in Thessalonica were trying to figure out what their new faith meant. Some undoubtedly had promiscuous sexual histories and were carrying around all kinds of sexual baggage. They reasoned that they ought to be able to indulge their passions and pursue sexual pleasure, and that it was completely acceptable to do so outside the confines of marriage. Though they had accepted Christ, they still had a very ungodly perspective on sex. Paul challenges them to bring their thinking and behavior in line with the gospel of Jesus Christ. He reminds them of five things the Lord wants believers to do: (1) abstain from sexual immorality, (2) aim for increased sexual purity, (3) control your body in holiness and honor, (4) don't sexually defraud others, and (5) don't disregard the importance of sexual conduct.

Abstain from Sexual Immorality

Immorality translates as the Greek word *porneia*, from which we get our English word *pornography*. It means sexual unfaithfulness. It refers to any type of illicit sex that takes place outside of a marriage covenant. Paul tells the believers to abstain from sexual immorality. In other words, he says, "Christians don't sleep around outside of marriage! Staying out of bed with someone you aren't married to is the bare minimum, Christianity 101, baseline sexual standard for followers of Jesus. If you've been sleeping around, stop sleeping around. Abstain. Give it up. That's what Jesus expects you to do."

Aim for Increased Sexual Purity

The Lord doesn't just ask us to refrain from illicit sexual intercourse. He asks us to aspire to increasingly higher standards of sexual purity. That's why "How far is too far?" really isn't the right question. He doesn't want us to ask how close to immorality we can get without crossing the line. He wants our sexual conduct to become more and more holy. Paul encourages the Thessalonians to pursue sexual purity—and to "do so more and more."

Sexual impurity is a sin that the Lord often lists alongside the sins of immorality and sensuality. The word *impurity* literally means "uncleanliness." It means dirty, common, and ordinary. *Purity* is the exact opposite. It means clean, uncommon, and extraordinary—set apart. As we grow in Christ, our understanding of and desire for sexual purity will also grow. It won't happen overnight, but as we are sanctified to become more like Jesus, our sexual conduct will become increasingly clean, extraordinary, and set apart for Him. The Lord doesn't want you to settle for dirty, common, ordinary sex. He wants you to reach higher. He wants you to nudge the bar up from where it is now. He wants you to constantly aim for increased sexual purity and increasingly higher standards.

Control Your Body in Holiness and Honor

Sexual purity takes self-control. It requires that we don't mindlessly follow our sexual passions, like people who don't know God. The Lord wants us to control our sexual impulses. He wants us to intentionally rein them in and submit them to Him. He has bestowed His Holy Spirit upon us—the Spirit of power, love, and self-control—to help us discipline ourselves and control our bodies and sexual passions in a holy and honorable way (2 Timothy 1:7).

Don't Sexually Defraud Men

Paul advises the Thessalonians to ensure "that no one transgress and wrong his brother in this matter." The Greek word used here for "transgress" is also translated as *defraud*. It means to overreach or overstep; to go beyond. It carries the implication of selfish personal gain. Defrauding a brother is overstepping the line to take something that is not yours to take. The Girl-Gone-Wild of Proverbs 7 defrauded the young man. She seized him and kissed him when she had no right to. His compliance or approval is inconsequential. She still wronged him. She wronged him when she overstepped *God's idea* of what was appropriate sexual behavior. Whenever you interact with a man who is not your husband in a way that you should only interact with your spouse, you not only sin against God, you also wrong your brother.

Don't Disregard the Importance of Sexual Conduct

Sex is a big deal to God. Paul warns the new believers not to underestimate or disregard the importance of their sexual conduct. He told the believers in Corinth the same thing:

> The body is not meant for sexual immorality, but for the Lord, and the Lord for the body. . . . Do you not know that your bodies are members of Christ? Shall I then take the members of Christ and make them members

of a prostitute? Never! Or do you not know that he who is joined to a prostitute becomes one body with her? For, as it is written, "The two will become one flesh." But he who is joined to the Lord becomes one spirit with him. Flee from sexual immorality. Every other sin a person commits is outside the body, but the sexually immoral person sins against his own body. Or do you not know that your body is a temple of the Holy Spirit within you, whom you have from God? You are not your own, for you were bought with a price. So glorify God in your body. (1 Corinthians 6:13–20)

Wrongful sexual conduct violates your covenant relationship with Jesus. It's serious stuff. It has serious consequences. Paul implies that it has greater consequences than other types of sin. Over my years of ministering to women, I have found this to be the case. Because sexual immorality is an assault on your personhood and a severe violation of covenant, it damages you in a way that other sins do not. When you sin sexually, you sin against your own body. You fracture your God-given identity. There is always great hope in the power of Christ's redemption. But those who engage in sexual sin dig themselves into a very deep pit from which it is often exceedingly difficult to climb out. In my experience, Satan capitalizes on sexual sin and establishes spiritual ties, footholds, and strongholds that require extensive spiritual warfare to overcome. So if you haven't wandered down the path of sexual sin, please don't. If you have, realize that God has the power to heal, and that He will fight with you to redeem what you have lost. But realize, too, that the scars will remain for some time, and that you will face battles that you would not have had to face if you had remained sexually pure.

FOR THE SAKE OF SEX

Some will claim that narrowing and confining physical intimacy to marriage will decrease the pleasure of sex. But quite the opposite is true. Narrowing the boundary to its God-given parameter increases the power, passion, and pleasure of sex. It allows sex to be everything God created it to be. The boundary creates the beauty. The following illustration captures the idea:

The pleasures and goodness of sex are heightened, not lessened by proper restraint, in the same way the Colorado River is made more powerful by the walls of the Grand Canyon. The very narrowness of the river's channel there makes for a greater river. Farther south, as the river flows through the deserts of California and Arizona, it is shallow, wide, and muddy, even stinky in spots. Wider boundaries diminish the river; sharper, stronger, and narrower boundaries strengthen it. Less is more. The boundaries and proscriptions of sex in the Bible are for the sake of sex. Again, less is more—at least less as understood by one man and one woman together exclusively till death parts them.[3]

God wants Christians to experience great sex. We haven't even brushed the surface of what that looks like. God is so supportive of good sex that He devoted an entire book of the Bible, the Song of Solomon, to the joy of passionate sex between a husband and wife. Make sure to read it sometime. I hope that this chapter has given you a vision of sex that is bigger and more wonderful and more astonishing than anything you have ever dreamed. I hope that it inspires you to give up the cheap sexual trinkets of a Girl-Gone-Wild and open your hands to reach for God's pure, solid gold locket of uncommon, set-apart sex. Don't settle for less.

(Download the chapter questions from GirlsGoneWise.com. They'll help you evaluate whether your outlook on sex is the one God wants you to have.)

BOUNDARIES
Her Hedges
and Precautions

Girl-Gone-Wild:	Girl-Gone-Wise:
Leaves Herself Susceptible	**Safeguards Herself**

". . . in the twilight,
in the evening,
at the time of night
and darkness."

(Proverbs 7:9)

She foresees danger
and takes precautions.

(Proverbs 22:3)

Espresso macchiato. Extra foamy." That's what Kyle ordered the day he came into the college coffee shop where Jennifer worked. He came back the next day. And the next day after that. For their first date, they went to a movie. For their second, Kyle took her on a long walk through the autumn leaves in the river valley. Jennifer was smitten. He was handsome. Funny. Engaging. He made her feel special. They had known each other a scant two weeks when Kyle invited her to a party at a club. She had never been to one, but he assured her it would be a lot of fun. He'd teach her to dance. Jennifer didn't normally go to such places, but Kyle was so kind and sweet. What harm could it do? She'd make an exception —just this time. It would be a great opportunity to witness to him some more.

The morning after the big party, Jennifer woke up in her apartment with a smashing headache and aching all over. She remembered having a drink, but little else. She couldn't shake the gnawing, dark suspicion that something bad had happened. She was too confused and embarrassed to confront Kyle when he dropped by the coffee shop later that day with a bouquet of flowers. She could tell that something had changed between them. He came by a couple more times, and then his visits abruptly stopped. Several weeks later, a pregnancy test confirmed her deepest fear. Kyle had drugged and date-raped her.

Jennifer couldn't bring herself to tell her parents. Her pregnancy would bring shame and embarrassment on her family, who were prominent in the church and community. She couldn't tell any of her friends. She was the Bible study leader—the one who challenged them to follow God's ways. How could she face them? How could she face the whispers and stares and all the other consequences of an unplanned pregnancy? Overcome with shame, Jennifer quietly went for an abortion. When I met her—five years later—she had undergone counseling and had dealt with the emotional aftermath of the rape. But she still hadn't told anyone about the baby. Her guilt over aborting the baby had emotionally crippled her. She couldn't accept God's forgiveness. Her walk with God, her desire to talk to others about Jesus, and her hope for the future had all but shriveled up. She asked me to pray to help lift the dark cloud that had settled over her life.

Sarah was a thirtyish single woman who inadvertently fell in love with a coworker, Paul. The only problem was that Paul was married. Their relationship had started innocently enough. Their boss had assigned them to work together on a project. At some point their e-mails, lunchtime meetings, and backroom network programming took a romantic turn. They crossed all boundaries one weekend, in a hotel room in California, when they attended the computer analyst conference together. The affair had been going strong ever since. Sarah wanted Paul to leave his wife. But they had three children, and he was reluctant to break up his home. He was beginning to waver. Sarah was turning into an emotional wreck. It was an impossible, no-win situation. With tear-filled eyes, she wondered, "How could this have happened to me?"

To her credit, Amanda could see it coming. She had gone to talk to her pastor, Mike. He was such a good listener and empathized with the struggles in her marriage. She was surprised to learn that his marriage wasn't as wonderful as it appeared on Sundays. He, too, felt deeply alienated from his spouse. Their "counseling" sessions ignited a spark between them. Amanda started thinking and daydreaming about Pastor Mike. At church, their looks grew deeper and their touches started to linger. He was finding reasons to call and ask if she could volunteer in the office. She could feel the chemistry intensify. They had already crossed many small boundaries. The ball was rolling downhill and gaining speed. Against such strong momentum, the remaining barriers provided little resistance. She could already imagine them giving way. Amanda came for prayer because she knew that if she didn't turn back immediately—and rebuild some stronger hedges—she would ruin two marriages, destroy a church, and bring scandal to the community. She knew what she needed to do, but didn't have the desire or the strength to do it. I prayed with her, but had the uneasy feeling that Amanda was more enthralled about the prospect of intimacy with Pastor Mike than she was about her relationship with Jesus Christ. She was holding the forbidden fruit up to her mouth, ready to bite.

What do these stories have in common? All three of these women went off track because they crossed proper boundaries. They experienced difficulties they would have avoided had they faithfully observed the boundaries. Minding them would have protected them from harm.

In Jennifer's case, the sin was not her "fault." That is, she was not complicit to it. Kyle committed a criminal offense against her. But by failing to maintain protective boundaries, Jennifer increased her vulnerability to this type of attack. Please don't misunderstand me. I am not saying she asked for what she got. The crime was heinous and unjustified and deserving of punishment. Leaving your car door unlocked doesn't justify the theft of the laptop you left on the seat. The person who steals it from an open vehicle is just as guilty as one who steals it from a secured one, and ought to receive as severe a sentence. But if you had hidden the laptop in your trunk and locked your vehicle, chances are you would not have become the victim of theft.

Failure to safeguard yourself increases your vulnerability. If Jennifer had observed the boundaries of not going out with unbelievers and not going to a place conducive to sin, she would have avoided or at least minimized the opportunity for Kyle to sin against her.

Sarah and Amanda, on the other hand, were complicit to sin. They progressed down the road of immorality of their own free will. Each did so by failing to put up hedges to protect her sexual purity. In the absence of protective boundaries, they became more and more vulnerable to sin. It probably happened the same way for the Wild Thing of Proverbs 7. She likely didn't begin her marriage planning to commit adultery. But bit by bit, she got to that point. One small compromise led to another until finally she ended up in an immoral situation that she would have never envisioned at the start.

Proverbs says the woman came out of her house to meet the young man "in the twilight, in the evening, at the time of night and darkness." The author implies that she shouldn't have been out at that time of night. It was inappropriate. In being out that late, her behavior crossed the boundary between appropriate to inappropriate conduct. You couldn't exactly call it sinful conduct—there are no "thou shall not go out after midnight" directives in the Bible. But it was definitely unwise. It opened the door to sin. If she had had a policy about not going out late and had abided by that policy, she would not have continued down the track of compromise. After she crossed the first boundary of going out late at night and the second boundary of secretly meeting the young man alone, she crossed the boundary of appropriate touch—by kissing him. She crossed another boundary when she engaged in inappropriate flattery and flirtation, and another when she invited him over to her place. Before she knew it, she had violated all the boundaries she should have observed.

A Girl-Gone-Wild disregards boundaries and leaves herself susceptible to the danger of sexual sin. Her counterpart, the Girl-Gone-Wise, safeguards herself. Her hedges are appropriate, clear, definitive, and strong.

HEDGING YOUR PURITY

When you hear the word *hedge*, you might imagine a row of shrubs that form a boundary around a yard. Hedges marked off several boundaries of the yard of my childhood home. They lessened the risk of us six kids wandering out and of big dogs wandering in. In a figurative sense, the word *hedge* refers to a protective method that lessens the risk of something negative happening. In the financial world, a hedge is a strategy to minimize exposure to an unwanted business risk. It defends against loss. And that's exactly what a clear boundary for sexual purity does. It protects against sexual injury and loss. For our purposes, a hedge is a personal rule that minimizes a woman's exposure to an unwanted sexual risk. It's a boundary that helps her protect her own sexual purity as well as the sexual purity of the men around her. It's a strategy whereby she lessens the opportunity for sin.

The Sage Father instructed his son that a sensible person "sees danger and hides himself, but the simple go on and suffer for it" (Proverbs 22:3). He repeats the exact same warning in Proverbs 27:12. "Danger" is literally the threat of evil. It's anything that could be a potential source of injury or harm. "Hides himself" means that the person takes action to guard from danger, or to escape or avoid it. This foresight is contrasted with the stupidity of those who ignore potential dangers and who end up getting themselves in trouble because of their lack of caution.

The father voices a similar sentiment in Proverbs 14:16: "One who is wise is cautious and turns away from evil, but a fool is reckless and careless." To be cautious is to be "careful," "alert," "on guard." It means to be apprehensive about the potential for sin. A wise person takes precautions to avoid being entrapped by sin. A fool doesn't take precautions. This person is reckless and careless. The Hebrew has connotations of arrogance, overconfidence, and throwing off restraint. The Latin translation uses the image of a person who overconfidently neglects and "leaps over" restrictions, thinking he won't get hurt.

A Girl-Gone-Wild crosses boundaries and plunges ahead with reckless confidence. She scoffs at the danger, believing that she's in control of the situation. A Girl-Gone-Wild doesn't believe that she's vulnerable to falling ("It won't happen to me!") or that the danger is substantial ("It can't hurt!"). So she doesn't put up hedges and precautions to safeguard her sexual purity.

TEN TYPES OF HEDGES

How can a woman keep her way pure? By "guarding" (hedging) it according to God's Word (Psalm 119:9). Practically, this means that we identify the common pitfalls of sexual sin and guard ourselves from stepping into those traps. We save ourselves "like a gazelle from the hand of the hunter, like a bird from the hand of the fowler" (Proverbs 6:5). We stay far away from the "thorns and snares" that entangle sinners (Proverbs 22:5). The Proverbs 7 woman did not do this. She did not establish hedges to protect herself from sexual sin. She overstepped ten boundaries that any woman who wishes to keep her way pure ought to hedge.

I. Location Hedges: Unhealthy Versus Healthy Environments
A Girl-Gone-Wise avoids unhealthy environments.

It always amazes me that women think they can expose themselves to immoral ideas, go to immoral environments, and constantly hang out with immoral people and suffer no ill consequence. The Sage Father asks, "Can a man carry fire next to his chest and his clothes not be burned? Or can one walk on hot coals and his feet not be scorched?" (Proverbs 6:27–28). A wise woman is not deceived. She recognizes that "bad company ruins good morals" (1 Corinthians 15:33). She resolves that she will not go to places that will potentially harm her. She puts up hedges such as these:

- I will not go to bars, lounges, or clubs.
- I will not go to strip shows or lewd bachelorette parties.
- I will not go to any parties that involve heavy drinking, drugs, or sex.
- I will not go to X-rated movies.
- I will not go to restaurants that encourage servers to dress and act provocatively.

- I will not go to comedy clubs that feature foul language and crude sexual humor.
- If I find myself in an unhealthy environment, I will quickly leave.

2. Pairing Hedges: Dual Versus Group Interaction
A Girl-Gone-Wise avoids inappropriately pairing herself with men.

The Wild Thing of Proverbs 7 was a married woman. She shouldn't have socially paired up with the young man. It was inappropriate for her to hang out with a man who wasn't her husband. If either individual in a male-female combination is married, then it is unwise for them to interact on a "paired-up" basis. It's also unwise for unmarried individuals to unreservedly pair off with each other. Scripture warns us, "The righteous should choose his friends carefully, for the way of the wicked leads them astray" (Proverbs 12:26 NKJV). Group interaction, involving three or more people, is a hedge that protects a pair from sexual temptation. Here are some suggested pairing hedges:

- I will interact with men in a group rather than one-on-one situations.
- I will not meet up, dine, or travel alone with a man if one of us is married.
- I will try to avoid being paired up with men in work projects, school assignments, or volunteer work. If pairing up is unavoidable, I will strengthen and emphasize other hedges to compensate for this.
- As an unmarried woman, I will not pair off with an unmarried man (one-on-one) until I have had ample opportunity to get to know him in a group context.

3. Seclusion Hedges: Private Versus Public Venues
A Girl-Gone-Wise avoids being in private, secluded places with men.

The Wild Thing of Proverbs 7 had no business inviting the young man into her home while no one else was there. It's inappropriate for a man and woman who are not married to each other to be together in a private, secluded place. That privilege belongs to married individuals. Men and women who desire to guard their sexual purity interact in places that are open to the view of others. Here are some suggested hedges that protect a woman from the sexual temptation and dangers of seclusion:

- I will not be alone with a man in a bedroom, an apartment, a house, a hotel room, a cabin, or any other place that is cut off from public view.
- I will interact with men in places where other people in the vicinity can potentially observe our interaction.
- If I am meeting alone with a man in a business context, I will ensure to keep the door of the room open or to meet in a room with glass walls or windows.
- If I am meeting with a man by webcam (e.g., Skype), I will observe these same precautions.

4. Communication Hedges: Inscrutable Versus Open Interaction
A Girl-Gone-Wise avoids secret communication with men.

Sin loves to remain hidden. It flourishes under the cover of secrecy. Do you think the Proverbs 7 woman would have said the same words to that young man if her husband had been standing there? Of course not. Today, many women get themselves into trouble by engaging in chat, e-mail, and text messages that are inappropriately personal or sexual in nature. They send secret messages that they would be ashamed to have others see. Girls-Gone-Wise hedge themselves by avoiding "for your eyes only" communication. They keep their communication with men as "above board" as possible. They do not keep secrets from spouses or send messages that they would be embarrassed about if intercepted. Here are my suggestions for some communication hedges:

- I will keep my electronic communication clean and pure, and free of all sexual flirtation, innuendo, and other sexual content.
- I will copy my spouse, the recipient's spouse, or other recipients if e-mails contain interaction of a personal nature.
- I will not communicate anything verbally or in writing that I would be hesitant to share with my spouse or a godly mentor.
- If I receive an inappropriate message, I will forward the message to my spouse or godly mentor and copy him or her on my response.

5. Contact Hedges: Copious Versus Controlled Contact
A Girl-Gone-Wise controls the frequency and amount of contact with men.

The more contact a man and woman have with each other, the more careful they need to be to guard against sexual impropriety. The "pull" to be together goes hand in hand with the "pull" toward sexual intimacy. Limiting contact goes a long way to diminishing the chance of falling into sexual sin. Here are some hedges that might help. Some are for married women, and some relate to interaction between unmarried couples.

- I will not initiate or reciprocate inappropriate contact with a man if one of us is married.
- If I feel "pulled" toward an adulterous relationship, I will immediately pull back and break off, or minimize contact with him.
- Before I am married, I will resist the pull to spend time with a guy as though I were married to him. I will resist the pull to be constantly together just as I resist the pull toward sexual intimacy. (You may want to limit the number of times you are together each week, based on what's appropriate for your age and circumstance.)
- I will not monopolize a guy's time or attention.

- I will not clamor for a guy's attention by sending him excessive texts or messages.
- I will not needlessly interrupt and distract him by calling and texting him when he is busy.
- I will not allow a guy to monopolize my time or attention.
- I will not neglect my obligations, responsibilities, or ministry opportunities.
- I will encourage him to attend to his obligations, responsibilities, and ministry opportunities.
- I will not neglect my family relationships or other friendships.
- I will encourage him not to neglect his family relationships or other friendships.

6. Curfew Hedges: Cover of Night Versus Light of Day Parameters
A Girl-Gone-Wise abides by curfew and nighttime boundaries.

Last summer, a female acquaintance of my son proudly told me, "I hardly ever get to bed before three!" All kinds of red flags went up in my mind. Really? I was thinking what is it that you do every night until three? I suspect it isn't anything healthy, like reading your Bible. I suspect that you're getting physical with someone you shouldn't be getting physical with, surfing to Internet sites you shouldn't visit, having conversations you shouldn't have, watching things you shouldn't watch, thinking thoughts you shouldn't think, and wasting time you shouldn't waste. Can you look me in the eyes and tell me that you do a good job of avoiding sexual sin—immorality, impurity, sensuality—in those hours between midnight and three?

My editor, who assures me she is a "chaste, middle-aged single woman," laughed when she read this passage at 2 a.m. and reminded me that some people are simply "night owls" by the way their body clocks naturally operate. If this describes you, you still need to be aware of whether the night hours induce you to sin and change any habits that you need to change.

My mom once told me, "Nothing good ever happens after midnight." I'm sure it's not literally true, but the point is well taken. The later it gets, the more tired we get, and the more we drop our guard. The more our guard drops, the more susceptible we are to sexual sin. The Bible draws a very strong connection between night, darkness, and sin. It warns us to shun darkness and love the light. This means that we must be very careful to hedge our purity by abiding by curfew and nighttime boundaries like this:

- I will keep the lights on when I am in a room with a man I am not married to.
- I will not sleep over at a man's apartment or house.
- I will be home before . . . (11 p.m., midnight, 1 a.m., etc.).
- I will turn off my computer by . . . (10 p.m., 11 p.m., midnight, 1 a.m., etc.).
- I will not send texts after . . . (9 p.m., 10 p.m., etc.).
- I will get to bed by . . . (10 p.m., 11 p.m., midnight, 1 a.m., etc.).

7. Disclosure Hedges: Deep Versus Casual Disclosure
A Girl-Gone-Wise doesn't inappropriately confide in men.

For most women, emotional intimacy precedes physical intimacy. The more emotionally connected a woman feels to a man, the greater the chance that this emotional intimacy will lead to physical intimacy. In order to guard against inappropriate sexual conduct, it's important that a woman hedges herself against deep, personal disclosure. Before marriage, she will resist disclosing too much, too soon. After marriage, she will resist disclosing her inner self to a man other than her husband. I suggest the following disclosure hedges:

- I will not disclose my inner self to a man when it is inappropriate to do so or (in the case of unmarried individuals) premature to do so.
- If I feel an emotional pull toward an illicit relationship, I will confess that pull to a trusted godly friend or mentor, so she

can pray for me and hold me accountable to maintain boundaries.

- Unless there is another person present, I will not allow a man to confide in me about difficulties he is having with his wife.
- I will not offer a man the emotional support he ought to receive from his wife.

(The following hedges are specific to married women.)

- I will only express admiration or compliments for a man in a group setting, where others can hear my remarks.
- Unless there is another person present, I will keep conversations with men on a superficial level.
- If I need to talk about struggles in my marriage, I will seek out a godly female friend or mentor and will not speak of them to another man.
- I will not seek from another man the emotional support I ought to receive from my husband.
- If I feel an emotional connection with a man that tempts me to cross any boundaries, I will immediately pull back, and tighten and strengthen the boundaries.

8. Encroachment Hedges: Wide-Open Versus Guarded Demeanor
A Girl-Gone-Wise doesn't leave herself open and unguarded.

To encroach is to exceed the proper limits of something. An encroachment hedge ensures that a woman does not invite a man to encroach on her purity. She sends the message with her appearance and body language that sexual sin is off limits. She guards her purity by the way she dresses and acts. Here are some ideas:

- I will not sit or stand too close to men.
- I will not provocatively position my body.
- I will not tease men with provocative body language.

- I will not wear revealing clothing.
- I will physically distance myself from men who encroach on my personal space.
- I will distance myself from men who fail to respect me or my standards for purity.

9. Touching Hedges: Improper Versus Proper Physical Contact
A Girl-Gone-Wise maintains strict boundaries of physical contact with men.

In the last chapter, we spent a lot of time discussing appropriate boundaries of extramarital physical contact. It's important for you to establish and maintain hedges that will help you honor those boundaries. The hedges that you decide on will help protect you when your emotions are screaming to take things further. I'm going to give you a variety of suggestions for hedges. You might come up with more on your own. Some of my suggestions relate only to unmarried women; others relate to married ones. Some are more and some are less restrictive. Some are more protective and closer to the heart of purity than others are. I hope you will aim for increasingly higher standards of purity. I challenge you to take God seriously and seek the desire of His heart. But if you disagree with the standard we discussed last chapter, or can't or won't attain it, I challenge you to put up hedges that will at the very least protect you from completely crossing over from impurity to immorality or adultery.

- I will restrict my physical contact with men to socially appropriate forms of greeting such as a handshake, hug (from the shoulders up), or, in the case of close friends or family, a peck on the cheek.
- I will not allow a man to touch parts of my body other than my hands, arms, upper back, and shoulders.
- I will dress modestly and always keep all of my clothes on when I'm with a man.

- I will not allow a man to touch parts of my body that I have covered with clothing. (Note that in Ezekiel 23:21, the Lord identifies pressing or touching breasts as lewd conduct.)
- I will not unbutton or unfasten articles of clothing and expose my nakedness to a man.
- I will not allow a man to look at or touch my private parts.
- I will not allow a man to kiss me anywhere except on the face and lips.
- I will not look at or touch a man's private parts.
- I will not lie down on a couch or bed with a man.
- I will not lie under or on top of a man, or position myself against him in any way that mimics the posture of sexual intercourse.
- I will only hold hands, kiss, and hug (from the shoulders up).
- I will save my first kiss for marriage.
- I will not touch a man in private in any way that we would not touch in public.

10. Covenant Hedges: Dishonoring Versus Honoring Marital Unions
A Girl-Gone-Wise does everything she can to honor and affirm marriage covenants.

The final type of hedge affirms and honors the sacredness of the covenant of marriage. It helps you interact with men in a way that acknowledges and affirms the vows that each of you have made. These hedges show that you have the same sort of value and respect for marriage that God does, and that you will never say or do anything to dishonor this holy institution. Here are a few, final suggestions for some covenant hedges you can establish. Again, some will apply to married, and some to unmarried women.

- I will always wear my wedding ring.

- I will reinforce the fact that I am "one" with my husband by mentioning him and by using inclusive words like "we," "us," and "our" when I talk about my personal life.
- I will affirm and support the marriage of others by inquiring about their spouses and acknowledging them in verbal and written conversation.
- I will try to get to know the wives of men I interact with and, whenever possible, relate to the husband and wife together, as a couple.
- I will never say or do anything to threaten or diminish the sanctity of marriage.

A GOLD RING IN A PIG'S SNOUT

Miguel De Cervantes, the author of the classic novel *Don Quixote*, once said, "No padlocks, bolts, or bars can secure a maiden better than her own reserve."[1] He lived in the 1500s, when society expected fathers to guard the purity of their unmarried daughters. Cervantes argued that the personal hedges a woman puts up around her sexual purity protect her far more effectively than her father or anything else ever would or could. That was certainly in line with the thinking of King Solomon, the Sage Father. He said that people fall into sin because they don't take the necessary personal precautions to avoid it. They lack discretion.

Discretion is exercising good judgment and foresight to avoid danger and do the right thing. Solomon told his son that a beautiful woman without discretion is like a gold ring in a pig's snout (Proverbs 11:22). Given that the Jews regarded pigs as filthy, unclean animals, this is a shocking image. It implies that women who lack discretion are shameful. Solomon wanted his son to avoid them at all costs. In essence he said something like this, "Son, a woman may be exceedingly beautiful, but if she lacks discretion, she'll pull you down in the mud where you'll wallow like disgusting pigs. Be on guard against beautiful women who fail to discern and maintain proper boundaries."

When you establish a hedge, you choose, ahead of time, to live by that protective policy. You choose to exercise discretion. Knowing what your hedges are will help guide you when you encounter a potentially compromising situation. For example, if a male colleague asks me to lunch, I might say, "Can Susan join us? I have a policy that I don't do lunch alone with men." The hedge gives me the freedom to relate to the colleague within appropriate boundaries. It helps keep the relationship pure. It honors my marriage and my colleague's too. It keeps the relationship on track and prevents it from taking a wrong turn.

I've suggested numerous ideas for ways you can hedge your sexual purity. If you have a few years of womanhood under your belt, you've probably already figured out that you need to have hedges. If you're like me, you figured it out by bumping your nose against situations where someone misunderstood your intent or where you naively left yourself in an exposed position by not having a clear hedge. It took me quite a while, as a newlywed, to figure out that I couldn't hang out and be friends with guys in the same way I did before I was married. Other than the general encouragement to remain a virgin until marriage and not to cheat on my husband after marriage, no one ever sat me down and challenged me to think through and establish clear protective hedges in my relationships with men. So now that I've figured some things out, that's what I am challenging you to do. Far too many women are careless and overconfident, and foolishly leap over restrictions. I think of the untold pain and heartache that women I've ministered to would have saved themselves if only they had exercised discretion and guarded their sexual purity. So I challenge you to come up with a list of personal hedges. Write them down. Have a friend hold you accountable.

I'll borrow the words that the Sage Father spoke to his son and speak them as though I were a sage mother: "My daughters, do not lose sight of these—keep sound wisdom and discretion" (Proverbs 3:21). "Discretion will watch over you, understanding will guard you, delivering you from the way of evil" (Proverbs 2:11–12). Hedge your sexual purity. Be a Girl-Gone-Wise.

(Do you have a comment or question about boundaries? You can visit the website GirlsGoneWise.com and post it there.)

Point of Contrast #12

AUTHENTICITY
Her Public Versus Private Persona

Girl-Gone-Wild: Two-Faced	Girl-Gone-Wise: Genuine
"With bold face she says to him, 'I had to offer sacrifices, and today I have paid my vows.'" (Proverbs 7:13–14)	"She who walks in integrity walks securely." (Proverbs 10:9)

M r. Facing-Both-Ways. His name says it all. This allegorical character in John Bunyan's classic book, *Pilgrim's Progress*, was two-faced. One face pointed toward the Celestial City, and the other pointed toward the City of Destruction. Scripture talks about people who have a double heart, and are double-minded, double-tongued, and double-faced. The Proverbs 7 woman is a prime example of this kind of individual. As the story unfolds, the narrator tells us that she seizes and kisses the young man, "and with bold face she says to him, 'I had to offer sacrifices, and today I have paid my vows.'" The face she showed when she worshiped together with people at church wasn't the same brash face she showed after church, on that back lane, hidden in the shadows. She was duplicitous. A hypocrite. Ms. Facing-Both-Ways.

Authenticity is another point of contrast between a Girl-Gone-Wise and a Girl-Gone-Wild. A Girl-Gone-Wise is genuine. Her public persona is congruent with her private one. The outside matches the inside—the visible matches the unseen. She is a woman of integrity. Her counterpart, the Girl-Gone-Wild, is two-faced. She wants people to think she is something that she is not. She puts on a religious face to impress, but secretly behaves in a way that is totally at odds with the faith she professes. She's the type of girl who religiously attends Saturday-night service with her boyfriend, sings on the worship team, and then sleeps with him in the back of the car after the church parking lot has emptied.

TWO-FACED HYPOCRISY

The rendezvous between the Proverbs 7 woman and the young man took place in the evening. She tells him that she had "paid her vows" earlier that day. Paying vows indicates that she had asked God for something and had promised to express her gratitude when He answered her prayers. She obviously got whatever it was she asked for, because on the day they met up, she fulfilled her promise. She went to the temple to offer a special kind of sacrifice to God—a vow offering (Leviticus 7:16).

The vow offering differed from other offerings in several ways. First, unlike a sin offering, a vow offering wasn't required. It was a voluntary offering, which an Israelite could offer at virtually any time. Second, the giver was to bring loaves of freshly baked leavened bread, unleavened pastries, and cakes to accompany the meat sacrifice. Third, while some offerings belonged completely to God and others were apportioned to the priests, the vow offering was a fellowship offering that everyone shared. The Lord got the inner, fatty portions of the animal, the priest got the breast and right thigh, and the person offering the sacrifice got the rest of the meat to take home. Each party also received loaves, pastries, and cakes.

Finally, this type of offering was unique in that there was a celebratory meal associated with it. The entire family joined in eating it.

The communal feast symbolized fellowship with God and with one another. Since the meal was holy, the guests had to be ceremonially holy in order to partake. They had to clean themselves up, and wash and change their clothes and dress up for the occasion. Impurity excluded them from participation. The celebration could last a couple of days, but the rules stipulated that on day three, all leftovers had to be burned (Leviticus 7:11–21; 19:5–8; 1 Samuel 20:26).

The vow offering was supposed to be a holy symbol of communion with God, but this woman used it as a crafty ploy to entice the young man over to her house. I suspect she let him know ahead of time that she was going to make this type of sacrifice. Perhaps she flattered him by telling him that his friendship was the answer to her prayers—*he* was the reason for her vow offering. She probably informed him that if he didn't join her, she would be left to celebrate the feast alone, and the food would go to waste. She likely pressured him by implying that if he didn't help her fulfill her obligation to partake in a communal meal, her hopes would be dashed, all her work would be for naught, and her offering would be ruined.

It's quite obvious that the woman's sacrifice was motivated by her desire to fellowship with the young man more than her desire to fellowship with God. Her husband was gone, so why else did she choose that day to make the type of sacrifice that required a communal meal? Why would she go to the trouble of preparing the bread, pastries, cake, meat, and other delicacies for the feast if she was the only one who would partake? Why go to the temple that day if she didn't already have the seduction in mind? And why did the young man wander over to her neighborhood on that particular night if she hadn't made the invitation clear? When she saw him, why did she confirm that the fellowship meal was waiting on her table? It didn't all happen by chance. It's clear to me that the sacrifice was part of her crafty, manipulative plan.

The Proverbs 7 Wild Thing was a hypocrite. Her religious behavior was a farce. A hypocrite is a person who deliberately and habitually professes to be good when she is aware that she is not. The word itself is a transliteration of the Greek word *hypokrites*, which means *play actor* or *stage player*. In ancient Greek comedies and tragedies, *hypokrites* wore masks. The mask was the most essential part of the *hypokrite*'s costume. The *hypokrite* hid behind the mask, and the mask projected the necessary image. Hiding their true selves behind a mask is what hypocrites do.

SIGNS OF HYPOCRISY

Jesus had an ongoing conflict with His two-faced religious opponents, the scribes and Pharisees. He repeatedly called them to task for their hypocritical behavior. His run-ins with them demonstrate how much the Lord hates it when people playact at loving God. Their interactions with Christ reveal seven signs of hypocrisy, many of which are evident in the life of the Wild Thing of Proverbs 7.

Contradiction

The first sign of hypocrisy is contradiction. A hypocrite is a pretender who honors the Lord with her lips, but her heart is far from Him (Matthew 15:8). There's a fundamental contradiction between who she is when people are looking and who she is when they aren't. Jesus said:

> Woe to you, scribes and Pharisees, hypocrites! For you are like whitewashed tombs, which outwardly appear beautiful, but within are full of dead people's bones and all uncleanness. So you also outwardly appear righteous to others, but within you are full of hypocrisy and lawlessness. (Matthew 23:27–28)

This type of incongruence is evident in the Proverbs 7 woman. She knew that partaking in a vow offering demanded that she be outwardly and inwardly clean. She pretended to be pure, but all the while was planning that night's illicit encounter. Her words and behavior didn't match up. There was a contradiction. Just like Melissa, the young woman who had a long chat about sexual purity with her boyfriend's mother, Nicole. Melissa feigned concern that the girls in her class were losing their virginity, but just a few hours later, she stripped down naked on screen for her boyfriend in their nightly sex-video encounter. The contradiction mortified Nicole when she took a load of laundry into her son's bedroom and happened upon the scene.

What Melissa said didn't add up with what she did. Her life was a contradiction.

A wild, two-faced woman is extremely clever at deception. She is often successful in keeping the contradiction hidden. But someone who is discerning can usually sense that things in her life aren't quite right. She is not who she makes herself out to be. She acts like a good girl, but a naughty bad-girl streak percolates under the surface. The double-minded woman is actually dishonest with herself and others. She uses truth and lies in whatever way they will best benefit her. Godly people who interact with her have the uneasy feeling that she's not being totally honest and up front. Incongruities exist.

Although a two-faced woman is usually an excellent pretender, the Lord won't tolerate her behavior forever. At some point in time, He'll expose her—just like He exposed Melissa's true nature to her boyfriend's mother, Nicole. Jesus warned, "Beware of the leaven of the Pharisees, which is hypocrisy. Nothing is covered up that will not be revealed, or hidden that will not be known. Therefore whatever you have said in the dark shall be heard in the light, and what you have whispered in private rooms shall be proclaimed on the housetops" (Luke 12:1–3).

A Girl-Gone-Wise isn't afraid of being found out. She's authentic. She's honest about her struggles, and does not try to hide. Who she is in public is the same as who she is in private. There is no deceit and no contradiction.

Self-Indulgence

The second sign of hypocrisy is self-indulgence. Jesus said, "Woe to you, scribes and Pharisees, hypocrites! For you clean the outside of the cup and the plate, but inside they are full of greed and self-indulgence" (Matthew 23:25). A hypocrite is a lover of pleasure rather than a lover of God (2 Timothy 3:4–5). She treats God like a vending machine. She puts her coins of religious conduct into the slot and expects Him to dispense the goods she wants. The Proverbs 7 woman fulfilled her vow to God, because in her opinion, He was giving her exactly what she wanted to get. The problem is, she expected God to do what she wanted, but didn't have any intention of doing what He wanted.

According to Scripture, this self-indulgent vending machine perspective is common among double-minded people. They constantly ask the Lord for things, but they ask for the wrong things, to indulge their worldly passions. They also have a wrong perspective about God. They suspect that He's stingy, vengeful, and withholds from them the very things that would bring them happiness. They question whether He really has their best interests at heart. A double-minded person "must not suppose that [she] will receive anything from the Lord" (James 1:7). This isn't because God doesn't want to give—but because she doesn't want to receive what He wants to give. She doesn't want to change her sinful behavior and desires. James explains:

> You ask and do not receive, because you ask wrongly, to spend it on your passions. You adulterous people! Do you not know that friendship with the world is enmity with God? Therefore whoever wishes to be a friend of the world makes himself an enemy of God. . . . Draw near to God, and he will draw near to you. Cleanse your hands, you sinners, and purify your hearts, you double-minded. (James 4:3–4, 8)

Focus on Externals

The third sign of hypocrisy is a focus on externals. The scribes and Pharisees "do all their deeds to be seen by others" (Matthew 23:5). They draw people's attention to their "goodness" so that "they may be praised by others" (Matthew 6:2). Two-faced people want others to think that they are very spiritual and have enviable morals. They are very concerned about outward appearances—how they look to others and what people think about them.

The Proverbs 7 woman was concerned about appearances. Otherwise, she wouldn't have bothered going to the temple that day. The priests and the other people milling around probably thought she was very devout. And from all outward appearances, she was. She was careful to draw attention to the good things she did in order to cultivate her "good girl" image.

Partial Obedience

Jesus criticized the scribes and Pharisees for partial obedience. They did some small things right—like tithing everything, down to mint and dill and cumin—but "neglected the weightier matters of the law: justice and mercy and faithfulness" (Matthew 23:23–24). Because they didn't wholeheartedly obey the Lord, their religious behavior was worthless. They totally missed the point.

The Proverbs 7 woman missed the point when she got the particulars of her vow offering right, but failed to address the glaring sin in her heart. Outwardly, she was clean—but because she neglected the weightier matter of inner purity, she totally missed the point. Two-faced people are very selective about which parts of Scripture they choose to obey.

Rationalization

Rationalization of sin is the fifth sign of hypocrisy. The scribes and Pharisees were masters at rationalizing sin. They came up with elaborate loopholes and arguments to justify disobeying God. Jesus accused them of "void[ing] the word of God" with their clever rationalizations (Matthew 15:3–6).

Over the years, I've heard innumerable rationalizations for immorality and impurity: "If God is love, how can our love be wrong?" "My husband doesn't love me." "We're going to get married anyway." "I prayed about leaving my husband." "God made us with sexual needs that must be fulfilled." "It isn't wrong if we don't go all the way." On and on the rationalizing goes. Hypocrites always find a way to justify their two-faced behavior. The Proverbs 7 woman undoubtedly rationalized her behavior. The Sage Father said, "This is the way of an adulteress: she eats and wipes her mouth and says, 'I have done no wrong'" (Proverbs 30:20).

Contempt

Hypocrites are full of contempt. They look down on others (Luke 18:11–12). They see the "speck" in another person's eye, but fail to notice the log in their own (Matthew 7:5). They have unrealistically high expectations of what other people should do, but aren't willing to apply that same standard to themselves (Matthew 23:4). They are highly critical when other people fail. They self-righteously think that they are beyond such weakness (Matthew 23:29–30). They feel malice toward anyone who tries to teach or correct them (Matthew 22:18). They easily take offense (Matthew 15:12).

Chameleon-Like Conduct

Hypocrites are like chameleons. They change color depending on which environment they are in. My friend Nate said of a common friend, "The Krista you get at a party is different than the Krista you get at church. She's only as spiritual as the people she's with." The scribes and Pharisees were like that. They were different people when they were out in public than they were at home (Luke 13:15). Their conduct changed depending on their environment. The Proverbs 7 woman was also guilty of chameleon-like conduct. Like Krista, she was only as spiritual as the situation demanded. The woman the worshipers saw at church in the light of day presented herself in a much different way than the woman who emerged dressed like a prostitute to seduce her prey at night.

ABOUT FACE

Two-Face is a fictional DC Comics super villain who first appeared in the classic Batman comic book series in 1942. He goes insane and becomes the crime boss Two-Face after sulfuric acid hideously disfigures the left side of his face. Two-Face does not consistently do evil. Every time he contemplates a crime, he flips his two-headed coin. If the coin lands unmarred side up, he refrains from evil and resigns himself to doing good. He turns his good face to the world. If it lands defaced side up, he boldly goes ahead and commits the crime. The Girl-Gone-Wild is like that. She flips the coin of public opinion to determine what she should do. If the situation demands that she show a good face, she displays that side of her persona. But if it doesn't, she boldly goes ahead with the sinful desires of her heart.

The Lord despises hypocritical behavior. He says, "I cannot endure iniquity and solemn assembly" (Isaiah 1:11–17). For Him, an unrepentant heart and religious behavior don't mix. Do you recognize any of the signs of hypocrisy in your life? If you are honest, I think you'll be able to identify tendencies toward contradiction, self-indulgence, focus on externals, partial obedience, rationalization, contemptuousness, or chameleon-like conduct in yourself. At least I hope you do. I can certainly see some of those sins in my life. The problem is not when we fight against hypocrisy in our lives—but when we don't. All of us have a long way to go when it comes to true authenticity.

The passage in James 4:3–8 explains that the way to combat double-mindedness is to draw near to God, to examine our lives constantly for sin, and to humbly repent. "Cleanse your hands, you sinners, and purify your hearts, you double-minded." A Girl-Gone-Wise is concerned about keeping the inner, hidden parts of her life just as pure as the outer, visible ones. She fights against hypocrisy in her life. She knows that the two-faced woman will be found out, but one who walks in integrity walks securely (Proverbs 10:9).

Point of Contrast #13

NEEDINESS
Whom She Depends on to Fulfill Her Longings

Girl-Gone-Wild: **Depends on Man**	Girl-Gone-Wise: **Depends on God**
"So now I have come out to meet you, to seek you eagerly, and I have found you." (Proverbs 7:15)	She delights in the Lord, and He will give her her heart's desires. (Psalm 37:4)

H e's out with a terrible case of CGS." That's what my son's twenty-year-old neighborhood friend, Warren, said, dropping himself into a wing chair in the family room. Jonathan sighed and nodded his head knowingly, disappointed that their friend had to miss the evening's planned activities.

"CGS?" I asked, alarmed, "What's CGS?" I had visions of their friend lying quarantined in a hospital room, hooked up to a respirator, with tubes sticking out from all over his body, surrounded by masked doctors and nurses talking in hushed tones. I asked, "Is it serious? Is he going to be OK?"

Warren looked at me with a deadpan expression and explained, "CGS—Clingy Girlfriend Syndrome. It is serious, and *no*, he's not OK. He's suffocating to death." I just about fell out of my chair laughing. I knew exactly what he was talking about. And so do you. Some women are so needy for attention and affirmation that they cling to men like plastic wrap to a piece of raw meat. The young man couldn't come to his scheduled outing because his girlfriend didn't want to spend the evening alone. She insisted that *her* needs take precedence over his wanting to spend time with his friends.

As the Proverbs 7 narrative unfolds, we see the woman expressing her ardent desire to be with the young man. She hopes and expects that he will come to her house and meet her needs. She's spent the whole day preparing for this possibility. She says, "So now I have come out to meet you, to *seek you eagerly*, and I have found you." She strokes the young man's ego by emphasizing his importance to her: "I have come out to meet *you*, to seek *you* eagerly . . . *You* are the man of my dreams! *You* are so amazing, so strong, so handsome, so right for me! *You* are the only one who can help me! *You* are the one I've been waiting for! I'm so glad that I found *you*!" She puffs up the young man's head to think that he is the only one who can rescue her from her loveless plight. He's her knight in shining armor, her savior. But the truth is, her flattery has very little to do with him being sensational and very much to do with her being needy. He is merely a means to a perceived end. She's only interested in him because she thinks he will satisfy her desires.

A Girl-Gone-Wild looks to men to fulfill the deep longings of her heart. She relies on them for her sense of self-worth. She is needy and dependent. A Girl-Gone-Wise knows that no man on the face of earth could ever fill the God-shaped vacuum in her heart. She doesn't depend on men for her sense of self. She delights in the Lord and depends on Him to give her the desires of her heart.

LOOKING FOR LOVE

The prophet Jeremiah tells the story of a woman desperate for love. As a young bride, she loved her husband—she delighted in him as he delighted in her. Then, her commitment was tested. Other men enticed her with the passion, thrill, and adventure of illicit sex. She took the bait. Lover after lover passed through her arms. With each one, her level of satisfaction decreased, and her level of desperation increased. She ended up so needy and so skilled in the art of pursuing illicit love, that even the most experienced whore could learn new secrets of seduction by observing her tactics. "How well you direct your course to seek love! So that even to wicked women you have taught your ways" (Jeremiah 2:33).

Who is this needy woman? It's God's bride, the nation Israel. In Jeremiah's time, she turned her back on her exclusive devotion to God and made alliances with the surrounding nations, embracing their morals and their gods. She played the whore by forsaking His love and pursuing relationships with them. She looked to them instead of Him to meet her needs. But the meaning of this allegory is much broader than that particular historical situation. It's also a lesson for women today.

Martin Luther once said, "Whatever your heart clings to and confides in, that is really your god."[1] Most women yearn to find love in the arms of a man. Their heart yearns for earthly romance more than it yearns for the reality to which it points. Romance is the hope they cling to and confide in. Romance is their god. Jeremiah's narrative portrays their story. It speaks to all of us who "direct our course to seek love"—and who turn to men rather than God to find it. It tells the parable of every woman who feels deep desires, longings, and needs, and tries to fulfill them in the wrong place and in the wrong way.

The tragedy in Jeremiah's tale is that the woman foolishly turned her back on the true lover who could meet her needs and embraced false lovers, who couldn't possibly satisfy the desires of her heart. The Lord told His bride that it was as though she had spurned a natural spring of pure, fresh water and sought instead to satisfy her thirst with the stagnant water from a self-made, leaky cistern. He says, "My people have committed two evils: they have forsaken me, the fountain of living waters, and hewed out cisterns for themselves, broken cisterns that can hold no water" (Jeremiah 2:13). Later He even curses those who would make such a choice:

Cursed is the man who trusts in man and makes flesh his strength, whose heart turns away from the Lord. He is like a shrub in the desert, and shall not see any good come. He shall dwell in the parched places of the wilderness, in an uninhabited salt land.

Blessed is the man who trusts in the Lord, whose trust is the Lord. He is like a tree planted by water, that sends out its roots by the stream, and does not fear when heat comes, for its leaves remain green, and is not anxious in the year of drought, for it does not cease to bear fruit. (Jeremiah 17:5–8)

The most reliable and refreshing sources of water in the land of Israel were its natural springs. This water was dependable, and its clear, cool consistency was satisfying. In contrast, the most unreliable sources of water were cisterns. Cisterns were large pits dug into porous limestone rock and coated with plaster, to prevent leakage. These pits gathered rainwater. The water was brackish and stale, and if the rains didn't come, they could dry up. Worse yet, if a cistern developed a crack, it wouldn't hold the water. The water leaked through the plaster into the limestone beneath. To turn from a dependable, pure stream of running water to a broken, briny cistern was idiotic. Yet this is exactly what the woman in Jeremiah's account did. She turned away from what would undeniably quench her thirst to what could undeniably not.

This text presents a picture of the contrast between a Girl-Gone-Wise and a Girl-Gone-Wild. A Girl-Gone-Wild relies on her own devices to quench her thirsty heart. She hews out a relationship and expects that it will meet her needs. She scoops out as much water from the leaky cistern as she can, but at some point, realizes that she's still not satisfied, and that the water she has greedily sipped has left a bitter taste in her mouth. Her heart feels parched—like a dry, brittle bush in a desolate desert. She has no roots. She feels her spirit wither up. But instead of planting herself next to the stream, she desperately tries to suck more water from her cistern, or she hews out another cistern with the unrealistic hope that there she will find water that is plentiful and sweet.

The Girl-Gone-Wise does not "trust in man and make flesh her strength." Her heart relies on the Lord. She is "like a tree planted by water, that sends out its roots by the stream, and does not fear when heat comes, for its leaves remain green, and is not anxious in the year of drought, for it does not cease to bear fruit."

The image is a powerful one. It's not that the wise woman never experiences pressure-cooker "heat" in her relationships—or that she never faces a year of relational drought. But she withstands those tough times. She doesn't get fearful or anxious when they come, because her relationship with the Lord nourishes and sustains her. She doesn't rely on the cistern. She doesn't dry up spiritually or emotionally when a man disappoints her. She doesn't have to hew out cistern after cistern after cistern, desperately trying to find the water she needs. Her roots go deep. If the love of her life disappoints, betrays, and wounds her—or even if she never marries—she will not dry up. Her leaves will remain green, and she will not cease to lead a spiritually productive and satisfying life. Her well-being does not depend on a man.

The passages in Jeremiah (2:13; 17:5–8) demonstrate that looking for love the wild way differs substantially from looking for it the wise way. Here are two lists that summarize how:

LOOKING FOR LOVE THE WILD WAY

- She forgets or neglects her relationship with God ("whose heart turns away from the Lord").
- She thinks that a relationship with a man will (or ought to) meet her emotional needs ("trusts in man and makes flesh her strength").
- Her heart feels lonely and needy ("uninhabited salt land," "parched places").
- She hacks and digs at the relationship, and makes demands of her man to get him to fill her perceived need ("hew[s] out cisterns for [herself]").
- She demands that the relationship provide her with something it cannot possibly provide ("cisterns that can hold no water").
- Her relationship repeatedly disappoints her ("broken cisterns").
- She feels anxious and afraid when the relationship falters ("fears when heat comes," "anxious in the year of drought").
- Her heart slowly shrivels and dies ("like a shrub in the desert").

- Her life is spiritually barren and unproductive ("shall not see any good come").

LOOKING FOR LOVE THE WISE WAY

- She faithfully pursues a relationship with God. (She "trusts in the Lord." She has not "forsaken" Him.)
- She knows that only a relationship with God can meet her deepest needs. She does not depend on men to do this ("whose trust is the Lord").
- Her relationship with God nourishes her spirit ("like a tree planted by water").
- She sends her roots deep into God's stream to meet her emotional needs. She does not demand emotional satisfaction from people ("sends out its roots by the stream").
- She knows that the Lord will sustain her if a love relationship goes through difficult times or in the absence of such a relationship ("does not fear when heat comes"; "is not anxious in the year of drought").
- Her heart remains alive and grounded in God's love, regardless of the state of her earthly relationships ("leaves remain green").
- Her life is spiritually fruitful and productive, regardless of the state of her earthly relationships ("does not cease to bear fruit").

Which way best characterizes the way you look for love? The Girl-Gone-Wild puts her trust in man—she looks for some guy to be her savior. She tries to monopolize his time and attention and makes demands to try to get what she wants. The Girl-Gone-Wise trusts in the Lord. She has a Savior, so she doesn't need or expect a guy to meet her deepest needs. She is not desperate for a man. It's not that she wouldn't enjoy a healthy relationship. She would. But she draws her identity and strength from a much more reliable source.

DESPERATE GIRLFRIENDS—
DESPERATE HOUSEWIVES

To introduce a talk, I once showed the classic Walt Disney clip of Snow White singing "Someday My Prince Will Come" to a roomful of college-aged girls. Their response was dramatic. Many raised arms in the air and shouted, "Yes!" Some stood on their chairs with their hands clasped over their hearts. Some whooped. Some cheered. Some hollered. Some pretended to swoon. One or two had tears streaming down their cheeks.

The response when I showed the same clip to a room full of mostly married middle-aged women, several weeks later, could not have been more different. Most looked disinterested. Many laughed and sneered. Some rolled their eyes. Some shrugged a shoulder and went back to having conversations with their girlfriends. Not one woman pumped her arm and shouted, "Yes!" Not one.

The reactions were telling. The college girls had hearts filled with hope of meeting their Prince Charming and living happily ever after. They eagerly anticipated that marrying Mr. McDreamy would fulfill their desire. The middle-aged women had hearts filled with cynicism because their Prince Charming hadn't delivered the happily-ever-after ending they had hoped for. Mr. McDreamy had turned into Mr. McDreary and Mr. McDumpy. They had the gut-wrenching suspicion that no one would ever meet the longings of their hearts. The nods, tears, and "yeses" for these women came when I talked about the pain of disappointment. It's not that their desire had died. It's just that they were wearied and wounded from all the years of hoping and yearning. They were tired of trying to squeeze water out of a broken, empty cistern. They still hadn't found what they were looking for.

So what are we to make of all the longing? To quench their thirst, many women spin themselves around in endless circles of desire, dissipation, and disappointment. I think of my high school girlfriend, Michelle, who has experienced numerous failed relationships: two or three serious boyfriends, two common-law relationships, one broken engagement, and one failed marriage. When we had dinner several years ago, her desire and desperation had reached a frenzied level. This forty-year-old was dating and sleeping with three different guys at the same time. "I just wish I could find someone to love me," she lamented, with eyes brim-full of tears.

C. S. Lewis once wrote, "What does not satisfy when we find it, was not the thing we were desiring."[2] He suggested that we can best describe the restless desire that exists in the human heart with the German word *Sehnsucht*. My parents were German immigrants, and my first language was German, so let me try to explain the word. There really is no adequate English equivalent. It's a quasi-mystical term that melds ardent inner longing or yearning (*das Sehnen*) with obsession or addiction (*die Sucht*). *Sehnsucht* is a deep, driven, inconsolable inner longing for something of monumental importance.

Sehnsucht compels us to reach for an ultimate answer that remains just beyond our reach. Some people experience it as a type of nostalgia, others as a type of homesickness. Others think that it's a longing for someone they have not yet met or something they have not yet attained. They think that if they only meet that "someone" or get that "something," their desire will be satisfied. The majority of people who feel *Sehnsucht* are not conscious of who or what the longed-for object might be.

King David knew. He said, "As a deer pants for flowing streams, so pants my soul for you, O God. My soul thirsts for God, for the living God. When shall I come and appear before God?" (Psalm 42:1–2). *Sehnsucht* is the deep, inner "panting" of our spirits for God. The human soul was made to enjoy something that is never fully given—that cannot even be imagined as given—in our present mode of existence. *Sehnsucht* is a longing for God that only God can fill, but cannot fill completely until we see Him face-to-face. Even the satisfaction and joy we can taste in His presence now is shot through with longing. It's like a woman enthralled to hear the voice of a distant lover, but craving the moment he will hold her in his arms. *Sehnsucht* beckons and whispers, points and draws us to the time when we will finally be united with the lover and redeemer of our souls.

When women feel *Sehnsucht*, many identify it as a desire to be the leading lady in a passionate romance. They think that finding a soul mate is the only thing that will fulfill their longing. That's what my friend Michelle thinks. In one sense, she's right. Her *Sehnsucht is* beckoning her to take part in a passionate romance—but not the one she's obsessed with finding. It's beckoning her to look past that image and reach for the reality it represents. Earthly romances are to the Cosmic One like sparkling reflections of light dancing on water are to the blazing sun. They are not the fiery light. They only reflect fleeting glimmers of it.

Michelle's neediness is not, in and of itself, a bad thing. She's just pinned it to the wrong hope. Looking to man to give what only God can supply is an exercise in futility, frustration, and pain. And it can lead farther and farther away from the place where that longing can truly be fulfilled. The Girl-Gone-Wise knows what the deep longing in her spirit is all about. So when she feels needy, she directs her longing and sighing Godward (Psalm 38:9). She understands that only as she delights herself in the Lord, will her needs be met. He is the One who gives her the desires of her heart.

Point of Contrast #14

POSSESSIONS
How She Handles Her
Money and Resources

Girl-Gone-Wild: **Indulgent**	Girl-Gone-Wise: **Circumspect**
"I have spread my couch with coverings, colored linens from Egyptian linen; I have perfumed my bed with myrrh, aloes, and cinnamon."	"She opens her hand to the poor and reaches out her hands to the needy. . . . She makes bed coverings for herself . . ."
(Proverbs 7:16–17)	(Proverbs 31:20–22)

S mart Girls Get More" is a wildly successful ad campaign that promotes the United Kingdom's bestselling young women's magazine, *More*. The message shouts from billboards, buses, TV commercials, radio spots, sponsorships, and competitions. It inundates British women with the idea that if they are smart, they will get more—more men, more sex, more celebrity gossip, more beauty, more fashion, more products, and, of course, more of the magazine that supplies all the latest and greatest information on these pleasures. "Cuz Smart Girls Get More!"

Although that particular ad campaign hasn't run in North America, it's the clandestine message of virtually all mass-marketing efforts. Merchandisers want to convince us that we need more of whatever it is they are selling. The Bible's perspective differs from the world's. Constantly buying more stuff isn't a trait of a woman who's smart; it's a hallmark of a Girl-Gone-Wild. The Wild Thing is an indulgent, voracious consumer who pursues pleasure through the purchase of material goods. A Girl-Gone-Wise thinks differently about the way she spends her money. She's circumspect. She understands that everything she has comes from God. She tries to honor Him by being a good steward of all her resources. She treasures the riches of the Kingdom more than the riches of the world.

DESIGNER LABEL DESIRE

As we rejoin the story of our Proverbs 7 woman, we see her trying to pique the young man's interest by describing her bedroom: "I have spread my couch with coverings, colored linens from Egyptian linen; I have perfumed my bed with myrrh, aloes, and cinnamon."

When the woman tells the young man about her couch and then later mentions her bed, she's not talking about two separate pieces of furniture. In Palestine, people commonly slept on the floor on mats that they could roll up and store during the day or they slept on multipurpose mud-brick benches. But if their beds were pieces of furniture with legs, they could also use the word *couch* to describe them (Job 7:13; Psalm 6:6). A couch was a specific type of bed—just like a recliner is a specific type of chair. The woman uses the word *couch* to let the young man know exactly what type of bed she has. Given the space restrictions of most homes, a couch-bed was an impractical extravagance that few could afford or would allow themselves to indulge in. She wanted to let him know that she didn't sleep on a pallet on the floor like a lowly commoner. Her bed was a couch. It was a luxury item.

The woman also makes sure to mention that she had spread her bed with coverings of delicate cushions and with linens imported from Egypt. Egyptian linen was the finest and most desirable cloth in the world. Its coolness, luster, softness, and strength set it apart from less expensive material. The woman emphasizes that her linens are colored—they're even more splendid and exclusive than uncolored ones. The dyes used in antiquity were costly, since artisans obtained them from the bodies of insects or mollusks, or from the petals and heads of flowers. Colored Egyptian linens were a particularly opulent indulgence.

The Proverbs 7 woman was undoubtedly trying to impress and allure the young man with the description of the exquisite designer label décor in her bedroom. I'm sure he was "wowed." His eyebrows probably rose even farther when he heard that she had perfumed her linens with myrrh, aloes, and cinnamon. Myrrh was a spice native to Arabia, aloe came from India or China, and cinnamon came from the east coast of Africa and Ceylon. These imported fragrances were exotic and pricey. She makes it clear that she spared no expense in preparing for their night of romance. She had prepared a sumptuous feast for his palate and for his senses, and was inviting him to indulge.

The fact that the woman takes such care to detail the extravagant luxury of her possessions gives us a clue as to her attitude toward them. It's clear she has an underlying attitude of self-importance and self-indulgence. She wants the young man to be impressed and to hold her in high regard. She wants him to admire her and desires to charm him with all her finery. She wants him to affirm that she is really something. She's like the harlot, Lady Babylon, who indulged in the "power of her luxurious living" and in the "passion of her sexual immorality," and seduced nations to "drink [her] wine" (Revelation 18:3).

The passage in Revelation informs us that Lady Babylon was a greedy consumer. She was a shopaholic who bought all sorts of exotic imported merchandise:

> gold, silver, jewels, pearls, fine linen, purple cloth, silk, scarlet cloth, all kinds of scented wood, all kinds of articles of ivory, all kinds of articles of costly wood, bronze, iron and marble, cinnamon, spice, incense, myrrh, frankincense, wine, oil, fine flour, wheat, cattle and sheep, horses and chariots, and slaves, that is, human souls.

She was extremely fond of these "delicacies" and "splendors." In her mind, they were status symbols—must-have items. The latest and greatest in Babylon's *More* magazine was "the fruit for which [her] soul longed" (18:12–14).

Nowadays, we've substituted designer jeans for purple cloth, satin sheets for fine linen, French perfume for frankincense, five-star restaurants for cattle and sheep, BMWs for horses and chariots, nannies and housekeepers for slaves, but we're just as greedy and self-indulgent. Like Lady Babylon and the Proverbs 7 woman, we're caught up in the endless quest for more. We spend and spend, even if we don't have the money.

A Girl-Gone-Wild is a voracious consumer. She treasures the things of this world more than she treasures Jesus Christ. She settles for fleeting pleasures that do not satisfy her deepest needs, and that, in the end, ultimately destroy her soul. The world tells us that smart girls get more. But Scripture says that if we're truly smart, we won't settle for the "more" the world can offer. We'll want immeasurably more than its cheap, temporary thrills. The problem is not that we desire beautiful and precious things, but that we have a faulty perception about what is most beautiful and most precious. We settle for treasures that wear out, break down, and can be stolen, when we ought to set our hearts on riches that last forever.

RESOURCE MANAGEMENT

Jesus told a parable in Luke 16 that illustrated what our attitude toward possessions ought to be. The story focused on a manager who was in charge of running a wealthy business owner's company. The owner heard that the manager was being irresponsible and reckless, wasting company resources. So the owner called him up, asked for a record of accounts, and gave him notice that his job would soon end. Upon hearing this, the manager decided he'd do his best to secure his future by doing a big favor for some of his boss's clients. The manager offered to write off a large portion of their debts if they immediately settled their accounts. He hoped that they'd remember the favor and be kind to him when he became unemployed. The business owner admitted that the manager was very shrewd in making sure he'd have friends after his job ended. Even though the manager was wasteful and irresponsible, the owner commended him for this. Jesus wraps up the story by saying:

> I tell you, use worldly wealth to gain friends for yourselves, so that when it is gone, you will be welcomed into eternal dwellings.

Whoever can be trusted with very little can also be trusted with much, and whoever is dishonest with very little will also be dishonest with much. So if you have not been trustworthy in handling worldly wealth, who will trust you with true riches? And if you have not been trustworthy with someone else's property, who will give you property of your own?

No servant can serve two masters. Either he will hate the one and love the other, or he will be devoted to the one and despise the other. You cannot serve both God and Money. . . . What is highly valued among men is detestable in God's sight. (Luke 16:9–13, 15 NIV)

Jesus' teaching contains several lessons for us about how we should manage our resources. The first lesson is about ownership. We often think that if we give the Lord a portion of our earnings, the rest of the money is ours to spend as we wish. But this parable teaches that everything we have belongs to God. Everything. Nothing is really "ours." We are just managers, not owners. And God doesn't like it when we're reckless and wasteful with His resources. We will answer to Him for the way we spend the money, time, talents, and gifts that He entrusts to us. So if I'm considering buying another cute skirt, one of the questions that ought to be at the forefront of my mind is, "Lord, is this the way You want me to spend Your money?"

The second lesson is about investment. The parable teaches that we ought to invest earthly resources—but not with a view to making more money. The owner commended the manager when he used money to gain friends for the future, for the time when his job would be over. Someday, our job on earth will end. Jesus' point is that we should invest our resources in heavenly things. The way we use our money on earth ought to help us gain friends who will join us in eternity. We should spend with a view to sharing the gospel and influencing people for the kingdom of God. The question for me is this: "Am I investing my money, time, talents, and gifts in eternal things?"

Third, the story contains a lesson about responsibility. Jesus said, "Whoever can be trusted with very little can also be trusted with much. . . . If you have not been trustworthy in handling worldly wealth, who will trust you with true riches?" In other words, the way you spend your money and resources is very, very important. The

Lord will not entrust you with handling the true riches of His kingdom until you've learned how to manage worldly wealth. The question is, "Am I being responsible with my money? Am I being careful not to waste it with costly, self-indulgent, or irresponsible purchases?"

The fourth lesson contained in Christ's teaching is about valuation. Valuation is the act of determining the value of something, established by appraising its quality, condition, and desirability. It answers the question, "What's it worth?" A woman in Scotland once bought an odd-looking vase at a sale for a pound (about a dollar). After the plant she kept in it died, she dumped it in the attic, and was about to throw it away when *Antiques Roadshow* came to town. On a whim, she took it for valuation. "The vase turned out to be a 1929 work— Feuilles Fougeres—by the renowned French designer and major Art Nouveau figure Rene Lalique." It sold at a Christie's auction for the equivalent of more than $50,000.[1]

The woman disregarded the vase until an expert told her the item's true worth. That's when she began to treasure it. The Lord wants to educate us about the true worth of earthly things. He gives us His expert valuation. He says, "What is highly valued among men is detestable in God's sight." He wants me to trust His valuation and esteem what He esteems. So what if I find a Feuilles Fougeres vase kicking around in my attic? Do I throw it in the garbage? No. I recognize its true eternal value. And I do my best to use its monetary value to invest in that which is of far greater worth in God's eyes. The question I need to ask myself is, "Do I treasure things based on God's assessment of their true worth? Is my valuation the same as His?"

The final lesson in the Luke 16 passage is about devotion. "No servant can serve two masters. . . . He will be devoted to the one and despise the other. You cannot serve both God and Money." How we spend our money indicates what's in our hearts. It reflects whether we're devoted to money or devoted to God. It reflects whether we've set our hearts on earthly goods or on Him. The rich man went away dejected when Jesus told him he would gain the kingdom if he gave away all his money (Luke 18:18–28). Jesus' challenge revealed what the young man truly treasured. If he had had the same perspective toward earthly riches that Jesus had, he would have gladly parted with what was less to gain what was more. As I consider the money and "stuff" that I have, I need to ask myself, "Is there anything that I would hesitate to give up for the sake of the kingdom? Is there anything that I'm clinging to more than I'm clinging to Jesus?"

RIGHT ON THE MONEY

You can tell a Girl-Gone-Wise from a Girl-Gone-Wild based on her attitude toward money and the way she manages resources. The Proverbs 7 woman was obsessed with spending her money on things that would make her desirable and enviable, and indulge her own senses and pleasures. The attitude of the Proverbs 31 woman was markedly different. She purchased quality goods like linen, but it wasn't so she could self-indulge. Her purchases were aimed toward best meeting the needs of those in her household and the needs of those around her.

In the narrative, we see the Wise Woman opening her hand to the poor, reaching out her hands to the needy, and making bed coverings for herself (Proverbs 31:20–22). She didn't buy exclusive, designer-brand, colored Egyptian linens like the Proverbs 7 woman did. She was much more careful and circumspect about the way she used her money. She probably could have afforded the same luxuries. If she had kept the money instead of giving it to the poor and needy, she likely could have bought the Egyptian linens for bed coverings instead of making her own. The problem is not that we have money, but that we use it for our own selfish ends, invest in worldly things, and neglect to invest in the kingdom. The Lord tells Israel, "Behold, this was the guilt of your sister Sodom: she and her daughters had pride, excess of food, and prosperous ease, but did not aid the poor and needy" (Ezekiel 16:49).

So what does this mean for you? It means that you should generously give money to your church, ministries, and missions to further the gospel of Jesus Christ. But it also means that you generously give your home, your food, your possessions, your time, your energy, your affection, and all the other resources God has entrusted to you. The Lord wants you to use all your resources to invest in the kingdom. The rich man Job is a good example. He tells his friends that he never "withheld anything that the poor desired," nor did he cause "the eyes of the widow to fail." His home was open to the needy. They always dined at his table. He says, "From my youth the fatherless grew up with me as with a father, and from my mother's womb I guided the widow." He fed the hungry. He warmed those who were cold with the fleece of his sheep. Whenever he saw a need, he generously used his resources to meet it (Job 31:16–21).

Job mentions that he was a "father to the fatherless and guided the widow" from the time he was very young. That indicates that what he provided the needy was much more than material goods. He provided spiritual oversight and guidance. You can follow his example by being a spiritual mother to your friends, relatives, neighbors, and work colleagues. Even if you are young, you can begin to spiritually parent girlfriends and to invest your resources in eternity.

The Bible teaches that what you do with money—or desire to do with it—can make or break your happiness forever. The Girl-Gone-Wild who makes material riches her goal in life has the wrong values. However wealthy she may appear, she is poverty-stricken in God's sight. In His economy, the truly rich woman is the one whose main aim in life is to serve Him as King. Her wealth lies in the currency of faith and good works, opening her hand to the poor, and reaching out her hands to the needy. She has a heavenly bank balance that no one can steal and nothing can erode. She lays up for herself treasures in heaven, "For where your treasure is, there your heart will be also" (Matthew 6:21). The Girl-Gone-Wise knows that heavenly treasure is the kind that smart girls get more of.

Point of Contrast #15

ENTITLEMENT
Her Insistence
on Gratification

Girl-Gone-Wild: Demands Gratification	Girl-Gone-Wise: Forfeits Gratification
"Come, let us take our fill of love till morning; let us delight ourselves with love." (Proverbs 7:18)	She denies herself and takes up her cross daily and follows Jesus. (Luke 9:23)

Last year, an Eritrean Christian woman, Azieb Simon, died of malaria in the Wi'a Military Training Center after being imprisoned and tortured for months. In Saudi Arabia, a member of the religious police cut his college daughter's tongue off and burned her to death for converting to Christianity. A twenty-year-old Christian Pakistani woman, Sandul, falsely accused of ripping pages from the Quran, was thrown into jail after an angry mob from the local mosque threw stones and set fire to her home. In Iran, thirty-year-old Marzieh and twenty-seven-year-old Maryam became very ill after languishing for months in a prison notorious for its harsh treatment of inmates. In the Shandong province of China, Christian youth camp workers, including a sixteen-year-old, were arrested, interrogated, threatened, beaten, and kept in detention.[1] All suffered greatly because they refused to recant their faith in Jesus.

At a conference for ministry women in Thailand, I met many such women. They came from all over Southeast Asia and the Middle East. One was deaf in her left ear because of a bomb that attackers had thrown into her house-church several weeks earlier. Her son had narrowly escaped death. They were still picking shrapnel out of his head. Another was weary from the police constantly harassing and threatening her children. Another, a former student of mine—a brilliant woman who was working on her doctorate in theology—was planning another move. Their names were on the Chinese government's wanted list. They had to move every three to four months when their evangelistic efforts alerted local police to their presence. They could have returned to North America, but chose not to. Another woman trembled as she worshiped, and tears poured down her face as she lifted her hands. At home, she was only able to whisper the name of Jesus, and it had been years since she was able to raise her voice and sing it aloud.

The most striking thing about all these women is not that they suffered for the name of Jesus—but that they suffered so gladly. They had the same attitude as the martyrs burned at the stake in the 1500s. When the sheriff put the rope about Ann Audebert, she called it the wedding-sash wherewith she would be married to Christ. With joy on her face she exclaimed, "Upon Saturday I was first married, and upon a Saturday I shall be married again." Or Elizabeth Pepper and Agnes George, who kissed and embraced the stake before they were burned. Or Elizabeth Folkes, who shouted, "Farewell all the world! Farewell faith! Farewell hope!" and taking the stake in her arms joyfully exclaimed, "Welcome love!" With fire licking and consuming her flesh, she clapped her hands for joy and raised her arms in exuberant praise.[2]

They were like the women in the Hebrews 11 faith hall of fame who "received back their dead by resurrection."

Some were tortured, refusing to accept release, so that they might rise again to a better life. Others suffered mocking and flogging, and even chains and imprisonment. They were stoned, they were sawn in two, they were killed with the sword. They went about in skins of sheep and goats, destitute, afflicted, mistreated—of whom the world was not worthy—wandering about in deserts and mountains, and in dens and caves of the earth. (Hebrews 11:35–38)

Or like the apostles, ten of whom, according to tradition, were martyred by various means, including by beheading, by sword and spear, and, in the case of Peter, reportedly by crucifixion upside down.

Entitlement is the next point of contrast between a Girl-Gone-Wild and a Girl-Gone-Wise. A Wild Thing is intent on immediate gratification. She feels she has a right to be comfortable, be happy, have fun, get what she wants, and indulge in all sorts of pleasures. Enjoyment, comfort, luxury, and ease are what she feels she deserves and what she constantly seeks and demands. A Girl-Gone-Wise, on the other hand, knows that the highest pleasure exists in denying self and willingly bearing the cross of Christ. She forfeits earthly gratification for the eternal joy that God has set before her. She sacrifices lesser joys for infinitely greater ones. She knows and accepts that on this side of heaven, Christian discipleship is a costly, uncomfortable, painful, and even bloody business.

INSTANT GRATIFICATION

The stage was set. She had primped herself to look provocative, seductively kissed him, told him about the sumptuous feast she had prepared, and described the lavish, sensual décor of her bedroom. She could tell he was tempted. Her subtle hints paved the way for her shameless proposition: "Come, let us take our fill of love till morning; let us delight ourselves with love."

"Take our fill" is literally "drink our fill." The Proverbs 7 woman was using a figure of speech that likened sexual relations to drinking from a fountain (Proverbs 5:15–19). The word signifies to drink something copiously in full draughts—to slurp it up without restraint. The verb in the second part of the sentence, *delight*, means to enjoy oneself fully, to "roll in" pleasure, or to give oneself up to it. She was brashly proposing, "Let's indulge. Let's make love all night. Let's play and pleasure ourselves to the max."

The Proverbs 7 woman was a "lover of pleasures." She was like the

Lady Babylon, whom Isaiah called to account for her attitude of entitlement:

> You said, "I shall be mistress forever," so that you did not lay these things to heart or remember their end. Now therefore hear this, you lover of pleasures, who sit securely, who say in your heart, "I am, and there is no one besides me; I shall not sit as a widow or know the loss of children": These two things shall come to you in a moment, in one day; the loss of children and widowhood shall come upon you in full measure, in spite of your many sorceries and the great power of your enchantments. You felt secure in your wickedness, you said, "No one sees me"; your wisdom and your knowledge led you astray, and you said in your heart, "I am, and there is no one besides me." But evil shall come upon you, which you will not know how to charm away; disaster shall fall upon you, for which you will not be able to atone; and ruin shall come upon you suddenly, of which you know nothing. (Isaiah 47:7–11)

The passage reveals that Lady Babylon had several faulty ideas about the things to which she was entitled. First, she assumed she was in control and had the right to do as she wished ("I shall be mistress forever"). Second, she felt entitled to self-indulge and put her own happiness first ("I am, and there is no one besides me"). Third, she considered her indulgence a private matter ("No one sees me"). And fourth, she denied that any harm could come of enjoying herself ("I shall not sit as a widow or know the loss of children").

The attitude of the seductress of Proverbs 7 was undoubtedly quite similar, and so is the attitude of a pleasure-seeking Wild Thing of this generation. The Girl-Gone-Wild thinks she is in control and can do whatever she wants. She denies that she is vulnerable to sin or accountable to anyone else for her behavior. She feels entitled to have fun and pursue her own happiness, feel good, gratify her desires, and indulge. She considers her sexual behavior a private matter. She rationalizes that it's no one else's business what she does behind closed doors. And she denies that any harm could come from enjoying herself. If it doesn't hurt anyone, what difference does it make? What's wrong with self-gratification?

The self-indulgence of the Girl-Gone-Wild isn't limited to illicit sexual affairs. A Wild Thing can self-indulge through emotional affairs, romance novels, fantasies, pornography, masturbation, sensuality, flirtation, and other types of sexual impurity. What's more, self-indulgence can, and usually does, show up in other areas too. The Proverbs 7 woman indulged in designer-label luxuries. The text implies that she indulged in her wardrobe, in food, in going out, in staying up late and sleeping in, and in neglecting her home. If she lived today, she'd probably indulge in beauty treatments, entertainment, fine dining, travel, and all sorts of luxury items. All of these indulgences point to an underlying attitude of entitlement. A woman indulges because she thinks, *I deserve this!*

Isaiah warns Lady Babylon that her sensual, self-gratifying behavior would only lead to disaster and ruin. The apostle Paul agrees that this is the case for all Christian women who have an attitude of entitlement: "She who is self-indulgent is dead even while she lives" (1 Timothy 5:6). He predicts that in the last days, self-indulgence will run rampant. People will be lovers of self, without self-control, "lovers of pleasure rather than lovers of God. . . . Avoid such people" (2 Timothy 3:1–5). James likewise condemns people who spend their time on earth luxuriating and self-indulging. He accuses them of foolishly fattening their hearts in a day of slaughter (James 5:5). The sarcastic illustration was vivid for Jewish believers who had seen many sheep and oxen happily fatten themselves on rich food, not knowing that their fatness singled them out as prime candidates for the butcher's knife.

RADICAL SELF-DENIAL

Do you remember what Peter did the night of Christ's arrest? Someone in the crowd recognized him as a friend of Jesus. Rather than suffer embarrassment, discomfort, harassment, or abuse, Peter denied it. Not once. Not twice. But three times he put his own comfort above his loyalty to Christ. The episode apparently taught him a thing or two about self-denial. At the end of a life of self-sacrifice, Peter paid the ultimate price when he refused to renounce Christ. Tradition says he was crucified upside down at his own request, as he did not feel worthy to die the same way as Jesus.

In his letter to the persecuted Christians dispersed throughout Asia Minor, Peter talked extensively about suffering and self-denial. As you read the following passage, notice how he suggests that a person's willingness to deny self and suffer like Jesus is a requisite for that person overcoming sins of sensuality, passions, and self-indulgence (debauchery):

> Since therefore Christ suffered in the flesh, arm yourselves with the same way of thinking, for whoever has suffered in the flesh has ceased from sin, so as to live for the rest of the time in the flesh no longer for human passions but for the will of God. For the time that is past suffices for doing what the Gentiles want to do, living in sensuality, passions, drunkenness, orgies, drinking parties, and lawless idolatry. With respect to this they are surprised when you do not join them in the same flood of debauchery, and they malign you. . . . Beloved, do not be surprised at the fiery trial when it comes upon you to test you, as though something strange were happening to you. But rejoice insofar as you share Christ's sufferings, that you may also rejoice and be glad when his glory is revealed. (1 Peter 4:1–4, 12–13)

Peter observes that refusing to gratify oneself with sinful, worldly pleasures often leads to suffering. People will malign and mock the one who refuses to self-indulge. Self-denial leads to suffering, which leads to a greater capacity to say no to sin, which leads to increased self-denial, which leads to more suffering. A Christlike mind-set toward self-denial and suffering causes sin to lose its power over us. But it also leads to more suffering. "Indeed, all who desire to live a godly life in Christ Jesus will be persecuted" (2 Timothy 3:12).

Peter says that those who are godly will share in Christ's sufferings. If a woman stands against the tide of popular opinion and boldly follows Jesus, she will suffer what He suffered. She will be despised and rejected, acquainted with grief and sorrow, insulted, scorned, mocked, ridiculed, afflicted, oppressed, humiliated, reproached, dishonored, deserted, estranged from friends and family. She will be stared at, gloated over, and be the object of gossip and slander. She will feel distressed, anguished, humiliated. Her heart will melt like wax. Her strength will dry up. She will be exhausted—utterly burdened beyond her own strength. She will weep and humble her soul with fasting to find the courage and strength to endure. In some hostile environments, opponents of Christ might physically attack and harm her, and in some cases, the Lord may ask her for the ultimate sacrifice of laying down her life for the sake of the gospel (Psalm 22:6–8, 13–18; 69:7–9, 19–21; Isaiah 53:2–5, 7–10; Matthew 10:22).

It costs to follow Jesus. Girls-Gone-Wise will pay a price for their obedience. In this culture, they will suffer for taking a stance on Christ's teaching about gender and sexuality. Like Amy, who endured stares, snickers, and whispers after she took a stand on morality in her social science class. Or Lisa, whose friend secretly dared three young men to enter a competition to get Lisa to lose her virginity. Or Samantha, who broke off her relationship with Jim because he didn't share her conviction on sexual standards. Or Christina, who was ostracized from her church group for having views that were far too radical. Or Kimberly, whose husband tried to force her to watch pornographic movies and relentlessly mocked her when she wouldn't. Or Alison, who lost her job because she refused her boss's advances. Or Rebecca, whose tires were slashed and house vandalized with graffiti when she said that homosexuality went against God's design. Or my fellow author who was stalked because she publicly took a stand on purity. Or Natalie, whose heart aches for a husband, but who refuses to settle for a man who isn't sold out to God. The price of obedience is suffering and self-denial. It's costly.

Christ's call for self-denial is radical. Jesus said, "If anyone would come after me, let him deny himself and take up his cross daily and follow me" (Luke 9:23). A Girl-Gone-Wise answers Christ's call to radical obedience. Every day, she takes up her cross and resolves to follow Jesus—no matter the cost.

FOR THE GREATER JOY

One of my favorite parables is the one about the pearl of great price. Jesus said that the kingdom of heaven is like a merchant in search of fine pearls, who, on finding one pearl of great value, went and sold all that he had and bought it (Matthew 13:45–46). He was so ecstatic about the prospect of getting the spectacular pearl that he gladly gave up everything else. It was worth more to him than the combined value of all his other possessions. That story pretty much sums up the reason that we ought to be willing to deny self and suffer for

Christ. It's not because we sadistically enjoy discomfort and pain, but because the treasure we've set our hearts on is worth the cost. The sufferings of this present time are nothing compared with the glory that we will enjoy in Jesus.

If there was ever a young man who knew how to indulge self, it was the first-century philosopher Augustine. He lived a hedonistic lifestyle, drinking, partying, and sleeping around with women. He felt himself drawn to the Lord, but hesitated to become a Christian because he thought he could never live a sexually pure life. He is famous for uttering the prayer, "Lord, grant me chastity and continence, but not yet."

Augustine was radically converted when he read Romans 13:13–14: "Let us walk properly as in the daytime, not in orgies and drunkenness, not in sexual immorality and sensuality, not in quarreling and jealousy. But put on the Lord Jesus Christ, and make no provision for the flesh, to gratify its desires." After he gave his life to Christ, he discovered, much to his surprise, that self-denial led to a far greater joy than self-indulgence ever did. The joy of Christ was sweeter than all other pleasures:

> How sweet all at once it was for me to be rid of those fruitless joys which I had once feared to lose! . . . You drove them from me, you who are the true, the sovereign joy. You drove them from me and took their place, you who are sweeter than all pleasure. . . . O Lord my God, my Light, my Wealth, and my Salvation.[3]

Do you believe it? Do you believe that treasuring Christ holds greater pleasure than sex, wealth, power, and prestige? Are you willing to forego worldly gratification? Are you willing to deny self and suffer so that the True and Sovereign Joy, "sweeter than all pleasure," can take the place of all lesser pleasures? It will cost you. For some, it will cost a great deal. But it's a price that a Girl-Gone-Wise is willing to pay.

Point of Contrast #16

RELIABILITY
Her Faithfulness
to Commitments

Girl-Gone-Wild: Undependable	Girl-Gone-Wise: Dependable
"For my husband is not at home; he has gone on a long journey; he took a bag of money with him; at full moon he will come home." (Proverbs 7:19–20)	"The heart of her husband trusts in her." (Proverbs 31:11)

Shibuya Station is located in the midst of one of the busiest and most colorful shopping and entertainment districts in Tokyo. If you were to visit, you'd see hordes of commuters bustling around a plethora of fashion stores, boutiques, nightclubs, and restaurants. The corner is lit up with neon advertisements and giant video screens—including one that covers half a skyscraper. But nestled among all the glitz, glamour, and movement is a simple bronze statue of a dog, Hachiko. Because of his loyalty, faithfulness, and love, little "Hachi" earned a place in the hearts of all Japanese people and has kept that place for the past seventy-five years.

Hachi used to accompany his Japanese master to the Shibuya Train Station each morning when he left for work. Upon returning, the master would find the dog with his tail wagging, patiently waiting for him. One day, the man died in the distant city and did not come back. That night and every night thereafter, Hachi went to the station and waited faithfully for him—sadly trotting home again when his friend didn't appear. The dog became a familiar sight to commuters as he kept up his vigil for more than ten years. On March 8, 1835, Hachi died on the very spot he last saw his friend alive. His loyalty so impressed the Japanese people that they erected a statue of the dog at the place where he had faithfully waited.

The story behind the statue is one that has endured. Though Hachi stood only two feet tall, the message he left is enormous. People yearn to have friends that are as loyal, reliable, and trustworthy. As the Sage lamented, "Many a man proclaims his own steadfast love, but a faithful man who can find?" (Proverbs 20:6).

Reliability is another point of contrast between a Girl-Gone-Wise and a Girl-Gone-Wild. The Wild Thing of Proverbs 7 wasn't loyal to her marriage vows—she wasn't a woman of her word. When her husband was out of town, she cheated on him. She betrayed her commitment. In the text, we see her enticing the young man with the fact that the coast was clear: "For my husband is not at home; he has gone on a long journey; he took a bag of money with him; at full moon he will come home" (Proverbs 7:19–20). In contrast to the untrustworthiness of the Girl-Gone-Wild, the Girl-Gone-Wise is faithful, loyal, and dependable. "The heart of her husband trusts in her" (Proverbs 31:11). She's a woman of her word. He knows that she will be true.

BREAKING FAITH

The husband of the Proverbs 7 woman appears to have been a merchant who often took long trips out of town, as was the custom of merchants those days. The woman assured the young man that there was no chance of him returning unexpectedly to catch them. Her choice of words is interesting. She literally says, "because the man is not in his house." She uses the impersonal "the man" instead of "my man" and "his house" instead of "our house." It's as though she's distancing herself from her husband, disparaging him, and making their relationship appear very cold and impersonal.

The indifferent, detached manner of referring to her husband is the only clue the woman gives about the state of their relationship. We can only speculate as to what it was like. Perhaps she felt trapped in a loveless marriage. Perhaps her husband was a rude, inconsiderate boor who constantly criticized and belittled her. Perhaps he was so busy in his business ventures and spent so much time out of town, that she felt ignored, isolated, and lonely. Maybe she suspected that he had been unfaithful too.

Earlier in Proverbs, the Sage tells us that this type of woman "forsakes the companion of her youth and forgets the covenant of her God" (Proverbs 2:17). The phrase "companion of her youth" indicates that the woman once loved her husband. When they first married, they were close confidantes, soul mates, and devoted companions. We don't know for sure what happened to contribute to the deterioration of their relationship. But whatever it was, I'm convinced the woman would have had a compelling story to justify why she was breaking her commitment. The young man probably empathized with her reasons. Her explanation would probably tug at our heartstrings too. But there's no reason that could ever justify her behavior in the eyes of God. Covenant unfaithfulness is reprehensible to Him. God expects that we will keep our word. When the woman cheated on her husband, she essentially abandoned "the covenant of her God."

Marriage is much more than a human covenant. It's a covenant with God. When a woman breaks faith with her husband, she doesn't just sin against her husband, she also sins against God and, as we'll soon see, against the entire covenant community of believers. She breaks and profanes covenant in multiple relationships and on multiple levels. Before we look at the passage that links all these covenant relationships together, I want to make sure that you understand what a covenant is.

A covenant is an arrangement between two or more parties involving mutual obligation. It's an agreement, a binding promise, or a standing contract that links or brings them together and unifies them in some way. Covenant is one of the central themes of the Bible, where some covenants are between humans and others between God and humans. The word *testament* is another word for *covenant*. Our Bible is divided into Old and New Testaments, which correspond to the old and new covenants that God made with humanity.

A covenant is essentially a mutual commitment. A variety of human relationships, from profoundly personal to distantly political, can be described as covenantal. Best friends David and Jonathan made covenant promises to each other (1 Samuel 18:3). A husband and wife enter into a covenant of marriage (Malachi 2:14). The elders of Israel made a national covenant with King David (2 Samuel 5:3). King Solomon entered into a covenant with Hiram, king of Tyre (1 Kings 5:12).

A covenant is an interpersonal framework of trust, responsibilities, and benefits. It stipulates that we have responsibilities to fulfill obligations toward others and to behave in a certain way toward them. The key word in Scripture to describe covenant responsibility is *faithfulness*. Faithfulness is maintaining faith or allegiance. It's being responsible to fulfill a commitment. It means that I do what I say I'm going to do and what our agreement obligates me to do.

Scripture emphasizes that faithfulness is an attribute of God. He always does what He says He's going to do. If He makes a promise, He keeps it. If He makes a commitment, He never turns His back on it. He is faithful to fulfill His responsibility. He keeps His word. He's totally and completely trustworthy. When He made a covenant with the Hebrew people, He told them, "Know therefore that the Lord your God is God, the faithful God who keeps covenant and steadfast love with those who love him and keep his commandments, to a thousand generations" (Deuteronomy 7:9). God remembers His promises forever (Psalm 111:5). He is never unfaithful. Not ever! "If we are faithless, he remains faithful—for he cannot deny himself" (2 Timothy 2:13).

The covenant-keeping nature of God is the foundation for faithfulness within human relationships. His faithfulness places a responsibility for faithfulness on our shoulders. He expects us to keep faith with Him, with our spouses, and with other people. He wants us to be as reliable to our commitments as He is to His. The prophet Malachi was upset that the people of Israel broke faith with each other. He claimed that when they broke their commitments, they profaned their covenant with God.

Have we not all one Father? Has not one God created us? Why then are we faithless to one another, profaning the covenant of our fathers? Judah has been faithless, and abomination has been committed in Israel and in Jerusalem. For Judah has profaned the sanctuary of the Lord, which he loves, and has married the daughter of a foreign god. . . .

You cover the Lord's altar with tears, with weeping and groaning because he no longer regards the offering or accepts it with favor from your hand. But you say, "Why does he not?" Because the Lord was witness between you and the wife of your youth, to whom you have been faithless, though she is your companion and your wife by covenant. Did he not make them one, with a portion of the Spirit in their union? . . .

So guard yourselves in your spirit, and let none of you be faithless to the wife of your youth. "For the man who does not love his wife but divorces her, says the Lord, the God of Israel, covers his garment with violence, says the Lord of hosts. So guard yourselves in your spirit, and do not be faithless." (Malachi 2:10–11, 13–16)

Let me give you a bit of background as to what was going on here. The Lord made a covenant with Abraham, his son, Isaac, and his grandson, Jacob—to whom He gave the new name "Israel." Israel had twelve sons, who became the heads of the tribes of the nation of Israel. These people were the covenant community of God. Soon after the death of King Solomon, infighting broke out, and the community split into two kingdoms: the northern kingdom, Israel (ten tribes), and the southern kingdom, Judah (two tribes). Instead of sticking together, the two groups began to make alliances with surrounding nations.

In the passage, Malachi condemns Judah for making such an alliance ("marrying the daughter of a foreign god"). Judah was "faithless" because it "cheated" on God by forsaking its covenant partner, Israel. What's more, the covenant breaking wasn't just a problem on the national level; it was a problem on the personal level too. Men were divorcing their wives to marry foreign women. The people were being unfaithful to their Jewish spouses as well as to the Jewish community. Malachi argued that this was a very serious matter. When they were unfaithful to each other, they were unfaithful to God and His covenant. Based on the Malachi passage, we can deduce some key concepts about covenants and faithfulness:

Covenants Are Based on the Character of God

God created the first covenant. He made a covenant with Adam, and then He performed a marriage ceremony to join Adam and Eve in covenant with each other. Malachi points out that bringing parties together and making them one is an act of God—"with a portion of His Spirit" in the union. There's something about the uniting of individuals that reflects God's nature. God, the united Three-in-One, created us in His image. A pure, faithful, unbreakable union is what He is all about. And that's what He wants us to image in our covenant relationships. When we are faithful to a covenant, we put God on display.

A Covenant Unites

A covenant connects or joins parties together in some sort of association. The purpose of a covenant is to unite. The language of "oneness" is foundational to the idea of covenant. The passage speaks of one Father. One God. One another. One flesh. One family. One nation. In the New Testament, the concept is enlarged. One Mediator. One faith. One baptism. One church. One body. One people. One heart. One soul. One mind. One Lover. One love.

Unfaithfulness to a Covenant Profanes God

The marriage covenant is a covenant of God, as is the covenant relationship between believers. When we are "faithless to one another," we violate our covenant. This isn't just an offense against an individual. It's an offense against the entire faith community. Even worse, it's an offense against the Lord. Malachi is emphatic that breaking faith in a human relationship damages a person's relationship to God and "profanes" His covenant.

Marriage Mirrors the Nature of God's Covenant

God is particularly disturbed by faithlessness in the covenant of marriage. He hates divorce. Why? Because marriage is a covenant of love. Marriage is the human relationship that most closely images God's covenant of love. Marriage best tells the story. When we are unfaithful in marriage, we tell a lie about the true nature of God's covenant. We misrepresent what it's all about.

Breaking Faith Rips Apart What God Has Joined

Faithlessness destroys unity. This is the case in all interpersonal relationships, but especially in marriage. Malachi says that those who fail to faithfully love a covenant partner "cover their garments with violence." They tear apart what God has joined.

Guarding against Faithlessness Is Critical

Being faithful to God requires that we be true to all our promises and commitments to one another. God is witness to all covenants. When we enter into a covenant, we are not only responsible to the other individual, we are also accountable to God. Malachi warns God's people to take care to guard their spirits against being unfaithful to each other. Faithfulness is critical, because it's the glue that makes a covenant work. Without faithfulness, a covenant relationship falls apart.

"I WILL . . . I DO"

When people get married, they make promises to each other with God, family, and friends as their witnesses. The difference between an ordinary promise and an oath is that, with an oath, a person appeals to or acknowledges a sacred witness. To take an oath before God is a very serious matter. A person who does this says, "I want you to know I'm telling the truth, I want God to witness I'm telling the truth, and I want God to punish me if I'm not telling the truth." The Jews understood that it was a very solemn thing to call God to witness a covenant. They knew that if they defaulted on the promise, He would punish them. That was part of the deal. Once they made an oath before God, breaking their commitment was out of the question. The promise was binding. For this reason, God warned them to be very careful about taking oaths, and to be very careful to do all that they promised to do (Numbers 30:2; Deuteronomy 23:21–23).

The Jews of Jesus' day put an interesting twist on the matter of covenants, oaths, and promises. They realized that if they swore before God to do something and then didn't do it, they'd be in a lot of trouble. Wanting to avoid this, they began swearing oaths by everything except God. They wanted to add some kind of force to their promises to make their words more credible, but they didn't want to incur the judgment of God by swearing something in His name, especially when they didn't fully intend to keep their word. So they swore oaths on heaven, on earth, on Jerusalem, on their own heads, and on all sorts of other things (Matthew 5:34–36). Apparently, it got pretty silly. For instance, the Pharisees argued that if you swore by the "the Temple," your word was not binding, but if you swore by the "gold of the Temple," you had to fulfill your obligation. If you swore by the altar, it was like having your fingers crossed behind your back, but if you swore by the offering on the altar, you had a duty to do what you said (Matthew 23:16–22).

Jesus chided the Pharisees for thinking they could get away with being unfaithful to their word. He pointed out that each of the items they were swearing by ultimately belonged to God. So in essence, they were still calling God as their witness. If they defaulted on their promises, they'd still fall under condemnation. God was a silent witness to every word they spoke. Jesus challenged them to stop using oaths to indicate when they were telling the truth, and to start telling the truth all the time. "Let what you say be simply 'Yes' or 'No'" (Matthew 5:37; James 5:12). He wants His followers to be people whose words are so characterized by integrity that others need no formal assurance of their truthfulness in order to trust them. He wants you to be as reliable with your word as He is to His (Ecclesiastes 5:4–5).

Last Thursday, my husband asked me to call someone and stressed how important it was that I do so that day. I said I would. But I procrastinated and didn't make the call until Sunday. I broke faith. I didn't do what I said I was going to do. I sinned, and needed to apologize to Brent for letting him down. I could write it off as "not a big deal," but faithfulness to my word *is* a big deal. Faithfulness is the foundation of my marriage covenant and of all my other relationships too. Being faithful in "little things" is extremely important. Jesus said, "One who is faithful in a very little is also faithful in much, and one who is dishonest in a very little is also dishonest in much" (Luke 16:10).

The Wild Thing of Proverbs 7 cheated on her husband. She was unfaithful to the solemn covenant promise she made. But I think it's fairly safe to assume that she broke faith with him, and others too, in many little ways every day. She was unreliable. She was the type who thought that going back on a promise or commitment, or failing to do what she said she would do, was "no big deal." It didn't matter if she said she would be there, and then wasn't. Or if she said she'd do it, and then didn't. Or if she said she wouldn't, and then did. Or if she said she was in, and then backed out.

How about you? Are you reliable to your commitments? Like the faithful dog, Hachiko, do you show up and continue to show up, even if the other person doesn't? Do you take your covenants and commitments as seriously as God does? The Wild Thing of Proverbs 7 felt justified in breaking faith. But the Girl-Gone-Wise knows that God is witness to the commitments she makes. Keeping faith with Him means keeping faith with others. His trustworthiness obliges her to be trustworthy. In a world where people continually break faith, her yes is yes, and her no is no. She is totally and utterly dependable.

Point of Contrast #17

SPEECH
Her Speech Habits

Girl-Gone-Wild:
Excessive, Duplicitous, Manipulative

Girl-Gone-Wise:
Restrained, Sincere, Without Guile

"With much seductive speech she persuades him; with her smooth talk she compels him."

(Proverbs 7:21)

She keeps her tongue from evil and her lips from speaking guile.

(I Peter 3:10)

S
he could see the hesitation in his eyes. He knew it wasn't a good idea. Even though her husband was out of town, the thought that she was married reminded the young man that a liaison with her was terribly wrong. She could see him begin to waver, so she pulled out all the stops. If her provocative appearance, body language, kiss, and scintillating invitation weren't enough, she'd use her last and most powerful weapon—verbal arsenal. "With much seductive speech she persuades him; with her smooth talk she compels him."

The way a woman uses her mouth is the next point of contrast between a Girl-Gone-Wise and a Girl-Gone-Wild. A wise woman is very careful about what she says. She ensures that her speech is restrained, sincere, and without guile. Cultivating godly speech is a challenge. I've written an entire Bible study and book to help women develop some "Conversation Peace." Visit GirlsGoneWise.com, take the twenty-question "Conversation Peace Quiz," and evaluate how your speech measures up to the Bible's standard. I think you'll see that when it comes to speech, "we all stumble in many ways" (James 3:2).

Controlling our tongues and learning to speak in a godly manner are things that virtually all of us need to work on. It would·be impossible to address the topic of godly communication adequately in one short chapter, so we're just going to discuss the three types of sinful speech that this passage identifies as characteristic of a Wild Thing. Her speech is excessive ("much"), duplicitous ("smooth"), and manipulative ("seductive").

UNZIPPED LIPS

Have you ever heard the statistic that a woman uses about twenty thousand words per day while a man uses about seven thousand? Some researchers claim that this commonly cited figure is inflated and is not based on proper scientific research. Nevertheless, the perception of most people is that women talk more than men do. I just asked my husband whether he believed this to be true. He thought for a moment, and then answered my question with a question.

"If I had three or four of my buddies over and we were outside in the hot tub, and you walked outside and noticed we were sitting in silence, would you think something was wrong?"

"No. I wouldn't. That wouldn't surprise me at all." I smiled. I thought I knew where he was going.

Brent continued, "If you had three or four girlfriends over and you were outside in the hot tub, and I walked outside and noticed you were sitting in silence, would I think something was wrong?"

The answer was self-evident. He would think something was terribly wrong if a group of women was sitting together in silence.

"So," he concluded triumphantly, "that should tell you something!"

I don't know if Brent's little parable demonstrates that the quantity of words men and women speak is different, but it does seem to indicate that there's a difference in the way we use words. For women, intimacy is the fabric of relationships, and talk is the thread from which it's woven. Women regard conversation as the cornerstone of friendships. The bonds between men are based less on talking, and more on doing things together and on common shared experiences.

Women are generally more adept at using language in interpersonal communication. They're better at discerning emotions, reading body language, interpreting nonverbal cues, and expressing thoughts, impressions, and feelings. In male-female interpersonal relationships, the woman is usually the one who has a higher threshold for verbal interaction. If she wants to, she can talk circles around the man. Linguistically and emotionally, he can rarely keep up. A woman will often use this to her advantage. She'll talk and talk until the guy gets overwhelmed, thrown off balance, befuddled, frustrated, or discombobulated, and agrees with her or gives in to her demands. Like Delilah, who cajoled Samson with her incessant yapping. "When she pressed him hard with her words day after day, and urged him, his soul was vexed to death. And he told her all his heart" (Judges 16:16–17).

The Proverbs 7 woman was a talker. When she wanted to bag the young man, she resorted to "much" seductive speech to overcome his resistance. Toward her forbidden lover, her many words were sweet. Her lips "drip[ped]" honey (Proverbs 5:3). But toward her husband, her incessant talk had probably morphed into constant nagging and criticism. Her speech still "dripped," but instead of honey, it was like the annoying drip of a leaky roof on a rainy day. "A continual dripping on a rainy day and a quarrelsome wife are alike; to restrain her is to restrain the wind or to grasp oil in one's right hand" (Proverbs 27:15–16).

The Sage says that trying to restrain the incessant "dripping" words of a contentious woman is an exercise in futility. It's like trying to restrain the wind or grab a handful of oil. Her words are many, and they're extremely slippery. He can't seem to pin down exactly what she means. And he can't stop the verbal barrage. The Bible is clear that excessive speech is usually sinful speech. "When words are many, transgression is not lacking, but whoever restrains his lips is prudent" (Proverbs 10:19). When words constantly drip out of a woman's mouth, chances are she's guilty of some sort of sin: misleading, corrupting, criticizing, gossiping, slandering, feuding, exaggerating, deceiving, clamoring, or a host of other speech sins.

A Wild Thing talks "much." She doesn't exercise restraint. She makes sure the guy is the constant beneficiary of her flattery, her opinion, and her attempts to influence and control him. The Proverbs 7 woman convinced the young man to sin with all her sweet talk and gabbing. The Sage says that the woman who multiplies words is a fool, but the one who restrains words has knowledge (Ecclesiastes 10:14; Proverbs 17:27). A Girl-Gone-Wise doesn't yap. She bridles her mouth and restrains how much she speaks and what she says.

Restraining words means that you don't have to have an opinion on everything. You don't have to comment on everything that happens. You don't have to answer every question. You don't have to constantly make your thoughts known. You don't have to be proved right. You don't have to show off your superior knowledge. You don't have to constantly offer advice. You don't have to nag. Restraining words means that you carefully weigh an answer before you speak, and that you hold back from constantly weighing in. It means that you are quick to listen, but slow to speak (James 1:19).

LIP GLOSS

The second quality of the Wild Woman's speech is that it is smooth. She compels the man with her "smooth talk" (Proverbs 7:21). The Sage warns his son several times about smooth-talking women. He wants to preserve him from the "smooth tongue of the adulteress"—from the woman whose speech is "smoother than oil" (Proverbs 6:24; 5:3).

Smooth talk is conversation that sounds sweet, pleasant, and affirming but is actually slippery, deceitful, and hypocritical. It's dishonest and insincere. It uses flattery, praise, adulation, and gentle pressure to manipulate a person into giving what the talker wants to get. People love to be praised and held in high esteem. They like compliments. They enjoy hearing good things said about themselves. They feel good when people stroke their egos. As a French author once said, "A man finds no sweeter voice in all the world than that which chants his praise."[1] People are much more inclined to respond favorably to those who make them feel good about themselves. A smooth talker takes advantage of this basic fact of human nature. Women are particularly good at sweet talk.

We've all heard the old saying, "Flattery will get you nowhere." But the truth is, flattery works, and works remarkably well. Call it what you will—apple-polishing, boot-licking, back-scratching, soft-soaping, currying favor, toadying, candy-talking, buttering up, kissing up, or managing up—smooth talk can and often does pay off. In the hands of someone who knows how to use it, it can be a dangerous manipulative weapon. Just think of the salesperson who offers a prospective customer profuse compliments on how good an expensive outfit makes her look. Or the subordinate who ingratiates herself to her boss to obtain a promotion or raise. Or villains like Grima Wormtongue in Tolkien's *The Lord of the Rings*, or Iago in Shakespeare's *Othello*, who flatter, deceive, and manipulate their superiors. Or the woman who uses sweet talk and flattery to charm, ensnare, and control a man.

Last week, my son expressed his disgust at the behavior of a girl in his class who was in the habit of apple-polishing the professor. What bothered him most was that everyone in the class could see through her scheme. Everyone, that is, except the professor. He seemed enamored and delighted by all her effusing. Smooth talk is often obvious to everyone except its target. Have you ever seen a man taken in by the smooth talk of a deceptive woman? Did you wonder how he could be so blind to what his family and friends could clearly see?

Flattery characteristically deceives. That's exactly what it's supposed to do. The apostle Paul maintained that those who resort to these tactics "do not serve our Lord Christ, but their own appetites, and by smooth talk and flattery they deceive the hearts of the naive" (Romans 16:18). He and the other apostles were extremely cautious never to resort to flattery when they interacted with people (1 Thessalonians 2:3–4). They did not want to use this deceptive tactic—even for a purpose as noble as furthering the gospel.

Smooth talk is deceptive talk. The Bible equates flattery with lying (Psalm 12:2). Flattery is dishonest because it masks a hidden agenda. It lies about a person's true intent. It glosses over the truth. A smooth talker doles out compliments and strokes a man's ego for personal gain. She butters him up so she can "take" something from him. William Penn, the Quaker colonizer and founder of Pennsylvania, once said, "Avoid flatterers, for they are thieves in disguise."[2] A smooth-talking seductress "lies in wait like a robber" (Proverbs 23:28).

The difference between a legitimate compliment and flattery is accuracy and motive. A legitimate compliment is not false, exaggerated, or motivated by self-interest. It's simply intended to encourage and give credit where credit is due. Flattery is self-serving and insincere. "Sincere" implies an absence of deceit, pretense, or hypocrisy, and an adherence to the simple, unembellished truth. It's derived from the Latin *sine ceras*, which means *without wax*.

When artisans in ancient times made a clay pot, it sometimes cracked due to the heat. Dishonest tradesmen disguised their inferior pots by covering the cracks and blemishes with beeswax before selling them. Picking out a good-quality clay pot wasn't an easy task. On the outside, a patched-up pot looked perfect. A woman wouldn't find out just how flawed it was until she tried using it. As soon as she poured in hot water, the wax melted and the pot began leaking. Honest artisans began labeling their pottery with the words *Sine Ceras*, without wax. A woman who bought a *Sine Ceras* pot knew that the clay had no hidden faults. If there were any imperfections, the artist left them visible. To be sincere is to be genuine, honest, and authentic—without pretense or disguise.

The Girl-Gone-Wild subverts her words. She speaks with flattering lips and a double heart. She's perfected the art of "sweet-talking him" and habitually uses this tactic to get what she wants. The Girl-Gone-Wise does not resort to flattery. Like Lady Wisdom, she can say, "Hear, for I will speak noble things, and from my lips will come what is right, for my mouth will utter truth; wickedness is an abomination to my lips. All the words of my mouth are righteous; there is nothing twisted or crooked in them" (Proverbs 8:6–8).

LIP STICK

We've covered the first two characteristics of the Wild Thing's speech—it is "much," and it is "smooth." The third descriptor the Sage mentions is that her speech is "seductive." To seduce is to win somebody over, to persuade or manipulate someone into agreeing. In this instance, her seductive talk persuaded and compelled the young man to have sex. But she could have used it to get him to agree to something else. Seductive speech is manipulative speech. It's wily speech. It seeks to control another person's behavior—it carries a hidden "stick." Seductive speech includes smooth speech, but it's much broader than that. It can also include criticism, put-downs, and all sorts of subtle innuendo and threats. It uses whatever type of speech is necessary to force the other person to comply with the hidden agenda.

For example, a woman might pout, "You're the only man who hasn't disappointed and hurt me. I put my trust in you. How can you be so self-ish as to not give up your football tickets to go to my friend's party? You've been so dependable. You're not going to let me down like those other jerks, are you?" Her lip "stick" strokes his ego, stabs him in the back, and backs him into a corner, and all at the same time. Why? So she can seduce him into doing what she wants. She bombards him with all sorts of slippery talk so that her opinion and desires will prevail.

The Psalmist said this about seductive talkers, "Everyone utters lies to his neighbor; with flattering lips and a double heart they speak. May the Lord cut off all flattering lips, the tongue that makes great boasts, those who say, 'With our tongue we will prevail, our lips are with us; who is master over us?'" (Psalm 12:2–4). If this passage were person-alized and paraphrased for a Wild Thing, it might say, "She is conniv-ing and insincere. Her smooth talk masks a deceptive heart. May the Lord slice the lips off her face—pull from her mouth the bragging tongue that says, 'I have the power of persuasion. I can talk anyone into anything. I'm in control.'"

The Wild Thing is skilled at using smooth talk to seduce. She talks a lot. She sweet-talks, criticizes, coaxes, and cajoles. She says whatever is necessary so that her wish will "prevail." She's a control freak. She's determined to get what she wants. On the surface, she seems all sweet and nice, but cross her and she'll start to show her true colors. The Sage says that her lips drip honey, and her speech is smoother than oil, but in the end she is bitter as wormwood, sharp as a two-edged sword (Proverbs 5:3–4). She's like David's friend, whose "speech was smooth as butter, yet war was in his heart; his words were softer than oil, yet they were drawn swords" (Psalm 55:21).

What if the young man had resisted the woman's advances? What if he had said, "Listen. This is a really bad idea. I'm not going through with it. I'm going to stand firm and do what's right. Please take your hands off me. I'm going home now"? How do you think she would have responded? Would she have hung her head in shame and said, "Yeah, you're right! I'm so sorry!"? I doubt it. My guess is that she would have thrown a hissy fit. Her sweetness would have quickly transmogrified into bitter venom. She'd drop the verbal candy jar, pull out the daggers, and viciously attack. Instead of flattery, he'd be hit with a sharp barrage of accusing, scoffing, mocking, deriding, scorching, demeaning, angry, abusive words.

The Wild Thing uses words to control and manipulate. But the Bible says that whoever desires to love life and see good days will keep her tongue from evil and restrain her lips so that they speak no guile (1 Peter 3:10 KJV). *Guile* is an old-fashioned word that means deceit. It's cunning, tricky, crafty, or wily speech. The Greek word meaning *guile* translates as *bait for fish*. Like an angler baits a hook to catch a fish, so a guileful woman hangs her words to bait a man. She conceals her true thoughts and intentions while trying to hook him into doing what she wants. A Girl-Gone-Wise does not do this. Her speech is not cunning, tricky, crafty, or wily. She examines it and rids herself of all insincerity and guile (1 Peter 2:1; Psalm 34:13).

MIND YOUR MOUTH

How's your speech? Is it more wise or more wild? Do you talk lots? Are you insincere with compliments? Do you use flattery, smooth talk, or sweet talk to ingratiate others to you? Do you use words to manipulate or control? Cultivating godly speech is one of the biggest challenges for women today. Pop culture encourages us to sin with our speech. It encourages us to talk lots and loudly, to speak up and make ourselves heard, to gain favor with flattery, to be cunning, to manipulate, to be brazen, and to demand that others give us what we want. But the Bible says that excessive, duplicitous, and manipulative speech only leads to strife, iniquity, ruin, and trouble (Psalm 55:9–11). God's way is very different from the world's way and, paradoxically, much more effective. Do you want to enjoy life and see good days? Then work at restraining your words, and at speaking with sincerity, clarity, and honesty. Rid yourself of all insincerity and guile. Mind your mouth, and exchange your wild speech habits for those of a Girl-Gone-Wise.

Point of Contrast #18

INFLUENCE
Her Impact on Others
and Their Impact on Her

Girl-Gone-Wild: **Negative Influence**	Girl-Gone-Wise: **Positive Influence**
"She persuades him. . . . She compels him. All at once he follows her, as an ox goes to the slaughter. . . . He does not know that it will cost him his life." (Proverbs 7:21–23)	"Whoever walks with the wise becomes wise, but the companion of fools will suffer harm." (Proverbs 13:20)

S he's so good for him. He's more 'Ryan' than ever before!" More Ryan? What did the mom of this twenty-three-year-old young man mean?

"More kind. More considerate. More gentle. More strong. More responsible. More good-humored. More focused. More all the good things that make Ryan, Ryan. More of the man God made him to be," she explained. "She brings out the best in him and makes him 'more.' I think she's *the one*."

I'd say that's a fairly high commendation from a potential mother-in-law! The godly influence his girlfriend exerted on her son convinced my friend that this young woman was pure gold. I got the chance to observe firsthand what she meant when, a few months later, my son started dating Jacqueline, and I watched Clark become "more Clark." When Clark asked for our blessing to marry her, Brent and I were able to give our wholehearted approval. Her positive godly influence had demonstrated to us that she was pure gold. She was the type of woman who would do her husband "good, and not harm, all the days of her life" (Proverbs 31:12).

This is often not the case. Many women have the opposite effect. They have a negative influence on men. They make him less and not more. Less responsible. Less considerate. Less reasonable. Less strong. Less good-humored. Less focused. Less committed to Christ. Less grown-up . . . less of the man God made him to be.

Influence is another point of contrast between the wise and the wild. Influence is the power to sway. It's the power that somebody has to affect another person's thinking or actions. A Girl-Gone-Wild exerts and is affected by negative influence. A Girl-Gone-Wise exerts and is affected by positive influence.

FATAL ATTRACTION

Back to our story . . . "With much seductive speech she persuades him; with her smooth talk she compels him." Her seductive words take hold. She succeeds in getting him to go home with her. "All at once he follows her, as an ox goes to the slaughter, or as a stag is caught fast till an arrow pierces its liver; as a bird rushes into a snare; he does not know that it will cost him his life" (Proverbs 7:21–23).

The woman succeeds in "persuading" and "compelling" the young man to sin. *Persuades* translates as a Hebrew verb meaning *to bend or turn*. It indicates that the woman turned the young man away from the direction he was headed. The other verb, *compels*, in Hebrew means to forcibly drive a flock of sheep away. It's used, for instance, for a lion or other predator that hunts and scatters them (Jeremiah 50:17; Isaiah 13:14). It's also used for inept shepherds who are guilty of doing the opposite of what they are supposed to do. Instead of compelling them to move in the right direction, the irresponsible shepherds scatter and/or lead the sheep astray (Ezekiel 34:4). The Old Testament uses both verbs repeatedly to refer to those who influence God's people to follow other gods (1 Kings 11:2; Deuteronomy 13:5).

That's exactly what the Wild Thing did. She seduced the young man to reject the true God for a false god of self-indulgence and sex. She was the negative influence that compelled him to sin. That's not to say the young man wasn't responsible for his behavior. He was just as guilty as she was. When he followed the seductress instead of God, he became a "traitor" (Proverbs 23:28). The Bible says that such a man will find himself "under the Lord's wrath" (Proverbs 22:14 NIV). Falling for a forbidden woman is a fatal attraction that will cost him his life.

The young man's illicit relationship leads to spiritual death. He falls into a deep dark pit. But the woman sets the trap. She "lies in wait like a robber and increases the traitors among mankind" (Proverbs 23:27–28). She robs the young man of his allegiance to God, his commitment to follow God's ways, his purity, his future, and ultimately his eternal destiny. It would be impossible to overstate how heinous her destructive influence is in God's eyes. Bad influence is a sin so wicked that God commanded the Israelites to put to death anyone who enticed a brother or sister to turn away from the ways of the Lord.

> If your brother, the son of your mother, or your son or your daughter or the wife you embrace or your friend who is as your own soul entices you secretly, saying, "Let us go and serve other gods" . . . you shall not yield to him or listen to him, nor shall your eye pity him, nor shall you spare him, nor shall you conceal him. But you shall kill him. . . . And all Israel shall hear and fear and never again do any such wickedness as this among you. (Deuteronomy 13:6–11)

Do you think God was being a bit harsh? Do you think He was over-reacting? Is bad influence truly a sin deserving of death? Is it a threat so dangerous that it requires total annihilation? Or is the problem with us—that we're just too trendy to "get" how wrong it is to influence someone to sin? This passage is talking about leading someone to idolatry. A false god of sex is what the Wild Woman is ultimately calling her prey to. She is calling him to care more about illicit sexual pleasure than about God. Jesus also taught that bad influence was deserving of death. In Matthew 18:6 He said, "Whoever causes one of these little ones who believe in me to sin, it would be better for him to have a great millstone fastened around his neck and to be drowned in the depth of the sea." And let's not forget that in the Old Testament, the penalty for adultery was death (Leviticus 20:10).

Christ's death paid the penalty for our sin. He died so we might live. When the Pharisees caught a seductress in the act and asked Jesus if they should kill her as stipulated in the Law, Jesus directed that the person without sin should throw the first stone. Her accusers soon disappeared. Jesus asked, "Woman, where are they? Has no one condemned you?" She said, "No one, Lord." And Jesus said, "Neither do I condemn you; go, and from now on sin no more" (John 8:4–11).

God's grace is amazing. He didn't send His Son into the world to condemn us, but to save us from sin's condemnation (John 3:17). Jesus knew that the adulteress standing in front of Him deserved death. He knew that the man who succumbed to her charms also deserved to die. She sinned. He sinned. We all sin. We all deserve death. The fact that Jesus bore our punishment is the essence of the gospel and the great hope to which we cling. But the sad fact is, we often take His sacrifice for granted. We fail to appreciate the seriousness of sin. We fail to understand that a sin like negative influence is a "big deal." I hope that you're beginning to figure out how much God hates it when people entice others to sin. The sin of seduction is abhorrent to Him. I hope that you're starting to get it. He wants us to expropriate this wrong from our lives and from the Christian community. Does He extend grace? Yes, absolutely. However, He expects that those who receive it will "go, and from now on sin no more."

THE COMPANY YOU KEEP

I wonder if the young man thought he was immune to the Wild Thing's negative influence. I wonder if he rationalized that he'd just hang out for a short while and keep her company that evening. She was obviously lonely, unhappy with her marriage, and in desperate need of a friend. Maybe he thought he could help her—maybe he thought he could be a positive influence in her life. The fact that she had to persuade, compel, and sweet-talk him into the affair, and that he hesitated before giving in, indicates that his standards for sexual conduct were higher than hers were, and that he wasn't planning on having an affair.

Negative influence is very powerful. Not only does the Bible want us to stop being a negative influence on others, but it also wants us to avoid people who might exert a negative influence on us. The Sage says, "A righteous man is cautious in friendship, but the way of the wicked leads them astray" (Proverbs 12:26 NIV). A Girl-Gone-Wise chooses her friends carefully. She does not take on just anybody as a friend. Being "cautious" means that she searches out and investigates a person's character. She knows that if she constantly and exclusively hangs out with people who don't love the Lord, chances are they'll have a greater influence on her than she will have on them. They will affect her negatively.

Paul warned the Christians in Corinth that hanging out with the wrong people would have a bad effect on their behavior. Just because they'd become Christians didn't mean they were immune to negative influence. They were still susceptible. Paul cites a proverb that was in popular circulation in his day. His point is that *everybody*—even unbelievers—knows that the saying is true. It's common knowledge. The young believers shouldn't be deceived: "Bad company ruins good morals" (1 Corinthians 15:33).

Have you ever heard that saying? Or how about, "Tell me your friends, and I'll tell you who you are," or, "Birds of a feather flock together," or, "A man is known by the company he keeps"? That last one was in a *A Preparative to Marriage* book published in the year 1591: "If a man can be known by nothing els, then he maye bee known by his companions."[1] The saying has endured for centuries. In 1967, recording artist Dolly Parton used it as the basis for her breakout hit, "The Company You Keep."

You say you're doin' nothing wrong
I don't believe you are
I'm only trying to help you, sis
Before you go too far
'Cause I think you're an angel
But folks think that you're cheap
'Cause you're known by the company you keep

The company you keep keeps you out too long
Mom and Dad don't go to sleep until you get home
Sis, you're gettin' in too deep
You'd better look before you leap
'Cause you're known by the company you keep.[2]

The lyrics indicate that it's not just the little sister's reputation the big sister is worried about. She's worried that her little sister is "gettin' in too deep." She's afraid that the friends are going to influence her little sister negatively and make her stumble. *Everyone* knows that that's usually the case. Not only are you known by the company you keep, you're also shaped by the company you keep.

Paul was aware of the incredible power of negative influence. He told the Corinthians not to associate "with anyone who bears the name of brother if he is guilty of sexual immorality or greed, or is an idolater, reviler, drunkard, or swindler—not even to eat with such a one" (1 Corinthians 5:11).

That's pretty radical talk in our "I'm OK—you're OK" culture. But Paul knew that the people who have the most negative influence on believers are other people in the community of faith who profess to follow Christ, but who are hypocrites. There's less danger in associating with those who openly reject Jesus than those who claim to follow Him but who promote mediocrity and compromise.

IT WON'T HAPPEN TO ME

The Sage Father said, "Whoever walks with the wise becomes wise, but the companion of fools will suffer harm" (Proverbs 13:20). What's really sad is that later in life, he ended up going against his own advice. He started keeping the wrong kind of company. The women he associated with were a negative influence on him and turned his heart away from wholeheartedly following the Lord.

Now King Solomon loved many foreign women . . . from the nations concerning which the Lord had said to the people of Israel, "You shall not enter into marriage with them, neither shall they with you, for surely they will turn away your heart after their gods." Solomon clung to these in love. . . . When Solomon was old his wives turned away his heart after other gods, and his heart was not wholly true to the Lord his God, as was the heart of David his father. . . . And the Lord was angry with Solomon, because his heart had turned away from the Lord, the God of Israel, who had appeared to him twice and had commanded him concerning this thing, that he should not go after other gods. But he did not keep what the Lord commanded. (1 Kings 11:1–4, 9–10)

Solomon was probably tripped up by the classic, foolish assumption that "it won't happen to me."

I'm amazed at the number of women who think they are immune to the power of negative influence. They think they're strong enough, and that they've walked with the Lord long enough, to be above the threat. So they start taking foolish risks in relationships. They let down their defenses, transgress boundaries, and crash and burn—and then wonder how it happened to them.

Scripture repeatedly warns against the assumption that we are beyond being affected by negative influence. "Therefore let anyone who thinks that he stands take heed lest he fall" (1 Corinthians 10:12). "Beware lest there be among you a root bearing poisonous and bitter fruit, one who . . . blesses himself in his heart, saying, 'I shall be safe, though I walk in the stubbornness of my heart'" (Deuteronomy 29:18–19).

If you are wise, you will walk in humble dependence on the Lord and avoid people who exert negative influence. You'll recognize that it could indeed happen to you, and that you are not beyond becoming a Girl-Gone-Wild . . . not at any stage in life.

POSITIVE INFLUENCE

The Lord created women with a unique relational bent. Therefore, women are powerful influencers—particularly in their relationships with men. How do we use this gift wisely? How can we make sure that we are influencing others in a positive way? The Bible gives some suggestions:

Choosing Positive and Not Negative Influence

Positive influencers seek out the company of those whose hearts are wholly inclined toward the Lord. Daniel 3 records the story of Shadrach, Meshach, and Abednego. It's an example of good friends who

227

were a positive influence on each other. They stuck together as friends and positively encouraged one another to obey God, even in the face of difficulty and opposition. Queen Esther, one of the most prominent female influencers in the Bible, was careful to seek out godly input from her uncle and to surround herself with friends who supported and joined her in godly spiritual disciplines. Wise Women will make sure that their best friends are wise women.

Positive influencers not only surround themselves with positive influence; they are also careful to avoid negative influence. They are acutely aware of their own susceptibility to sin, so they do not form close associations with people who will influence them to compromise their obedience to God (Proverbs 13:20; 14:7).

Affecting Others through Strength of Character

Peter told female believers that the best way to be a positive influence was through their strength of character. He said, "Likewise, wives, be subject to your own husbands, so that even if some do not obey the word, they may be won without a word by the conduct of their wives, when they see your respectful and pure conduct" (1 Peter 3:1–2). The "respectful" and "pure" conduct of the women is what would have the greatest impact.

A wise woman knows that it's not her words, but her behavior that carries the biggest clout when it comes to compelling change. The more Christlike you are, the more positive your influence will be. If you truly want to influence someone else for good, you won't focus on changing *his* behavior. You'll focus on changing *your* behavior. You'll work at becoming more godly, and on interacting with him in a more godly way.

Judicious with Words

A positive influencer is very wise and careful with words. She wins others over "without a word." She's not a blabber, jabber, nagger, whiner, complainer, or yammerer. Nor does she use wiles, charms, smooth talk, or sweet talk to manipulate. She gives very little in the way of advice—so the little she says is extremely powerful and effective. "The heart of the wise makes his speech judicious and adds persuasiveness to his lips" (Proverbs 16:23).

Relying on God to Effect Change

A positive influencer knows that ultimately it is God, and not she, who effects positive change in a person's life. So she relies on Him and on her most potent, influential tool—prayer. Take Queen Esther, for example. When she wanted to influence King Ahasuerus, she didn't self-confidently burst in and start making demands. Nor did she try to influence him with crying, nagging, or pouting. What did she do? She called a fast. She asked her family and friends to fast and pray with her for three solid days. Only then did she approach the king. And she approached him with humility, few words, and much wisdom, knowing that in the end it was the Lord, and not she, who had the power to turn the king's heart.

How about you? Are you a positive influence? Are you surrounding yourself with positive influences and avoiding negative ones? Are you working on your strength of character and at controlling your mouth? Do you pray and rely on God to effect change? When it comes to the influence you accept and exert in your life, are you living wild or wise?

If you haven't already done so, download the chapter questions from GirlsGoneWise.com. They'll help you apply the Word to your life and influence you to be increasingly wise.

Point of Contrast #19

SUSTAINABILITY
Her Ability to Nurture
and Sustain a Relationship

Girl-Gone-Wild: **Relationships Deteriorate**	Girl-Gone-Wise: **Relationships Grow**
"For many a victim has she laid low, and all her slain are a mighty throng." (Proverbs 7:26)	"The wisest of women builds her house, but folly with her own hands tears it down." (Proverbs 14:1)

What's your sexual history? How many sexual partners have you had?"

"Three. No, wait . . . make that four, including my fiancé." Emily's blue eyes blinked. "But I don't sleep around," she added, as though that somehow added an element of integrity to her pattern of behavior. Not sleeping around meant that she remained sexually faithful to her current love interest. That, and the fact that her number of partners hadn't yet reached the double digits, indicated to me that she considered her conduct to be respectable, and not promiscuous or whorish.

I sighed and silently asked the Holy Spirit how to start praying for this twenty-something Christian young woman. I felt as though I was looking at a massive, tangled ball of string with ends sticking out all over the place. Pulling on one would do little good, since it was attached to all the others. It would take years of prayer ministry and discipleship training to unravel the tangled knots. I only had a few short minutes.

As I prayed, the Lord met Emily in a significant way, but my heart was heavy and ached for her as I watched her walk across the room and out the door. I could tell she was carrying around a father-wound, a demonic stronghold, wrong patterns of thinking, bitterness, deception, and bondage to sin. I turned and asked a friend, "Is it just me? Or is the amount of sexual sin and bondage in the average woman's life piling up higher and higher?" Twenty years ago in women's ministry, it was extremely rare for me to encounter someone who had experienced so much relational dysfunction and sexual sin. Today, I am routinely seeing in women in their twenties more carnage than most women of the past accumulated in a lifetime. A woman who hasn't burned through a string of ugly, fractured relationships and had a succession of men in her bed, is now the exception rather than the rule.

Serial monogamy, the repeated leaping from one sexually monogamous relationship to another, has become a popular relationship trend of this generation. According to the Urban Dictionary, the most popularly accepted definition of a serial monogamist is this:

> One who spends as little time as possible being single, moving from the end of one relationship to the beginning of a new relationship as quickly as possible. Although the relationships in which many serial monogamists find themselves are also often short lived, the defining aspect of serial monogamy is the desire and ability to enter new relationships very quickly, thus abbreviating any period of single life during which the serial monogamist may begin to ask questions of an existential nature.[1]

Serial monogamy involves a succession of intense "committed" relationships, separated by tragic breakups. Take Karin, for example. This girl breaks up with Brad, whom she's been going out with for a year and a half, to go out with Scott. After a couple of months, she moves in with Scott, and they live together for two years. When her relationship with Scott seems irreparable, she starts dating Adam, who she then dumps after a few months because Harry has asked her out. She's sure Harry's the one. She convinces him that he is. They get engaged, move in together, and soon thereafter get married. But three years later, she's got a list of grievances. Her coworker, Bryan, lends a sympathetic shoulder and helps her through the divorce. Not long after, she moves in with Bryan. By the time she's twenty-five, she has cohabited with three men, married and divorced one of them, and slept with two others. She's had five serious, "committed" relationships.

I see it all the time. Older women aren't much better. They're into chain marriages. Perhaps they've been able to sustain a marriage for ten or twenty years before moving on to the next, but whether it's two or twenty-two sexual relationships a woman has in her lifetime, it's still serial monogamy. It goes against God's plan for one love between one man and one woman for life—an exclusive, permanent, "till death do us part" union.

The Proverbs 7 woman cheated on her husband. So she obviously wasn't monogamous. But that wasn't always the case. The Sage says that this type of woman "forsakes the companion of her youth and forgets the covenant of her God" (Proverbs 2:17). That indicates that she was committed to her husband and to monogamy at the start of her marriage. She didn't plan on being unfaithful. We don't know what her premarital sexual history was, but perhaps she had a number of "committed" relationships prior to getting married. Perhaps she was serially monogamous with one or more boyfriends prior to marriage. Perhaps her husband was one of them. Maybe she had remained faithful to him for a number of years and had only recently started having flings behind his back. We do know that by the time we encounter her, she had had several sexual partners, and the revolving door of men was a well-established pattern. "For many a victim has she laid low, and all her slain are a mighty throng."

Sleeping with one man at a time, in one "committed" relationship after another, is not substantially different from promiscuously sleeping with more than one at a time. The timing and the intent is different (the serial monogamist doesn't "intend" to sleep with anyone but her current partner), but the offense and the effect are the same. Both patterns involve sexual sin and leave multiple victims in their wake.

The ability to sustain and nurture a relationship is another point of contrast between a Girl-Gone-Wise and a Girl-Gone-Wild. Wise Things guard their hearts. They choose friends and a life companion very carefully and are usually able to make relationships work. Wild Things rush in and suffer through one tragic relational breakdown after another. Wise Things nurture and grow their relationships. Wild Things behave in such a way as to destroy them. They "shoot themselves in the foot," tragically crippling and sabotaging the very thing they hope to gain. As the Sage observes, "The wisest of women builds her house, but folly with her own hands tears it down" (Proverbs 14:1).

The reason a Wild Thing's relationships break down are many and varied, but I think they generally boil down to one thing, disrespect —disrespect for God and disrespect for others.

DISRESPECT FOR GOD

Many women think that God's plan for relationships and sexuality is prudish, repressive, and seriously outdated. Just yesterday, I received a comment on my blog from Christy. She said that encouraging girls to be pure and holy virgins promotes sexual repression. She argued that I was creating problems for women by bestowing a Madonna/whore complex on their sexuality. Christy wasn't against morals, she just thought God's standards were extreme. They're "damaging" to women. And by teaching what the Bible says about sexuality, I am "part of the problem."[2] Christy obviously doesn't have a very high regard for God or for His Word. She wants to come up with her own set of standards. She thinks she knows better than God does. While most Christians wouldn't come right out and say it, their behavior indicates that they have this same attitude of disrespect.

We disrespect God when we reject His pattern and purpose for our lives. God is our Creator. He knows what's best for us. God says, "You turn things upside down! Shall the potter be regarded as the clay, that the thing made should say of its maker, 'He did not make me'; or the thing formed say of him who formed it, 'He has no understanding'?" (Isaiah 29:16). God is not a mean ogre trying to rain on our parade. When He tells us how we ought to behave, it's because He knows and wants what is best for us. He has all wisdom and understanding. He is the Creator. He is God!

We respect God by respecting what He says we ought to respect. He tells us to respect the institution of marriage and not to sleep around outside of it. "Let marriage be held in honor among all, and let the marriage bed be undefiled, for God will judge the sexually immoral and adulterous" (Hebrews 13:4). He tells us to honor the fact that our bodies are the temple of the Holy Spirit, and to glorify Him with our bodies by keeping them sexually pure (1 Corinthians 6:15–20). He tells us to control our bodies in holiness and honor, not in the passion of lust (1 Thessalonians 4:4). He tells us not to marry unbelievers (2 Corinthians 6:14). He tells us that marriage is a permanent union, and in God's eyes, divorce and remarriage isn't an option (Mark 10:4–12). The woman who thumbs her nose at His plan and does things her own way is foolish. She will undoubtedly suffer negative consequences.

Sherie Adams Christensen, a student at Brigham Young University, did an extensive survey of research on premarital sex and marital satisfaction. The results are staggering. In study after study, premarital sex correlates negatively with marital stability. In other words, those who don't have premarital sex have more stable marriages. Women who were sexually active prior to marriage face a considerably higher risk of marriage breakdown than women who were virgin brides. Premarital sexual activity, even with one's future spouse, can decrease future marital satisfaction, and increase the chance of infidelity and divorce by up to almost 80 percent. The risk of divorce for women engaging in premarital sex with someone other than their future husband was 114 percent higher than those who did not!

Premarital cohabitation significantly lowers subsequent marital quality and happiness. Premarital cohabiters had significantly lower levels of problem solving and support behaviors than those who had not cohabited before marriage. On average, cohabiting relationships only last about a year. The statistics also show that sex is more satisfying in marriage than in any other context. Christensen concludes that "premarital sexual promiscuity must be considered among other documented 'risks' that negatively affect marital and sexual satisfaction."[3]

That's not to say that doing things God's way guarantees that you will never face serious problems or difficulties in your marriage. But the girl who commented on my blog is wrong when she maintains that following God's plan "damages" women. Women are far more "damaged" when they disrespect God and do things their own way. Following His plan for manhood, womanhood, relationships, marriage, sex, and family is not only good—it's also good for you. If you want a lasting, fulfilling relationship, you will go about it in God's way. You will respect Him.

DISRESPECT FOR OTHERS

The Proverbs 7 woman didn't respect men. She just wanted to have a good time. She didn't care if anyone got hurt in the process. She didn't care that her fling would wound her husband, or that her behavior would have negative consequences for her lover. She was too selfish to be concerned about hurting them.

"For many a victim she laid low, and all her slain are a mighty throng" is military language. Several commentators think the Sage used this description to bring to his son's mind the familiar image of the Phoenician goddess, Astarte. Astarte is queen of the Morning Star, goddess of war—a wild and furious warrior who sadistically "plunges knee-deep in knights' blood; hip deep in the gore of heroes."[4] She is also Queen of the Evening Star, goddess of sensuality and passion. She is beautiful, desirable, sexual, savage, and deadly. She's a ruthless conqueror who leaves the battlefield strewn with corpses. Solomon hoped the allusion would help his son grasp the danger of associating with such a woman.

The seductress causes the downfall and destruction of many men. From all outward appearances, she's just a beautiful woman looking for a friend. But in actuality, she's a "man-slayer." She uses men. She hurts them. She's not a builder, she's a destroyer. She tears her "victim" down and "lays him low." The fact that she uses him to meet her own selfish ends, disregards that it will affect him negatively, and discards him when he no longer serves her purposes demonstrates contempt and a severe lack of respect.

Have you noticed how prevalent disrespect toward men has become? In the sixties, women complained that men victimized and disrespected them. Now the tables have turned. Our sons, husbands, fathers, and men-friends are subjected to malicious jokes and attitudes that wouldn't be tolerated toward any other group. Women portray them as selfish, lazy, inconsiderate, hormone-crazed buffoons.

They gleefully slander and tear them down simply because they are male. Women today are like the Phoenician goddess. One moment, they entice men with their beauty and sexual prowess, and the next, they pull out their swords and slice them down.

Christians are not innocent of this sin. I am astonished when I see the haughtiness and contempt with which Christian women treat men. I feel grieved when I hear them tell jokes, mock, deride, put down, and criticize their male colleagues, friends, boyfriends, and husbands. I wonder how they can have the audacity to disrespect and hurt those whom God has created. Sadly, the church is filled with man-slayers. Instead of building men up, we attack, destroy, and bring them down. We use the sword of our tongues to lay them low. Disrespect is one of the main reasons relationships break down. Can you imagine how much longer they'd last if we treated our husbands and friends with respect and didn't lash out to wound them? If, instead of criticizing, complaining, whining, and demanding that they live up to their responsibilities, we took care to ensure that we lived up to ours?

The following list summarizes some of the Bible's directives on how we ought to regard and respect others. They represent the nuts and bolts on what God requires of us in our relationships with one another:

- "Do nothing from rivalry or conceit, but in humility count others more significant than yourselves. Let each of you look not only to his own interests, but also to the interests of others. Have this mind among yourselves, which is yours in Christ Jesus." (Philippians 2:3–5)
- "Love builds up." (1 Corinthians 8:1)
- "Let each of us please his neighbor for his good, to build him up." (Romans 15:2)
- "Encourage one another and build one another up." (1 Thessalonians 5:1 1)
- "Let no corrupting talk come out of your mouths, but only such as is good for building up, as fits the occasion, that it may give grace to those who hear." (Ephesians 4:29)

- "See that no one repays anyone evil for evil, but always seek to do good to one another." (1 Thessalonians 5:15)
- "Do not grumble against one another." (James 5:9)
- "Bear one another's burdens." (Galatians 6:2)
- "With all humility and gentleness, with patience, bearing with one another in love." (Ephesians 4:2)
- "Be kind to one another, tenderhearted, forgiving one another, as God in Christ forgave you." (Ephesians 4:32)
- "Bearing with one another and, if one has a complaint against another, forgiving each other; as the Lord has forgiven you, so you also must forgive." (Colossians 3:13)
- "A new commandment I give to you, that you love one another: just as I have loved you, you also are to love one another." (John 13:34)
- "Let all things be done for building up." (1 Corinthians 14:26)

The thing about these commands is that they have no qualifiers. They're not dependent on how our partner behaves. They don't say, "Let no corrupting talk come out of your mouth *if* no corrupting talk comes out of his." Or "Build him up *if* he builds you up." Or "Be kind and tenderhearted, forgiving him *if* he is kind and tenderhearted, forgiving you." God doesn't give us the option of respecting only those who are respectable. He commands, "Honor *everyone*!" (1 Peter 2:17). The reasons most relationships break down is that the parties spend more time pointing fingers at how the other person is failing to be honorable, rather than making sure that they themselves are.

It breaks my heart when I see wives "man-slaying" their husbands—cutting them down instead of building them up. Women, don't ever forget that when you hurt your husband, you hurt yourself. "The wisest of women builds her house, but folly with her own hands tears it down" (Proverbs 14:1). A Girl-Gone-Wise does not tear down. She is a builder and not a destroyer. She demonstrates respect.

DEMANDING RESPECT

You might ask, "What about me? Don't I deserve some respect?" Pop culture incessantly chants the "you-deserve-it-so-demand-and-take-it" mantra. It teaches women to demand that others respect them before they will give respect in return. But that's not the way of Christ.

Peter anticipated that believers would ask the "Don't-I-deserve-respect?" question, when he instructed them to honor everyone. He knew that some of his friends would face situations where people would respond to good with evil. He told them that they should be honorable and respectful nonetheless.

> If when you do good and suffer for it you endure, this is a gracious thing in the sight of God. For to this you have been called, because Christ also suffered for you, leaving you an example, so that you might follow in his steps. He committed no sin, neither was deceit found in his mouth. When he was reviled, he did not revile in return; when he suffered, he did not threaten, but continued entrusting himself to him who judges justly. (1 Peter 2:20–23)

What did Christ do when others disrespected Him? Did He "demand" respect? Did He scream, yell, and attack them with caustic remarks? No. He responded by "entrusting himself" to God. That's what we're to do too. That's not to say that we don't have protective boundaries, or shouldn't clearly express our opinions or work to change our circumstances, but that everything we say and do is honorable and respectful. Entrusting ourselves to God means that we don't try to control how the other person responds. We behave in the right way and leave the rest up to the Lord.

How are your relationships doing? Are you nurturing and sustaining them? Are they growing? Or are you stuck in a revolving door of broken ones? If you are married, is your love growing deeper? Are you more in love with your husband now than you first were? If you're not, you may need to take a serious look at whether you're behaving with the proper respect toward God and toward your husband. Evaluate your other relationships too. For them to grow, you need to behave in an honorable and respectful way. Remember: Girl-Gone-Wise builds her house—but a Wild One with her own hands tears it down.

Point of Contrast #20

TEACHABILITY
Her Willingness to Be Corrected and Instructed

Girl-Gone-Wild: **Scornful**	Girl-Gone-Wise: **Teachable**
"Woe to her who is rebellious and defiled. . . . She listens to no voice; she accepts no correction. She does not trust in the Lord; she does not draw near to her God." (Zephaniah 3:1–2)	"The ear that listens to life-giving reproof will dwell among the wise." (Proverbs 15:31)

Sadly, the man falls for the seduction. He follows the woman home and they spend the night together. The "stolen water is sweet, and bread eaten in secret is pleasant," but the story doesn't have a happy ending (Proverbs 9:17–18). The young man didn't realize that when he went to her house, he went to his grave. Maybe her husband finds out. Maybe she gets pregnant. Maybe he gets an STD. Maybe he loses his reputation. Maybe he's overcome with guilt and shame. Maybe she breaks his heart. Maybe he gets drawn deeper into sin. We don't know the details, but we do know that his decision disrupts his relationship to God. It leads to spiritual death. She promises him a slice of heaven, but he ends up in the pit of hell.

We've come to the end of the story, and to the last point of contrast between the wild and the wise. The simple young man who lacked sense and the wily seductress who caused his downfall are examples of two individuals who failed to walk in the way of wisdom. The Sage urged his son to pay close attention to their mistakes, so that he might learn from them. That's why he told the story. And that's why he wrote his book. The dad wanted his son to become wise. He wanted him to understand words of insight, to receive instruction, to be discerning and not naive, and to advance in knowledge and discretion. The Sage figured that everybody who was wise would pay attention to the meaning of the story and to all the proverbs that he wrote down. His wise words would help readers increase in learning and knowledge. They would make the wise increasingly wise (1:2–5).

SIMPLE, FOOLISH, OR SCOFFING

The final point of contrast between wise and wild is teachability, which is a woman's willingness to be corrected and instructed. A Girl-Gone-Wise is teachable. She's eager to grow. She welcomes correction and training. A Girl-Gone-Wild scorns instruction. She doesn't think she needs input. She resists change. In the book of Proverbs, the Sage profiles three types of individuals who turn their backs on God's invitation to become wise. They are the simple, the fools, and the scoffers. Proverbs 1:22 mentions all three. Wisdom asks, "How long, O *simple ones*, will you love being simple? How long will *scoffers* delight in their scoffing and *fools* hate knowledge?" (italics added).

The three categories aren't mutually exclusive. The characteristics of simple people, fools, and scoffers overlap. At times, the Sage uses the word *fool* in a general way to refer to anyone who resists wisdom. He sometimes calls a simple one a fool, and sometimes accuses a fool of scoffing. Nevertheless, he seems to make a distinction between these three types of foolish people—a distinction based on their likelihood to learn. The three represent a continuum of teachability. The simple person is somewhat open to instruction; the fool, less so; and the scoffer, completely closed to attaining wisdom. From the simple one to the fool to the scoffer, there is an increasing hostility and resistance to learning, and to doing things God's way. A Wild Thing will fall somewhere along this continuum. She will be like Simple Sally, Foolish Fran, or Scoffing Sue.

Simple Sally

Simple Sally is the female version of the young man in our story. The Sage described the victim as "young," "simple," and "lacking sense." "Young" refers to age, but also, and more importantly, to a lack of life experience. To be simple means that a woman doesn't have the necessary know-how. She doesn't clearly understand the implications or consequences of her actions (Proverbs 22:3). She doesn't see the danger, so she's easily taken in (27:12). She naively "believes everything" and fails to give thought to her steps (14:15). Unfortunately, this means that she's open to negative influence and that she'll likely get burned. Since she can't tell the difference between good and evil, folly and wisdom, she'll fall prey to the wicked.

The simplemindedness of the young man prevented him from seeing through the Wild Thing's wily scheme. He was naive. He didn't fully grasp that meeting up with the woman and having an affair would be bad for him. He hadn't bothered to think things through and to educate himself in the ways of wisdom.

Like him, Simple Sally is uninformed. She doesn't think that learning is all that important, so she doesn't make the effort to figure out what's wild and what's wise. She's blissfully ignorant. She "loves being simple." In short, she's childish. Children are open, trusting, and naive. This mind-set is to be expected in a child, but for a grown woman, it's a recipe for disaster. The danger is that Simple Sally will listen to the instruction of fools (Proverbs 16:22). She'll get mixed up with the wrong crowd and start taking the wrong advice. She'll believe the guy who tells her he loves her or who makes hollow promises so he can get her into bed, or she'll believe the girlfriend who tells her that going to the bar or strip club is a good idea, or she'll believe the ad that entices her to look at porn. If she fails to seek wisdom, she'll inevitably "inherit folly" (14:18). She'll be killed by inadvertently turning away (1:32).

The Sage says Sally needs to give some serious thought to her steps (Proverbs 14:15). She needs to learn how to think things through and behave with knowledge and discretion (1:4). In order to succeed in life, she needs to grow up and stop being so naive—to stop and look before she leaps. The Sage urges, "Leave your simple ways, and live, and walk in the way of insight" (9:6). To grow in wisdom, Simple Sally has to accept the challenge to learn. She must eagerly study the Word of God, pay attention to the pitfalls and dangers of sin, and learn from the mistakes and failures of others (19:7; 21:11). Sally has to stop being so simple. If she doesn't, she'll become like her sister, Foolish Fran.

Foolish Fran

Unlike Sally, Foolish Fran isn't uninformed. Fran has heard the message of wisdom. But she's unconcerned. She just doesn't care. She thinks she's got life figured out and under control. Fran is overconfident (Proverbs 14:16). She doesn't take God seriously (14:9). She takes no pleasure in understanding, but only in expressing her own opinion (18:2). Fran knows best. Her way is right in her own eyes (12:15). If a friend warns her about the consequences of sin, Foolish Fran tells her to "just lighten up." Doing wrong is like a joke to her (10:23). Nothing bad will happen! She'll be able to stop before going too far. She's got the situation under control. The thing that matters most to Fran is that she enjoys herself and has fun (Ecclesiastes 7:4).

Fran's problem is that she's reckless and careless (Proverbs 14:16). She despises wisdom and instruction, and especially the advice of her parents (1:7; 15:5). What do they know? Fran doesn't need another lecture. She knows what could happen; she just doesn't think it could happen to her. So she doesn't turn away from evil (13:19). If it looks like fun, she wades right in. She sins and makes mistakes. But she doesn't learn from them. Like a dog that returns to his vomit, she repeats her folly (26:11). She promises herself she won't, but she ends up making the same mistake over and over again.

Foolish Fran denies the danger of sin. She doesn't really believe that folly leads to more and greater folly (Proverbs 14:24). She thinks the consequences of sin are way overblown. She won't get sucked in. She can handle it—she's got things under control. Fran's lack of concern will lead to her ruin (10:14). She'll be destroyed by her complacency. The more she sins, the more she'll be enslaved to the bondage of sin.

Sin will lead to more sin. Much like Israel, who paid an awful price for depending more on other countries' military power than God's, the more she sins, the more the bonds will "be made strong" (Isaiah 28:22), until she becomes a scoffer. Her heart will get increasingly hard. Eventually, Foolish Fran will pass the point of no return. She'll get to the place where she is so enslaved to sin that she is unable and unwilling to change (Proverbs 27:22). In the process, she'll make a mess of her life.

What does Foolish Fran need to do to break out of this destructive pattern? The Sage says she needs to learn to love God's ways (Proverbs 1:22–23). She needs to stop feeding on folly (15:14) and start developing some self-control (18:7). Fran needs to have more respect for God (1:7). Usually a woman like Foolish Fran won't be motivated to change until she reaches a crisis point (3:35). She'll run headlong after the pleasures of sin until she hits a wall and the consequences beat her down (19:29).

If she's too far gone, even this won't bring change (Proverbs 27:22). But if she humbly repents and learns some sense, the Lord will help her get her life back on track (8:5). In either case, she'll have to live with the consequences of her sin. For example, she will never regain her virginity, her relationship will still break down, the STD will still flare up, the baby will still be born, the memories will still haunt, the dark temptation will still knock, bad thoughts will still nag, and new relationships will live under the shadow of it all. If she repents, the Lord will redeem what Satan intended for harm and bring good out of it, but the damage will rarely be completely undone.

Scoffing Sue

Scoffing Sue isn't interested in learning the way of wisdom. While Sally is uninformed, and Fran is unconcerned, Sue is unashamed. She unabashedly insists that God's way is wrong. Like the Babylonian army in Habakkuk, she makes believe she has the power to be her own god (Habakkuk 1:10–11).

She is proud, arrogant, and insolent (Proverbs 21:24). She doesn't hesitate to "stick her tongue out" and thumb her nose at the Lord (Isaiah 57:4). She doesn't care what He thinks, nor does she care what others have to say about it (Psalm 74:10; Proverbs 15:12). She hates people who think she's doing something wrong. If someone tries to correct her, she lashes out to injure and abuse (9:7–8).

Scoffing Sue is a slave to her own sinful desires (Jude 18). What's more, she's intent on seducing others to indulge in sin with her (Proverbs 7:21). She doesn't care if she hurts or exploits them in the process (7:26; 29:8). When Scoffing Sue is presented with wisdom, she doesn't "get" it. She can't grasp truth (14:6). She's convinced her way is right, so she refuses to change (13:1).

The danger of being a scoffer is profound. Sue is spiritually dead, condemned, cut off from God (Proverbs 19:29; Isaiah 29:20). Her life will be tough. She won't be able to sustain relationships, and the consequences of her sin will come back to haunt her, bringing pain and suffering down on her head (Proverbs 9:12; 22:10). Scoffing Sue won't escape God's punishment (Isaiah 29:20). Scripture says she'll come to nothing (Isaiah 29:20).

We don't know exactly where the seductress of Proverbs 7 was on the continuum of the three profiles, but I think it's safe to say that if she hadn't already crossed over from being a Foolish Fran to a Scoffing Sue, she was extremely close to doing so. What a woman like this needs is to encounter Christ. She has no desire to change and no inherent ability to do so. Apart from God's intervention and the regenerative work of the Holy Spirit, she's doomed. The Lord will let her "eat the fruit of her way, and have her fill of her own devices" (1:31).

A Girl-Gone-Wild, like the city of Jerusalem in the days of Zephaniah, "listens to no voice; she accepts no correction. She does not trust in the Lord; she does not draw near to her God" (Zephaniah 3:1–2). Simple Sally can't be bothered to listen, Foolish Fran doesn't see a reason to, and Scoffing Sue brashly refuses. The following chart summarizes their three profiles. As you read and compare them, think about whether you fit into any of the categories. (Note: Unless otherwise indicated, all references on this chart are from the book of Proverbs.)

	Simple Sally	Foolish Fran	Scoffing Sue
Trait	She's uninformed—she doesn't make an effort to learn.	She's unconcerned—she thinks she's got it all figured out.	She's unashamed—she insists God's way is wrong.
Attitude	She doesn't think that learning is all that important (9:4–6). She likes not having to think about serious things (1:22).	She doesn't take God seriously (14:9). She's overconfident (14:16). She thinks she knows better (13:16; 18:2). Her way is right in her own eyes (12:15). Doing wrong is like a joke to her (10:23). She just wants to have fun (Ecclesiastes 7:4).	She is her own god (Habakkuk 1:10–11). She sticks out her tongue at God (Isaiah 57:4). She is proud, arrogant, and insolent (21:24). She doesn't care what God thinks (Psalm 74:10). She doesn't care what wise people say (15:12). She hates those who say she's wrong (9:8).
Problem	She lacks sense (7:7). She fails to see the danger (22:3). She doesn't understand the implications (27:12). She's gullible (14:15).	She's reckless and careless (14:16). She despises wisdom and instruction (1:7), especially of parents (15:5). She doesn't turn away from evil (13:19). She repeats and doesn't learn from her mistakes (26:11).	She's a slave to sin (Jude 18). She seduces others to sin (7:21). She doesn't care if she hurts and exploits (7:26; 29:8). She can't grasp truth (14:6). She refuses to change (13:1).
Danger	She'll listen to the instruction of fools (16:22).	Her folly will lead to more folly (14:24).	She's spiritually dead (9:18).

	Simple Sally	Foolish Fran	Scoffing Sue
Danger (cont'd)	She will inherit folly (14:18). She will be killed by inadvertently turning away (1:32).	She'll ruin her own life (10:14). She'll be destroyed by her complacency (1:32). Her bondage will be made strong (Isaiah 28:22). She'll pass the point of being able to change (27:22).	She is condemned (19:29). She will be cut off (Isaiah 29:20). She'll be unable to sustain relationships (22:10). She'll suffer (9:12). She'll be punished (21:11). She'll come to nothing (Isaiah 29:20).
Need	She needs to give thought to her steps (14:15). She needs to leave simple ways (9:6). She needs insight (9:6). She needs to be cautious (1:4).	She needs to appreciate knowledge (1:22). She needs to stop feeding on folly (15:14). She needs to develop self-discipline (18:7). She needs to start hearing God (1:7).	She needs to encounter Christ.
Corrective	She accepts the challenge to become wise (9:4). She eagerly studies the Word (Psalm 19:7). She learns from the failures of others (21:11).	She reaches a crisis point (1:31; 3:35). She experiences the consequences of her sin (19:29; 26:3). She humbly repents and works at change (8:5).	She has little or no desire to change. Change will only come through God's intervention (1:20–33).

THE BEGINNING OF WISDOM

One of the best-known verses in Proverbs is "The fear of the Lord is the beginning of knowledge; fools despise wisdom and instruction" (1:7). These words have been used as a motto and inscribed over the entrance of many schools and colleges. The Sage probably would have approved. This concept was so important to him that he mentioned it at the outset of his first collection of proverbs, and then repeated it, with a slightly different twist, at the end of it (9:10). This was his way of emphasizing that the fear of the Lord was the all-important idea behind all the sayings in the section and the all-important idea behind the lesson of the Wild Thing of Proverbs 7.

The "fear of the Lord" is an important theme throughout Scripture. The Lord is infinitely good and loving, but fear is the natural and appropriate response of all who catch a glimpse of His glory. When the Lord appeared to Moses, Moses trembled with fear and did not dare look at the spectacular sight. Isaiah came undone. Daniel fell trembling on hands and knees. Ezekiel fell on his face. John dropped down as though dead. Even the disciples, who were good friends with the incarnate Lord, were terrified of Jesus when He calmed the storm. Scripture reports that they felt more frightened of Him than they had of the raging wind and waves.

To know God is to know fear. The fear of God is a heart-pounding, knee-trembling, spine-tingling, shuddering recognition that God is infinitely more good, powerful, and important than I. It means that I live, think, act, and speak with a keen awareness that He is the Creator and I am the creature; He is holy and I am not; He is wise and I am a fool; He is powerful and I am weak; He is ruler and I am servant; He is self-sufficient and I am utterly dependent.

To fear God means to be ever aware of His all-pervasive presence, conscious of my absolute need for Him, mindful of my responsibility to follow His way, determined to obey Him, cautious of offending Him, and overwhelmed in amazement and gratitude at His incredible goodness and grace. As the early-twentieth-century philosopher Rudolf Otto said, "It is the emotion of the creature, submerged and overwhelmed by its own nothingness in contrast to that which is supreme above all creatures."[1]

So how is the fear of the Lord the beginning of wisdom? A woman won't figure out what's right if she starts at the wrong point. God is the starting point. We aren't. It's impossible for us to understand how we should live apart from our Creator. He knows the purpose and plan for our existence. If we follow His rules and His precepts, then we will live wisely. *Beginning* also means the capstone or essence. The fear of the Lord is wisdom's choicest feature, its foremost and most essential element.

Do you fear God? Do your knees knock when you think about His greatness? Do you tremble when you consider His holiness? Do you respect Him enough to listen and obey? Do you have any idea who He is? The fear of the Lord is twofold. First, it involves knowing who God is. Second, it involves obedience—loving righteousness, hating sin, and humbly following His way. The Sage says, "The fear of the Lord is the beginning of wisdom, and *the knowledge of the Holy One is insight*," and, "The fear of the Lord *is hatred of evil*" (Proverbs 9:10; 8:13, italics added). If you want to be wise, you'll start by getting to know God and doing what He says. You'll love the things He loves and hate the things He hates. You'll be humble and teachable, willing, eager, and determined to learn His ways.

He promises that those who do this will reap the rewards. He will pour out His Spirit on them, make His words known to them, guide them, and protect them. They will dwell securely, be at ease without dread of disaster, walk in the way of insight, and truly live.

LADY WISE CALLS

The Sage presents another idea at the beginning and end, and peppered throughout this section of his sayings—the concept of a personal invitation. A personification of the trait of wisdom, Lady Wise invites you to her feast. Above the din and bustle of daily life, she cries out and summons you to sit down at her table and listen to her correction and counsel.

Wisdom cries aloud in the street, in the markets she raises her voice; at the head of the noisy streets she cries out; at the entrance of the city gates she speaks: "How long, O simple ones, will you love being simple? How long will scoffers delight in their scoffing and fools hate knowledge? If you turn at my reproof, behold, I will pour out my spirit to you; I will make my words known to you. . . . For the simple are killed by their turning away, and the complacency of fools destroys them; but whoever listens to me will dwell secure and will be at ease, without dread of disaster." (Proverbs 1:20–33)

Does not wisdom call? Does not understanding raise her voice? . . . Take my instruction instead of silver, and knowledge rather than choice gold, for wisdom is better than jewels, and all that you may desire cannot compare with her. (Proverbs 8:1, 10–11)

[Wisdom] has slaughtered her beasts; she has mixed her wine; she has also set her table. She has sent out her young women to call from the highest places in the town, "Whoever is simple, let him turn in here!" To him who lacks sense she says, "Come, eat of my bread and drink of the wine I have mixed. Leave your simple ways, and live, and walk in the way of insight." (Proverbs 9:2–6)

Hers is not the only, nor the loudest, voice you'll hear. Lady Wild is also extending an invitation for you to go over to her place.

The woman Folly is loud; she is seductive and knows nothing. She sits at the door of her house; she takes a seat on the highest places of the town, calling to those who pass by, who are going straight on their way, "Whoever is simple, let him turn in here!" And to him who lacks sense she says, "Stolen water is sweet, and bread eaten in secret is pleasant." But . . . the dead are there . . . her guests are in the depths of Sheol. (Proverbs 9:13–18)

Lady Wise and Lady Wild both call for guests to come and dine at their tables. Lady Wise has slaughtered a beast and served up bread and wine. She serves up a rich and bountiful feast that will be sure to satisfy. Her only stipulation is that her guests be willing to forsake foolishness and walk in the way of wisdom. The "feast" of Lady Wild is a cheap imitation. She offers stolen water and bread—a veiled reference to illicit sex and everything else that God says is off limits. Lady Wild invites you to indulge in foolishness. She entices you with the idea that sin is sweet and pleasant, that you don't have to listen to God—that you can do whatever you want. But the simple young man who accepted her invitation discovered it was a ruse. Her seductive invitation leads to spiritual death.

The choice is up to you. Are you teachable? Are you willing to listen and accept God's wisdom for your life? Are you committed to learning and making the necessary adjustments? "The ear that listens to life-giving reproof will dwell among the wise" (Proverbs 15:31). The three Wild Things would refuse the invitation. Scoffing Sue would respond with, "How dare you suggest my way is wrong?" Foolish Fran would say, "No, thanks. I've got it all figured out." And Simple Sally would pipe in with, "Not right now. Maybe later." How about you? How will you respond? Lady Wise and Lady Wild are calling you to their tables. You will dine with one or the other. Whose invitation will you accept? Will you be a Girl-Gone-Wild or a Girl-Gone-Wise?

Conclusion:

WILD TO WISE

"The beginning of wisdom is this: Get wisdom,
and whatever you get, get insight.
Prize her highly, and she will exalt you;
she will honor you if you embrace her.
She will place on your head a graceful garland;
she will bestow on you a beautiful crown."
—Proverbs 4:7–9

D o you remember the seventy-year-old woman I told you about
in the introduction? She came up to me after a workshop with
tears streaming down her face saying, "I came to your workshop
to get some ideas about how to help my granddaughter, but I see now
that it's me who is a Girl-Gone-Wild."

I hope as you've worked your way through the twenty points of
contrast, that you've noticed areas in your life where you need to
learn and grow—and become less wild and more wise. I know I have.
To refresh your memory about the ones you need to work on, you can

go to GirlsGoneWise.com and do the "Wild or Wise?" twenty-question survey. The questions correspond to each point of contrast between a wild woman and a wise woman. Your answers to the survey will help you determine which wild parts of your character the Lord wants you to tame.

Being a Girl-Gone-Wise in a world gone wild isn't easy. In our culture, Lady Wild cries out more loudly and clamorously than ever before. Women are congregating at her table in droves. That's where the party is. That's where all the noise and commotion is. All the popular girls are members of her sorority. All the celebs are endorsing her club. All the guys are ogling her guests. I pray that you've grown wise to the ruse. I hope that you've seen through her deceptive scheme and you understand the danger of setting foot in her house. I hope that you've realized that the dead are there—that "her guests are in the depths of Sheol."

Throughout the pages of this book, a quieter voice has been calling. Lady Wise is asking you to come to her house instead. If you accept, you'll have to say no to the conflicting invitation. You'll have to leave Lady Wild's party. You'll have to choose to be different. You'll have to stand against popular opinion and also, perhaps, against the opinion of family and friends. Joining Lady Wise means thinking differently, speaking differently, dressing differently, and behaving differently than the throng of women around you. As you've seen in the Twenty Points of Contrast, being obedient to Christ affects every area of our lives. Like my son exclaimed, "Everything about a woman who loves God is different!"

In the past fifty years, we have witnessed a monumental shift in our culture's idea about what it means to be a woman. Feminism infused us with the idea that womanhood means deciding for ourselves what womanhood, manhood, marriage, sex, and sexuality are all about. The carnage of this way of thinking is almost beyond belief. Marriages and families are breaking down. STDs are rampant. Pornography has gone mainstream. Sexual identity is becoming a matter of choice. Gender confusion is on the rise. We live in a world of women who have had sex changes and make the headlines as pregnant "men," and men who manipulate their hormones to lose their beards and become "women," adolescents seeking to figure out their gender identity and "preference," and same-sex couples necking on TV.

Women and men are having a crisis of identity. Few people know, anymore, what it really means to be a woman or a man. What's worse is that even fewer care. They have no idea how important our God-given design is to our personal identity, our purpose, our wholeness, our well-being, and our capacity to enjoy healthy, fulfilling relationships. It matters how you live your life as a woman. It matters a great deal!

THE ALTERNATE ENDING

The Proverbs 7 woman messed up big time. Her story didn't have a happy ending. Scripture talks about another Wild Thing whose story was very similar, but had an alternate ending.

Have you ever read one of those kids' Choose Your Own Adventure books? They were quite popular in the eighties and nineties. Our kids constantly clamored for Brent to read them one. Each story was written from a second-person point of view, with the reader taking on the role of the main character and making choices that determined the main character's actions. Depending on the reader's choice, the plot and its outcome would change. At the end of each scene, the reader stood at a crossroad and had to determine the protagonist's next course of action. For instance, "If you decide to call the police, turn to page 24. If you decide to go after the intruder, turn to page 8." The plot branched out and unfolded, leading to more decisions and, eventually, to some alternate endings—some good and others bad.

There was a Wild Thing whose Choose Your Own Adventure story followed the same basic pattern as the Proverbs 7 woman. She was a party girl—incredibly beautiful and personable—but as her life unfolded, she just couldn't seem to make life work. Every relationship started out with a lot of promise, but then inevitably broke down. She could have been called "The Woman Who Had Five Husbands" or "The Woman Who Changed Husbands Like Vacuum Cleaner Bags." Nowadays, she'd have made an interesting guest on Jerry Springer's talk show, on a sleazy episode entitled something like "Break-up and Pick-up Techniques of Serial Seductresses." But we know her by less sensational titles: "The Samaritan Woman" or "The Woman at the Well."

Up to the point where we meet her, the plot in her Choose Your

Own Adventure story had been essentially the same as her Proverbs counterpart. In each scene, at each crossroad, she made the same sort of decision. But in this scene, her story takes an incredible twist. The choice she makes changes everything. Instead of the deadly ending for which she and the Wild Thing of Proverbs 7 were both destined, her choice leads to a happily-ever-after ending. You've probably heard her story. The Samaritan woman was looking for that which would satisfy her thirst. Her bucket was empty. And she had come to the well hoping to fill it up.

She came to the well alone. Women normally came to the well in groups. And they came either earlier or later in the day, when the heat wasn't so intense. But the Samaritan woman came alone in the blistering heat. She was lonely, isolated, and excluded from regular social contact with other women. Her public shame about her relationships with men likely contributed to this. She didn't belong to the group. She also had identity issues. When Jesus approached her, she immediately cited their differences: "Hey, why are you talking to me? You are a Jew, and I am a Samaritan *and* a woman." Right at the onset, she was anticipating conflict and rejection. It was what she was accustomed to. She thought Christ wouldn't accept her once He knew who she really was. She was suspicious of His friendliness. And she was even more suspicious when he implied that He could give her what she was really looking for. Yeah, right! She had heard *that* from men before!

The Samaritan woman thought that Jesus wasn't quite telling the truth when He offered her living water. But at the same time, underlying her caution, her interest was piqued. That's because she was acutely aware of her longing. Jesus' offer had touched a chord in her heart. She had come to the well feeling empty. Every day she felt dry and thirsty on the inside. She wanted to belong. She wanted to feel worthwhile, respected, and loved. She wanted purpose and meaning. She wanted to know truth. She wanted to find someone worthy of trust. She was so tired of the emptiness. She wanted to find fullness and satisfaction instead of constantly carting around an empty bucket.

No matter how she tried to fill it, her bucket remained empty. To satisfy her longings, she had engaged in a lifestyle of pursuit and indulgence. She went after everything that she thought would satisfy her desires. She had had five husbands and hadn't even bothered to marry the man she was living with now. When Jesus met her, she was on serial monogamy relationship number six. She was undoubtedly very alluring to have attracted all those men. She knew how to turn on the feminine wiles and charms. And the men provided her with what she thought she wanted—power, affirmation, marriage, sex, material provisions, a home, and a family. But it was all empty. It didn't satisfy.

Her story is all too familiar, isn't it? How often do we pursue and indulge in that which we think will satisfy? We try to fill our buckets with sex, romance, getting a husband, having kids, having a perfect husband and perfect kids, perfect looks, perfect friends, a perfect house, a perfect wardrobe, or car, or job, or education, or income, or holiday, or retirement, or a host of other things. We pour those things into our buckets, seeking to fill them up, but the water keeps running out. And on the inside, we begin to wither and die of thirst.

The Samaritan woman was tired of trying to fill her bucket. Jesus looks right into her heart, puts His finger on that tender place of all her shattered dreams and failures, and promises to quench her longing with living water. She pleads, "Sir, give me this water, so that I will not be thirsty or have to come here to draw water" (John 4:15). As the conversation unfolds, Jesus reveals that He is the living water—the Messiah, the deliverer. He is the object of all her longings and dreams. He is the only One who can fill her bucket. He reiterates the age-old invitation that the Lord extended in the pages of Proverbs through Lady Wisdom—the same invitation He extended through the prophet Isaiah:

> Come, everyone who thirsts, come to the waters; and he who has no money, come, buy and eat! Come, buy wine and milk without money and without price. Why do you spend your money for that which is not bread, and your labor for that which does not satisfy? Listen diligently to me, and eat what is good, and delight yourselves in rich food. Incline your ear, and come to me; hear, that your soul may live. . . . Seek the Lord while he may be found; call upon him while he is near; let the wicked forsake his way, and the unrighteous man his thoughts; let him return to the Lord, that he may have compassion on him, and to our God, for he will abundantly pardon. (Isaiah 55:1–3, 6–7)

The Samaritan woman made the decision to believe and follow Christ. He offered to fill her bucket brimful. In Him, she'd find forgiveness and life. Instead of the poisonous "stolen water and bread" of Lady Wild, she'd find good, rich, delightful, and satisfying food and drink. Jesus promised that she would find all this and more at His banquet table. So she left the house of Lady Wild and sat down under the correction and counsel of Lady Wise. Her choice at that crossroad made all the difference. It led to the alternate ending.

Now that you've read this book about the Wild Thing of Proverbs 7, who chose the house of Lady Wild over Lady Wise, and heard the story of the ex-Wild-Thing-at-the-Well, who met Christ and left the house of Lady Wild for Lady Wise, you are at a crossroad. You have a decision to make. It doesn't matter how wild you've been in the past, Christ is extending you an invitation. Today, you can make a choice that will lead to the alternate ending. God is giving you the opportunity to choose your adventure.

The message of the gospel is that Jesus Christ died to pay the penalty for our sins and restore us to a right relationship with God. All of us fall short of the glory of God. We all fall short of who He created us to be. As our study of the Proverbs 7 woman indicates, we all fall short of being the *women* He created us to be. All of us have messed up. Our guilt before God is undeniable. We are not worthy to be in a relationship with Him. Our sin and guilt condemn us. Yet Christ pours out His marvelous gift of grace on all who respond in faith to His offer of forgiveness and an eternal relationship with God. "For all have sinned and fall short of the glory of God, and are justified by his grace as a gift, through the redemption that is in Christ Jesus" (Romans 3:23–24).

The Wild-Thing-at-the-Well recognized her sin and her need for a Savior. Can you imagine how she felt when she met Jesus and He filled her bucket to the brim with living water? Can you imagine the emotions that flooded her heart when she realized that Christ would forgive her sin and quench her thirst? Can you imagine the joy? Can you imagine the overwhelming gratitude? Can you imagine the resolve to change and follow His ways? Can you imagine the transformation that took place in her life?

Maybe this book has been difficult for you to read. Maybe it has opened your eyes to the sin in your life. Maybe it's highlighted just how much you've messed things up. I hope you understand that God's grace is bigger than all your sin. I hope you understand that Jesus Christ was killed on a cross to cancel your debt to God, take away your sin and shame, and help you live the right way. I think of Christ's words to the adulterous Wild Thing who was thrown down at His feet by the self-righteous Pharisees who wanted to stone her to death.

The Pharisees were right—according to the law, she deserved death. But God did not send His Son into the world to condemn the world, but in order that the world might be saved through Him (John 3:17). When Christ saw the Wild Thing trembling in shame and fear, He did not condemn her, but extended undeserved grace. He said, "Neither do I condemn you; go, and from now on sin no more" (John 8:11). I suspect that that's what she did. Author Nancy Leigh DeMoss says, "Undeniable guilt, plus undeserved grace, should equal unbridled gratitude."[1] Wild Things who recognize their guilt and encounter the amazing love and grace of God, will respond to Him with gratitude and a resolve to become a Girl-Gone-Wise.

For all you Wild Things, I'd love to reach past these pages and embrace you as daughters, sisters, and mothers. I'd look you in the eyes and plead with you to respond to Wisdom's call. Listen, and live. Leave the way of wildness, and follow the way of Christ. Obey Him. Live your life the way He says you ought to live, and trust that *He* will fill your bucket. He will. Your thirst will be quenched at His table.

For those of you have already made the decision to ditch the Wild sorority and dine with Lady Wise, I urge you to stand strong. Follow the way of wisdom. Grow in wisdom. Do not flinch. Do not waver. Do not get careless as you get older. Be salt and light to a generation of women who are broken, floundering, and looking for answers.

For you older women, I challenge you to take up the mantle of sage motherhood and speak truth to the young. Mentor them in how to be a Girl-Gone-Wise. A sage mother "opens her mouth with wisdom, and the teaching of kindness is on her tongue" (Proverbs 31:26).

For you young women, it's never too early to start exerting some "motherly" influence. Remember Job? He said, "From my youth the fatherless grew up with me as with a father" (Job 31:18). He exerted a fatherly influence on his fatherless friends. The girls of this generation are "motherless." I challenge you young women to start spiritually mothering them. Your girlfriends desperately need input on how to live wise and not wild.

As I've said before, "I believe the time is ripe for a new movement—a seismic holy quake of countercultural women who dare to take God at His word, those who have the courage to stand against the popular tide, and believe and delight in God's plan for male and female."[2] Women are looking for something to fill their buckets. Christ is the only answer. Will you join the quiet counterrevolution of women who are committed to living according to God's design?

THE MOST BEAUTIFUL WOMAN IN THE WORLD

After hearing me on the radio, speaking about the points of contrast between Wild and Wise Women, a young man e-mailed me. He said he was so "wowed" that he shared the script of the radio show with all his buddies and posted it on his Facebook page. He said it was refreshing to hear something that wasn't "man-bashing" and would build, rather than destroy, male-female relationships. He wished every woman would encounter the material and learn the way of wisdom. He concluded with this statement: "My impression is the woman who has this [wisdom] would be the most beautiful woman in the world!"

I think the young man has the right impression. No woman is quite as beautiful as a Girl-Gone-Wise. So, look carefully how you walk, not as wild but as wise. Get wisdom! Prize her highly, and she will exalt you; she will honor you if you embrace her. She will place on your head a graceful garland; she will bestow on you a beautiful crown. Lady Wisdom will make you over, head to toe. Amazingly, she extends this opportunity to everyone. Any woman can become a Wise Thing. Any woman can become that most beautiful woman in the world. The choice is yours. Will it be you?

NOTES

Wild Thing

1. "Wild Thing," Words and Music by Chip Taylor ©1965 (Renewed 1993) EMI BLACKWOOD MUSICE INC. All Rights Reserved. International Copyright Secured. Used by Permission. Reprinted by permission of Hal Leonard Corporation.

20 Points of Contrast

Point of Contrast #1. Heart

1. Quotes from "A Faithful Narrative of the Surprising Work of God." By Jonathan Edwards. http://www.iclnet.org/pub/resources/text/ipb-e/epl-10/web/edwards-narrative.html.

Point of Contrast #2. Counsel

1. Data and calculations based on statistics by the U.S. Census Bureau. Table 1089. Media Usage and Consumer Spending: 2001 to 2011. http://www.census.gov/compendia/statab/tables/09s1089.pdf.
2. A. W. Tozer. http://christianquotes.org/search/quick/heart/30.
3. Nancy Leigh DeMoss has a great book and Bible study that expands on this concept of women being deceived: *Lies Women Believe: And the Truth That Sets Them Free* (Chicago: Moody, 2001).
4. Joshua Harris, "Like to Watch." http://www.boundless.org/2005/articles/a0001258.cfm.
5. C. S. Lewis, *The Silver Chair* (New York: HarperCollins, 1994), 181–82.

Point of Contrast #3. Approach

1. Hugh Kenner, *Chuck Jones: A Flurry of Drawings, Portraits of American Genius* (Berkeley: Univ. of California Press, 1994). http://ark.cdlib.org/ark:/13030/ft6q2nb3x1/, http://www.escholarship.org/editions/view?docId=ft6q2nb3x1&query=&brand=ucpress.
2. Ten-Year Magazine Readership Trend. 1997-2006 by the Magazine Publishers of America (MPA). http://www.magazine.org/content/Files/TenYrReader Trend97-06%2011-27-06.doc.

3. Eric and Leslie Ludy, *When God Writes Your Love Story: The Ultimate Approach to Guy/Girl Relationships* (Multnomah, 1999), 13.

Point of Contrast #5. Habits

1 . Eric Zorn. http://www.great-quotes.com/cgi-bin/viewquotes.cgi?action=search& orderby=&keyword=priorities&startlist=45.

Point of Contrast #7. Appearance

1 . Patrice A. Opplinger, *Girls Gone Skank: The Sexualization of Girls in American Culture* (Jefferson, N.C.: McFarland & Company, 2008), 1.

2. "What's the Problem with Nudity?" *Horizon*, aired Saturday, March 3, 2009, http://www.bbc.co.uk/programmes/b00j0hnm, and "Can People Unlearn Their Naked Shame?" by Paul King, http://news.bbc.co.uk/2/hi/uk_news/ maga-zine/7915369.stm.

3. John Piper, "Nudity in Drama and the Clothing of Christ." Sermon preached on November 20, 2006. http://www.desiringgod.org/ResourceLibrary/TasteAnd See/ByDate/2006/1884_Nudity_in_Drama_and_the_Clothing_of_Christ/.

4. John Piper, "The Rebellion of Nudity and the Meaning of Clothing." Sermon preached on April 24, 2008. http://www.desiringgod.org/ResourceLibrary/ TasteAndSee/ByDate/2008/2737_The_Rebellion_of_Nudity_and_the_ Meaning_of_Clothing/.

Point of Contrast #10. Sexual Conduct

1 . W. Barclay, *The Letters to the Philippians, Colossians, and Thessalonians*, The Daily study Bible series, rev. ed. (Philadelphia: Westminster Press, 2000), 198.

2. Ibid.

3. Ben Patterson, "The Goodness of Sex and the Glory of God." In *Sex and the Supremacy of Christ*, Eds. John Piper and Justin Taylor (Wheaton, Ill.: Crossway, 2005), 52.

Point of Contrast #11. Boundaries

1 . Miguel De Cervantes, cited in http://www.cybernation.com/victory/ quotations/.

Point of Contrast #13. Neediness

1 . Martin Luther, http://www.brainyquote.com/quotes/authors/m/ martin_luther_3.html.

2. C. S. Lewis, *The Pilgrim's Regress* (Grand Rapids: Eerdmans, 1981), 123.

Notes

Point of Contrast #14. Possessions

1 . "The vase that dreams are made of," by Giancarlo Rinaldi, South of Scotland reporter, BBC Scotland News website, http://news.bbc.co.uk/2/hi/uk_news/scotland/south_of_scotland/7789458.stm.

Point of Contrast #15. Entitlement

1 . 2009 News Releases from Voices of Martyrs, http://www.persecution.com.

2. *Foxe's Book of Martyrs* (Grand Rapids, Mich.: Revell, 2008).

3. Augustine, *Confessions*, 181 (IX.1).

Point of Contrast #17. Speech

1 . Bernard de Bovier de Fontenelle, http://www.giga-usa.com/quotes/topics/flattery_t002.htm.

2. William Penn, http://www.giga-usa.com/quotes/authors/william_penn_a001.htm.

Point of Contrast #18. Influence

1 . H. Smith, *A Preparative to Marriage*, 1591, p.42, cited on http://www.answers.com/topic/a-man-is-known-by-the-company-he-keeps.

2. Dolly Parton, "The Company You Keep." Lyrics copyright 1967, Monument Records. Used by permission.

Point of Contrast #19. Sustainability

1 . Urban Dictionary, Definition for Serial Monogamist, http://www.urbandictionary.com/define.php?term=serial%20monogamist, October 2009.

2. You can read Christy's comment at http://www.marykassian.com/archives/1136#comment-1417. You can also leave a comment on the GirlsGoneWise.com blog.

3. "The Effects of Premarital Sexual Promiscuity on Subsequent Marital Sexual Satisfaction" by Sherie Adams Christensen. A thesis submitted to the faculty of Brigham Young University, Marriage and Family Therapy Program, School of Family Life, Brigham Young University, June 2004. http://contentdm.lib.byu.edu/ETD/image/etd454.pdf.

4. Duane A. Garrett, *Proverbs, Ecclesiastes, Song of Songs*, electronic ed. (Nashville: Broadman & Holman, 2001), c1993 (Logos Library System; The New American Commentary 14), S. 104.

Point of Contrast #20. Teachability

1 . Quoted by Mary Kassian in *Knowing God by Name: A Personal Encounter* (Nashville: LifeWay, 2008), 114.

Conclusion: Wild to Wise

1 . Betsey Stevenson and Justin Wolfers, "The Paradox of Declining Female Happiness," *American Economic Journal*: Economic Policy 2009, 1:2, 190–225, http://www.aeaweb.org/articles.php?doi=10.1257/pol.1.2.190, http://bpp. wharton.upenn.edu/betseys/papers/Paradox%20of%20declining%20female%20 happiness.pdf.

2. Mary A. Kassian, *The Feminist Mistake: The Radical Impact of Feminism on Church and Culture*, rev. ed. (Wheaton, Ill.: Crossway, 2005), 299.